Fallen

Book II

I. R. Harris

10 digit ISBN 147744615X

13 digit ISBN 978-1477446157

For Ada who inspired Lucie to be as courageous as she is, and for Kate who has inspired me since the day we met...

THE BOUND TRILOGY

To Ana, the Bonding ritual is a dangerous part of being human. She herself hasn't been chosen--yet. However, her dear friend Kai has, and on the surface he seems happy. However, Ana knows that Kai was lucky; his Bonder didn't make the choice to kill him. When it is her time, she might not be so fortunate. As it so happens, the choice to take Ana as a Bond was made years ago and her time is now. When Ana's peaceful life in Indonesia is suddenly intersected by a Bonder Demon named Nathanial, she is thrown into a roaring tempest of choices, of love, of ever changing loyalties, and of lies. She quickly realizes that loving someone is not the same as knowing them, and that having either of those things offers no guarantee that her heart will be protected or her life will be spared. For Ana, does being Bound mean to live in the absence of love, of autonomy, of trust or does it mean she will have to make the ultimate sacrifice in order to reclaim who she is and to save not only herself, but also the lives of those to which she is forever tied?

BOUND BOOK I

FALLEN BOOK II

AWAKENING BOOK III

Part I

Chapter One

Ana

Six months and not a single decision about my death had been made. Six months since I'd left Nathanial, six months of me living with my assassin Stephen, and six months of me trying to scrape the pieces of myself back together. It was an uncomfortable knowledge that I would never be quite whole again. I hadn't seen or spoken to Nathanial since I found out that he'd lied to me, that for whatever reason, he had decided to indulge his fantasies with other women and perform the most sacred of Bonding rituals with strangers, instead of with me. Apparently, he had been depressed, not acting himself, possibly drugged by one of the Vampires with whom he had been working. It actually didn't matter so much anymore, I had a very serious problem and my issues with Nathanial were not at the top of my "things to fix" list. I was waiting to die. Well actually, I was waiting for Stephen to decide if my fire wielding ability was worth sparing my life. My particular talent had defied the rules that both Demon-Bonders and Vampires had established amongst themselves; no human could ever possess a power that either species had difficulty obtaining, much less controlling or that had the potential to destroy the Demons and the Vampires. The fact that it was a human in possession of such ability just made matters worse. Most Vampires hated humans, Bonders didn't trust humans and now here I was, with the one thing that both groups feared and wanted and the one thing that I could care less about. I hated fire.

The Vampires were quick to act. Upon hearing about the demise of one of their highest-ranking individuals, Devon, mostly by my hand, they sent someone to handle me. As far as assassins go, Stephen was probably the most low-key. We already knew each other a bit, so that made our arrangement somewhat easier to endure. Due to the nature of my current situation, being a marked woman, Stephen insisted that I stay with him. Unseen Vampires from his coven protected his apartment and most Bonders could not shimmer in or out of the space we occupied. Such protections didn't quite matter so much out in the real world. Both groups wanted me dead and the chances of an attack were always high. The Vampires had gotten to me first and therefore they wanted to relish in the rewards that came with my untimely demise. I was pretty sure that if Stephen's coven did not decide to utilize my skills and turn me like I had asked, then by killing me, Stephen would most likely hold an even higher rank of power and influence in his coven. My proposition to work with the Vampires in their war against the humans and the Bonders was completely absurd; I knew nothing about war and of all the groups involved, I disliked the Vampires the most. However, I had decided that I was not, in fact, ready to die and certainly not for a power that I had never wanted; it was the only compromise that I could offer that might prove alluring enough for the Vampires to want to keep me around. So far, no decision had been made.

My days were pretty mundane, besides the fact that I was waiting for someone to jump out from behind every corner and blow me up, but other than that, I had a somewhat normal routine. Stephen took a sabbatical from his teaching position and escorted me back and forth to work every day. He took me to the gym, to my rowing meets, to the grocery store and clothes shopping. If people didn't know that he was poised to kill me, they might think that we were the most attached couple on the planet. I couldn't help but laugh at the bizarre familiarity my current situation posed; it was almost the exact replica of my time with Alec and Patric, after Nathanial left the first time, and Alec had taken to becoming my personal chaperone. Most days I didn't allow myself to think about anything that had occurred in my life before coming here to live with Stephen; it was just too much for my head and my heart to remember and to feel.

Living with Stephen was proving to be an interesting distraction from my deep moments of depression and malaise. He played music in various clubs around the city and his paintings were constantly being exhibited in local art galleries. I would follow him to some of his shows, even bringing a few of my friends from work, and I almost always went to his art openings—it was as close to normal as Stephen felt comfortable allowing. I actually liked him very much. He was Irish and had a wicked sense of humor that I remembered from my days studying in Dublin. His style was rugged and casual, opting for layered t-shirts, jeans and boots. His hair was short as far as Vampires went and he had just gotten it cut so that it fell over his ears in thick, chestnut brown waves. He was tan, which was an odd occurrence for an Irishman, but he spent so much time down at the beach painting and taking photographs, that his skin had taken on the deep burnished glow of a bronzed surfer and it only served to make his marine-blue eyes more luminescent and clear.

Stephen liked to talk… a lot. He had a ton of creative energy and sometimes when we'd be together shopping or driving, I felt as if we were both sixteen, watching him laugh and sing in his car. Every so often, mainly at night, I would hear him strumming on his guitar in the dark, the melodies solemn and moody. I would also catch him staring at me sometimes, when our eyes would meet, he would look away shyly, blushing. I hadn't known that Vampires could blush, but there it was. He would let me paint along side him, mostly when I was suffering from a bout of insomnia or nightmares. I wasn't an artist, but I had always enjoyed playing with colors and patterns and Stephen indulged me. It was during those times, the times late at night when we'd be sitting on the hardwood floors, canvases and paints spread out before us, that I would notice he was his most quiet, his most contemplative. Sometimes he would just sit against the back wall and watch me splattering paint all over the place. His eyes would follow my every move and I would wonder if he was thinking about how to kill me and if I would try to fight him if he did attack. He'd read my mind and see what I was thinking and then he'd get upset. I would apologize and tell him that it seemed only natural that my thoughts should allow for me to have a healthy dose of fear from being around him—he was, after all, instructed to kill me.

Currently, I was headed to meet him at an art gallery across town. This was one of those rare times that I was actually allowed to drive myself, but I was pretty sure that I was being followed nonetheless. His work was to be part of an exhibit that featured local artists and photographers who used humans, Bonders or Vampires, as their subjects. The gallery itself was a bit counter-culture; it had great energy and lots of progressive and unique art programs for the youth in the city and it was probably one of Stephen's favorite places to exhibit his pieces. I pulled up along the street and crudely paralleled parked. The gallery was only a block away from my parking spot and I was all too happy to walk outside by myself for a bit. The air was warm, but not heavy and I was glad that I had opted for a sleeveless tank, dark jeans and motorcycle boots. Thank god the gallery didn't have a posh dress code. I rounded the corner and I immediately could see the crowd outside milling around drinking, smoking and taking pictures. They had a band playing from somewhere inside and the music was upbeat but not intrusive. The gallery itself was amazing, it had been an abandoned meat warehouse and the primal and organic feel was still very much a part of the space. It was always relatively dark with just the right amount of subtle lighting to display the different pieces on the brick walls or out in the center of the floor. Long red couches were placed in various corners, with bistro tables and small votive candles providing the ideal place to sit and admire the atmosphere. It was packed. I headed to the bar for a drink and to get my bearings.

Immediately I could tell where Stephen was, mainly because you couldn't miss his extreme physicality, but also because wherever Stephen went, women followed—in droves. Tonight was no exception. He was sitting on one of the couches surrounded by what appeared to be supermodels. They all were scantily dressed, had long flowing hair, lots of make-up and they were groping him incessantly. I laughed. I was used to the parade of women that came by the apartment, the women that showed up to hear him sing and the women who came to his exhibits. There were always a lot of women in Stephen's life and I was grateful that he kindly offered to convert his study into a second bedroom. I didn't want to think about what went on in his room when I was at home. I shook my head, took my ginger ale and headed up to the second floor where Stephen's photographs were displayed.

From the looks of things, everyone was downstairs with the artists so I had the space to myself for a bit. The lighting was dim and tiny candles were placed along the mantels that connected wall-to-wall. Stephen had submitted ten photographs, all black and white and they were sporadically hanging expertly from the meat hooks in the support beams. I hadn't seen anything that he had been working on for this exhibit so viewing his choices would be a new experience. The first five were of the ocean at night. Somehow he had managed to capture the movement of the tides with such precision and light, that the waves almost appeared to be shifting and lapping up on the shore. Each photograph also depicted the phases of the moon, waxing and waning, and the stars in their infinite depths and brilliance. I was stunned at the amount of detail he was able to reflect. The back of my neck grew warm as I passed the nightscapes. I absently ran my fingers over the metal and stone imprint secured in my flesh. Surprisingly, the bonding held firm, there had been no separation of the metals since I left Nathanial. I felt my heart seize at the thought of him. I shook my head, took a deep breath and continued to walk between the pictures, arriving at the next grouping. Here was the heart of his theme, people, or actually, it seemed to be just one person. The first photograph was taken at a great distance. All I could make out was a single figure standing on a cliff, looking up at the moon. The next two pictures took the viewer in just a bit closer and I could see that the figure was definitely a woman. She was wearing a loose dress and her hair was blowing back off of her shoulders. Her face was intentionally blurred, but I found myself frowning as my eyes roamed over her figure. The last two pictures completed the journey and I gasped. I saw the same woman, now fully up close in the lens, her profile clear and sharp. She was standing on the cliff, her face turned toward the ocean in the second to the last picture, and in the tenth photo, the woman was looking down, her feet so close to the edge that I wanted to reach out and grab her. The photos were of me! I was looking at myself standing on the edge of the cliffs not far from my old house, the house that had burned to the ground, the house where I had fought Alec and Devon, the house that I had shared with Nathanial and that Patric would visit, the house that Kai would come to drink and eat and watch movies; those were the cliffs that I had looked down from and seen Kai's body lying cold and dead in the sand. Stephen had somehow captured those extremely private moments. Once a month for six months, I pretended that I needed some "alone time" and I would take my jeep and drive back to the coast, and I would go out to those cliffs and try to convince myself not to jump; I would remind myself that Nathanial had betrayed me, that Patric, Kai and Alec were dead and that once again my life was in the hands of someone who did not care about me as a breath in this world. Those were sobering moments for me, and the only time that I ever allowed myself to cry. Apparently I had not been alone.

"Ana," a quiet voice penetrated my stunned silence. I whipped my head around but I couldn't see anyone. Suddenly, a movement from across the room caught my attention and I saw Stephen emerge from the shadows. How long had he been watching me? "Since you came upstairs," he spoke slowly, walking tentatively toward me.

7

"You took pictures of me?" That was all I could actually manage to blurt out. I felt violated to know that he had been right there, watching me in my most vulnerable state; that he had seen me crying, debating with myself, trying desperately to convince my mind that I should just hang on—but to what, to whom? I didn't know if I wanted Stephen, of all people, to see just how weakened I felt, just how fractured I had become. It made me seem like such easy prey and that's what I was— prey. His eyes were on me, and he took another step closer. I was terrified, desperate. "Please," I choked out. "Please. Just leave me alone." Fear and a crushing sadness washed over me and I ran past Stephen, down the stairs and out into the street.

I had nowhere to go, no one to go to. I thought of Nathanial, of driving to his home, of seeing him one more time, of asking him to help me; I was sure that he had left, left the country, left our house, left me. I drove back to the apartment, turned off all the lights, curled up in my bed, my body shivering. I turned on the stereo, trying to filter out the deep black fear that was now filling my mind. Tears streamed down my face and soon the sobs came, retching and heaving in my throat. A sharp pain ripped through my chest, sending a splintering fissure into my heart and I gasped into my pillow. Nathanial's face appeared in front of me and I closed my eyes, trying to desperately hold onto the image. It swirled away from me, drifting and blurring into the cold black that was now shrouding my mind. What had I done? I had walked away from him feeling betrayed, not letting him explain, not fighting for us after everything we'd been through, after fighting our way back to each other; I had not chosen to fight for us. I ran, scared and angry, and I ran straight into my own certain death. Nathanial said he would protect me, if I had just stayed, if I had just let him talk to me; I ran—

just like I always did, like I've always done and now, I was alone, bound to die at the hands of a Vampire or of a broken soul, a shattered heart; either way, I was dead.

Nathanial

I couldn't remember how many drinks I had. I didn't really care. I rolled off the naked woman lying beneath me and tried to avoid the blood on the sheets. I heard her groan in her sleep as I pulled on my pants and took another swig from the bottle of scotch on the table. Blood and alcohol coated my lips and I tried not to gag. I buttoned my shirt and opened the door. Smoke and loud music assaulted my already dulled senses and I grasped the bottle and stumbled out into the hallway and back into the main part of the club. How many women had it been tonight? Five? Six? I lost count but I could already see another one waiting in my seat. They all looked the same, all around 5'3 with curly brown hair and brown eyes, flat brown eyes that I made them shut. I had enough reminders of her, too many nightmares, too many fantasies that she would come back, that I would hear her jeep tossing gravel into the grass, too many nights walking along the shore, wondering if she missed me or if she was already dead. My gut retched and I chugged another sip from my bottle and went to sit down at the bar, I needed a few moments to recover. I laid my head down on the counter, trying to quell the dizziness and nausea.

"Nathanial." I heard someone sit down beside me. I ran my fingers through my hair and turned my face to the side. It was Stephen. "You

9

look like hell," he said quietly as he ordered a drink. I stood up to leave, but his hand shot out and pressed me back down in my seat. I felt my muscles tense at his gesture. He chuckled. "I really don't think either of us is up for a fight this evening do you?" He stirred his drink. "Besides, I think you're going to want to hear what I have to say." I doubted that. If it hadn't been for Stephen, Ana would have never known about what happened while I was with Patric; she didn't need to know. I felt my chest heave. "Well, I'm no relationship expert, but I'm guessing that lying to someone that you claim to love is not the best foundation to build," he said, turning his eyes on me.

"I didn't lie to her." I sighed, trying to breathe calmly. Stephen waved his hand.

"Whatever, that's neither here nor there. We have more important issues to discuss Nathanial. I had actually hoped that you would be fully sober when hearing this, but I suppose your current condition will just have to suffice." He took a deep breath as he looked me over. I turned my attention to my drink, lowering my eyes.

"I have Ana. She's living with me, she's safe as of tonight and she's a mess," he spoke softly, but with a slight commanding tone. I felt my body tense and relax all at the same time. She was alive, that was good, but what the hell was she doing with Stephen? "She came to me for help Nathanial, with a request. Unfortunately, she had no idea just what it was that she was doing. She had just left you, she was hurting and grieving and I truly do not think that she was quite in her right mind." I shook my head.

"What does it matter to me what Ana does anymore Stephen? I asked her to stay, she left me and now what she decides and the consequences of those decisions are her sole accountability." My voice sounded flat, dead. Stephen took a slow sip from his drink, his eyes holding my face.

"We both know that's not how you really feel Nathanial." I saw his eyes flash and I looked away and shrugged.

"It's too late for her Stephen. She's made up her mind about what she wants. All I could ever hope for is that she realizes just what she's done, before she's killed," I said bitterly. I eyed Stephen warily. "Now, I have things to do, so if there is something you needed to tell me..." I waved my hand for him to get on with it and I took another drink from my bottle. He smirked at me.

"Yes, I can see you have lots to get too, trying to forget Ana and all that." He eyed the short brunette waiting for me. I stood. "Sit down Nathanial, we're not done." Stephen's tone had turned icy and his eyes went black. I felt chills filter in my chest, penetrating the metals in my flesh over my heart. I looked at him, fear creeping into my bones. "I've been given the honorable task of killing Ana, Nathanial. That is, if my coven does not choose to oblige her request to join the vampires against the Bonders and the Humans, if they don't decide to turn her and utilize her power. That's the deal she's asked for. She's quite a negotiator and her request has managed to ignite a debate within my brethren; that's why she's still alive of course, otherwise I would have killed her the moment she stepped foot in my apartment." He paused, letting his words sink into my soul. I stopped breathing and my heart began slamming against my chest. This wasn't happening. This

11

couldn't be happening. "It is happening Nathanial and beyond all of this, war is happening too and I'm sure that you will be called to service, being as valuable as you are. I felt somewhat obligated to inform you about Ana, before you left to go back to South America." He glared at me. How had he known? "We're having you watched of course." He sighed. "Look, I'm not telling you any of this because I expect you to try to save her, you can't, you won't win; between the covens that want her annihilated for Devon and Alec's deaths, and your own Bonders who don't want her to be in possession of this fire power she has, you're out numbered. Someone would have gotten to her eventually, I just made it there a bit sooner." His voice became quiet and solemn.

"You're going to kill her?" I couldn't believe what he was saying.

"No decision has been made yet, but the alternatives don't look too pleasant either. I'm not actually sold on Ana becoming a vampire, I would much rather she stay Human…she's unique, different…" His voice became barely audible. He took a sip from his glass and I noticed that he was having difficulty swallowing. He turned to look at me, my face in my hands. "I don't know what's going to happen…I can promise you that if they decline her offer…I can promise you that I won't…" he paused and took a breath, "I'll promise you that I won't make it painful for her, it won't hurt her Nathanial." My head shot up and I grabbed him around the neck, but I was too overcome in despair and liquor to do any damage. I pulled my hand away and ran my fingers through my hair.

12

"You can't do this Stephen, you can't. You like Ana, you respect her, I know. I saw the way you looked at her when we were all together; she affects you. You can't kill her!" I was begging him, pleading.

"I like Ana very much Nathanial, but I'm not conditioned to feel the same things for Humans that your species does. I would prefer not to kill her, as far as Humans go, she's one of the most special people that I've ever met; it's a shame really. I'm sorry, but there's nothing more that I can do." He finished his drink and turned to look at me. "Look, I don't know if she'll see you, but you are welcome at my apartment any time you want. No harm will come to you, I can promise you that." He put his hand on my shoulder and lifted my head to meet his gaze. "Nathanial, if you weren't on the side that I was trying to eviscerate, I think that I might actually find your company tolerable." His eyes flashed once more and then he was gone.

Ana

I put Stephen's card on his bed as I gathered my gear; I had a rowing meet out of the city, but it was his birthday soon and I didn't want him to think that I had forgotten, not that he had ever celebrated the event—he was over five hundred years old. I had purchased him tickets to see one of his favorite singer/songwriters and one of mine too, although I wasn't expecting him to take me. I thought maybe he could go with a friend or perhaps one of the many women that he courted. I sighed. I was happy to get out of the house by myself for a while. My rowing and the various other events that I needed to attend seemed to be quelling the massive depression that clung to the edges of my mind. Like a thick cobweb, it threatened to encase the very core of my existence; I was working very hard to not give in. I wasn't mad at Stephen anymore for the pictures. I wasn't even mad at Nathanial, I was just emotionally drained. I lugged my giant bag down the hallway and into the living room where Stephen was writing some music. He jumped up to help me. "It's ok, I've got it," I said, as cheerfully as I could. He took the bag from me anyway and carried it effortlessly to the door.

"Your teammates are picking you up?" he asked, his eyes wary. He didn't like putting my life in the hands of what he considered "irresponsible and weak Humans", but I had insisted that traveling two hours out to the University was not something that he needed to engage in, plus, I reminded him that he had a date. "I don't have to go, it's not important, it's just an evening out…" He looked at me, his eyes brilliant and clear.

"What, and have you forgo an evening with yet another beautiful woman so that you can escort me to a rowing meet out in the middle of nowhere? Now what kind of friend would I be if I let your reputation suffer on account of me?" My tone was sarcastic, but light. He rolled his eyes and slid open the door. "Have fun!" I called, as I headed for the elevator.

"What time will you be back?" he asked, sounding like a concerned father. He chuckled.

"Umm, well if we place, then it won't be until the evening, but I'm guessing that you'll still be gone? I'm happy to stay out later if that would work better for your plans?" I asked, hinting at his tendency for sexual promiscuity.

"That won't be necessary Ana, but thank you for your consideration." He smirked at me and held the door to the elevator. "I'll see you this evening and good luck." He pulled the door back allowing for me to pass him. I met his eyes and nodded, closing the door and stepping into the elevator.

It was a very long day. We'd won our meet and decided to celebrate at one of the local pubs and it was after eleven at night when I returned to the apartment. My muscles ached, my skin felt raw and dry and I was in desperate need of a long shower. I turned the key and clumsily slid back the door, kicking my bag inside. It was dark except for the glow of the kitchen light above the stove; I had guessed that Stephen was still out on his date. I dragged my bag behind me as I came into the living room and immediately I felt my blood go cold. There was someone standing by the large window in the far corner of the room; actually there were two people. They turned hearing my sharp intake of breath and I knew that they were Vampires, one man and one woman. The familiar swelling of my skin became apparent and my blood grew warm, slowly seething beneath the surface. My body tensed, waiting for the attack. Suddenly the woman came forward smiling, her hands behind her back.

"You must be Ana." Her accent hinted at some Latin American ethnicity. She was maybe my height, with long curly black hair that fell below her waist. She was curvy with deep, bronzed skin and glowing dark brown eyes. Her smile was wide and full and it illuminated her round face. Instinctively, I took a quick step backward, eyeing her.

"Carmen," the other figure spoke, as he stepped from the shadows. His eyes struck me first; they were clear and brilliant blue, deep sea blue. He was tall and lean, but muscular with sandy brown hair that he wore pulled back into a long plait that cascaded down his back. His skin wasn't as dark as the woman's, but it had a definite tanned appearance. He wasn't dressed as ruggedly as most Vampires, but more professional, and he was clean-shaven, showing off a strong jaw line and his youthful yet worn face.

"Oh, I'm so sorry, we must have frightened you." Carmen stepped back from me smiling shyly and looking toward the man apologetically. I was waiting for my heart rate to slow down and for my body to relax; so far that seemed highly unlikely. Suddenly I saw something out of the corner of my eye, something small, walking slowly down the hallway from my bedroom. I turned to see a tiny girl, maybe two or three, teetering unsteadily, trying not to slip on the hardwood floors. She was holding a small doll and laughing. What the hell was going on? Carmen ran and scooped up the girl, holding her tightly against her chest. All I could do was stare. Had I walked into the wrong apartment? Was that possible?

"Ana, I'm Liam, I'm Stephen's brother and this is my wife Carmen and our little girl Lucie." He smiled at me and went to put his arms around Carmen. I felt my eyes widen. Liam laughed, clearly expecting my reaction. "We came looking for Stephen, do you know where he is?" I swallowed as my brain tried to process the scene in front of me.

"Umm, well…" I was trying to formulate words. "I think he's out on a date, maybe; he goes out quite a bit…" I laughed nervously. "I've been gone since this morning…" I moved to lean against one of the bar stools, trying to steady the massive amounts of adrenaline coursing through my veins. I fingered the metal hanging around my neck, its gold gleam catching the light from the moon. The little girl cooed and squirmed to be let down. Carmen smiled at me and placed Lucie gently on the ground. She bolted and made a beeline straight for me. She stumbled, losing her footing and I reached out to catch her. She wrapped her arms around my neck and pressed her face to the gold metal, looking intently at its shape.

"Lucie!" Liam scolded. I smiled at him, letting him know that what she was doing was fine. I looked at the tiny girl in my arms and immediately I thought of Maria, the girl that had been murdered down in West Papua. Lucie had the same black hair, the same deep skin tone, but perhaps the most startling similarity was in her eyes; they were sparkling brown, deep and luminous. I smiled at her and shifted my weight, holding her against my hip. I decided that neither Liam nor Carmen were most likely to try and kill me, so I allowed my body to unclench slightly.

"Can I get you anything or would Lucie like something?" I had no idea what sort of things I could offer a family of Vampires, but I felt rude not offering anything. Liam laughed and sat down on the sofa.

"We're fine Ana, but thank you for being so hospitable. It looks like Stephen is doing well?" He surveyed the room, his eyebrows raised as he looked at the myriad of paintings and photographs scattered haphazardly around. I wondered if they knew that Stephen was waiting around to kill me. I heard Carmen make a small hiss as her head shot up, her eyes searching my face. "Yes Ana, we know," Liam said quietly, putting his arm around his wife. "Carmen has some problems

17

with what Stephen does, shall we say…?" He looked at Lucie and me. For some reason I hugged the little girl closer to my chest.

"I didn't think he had a choice in the matter," I said flatly. I heard Carmen make a huffing noise and roll her eyes.

"That's debatable." Liam sighed as he stroked the length of Carmen's hair. The gesture was so tender, so intimate, that I felt utterly and completely shattered. I tried to swallow the tears that were threatening to overflow.

"I offered to…to help," I said, my voice barely a whisper. "I offered a compromise of sorts." Lucie put her hands on my face and laughed. Absently, I kissed the top of her forehead, inhaling the sweet smell of her skin.

"I know you did Ana." Liam chuckled. "And might I add, what a compromise it is. You have to understand that this is very new to our species and to the Bonders as well I'm guessing; we don't know how to best deal with you or your powers or this situation. It's proving very complicated." He sighed again and smiled at me.

"It doesn't matter…" I whispered. "What happens, happens; it just doesn't matter anymore." I walked over to the window and gazed up at the moon. Just then I heard a key in the door. Liam and Carmen looked up to see Stephen, unaccompanied, thank god, walking down the hallway towards us. Immediately, I saw his body tense before his recognition of his brother kicked in and his eyes locked onto mine, roaming over my face and down the length of my body, checking to see if I had been harmed I guessed. Liam broke the tension.

"Good god Stephen, do you honestly think we'd attack Ana?" He laughed and went to hug his brother. Stephen's eyes had yet to leave my face. I moved to hand Lucie back to Carmen. I smiled at her and I thought I saw the glimmer of tears in her eyes as I placed her daughter into her arms. I turned to face Liam and Stephen, who were now pouring a bottle of scotch into thick, glass tumblers.

"Um, I'll let you guys catch up," I said awkwardly, as I grabbed my gym bag and hoisted it over my shoulder. "I need to take a shower anyway." I turned toward Liam and smiled. "It was really nice to meet you, all of you," I said, smiling at Carmen and Lucie. I nodded at Stephen who was now starring at me so intently, that I felt my bones go shaky. I moved down the hallway, grateful to get to the sanctuary of my room.

I took the longest shower that my skin could handle, trying not to wonder what Stephen and his family were discussing. Perhaps the most humane way to go about killing someone who seemed somewhat nice? I laughed to myself as I pulled on my favorite sweats; they were actually Nathanial's sweats, and I settled into twisting my hair into wet waves and curls. I turned on my stereo and tried to concentrate on the somber and dark melodies filtering around my room. I finished with my hair and went to sit on my bed, slowly unpacking my rowing gear and clothes. There was a soft knock at my door.

"It's open." I sighed and heaved my bag onto the floor. Stephen was standing in the doorframe, hesitant. "Come on in." I motioned at him. I couldn't remember if he had ever been in my room before. He drifted silently into the space and came to stand next to my bed, leaning against one of the posts, watching me. "I didn't know that you had a family, that you were an uncle," I said, keeping my eyes on my clothes.

"Hmmm," he murmured.

"Did you have a nice evening?" I asked, smirking up at him. He pulled something out of his jacket pocket. He was holding a small white envelope, the one that I had placed on his pillow before leaving this morning, the one for his birthday. He raised his eyebrows at me. "What?" I said, not sure if I had somehow offended him with my gesture.

"Ana, I can't for the life of me, understand who you are. For months now, I've been trying to decipher your persona, your psyche and just when I think that I have it, you surprise me. You utterly surprise the hell out of me." His voice was rough and somewhat harsh in tone. He flung the card on the bed, his eyes searching my face.

"I'm…I'm sorry Stephen," I stammered, not understanding the source for his frustration. He sighed and turned away from me, pacing around the room. My chest began to hurt. I fingered the card gingerly as if it was diseased.

"Have you seen Nathanial?" he asked, rounding on me. The pain in my chest grew sharper and I was having trouble breathing. Why would I have seen Nathanial? Stephen shook his head and turned away from me again, his dark shadow filling the blank space on my wall.

"I went to see him Ana, to tell him about you, about us, about what I am waiting to do…" I felt myself wince as I tried to suck in the air around me. Stephen turned and came to sit next to me on the bed.

"Ana, I told him that he could come, that he should come to see you, to talk to you, before…before anything happens. He's leaving for South America, I was hoping that he would've come by…" his voice trailed off to barely a whisper. I took a shaky breath in and slid back against my pillows, shaking my head.

"No," I said quietly. "No, he would never come Stephen, not now, not anymore. We've hurt each other too much, and now things are beyond repair and it wouldn't matter anyway; my life is…well, it's not destined to be much of a life no matter what happens." I laughed softly, leaning my head back and looking up at the ceiling. I repeated my current mantra to myself; *it just doesn't matter, it is what it is.* "I'm very sorry that I've upset you with the card, I didn't mean to be intrusive or disrespectful or anything. I just thought that you might like to do something special for yourself that's all… and to show you that I'm grateful to you for allowing me to come and disrupt your life, your routine…" I sunk deeper into the mattress, feeling rather embarrassed. He sighed loudly.

"Would you like to go?" he asked, his gaze on my face. I looked at him, confused.

"Go where?" I said, turning on my side so that I could see him. He rolled his eyes.

"To the concert, you ridiculous and intriguing woman." He moved toward the door.

"Oh, well sure, if you want," I said hesitantly. "What about your date tonight, don't you want to bring her?" I asked, smiling weakly. He turned to look at me, his face serious.

21

"No Ana, I don't want to bring her, I want to go with you. Do we have a plan then?" he asked, still looking solemn.

"Sure, sure, I'd love to go, thanks Stephen, that would be great." I smiled, trying to break the seriousness of his gaze. He braced his hands on my bedposts.

"Carmen likes you a lot. She doesn't have many female friends and no Human female friends that I'm aware of…she likes you." His head was bowed.

"I like her too, and your brother and Lucie—you're very lucky to have such a nice family," I said, wanting him to raise his eyes. He smiled and shook his head again.

"Good night Ana, I'll be home around six tomorrow and then we'll leave for the concert alright?"

"Sounds good," I replied softly and watched as he quietly shut the door behind him.

I decided that I needed to go shopping, that I needed to try not to think about Nathanial, about him not coming to see me, about how I most likely would never get to say goodbye or to tell him just how sorry I was for everything; it was too much. I cleared my venture out with Stephen, although I was sure that he had someone following me to my destination. I made the most of it. I ate lunch, had tea and strolled in and out of my favorite shops. I bought something appropriate for the concert and a bit more daring than my usually sporty wardrobe. I opted for a backless tunic that was also low cut at the neck and skimmed to my waist. I also splurged and purchased some exceptionally skinny dark jeans that were so tight, I was sure my organs were going to be crushed, but with the stiletto black boots I had, the outfit was close to perfect. By the time I made it home, I had a little over an hour to change and try to make myself presentable. I started to feel somewhat self-conscious that I would be seen out with Stephen. I had yet to see him have anyone less than some Brazilian supermodel on his arm and I was feeling anything but supermodelesque. I sighed and turned up my stereo, loud. I was opting for a bit of a darker look this evening and took to applying some dark gray eyeliner and smoky shadows. The shimmering gray color always seemed to bring out the gold and copper in my brown eyes and I almost liked the way they looked if they weren't so plain. I wore my hair long and loosely curled, opting for a more bed-head feel, fitting for a casual acoustic concert. Nathanial used to call me a chameleon, for my ability to take on any look and apparently make it my own. The sudden thought of him made the back of my neck grow warm and I cleared the tightness in my throat. I thought I heard the clinking of a glass, so I grabbed my purse, turned off the stereo and headed out into the living room. Stephen was in the kitchen pouring himself a drink when I appeared, digging through my purse for my lip balm.

"Shit!" I heard him say, and I looked up to find that he had missed his glass entirely and caramel colored liquid was now dripping down the side of the bar. He had been staring at me. I laughed.

"Well, I know I'm not what you're used to in terms of the normal goddesses that you date, but maybe you won't be too ashamed to be seen with me," I said watching him reach for a paper towel. He sopped up the spill and turned to look at me. His eyes flashed and I took that as a sign that my choice in outfit was pretty spot on. "Ready?" I asked, still chuckling.

"Hmmm, yeah." His eyes wandered slowly down my body. I rolled my eyes. Vampires were so one-track-minded. I turned my back to him to grab the tickets off the end table and I heard him whistle low and deep.

"What?" I said, somewhat alarmed.

"I hadn't seen the back yet." He laughed, but his eyes had grown a few shades deeper and I saw him lick his lips. I sighed and shook my head.

"Behave." I pointed my finger at him jokingly. "I live with you, so none of your normal seductive tactics will work on me; I know that you're a womanizer and far from monogamous." I laughed at him and went to open the door, motioning for him to get a move on; at this rate, we were never going to arrive on time.

Stephen surprised me with dinner reservations at my favorite Cuban restaurant. It was a very nice gesture considering that he didn't eat and a bit odd, given our relationship. Still, it was nice to just be out for once; for me it had been awhile and Stephen seemed content to sit across from me and drink his wine and stare at my exposed chest. He knew a lot of people at the place and most of them had no problem coming up to our table to chat. The majority of them were women. I felt awkward. They all eyed me as they approached, I'm sure trying to determine the nature of our relationship, if we were on a date or if we were just friends. One woman who approached our table was one that

24

I had seen groping him the night of his gallery exhibit and she seemed less than pleased to see me. I was pretty sure that she was human, but I couldn't tell anymore. Stephen introduced us.

"Ana, this is Alessandria, Alessandria, my date, Ana." I looked up at him, my eyes wide. Date? I quickly composed myself and stood to shake her hand. She was having none of it and I saw her eyes turn stormy as she looked at me.

"Hmmm." She eyed me and turned back to stroking Stephen's hair. I decided that since I was already up, that perhaps now would be a good time for me to use the restroom. My chest felt tight as I watched Alessandria run her fingers along his jaw, caressing him. Ugh, what was with these people? As I made my way to the back of the restaurant, I caught the eye of an extremely handsome man sitting at the bar. I didn't think he was a Vampire, mainly because he was dressed in the Bohemian style that the Bonders usually wore. His hair was coiled into dark blond dreadlocks and something about his face reminded me of Alec; his stare perhaps, it was stern and composed. I smiled at him as I passed. He continued to stare at me as I walked to the back of the room. Suddenly I felt chills run up the back of my neck. Upon leaving the bathroom, I noticed that the man or Bonder, was no longer in his seat. I scanned the room, but failed to notice his presence. More chills broke out on my skin as I headed back to our seating. Alessandria was now in my seat, leaning so far across the plates that she was practically crawling across table. The tightness returned in my chest. I stepped right beside her and cleared my throat.

"Excuse me," I said calmly, but my voice was surprisingly commanding. Stephen looked at me, and Alessandria's eyes narrowed at my tone. "Do you mind?" I said, taking a step closer to her, my muscles flexed. I wanted to shove her perfectly make-uped face into my Cuban sandwich.

"Actually," she said, her tone catty, "we were having a private conversation. Why don't you go and play nice, until we're done." She smiled at me. That did it. My blood started to boil and my skin throbbed. I leaned down close to her face, so that she could see my eyes, which I was sure had gone black at this point.

"Alessandria, I'm only going to say this once," my tone was diplomatic but deadly, "if you don't get your pathetic, whoring ass out of my seat, I'm going to show you just how *not* nice, I can play." I brought my hands down around her wrists, bracing them to the table.

"Ladies, this is not necessary." Stephen laughed, but I could tell that his voice was dark. I'd forgotten he was there. I pushed off of her and stood, waiting for her to get up. She glared at me as she collected her purse and shoved her way past me. I sank back down into the booth and picked up my sandwich. Stephen was eyeing me over his glass of wine, his eyebrows raised.

"What?" I said, taking a bite of my food. He pursed his lips as if to say something, but thought better of it; instead he took to gazing at my face, his blue eyes, piercing.

We made it to the concert with thirty minutes to spare and navigated our way into the performance hall to find our seats. I couldn't help but feel as though someone was watching me, and I took to scanning the room as we entered. Everything seemed normal, but what did that mean, I mused. Stephen hadn't said a word since my little display of aggression at dinner and I wondered if he was mad at me. I saw him smile as he read my thoughts and I relaxed a bit. I had gotten us third row center seats and ours were the only two places left open. I felt Stephen place his hand on my back as he moved me in front of him to enter our row. The sudden touch of his fingers on my bare skin sent a tremor of heat and electricity up and down my spine and I felt my back arch involuntarily. He jerked his hand away as if he'd been shocked as well. I made it to my seat and turned to look at him. His eyes were already on me. This time it was my turn to raise my eyebrows at him. I held his gaze, wondering what he was thinking or feeling. Out of the corner of my eye, I caught a glimpse of a dark blond head of dreadlocks moving down one of the aisles. I tore my eyes from Stephen and turned to see the man from the restaurant sitting not two rows in front of us, to my left. Again, chills erupted over my skin as I tried to reason with myself over his presence. I felt Stephen's warm touch caress my back.

"What is it?" he asked, his eyes following my stare.

"It's nothing," I replied, not taking my eyes off the man. "That man was in the restaurant earlier, he…he noticed me," I said, frowning, unease growing in my stomach.

"Of course he noticed you Ana, how could anyone *not* notice you?" he said as he ran his fingers gently up and down my spine. Stephen had never, ever touched me like this and he'd never really touched me since holding my hand to paint on my first night at the apartment. It was a different sensation, but it felt nice, calming and not threatening like it had been with Devon. I turned to look at him.

"Thanks," I said shyly. He laughed and kept his hand on my back, moving to stroke up under my hair, his fingers tracing along my metal tattoo. I felt every muscle in my body turn to liquid, yet at the same time, I felt a surge of energy course through my veins. Bewildered, I looked at him and he laughed at my reaction to his touch. I jabbed him lightly in the ribs as the lights dimmed and our concert began. I moved to look once more for the man with the dreadlocks, but I didn't see him, he had disappeared yet again. My anxiety heightened, but I tried to relax and listen to the music. When the familiar dark and somber chords of my favorite song started to play, I felt the tips of Stephen's fingers begin to caress all the way down my back. Moving slowly, he swept the locks of hair that blocked my bare skin from his touch, shifting them over my shoulder. I felt him staring at me and my pulse quickened. He shifted in his seat and moved so that the back of his hand was now traveling the length of my arm, his eyes on my face. Heat rushed underneath my skin and suddenly I could smell Stephen's fragrance. He had rarely emitted it in my presence, mainly because it was a predation tool for the Vampires; their fragrances displayed only the things that most attracted their prey—the scents that their victims found most arousing. For me, it was a combination of things; a layered musk with hints of the ocean and patchouli oil, sometimes vanilla and sandalwood and of course woods, honey and lemon. Any combination of those fragrances made my heart stir and I was constantly trying to find a perfume that I could wear that came close to one of those notes. Stephen's scent was, of course, exactly what I found the most arousing and I tasted just a hint of desire begin to move inside my body. I sighed and let the heady perfume from his skin, surround me. Surprisingly, I wasn't in the mood to fight off any attraction to him that I was having at the moment, my emotions had been so close to the surface lately, that I was thinking of just letting them flow, not fighting against the tides anymore. He bent his head close to my ear and I felt his breath on my neck.

"Maybe we should leave a bit early?" he murmured, stroking his finger from my jaw to my neck. I shuddered. This was so weird. I didn't think that Stephen was attracted to me one bit; he was, after all, supposed to be the one to kill me at some point. How could he possibly want to be with me? I felt him pull back from me. I turned my face to his and saw that his eyes were full of emotion; I knew he had heard my inner monologue. He grasped my hands and he pulled me up from my seat, leading me down the aisle and out the side exit. I thought I saw someone else move down an aisle as well, but my head was feeling a bit loopy and my body a bit weak from Stephen's touch so I didn't bother to look. We were deposited into an alleyway that led out into the street, but Stephen was in no hurry to go anywhere. I could still here music from the concert, the song wafted into the street, the chords sensual and slow. He moved to lean his back up against the wall pulling me with him. He looked contemplative, as if debating what he wanted to do. He studied me, and moved to hold my face between his hands. The gesture was incredibly intimate and I felt my body warm at the closeness we both were experiencing. Stephen's eyes churned and I saw him take a deep breath.

"Tell me something Ana." His eyes locked on me, they were hypnotic and dark. "Why did you get so upset at the restaurant, why so angry?" I lowered my eyes and looked down at the street. Christ, what

29

was he getting at? "You know what I'm getting at." He cocked his head to the side, still holding my face.

"I don't know Stephen, I guess I've always disliked women like that, you know, the ones who think that they can have anyone at anytime just because of the way they look—it's obscene." I laughed, but I felt him move one of his hands up under my hair and begin to softly caress my back. I swallowed. He was studying my reaction to him. He had our bodies so close that I began to taste his scent on my lips. I was stunned at how much it seemed to both nourish and stir my hunger, my hunger for him; this was so new, these desires for Stephen. He began tracing his fingertips across my mouth, stopping to move gently over its shape. He parted my lips and my breath suddenly became very shallow. He moved from my mouth down to my throat and he slowly caressed across my collarbones, lingering on the hollow at the base of my neck. His eyes were watching me, taking me in. He wrapped his hand around my waist and pulled me so that our hips were touching. I couldn't get my head around this sudden display of physicality, but for some reason, it made sense and my body was not reacting as if it was under any sort of threat; it was just the opposite actually. My body was responding with an intense and very, very different arousal from anything that I'd ever felt; it was dark and penetrating and it seemed to hold deep inside of my bones and my blood. He stared at me as he heard me reasoning through what was happening between us. We had been talking about something...he pulled me closer and whispered in my ear and I felt both the softness of his breath and the sharpness of his teeth as they grazed my earlobe. My body trembled.

"Why does it matter if she thinks she can have me?" Stephen murmured. "What difference does it make to you Ana?" he asked softly, moving and raising my chin so that my eyes were level with his. "Hmm? Why does it matter?" I took a deep breath, not sure if I wanted to hear what I knew I was going to say—it was not what I had expected considering out situation. Suddenly, I saw a blur and a shift of movement to my left, down the darkest side of the alley and I pushed myself off of Stephen. "What!" he asked sharply. I turned my head swiftly to the side just in time to see a mass of blond dreadlocks come hurdling toward us through the air. Stephen flung me backward in the opposite direction and jumped lithely into the air colliding with the Demon. The Bonder flung Stephen off to the side, sending him soaring into the air and smashing into the concrete wall hitting his head. I screamed. I watched as Stephen sprung quickly to his feet, unscathed and propelled himself into the Demon, tackling him to the ground. I tried to run over to him, but I couldn't move, Stephen had paralyzed me on the spot. I saw them both shift and roll, changing positions on the ground. Stephen looked stronger and more experienced in ground fighting and I could see that he was easily winning, but then I saw something shiny reflecting off the wall. I followed the source of the light and gasped; the Bonder had a metal stake in his hand. Vampires could rarely be killed, but like Bonders, staking one in the heart would most certainly do the job. I didn't even think, I didn't even take a breath. I pushed hard through Stephen's hold on my body and ran down the alley toward the fight. I screamed a warning at Stephen, but by the time I reached them, the Bonder had Stephen pinned to the ground, the metal bar poised over his chest. Stephen turned to look at me, his eyes wide at my sudden appearance.

"Ana-get-out-of-here!" he gasped, trying to pry one of the Demon's hands from around his throat. I knew from the scene that Stephen's life was now in danger; that the very person who was supposed to be responsible for my death, was now fighting for his life, perhaps to save mine, but that didn't matter. Stephen was not to perish, I couldn't let his life be taken by such violent means and all because the Bonder wanted me—it didn't make any sense. "Ana!" Stephen shouted out a warning to me, clearly having registered my current thought process. I caught his eye and without blinking, I turned and grabbed the Demon by his hair, sending him flying off to the side. I smelled something putrid and salty in the air and I whirled to see blood pouring from Stephen's hand. Somehow the guy had managed to get the sharp end of the stake through Stephen's palm and he was now writhing on the ground screaming. My skin pulsed and throbbed and I could feel my blood start to scald in the veins. The Bonder was walking slowly toward me, the metal shank coated with blood; he was smirking. I heard Stephen scream again and I stepped out to meet what I was sure to be the second major battle for my life.

The Bonder waved his hand in front of him and my body was jolted to the side; spinning, I crashed into the wall next to me, slamming my head against the stone. Nausea enveloped me and I struggled to keep vomit from filling my mouth. My vision was blurry, but I could see that my attacker was no longer coming for me; he wanted to finish the job he'd started with Stephen. I struggled to pull myself to a standing position, but my knees kept buckling. All I could do was watch as the Demon towered over Stephen, raising the stake over his chest. NO! I screamed to myself, no—this couldn't happen. I shoved my weight up against the wall and pushed myself forward, lunging out and grabbing our assailant around the knees with all my force. He teetered and I shoved my shoulder into his waist, throwing him off balance. He toppled to the side and I rolled with him, hooking my legs around and under his thighs. He hoisted his waist up and over, trying to shake me off, but I held strong, grasping his shoulders and slamming the wrist that held the stake, over and over into the pavement. Stephen was yelling, cursing and the smell of blood was getting stronger, more rancid. I was trying to calm my mind enough to feel the heat rising in my blood and allow myself not to resist the swelling in my skin, but I was being tossed around like a rag doll on top of a crazed Demon, my mind was anything but calm. I felt something hit me in the side of the head and I fell off to the side. The bastard punched me; that motherfucker actually punched me! I heard Stephen struggling to get up and I yelled for him to stay down. The Bonder was now on top of him again, plunging the stake repeatedly into the ground as Stephen rolled back and forth. Blood was dripping down from my lip and the side of my face. I spit and stood back up. Stephen was now on his feet but something was wrong, I watched as his body went rigid and his head whipped around looking right at me. His eyes were black flames and his teeth were barred. Christ! He smelled my blood and now he was in attack mode. I couldn't fight them both off; I would never win. Somehow, the lure of my blood added some superhuman strength to Stephen and I watched, awestruck, as he lifted the Demon by his neck and threw him to the ground, crunching the bones in his back. The attacker didn't move. In one breath, Stephen rounded on me and we stood facing each other in the dark alley, massive amounts of my blood now dripping down my face and onto my neck and chest. One more breath, and he had blurred directly in front of me, he was panting and color rose high in his cheeks. I stepped back, not knowing what to do, how to act. Was I going to have to kill him? Before I could even register my own thoughts, he was on top of me, knocking me to the ground. My blouse tore and I felt his fingers dig into my flesh, drawing more blood. I screamed at the pain; was it venom? Was I going to die? I saw a shadow appear behind him and a flash of metal against the dark sky. I screamed and Stephen turned to look just in time to see the metal stake come down towards his neck. In that same instant, the Bonder exploded into flames, sending Stephen and I flying backward, rolling together. I crawled away from him and got to my feet, sprinting down to the other end of the alley. I looked back to see a fire storm of light and flame ignite the sky, then a whoosh of air, a final scream, then nothing.

I collapsed against the side of the building, vomiting blood. My left eye had begun to swell and the pain in my head was debilitating. I had no idea where Stephen was, but I was sure that there would be no way that I could ever fight him off now, not in my current condition. The pain from his scratches made me feel as though I was burning alive from the inside and I screamed out loud falling to the ground no longer able to stand. I felt darkness behind my eyes and knew that someone was standing over me blocking what little light was coming from the moon. I was dead. It was over. I felt my body being lifted up and pressed into someone's chest. I was being carried. My body heaved and I lulled my head to the side and vomited again, my body convulsing.

"Ana!" someone was speaking to me, it sounded like they were crying. "Ana! Christ! I'm so sorry. God Ana! Please hang on! Please. I'll fix you, I promise. Please Ana, please!" I felt wetness over my face as someone's tears filtered onto my skin. My body seized again, the heat and the pain contorting my muscles. I screamed. "Ana! Hold on, it's going to be all right! Just hold on!" I felt a sudden gust of cold air and every organ in my body seemed to come detached. There was blackness swirling around me, but I knew that I was still pressed against someone; someone was still holding me. Another gust of wind and the pressure in my body seemed to quell, the darkness lifted.

"Liam!" someone shouted. "LIAM!" I felt my body shift and another set of arms wrapped around me, lifting me. I couldn't move; I wasn't even sure if I was breathing. I tasted bitter saltiness on my tongue and my stomach heaved again. "Help her Liam. I scratched her! We were attacked, she saved me and I attacked her! Please do something! Please don't let her die!" Someone was shouting as I felt something soft against my back, a bed maybe? I was thankful that my brain seemed to still be processing things; at least I was alive. My shirt was being cut and I could hear the fabric tearing. I felt something press into my flesh and I screamed again.

"The scratches aren't deep Stephen, but you definitely injected some of your venom into her system," an urgent male voice was speaking in an Irish accent. I knew that I recognized it, but I couldn't register the face or the name in my head, all I heard were the words.

"Was it enough? Is it too late for her?" someone asked; their voice desperate.

"I don't know, it's too early to tell." Someone sighed loudly and I felt the weight shift on the bed. " I can give her something for the pain, but that's all I can do right now. We won't know anything until the morning." I heard a door open and I thought I heard a woman crying.

Someone pressed his hands to my face, stroking my hair back and I could smell the ocean, the sea spray and a light musky fragrance. Ahh…it was Stephen; he was here—he had carried me to Liam. Things were making sense now. I heard the door open again and my veins began to throb; they pulsed and quivered deep below the skin, sending raw heat shooting through my limbs. I felt my body twist and writhe.

"Liam!" Stephen cried. "She's in pain, hurry." I felt someone grab my wrist, the one that housed my scar from Nathanial; god I was pathetic. I heard nothing, no one breathed, no one spoke, as they all must have been examining my scar.

"Jesus, what gave her this scar?" someone asked. More silence.

"Her Bonder. Nathanial attacked her last year," Stephen answered solemnly, his voice dark and menacing to my ears. I heard someone sigh, Liam I guessed. I felt fingers graze along the side of my neck, lingering along the two small bite marks I had just below my jaw line. Someone gasped.

"Stephen, did you bite her?" Liam asked, his tone sharp and infuriated. I heard Stephen sigh and another wave of nausea crashed over me. I felt blood and vomit spill out of my mouth. I couldn't move my arms to wipe it away.

"Christ Liam, we don't have time to discuss all of the ridiculous martyrdom rituals that Ana has carried out. Now give her the damn medicine," he commanded. I felt something sharp dig into my arm just above the inner crook in my elbow. I winced as the needle hit the vein. Someone was putting a cool, damp cloth to my mouth, wiping away the blood and vomit. They were whispering to me in Spanish. Carmen. Carmen was here. Something icy was filling my body and I shivered uncontrollably. A blanket was tucked up around my neck as my muscles convulsed. My mind was growing dark and I could no longer hear what anyone was saying. I seized one more time, and then darkness took me.

Chapter Two

Nathanial

The news was just getting to me. I had no details, no confirmations, nothing. My heart was beating so rapidly that I felt my chest begin to ache from the movement. I hadn't ordered the attack, but rumors were already spreading to the contrary; that I had a vendetta against Stephen, that I wanted him dead, that I wanted Ana dead…just having those thoughts in my head made my body heave with such despair, such pain, that I couldn't concentrate, couldn't breathe. I pulled up to the large iron gate, a man approached my vehicle. I showed my identification and unbuttoned my shirt to revel my metal imprint on my chest—the imprint of my mother and of Ana. He nodded and waved me through. I had returned to Peru at the request of my uncle, my mother's brother who was also a Bonder. The Vampires were staging massive attacks on Humans and demons and communities needed extra protection. I wasn't sure what, if any assistance that I could offer, but when Micah had called, it was just after Stephen had found me, drunk at the bar, when he told me that he was going to kill Ana and I wanted the distraction…I felt my heart stop for a moment as the memory filled my mind.

Micah was waiting for me. I brought the jeep to a screeching halt in his drive way and blurred to his side. "What do you know?" I asked, desperate for any information. Micah was the first person to hear about the attack; both he and I were high ranking demons, but Micah was more connected than I was and I had asked him to find out anything about what had happened to Ana…and to Stephen. He put his arm on my shoulder and held the door open to his house.

"Well, we know a bit more than we did yesterday, but it appears that the attacker was a rogue demon, trying to gain a higher rank by taking out a very skilled assassin Vampire and your fire wielder…your Ana." I winced at those last words. She wasn't mine anymore. Micah put his hands on my shoulders and looked deeply into my eyes. I turned away. "From what we can piece together, there was another Bonder in the area watching the whole thing, apparently too terrified to attack. He's told us some interesting details that I'm sure would surprise anyone but you, Nathanial." He smiled at me and motioned for me to take a seat in the chair across from him. "It appears that Ana had to not only contend with the Bonder trying to kill her, but it seems that this Stephen also attacked her." My blood froze.

"What! Stephen attacked Ana? Micah, what are you saying?" I was holding my breath. Micah sighed.

"It seems that the Bonder came prepared to kill a Vampire. He was armed with a metal shank. It appears that he had punched your Ana in the face drawing copious amounts of blood…" He stopped to look at me. My lips were pinched and my eyes were closed. "Stephen went into attack mode upon smelling the blood and I guess he was trying to kill her…funny thing is…" I opened my eyes, waiting for him to continue, "while Ana was being attacked by Stephen, the Bonder came up behind them and just as he was about to stab Stephen, he exploded into flames." Micah snapped his fingers. "Just like that, he burned on the spot." He glanced at me, his eyebrows raised. Of course, I thought. Of course Ana would save Stephen from being

39

killed, that's what she always did; it was everyone else's life over hers, even her own assassin deserved a second chance. Christ, she was unbelievable.

"Is she dead Micah? Did Stephen kill her?" Or worse I thought, did her turn her?

"I don't know the answer to either of those questions. It'll be a few days before we can get any information. Nathanial, I want you to know that if you want to return to Indonesia, if you want to find out for yourself, that I would of course support your decision." Again his eyes found mine and I could see my mother in them and Patric; they all shared the same brilliant shade of turquoise. My body trembled at the very thought of seeing Ana, dead or alive. I tried to breathe.

"No," I said flatly. "No. I'll stay here with you. We'll hear in a few days, then I can decide what to do…" I was whispering.

"As you wish," Micah said, still watching my face. He stood and took my face in his hands. "Your mother believed that no matter how much was lost; no matter how separated we became from ourselves or from the people we love, that we would always find our way back. That in the end, through the sheer force of courage and hope, we could find redemption, healing, salvation—that in the end, through love, our true destiny would be revealed. You will find your way back Nathanial, you will find your way back to your Ana. I believe as your mother did, that Ana is your true destiny." My head snapped up. "She knew, Nathanial. Your mother was a great Seer; she saw your path and your brother's and she saw Ana. You will find your way back my son and

40

you will be redeemed." He bent to kiss me on the forehead before turning and leaving me alone.

Ana

Everything hurt. There wasn't a place on my body that didn't feel as if I'd been slammed into the side of a brick building, which I had. The whole left side of my face felt numb and I was sure that opening my eyes would cause so great a fissure to open up in the skin, that I would start to gush blood. Blood. The word conjured a horrific image in my mind; Stephen on top of me, clawing, biting and scratching my skin, tearing my clothes, his eyes black flames. I shuttered and the movement caused a sharp pain to resonate down to the muscles and through my bones. I groaned and opened my one good eye. It was dark, but I could make out distinct shapes filling the space. A large window with gauzy curtains that filtered the moonlight was to my left and a dresser that looked to be hundreds of years old, possibly hand carved, was set into the wall directly across from my bed. Small side tables held dim lamps that gave the room a warm and gentle glow. When I turned my head to the left, directly next to the window, there was a large cushy chair angled in toward the top bedpost. A figure sat watching me, still and silent, his chin resting in his hands. It was Liam. "Where's Stephen?" I croaked, my throat was dry and my voice sounded like it had been coated with gravel.

"He needed some time. His injury needed tending to by someone more skilled than myself." Liam stood and moved to sit on the edge of my bed, his blue eyes never leaving my face.

"Is he going to be ok?" I asked, trying to sit up. Liam grasped my hands and helped me shift my weight so that I could prop myself against the pillows. My limbs were not cooperating and immediately, I sank back down, lying flat.

"He should be," Liam said, his fingers caressing over my swollen eye. I felt something cool begin to penetrate my skin, numbing the ache in the side of my head. "But you don't need to worry about him, Ana. Stephen is a quick healer, physically." Liam caught my eye and suddenly I felt worried for Stephen's mental health. I didn't want him to feel guilty about what happened; it would be a waste of energy.

"Is he going to be in trouble because he didn't kill me when he had a chance?" I figured that Stephen's coven would have been fine with him finishing what the Bonder tried to start. It would put a stop to all of their debating. Liam sat back, his lips pursed and his brow furrowed.

"No Ana, Stephen will not be punished for the circumstances that befell both of you. He's highly ranked amongst our coven and considered to be respected in most other covens, as much as vampires can offer respect towards one another; his life is in no danger." He was still frowning at me. I looked away, feeling somewhat relieved.

"Well, what's wrong with him then? Why did he have to leave?" I asked, my voice high and tight. Liam pulled me gently up to a sitting position and lifted my top up over my stomach, surveying the scratches from

42

Stephen. He stood from the bed and went to the giant dresser, pulling out various vials and syringes. He stood over me, staring.

"Aren't you the least bit curious about what's happened to *you* Ana?" Liam asked. He was grinning slightly, but there was an edge to his voice. "Since you've woken up, all of your concerns have been for my brother, not a single question about your own wellbeing or about what he did to you..." His voice became quiet and his eyes studied me. I shrugged.

"Does it really matter?" I replied. "I mean, what difference does it make what I do or don't turn into? The way I see it, I haven't had much of a human life since Nathanial left the first time and I'm sure shortly, whatever is left, will be altered—either through my own death or by becoming like you. I stopped caring a while ago." I laid back and stared at the ceiling. "But thanks for taking care of me, I know you don't have to—it's really very kind of you." I closed my eyes as I felt the sharp prick of a needle into my abdomen.

"Mmm, well, if it's any consolation, I don't think my brother managed to get enough of his venom in your system to instigate the Change and you were lacking his blood to complete the transformation at any rate," Liam said, as he wiped gauze over my wounds. Then something occurred to me.

"Hey Liam, may I ask you something?" I tried to sit up. He nodded as he put the needles and vials in the trash. "How come when Patric bit me, how come that didn't instigate the Change. I mean I did have some of his blood in my system, he was using it to keep me alive after...after," I sighed, struggling with the memories, "after Nathanial

43

attacked me." Liam looked at me and cocked his head to the side, his eyes finding the tiny puncture marks on my neck. I saw his eyes flash and grow dark.

"Yes, well, as you know, Patric was only a half-vampire and his Bonder blood diluted whatever venom he did have in his system. Of course, you didn't get away with nothing though, right?" he said smiling, referring to my "ability" with fire, I guessed.

"Are you going to tell me why Stephen is gone?" I asked, not wanting to let him off the hook. He smiled at me again, but his eyes showed a small amount of wonder as he surveyed my face. He crossed his arms and leaned up against the window, his hair flowing over his shoulders to his waist.

"Hmm, yes, that's an interesting question..." he mused. "It appears that my brother seems to be grappling with some very distinct Human emotions at the moment, emotions that are not normally part of our evolution as a species."

"What kind of emotions?" My voice was quiet. Liam sighed and tossed his hair back, the moonlight making the strands sparkle.

"Like guilt," he laughed softly, "and regret, two things that we are not quite accustom to feeling when it comes to revealing our true nature as predators." His eyes were shining.

"But you feel love though, I mean you love Carmen, she's your wife and you love your daughter; love is a human emotion, why couldn't you feel guilt and regret as well—you were all human once." I said defiantly. Liam chuckled and he turned to look out the window.

44

"Hmmm, I'm not sure if 'love' is the most accurate term to describe my relationship with Carmen or with Lucie for that matter. I suppose our mutual companionship is the closest semblance to love that we could manage for vampires. Having Carmen as my wife is really just to make our interactions with Humans more comfortable—it's an accessible label." He turned back to face me, his face smooth and calm.

"Well what about Lucie, she's your daughter right? You must love her." I didn't know why it was so important for me to hear that Liam loved Lucie. Perhaps I just needed to know that some father, somewhere out there actually loved their child, thought that their daughter was the most beautiful, the most precious gift—my father had thought none of those things about me, so maybe I felt that Lucie deserved what I never had—she deserved a father who loved her more than he loved himself. Tears pricked at the corners of my eyes and I quickly tried to wipe them away.

"Ana," Liam said softly, his eyes watching and his mind reading my thoughts. He shook his head slowly. "Christ, Stephen wasn't kidding. You have this innate ability to resonate in the deepest parts of someone, even someone who has had their humanity stripped away, who wouldn't recognize themselves as Human anymore…" He moved toward the door.

"I don't think that your humanity has been stripped away Liam; I would never think that, not about you or Carmen or Stephen, not about Patric or Nathanial or even Alec; I just think it gets lost. It becomes rusted and corrosive and we make the easier choice, the choice that says we don't have to care about anyone or anything— not even about ourselves. But it's always there, waiting to be acknowledged, to be given a different choice, the much harder choice, the choice that Patric made for me and for his brother. In the end, it was Patric's humanity that surfaced; it was the love of his mother and his father mixed with a little boy and a man who just kept making bad choices, kept losing his humanity. He fought for it, he remembered it and he made the hardest decision that anyone could ever be asked to make…." My voice was harsh and strong and I held Liam's gaze. He didn't move, he just stared at me and I stared back, believing every word that I had spoken as the truth, as the irrevocable and unyielding truth. Liam looked at me, his eyes wide. He bowed his head and quietly left my room.

****

I was ready to go home. Two weeks had passed and no sign of Stephen. I was pretty sure that I had disturbed Liam with my little speech about his humanity, so he was effectively avoiding me. Physically, I was feeling much better. My left eye was now almost healed thanks to something that Liam had administered and my scrapes from Stephen were fading into jagged, puckered scars; god, I supposed it was a good thing that I didn't have too much attachment to how my body looked. I was covered in scars and bite marks and I was pretty beaten up. Lucie had taken to visiting me while I rested and we spent time on my bed reading and playing her princess card games. She was the sweetest child that I had ever met. She laughed all the time and she was in constant need to be snuggled down in the bed with me. For a toddler, Lucie was as verbose as most thirty year olds, a trait that I guessed came from having two Vampire parents. She'd ask me questions about what books I liked to read, what make-up colors were my favorite and if I had a boyfriend. Sometimes Carmen would come in, although she was always hesitant in her approach to me. I didn't think for a minute that Carmen would ever attack me, so I tried to engage her as much as possible; I wanted her to feel comfortable. I hadn't talked to a woman in a very long time and I'd forgotten just how nice it was to have that female companionship. I learned that Carmen and Liam owned several boutiques in the city; they were trendy and catered to a somewhat counter-culture of customers. She blushed when I asked her if they were "adult" in nature, but nodded her head "yes". We laughed out loud when I asked to see a catalogue. God, I couldn't remember the last time that I had laughed so much; it felt wonderful, but it also made me sad. I missed this, missed the joking, the new friendships, the talking. We were still laughing and looking through one of her brochures when a soft knock came at the door.

"Am I interrupting?" a shy but steady voice called into the room. It was Stephen. Carmen glanced at me, her eyes wide. I smiled at her and leaned in to give her a kiss on the cheek. I noticed Stephen's body stiffen at my gesture of intimacy, but Carmen kissed me back and turned to walk out of the room stopping just long enough to give Stephen a stare that could shatter glass. He came in slowly and closed the door behind him. He looked like hell. His hair was long and shaggy and his face was waxy and pale. He had more than his normal five o'clock shadow and his clothes looked in dire need of a washing.

He still smelled good though, I thought, smiling to myself. " You look like crap." I said, lying back on my pillows. He smirked at me.

"Hmmm, look who's handing out judgments on physical appearance." He moved to stand near the edge of the bed, his eyes searching for something in my face. Permission maybe? I patted the bed next to me. He took a deep breath and sat down facing me.

"May I go home now?" I asked him, sounding a bit like an aggravated child who'd been kept in the car for too long. It was also interesting to me that I had taken to referring to Stephen's apartment as "home"; I supposed it was the closest thing I had to normal home life over the last six months. He bowed his head, hiding his eyes.

"I don't know if that arrangement is going to work out anymore, Ana." His voice was flat. My heart skipped a beat and I felt something begin to push down on my chest. I ran my fingers through my hair and exhaled.

"Sure, sure. I get it. So, what do you want to do then Stephen? Would you like for me to just sit here and you can just get on with killing me now, or would you like to wait a bit until I get my own place." My voice was sharp and I moved to get up off the bed. He raised his head, pain reflected in the deep oceans of his eyes.

"I'm not going to kill you, Ana. I can't kill you. I won't do it." He put his head in his hands. I wasn't feeling particularly sympathetic at the moment.

"Fine. That's fine. Whatever Stephen. I'll just wait for someone else to finish the job or perhaps I could just do everyone a favor and do it

48

myself!" I shouted at him. "For Christ's sakes, can anyone on this planet make a fucking decision? Kill me, don't kill me—I'm a broken record at this point. Do you know how many times in the last year and half that I've said that?" I was storming around the room and I was sure that Liam and Carmen could hear the argument. Stephen rubbed his face, his eyes pleading.

"What do you want me do Ana? What the hell do you want me do?" He stood and blocked my frenzied pacing.

"I want you to honor the truce we made. I want you to do your part. I came to you and asked you to help me; I offered you the only thing that I have that's worth offering—my life. Either turn me or kill me; those are your two choices!" I screamed at him.

"No," he said quietly. "No, I won't do either, Ana. I won't do it." He was shaking his head furiously back and forth. I heard the door open and turned to see Liam coming into the room, his face anxious.

"Fuck you Stephen! You can go to hell!" I shoved him as hard as I could and he stumbled backward into the wall. "You're a coward! Nathanial, you; you're all cowards!" I was standing over him, screaming and panting, my blood beginning to boil. I felt arms encircle my waist and I turned to see Liam holding me back.

"Ana, you need to calm down," Liam spoke in my ear.

"Get off of me!" I rounded on him. "You know what, this is fine, but I'm not going to wait for someone else to finish job, that's for damn sure! Thanks so much Stephen for all of your help, all of your lobbying for what I want, thanks for breaking your promise to me and thanks for making the decision an easy one for me now." I turned and walked back to stand and face him. "Don't you ever, ever talk to me again, it's done. You won't have to live with any guilt or regret, because you've passed the buck and just like always, it stops with me, with my sacrifices, with my life. Well, that's it now. Nathanial and Alec aren't here to bring me back from the brink of death and this time I will make sure that I end things on my own terms without any interference from people who end up betraying me. Thank you Stephen for allowing me to regain my own accountability." My voice was icy and I could feel my eyes darken. I grabbed my bag and whatever clothes I could find and exited the room, leaving Stephen and Liam watching my back as I slammed the door.

I was headed back to the apartment. I hoped that it was still protected, but really, it didn't matter if it wasn't. I had no plan except to get out of Indonesia. I wanted to go back to Idaho and see Noni, touch her face and kiss her cheeks. I just needed a little more time to be with her, to tell her how much I loved her. If I was really being honest with myself, I also wanted to see Nathanial one more time. I wanted him to know how sorry I was and that I didn't hate him for what happened, for what he'd done and that I wanted him to be happy. Tears were streaming down my face and I was having difficulty seeing the road. I made it downtown and parked in the garage, sprinting out of my jeep. My mind was racing. I needed my passport, my credit cards, some clothes; everything that I could put in my backpack, that's everything that I would take. I had to be quick. I was pretty sure that I could fight someone off enough to at least get to the airport, but more than one, then I was shit out of luck.

50

The elevator seemed to creep along and I found myself jumping up and down, pressing on the button for my floor. I squeezed out the barely opened door and rammed my key into the lock. I heaved the door aside and stumbled into the hallway, skidding on the slippery wood floors. I cursed Stephen for always waxing them and slid down to my bedroom. I grabbed my backpack and began cramming it with jeans and t-shirts, make-up, whatever seemed like I may need for a long trip. I tore open my top drawer where I kept my passport and the one credit card that I used for emergencies. Nothing. The drawer was empty except for a few ponytail holders and lip balm. Frick! Where the hell did I put them? I proceeded to open every drawer in my dresser, spilling out the contents onto the floor. Frick, frick, frick! Maybe I put them in the roll top desk, the one where Stephen kept all of his checks and his passports, he had ten or more of them. I ran down the hallway at full sprint and went straight for the desk in the living room. I began rummaging through his files and all the drawers. Suddenly I noticed that the sounds I was making with the papers and the shutting of the drawers, were not the only sounds in the room. Music was softly playing in the background, music that I loved, my favorite song. Had Stephen left the stereo on? My muscles tensed as I slowly turned around looking for the source of the sound. I wasn't alone.

A dark figure was standing near the window, his face shrouded in shadow. I felt sick, but adrenaline was coursing through my veins and I felt the familiar swell of my skin. I was preparing to fight for my life— yet again. A heartbeat passed and he stepped from the open window, his hair, a dark curtain of satin, billowing in the breeze. His skin glowed with a deep copper sheen and it filled the dark space between us,

51

illuminating his face and his eyes, his beautiful midnight blue eyes. Nathanial.

Without thinking, I took a step forward. I wasn't sure if he was real. His eyes roamed over my face, taking in every bruise, every cut, every scratch. I must have looked horrible to him. "Nathanial? What are you doing here?" I asked softly, my voice shaky. He didn't move toward me, but stood still, his arms crossed on his chest. He looked huge and menacing.

"I had to come to see if you had survived the attack Ana." His voice was flat, emotionless, almost harsh. Of course he had heard, he would know if a Bonder had attacked me; he always knew.

"Oh," I said, my voice barely a whisper. "Oh, well yes, I guess I did." It didn't really matter that I had survived and he knew that, he knew that someone was going to kill me at some point, so my survival really wasn't of much concern. My current condition was just delaying the inevitable. The music filtered around me and I closed my eyes. I was falling apart and I could feel it. Nathanial had turned back to the window, his hair blowing back behind him, sending his fragrance wafting through my pores. The taste of honey coated my tongue and I swallowed greedily knowing that this was probably the last time that I would see him. I choked back my sobs and I leaned against the desk. "I-have-to-go," I said, my words halted. "I don't have much time." Nathanial bent his head, his arms still crossed. I took a deep breath and moved closer to him. "Listen, Nathanial. I just want you to know that…" Tears were coming now, thick and heavy, they ran down my cheeks and down my neck. He turned to look at me. "I just want you to know, that I don't hate you; I could never hate you. We got lost, from ourselves, from each other; we disappeared from what we knew to be real…I'm so sorry for everything, for all of the horrific things that happened, for leaving you." My voice was heavy and I could feel my heart crumbling, shattering into a million pieces. "I love you, I have always loved you and I want you to be happy. You deserve to be happy. I'm sorry that I lost my way, that I forgot who you are to me, that I doubted who you wanted to be for me." I heard thunder in the distance and rain began to fall heavily outside the window. I needed to get through this; I had to get through this. "Nathanial." I moved and touched his shoulder, turning him toward me. "I need to say goodbye, I need to say that I love you, and I need to say that I'm sorry." I reached to stroke his face. I searched his eyes, memorizing their color, their shape, their intensity. I touched his lips, closing my eyes and filling my head with all the memories of when he kissed me. I grasped his hands, placing them to my heart; I breathed, feeling their heat.

"Ana," a voice whispered from behind me. I turned to see that Stephen had moved into the living room, his shadow merging with the darkness now filling the space. Lightening flashed and Nathanial reached to take his hands away from my heart; he turned his back to me. I bowed my head and stepped back from him, broken. I felt cold. I turned toward Stephen, eyeing him.

"Where's my passport?" I asked, my voice steady, but hollow. Stephen looked at Nathanial, then back to me. He moved to the desk and took out an envelope that had my passport and my credit card along with a roll of cash. He held them out for me to take. I didn't meet his eyes. I went to stuff everything in my purse and hoisted my pack around my shoulders. Keeping my back to them, I headed for the door. I paused. "Tell Carmen that I'm sorry and that I love her and Lucie too," I said quietly, sliding back the door. "And tell Liam that in spite of all that's happened, I'm still right—he'll know what you mean." I exhaled and closed the door behind me.

Nathanial

"Where's she going?" Stephen asked, moving to sit on the couch. I turned from the window, numb and cold.

"Idaho," I said, joining him on the couch. "How much time do you think she has?" I rubbed my face, trying to clear my head. Stephen leaned his head on the back of the couch and sighed loudly.

"Depends. Your brethren have her tracked; Liam has ordered our coven not to touch her, but what the other covens do… well, they have their own autonomy. I'm guessing that she'll manage to do it herself before any of us can get to her." He turned to look at me. Blackness was creeping into my bones; I felt sick. "How are things in Peru?" he asked; I glared at him. "That bad eh?" I stood up and paced around the room.

"Your covens have managed to slaughter hundreds of Humans and remove the imprints from several dozen Bonders. They're burning people and demons alive…it's getting out of control." My voice was cold. He smirked at me.

"Well, what do you want me do about it Nathanial?" His tone matched mine.

"I want you to tell Liam that the violence has to stop, that neither side can afford to engage in a war and Humans have no capabilities to support such attacks on their communities. I want you to tell your brother, that the Vampires are not going to get what they want and that negotiation is the only way to give them some semblance of status amongst the rest of us." Stephen leaned forward on the couch, his eyes watching me.

"Nathanial, Liam doesn't negotiate, you know that. My brother is extremely calculated, vigilant and unyielding in his views on Humans, Bonders and the superiority of my species. He'd welcome war, compromise is for the weak; it's a Human fragility that serves no purpose... his words, not mine, although I do share his vision for the regaining of our power and status." He moved from the couch and over to the bar to pour two glasses of scotch.

"He allowed for Ana to stay alive, at least while she healed from your brutality," I scoffed at him. He raised his eyebrows at me and shook his head.

"Do you really want to go down that road Nathanial? Do you want to see just which one of us has inflicted the most damage to Ana?" He sipped his drink, watching me, his jaw tight. I bowed my head. "That's what I thought," Stephen said quietly. "As far as Liam goes, he knows that Ana could be an asset. He decided that she could be turned, that she would work well with us—with me." I could barely hear him. He was whispering. "I said no, that I didn't want that for her, that I rather she die than be like me, like any of us." He waved his hand and took another sip from this glass. "My decision effectively sealed her fate. Liam listens to me, he respects me, he's my brother and most of the time he does what I ask, but I can't ask him to compromise on his beliefs, on what he feels and knows our species deserves, Nathanial. I won't do it." I finished my drink in one swallow.

"So that's it? Liam is calling for all out war and you aren't going to do anything to stop it?" I was incredulous.

"War is already here. I couldn't stop it if I wanted to—which I don't." He bent his head.

"And what about Ana, do you wish to see her die Stephen, do you wish to see her tortured, brutalized at the hands of your kind or by my brethren? Are you so past any shred of humanity that you have not a single thought about what's coming for her? Neither side is going to make it a pretty scenario Stephen. If we're at war, then everyone, everyone is fair game and violence is just one tactic—one of many. Do you think Ana will be spared what your brother is now proposing? Do you think that the Vampires will make it quick and painless? You better hope to whatever god you pray to Stephen, that Ana kills herself first, that she dies without having to endure the hell that she is destined to experience." I was spitting at him, my anger and desperation brimming over. I heard something shatter. Stephen's fist was holding thick, broken pieces of his glass, his knuckles bleeding.

"Don't talk to me about what I want for Ana, Nathanial! You're such a fucking hypocrite. You gave strangers a better chance at life than your own fiancé; you chose to offer your blood to make Humans,

Humans who aren't even as special as Ana, more like you; you gave them strength and power and life beyond what they deserve. You have handed down a death sentence to Ana twice Nathanial. You are no less guilty for what happens to her now than I am!" Stephen's voice had turned deadly and I saw that his eyes were stormy. My heart cracked upon hearing his words; he was right and he knew it. Even with the blood that I'd given Ana when we were together, when Patric had made me complete the exchange; it wasn't nearly enough to give her the benefits that I had allowed the other women to experience—it wasn't enough. I felt my stomach heave.

"There's nothing either of us can do now, not about the war, not about Ana; things are already set in motion, it's a perfect storm. I guess we'll just have to see who's left standing when that storm clears," Stephen said, as he looked at me, our eyes meeting. I nodded once and shimmered out into the night.

Chapter Three

Ana

It took me over a week and many late nights over tea, to catch Noni up on everything that had been happening in my life; like always, she was contemplative, non judgmental and very, very kind. When I told her that I was unsure just how much time I had left, that I hadn't decided what to do about ending things myself just yet, she held my face in her hands saying; *"My beautiful bambina, my heart song; in the end, he will come, he will make the right choice and your life shall be spared. This I know, this I have seen."* I wasn't sure whom exactly that Noni thought would come and be able to spare my life. No one I knew was in any position to make that decision anymore. I was on my own.

Noni had rebuilt the Wolf Sanctuary and I spent everyday working with her, feeding, running and caring for the wolves. I had to leave Kuckuc and Piyip behind; there wasn't enough time for me to round them up from Rene and prepare them for a flight back to the U.S. I knew she would take good care of them. She would love them and they would protect her and love her. I was severing ties in a way. Being able to say goodbye to Nathanial, to see his face and touch him again, that was the finality that I needed. I felt guilty for the way I left things with Stephen. I hadn't meant to be so cruel, or so angry. Like so many times in my life, my emotions were coming from a deep sense of anger and disappointment that I felt within myself. I wasn't angry with Stephen; I cared a great deal for him, more than I would allow myself to acknowledge, but that didn't matter anymore—nothing did.

Noni was gone a lot; she was a community elder and mediator between the local Bonder populations and the Nez Perce Indian Tribe. The chaos that seemed to be engulfing the globe; the violence between the Vampires, the Bonders and the humans, had yet to make an impact here in Idaho, but Noni felt that it was just a matter of time— she wanted to be prepared. As the days turned into weeks and the weeks into months, I began to settle into a routine. My guard was constantly up, but for the time being Noni kept my body extremely busy and my mind occupied with all the work at the Sanctuary. I was exhausted and most nights I would fall into bed, still fully clothed and sleep the entire night, something that I have never done in my life. Some evenings, when my work was finished and Noni had returned from her council meetings, she would ask me to walk with her into the mountains. The Sawtooth Range was a very spiritual place for her and I could see both the physical and emotional transformation happen in her eyes the moment we began our ascent to her favorite overlook. This particular evening we were sitting in a grassy field that sat in the shadow of the mountain range. Noni was meditating and I was staring at the sunset, thinking of Nathanial, Stephen, Kai, Alec and Patric. Suddenly, I heard Noni gasp, breaking her trance and mine. I turned to look at her, but immediately my instincts told me to look around, to look into the trees, to look behind us and to our sides. I whipped my head in every direction, searching and scanning. Nothing. We were alone. I moved to sit next to her and noticed that her eyes were closed and she was rocking slowly back and forth, her breath coming in short, shallow movements. I grasped her hands gently, not wanting to disturb her vision, but needing to touch her. She opened her eyes and they found my face. I smiled. "Are you ok Noni? Did you see something?" I asked, quietly, respectfully. She looked at me, seeing and not seeing, as I could tell that she was still experiencing the effects from her vision.

"You need to go back my precious bambina. You must return. You have not completed the journey; you have not helped all those that you can. There is still someone left to save—they too need to remember who they are..." Her voice was low and quiet and chills broke out on my skin.

"Who Noni? Who needs to be saved? I don't understand. I don't want to go back." The tenor of my voice was raised and I could feel my chest tighten. Noni stood, her eyes clear and her voice steady and strong. The vision was over and I knew that I no longer had a choice in the matter; I was going to have to go back to Indonesia. Noni didn't allow for one to not follow her visions; it was a matter of respect to do what a Seer asked of you and I was no exception. I was grief-stricken and I had no plan, no idea of just what the hell I was supposed to do in Indonesia; see Stephen? See Nathanial? I was clueless.

****

Back in Indonesia, as I rode in the cab, I watched the rain streak down the windows. I heard Noni's last words to me as she left me at the airport. "*You will do what you know to be right, my beautiful, courageous child, my bambina. You will honor who you are and through your love, the path back will be revealed. You will find the way again and when it is time, you will know who you are truly meant to be*".

I wiped the tears from my cheeks and stifled the sobs that were now threatening to overwhelm me. I pulled my pack from the seat and exited the cab. I stood in the pouring rain in front of the warehouse and looked up to see a dim light shining down from the fourth story. I sighed heavily and stepped out of the rain and back into what I was now sure was going to be my final end.

I heard music playing; a quiet strumming of guitar filtered out from behind the heavy door. Stephen was playing. I recognized the song that we loved, the one that was playing at the concert when we decided to leave early. I sighed again and took out my key, sliding it into the lock and hearing the click. I listened for the guitar to stop, but he continued to play. I pushed the door aside and stepped into the familiar hallway. It was dark, except for a few candles that were lit along the bar and on the roll top desk. I walked slowly into the living room and stood, listening to Stephen as he played and sang through the song. His voice was quiet but strong and passionate. I felt my chest relax and I took a breath, tasting his fragrance; sea and musk, sand and air; they swirled around, nourishing me and giving me courage. Music continued to play in the background, but Stephen had stopped playing, his eyes on me. He didn't look surprised, but instead his face registered such a deep sadness that it made my gut wrench. Immediately he was at my side, his hands cupping my face. His eyes were so startling, so blue and intense, that I had to look away. He grasped my face harder, not letting me turn my head.

"Ana. What are you doing here? Why have you come back?" His voice was rough and deep and he was still gripping my face. His questions were good ones. I had no idea why I was back in this stupid apartment. What was I going to tell him, that Noni had a vision, that she's an old

Seer and a Healer and when she has a vision, you don't question it, you just do what she says? That sounded absurd, even to me and I grew up with her. His eyes registered my thoughts and he pushed himself away from me and started to pace around the room. "You shouldn't be here. It's not safe anymore; this place is not safe." He ran his fingers through his hair and using the break in his dialogue, I took a quick survey of the apartment. Something was off. Scanning the room, I could see dust coating the usually shiny hardwood surface. Papers and maps were scattered all over the floor and on the coffee table. There was a musty odor, as if the place had been closed up for many months—perhaps the several that I had been gone? Even more disturbing was the lack of art on the walls. There was nothing; no canvases, no photographs, no paint—everything was gone. My stomach turned.

"Stephen, what's happened here? Where are all of your paintings? Why is the place such a mess?" I almost laughed at my tone. I sounded like a mother scolding a child for not keeping their room clean. Stephen was at the window, his hands on his hips and his back to me.

"Things are bad Ana. War has started and you are not safe; you're a Human and you are not safe." He was shaking his head. I looked around the room again, a disturbing feeling creeping into my soul. "If Liam knows you're here, if Christopher or Andres; if they find out you've returned…" His voice stopped short. I didn't understand what Liam had to do with anything and I didn't know that Christopher and Andres were part of Stephen's coven. I supposed that explained why they were all together down in West Papua when I first met them. Stephen turned to face me, his eyes now dark. "Ana, Liam is one of the highest ranking vampires there is; Devon, Patric, Alec—me, we're nothing compared to what Liam can do, the power that he has; it makes the rest of us look like inexperienced teenagers." I felt my eyes grow wide. "Any Human, *any* Human not having been proven to be working with us," he looked at my face, his eyes burning and fierce, "if they are found in the presence of a vampire, they are to be killed and the Bonders have the same rule. They have been ordered to execute any person that is even seen with a vampire. Your ex is responsible for that set up," he scoffed at me. "They trust no one, and neither do we. Liam has offered no exceptions, no compromises and no Human life is to be spared." His voice cracked and I felt myself take a step backward. I was in disbelief. Nathanial was always so gentle, so compassionate towards humans. I had always felt that he respected human life and now he was ordering people to be murdered? What happened to him? "Nothing happened to him Ana. Nathanial is a warrior by birthright; he's a Demon and he is not Human. He, just like Liam and myself, will fight for their very survival, even if that means killing a population that we've been a part of for our entire existence, even if that means killing a member of that same population that we love and we care about; thus are the rules of war Ana." He chuckled darkly and moved a step closer to me. I suppose that I should have been surprised by all of this information, but after Alec, after Devon, nothing seemed quite so shocking anymore. Stephen laughed again, taking another step toward me. "No, no I guess it wouldn't, not after all you've been through Ana." I moved back, something met my body with resistance—a wall.

We stood facing each other, just like we'd done that night in the alley, just before he'd attacked me. My life was full of so many redundancies that it was almost comical. I didn't want to fight with

Stephen, I didn't want to have to harm him, but I could feel my skin tighten and swell and the heat in my blood rise to the surface. I tried to take a deep breath, tried to calm my fear and my instinct to attack first. Stephen's face was smooth and calm, too calm and he stepped closer to me, forcing my back to press even harder against the wall. His eyes were black and fire burned in their depths. There were only inches between us now. I heard our song begin to play again, soft and low, it swam through my ears and made my heart pound. I bowed my head, my hair falling over my face, shielding my eyes. I felt him sweep the locks back, gently letting them fall down my shoulders and over my back. He lifted my chin to raise my face to his. His eyes pulsed in their hunger and their bloodlust. It could have been worse. A more violent Vampire or Demon, one who wanted to see me suffer, one who wanted to brutalize me, could have cornered me. Stephen closed his eyes hearing my thoughts. His fingers reached to stroke my face and down my throat; he stopped to feel the throbbing of my pulse and I felt the blood rush into my cheeks, the heat from his touch spreading through my skin and into my bones. I met his eyes. I didn't know what in the world possessed me, but I leaned in toward his face, hesitantly, slowly. I brought my lips close to his, not touching, but lingering in the space between our mouths. His eyes burned and widened. Not taking my gaze from his, I moved slowly, pressing my mouth gently to his. He didn't move, he didn't breathe, and so I did both for him. I softly pulled his waist to mine and let my breath penetrate between his lips. His body trembled in my arms, but he didn't pull away. Suddenly, I felt a gust of cold air and the room was jerked away from me, from us. My body contracted and my heart and brain felt as though they were being squeezed and torn to shreds. I tried to gasp, but there was no air in my flattened lungs. Someone was holding me tightly. Another gust of air and my body heaved forward, shoving itself through space. I felt hands around my waist catching me as I began to tumble forward onto a floor. I opened my eyes and realized that we were no longer in Stephen's apartment; we were in a house, a house that I knew.

"Where have you been...?" a steady voice broke through the haze that was fogging my mind, but the voice quickly broke off in mid sentence. It was coming from behind us. I felt Stephen turn and push me behind him. I stepped out from behind his back, not wanting him to hide me, and I saw Liam, with Christopher and Andres flanking his sides; they were smirking. "Ana," Liam said quietly as he stepped forward, his eyes on his brother. I felt Stephen's arms reach out and push me back from Liam's advancement. "Christ Stephen. I'm not going to hurt her," Liam said, clearly offended by his brother's reaction. I saw Stephen's body relax, but just barely. His arms were still tensed and his jaw was locked. Liam sighed and looked back behind him. "Christopher, Andres; will you please go and find Carmen, tell her that I need her and Lucie to return immediately." Christopher nodded, but Andres was staring at me, his gaze was leering and his eyes black. I saw a wry smile begin to spread across his face; he licked his lips. A low snarl erupted from Stephen's chest and I saw him begin to crouch. Liam shot Andres a sharp look and immediately, he turned away from me and shimmered out of the room. I saw Liam and Stephen exchange glances and I thought I saw Liam nod once, and then he turned to me. "Ana, I'm sorry, but due to current circumstances, I can't let you leave now. I know that Stephen has explained what our position is as far as Humans are concerned, but considering your unique relationship with myself and my brother...well, it's better if we can keep you with us for the time being.

65

I can assure your safety within my coven." He gave me a subtle smile. "Carmen has returned and I will leave her to make sure that you have everything that you need. We'll make some decisions about what to do with you later, but right now, I need to speak with my brother privately." He looked past me and I turned to see Carmen holding Lucie, standing in the doorway. Lucie clapped and I heard her laugh my name out loud. I nodded at Liam and thanked him silently, knowing that he would hear. I turned to look at Stephen, his eyes were clear, ocean blue and he lifted his finger to trace the shape of my lips, looking astounded and slightly confused. I heard Liam clear his throat and I stepped back from his touch, crossed the room to Carmen and Lucie and left the two brothers alone.

****

The city was burning. Every day for weeks, there were new explosions as the Bonders launched their attacks on any Vampire strong holds. Two large covens had been completely eviscerated and the fires from their deaths caused the entire city to be plunged into blackness. I could sense how frightened Carmen had become. She spent more and more time pacing through the house waiting for any sign from Liam or from Stephen. They were both gone, mostly out fighting or trying to rally others to fight and we spent hours together, playing with Lucie, both of us trying not to let the other see how worried we were. I *was* worried about Stephen, more so than I was about what was going to happen to me when this was all over. I wanted him to be protected, to be safe. I was pondering this sudden wave of anxiety over his wellbeing, when I heard my door crack open, letting the dim light from the hallway spread into the room. Carmen was standing in the doorway, Lucie curled in her arms.

"May we come in?" she asked quietly.

"Of course, please," I said, motioning for her to come and sit on the bed. She scooted herself next to me lying Lucie between us, sleeping. Resting her head back against the pillows, she sighed and closed her eyes.

"You have such a wonderful energy, Ana. When you're around, I feel as though everything I've done in my existence is valued, even my very darkest mistakes."

"Carmen, I do value you." I turned to look at her face. "When I think about what happened to you, before…before your Change; it makes my heart hurt." Carmen had been raped brutality by the Vampire who bit her and I thought in some ways that was why I felt such a connection to her; we had both been violated, traumatized and left feeling worthless and demeaned. I sighed. "I know, in some ways, what you must have been feeling, but I would never be so arrogant as to say that I understand your experience, your journey. I do think that you are a courageous person. I see that you truly love Liam and Lucie—no matter what Liam believes about your species' capacity for love, I see it in your eyes. It takes great courage to love, Carmen, especially coming from everything that you have had to endure." Her eyes were on me, wide and bright. "Your daughter will know to never fear love because of you." I turned to see tears falling gently down her cheeks.

67

She was sobbing and she put her head on my shoulder. I kissed the top of her head and closed my eyes. Lucie stirred, murmuring in her sleep. I looked at the little girl, at her curly hair and pink lips. I had made the decision when I was a teenager, to never be a mother; I was way too damaged at that point to even consider trying to raise and love another human being. By the time I was engaged the first time, the damage was somewhat repaired, but I was nowhere near being fixed. I thought it would be selfish of me to bring a child into the world when I had too many wounds that still were not healed. Now of course, those old wounds were manageable, but new, deeper ones had taken their place—I was damaged in a different way, a more complete way; there was no coming back from that kind of disrepair. Carmen lifted her head and looked at me, her eyes fierce.

"That's not true Ana. You believe that all of us, all of us, with our faults and selfish behavior—you believe that we deserve happiness, that we can be redeemed, that we have the capacity to love and to be loved. Why do you not reserve that belief for yourself? Why do you fear that you are too broken, too damaged to find your own redemption, or to allow someone else to carry you or catch you when you fall? Is your life worth so little in your eyes, that you've lost your own capacity to love who you are, to love this beautiful, beautiful soul; a soul that I know has affected all of us, even Liam and especially Stephen, a soul that allowed someone as jaded and too far gone as Patric, to remember himself in the end—to fight for you and his brother?" Her voice was shaking. She looked at Lucie and stroked her hair. A thought occurred to me as I watched her touch her daughter.

"Carmen? Did you give birth to Lucie?" I had no idea if Vampires could actually conceive; I didn't know that much about the intimate behaviors of the species. She smiled, but sadness spread across her face.

"No. We found Lucie about three years ago in my village in Colombia." She stopped to look at me, her face hesitant.

"What do you mean, you 'found' her?" I asked warily. Carmen sighed.

"She'd been bitten, attacked, but they were sloppy and didn't inject enough venom for her to Change completely; they didn't give her their blood. Liam and I debated about whether to just make the Change fully, but when I looked at her, when I saw her eyes, I knew that I would want for her to have a life, to grow up, to wear dresses and go out with her girlfriends, maybe even go to college, not to be stuck as an infant for eternity. I wanted her to complete the life of mine that was cut short—we gave her enough of each of our blood and venom to save her life; we wanted her to have the blood of two beings who cared for her and Liam was able to inject a bit of venom to heal some of her more deadly wounds. We weren't actually sure if she would even survive what we'd done, but when she awoke, we knew immediately that we'd made the right decision; it's different with everybody. People respond in different ways from being bitten, to venom and blood—it can be a bit of a crap shoot on how they will turn out." She caressed Lucie's cheek. God, who on earth would ever, ever make a child suffer like that—the very thought of someone choosing to bite a little girl, a baby, it made my stomach turn. Carmen sighed again. "I know Ana, but most vampires are uncivilized and don't decipher between a child and an adult—blood is blood," she said quietly. I shuddered.

"So, Lucie is half…she's half a Vampire?" I wasn't sure if that was the respectful title to give to this little girl, but I didn't know another term. Carmen laughed softly and tousled my hair.

"Yes, she's half and you are always respectful Ana. She'll have a very, very long life, longer than most Humans and I think she'll have some enhanced abilities—maybe fire wielding." She smiled at me and tossed her head back to laugh. I smirked at her. "But more importantly, she'll get to grow up, hopefully fall in love many, many times, even have her heart broken so that it becomes stronger and more resilient, so she learns what a gift she is; maybe she'll be like you." Carmen looked at me and held my face in her hands. "Maybe she'll be just like you, Ana." Poor kid, I thought. Carmen laughed again and scooped Lucie gently off the bed. "You need to sleep now. Maybe we'll hear from the men tomorrow." She stood in the doorway and blew me a kiss goodnight. For the first time since I'd come back to this place, this place with so many memories, with so much pain and love, I finally slept through the night.

Another week passed before we heard any news from Liam and Stephen. It was Andres who came back through the house to report that the coven had managed to over take some crucial land that the Bonders had inhabited; they left no one alive. I cringed upon hearing the news. I wasn't one to enjoy violence and hearing the ecstatic emotion coming from Andres at the mention of slaughtering hundreds of Bonders and humans; it made my stomach turn. Plus, I didn't like Andres and I didn't like the way he was constantly staring at me, sizing me up and looking me over. He was tall and muscular with thick black hair and dark olive skin. He was from Portugal and his accent made him seem that much more exotic and menacing. I also noticed that Carmen always seemed to stand a bit taller when he came into the room. She was small, but extremely powerful and a lethal killer if she had to be. Apparently, Liam had trained her for combat and she was a natural. I wouldn't want to ever go up against her in the ring.

I took Lucie from Carmen on this particular evening when Andres arrived, excusing myself and heading into the living room. I put Lucie up on the couch next to me and she handed me her favorite book; we'd read it at least fifty times since I'd gotten here, but the stories about princesses and fancy crowns always seemed to captivate her. We made it halfway through when she started snoring and I carried her upstairs to her room, placing her gently in her bed and leaving the door cracked. I backed into the hallway and stumbled right into the arms of Andres. He had been standing in the hallway, watching me. I wondered where Carmen was.

"Her services were needed elsewhere for the moment. She asked me to tell you that she should be back before the morning, but if you could look after Lucie for a while," he said softly, his eyes roaming over my face and to the bite marks in my neck. I saw his eyes flash and something in my gut told me that I was not in a good situation. He laughed softly. "You don't trust me?" he asked, raising his eyebrows and grinning.

"Not really," I said forcefully, moving past him and walking down the stairs, of course he followed.

"You trust Stephen and he almost killed you—twice," he mused. I went to the refrigerator and grabbed a ginger ale. I didn't have the energy to engage in a philosophical debate about the merits of trust this evening.

"I don't really trust anyone anymore Andres, Stephen included, but I don't actually have a choice at the moment," I said, taking a sip from my drink, meeting his gaze.

"Hmmm, no I guess you don't. I'm sure you are wondering what Liam has decided to do with you as far as your life is concerned, I mean." He smiled at me and pursed his lips. Christ, why must people always try to bait me? He laughed, reading my thoughts. "I'm not baiting you Ana, I'm just saying, if it were me, I'd want to know." He moved a fraction of an inch closer to me. The motion was so subtle that I wasn't actually sure if he had even stepped forward. He raised his head so that his eyes were looking down upon my face. I sighed.

"What do you want Andres? Is there something that I can do for you?" I asked, my tone icy.

"Actually, now that you ask, I am curious about something." My eyes narrowed and I stepped to the side, not so subtly.

"What?" I replied, feeling my heart begin to race.

"Well, it's just that I was privileged enough to catch a glimpse of your...your tryst with Patric before his unfortunate demise and I couldn't help but be completely intrigued by his experience. His memories were so detailed, so rich, that it felt as if I too had tasted your blood. Of course, I didn't get such an experience, but the effects that your nourishment had on Patric… well it made him the envy of most of the coven—even Nathanial." Adrenaline surged in my veins and I felt a dark wash begin to color my eyes. Andres chuckled. " I see you still have an attachment to the Bonder." He waved his hand nonchalantly. "As soon as you can get over those ridiculous Human contrivances, you'll be so much better off Ana." He moved again, this time to the side, lining his body up with mine. Again, arguing with him just seemed to be a waste of energy, so I just shrugged and turned to walk into the living room. Immediately I felt him wrap his hands around my waist, pulling me back so forcefully against him, that I lost my footing. He took one arm and looped it around my neck, holding me in a death grip. I struggled to breathe, but my windpipe was constricted. I felt him breathing in my ear.

"I really don't think that Patric should be the only one to benefit from your exceptional blood Ana—it just doesn't seem fair that someone so weak, someone who had no idea how to use such a gift, should be the one to experience the power, the energy." His tongue traced around my ear and over the bite marks, making them burn. I tried to flip him off of me, but he was unbelievably strong and instead he flung me onto the kitchen floor. He struck the side of my head, leveling me and instantaneously, he was on top of me. I heaved my hips and tried to twist my body enough to throw him off balance, put he was unmovable, his bloodlust giving him power beyond anything that I could fight. He ripped off my shirt and slashed through my jeans, exposing my groin. He was snarling and growling and I felt him tear the fabric on my legs clean off. He had both my arms pinned with one of his hands and he was using the other one to undo the belt on his pants, pulling them down past his waist. I felt his hand slip from around my wrist and I jerked away, punching him across the jaw, splitting his lip and sending a cascade of black blood spraying onto my face. He snarled and yanked my hair, snapping my neck back. I couldn't concentrate enough to conjure any more retaliation, but I could feel the throbbing and swelling of my skin, the sign that my anger and my survival mode was ready to ignite. He brought his face down on my neck and I felt his fangs skim the flesh under my jaw. His hips were pressing so hard against me that my tailbone began to throb. I felt his hand move my underwear aside, as his fingers pressed down on the bite marks in my groin. He started to thrust as he moved himself closer to me. A surge of energy pulsed through my limbs and I screamed and shoved him off, sending him soaring backward, crashing through the kitchen door and landing on the coffee table, shattering the wood and glass. I struggled to get up, my head was dizzy from his hit, but I managed to sprint through the living room to the front door. He was there, blocking my way. My mind cleared and I locked eyes with him as he lunged for me, he knocked me to the ground, but I flipped him over my head and his back slammed down onto the floor, sending fissures through the wood. I thought I felt a gust of cold air, but I didn't have time to assess. While Andres was on the floor, I sent a circle of flames around his body, keeping him locked down. I wanted Liam to see what had happened; I wanted him to know. I heard Andres snarl and try to spring from the circle, but I sent the flames shooting into his face—I wanted him to die. He yelled and fell back down to the ground. Suddenly someone grabbed me from behind, lifting me clear up in the air before I could deliver a final blow. I was being taken upstairs, away from the fire, away from Andres. I struggled to see who it was; my mind was telling me to fight.

"Ana, it's ok, it's ok," a strong, but distinctly feminine voice was whispering in my ear. Carmen. I was panting and gasping. "It's ok, you're ok; you're safe Ana. It's over, it's ok." Her voice was firm, but there was an undercurrent of ferocious anger. She carried me effortlessly to my room and placed me on the bed, shutting the door behind us. "Liam is on his way." I heard Andres still snarling downstairs and I began to shake. Carmen put her arms around me and began rocking me back and forth like a small child. Lucie, I thought— was she all right? Where was she? "She's fine Ana, no one will hurt her, I promise." Carmen's voice still sounded black. I hoped she wasn't upset with me; I ruined her house. I heard her chuckle, still rocking me back and forth. Suddenly she sprung from the bed and ran to the door. "Liam is here, I'll be right back Ana." She sprinted into the hallway and I heard her descend the stairs. I moved back against the pillows and pulled the quilt up over my chest. I could feel the blood from Andres' lip beginning to dry. It stung and burned on my skin. Christ, I thought. That was the last time that I ever listen to any vision of Noni's. Foolish woman. I didn't know how long I laid there, the convulsions giving way to sheer exhaustion. I must have dozed off, because when I came to, there was a figure sitting on the edge of my bed. I jerked my head off the pillow and spun out onto the floor, my hands guarded—ready to fight.

"Ana. It's ok, it's me." Stephen. Stephen had come. I reached to turn on the little bedside lamp; it's light illuminating his face in a soft amber glow. He gasped as his eyes surveyed my torn clothes and the blood caked and dried on my face. I tried to pull the shredded garments around my body, but there was nothing left to hold on to—how ironic, I thought bitterly and sank back down on the bed. Stephen stood and went quietly to the bathroom. I heard water run and a cabinet being opened and closed. He came back holding a washcloth and some antiseptic. He sat close to me, his eyes meeting mine. I started to shake. He reached out his hand and smoothed back my hair. "You're ok, Ana. I'm not going to hurt you." He took the damp cloth and began gently to wipe the blood from my face. I closed my eyes, letting his tender caresses quell the shock in my body. He didn't speak, but I watched his eyes carefully. They never left my face. I shivered and his gaze reluctantly ran over my torn clothes. I saw him shudder, but he composed himself. "May I take a look or would you rather me get Carmen?" he asked quietly, his voice even, but there was ferocity to it that mirrored Carmen's and it sent chills down my back. I shook my head "no" and let the quilt fall off to the side revealing my torn jeans and the massive blood bruises now forming around my inner thighs and my groin. He took a sharp breath in, holding it. Gently, softly, he moved his hands over my wounds. My throat was swollen and I tried to swallow, but I ended up choking. His head jerked up and I saw his eyes widen as he saw where Andres has tried to crush my windpipe.

"Jesus," he said, his voice low and dark. He stood and went to open the door. "Liam!" Stephen called down the hallway. I didn't hear anything and I wondered what had happened to Andres. Had they killed him? Liam appeared in the doorway and suddenly I felt terrified. I didn't know whom to trust anymore; perhaps I should just stop fighting back and let someone kill me the next time. Before I could even finish my thought, Stephen had whipped his head around, his eyes flashing. "Don't you ever think that Ana, not ever. Do you hear me! Not ever!" His voice sounded unhinged and I sighed deeply, shaking my head. He turned back to Liam. "Do you see what he did to her, he was going to rape her Liam; he almost crushed her throat, the bruises to her groin are massive… he was going to rape her then kill her!" I wished he would shut up; I didn't like hearing what had almost happened, it made it too real and too close. I heard him sigh and move aside as Liam stepped into the room.

"Ana, I need to have a look at you. Do you mind?" Liam was studying my face.

"No," I said quietly. Carmen suddenly appeared at my side and she put her arm around my shoulders. I trusted Carmen; yes of course I could trust Carmen. Her eyes found mine and she nodded to me, our silent bond understood. Liam placed his hand on all of my bruises, but when he moved toward my hips, I pulled away from him, shaking. He looked at Carmen and she held me tighter, pressing her lips into my hair as she began to sing softly. Liam gently pushed back the torn fabric around my groin and touched his hands softly to the battered and swollen skin. I couldn't stop shaking, but I didn't pull away. I felt deep warmth begin to rush over my skin then a numbing sensation flooded into my veins. I felt tired and my body was weak. Liam looked at my face, his expression smooth.

"Ana, did Andres scratch you or bite you? I can't see anything, but your bruises are quite extensive and I want to make sure that I didn't miss anything." He sounded so clinical, so practical.

"I punched him before he could bite me," I said quietly. Liam chuckled, but I could see another expression in his eyes, wonderment, maybe?

"Of course you did," he said, patting my leg and standing up. "I think you will be quite sore, but otherwise you were lucky. Andres is a skilled fighter and most of our coven, with the exception of my reckless brother, refuse to spar with him." He shook his head and smiled at me. "I'm very sorry for this Ana; Andres will not be anywhere near you in the future. I promise you that." They didn't kill him? How stupid were these people? I should have finished him when I had the chance. "Andres is a valued asset to our coven Ana, and while his behavior was certainly less than civil, we need his particular skill set." I glared at Liam, *less than civil*? Was he serious?

"Tell me something Liam," my voice was cold, "would you feel the same way if Andres had tried to rape your daughter? Would you see his skill set as valuable then?" I heard Carmen gasp and Liam's eyes flashed in anger, but I could also see something deeper move across his face; I saw pain and fear. Stephen moved in front of his brother.

"I think that's enough for tonight," Stephen said quietly. Liam and I stared at each other and I let him see the one memory that I had never let anyone know. I showed him a little girl with long hair tied into two braids. I showed him that little girl on her back and a teenage boy hovering over her, looking possessed. I showed him what was taken from me, what I should have been protected from by my father, by my mother and I showed him just how alone that little girl was, alone with a monster that would never, ever leave her memory. I heard Carmen begin to cry and Stephen bowed his head, but Liam stared at me, our gazes unyielding. He nodded his head and turned to walk out of the room.

Chapter Four

Nathanial

I had ordered five Humans to be executed for treachery; five today, ten yesterday...I felt numb. The Humans had sworn an oath to work with us, to fight alongside us and in return, we promised that we would protect them. They were a disgrace. So many of them were falling victim to the Vampires' promises of an eternal life, of power...of status; Humans were cowards and they allowed for fear to rule their lives. We couldn't afford to have such cancers invade our mission; the malignancies of Human fragility would not be tolerated. I was staring into the fire in my hut, trying not to think about her, trying not to wonder if she was still alive; I was trying to forget her.

"Nathanial," a voice came from behind me. I watched as my uncle came quietly into the room, his face smooth and the turquoise eyes he shared with my mother, clear and bright. "How are you feeling?" he asked, sitting next to me. I shook my head and turned back to the fire. "I know. What's happening here, what you are being asked to do, it's not civil and it's not humane, but what other choice do we have?" He sounded frustrated and sad. At his mention of the word "choice", a picture of Ana filled my mind; she was always hoping that people would make different choices, and she was always being disappointed. I didn't want to think about how she would view me now; after everything I had done, everything that I was doing, the lives that I was choosing to destroy—even my own, she would be disgusted. "Nathanial, there was another attack, a very severe attack in

Indonesia." Micah put his hand on my shoulder and I turned to face him.

"Who was attacked?" I asked. We had several hundred Bonders in Indonesia and so far, we were managing to maintain some land and several strong holds within a few of the indigenous communities. It was becoming a fairly even fight. Micah sighed.

"On Ana, Nathanial. There was a very brutal attack on Ana." I stood up, not understanding.

"What the hell is she doing back in Indonesia?" I said, my voice rough. "She was supposed to be in Idaho; what the hell is she doing?" Micah stood and moved to pour us a drink.

"I don't know the details of her return; I only know that a Vampire you know well, attacked her, and that's being diplomatic." He handed me a glass. The only face that I could conjure was Stephen's, but it just seemed unlikely—he wouldn't harm her again. "Not Stephen, although I think he was primed to kill her directly upon her return. However, Liam interrupted what I am sure was to be her demise... it was Andres who attacked her Nathanial. You know him, yes?" Micah raised his eyebrows. Andres? Of course he would attack her; he was violent, never listened to orders and lived only by his instincts. I knew how powerful a fighter he was. I knew who trained him, a Vampire so vicious, so hell-bent on violence and one that I knew I would have to fight eventually; Carlo, his coven was behind all the current mayhem in Peru. This Vampire had created armies of fighters like Andres. Ana couldn't survive; my heart began to sink. There would be no way that

Ana could ever fight him off, not even with her abilities—he was that strong and that skilled. I looked at my uncle.

"What happened Micah?" I spoke forcefully. "Did he kill her? Is she dead?" I heard my voice crack. That was the second time I had to ask that question and it made my heart break. Micah shook his head and met my gaze.

"He tried to rape her Nathanial, he wanted her blood and he tried to rape her, he hurt her severely, physically; apparently she fought him back and managed to keep him restrained until Liam could arrive. He did extensive damage, but she's alive and he didn't manage to..." he sipped his drink, his voice trailing off, "he didn't manage to violate her." Bile filled my throat and I lurched forward, gasping, my hands on my knees. "There's more," Micah said, coming over to put a hand on my back. Christ, how much more did I want to hear? "Liam did not kill Andres, he ordered him not to touch Ana, but Andres being Andres, well he's feeling a bit retaliatory; he's not in agreement with Liam that Ana should be kept alive and some in Liam's coven are worried that Andres may want revenge on Liam, and on Ana..." His voice faded. My head snapped up. Micah moved away and sat back down on the couch. "Some of our brethren are watching Liam and his coven; they have the greatest strongholds of land and the best fighters, but we are poised to destroy him Nathanial, however, Ana is still with his family; she's living at the house." This couldn't get any worse. How could one person continue to get herself into possibly the worst situations of her life; she couldn't keep surviving, she couldn't keep fighting. "Your orders still hold true Nathanial; Bonders will not disobey what you have told them to do in regards to Humans being found in the presence of Vampires...they will carry out what you and

81

the Council have set in motion." My body went weak and I sank back into the couch, running my hands through my hair.

"She's not to be touched, Micah. If she's found, she's not to be touched. I don't give a damn about the fucking Council. She's to be brought here and I swear, if a single curl on her head is out of place, I will kill whoever is responsible." My voice was fierce. Micah nodded.

"I will do what I can Nathanial, but there's no way for me to make any promises. I have no idea what the group in Indonesia has planned for Liam's coven or when they are to strike, but I will tell them what you have ordered." He patted my leg and I saw his form shimmer once and then disappear.

Ana

Lucie and I had been left alone for weeks now. Stephen, Carmen and Liam were out organizing and fighting the Bonders and the humans on some of the outer communes, and I was just trying to stay sane. Surprisingly, I was holding up quite well after Andres' attack; it wasn't anything that I hadn't had to confront before and my emotional state seemed relatively strong, all things considered. Still, I contemplated asking Carmen to help me get back to Idaho, to leave the hell that was now burning around me, but I knew that she would never betray Liam and in some way, I respected that. I had yet to endure any run-ins with Andres and it appeared, at least for the time being, that Liam had kept his promise that he would not harm me again. I was still always on edge, especially at night. Lucie had taken to sleeping in my bed and that's where she currently was, snoring gently next to me. I was trying to compose an email to Noni; I had called several times, but I wasn't getting an answer and I was worried. I started to type, when a sudden potent fragrance filled the room; salt water and musk, sand and sea air. I closed my laptop and tried to listen for anything out of place. A shadow appeared in the hall and I snapped my computer shut, waiting, my body tense. Stephen's form filled the doorway and I held my breath. I still wasn't sure if I could trust Stephen and my instincts told me to be wary.

"Hi," he said quietly, his eyes moving to glance at Lucie, her tiny body pressed so close to mine that you could barely make out her face. He smiled, and then looked back at me. "She loves you," he murmured as he came into the room, placing his hands on one of the bedposts. I looked at her face and shrugged.

"Maybe," I said, smoothing her hair, "but kids aren't known to have refined taste." I laughed softly.

"I disagree. I think that children have the most acute sense of a person's soul; they are the most honest in their feelings about people, much more so than anyone else...except you." He came around from the end of the bed and stood near my side. I could see movement deep within his eyes, like the sea during a storm. He bent over me and I felt my body tense; he stared into my eyes and gently scooped Lucie from the bed, holding her against his chest. I watched as he carried her down the hallway. It looked natural for him. He looked like a father. I thought I heard him chuckle as he reentered my room.

"What?" I said. "It does look natural for you, why is that funny?" I asked, my tone serious. He shook his head.

"May I?" He motioned to the space next to me and I nodded. He swung his legs up on the bed and moved back to lie against the pillows. He seemed exhausted. "I am," he said quietly, his face turning to look at me. "What are you working on?" He glanced at the laptop.

"Oh, I'm just emailing Noni; I've been trying to call, but I can't get in touch with her. I'm just a bit worried," I said, putting the computer on the floor. Stephen's eyes were closed.

"Do you want me to see if I can find anything out for you?" he murmured.

"Really? That would be great. Thanks Stephen," I said, feeling a bit better. He smiled, his eyes still shut. I settled back against my pillows and we just relaxed there, listening to the soft music I had playing. I let my body relax as much as I could. It felt nice, peaceful almost and I could feel my anxiety about his presence begin to ease. I didn't want to be angry with him anymore; I still felt horrible about leaving things the way we did when I returned to Idaho. Processing my thoughts, he shifted his weight and rolled on his side, propping himself up on his elbow.

"Ana, I'm so very sorry…I don't know what to say to make things right; I don't have the words to tell you how I feel." His eyes flashed across my face, their color luminous and fluid. I shrugged and closed my eyes.

"Don't worry about it; you're a male, communication is not a forte for your gender," I said, laughing. I opened my eyes to survey his reaction. He bowed his head.

"It's not funny," he whispered. "Nothing about what I feel for you is funny, Ana." He raised his eyes, searching my face. I saw him blush slightly and bite his lip. He looked so human in that moment, so much like a man, that I found myself smiling broadly. He rolled his eyes and fell back against the bed. "You have no idea, just how much your thoughts torture me," he mused.

"Well, quit listening then," I said rolling on my stomach, tucking my arms under my pillow, my head facing him. He laughed.

"Not a chance. Where would I get my entertainment from then?" he said, shifting so that our faces were close together. I felt him softly brush my hair off of my back, sweeping it to the side. I took a deep breath in. He traced his fingers lightly over my shoulder blades and down my back. He had touched me like this once, the night of the concert, and I was amazed at how familiar and safe it felt. My body relaxed as I let him stroke his hands down my body, pressing ever so gently into my muscles. Warmth flooded the tissues and into the bones and I felt every tendon turn loose and soft at his touch. "Is this ok?" he asked hesitantly. "Is my touching you ok Ana?"

"Hmmm," I murmured. That was all I could get out. He chuckled softly and continued to stroke down my spine, lifting my shirt and moving his hands over my lower back. He pressed deeply into the muscles above my tailbone and suddenly, I felt a surge of heat and deep longing. The feeling was similar in intensity to when Devon had pressed on Patric's bite marks, but this time it felt more intimate, more real and safe and much more powerful. I heard our song begin to play and I felt my heart beat faster.

"Why does this song always play when we're together?" he asked quietly and I heard him begin to sing softly along with the track as he pushed deeper into the depths of my back muscles. I tried to stifle a groan. I always thought Stephen sounded better than the guy actually singing; Stephen's voice was darker and it resonated with such passion that my heart had a hard time keeping its own rhythm whenever I listened to him. Stephen laughed and bent his head close to my ear, singing softly. An errant thought entered my mind. I wondered how many women Stephen had been with; he was over five hundred years old, so I was guessing thousands. I suddenly felt self-conscious and my body tensed under his touch; I was gross. He pulled back from my face. "Ana," he said in a hushed voice. I rolled onto my back and looked at his face. His fingers reached to trace over my lips and down my throat. A sigh escaped my mouth and our eyes met. He lowered his face to mine, watching me. He brought his lips within millimeters of my own and I could taste his scent. He breathed slowly into my mouth and I took a shallow breath in, feeling his intense heat and tasting his fragrance; still, our mouths did not touch. I wondered if Stephen actually kissed or if he too, was like Devon. I felt his chest rise and fall and he closed his eyes. He wrapped his arm around me and lowered me back down against the pillows, his body pressing gently against mine. Our foreheads touched and I felt his hips move slowly. We were both breathing hard as he lifted my shirt over my head, letting my hair tumble down my back. I moved to unbutton his shirt, letting it fall open, his tanned, smooth chest exposed. I ran my fingers along the deep ridges of his stomach muscles, feeling him quiver at my touch. A vast and deep passion began to rise in my heart and in my soul and I wanted to feel connected to him, to hold him close to me. Slowly, I reached to run my fingers across the plains of his thick muscles and down over his shoulders. He shuddered, our heads still pressed together. He pulled his shirt off and let his body lie fully upon mine. I ran my hands over his back, pressing deeply into his skin. He slid his hands down around my waist and in one breath he had my sweats off, flinging them to the side of the bed. His fingers moved gently over my stomach, caressing softly, slowly. I sighed and held his face in my hands. He held me so close, and so tightly that I wanted to cry. It was the safest that I had felt in a long time.

"You are safe Ana," Stephen whispered as he kissed my cheek. "I'll keep you safe," he murmured. I raised my face to his and pulled his mouth to mine, kissing him as deeply and slowly as I could manage. He moaned gently and I felt fire surge in his lips. Hovering above me, he kissed my throat, down my chest and I could feel him begin to move gently against me. He used his knee to slide open my leg, hitching it around his waist, his fingers tracing a fiery trail along the curve of my hip. My back arched as I pressed my hands into his lower back, pushing him closer to me. He was kissing me passionately now, not letting me breathe. We were both gasping as our bodies moved together in a perfect rhythm. He smoothed the hair back out of my face and pressed me tight to him, lifting my body from underneath. The pulse of his thrusting was slow, and he groaned, suddenly, moving off of me.

"What's wrong?" I asked, breathless. He swallowed and took a jagged breath in.

"I can't," he said, rubbing his face. "I can't do this Ana." He closed his eyes and took a deep breath in. I struggled to sit up, the blankets twisted around my waist.

"Why? Is it me, is it something that I did?" I asked, unsure about his sudden hesitation. I knew that Stephen had been with a ton of women, perhaps I wasn't as well versed in the things that pleased Vampires as they were. He laughed softly and pulled me back so that I was lying upon his chest.

"Your problem is that you are *too* well versed, Ana. You make it *too* hard for any being, man or vampire, to be able to control themselves." He ran his fingers down my spine. I shivered with desire

"Well, what is it then?" I asked, still confused about why he had stopped us. I heard him exhale.

"I'm not good for you Ana. I'm not right; I'm not who you think I am." His voice was tight and soft. I raised my head off of his chest and searched his face; he looked like he was in pain.

"Why would you think that Stephen; I don't think that about you at all. I've never thought that, even when you tried to attack me…"I drifted off, remembering. He sighed and met my eyes.

"I know," he said quietly. "And that is why you deserve so much better than me. I've done things Ana, terrible things and I can't change the decisions that I've made; I can't go back." He sounded so sad and so desperate, that I felt tears begin to prick in the corner of my eyes.

"We've all done things we're not proud of Stephen, been someone other than who we truly are, but it's what we do after those events have occurred, who we choose to be in spite of those decisions, that reveals our most honest selves," I said, wishing that I could shake him, make him see himself as I saw him.

"I wish I could believe that Ana, and maybe for others that wisdom holds true, but not for me, never for me," he said quietly. I wanted to ask him what he was referring to, what it was that he could have possibly done that made him feel that he was beyond redemption, that he didn't deserve love, my love. He raised my face up so that our eyes met. He looked shocked.

"You've been my best friend; I know that may sound odd, but it's true Stephen, of course I love you," I said, not blinking, but knowing just how true that statement was; how much I knew now that I did love him and perhaps as more than just a friend—I wasn't quite ready to go down that road with myself just yet.

"You have lousy choices in friends, Ana." He smiled at me.

Finally, we remained still and silent, our arms bound in a tight embrace. Stephen shifted and situated himself so that his head could lie against my chest. I ran my fingers through his hair, feeling its softness and smelling his scent. He hugged himself closer to me and sighed. I kissed the top of his head, breathing him in deeply.

"Will you stay with me tonight?" I asked, quietly, not wanting to disturb the calm of the moment. He turned to raise his face so that he was looking at me.

"You want me to stay?" he asked, sounding surprised.

"Very much," I said, bringing my mouth to his and kissing him softly. "Very, very, much," I murmured, letting my tongue part his lips. He moaned and kissed me harder.

"Christ Ana," he said, pulling his face back. "You are the most dangerous woman I have ever met."

"Is that because I can wield fire and kick your ass, or is it because you almost found out just how good in bed I actually am?" I said, laughing and moving forward to kiss him.

"Hmmm." His lips moved over my neck. "I don't think the two are mutually exclusive." And I felt his teeth grasp my earlobe, biting it teasingly. He settled himself against my chest and I felt his body relax. Stephen didn't actually sleep, but he went into more of a deep meditative state, so when I awoke to the smell of smoke, it took a few violent shakes to snap him out of his trance.

"Stephen! Get up! Stephen!" I shoved against him, moving his head back and forth. His body shuddered and I saw his eyes begin to focus. He studied my face.

"What's wrong?" he asked, sitting up suddenly. "Is that smoke?" He threw the covers off and jerked on his pants, throwing me my top and sweats. He slammed open my door and thick curls of black smoke began filling the air around us. He coughed and grabbed the quilt off the bed wrapping it around my face and pulling me through the door.

"LUCIE!" I screamed and broke away from him, sprinting down the hallway to her room. She was sleeping soundly and I grabbed her from

90

her bed. Where were Carmen and Liam? We didn't have time to call for them. Lucie stirred and began to cry. "It's ok baby, it's ok!" I ran back down the hallway to where Stephen was standing against the wall. He pulled us in tight and tired to shimmer us away from the fire, but we didn't move, nothing happened. He cursed. Suddenly the rooms down the hall exploded into flames blocking our access to the windows. My heart stopped; I had barely gotten Lucie out in time. The smoke was moving up the stairway and filling the hall; I began to feel the heat from the flames warm my skin. Lucie was still crying, pressing her face against mine. Stephen turned to me, his eyes fierce.

"Ana, you are going to have to listen to me very closely." I nodded, ice spreading into my heart. "You need to take Lucie, you need to move the fire enough to let the two of you by, you need to take the car and drive as quickly as you can to the airport." He was flinging money and credit cards at me and pulling an envelope out of a drawer in the hallway, as he covered his nose and mouth with his shirt. He handed me two passports and some other paperwork. I looked at him not understanding what he wanted me to do. "I need you to concentrate Ana; you need to use all of your energy. This fire is not Human made so you must concentrate!" He was holding my face in his hands. "Do you understand me?"

"NO!" I said, shaking my head; the reality of what he was telling me to do, finally registering. "NO! I won't leave you, I won't! I'm strong enough for all three of us to escape Stephen! I won't do it!" I was crying. He pulled me close to him, hugging me violently; he kissed my cheeks and kissed Lucie.

"I have to stay, Ana, I can't abandon Liam." I cut him off.

"You can get to him once we're away from the fire, you don't have to stay in the house Stephen." Suddenly, I heard voices, shouts coming from downstairs. Bonders, they had come and now Stephen was going to stay and fight in this hellish inferno. He was shoving me down the back stairway, the one that led into the kitchen. He looked at me, his eyes clear and bright. No! Not again; how much was I going to have to lose before I completely crumbled, before all the love I had in my heart was ripped away? I wasn't going to let Stephen die, I needed him; we needed each other.

"I do need you Ana, and I love you more than I ever thought I was capable of loving anyone. You must do this for me, for Lucie. Carmen needs you to do this for her and for her daughter." He was dragging me through the kitchen, the voices and shouts getting louder. He turned to look at me. "When I open the door, I can give you a few seconds, but just a few. You are going to have to be quick Ana, faster than you have ever been before. There is no time for you to be thinking about me, about what's happening behind you; do you understand?" I was sobbing, but I nodded my head. He kissed me and whispered in my ear. "Ana. You always fight; do you hear me? You always fight for yourself, for your life—no matter what!" He touched my face and I saw his eyes grow dark and fill with a fire that I had never seen before. "Ready?" he asked as he took his place by the door. I held Lucie close to me and whispered to her.

"Hold on to me Lucie, hold on to me very tightly ok?" I felt her arms press around my neck in an unnatural display of strength for a three year-old. She looked at me and smiled.

"Yes," she said. I nodded to Stephen and he looked once more at my face and flung open the door. Flames exploded in my face and I heard Stephen yell for me to hurry. I let my mind go calm and tried to block out the sounds of fighting going on around me. I felt the surge and swell of my skin and my blood boiled over, filling my eyes in a red haze. I shifted my eyes a fraction of an inch and I saw a small opening in the wall of fire, a break in the storm.

"GO!" Stephen shouted. I turned to see him on the ground punching a Demon. Our eyes met. I pulled Lucie to me and jumped through the flames, leaving Stephen to battle both Demons and fire. I sprinted to the car and flung Lucie into the back seat. I didn't have time to get her strapped into her car seat, so I yelled for her to lie down on the floor. I jumped into the front and started the engine, but before I could put the car in gear, the window smashed open and the door was suddenly ripped from its hinges. Someone grabbed me around the neck and yanked me from the car and threw me onto the pavement. Andres. He was looming over me, his teeth barred and his lips slick. I thought of Lucie and hoped to god that she would stay where I put her.

"We're going to finish what we started Ana. We're going to finish *everything* that we started." He smirked at me and he put his boot to my chest. Just before he could stamp down and crush my lungs, he heaved forward, blood seeping through his chest and splattering out onto my face. I crawled away as he tumbled forward, landing face down. A large metal shank was sticking out of his back, and it gleamed with black blood in the moonlight. I tired to get up, but someone was pulling me by the hair. I focused my energy and shot a line of flames out toward the hands that were dragging me.

"It's her!" someone shouted. "We got her, it's her!" The hands jerked me into a standing position and I turned to face my assailant.

"Ana!" a tiny voice cried behind me and I turned back around to see Lucie standing by the car, her thumb in her mouth. Frick!

"What the fuck is this?" The Bonder holding me asked. "Is that a kid?" He spun me around to look at him. "Jesus Christ! We don't have time for this bullshit," he fumed.

"What's the hold up, why haven't you killed her already? What are you, a fucking pussy? Let's just do this and get the hell out of here," another Demon spoke as he stepped from the shadows and suddenly a huge sonic boom erupted around us, leveling the Bonders and me to the ground. We all looked up to see the house shoot a stream of sparks into the night, the roof blowing off in massive chunks. My heart stopped as I thought of Stephen. The Bonder grabbed me around the neck again and pulled me to my feet. He rounded on the other Demon, the one that stepped out just before the explosion.

"Look you fuckhole; maybe you're ok murdering women and children but I'm not. They're coming back with us; he'll decide what to do. I don't want the murder of a little girl on my conscience. Now get the fuck out of my way." He grabbed me around the waist and pushed me toward Lucie. "Get her!" he said. I held out my arms and Lucie ran and jumped into my chest, wrapping her hands into my hair and nuzzling her face in my neck. The Bonder grabbed my arm, squeezing me hard and I felt the sudden flattening of my organs as we spun away into ice and blackness.

I had no idea where we were. I was disoriented from shimmering and my head had yet to stop spinning. Darkness penetrated every corner of whatever space we occupied, but I distinctly heard voices around me, whispering. I checked to make sure that Lucie was still with me. I reached around down by my legs and felt her soft hair. I breathed a sigh of relief. Why the hell was it so dark? As if on cue, a dim light began to pulse and glow, illuminating the shadows of figures along the barred walls. I scanned the room and counted six people, they all looked to be humans, and all were male, all prisoners. The men turned their eyes on us, looked us over then resumed their conversation. I picked Lucie up and moved us into the farthest corner of the room. I slid down the wall and pulled her into my lap, stroking her hair. Exhaustion seeped into my body and I wanted desperately to close my eyes, but instinct and adrenaline coursed through my veins, not allowing for me to lower my guard. Some of the men in the room were speaking Spanish and I could decipher that we were in Peru, or close to Peru. My Spanish was rusty. The prisoners had all been found working with Vampires and were now considered to have violated some treaty; they were considered traitors. Lucie squirmed in my lap and lifted her head, breaking my concentration.

"Ana, I'm hungry and I have to use the bathroom," she said softly. I nodded to her and stood up. There were guards standing outside our confines and I went to tap one on the shoulder.

"Perdóneme mi niña necesidades para usar el baño y también esta hambriento." I hoped that my Spanish was correct. The guard turned to me, his eyes roaming over my face.

"I speak English," he said quietly. "Someone is coming for you in a minute. Can she wait?" he asked, looking down at Lucie. She smiled up at him and nodded putting her thumb in her mouth. I took her hand and led her back to our corner. I twirled her hair absentmindedly, around my finger. I didn't know how much time passed, but I heard the guard speaking to someone and then the door slid open. A man appeared, his arms behind his back. I took a deep breath and stood up. I gasped upon seeing his face, well, upon seeing his eyes. They were bright turquoise and they gleamed deep, taking in my entire presence.

"Hello Ana." His voice was clear and full of emotion. "I've heard a lot about you." He smiled at me and his eyes looked at Lucie. He stooped so that he was even with her. "And who is this young one?" he asked. She moved to press herself to my leg, looking up at me.

"This is Lucie," I said, my tone quiet and wary. This man looked just like Patric. Actually, he looked just like the most perfect combination of Nathanial and Patric and that reality could not bode well for me considering Nathanial's reaction the last time that I'd seen him. I saw the man glance at me, cocking his head to the side, but he quickly returned to engaging Lucie. "Well hello Lucie, my name is Micah Ch'en, would you be so kind as to take my hand and come with me please? I won't hurt you." Ch'en, I knew that name; it was a Mayan name. I was thinking that the name "Ch'en" was for the Mayan Goddess of the moon, it was Nathanial's mother's maiden name. "You're right," Micah said, again his face registering an emotion that I couldn't place. "Nathanial's mother was my sister; I am Nathanial and Patric's uncle. I'll be escorting you somewhere more comfortable and of course we will get both of you some nourishment," he said, watching me. I nodded, trying to process what he had just said and staying close to Lucie as he led her out of the little room and into the night.

We drove in an open-air jeep along the coast to what appeared to be a well-established campsite. Small huts were erected in the dense forest and ground torches provided the only lighting. We parked along a small gravel road and I hoisted Lucie into my chest, holding her on my hip. I smelled fire from the campsite and the cooking of meat. I also heard quiet laughter and soft music being played and I immediately thought of Stephen. My chest constricted and I sighed heavily. Micah led us past the group of Bonders who had assembled around the campfire and I heard whispering; something about how I was supposed to have been killed, that I was a human with a power I didn't deserve. I hugged Lucie closer and followed Micah into a small hut set back from the rest of the housing. The place was small but cozy. A large quilted mattress coated in gauzy mosquito netting sat in the far corner and we had a small bedside table with a dim lamp. There were two chairs and a Mayan or Inca rug arranged in the center of the room.

"The outhouse is behind the hut. It's not much, but you have a shower and a compost toilet and you'll be safe using either." Micah said, registering my wariness about wondering out into the night with Lucie. "I have to ask that you stay here Ana, we'll move you with the rest of the prisoners tomorrow." He looked sad as he spoke. I nodded. "I'll have one of the guards bring you both some food." He turned and stepped off the ledge at the entrance.

"Thank you Micah," I said, meeting his gaze.

I spent the rest of the evening bathing myself and cleaning Lucie and making sure she ate everything on her plate. I was grateful to have the distraction. My mind was racing. I couldn't stop thinking about Stephen or about Micah. Where was Nathanial? Was he here? Did he know that I was here? Was he supposed to kill me? I shuttered at the mere thought of Nathanial ordering my death—I would never, ever fight Nathanial, not for my life, for Lucie's definitely, but not for my own. The morning came quickly, I hadn't slept at all and my mind felt jarred and my body tense. A guard came to take us in a large van with the other men from our first cell. We drove down winding paths and bumpy roads and the lack of windows made it a very desensitizing experience. I was trying not to throw up. The van eventually came to a skidding halt and the door slid open, plunging our eyes into the bright light of the morning. I squinted and picked Lucie up and stood with the other men. They lined us up against the van and began handcuffing us together. When they got to Lucie and me, they looked hesitant.

"I just need to be able to pick her up and carry her if necessary," I spoke calmly. The guard eyed me and then clamped one of my hands to the young man next to me, but he left the other one free. I nodded at him and we began walking up a steep hill. It was arduous and my back was hurting, the metal cuff on my restrained hand began to dig and rub the skin raw. Lucie hopped down and walked beside me. What a great kid, I thought. She hadn't complained once and she never asked what we were doing. I guessed that Carmen and Liam had disciplined her well. I smiled down at her. I didn't know how long we hacked our way through the trail, an hour maybe. Finally we arrived at what looked like a small compound. Several larger huts were joined together and there were people out in the main yard doing various manual labor tasks, a work camp possibly. The guards ordered us into the largest hut and we were told to wait inside. I picked Lucie up and carried her over the steep stairs into the compound. It was sweltering inside and the sweat began to drip down the back of my neck. I felt my imprint begin to shift, pulling and splitting the skin. I gasped and Lucie turned her face to mine.

"Ana?" she asked, her eyes wide.

"Yes, baby, I'm ok." I tried to smile at her, but the pain in my neck was making me nauseous. She pressed her lips to my cheek. We waited for what seemed like a lifetime, the men talking and Lucie and I sitting and staring at each other. Finally, I heard the door open and a guard ordered us to stand up. The sound of metal clanking and chains shifting made my skin crawl. For some reason, it reminded me of when I found Nathanial chained at the University. My heart thumped heavily in my chest. I watched as two men entered our holding space and then sighed out loud when I saw Nathanial move forward, his arms folded across his chest. He looked the most terrifying that I had ever seen him. His skin was so dark as were his eyes, that he resembled an entirely different race. His hair was tied back in a long ponytail and his muscles bulged tight and strong from the confines of his t-shirt. His jaw was locked and the normally smooth skin of his arms was now covered in burn marks and scars. I didn't know why, but I immediately bowed my head; I couldn't look at him. I pulled Lucie in tighter and fought back the tears that were brimming in my eyes. God, I was so tired. I listened as his heavy boots walked in front of us, his steps vibrating on the ground under my feet. He moved along each of the men, finally stopping in front of me. I took a deep breath in. I felt him

99

move his finger gently under my chin, raising my face. As he did, tears streamed down my cheeks and our gazes met. He closed his eyes and took a breath in. His expression was fierce and emotion raged beneath the surface, making the heat from his skin pulse out towards me. He dropped his hand and his eyes fell upon Lucie. He looked back at me, then back at her, and I could see that he was trying to figure out where I had gotten this child from and why she was with me. He motioned to Micah and he came to stand next to Nathanial. They looked so similar, yet there was such an ethereal look to Nathanial, that it made him seem like a god amongst children.

"Get the men set up in the barracks and working. Take Ana to the farthest part of the compound and make sure the doctor comes by to check the child," Nathanial ordered, his voice deep and clear. Micah nodded and motioned to the guard to unchain me. I watched Nathanial's face as the metal cuff around my wrist was released reveling a deep gash and fresh blood. I could see his body shudder just slightly.

"Ana." Micah moved to lead me outside and away from Nathanial and the rest of the men. I shifted Lucie to my other hip and she weaved her tiny fingers into my hair and kissed my cheek. Nathanial was watching us, his gaze captivated by the intimacy between Lucie and myself. I bowed my head, not wanting him to see my eyes and followed Micah out the door.

The doctor came by and did a thorough, but gentle examination of Lucie; he gave her an injection to prevent tetanus and some quinine pills for malaria. I was sure that a half-Vampire child wasn't as prone to human borne illness as other children, but who was I to argue. He cleaned and dressed my wound, leaving it stinging. I laid Lucie down on the bed and moved over to the window. I could see the ocean and the mountains and I cried until the sun set. So deep was I in my thoughts, that I didn't hear the door open.

"Ana," a strong but quiet voice spoke behind me. I wiped my eyes and turned to see Nathanial standing in the little room. He looked to the bed. "Did the doctor come by?" he asked, his eyes still on Lucie.

"Yes. Thank you. She's fine," I said, my voice rough and cracking. I sighed, so much for putting up a strong façade. He turned back toward me and moved over to my place at the window. He gently grasped my wrist, the one that had been shackled and traced his fingers along the bruise that was now forming; it seeped out from the bandage like some dark snake across my flesh. My metal tattoo shifted again and I winced.

"Are you hurt?" he asked, his face showing the first signs of concern and worry. He moved his hands along my wrist, stopping to caress over his scar. At his touch, my arm flooded with such an intense electric current that I jerked my hand away, unintentionally. His eyes widened at the sudden, violent movement.

"Sorry," I said. "You shocked me." I dropped my hand to my side and exhaled. He moved away from me, ice filled my soul as I watched him turn his back to me. The only thing that kept coming to me was how grateful I was that I had told him that I loved him and that I was sorry for everything; I was glad that he had heard me say those words. I guessed from his reaction in Stephen's apartment, that my gesture was too late, that he...that we, would be forever lost to each other;

that we were effectively strangers, bonded only in ritual, not spirit. He sighed, hearing my thoughts and I watched him pinch the bridge of his nose between his fingers.

"I thought you had gone to Idaho, Ana. What happened? Why did you come back?" His voice came out rough and soft. Funny, those were the exact questions that Stephen had asked me and I still didn't have an answer that sounded close to logical; Noni's vision had gone horribly, horribly wrong; unless…my mind was trying to navigate through all of the events that had occurred since my return. "Ana?" Nathanial was impatient and he wasn't willing to listen to my analysis of the musing of an old woman. I cleared my throat.

"It's a long story," I said, turning to look out the window, the impossibility of my situation threatening to overwhelm me. I tried to concentrate on the beauty of the Andes, rising like the spine of a dragon along the horizon. "What happens now?" I asked. "Aren't you supposed to kill me or something?" Oddly, the question didn't seem out of place to me; I knew what Nathanial had been ordering for any human found with Vampires. I couldn't be the exception; it would make him look weak. I looked over at Lucie sleeping in the bed, her hair spread out behind her like a black pool of ink across the pillow. "Not her," I said, my tone fierce. "My life for hers. You are not to touch her," I said, turning on him. He exhaled loudly and put his hands on his hips.

"Jesus Christ, Ana. Do you think that I have lost myself so much, that I would order an innocent child to be murdered? Do you think so little of me that you feel in your heart, that I could have the potential to commit such an egregious act?" I eyed him, taking in the hardness of his face and body, his scars and wounds from battles and his eyes. They were still dark, with no hint of the night skies; it was as if I was now staring into the abyss, a place that had no more need for light or warmth—I didn't know those eyes and I hadn't failed to recall that the last time I had seen him, when I had said goodbye, he didn't reciprocate. He never said that he had loved me or that he still loved me...he never said those words as I left; so yes, perhaps I did think he had lost himself, for I did not know this Nathanial, this warrior standing before me and I was pretty sure that he no longer *cared* for me to know him.

"Ana," he choked, his head bowed, "god, how could you even think..." His voice was cut off as a sharp knock sounded on the door. I watched him compose himself as Micah entered the room. I saw Nathanial's uncle survey us, taking in our expressions. He sighed and put his hand on Nathanial's shoulder.

"I have the men working on the road down to the coast; you'll need to make some decisions about..." Micah hesitated and looked at me, "about what to do with them; the Council has agreed to hear their stories and we'll need you to be present for that before any punishment is handed down." Again, he looked at me, his stare intense and penetrating. I moved to sit on the bed next to Lucie.

"Fine, yes, I'll be there," Nathanial said as he watched me stroking Lucie's hair.

"Nathanial." Micah's voice suddenly became low and slightly anxious. He looked at me and then back to Nathanial.

"No!" Nathanial exclaimed. His tone made my heart drop.

"Nathanial, you know the rules, you know that the Council will need to question her; there's no way around that. They of course will take into account your opinion of the situation and that you and Ana are still technically Bound, but procedure is procedure; as a General, you need to be seen not making exceptions. You know this." Micah sounded desperate and sad as he spoke and I could see Nathanial's body begin to slump under the weight of what he was being asked to do.

"Micah?" I asked, standing to face them both. "I've told Nathanial, that whatever decision is made, that Lucie will not be harmed; that it is my life that is being offered, not hers and I am prepared to fight you and Nathanial if necessary. I assure you, that neither of you know just what I am capable of. I, like Nathanial, do not fight fair and you won't win." My voice was so clear and the strength of my tenor rang with such certainty and truth, that I felt power and energy flood my body and I felt strong. I saw that both Micah and Nathanial took a fraction of a step back from me, Nathanial staring so hard at my face that I thought his eyes might explode from their intensity. "I am of course happy to oblige your 'procedure'," I said, maintaining as much diplomacy as I could. "I will answer whatever questions the Council and Nathanial deem necessary to ask, but Lucie is not to be present. Am I understood?" Again, my voice held steady, this time, however, ice flooded my tone.

"Of course, Ana. We wouldn't imagine having your Lucie in front of the Council. I will make sure that my housekeeper tends to her needs—you needn't worry," Micah spoke quietly, his eyes roaming over my face. I nodded and turned toward Nathanial.

"Are we of the same understanding?" I asked him, meeting his stare. He nodded, his eyes filling with questions and what looked like disbelief. "Good, then please feel free to come back when the Council has assembled," I said and motioned for the door. I could feel my anger begin to pulse and throb in my chest. They needed to leave. Nathanial looked once more at me and I thought I caught a flash of silver and blue move across his eyes. I set my jaw and this time it was *I* who turned my back on *him*.

Chapter Five

Nathanial

Fear gripped every bone in my body. Never once, in as long as I had known and loved Ana, had I ever thought about the possibility of her fighting me, and never had I seen the kind of power and strength that she exuded, come so forcefully from her entire being. Somehow, the course of events in her life appeared to only have made her more resilient, more courageous, more capable of love, if that was even possible. From my part, I was weaker, a shadow, a ghost; without her, I was nothing. She believed that I no longer loved her, that perhaps I never truly had loved her; she believed that her saying goodbye to me, her leaving to go to her death, was the end of the road for us, that we couldn't possibly find our way back to each other, not after so much bad had happened. It hadn't been all bad though; we were going to get married, we were living together, building a life...we loved each other, she was mine.

I sighed and walked further down the shore. I had to admit that I was curious about her time with Liam and Stephen, and how in the world she had become a surrogate mother to that little girl. I had been jealous of Stephen since he found me in that godforsaken bar, since he told me that Ana had come to him for help and that she was staying with him, and I felt betrayed by her. She hadn't given me a chance to explain anything and she left so quickly, so easily and then to go to a Vampire of all things. I stopped to stare at the waves, remembering her standing there with that stupid box in her hands; I remembered the way Stephen had looked when he said her name, when he told me what he'd been instructed to do— it was sheer pain. Stephen was decent as far as Vampires went, and I knew that Ana, yet again, had managed to infiltrate his armor; she affected him deeply. They relied upon each other, it was a very untraditional relationship, but then again, Ana was prone to non-traditionalist modes of bonding with people or Vampires or demons—that was just Ana. Now, now, here we both were, in this horrible place with her life, yet again, in my hands, in the hands of an unyielding and unforgiving Council. I knew the odds and they weren't good, they were far from good. My heart stopped beating and I felt a sudden wave of ice wash through my body, through my soul. I gasped and fell to my knees in the sand, sobbing.

Ana

Micah's housekeeper was a very pleasant and caring woman. She came to our little room laden with books and crayons and paper. She was plump, with a round face and glorious smile, but upon seeing us, upon understanding that we were prisoners, her face fell and tears brimmed in her eyes. I patted her on the shoulder and thanked her for watching Lucie. Beautiful, courageous Lucie… I didn't know what to do, what to say. I had no idea if I would be coming back. Who would take care of her, who would love her? I didn't know if Carmen or Liam were still alive or if Stephen had managed to escape; I knew nothing except that I too might have to abandon her. My throat closed and I tried to swallow the torturous amounts of pain that now filled my chest. I pulled her close to my face and kissed her cheeks. I heard the door open and Micah and Nathanial entered. I bent my head close to Lucie's ear and whispered, "I love you so much, you know that? And your mom and dad, they love you too. I want you to be brave for me; I want you to be strong. You are so special and so loved Lucie and you are the most precious thing in the world to me. You changed the very essence of who I am and I will be forever in you debt." I was crying, and she began to cry, our mutual tears mingling on our cheeks. "I love you, I love you, I love you," I whispered as I handed her back to the housekeeper. She reached out her arms and screamed for me. My heart seized and I thought, just for a moment, that it stopped beating. I looked and saw that Nathanial had a single tear moving slowly down his high cheekbone. I turned away from Lucie, still screaming and crying and I moved to walk out the door, Nathanial and Micah behind me.

We traveled back to the first camp where we had stayed. The little torches now lit as twilight began to seep into the forest. There was no campfire this time, no soft music, no whispering. I stepped from the jeep and followed along side Nathanial, not looking at him, not speaking. He was stiff and his jaw was flexed. We stood outside a large hut and I could see the men to whom I had been chained, assembling in front of a circle of chairs, a small fire lit in the middle of the room. Micah looked once at me, then at Nathanial and he entered the circle. Nathanial moved to follow him, but I reached out to touch his arm. A heated current swept through my veins and the back of my neck surged in a familiar electrical charge. He turned to look at me. "Lucie," I said, my voice quiet and low, "if Carmen and Liam or Stephen are dead, she'll need someone Nathanial." I stared at him, knowing that of course it should be him; I had always thought that if I had wanted to have children, that he would be the most amazing father. How lucky our child would be to have him. He closed his eyes and swallowed.

"Ana," he said.

"Please do this for me, please. If nothing else, if you no longer love me, that's ok, but *she* deserves to be loved; if nothing else, please, whatever feelings you still may have for me, give them to her, love her Nathanial like she was your own, like she was ours." I squeezed his hand and stepped into the hut. The Council was small, maybe six or seven Bonders, not including Nathanial and Micah; all were male and all looked like they each had seen too many wars, too much violence, too much betrayal. I sighed and took a place next to a young man, the one who I had been chained to with Lucie. His eyes widened at my appearance and I nodded to him.

"It ain't right," he whispered to me, his voice fierce. "Havin' you here, it ain't right. Us, it's different." He motioned toward the other men. "But you, you're a woman, you have a child. What's this world comin' to? It ain't right." His voice began to rise and I patted him on the shoulder, trying to quell his fear. We stood against the wall and watched as the council assembled and discussed various military business. Nathanial's back was to me, but I could see Micah; he was watching me. Finally, after what I was sure to be hours, the Council motioned for the guard to bring us forward. I quickly noticed that there were only three men with me in the hut and my stomach sank wondering what had happened to the others. Were they already dead? One by one the men stepped into the circle, standing near the fire and one by one they were all asked the same questions; did you know you were in the presence of Vampires? Did you willingly help the Vampires usurp the Bonders and the Humans? Did you reveal any information that may have helped the Vampires in their war against the Bonders and the Humans? Are you aware of the rule pertaining to all Humans who are found in the company of Vampires? Each man stood and answered the questions, and each one seemed defiant in their position; they all willingly had worked with Vampires.

The Council had yet to call me, so I tried to clear my mind and I stared into the fire, pulling the energy and the heat into my blood, letting my skin swell and stretch. I wasn't gearing up for a fight, but for some reason, being in the presence of the very element that had always frightened me, the one thing that had almost taken away my life as a child; being a part of it and having it be a part of me, was comforting. The Council turned to Nathanial and asked for him to render his opinion. I looked up, he was now standing, facing my direction and I caught his eye; flames danced in their blackness and I knew what his decision would be for these men. I continued to stare into the fire, trying to block my mind from processing what was going to happen. I heard concurrent "I", around the circle and the men were led out of the hut. Only I was left in the center of the circle now and I stood, my legs holding strong and my blood pulsing. Nathanial returned to his seat, his body stiff.

"Ana Tessatore, you were found and captured in the presence of Vampires in Indonesia. What was your business with that coven?" a handsome Demon asked me and I noticed that his eyes roamed slowly over my face. "You may speak freely," he said, his voice calm and even. I noticed that Nathanial sat up, his eyes intent, watching the male who was speaking.

"I was under the care of that particular coven," I said, my tone matching his, calm and even.

"I don't understand; the Vampires were taking care of you?" He sounded confused and he looked around the circle as if waiting for someone to explain the situation.

"Yes, but not because we were working together," I said patiently. Looking at each of the members in turn.

"Well, if you weren't working together, then what were you doing in their company?" another Bonder asked, this one sitting next to Micah. I took a deep breath and exhaled.

"I was waiting for them to decide when they were going to kill me," I said, flatly. "Or turn me. Those were the conditions I gave to them." Whispers broke out and people began talking over one another. I saw Nathanial wave his hand, asking for silence. The handsome Bonder, the one who spoke first, leaned in to stare at me.

"Are you telling me, that you offered your life to the Vampires?" he asked, he sounded almost to be laughing in his disbelief. I cocked my head to the side and met his gaze.

"In a way," I said, diplomatically. "As I'm sure you already know, both the Bonders and the Vampires placed a...a bounty of sorts on my head, because I have this ability." I paused, not wanting to go to fast. Everyone, including Nathanial leaned in towards the fire. "I thought that such an order seemed a bit extreme considering that I am just an ordinary human, who just happens to have this innate talent. I thought a compromise might be a better option, a mediation, if you will," I said, looking at the Bonder who had spoken.

"And you offered this...this compromise to a coven of Vampires? What was the compromise?" His face registered complete awe.

"That I would join with them, and they could utilize my talent, come to understand it, if they Changed me—sparing my life in a way." My voice was holding strong. More whispers broke out and the Bonders began to shake their heads, disbelieving. I knew that offering the truth of the situation would never score me any points, but what other choice did I have; if you were to never be honest in the moments before your death, then you could never be at peace with who you are—or were.

"Why were we not made aware of this compromise, why did you not offer such a negotiation with us?" another Demon asked. I smiled, remembering my last fight with Nathanial.

"I did," I said, my tone dark. I turned and stared at Nathanial. "I asked to be Changed, to have the blood ritual be done to its fullest, but I was denied," I said simply, still staring at Nathanial. His eyes widened. More gasps and chairs shifting closer to me.

"Who denied you?" The Bonder next to Nathanial asked, his chair so close to the flames that I was concerned it might ignite. I hesitated. I didn't want to get Nathanial into trouble.

"Is it crucial for your decision to know who?" I asked, quietly. I felt that I had betrayed Nathanial enough for an entire lifetime.

"Yes, it actually is," a rather large male answered, his tone aggressive. I met his stare, confidently. I stepped in his direction and I felt the entire circle shift to follow me.

"Well, then, I guess you will just have to be disappointed," I said, eyeing him. He stood up and moved toward me.

"Sit down Luke," someone called from behind me and the Demon grunted but returned to his seat.

"Ana, we can respect your decision not to betray confidences, but it is really crucial for your case if we can vouch for this information." Micah looked at me, his face smooth, but his eyes were on fire; he looked desperate.

"It was me; I denied her, I told her no." I whipped my head around and found Nathanial leaning forward speaking, his chin in his hands; he looked oddly relaxed and extremely powerful. Our eyes locked and I knew that we were both remembering the argument, and perhaps the intimate moments before, remembering how we held each other, how we had wanted one another. My eyes felt wet and I had to turn away. I concentrated on the fire, letting it fill me with heat and memory.

"Nathanial, that decision was not solely up to you. We understand that Ana is your Bond, but such an offer really should have come through the proper channels before any decision was made," a voice spoke from behind me. It was Micah. Nathanial raised his hands, clasping his fingers behind his head.

"Fine. I should have gone through the right series of procedures, let's say that I did; what would you have decided?" he asked, looking around the circle.

"There's no way for us to say, the offer was not brought to us, we can only go with what we do know and that is, she went to the Vampires and offered her talent and her life to them," the handsome Bonder said, his eyes never leaving my face.

"Well, she's not with the Vampires anymore, they assigned someone to kill her anyway. She's with us now and let's say the offer still stands. What would be our decision then?" Nathanial asked, his voice commanding and fierce. I saw several Bonders raise their eyebrows at his sudden sign of authority.

"Does the offer still stand?" Micah asked; he was watching Nathanial. I didn't say anything. I wasn't sure if he was speaking to me. "Ana? Does your offer still stand?" he asked, directing his gaze back to me.

"Yes," I said, my voice focused and clear. "Of course it still stands, I did come to you first," I replied.

"And what of your alliances with the Vampires, how do we know that you can be trusted," the Bonder named Luke asked. I saw Nathanial turn to examine my face. I moved and stood close to the fire. I placed my hands over the flames letting the sparks meld to my fingertips like I had seen Nathanial and Patric do so many times before. I brought my now fire-laden hand in front of my face and I began speaking very slowly, very calmly.

"Let me just say this," I said, moving my hand back and forth, watching the red-orange streaks cut through the air around me, "I will not kill for you; I will not harm Humans. I will not do anything that risks the lives of the coven in which I now hold a child in my care. I will not, under any circumstance, allow for them to be taken away from her, if they are in fact still alive." I shifted the fire from one hand to another. The silence in the hut was so deep it served to calm my mind even further. "I care not for my own life now except only as it pertains to Lucie, and it matters very little to me what you decide as far as I am concerned. I will however, fight for the life of that little girl and I will fight to make sure that she can be reunited with the parents who found her and the family who love her, and I will win." I tossed the flames back into the fire and stepped away, my head high. No one moved, no one whispered. I took a deep breath and looked at Micah.

"Ana, will you please wait outside for a moment?" Micah said, looking at Nathanial. I nodded and headed for the stairs outside.

"Just a moment," someone called to me. I turned to see the handsome Bonder standing, his hands behind his back. "Would you mind showing us this particular talent you have Ana?" I saw people nod and also begin to stand up.

"Excuse me?" I asked, my tone genuine and sincere. I had never been asked to display my abilities on cue before.

"I don't mean to be rude or intrusive," the Demon asked as he moved closer to me. Something in his gate and the way he spoke, he reminded me of Alec. I smiled to myself, but suddenly became aware that Nathanial had yet to see just how powerful I knew I had become; it was something that I could feel in the deepest places of my soul and my heart and it was more than what he had witnessed during my fight with Devon, so much more because I had so much more to fight for now, so many people that I loved. He was standing directly in front of me, his head cocked to the side, taking me in. "It's just that it might help for us to see just what you are capable of, we ourselves have yet to harness such an ability, such a gift. While we can use fire to fight, we cannot call fire, command it from nothing, bend it's powers to our will—take it inside of us. We'd like to see what's possible." He raised his eyebrows at me and I immediately looked at Nathanial. I didn't know why, but I felt as though I needed his permission or maybe I just wanted him to be ready; maybe it was both. Whatever the reason, I saw him subtly nod and he moved toward the back of the room with the rest of the Council. Only the Alec-type Demon and I remained in the center on either side of the fire. I could do it, that wasn't the issue. The problem was making sure that I didn't ignite the entire hut and eviscerate the entire Council including Nathanial. I thought about where I wanted the fire to go, what I wanted it to do. I looked across the fire at the Bonder and motioned for him to move. He obliged and I waited for him to take his place next to Nathanial. I looked once more at Nathanial and then I turned my gaze to the fire, extinguishing the flames as I inhaled.

My hair began to swirl around my face and I took a deep breath in, allowing myself to feel the heat within my skin. I didn't have to rush this time, not like when Stephen had asked me to escape. I could go slowly. I exhaled forcefully and I felt the air begin to surge and pulse around me, a low rumble emitted from the center of the room as flames began to dance off my body. Flashes of what looked like lightening appeared at the base of the fire that was once burning and another deep growl of thunder shook the hut. I was breathing hard and I lifted my eyes up toward the roof, sending fingers of flames shooting upward. They shifted from elongated ribbons to huge rolling clouds of fire, tumbling and growing in size and speed as the storm of fire surged around me. I stood, untouched in the middle of the lightening, the clouds and the thunder, my blood boiling over and my skin radiating in its own fire. My hands at my sides and with my fists clenched, I inhaled, expanding my lungs as much as they would allow and I gathered the entire storm within my body, engulfing myself in the surge of flames. I heard someone yell. My body lurched upwards and I sprung from my space on the ground and out from somewhere deep inside, the fire became my own breath and in a single heartbeat, I exhaled the entire storm in a ball of fire so vast that it plunged everything into darkness. There was no moonlight, there was no starlight, no tiny torches, only fire and breath; at that moment, they were one in the same.

I crashed to the ground, but I landed solidly on my feet. I raised my hand and called the fire into my palm, decreasing the storm to a single ball of flames and smoke. I tossed it casually back into the pit and watched as it reignited itself into a calm little camp-side fire, illuminating the hut in it's soft and peaceful glow. My breath was amazingly calm as was my mind, but as soon as I came back to myself, to my current situation—I was overwhelmed. I grasped my chest, trying to keep the pieces of myself together. I couldn't breathe; I couldn't speak. My foundation could no longer withstand the storms of what my life had become and I was collapsing under the weight of it all. Someone shifted and stepped forward. I gathered myself enough to see Nathanial moving, ghostlike, towards me. I sobbed and ran, jumping into his arms and wrapping my legs around his waist. I buried my head in his neck, holding him so closely, not wanting him to leave me, not wanting him to forget me.

He held me, and there we stood, in the middle of the hut, surrounded by Demons and fire and death, we stood, holding each other. I heard breathing begin and whispers start to penetrate the intimacy of our moment. He pulled his face back and bent his lips to my ear.

"Wait outside Ana." His voice was barely audible. Gently he disentangled me from around his body and set me down, not looking at me. Was there something wrong? Had I done too much? Not enough? Everyone was staring at me and I felt embarrassed, self-conscious. Nathanial motioned towards Micah and he whispered something in his ear as he stepped forward. Micah nodded and turned to me, offering his arm. I looked at Nathanial, but still he kept his eyes averted. I swallowed and let Micah escort me outside. We stood in the darkness, just the two of us and I turned to look at Micah. I saw Patric in his face, they had the same beautiful turquoise eyes and I smiled in spite of myself. Patric would have been proud of me tonight; he would have wanted to see what his blood allowed for me to do.

"No Ana," Micah said, reaching to hold my face in his hands. "What you experienced tonight, what you were able to do, that does not come from a few drops of blood, that comes from your very soul; it is everything that you are separate from Patric, separate from Nathanial. It is all of your journeys, all of your regrets, all of your memories, all of your love. The fire is only as powerful as the soul who commands it and it is only as destructive and corruptible as its wielder. The fire you conjured tonight was pure, it was strong and it was full of so much courage and love that it left none untouched." His eyes held mine and I could see images, pictures inside the very pupils, pictures of a beautiful woman holding two babies in her arms, pictures of two strong teenage boys, their arms around each other, a picture of Patric, his head in his hands, Nathanial at his side reaching for him, a picture of Nathanial on a beach, sobbing onto a lifeless body—my body, a picture of Noni and me in a meadow, me grasping her hands, a picture of me and Lucie and Stephen standing against a wall of fire, a picture of Nathanial and me, my legs wrapped around his waist, him holding me. I gasped and pulled away.

"Micah." Nathanial appeared outside, his eyes surveying me. "Take Ana and Lucie to the house, I'll be there shortly." His voice sounded sharp and tight and my stomach dropped. Micah nodded and put his hand on my shoulder, guiding me into the night.

Micah's house was small, but cozy and it sat at the base of the mountains. It took us over three hours to get there from the camp and Lucie slept the whole way with one of Micah's guards driving us. My body was tense and I had a deep foreboding that threatened to darken my mind. We were set up in a guest room, equipped with a soft bed and our own bathroom. If I hadn't been on the edge of complete panic, I would have allowed myself to relax within the quiet space. Instead, I laid Lucie down in the bed and followed Micah out into the living room where he was lighting the fireplace. I didn't want to be alone with my thoughts. Micah poured us each a glass of wine and he settled down on the couch next to me. We sat silently, sipping our drinks and staring into the flames. I broke the silence.

"Micah, I asked Nathanial to take care of Lucie for me, especially if her parents and Stephen were killed. Do you think he will?" I asked, not looking at him.

"Yes, Ana. Nathanial will do anything you ask," he said quietly.

"Not anything," I murmured, thinking about tonight's discussion.

"Ana, Nathanial knows that the chance of you surviving such an onslaught of blood to your system, with everything that you have already endured, is near impossible, you would most likely die in the transition. He's terrified of losing you, he does love you, no matter what you think." Micah turned the full force of his eyes upon me.

"I would survive the Change from the Vampires, what's the difference?" I asked.

"The difference is that changing into a Vampire essentially ends your Human life; for all intents and purposes, you die when you become a Vampire. The Bonder transition does not kill your Human self—it enhances who you already are, you become a better and sometimes, worse version of yourself; you would carry all of your best and worst qualities into the newer version of who you are, but you are still Human."

"At least Stephen gave my request thought; at least he thought of me as valuable enough to possibly consider keeping me with him," I said, my voice rising.

"Was that before or after he tried to kill you?" Nathanial spoke. I turned to see him enter the room. He crossed behind us and poured himself a glass of wine, his face showing just a hint of smirk. Anger and despair filled my muscles and I stood up, facing him.

"You tried to kill me as well, did you forget, or are we feeling that we've accumulated enough humanitarian points this evening to not acknowledge that incident?" I scoffed at him, the rush of desire and love that I had felt for him earlier, giving way to resentment at his criticism of Stephen.

"Ahhh, I see; you have feelings for Stephen, of course that makes sense. You can't help it. You keep choosing the partners that will never, that can never stay with you Ana." He took a sip of his drink and surveyed me over the glass. Why was he acting like this? Did he have some sort of multiple-personality disorder? My chest constricted upon hearing his words and I stepped closer to him, my hands balled into fists.

"I chose *you* Nathanial," I said quietly, trying to break his insane and hurtful tone. "I asked *you* to marry me, you, not Patric, not Stephen—*you*. Are you saying that you would have left me if we'd gotten married? Are you saying that by choosing you to love, to share my life with, that you would have not wanted to stay with me? Is that what you are saying, because when you speak of Patric and Stephen, you speak of very different kinds of love than what I felt, what I do feel for you still Nathanial, but perhaps you are just too jaded, to lost from yourself to understand what it means to feel compassion, to feel hope, to want someone to understand that you acknowledge their value even with their flaws, with their bad decisions; perhaps that's just too human for you, too weak. Perhaps *I* am just too weak for you," I said bitterly, my breath coming in short bursts. I wanted to

121

shake him, to wake him up from this bizarre person that was standing in front of me, but I didn't. Instead, I put my glass on the table, nodded at Micah and walked out of the room.

I curled up on the bed, pulling Lucie close to me, feeling the warmth of her tiny body, but even Lucie couldn't quell the utter despair and grief that I was experiencing. I felt so frigid, that all I could do was sit and stare without blinking, trying not to feel. Sometime during the night I rolled over to stare out the window and noticed that Nathanial was sitting in a chair, the wind blowing his hair like dark curtains around his face. He was startling to look at; his beauty and power amplified by his contemplation. Lucie murmured in her sleep, saying my name and I smoothed her hair back from her face.

"I'm sorry Ana, for what I said. I shouldn't have been so hurtful; it wasn't right." His voice pierced through the space between us and I shuddered trying to take a breath.

"What the hell is wrong with you?" I asked, my tone quiet but desperate. "Why are you being so awful to me? Did I hurt you that bad Nathanial? I tried to apologize to you, to tell you that I never meant to leave things the way I did—you had none of it, so why the attitude now?" I sat up, trying to get a better look at his face. He sighed and leaned forward in the chair.

"I suppose I'm a bit jealous Ana. I've seen Stephen in your mind, I know how you feel about him, what he's come to mean to you. Envy is a very destructive trait, but there it is nonetheless." He looked at me, grinning slightly. I bowed my head; I didn't want to feel guilty about the feelings I had for Stephen, but I did and no matter what happened to me, even if I was allowed to live, any person that I was with, I would always feel guilty about being with them; I still felt that I belonged to Nathanial despite the fact that he clearly no longer wanted to be with me. He studied me intently, processing my thoughts. His silence was making me nervous.

"So, what did they decide?" I asked, although my heart already knew the answer. He shifted away from me, leaning his head against the back of the chair.

"I'm sorry Ana. I did everything that I could; they don't understand you or your power. It frightens them and fear almost always leads to rushed and poor decisions…" His voice became soft. I nodded and sat back, pulling Lucie close to me.

"When?" I said, trying to breathe slowly. Nathanial looked at me, his face hard and his jaw set, his breath coming in rapid pulses. "Oh. I guess they don't want to wait around to see if I'll blow them up?" I laughed darkly. "Who?" I said, my heart sinking. Nathanial looked away from me, standing to stare out the window. "You?" I said, incredulous. How could that be? Nathanial sighed and kept his back to me.

"A punishment of sorts," he said bitterly, "for taking your request into my own hands, for not following procedure." His tone was black and I felt my skin crawl. I sighed. I couldn't help but to notice how Nathanial was like the book ends to my life. First his attack on me at the University, the one that should have most certainly killed me, the life that happened in between, and now Nathanial would be the one to bring every thing it's finality. It was funny, I recalled the first night I met him; I was so concerned that it would be *me* making the decision to end *his* life, and possibly mine, by not agreeing to the Bonding, and I remembered him saying that no matter what, our lives and our deaths would always be intrinsically bound—they were one in the same. Lucie stirred and opened her eyes, blinking wearily at me.

"Hey baby," I said softly. "Did we wake you?" She shook her head "no" and moved to crawl into my lap. Nathanial turned from the window and sat down on the end of the bed, watching us.

"Book ends…" he murmured, his face searching mine. Lucie eyed him, then smiled and started to suck on her thumb.

"Who are you?" she asked, drool dripping down her hand. Nathanial looked at me, clearly surprised by her verbal ability.

"She's advanced for her age." I laughed and grabbed a tissue to wipe her hand. Lucie laughed. "This is Nathanial," I said, dabbing her face. She leaned forward, trying to get a better look at his face.

"Are you taking care of us?" she asked, her words sounding clear and strong. Nathanial's eyes widened, seeing the irony of her question. She leaned forward more, falling on her stomach, laughing. Immediately Nathanial reached for her and she put her hands out for him to pick her up. He looked at me. I nodded and watched as Lucie tucked herself against his chest, playing with his hair.

"I thought you didn't think you'd ever make a good mother," he said, holding her close. I laughed.

"Well, sometimes what you think isn't possible within yourself, turns out to be the very thing that you need," I said quietly, turning to gaze out at the moon. I turned back to look at him, Lucie pulling his hair down around her face.

"You smell good!" she said, giggling and tossing his hair back over his shoulder. My throat closed and I tried desperately to swallow back a gut-wrenching sob. He pressed his nose to the top of her head and breathed in deeply.

"So do you," Nathanial said quietly, his eyes on me. "Is she...?" he trailed off as he spoke.

"She's half," I said, understanding his question. I let my mind finish the story, not wanting Lucie to hear about how she'd been found. Nathanial shook his head, seeing the images that Carmen had conjured for me, in what seemed like lifetimes ago. "Nathanial?" I asked, moving myself back against the pillows. He turned to me. "Will it just be the two of us?" I was hoping that if I was going to die, that it would be a private moment. He bowed his head.

"They want to be present, Ana. They don't trust me right now." His voice was dead. I nodded.

"You know how I always wanted to die? I wanted to be taken out in one of the Godfather moments, like with a big car explosion, you know when someone goes out to their car in the morning and they turn the key and the whole thing goes up in flames..." Nathanial looked at me, slightly stunned at my pop culture reference to how I wanted my own death to be emulated. I smiled at him and shrugged. A thought that I had been trying to keep at bay, managed to surface. "Will it hurt?" I asked him, the question sounded strange to my ears and I was surprised that I had said it out loud.

"BOOM!" Lucie declared and laughed, twisting herself around so she could look at me.

"Yes, boom!" I said, laughing at her. She turned back to Nathanial and began kissing his face. He looked at me, a wave of shock falling over his face.

"Christ, she's just like you," he said softly, moving his lips to kiss her forehead.

"Is that bad?" I said, smirking at him, both of us remembering how it took him months to get used to my rather affectionate nature.

"No, Ana, it's not bad...it's beautiful," he said, handing Lucie back to me.

"You haven't answered my question," I said, watching his face. He stood and ran his fingers through his hair, pacing.

"I don't...I can't talk about this with you..." He sounded angry, but not with me.

"Well, I'd rather hear it from you than anyone else Nathanial. I trust you not to lie to me..." I trailed off, thinking about our last argument, thinking about what he'd done with those other women, the women that Stephen told me about. He sighed loudly, clearly exasperated by my recollections. "Sorry," I said. "It's not like it matters anymore—it's not like it should have ever mattered," I said softly. He held out his hand for me to take. I shifted Lucie to the bed and let him pull me up. He placed me in front of him so I was staring out at the mountains and the moon. His fingers smoothed down the back of my head, weaving themselves into my hair, raking and combing the curls. Waves of heat began to lap over the back of my neck. He swept my hair to one side, exposing my neck and my metal tattoo. I couldn't remember the last time that I had looked at it, months maybe? It had been hurting me ever since we arrived here, but I refused to see what new configuration it was succumbing to at the moment. His fingers traced along the patterns, following the bonded lines of metal and stone. I shuddered and he turned me so that I was facing him. Slowly, he unbuttoned his shirt, revealing the hard lines of his chest. He pulled the sleeves down over his shoulders and I could see his own metal inscription, carved deeply right over his heart. It hadn't shown up until after the night at the University, but I had a recollection of its distinct yet familiar pattern. Nathanial's mark had the same combination of my silver and jewels, his midnight blue universe and the sharp turquoise stone of Patric and his mother, but it had something that mine did not. At the very center of the pattern there was what appeared to be an eye, liquid brown, with gold and bronze flecks framing the iris. The gaze that it emitted was so deep and penetrating that my finger automatically went to graze over its shape. As I stroked, Nathanial's chest began to flex and tremble and his eyes closed. I pulled away and looked at him

"What is that? Why do you have that?" I asked, still memorized by his new addition. He took my hand and placed it over his entire mark and I could feel the pulse and strength of his heart.

"Do you not recognize your own eyes Ana? Can you not identify with their beauty, their depth? Do you not see yourself in my heart?" I gasped, understanding gripping by body. My other hand shot around to my mark and I felt a familiar shape in the center of the entwined metals, an eye.

"Is it yours?" I asked, incredulous. He smiled at me.

"Well, sometimes it is," he said calmly, still pressing my hand over his heart.

"What do you mean?" I replied, not understanding his response.

"Yours seems to change color; it shifts, like the tides," he spoke quietly. He had said something similar about my mark before, when we were going to Patric's villa for that awful dinner, that dinner with the blood ritual discussion. "Hmmm, that's right, you have such a powerful memory," he said, turning me back around so he could examine my mark again. My body seized at his touch; a sudden realization began creeping into my soul.

"No," I whispered. "No, you can't take it from me." My voice was shaking. "You can't Nathanial; it's all I have, it's all I have of you, of Patric, of myself. You can do anything else, anything, but please, you can't rip this from me—it's all I have!" The sobs that I had been trying to quell suddenly burst forth from my chest and I fell to my knees. I heard the door open and Micah stepped in from the hallway.

"Nathanial," he said, his voice soft. His eyes found me on the floor, my head bent, my chest heaving. I looked up at Nathanial and saw him nod, then he turned and walked out the door, leaving me on the ground. Micah moved next to me, pulling me up gently. "Shhh, now. Ana, look at me." He brushed my hair back from my face and took my chin in his hand. I gulped and looked into his eyes. Pictures again began to swim in their depths and I felt the very essence of my soul being pulled forward. Fire, a huge storm of flames and lightening passed in front of my vision. I saw Nathanial and I standing and facing

128

each other, at least I thought it was me, the woman looked different somehow; she looked powerful, strong and fierce as fire danced around them. I saw the woman, bend on one knee and Nathanial moved to stand over her. The image shifted, and I saw a hut, burning, being consumed, exploding. A new picture, the woman holding a little girl close to her and gathering herself, her whole body, then she disappeared, whipped away in a blur, her body leaving behind the glow of embers and shadows. Then blackness. I gasped, breathless and pulled back from Micah. He was staring at me, his eyes wild in their movement. He was searching my face, wanting me to understand. He wanted me to fight.

Chapter Six

Nathanial

No one spoke, no one moved. I could hear every heartbeat in the room, except my own; mine had stopped. We waited, every second ticking by like a single breath from her soul, fleeting, disappearing— dying. Someone touched my shoulder and I jumped, startled by the movement. Nicholas, the demon who had asked Ana to demonstrate her power, he was standing next to me, his face somber.

"This isn't what we would have wanted for you Nathanial. You know how valuable you are to us, how much we depend on your skills, your insights…this is never something we would want you to do…never." His voice came out rough. I shrugged off his hand and went to walk by the entrance, waiting. More seconds passed, more breaths, then headlights pierced the darkness and my body went numb. I watched as Micah opened her door, as she walked with him, arm in arm, just like she had done with Kai the first day I had waited for her—too many lifetimes ago. They approached me at the entrance and I saw Micah take Ana's face in his hands, he was wiping tears from her cheeks and whispering to her. She nodded and her body suddenly went rigid, she took a deep breath and turned to look at me. As she passed in front of me, she reached out and ran her fingers gently over my heart, caressing my metal imprint, making it burn and scorch my skin. I inhaled sharply and looked into her eyes; they were black, black onyx and small embers pulsed and flickered inside their depths. I gasped. Immediately, my mind conjured images of Patric, when I had seen him angry, ready to fight, that's when the fire in his eyes burned the strongest, the brightest. I felt a sudden thudding in my chest—my heart had started to beat again as I stood watching Ana take her place back in the center of the circle; there was no fire lit this time. Micah stayed outside, pacing back and forth; he looked anxious. I moved to stand next to her, facing my brethren as they lined up in front of us.

"Ana, do you understand the nature of why you are here?" Nicholas asked, his eyes lowered. She nodded. "Could you please answer 'yes' or 'no'?" Nicholas asked her, his voice going tight.

"Yes," she said, her own tone, strong and even. "Yes, I understand why I am here." I felt a surge of heat so intense that I turned around, fully expecting to see something on fire behind me.

"Is something the matter, Nathanial?" Nicholas asked, his eyes darting over my shoulder. He was nervous.

"No," I said, my skin beginning to warm by the unknown source of heat. I looked at Ana out of the corner of eye. She was still, completely unmoving. I wasn't sure if she was even breathing.

"Ana, do you understand that your mark will be removed, effectively breaking the Bond you have with your Bonder?" Again, my heart stopped and I closed my eyes.

"Yes," she said and I felt another blast of heat disrupt the molecules in the air; they shifted.

"Nathanial, do you understand the nature of what your are being asked to perform here this evening?" Nicholas asked me, his eyes still lowered.

"Yes," I whispered.

"Nathanial, do you understand that by removing the mark from your Bond, that you are no longer Bonded to this Human and that any resulting powers that were inherited through such a joining may or may not be diminished by the Human's resulting death?" I couldn't speak, my throat closed and my breath stopped. "Nathanial? Do you understand the conditions as I have spoken them?" Nicholas asked again, his eyes narrowing upon seeing my face. I turned to look at Ana. She seemed taller all of a sudden and the shadow that she cast, overwhelmed my own. She didn't meet my gaze.

"Yes," I replied softly. "Yes, I understand." I wasn't going to do this; this wasn't going to happen. I would kill each and every one of them if I had to, but I would not take Ana's life; I would never take Ana's life. My heart started beating rapidly and my muscles tensed. Adrenaline flooded my mouth and I felt a low growl begin to vibrate in my chest. Nicholas' head shot up and our eyes met. He cleared his throat.

"Ana, would you please kneel in front of Nathanial." His tone was wary and his eyes were darting back and forth between Ana and me. I would have to be quick, precise. Any errant movement and I could kill her. I wanted to knock her out so I could get her out of here. I shot Micah a mental image of what I wanted and hoped that he would listen to me, that he would know what to do. She moved her body in front of me, her back to the line of the Council. She knelt down, her eyes

132

catching mine, but before I could show her what I was thinking, her voice penetrated into my mind; *I will protect you, just stay close to me and I swear on my life that I will keep you safe. Please forgive me Nathanial, I am so very sorry—for everything.* It was Ana's voice, but it was different, it was dark and menacing and full of violence and it shook me to my core. I took a step back from her, not comprehending what she was saying. Suddenly, a wave of heat broke through from somewhere deep inside my chest; it burned through my flesh and filtered its way to the metal over my heart—scalding me. I screamed and stumbled backward as I saw flames begin to shoot out from my mark. I was paralyzed. Ana rose from her spot on the ground and for the second time in our lives together—I didn't recognize her. She threw me backwards landing me in a circle of blue flames as my body writhed and burned under the intense heat. One by one, I saw each demon in the line explode, igniting the hut in a storm of blue fire. Screaming shattered the very atoms in the air as she lifted the entire line of demons straight up, spinning them, wrapping fire around their bodies. The smell of burning flesh flooded my nose and I gagged, trying to sit up. My chest heaved and my mark ignited on its own, sending a pain so vast and so intense into my heart that I called out, wanting her to make it stop.

She turned to look at me and I saw her face, it was shifting back and forth in form and for a brief moment I thought I saw a flash of bright turquoise appear in her eyes and I thought I saw my brother staring back at me, his face smooth and his eyes burning. I reached out to him, but Ana's body had begun to shimmer in and out of itself and his face disappeared. She turned once more to the line of burning and charred bodies now strewn across the hut. With one wave of her hand, they rolled together in a giant cloud of fire, raging and storming through the roof. I heard the ceiling explode from the force of her command and showers of flame began to rain down. She blurred to my side and suddenly I was able to stand. I rose up, still surrounded by the blue circle of flame, my chest burning, my heart on fire. She waved her hand and I felt a cooling and numbing wash over me. Fire was all around us, but it was quiet, still. The silence between the flames pulsed out toward our bodies, I wanted to go to her, to hold her, but I couldn't move forward.

"Micah!" she yelled, her eyes on me. Instantaneously, Micah came to her side, holding Lucie. "He'll need some care." She looked at me, her eyes dark as she took hold of the little girl. I noticed that none of the flames from the explosion were creeping towards us; they were burning the place down, yet we were all safe, protected. Lucie was crying, the only sound in the vast quiet of the fire. Micah nodded and he looked at her.

"Hurry!" he said. Ana nodded and hugged Lucie close to her. She spoke to the little girl as if speaking to a good friend.

"Remember last time? Remember with Stephen and the fire? Remember what we needed to do?" Ana's voice was commanding and Lucie shook her head, wrapping her arms around Ana's neck and kissing her cheek. Ana looked at me, "I love you Nathanial; I always have. I would die for you—I would have died for you. Maybe one day we can find our way back to each other, maybe it's not too late for us. Maybe you can love me again, I don't know." She looked at me, looked at Micah and moved to plant a gentle kiss on his cheek. "Thank you my dear friend, thank you for allowing me to find my own

134

redemption, for seeing me when I couldn't see myself, for acknowledging my love for Nathanial, for Lucie, for Patric." I saw her curve her body inward, so much so that I thought she might crush Lucie. I saw her form shimmer in and out, in and out, and then—she disappeared.

Ana

I couldn't stop throwing up. The effects of my lack in ability to shimmer were wreaking havoc on my body. As a human, I shouldn't have been able to escape like that; shimmering was a supernatural power, a power of Vampires and Bonders. Somehow Micah knew that I might just have enough of Patric and of Nathanial in me to make it happen, that I had enough love for Lucie and surprisingly, for myself, that I could do what I needed, to save us.

Noni was tending to me and keeping an eye on Lucie who, amazingly, had come through the whole thing unscathed. She was so strong. In between my vomiting episodes, I had managed to tell Noni everything that had occurred since she'd told me to go back to Indonesia. She wasn't surprised and she wasn't judgmental about me having to kill several Bonders in order to escape; she just wrapped her arms around me and whispered in my ear, *"I know my love, my precious bambina. You saved yourself, you saved this precious child like I knew you would do; there is no judgment here."* I wanted to ask her if I had done what her vision foresaw, if someone, besides Lucie, and myself had managed to be saved; I still didn't know who that could be.

135

Stephen might be dead and Nathanial... well, he seemed dead, he seemed not himself, and he still never told me that he loved me, not even when I was kneeling in front of him, waiting to die. Perhaps he was too far-gone now to ever find his way back and I wondered if he would have killed me that night; I tried not to think about that possibility.

Noni kept ushering cups of tea into my mouth; they tasted bitter and harsh, but after a week of drinking nothing but her concoctions, the waves of nausea and vomiting eventually subsided. Soon, I was up walking around and able to look after Lucie myself. Noni was in the depths of negotiating a peace agreement with the Vampires that had shown up on the Reservation. Amazingly, this particular coven did not kill the humans that they found living here or the Bonders; they were trying to find a way to establish a land agreement without resulting in violence. Every night Noni would come back frustrated and exhausted, as the talks stalled and compromises couldn't be agreed upon. She was working so hard to protect her people and I wished that I could help. If I was being honest though, I really didn't want anything to do with anyone right now except Lucie. I was just trying to get my bearings after so much horror had happened to me and I didn't want my attention to be diverted from Lucie. She needed me and I knew that she missed Carmen and Liam. All I could do, was try to love her as much as they did. I had protected her and I knew that Carmen's soul could rest easy knowing that I would always protect her daughter; for as long as I had a breath in this world, Lucie would be safe.

The care of the wolf sanctuary fell mainly to me and I had taken to getting Lucie used to being around the animals. I knew they wouldn't harm her and she quickly became one of their closest friends. I would give her a brush and plop her down in the middle of the food prep area and she would sit on the floor, two or three wolves nestled against her, and she would brush and comb their pelts, laughing and singing to herself while I prepared their meals. Every so often, I would stare at her and fear and panic would wash over me. I wasn't sure if we were now being hunted; five murders of Bonders by a human couldn't bode well for us. Noni, however, seemed confident that as long as we stayed on the Reservation, we would be safe. I would just have to trust her, no matter what my instincts were telling me.

It was a Saturday and Noni had offered to take Lucie for a short hike into the mountains and I was planning on cleaning up my old sculling boat from when I was a teenager, and going for a row. I needed the exercise. My body felt tight and my muscles were cramped; they needed to move.

The lake was a vast one, and it wound its way around the base of the mountains, with steep valleys opening up as it stretched its liquid curves into distant nooks and crannies. It was a good place to get lost for a while, a quiet place. I let my mind wander as I pulled the oars through the water, thinking about Nathanial and wondering if he hated me. The eye on the inside of my mark was still changing color and I had hoped that eventually it would settle on something, perhaps giving me an inclination about what was going to happen to me, if Nathanial would ever come back, if he would ever want to find me. I also let myself think about Stephen, about how we'd been so close to each other the night of the fire, about how much of a man he was to me, about how he had saved Lucie and me by believing in what I could do, by acknowledging my love for Lucie and for him. I was comfortable in my knowledge that I had grown to love Stephen. He'd been the closest thing to a friend that I had in the months after leaving Nathanial and I came to depend on him, on our quiet moments together, on what he had shared with me about the first woman that he had ever loved when he was human, on the way he sang to me, the way he looked at me when he strummed his guitar...and just like Patric, he was now embedded in my heart and in my soul. I thought that there was something very, very special about my feelings for Stephen, something unique and commanding that I had yet to understand. He'd changed me in a way, brought me closer to who I'd always wanted to be growing up, but could not attain due to my circumstances. Stephen let me laugh, he made me smile and there was an acute sense of the most soul stirring calm that I felt whenever he was near.

I finished my row and arrived back at house to find Noni pacing on the deck. She looked agitated. "Noni! What's wrong, did something happen? Where's Lucie?" My eyes darted back and forth between her and the inside of the house, searching.

"Lucie's fine, bambina, our Council needs a bit of help and I am trying to sort out if what I need is the best thing." She took a deep breath and centered herself.

"What do you need Noni? Is there anything that I can do? I'll do anything," I asked, still looking through the door, my heart uneasy. Noni crossed to stand in front of me, placing her hands on my face.

"My precious, my love, my child; I'm afraid that our negotiating skills have faltered somewhat and we are standing on the edge of a knife.

138

We need help." Her eyes met mine and I could see what she would never ask of me, what she would never allow herself to say that she needed. I grasped her hands and pressed my lips to her cheeks, kissing them gently. I nodded at her.

"Let's go," I said calmly. I called for Lucie and the three of us piled into Noni's jeep and made the journey into the township of the Reservation. She explained on the way that the Vampire coven was not willing to sacrifice the little land they had managed to acquire from the Bonders years ago, for a different, much larger acreage of land that was set away from the majority of the human population in the area. Of course, I thought, what Vampire would want to be kept away from the most dense blood supply—they could be lazy and unwilling to travel to satisfy their hunger. They were letting their bloodlust run their negotiations, not what they wanted in terms of status and land. I had seen this before and in fact, one of the first cases that Caleb assigned to me was to mediate between Vampires and humans over just such a scenario. It was one of the most arduous mental exercises that I had ever experienced and it took every ounce of my innate diplomatic skills to broker a deal. I could do this, mediation was when I was closest to my true self; I remember Noni telling me once, that my father had been an exceptionally skilled negotiator. Perhaps having me wasn't a total loss I thought, as we pulled up to the tribal council's house.

I hoisted Lucie onto my hip and took Noni's hand, and together we walked up the stairs. So many people greeted me that I remembered from my childhood, people that had watched me grow up in Noni's care, people who taught me about the Spirit of Nature, the glory and mysticism of wolves and the inner eye of knowing the soul. All these faces now turned to me, their smiles not reaching their eyes; they were scared. I hugged each one in turn, letting my hands hold their faces.

I took Lucie's hand and walked into the living room where a long table had been arranged in front of a blazing fire. I was looking down at Lucie as she was showing me a rock she'd found on her hike, and my attention was occupied. I felt the fire shift the air around us as fragrance that I knew, wafted into every pore, and my body froze to the ground. I raised my head and I saw a pair of clear, marine-blue eyes staring wide at my face, looking stunned and overwhelmed with emotion. Suddenly, my body lurched forward and I started to run towards Stephen, but I saw him shake his head subtlety and I halted mid-stride. Something was wrong. I quickly surveyed the table where Stephen was sitting and saw Christopher to his right, another Vampire that I didn't recognize next to him, and then to Stephen's left was Liam. I heard Lucie cry out to her father and dart forward. Liam's head shot up and I saw his face register his daughter, now running towards him. He looked to be in shock. Noni appeared behind me, her face solemn and smooth. She took my hand and led me around to the front of the table. I felt Stephen's eyes on me, but I didn't look at him. I did, however, look at Liam as I passed. Lucie was stroking his face and kissing his cheeks. As I moved by them, her little hands shot out and she reached for me.

"Ana," she said, shifting to stand in her father's lap. Liam stared at me, his eyes soft and I saw his mouth tremble.

"Stay with your dad for a moment, baby girl, ok? I'll just be right over here." I cooed to her, bending my face close to hers and kissing the top of her head. Liam took a shaky breath in and I saw him attempt to compose himself. It took a while to get everyone settled and to stop chatting and talking over one another, but after about twenty minutes, Noni stood to address the table. I noticed that Liam had moved Lucie to the floor next to him, but she looked uncomfortable. I caught his eye and I moved quietly to her side, picking her up and placing her on the couch. I fetched my purse and pulled out her favorite coloring book and a few crayons and smoothed her hair back. Liam nodded at me and he looked slightly shell-shocked as I walked passed him, but I also felt a rough hand reach out and graze my fingertips, heating my entire arm. Stephen. I didn't look at him and returned to my seat next to Noni.

After Noni introduced me, and after I had listened to all sides of the issue, we got straight to business. As far as mediators went, I was a bit unconventional. I had a very "lay all cards on the table" approach and I had very little tolerance for manipulative behavior—from any group. I was straightforward, patient to a point, fair and extremely well versed on the tactics used by Demons, humans and Vampires alike; it was impossible to pull any wool over my eyes because I had either seen it all, heard it all or, as with the events of my most recent past, I'd experienced it all. Of course the humans in the group were the most emotive and their passion for their needs was causing a bit of a volatile environment. I leaned forward as one of Noni's elders began to raise his voice, his tone angry. He was glaring at Liam. I stared at the man and placed my hand over his arm.

"Ok," I said calmly, my voice penetrating through the shouting. "Let's just take a breath for a moment," I said, squeezing the man's arm gently. He closed his eyes and sat back in his chair. "In case I forgot to mention at the beginning of this discussion," I said casually, but my tone was commanding and I saw Stephen raise his eyes to stare at me, "I do not tolerate raised voices during a mediation; they serve no purpose and it's the fastest way to ensure that no one will ever get what they want," I said, looking at each individual in turn, my eyes pulsing. "Are we understood." I spoke the words not as a question and I could see the Vampires all turn to look at Liam. I shook my head—apparently individualism within covens was not tolerated, unless you were like Andres, I thought. I glanced up and saw that Stephen was watching me, his eyes churning and turbulent. As it turned out, Stephen was an excellent negotiator and he and I, along with several elders and Bonders, were able to hash out a very tentative agreement—very tentative. It would take a few more meetings before anything official could be passed. I was exhausted.

I pushed my chair back from the table and shook the hands of everyone at the meeting, finally getting to Stephen and Liam. I nodded at both of them, showing no emotion in my face. Lucie had appeared at my side, clinging to my leg and begging for me to pick her up. I turned to speak to Liam.

"I'm sure she would love to spend some time with you Liam. Would you like to keep her with you?" I didn't know what kind of arrangement he would want now, I was unsure if he would be taking Lucie back with him, wherever he was living at the moment. I felt a wave of sadness crash over me at the thought of being without her, but I remembered the declaration that I had made in front of that stupid Council with Nathanial. I would fight to get her back to her parents, to keep her safe until they could be reunited.

"May we go somewhere private for a moment Ana?" Liam asked me, his voice quiet. I looked at Noni who was fully engrossed in conversation with several of the elders. I caught her eye and she nodded, but not before staring hard at both Liam and Stephen. I motioned for the two of them to follow me out to the back deck. I leaned my back against the railing, trying to keep as much distance between us a possible; I just wasn't sure what to expect from anyone anymore. Lucie tucked her head against my neck and I heard her sigh. She was sleepy. I waited for them to speak, but they just stood there staring at me and at Lucie. I decided to break the silence.

"I'm very glad that you both survived," I said, looking at Stephen. "I promised that I would keep Lucie safe, that I would protect her…" Lucie raised her head up and shouted,

"Ana go boom! Ana made a huge fire boom, daddy, huge!" She laughed and turned her face back into my neck. I saw Liam and Stephen exchange glances, worried glances.

"We received news of the explosion, that Bonders were killed in a massive fire…"Liam said, his eyes on his daughter. "Ana, was that you?" he asked, his voice steady on the surface, but I sensed an undercurrent of an emotion I couldn't decipher. I shrugged and kissed Lucie.

"I was pretty sure that Nathanial was going to kill me, what choice did I have," I said, nuzzling my face into her dark hair. Again, Stephen and Liam exchanged shocked glances.

"You were in Nathanial's care?" Liam asked. I laughed out loud despite myself.

143

"Umm, care, would be a bit of a stretch. We were prisoners, he looked after us though…" I trailed off, not wanting to be critical of Nathanial. "Lucie was well tended to, she's healthy, I promise." I looked at Liam and smiled.

"I don't understand, Ana," Stephen finally spoke, his eyes wide and clear. "Did you say that Nathanial was going to *kill* you?" The word "kill" falling from his lips. He seemed incredulous. I sighed.

"Look, it's a really long story, and I'd be happy to spend all evening catching you up on the horrors that have been my life for the last few weeks, but perhaps we should decide what to do about this little one first, no?" I said, looking at Liam. He was staring at me, penetrating my very core with his gaze.

"Would you mind if I took Lucie with me tonight, Ana? Although, I hate to separate her from you, she's so attached…" His voice became a whisper. I had never seen this side of Liam before, he was emotive and I could tell that he was struggling against the current of his feelings. I nodded. Stephen stared at me.

"I know you've had a long night Ana, but would you mind spending a bit of time talking with us—just for a while?" His eyes searched mine and I felt my bones go soft.

"Of course," I said, smiling at him. "Whatever you want Stephen." He motioned for me to follow them back into the house. I stopped to tell Noni what I was doing and she grasped my hands, Stephen stopped as well.

"Thank you my dear child, thank you for helping us. My precious bambina, my love." She then turned to Stephen and reached to touch his hand, her voice changed; it became dark and quiet. "If any harm comes to her, if any hurt befalls her heart, her body or her soul, you will suffer the consequences, you will never find the redemption that I know you seek and you will continue to live in the hell that you have tried to bury in your heart. If you love her as your eyes tell me that you do, you will protect her and offer her the very same grace that she so unselfishly offered to you." I gasped and moved Stephen away from her.

"Noni!" I scolded her. She looked at me and I could see that she was crying.

"She's right Ana, I deserved that, and she's right." Stephen moved and gently took Noni's face in his hands. "On my very existence, no harm will come to her," he said and Noni nodded, turning back to her conversation. I felt Stephen's hand on my back as we walked out of the room.

Stephen and Liam had a cabin not too far down from Noni and me, but the drive was rough and I was glad that I didn't have much on my stomach. Stephen drove, and I noticed that every few minutes his eyes would find mine in the rearview mirror and I wondered if he was glad to see me or maybe, like Nathanial, it was just too hard to care about me. I saw him shake his head as he heard my thoughts. Liam carried Lucie into the house and I touched his arm.

"Umm, she hasn't eaten much today," I said, not wanting to intrude into his parenting with his daughter. "She's been a bit picky, foodwise and I'm guessing she might be a bit hungry," I told him quietly. Lucie turned to me and pouted.

"I'm not picky, I'm refined," she said, laughing at me.

"Oh, you're right, I'm so sorry; you are refined." I laughed and ruffled her hair. Liam's eyes widened and I smiled at him. "Your toddler is refined." I said, turning to follow them into the kitchen. I couldn't imagine that they actually had food in the cabin. Liam and Stephen didn't eat, although Stephen was an excellent chef, I recalled.

"Well, let's see," Stephen turned to me and smiled, but his face was showing some emotion that was so intense, my heart stirred deep in my chest, "I think they stocked this place pretty good, so I'm sure we can find something suitable for a refined palette." He smirked at Lucie and bent to kiss her cheek. "Are you hungry Ana? You must be," he asked, as he opened cabinets and drawers. I was hungry, but I didn't want to put him out. He sighed and laughed softly. "How about omelets?" He looked at Lucie and she raised her hands over her head in a sign of triumph. Both Stephen and Liam looked at me, slightly aghast. I shrugged.

"She picks up on a lot," I said, raising my own hands over my head and cheering. She laughed at me and gave me the "thumbs up" sign. Liam stared at me. I wanted to ask him about Carmen, but I didn't want Lucie to overhear if something terrible had happened; god, I hoped that she was ok. Reading my thoughts, Liam nodded and smiled. I felt a rush of relief. Carmen was a much better mother than I was, thank god she'd be able to raise Lucie. She was way smarter than me I thought, looking at the little girl who had been my companion through some of the most devastating events in my life. I hoped that Carmen would know that I did everything to keep her safe; I was ready to die for her. I heard something crash into the sink as Stephen dropped the pan he was using, his hands gripping the edge of the counter, his head bent. He had heard my thoughts and so had Liam. I sighed. I knew that I was going to have to recall everything that we had endured. Liam was not one to have details left out and besides, maybe I wanted him to know what we had experienced...it was good for him to see humanity at its best and its worst. I met his eyes and they flashed.

Stephen made me my favorite omelet, Greek, with feta cheese; I couldn't believe he remembered. Lucie kept stealing bites off my plate, until Liam got up and sprinkled some feta on top of her own eggs. She gave him another thumbs up sign and Liam laughed. I couldn't remember if I had ever heard Liam laugh, not like this, it was a beautiful sound and I wondered if my father had ever laughed like that with me. Stephen reached across the table, his fingers brushing along my hand. Eventually, Lucie fell asleep and Liam put her down in his own bed. When he returned, I felt my chest tighten and my heart rate increased.

"Relax Ana." Liam looked at me as he poured us all glasses of wine. "Just start at the beginning." He handed me a glass and I took a sip, dreading what was to come. It all seemed surreal to me and maybe I was scared that retelling the story would just make it too close; it would hurt too much. Stephen sat back and stared at me, his face contemplative.

"What happened to you Ana?" he asked. I sighed and started recounting at the point after Lucie and I left him in the house. I told them about Andres and the Bonders. I told them about meeting Micah and our first holding cell and how good Lucie was and that she never complained once. I saw Liam close his eyes when I mentioned her. I told them about being shackled and about the other prisoners, the ones who were considered traitors. Liam and Stephen exchanged glances, so I paused for a moment and took a sip of my wine. "Go on, please," Liam said. I took a deep breath and recalled to them, me seeing Nathanial for the first time. I told them about the compound and how much he had changed, that he didn't look at all like the same person. Stephen's eyes flashed and I met his gaze, wondering what he was thinking. I turned to Liam and explained that Nathanial had a doctor come and check Lucie over, that she'd been given shots; that seemed like information a parent would want to know about their child, I thought. Liam smiled and nodded at me. The next part, I struggled with, it was hard to discuss what I had done during that first meeting, but I explained to Stephen and Liam that the Council had asked me to display my abilities, that really I wasn't being given a choice. So I did and *that*, according to Nathanial, made them very frightened.

"What exactly did you do?" Stephen asked, eyeing me. I sighed.

"It's probably easier if I can just show you, mentally, I mean," I said, my eyes lowered; I felt embarrassed for some reason.

"Ana," Stephen spoke, and I looked up to meet his stare. I nodded and closed my eyes trying to conjure up the memories. I wanted Liam to see what I had spoken to the Council about protecting Lucie and

148

that I would die for her first; I wanted him to know that his daughter was never in any danger. I did the best I could with the fire stuff and I felt bad having Stephen see the moment between Nathanial and me, when he was holding me. I felt guilty and confused. I sighed and opened my eyes. Liam was gripping the table so violently, that I saw a crack begin to seep into the wood. He was staring at me, his jaw was slack and his eyes watering. I looked to Stephen. He was shaking his head and his eyes were searching over my face rapidly.

"Do you want me to continue?" I asked, unsure if I had let them see too much.

"There's more?" Liam asked. "Christ," he said quietly. He had no idea. The next part I tired to keep to a bare minimum. I didn't think they needed to see what transpired in the room with Nathanial, with our marks. That was private and too painful for me to even let my mind recall. I showed him what Micah had let me see in his eyes and I heard Liam gasp. I showed them what Nathanial had explained to me about his punishment and I showed them the two of us standing, side-by-side, the Council asking us those stupid questions. Stephen took a sharp breath in as I flooded their minds with the image of me kneeling before Nathanial, his hands on my shoulders. The rest was pretty much fire and death and Lucie and I shimmering away from Nathanial and Micah. I heard the shoving of a chair being pulled away from the table and I opened my eyes in time to see Stephen storm out of the kitchen. I heard the front door open and slam shut and I jumped at the violence of the noise.

"What's the matter?" I asked Liam, my breathing coming in short bursts. "Did I do something wrong?"

"He's not upset with you Ana," Liam said, moving to sit closer to me. "He's infuriated with Nathanial."

"Oh. Well, if it helps, I really don't believe that he would have killed me, I mean I'm not sure what he would have done, but I just can't let myself think that he...that he would let that happen..." I said quietly. Did I believe that? Was that something that I felt beyond a shadow of doubt? I wasn't sure.

"That doesn't matter to my brother Ana. Nathanial had your life in his hands and he was poised to destroy it, whether he would have or not, is not really the issue; at least not to Stephen," Liam said, his eyes intent upon my face.

"Hmm, well I can remember when my life was also in Stephen's hands, when he was poised to take my life from me; the scenario isn't really that different Liam. It's a bit hypocritical for Stephen to be so judgmental of Nathanial; the Council didn't give him a choice." Liam looked into my eyes, holding my gaze.

"Perhaps, but Nathanial could have helped you long before any of these circumstances came about, he could have honored your request to join him as a Human-type Bonder, the risk it posed to your life was far less than what was to come for you Ana, far less. Stephen sees Nathanial as selfish, just as he sees himself. Neither one of them wanted to risk losing you or to make you like them, and so they left you to endure the consequences of their behavior. I think Stephen was hoping that Nathanial would redeem himself, that he would honor who Stephen knows Nathanial truly is, that he would die for you, protect you or even Change you, even if that Change meant killing

150

you. It was a far better alternative to what he let you experience; that knowledge that it would be him to break your Bond, to sever the most scared of ties, to Stephen, that was worse than killing you." Liam was now holding my face in his hands and the gesture was shocking. He was grasping me, his eyes searching my face. Suddenly, he bowed his head and I heard him begin to sob.

"Liam, what is it?" I asked gently.

"You, Ana, you, after everything we put you through, after Andres...after everything you endured...you saved her, you protected my little girl because you knew, you believed that I loved her, that I *could* love her. You kept her safe, you...were going to die for her Ana, for *my* daughter." He was gasping and sobbing uncontrollably. I heard a movement from behind me and I turned to see Stephen standing, watching his brother fall apart in my arms. I kissed the top of his head; I didn't know what else to do and that felt right. I lifted his head gently and waited for him to gather himself.

"You should go up and see her, she likes to snuggle quite a bit at night these days," I said smiling at him. He swallowed and nodded to me, pushing his chair back. I saw him look at Stephen, their eyes meeting in the most intense way, an intimate way that only siblings could have. I looked down and took a breath.

"Ana." I looked up and Stephen was holding out his hand. I sighed and took it, letting him lead me into the living room. He lit the fire and we sat side by side on the sofa, letting the silence fill the space between us. I had to stifle the sudden urge to move next to him, to have him put his arm around me, to be pulled in close to his body. I felt him shift and stroke the side of my cheek as he gently moved closer to me. I sighed and reached for his hand.

"I thought you might have died," I said quietly, looking into his eyes. "I didn't want to leave you there, I could have saved you," I whispered as I touched his face.

"You already have saved me, Ana—many times over and more than I deserved." He reached to remove my hand from his face and he wound it around his neck, pulling me in toward his chest. He brought his face close to mine and I heard him sigh as his lips parted. Something in me jolted my body and I grasped him roughly around his neck and pulled his mouth to mine, kissing him passionately, deeply— not letting him surface. He moaned and I felt him grip the sides of my waist tightly, pressing me against him. I had fallen in love with him. This I now knew to be true and it was the most pure love that I had ever felt, besides the love that I would always have for Nathanial. This was different even to the love that I had for Patric; Stephen was everything to me, friend, love, now a protector. He believed in me and he helped me to believe in myself. I wasn't lost anymore, not when he was holding me; it was in his arms that I felt the closest to myself that I was the strongest and the most alive. He pulled his face away from mine and he stood, taking me with him down the hallway.

"Ana?" He moved us near the window next to the bed, his hands on my waist.

"What?' I replied, moving to kiss him. He pulled back and stared at me.

"I want you to be with me. I want you to always be with me." His gaze was so deep that for a moment I got lost looking into his eyes. "I promise, that if you stay with me, I will keep you safe, I will try to be everything that you need, everything that you deserve. Ana, I can live with everything that I have done wrong in my existence, all of my regrets, but I cannot, and I will not move through this world without you—I don't want you to disappear Ana." He was kissing me, his mouth moving so roughly against mine that I couldn't breathe. What was he saying? I didn't understand. I felt a groan move through my throat as he pressed his hands into my lower back, my muscles reacting to the warmth of his touch, the pressure in his hands.

"Stephen," I whispered. "Of course I'll stay with you, I'm in love with you, I love you; what are you asking me?" It was hard for me to concentrate. He was moving me to the bed, pulling me down next to him, his mouth tracing under my jaw.

"Be with me, Ana, and let me be with you," he murmured again, moving his lips to my throat. Suddenly, familiarity struck and a memory of Patric and me in my bedroom swam in front of my eyes. My body tensed and I struggled to pull away from him, I needed to catch my breath.

"What are saying Stephen? Are you offering to Change me?" My voice was breathless.

"Yes," he whispered, his fingers tracing over my lips. "Yes. I want you Ana. I want us to be together and I can protect you, I can love you in ways you don't even know yet. I promise Ana, if you let us do this, I will make you happy, not nearly as happy as you make me, but I will try…" He brought his mouth to mine and I felt his tongue move in such a way that my whole body reacted, and I pressed myself against him.

"When?" I gasped, trying to unwrap myself from his grip. He was having none of it and he moved to pin me below him.

"Whenever you want," he whispered into my ear and I felt his teeth move over the wounds from Patric. A flash of Noni's face entered my mind, then Kai's and Alec's, then Patric's and finally Nathanial, his midnight blue eyes piercing through my inner eye. Stephen stopped moving and he looked at me. "I know," he said, his voice quiet and sympathetic. "I know you still love him Ana. That won't go away, he will always be yours and you will always be his. I understand that, but I love you; I'm in love with you and I'm here with you now and I know that you are too in love with me to let me go, to let us go. I've seen your heart Ana, and I know that I'm there, I'm there with him and all the others who you have had the courage to love, who you have changed, altered, transformed. I'm asking you, please, be with me, please let me love you Ana. Please." He was crying and as his tears streamed down his face, his eyes changed and I saw a picture of the man that he was, standing with a girl, with long dark hair, holding a child, holding each other. I saw the life that he wanted, the life that didn't come, that was to never come, until now, until he'd met me. I kissed his tears and held his face close, letting him cry for that life, for that man, letting him cry for what he was asking of me.

"I just need some time Stephen; this is a lot to take in after everything I've just been through, I just need some time," I replied and my voice was steady, clear and strong, he deserved honesty. "Stephen, I want to be with you, I want us to be in this world together, but I need to get my head around what you are proposing." Then, for some reason, I started to laugh; I had no idea why—it seemed terribly disrespectful and totally inappropriate, but I couldn't help it. Stephen pulled his face back and propped himself up so that he was hovering above me. He eyebrows were raised. "I'm sorry," I said, in between bursts of laughter. "I'm so sorry, I don't know why I'm laughing…" I said, my stomach beginning to hurt. I felt a sudden release wash over me, a calm so great and so deep that everything that happened to me, it seemed to be taken away by the tides from his tears and I knew that no matter what happened, that it was ok that I still loved Nathanial, that I would always love Nathanial…that we would always be Bound. Stephen respected that, he didn't try to suppress it, he honored that bond as scared and as a part of who I would always be—he loved me.

"I do Ana, I'm so in love with you…" he murmured, moving to lie beside me. "You can have as much time as you need, I'll always wait for you. I don't want you to feel pressured; I want you to want to do this feeling complete in you decision," he whispered.

"Can I talk to Noni first?" I asked, turning to lay my head on his chest.

"Of course you can Ana, whatever you want." He stroked my hair. "But know that she can't make the decision for you, you have to come to it in complete trust, trust in me and trust in yourself." He moved me so that we were eye to eye.

"Will it hurt?" I wasn't sure about the full transaction into a Vampire, Patric and I had only gotten so far. Stephen laughed.

"Hmmm…did he hurt you?" he asked, still running his fingers through my hair.

"No," I said, "No, he didn't," I whispered, letting my love for Patric fill my heart.

"I won't either Ana," Stephen spoke gently. "I won't ever hurt you." I shifted to look at his face.

"Can we go somewhere, just the two of us? I mean it doesn't require an audience of any kind does it?" I asked, laughing softly.

"We can go anywhere you want, where do you want to go?" he asked, staring down at me. I didn't even hesitate.

"Ireland, and not your crappy Northern Ireland that you are so attached to, the *real* Ireland, I said nudging him in the ribs. I actually liked the North, but I also liked to tease Stephen, he was sensitive about his heritage.

"Oh, I see, you want to tease me do you? Feeling a bit brave since you can create vast storms of fire now?" He laughed and rolled me over, pressing his hips against me. "Perhaps I should show you the true meaning of 'tease'," he said, winking at me. I felt him entwine our fingers as he pressed my hands above my head.

"Stephen," I said, my tone serious. He looked at me. "Thank you."

"For what?" He was confused.

"For having the courage to love me, to let yourself love me, and for understanding, for respecting me and my choices, my feelings," I said, watching his face. He shook his head and began kissing me in ways that I had never experienced. I gasped, pulling back from him, shocked at his sudden change of physicality with me. It felt sensuous and rough at the same time and the taste of desire and heat lingered deep on my lips and tongue.

"Hmmm… there's lot's more where that came from, you just wait," he said, smirking at me; then he laughed rolling off and watching me as I tried to come down from the sudden onslaught of passion he'd brought out. I could get used to this.

Chapter Seven

Nathanial

Something had changed; I could feel it in the air and in my bones, something had shifted. Ana's face came to me and I closed my eyes. Since she'd disappeared, since she'd spoken those last words to me, since she had knelt down in front of me, believing that I was to be the one to take her life; I knew that I must fight for her, that I must prove to her that I deserved her love, that I had enough courage in my heart to give her what she wanted, to keep her with me and for us to be together. My chest hurt and I unbuttoned my shirt. My metal inscription was unaltered, except for the eye at the center of the knot, Ana's eye; it was black now and it had been since she'd left. I sighed and went into the house to see my uncle.

"You're leaving," he said, not turning around, his face to the fire.

"I have to go Micah. I have to see her, to talk to her, to make her listen to me," I choked, my breath short and shallow.

"Of course that is what you must do Nathanial, of course. She is your Ana and you must find your way back to her." He turned to look at me. "I have seen that she is on the precipice of something in her life Nathanial; a huge tide is about to shift for the two of you and I have yet to see what she will decide to do, what you both will decide to do. I can tell you that you must trust in her, trust in her love for you, no matter what has happened, no matter what will happen. Trust what you know her to be. Your biggest fault, Nathanial, is that you allow for your jealousy, your desires, to cloud your ability to listen—to really listen to what is being said. Ana has tried to speak to you, she has tried to appeal to your heart and your soul and you have not listened. You cannot fault her for whatever actions she may be contemplating taking, or for those she has already chosen. You must support who she is and stand beside her in your own truth—you must offer her your unconditional love." He turned to stand before me. All I could do was nod. Micah placed his hand on my shoulder and gazed upon my face. "I will be here when you return." And with those words, he shimmered, leaving me to my tears.

Ana

Stephen and Liam were gone; some fights had broken out on one of the other reservations. Vampires were attacking the humans and Bonders, the violence had escalated and Liam's coven went to provide support. I was trying not to think about Stephen, about him fighting or about what he had asked me. I loved Stephen desperately, more than I ever thought I would be capable of, after Nathanial, but still, Nathanial was always there, always a part of my soul and his face was a constant image in my mind. But he had not come for me, he had not come to see if we were alright; he had not come to say how sorry he was or to tell me that he loved me… in months now, he had not come. I sighed and scooped Lucie up off the floor and placed her in her high chair so I could clean the floor. Noni was gone as well, lending her skills to the reservation that was in trouble and Lucie and I were left to our own devices.

Things on our Reservation were relatively calm. Stephen and I managed to negotiate a formal agreement between each interested party and it seemed that most everyone was happy with the settlement. I knew from my experience the extreme fragility that came with these peace agreements; again, they depended on foundations, on how well those structures were built and tended to and how carefully you treaded upon them whilst they were evolving. Finding peace was tenuous, at best.

Lucie and I had taken to going for walks in the evening, usually she wanted to take one of the wolves with us and tonight she chose Zanuck, a jet black wolf with deep blue eyes and I couldn't help but notice the resemblance between the animal and Nathanial. Zanuck was the perfect pairing for Lucie. He was patient and gentle, but he had a protective side and any time Lucie cried, Zanuck howled along with her, pacing back and forth, only letting me or Noni get close to her.

It was a clear evening, with a slight chill in the air, and I stopped Lucie to help her put on her pullover. We had been walking for over an hour and the temperature had begun to drop. It was past dusk as we made our decent back down to the house, but we were still fifteen minutes away. Zanuck trotted along side Lucie, keeping pace with her small steps. I could tell her legs were getting tired because she kept stumbling. I reached around and pulled her up onto my shoulders, laughing as she started to sing. Zanuck began to howl and we finally saw the top of Noni's chimney—it was lit. Lucie clapped and kicked me to get down so she could run the rest of the way. She beat me to the porch and shouted that Noni was back. I yelled for her to slow down and ran with Zanuck the rest of the way.

We bounded up the stairs and I pulled open the screen door to find Noni and Liam sitting, having a cup of tea. My heart was already elevated from the short run, but upon seeing him, it raced that much faster.

"Daddy!" Lucie yelled as she slid on the floor, reaching for his outstretched arms. Liam scooped her up and pressed his face to hers.

"My love," he said, smiling. He seemed happy, so I took that as a sign that so far, everyone was safe; that Stephen was safe. Liam nodded at me and pressed Lucie closer to his chest. Noni stood and headed to the stove to start another kettle for tea. I ushered her back down and took to assembling my mug and the water myself.

"We've been discussing the violence on the other reservation, Ana." Noni, looked at me as she sipped her tea.

"Hmmm," I replied quietly, not really wanting to hear about people being set on fire or their Bonds being ripped from their neck and chests. It made me sick.

"It appears that several covens are now fighting amongst themselves," she continued, both her and Liam shaking their heads.

"It's not unusual behavior for Vampires," Liam replied, letting Lucie stand on his legs. "We're selfish and driven by instinct, bloodlust and power, all things that don't meld well in terms of cooperation." He laughed. I rolled my eyes at his description of his species; both he and

I knew that wasn't always the case. I poured my tea and pulled out a chair next to Noni.

"How is Stephen?" I asked, not wanting to be too intrusive, but I had to know. Liam surveyed me over his mug and grinned.

"He's fine Ana. He sends his love to you." Liam touched my hand. I nodded and felt the breath I'd been holding, release.

"Ana," Liam turned to me, "I was wondering if I could take Lucie to see Carmen. She's...well, she's terribly grateful to you and wishes to speak with you about what you did for our daughter, but she's training some of our new recruits..." He trailed off, his bright blue eyes filling with emotion. I laughed at him.

"Liam, of course you can take Lucie—she's *your* daughter; you don't have to ask my permission. Lucie should be with you and Carmen; she should be with her parents. God knows I've probably screwed the kid up enough over these last months; she'll need a lifetime of therapy for sure!" I said shaking my head. I felt Noni put her hand on my back. She never tolerated my self-deprecating sense of humor; it bothered her that I was always so self-critical. I smiled and shrugged at her. "Let me get some of her things." I stood up and put my mug in the sink. I began gathering her clothes and some of her favorite toys and books. I took out her favorite pink backpack and carefully tucked everything where she could access it easily; books and crayons on top. I sat on the floor in our room and folded her clothes. I didn't know where Carmen was, so I figured Lucie should have some layers that she could take on and off. Suddenly, I felt my chest constrict. I sighed, trying not to be

162

so emotional; what a ridiculous thing, she wasn't my daughter I thought, wiping the tears from my face.

"Ana," a voice spoke from the door; it was Liam. I sniffed and stood up, zipping up the backpack.

"I've put some things in there that she's a bit attached to at the moment," I said, not wanting him to see how upset I was. "Um, clothes and another pair of shoes and her flower headbands are also in there," I said, swallowing and handing Liam the pack. He smiled at me.

"She's attached to you," he whispered, moving to take my hand in his. I shrugged and averted my eyes. He sighed and lifted my face. "Stephen has told me what he proposed to you." My eyes widened. I wasn't sure how Liam would react to Stephen taking matters into his own hands. Liam laughed softly. "Well yes, I usually like for my brother to council with me first, particularly with matters that deal with life and death." Liam's eyes narrowed. "However, I originally was for us taking your compromise when you first presented it to Stephen; he however, was adamantly against changing you." I frowned; I didn't know any of that information and I wondered why the sudden change of heart. "I'm wondering that myself..." Liam trailed off, his expression distant. "I fear it may have more to do with his issues with Nathanial, than it does with you," he said, his voice a bit stern. I stepped back from him, puzzled.

"What do you mean? What issues with Nathanial?" I asked, not quite following Liam's logic.

"Stephen loves you, that I am sure of; however, he also has quite a ramped retaliatory streak in his personality...something that carried over from his Human side." Liam moved to sit down on my bed. "Did Stephen ever disclose any information about Laura, the woman he was with before his Change occurred?" My mind went immediately back to the first night that I came to Stephen for help. I had seen that beautiful portrait of a woman sleeping, she was mesmerizing, and he looked so sad when I had asked him who she was. Liam, seeing my memories, nodded. "Yes, that was Laura; she was the love of his short Human life."

"He told me that she betrayed him, with…with his brother…" I whispered, thinking surely it couldn't have been Liam that she slept with.

"No, it wasn't me. We had a younger brother, Colin, who Laura had an intense chemistry with, I guess you could say, a chemistry that Stephen knew, that he'd observed. He told Laura that before they could be married, she needed to make a choice, to decide if she could withhold her feelings for Colin and have a life with Stephen or pursue our brother. But of course, Laura had already made her decision; she and Colin had already consummated their relationship while she was still seeing my brother," said Liam as he was studying me.

"They had a child," I said, more to myself than to Liam.

"Yes, a little boy, Finn," Liam said, still watching me. I suddenly felt unease with the conversation, but I wasn't sure why.

"That's when Stephen asked to be Changed, when he found them together, when he knew she was pregnant, right?" I moved to sit down next to him.

164

"No Ana. Stephen has managed to block out the events of that night, and when we become who we are, when we complete our transition from our Human lives into who we are as Vampires, most human memories fade; most, but not all," Liam said, turning to hold my gaze, his face smooth and emotionless. He waited for me to ask what he already knew was in my mind.

"What happened Liam?"

"Stephen murdered our brother," Liam said, simply, flatly. "Upon seeing them and hearing their conversation about the pregnancy, something became detached in my brother's heart, in his soul; he lost himself that night; he lost his humanity." Liam looked at me and I could see that he was remembering the conversation he and I had had about the human condition. "He was also poised to kill Laura and the unborn child, but something in her eyes allowed for him to regain some semblance of composure, something about the way she looked at him stopped Stephen from committing perhaps an even worse act of violence. Of course, upon realizing what he'd done, what he was about to do, I believe that Stephen's soul was lost. At that moment, looking at the body of our dead brother, looking into Laura's eyes, I think that the human Stephen died. Asking to be Changed, well, I feel that was purely ceremonial at that point." Liam bowed his head a bit, his eyes still watching me. I exhaled loudly.

"What does any of this have to do with Nathanial?" I asked, trying to regulate my breathing.

"Hmmm...well, I'm not for certain if my analysis of my brother's psyche is one hundred percent accurate, he keeps himself pretty well shut down, but I think that in Stephen's mind, he sees Nathanial as selfish and arrogant. He believes that Nathanial had the opportunity to keep you with him, to give you a chance for a different life, but instead, he hurt you, he caused you pain, he put himself in what Stephen considers the most unsacred of positions—poised to take your life when perhaps he could have fought for you. Stephen believes that Nathanial had everything, had the potential to have the life that my brother so desperately wanted, that he deserved. He sees Nathanial's indecision about you, his lack of willingness to listen to your apologies, to see beyond all that has transpired; Stephen sees those as weaknesses. I also think Stephen sees you and Laura as similar. Both of you loved Stephen, but both of you also carried or carry feelings for someone else in your hearts, and Stephen was already betrayed once by Laura. By convincing you to be transitioned, to be with him, he's in effect retaliating for everything that he lost. Nathanial represents a life that Stephen was on the precipice of having and Nathanial is treating you and your relationship with disrespect. I think that to Stephen, your history with Nathanial represents both the betrayal by Colin and Laura and the betrayal within himself. By taking you away from Nathanial, Stephen thinks that at least one half of those treacheries could possibly be avenged." Liam stood and paced around the room. I couldn't process what he'd just said; it was like a soap opera. Liam chuckled. I sighed, trying to wrap my mind around this Stephen that I didn't know.

"Well, ok, so he's not Nathanial's biggest fan at the moment," I said. "I'm not either, if I'm being completely honest, but I think that Stephen is over estimating Nathanial; just like Alec did and just like Patric— they all were so sure that Nathanial loved me enough to do what they wanted or to come through for me somehow; they were all wrong and so is Stephen. If he thinks that it will crush Nathanial when I'm Changed, that it will hurt Nathanial if I'm with Stephen, that's going to completely back fire on your brother. The hurt and pain he wants to see in Nathanial's eyes, the pain he wanted to see in Colin's eyes, it won't be there," I said laughing. "This is what all of you seem to be missing and I can't figure out why!" My voice was rising. "Nathanial does-not-love-me, not in the way Stephen is hoping, not in the way Patric hoped; it's not there. I told Nathanial that I loved him, that I was sorry and that I hoped we could find our way back to each other; I asked him to forgive me. You know what he said? Nothing! He just stared at me. He said nothing. I told him the night he was supposed to kill me, that I would of course protect him, that no matter what he was going to have to do, that I would always protect him. Do you think that provided any impetus for him to tell me that he was sorry too, that he really did love me? No, it did not!" I said storming around the room. "So Stephen is just going to have to find another way to exorcise his demons and need for revenge, because Nathanial won't provide the relief he's looking for Liam." I stood, hands on my hips as another realization occurred to me. "And by the way," I said, staring at Liam as he put his hands behind his back, "you can tell Stephen that his little proposal is off. I'm not Laura and I haven't betrayed him and apparently he's forgotten some of our previous conversations about just how much he was willing to accept Nathanial as being part of my life…he's not remembering things that he promised me—yet again! As much as I love him and I think that he loves me, I will not be anyone's means to an end—I've been down that road more times than I care to acknowledge. I really believe that after nearly three decades on this planet, that I deserve better, and if that means that I have to

167

be alone, that I spend every waking moment waiting for someone to track me down and kill me, well then it's better than the alternative; it's better than waiting for someone to realize they love me and it's better than letting someone Change me so that they can feel better about their own horrible mistakes!" I threw up my hands in exasperation. I wasn't angry with Liam, just so damn tired of listening to the same problems over and over again.

"I agree with you Ana," Liam said quietly. "You do deserve better, you deserve so much more than what you have endured and you deserve the most unselfish of loves in your life, the most unconditional love…this I know, because this is what you have shown my daughter, my wife and myself." He wrapped his hands around my waist and pulled me to his chest. I took a deep breath.

"Please tell him that I love him, I truly, truly do, but until he can come to me, without these ghosts, until he can be with me in the absence of so much anger and regret, then I cannot be with him the way he wants. I have to start valuing myself at some point Liam, otherwise, I too am at risk for losing *my* humanity." I exhaled and pulled back to look at his face. His eyes were brimming and he touched my cheek.

"You are an extraordinary being Ana and Stephen is so very lucky to have your love. Of course I will tell him; I think it will be good for him to hear and to know that he must find peace within himself, that he must be accountable for his own existence, that you have saved him enough now—he needs to save himself." I nodded and hugged Liam as Lucie patted into the room, her thumb in her mouth. She hugged on my leg and I picked her up, swinging her in the air.

"This won't be the last time that I see you or her, will it?" I asked, fear making my heart beat faster.

"I hope not Ana, but just so you know, if you ever need anything, anything at all; if you ever feel unsafe or threatened in any way, all you need to do is call to me or Carmen or Stephen and we'll be there—always." Liam kissed my face and I handed Lucie to him, pressing my lips to her forehead. "I will never be able to repay you for what you did for my daughter—there are not enough lifetimes..." I shook my head.

"Maybe you could try to be a little more affectionate with Carmen," I said laughing at him. "You know she's a Latin woman and they have a tendency to be a bit spicy—perhaps you could indulge her every now and then?" I said and Liam laughed so loudly, that it made Lucie jump. He shook his head and we walked out to the porch where Noni was waiting on us. Liam handed Lucie to Noni and she proceeded to bless her and kiss her cheeks.

"Thank you," Liam said, his eyes locking with Noni's. She nodded and moved to stand next to me, my heart beginning to break. Lucie reached for me and I leaned in to hug her.

"I love you, my precious bambina, my heart." The tears were coming fast now.

"I love you my Ana," she whispered as she wiped my cheeks with her tiny hands. I stepped back and found Noni's arms waiting for me and together we bowed at Liam and watched as he and Lucie shimmered off the porch.

Nathanial

It took three weeks before I felt comfortable leaving Micah in charge of the surrounding communities. Most of the violence had been quelled, but I was nervous about any additional uprising that may occur upon the Vampires hearing of my absence. Micah had taken offense at my lingering and eventually shoved me out the door. I knew that Ana was in Idaho. Micah informed me that both Ana and Stephen had managed to broker a peace agreement between the Nez Perce, the demons and the Vampires; I was uneasy about the possibility of facing Stephen and I had no idea if he and Ana were together. Micah was right, I would have to get my jealousy under control if I wanted Ana to listen to anything that I had to say.

I was driving through the Sawtooth Mountains and back to the cabin that I had occupied after the attack at the University. It was an odd sensation returning to this location again. The first time I came, I couldn't place the unquenchable desire to be in this particular area, but now it made sense to me, it was because she'd been here, she'd grown up here and it was the place she'd always return to, to feel safe, loved and protected. I had absolutely no strategy for finding and talking to Ana, and I wasn't even sure if she would see me; I just knew that I had to try, that I wouldn't leave until we'd talked, really talked. I pulled into the drive and unloaded my bags, wondering if it was too late for me to try and find Noni's place. I had directions in my mind from when we were planning the wedding and I was almost sure that the house was less than a mile away from me. I decided to wait, that I needed some more time to go over what I wanted to say, it needed to be perfect; I *wanted* it to be perfect.

Ana

Almost a month had passed since I said goodbye to Liam and Lucie. I had not heard from Stephen and I was guessing that he was pretty pissed at me for breaking off our relationship, if that's what you could call it. I was managing to stay busy. I wanted to work and I missed my career terribly. Noni suggested that I teach on the Reservation and I had leapt at the opportunity to flex some of my other skills besides fire wielding and trying to save Vampires and Bonders from themselves. The Reservation was in dire need of a youth counselor and it was a role that I had enjoyed taking on when I first graduated from college. For my current position, I was charged with about ten teens from the Reservation, mostly young pregnant girls who were in need of some academic and personal assistance. I loved every moment of it so far. The girls were great and my co-workers were a wonderful group of Bonders and humans who all had a passion for helping others—I couldn't have asked for a better fit.

Today was my day off, and I wanted to get out and hike in the mountains; I had been cooped up in my office the whole week meeting parents and having advising sessions—I needed some fresh air. Zanuck was with me and he was keen to take a bit of a longer route today. We had climbed about a mile up from where Noni's house was situated, but in a different direction than I normally went. I was content to let Zanuck lead the way; he seemed to have a location he was working towards and I was happy to let him make the decisions. Currently, he was pulling me up a steep path that veered off from the main trail; it looked like a private driveway and I wasn't keen to be trespassing on someone's vacation home. I tried to direct Zanuck back down the trail, but he was having none of it and he turned to howl at me. Christ, I thought... fine, but if we get shot at by some crazed Deliverance type man; it's on you! Zanuck barked and howled, registering my annoyance, I was sure. The drive had a huge grade, and it was full of switchbacks that cut and twisted as we climbed. Some sort of SUV was a definite must in the winter, I mused. I noticed that the path had tire tracks grooved into the dirt and I began to feel uneasy; I knew most of the people who lived up in the mountains, but I didn't know them all and I had never been in this part of the area before. I sighed as we rounded the final turn and came to a halt at the top of the climb. There was a small cabin nestled into the woods and a stream that ran through the front yard; something about the construction and the layout reminded me of the Hansel and Gretel story. I wondered if the person liked gingerbread, I laughed. Zanuck began to growl, low and fierce and I immediately looked to the front porch. I saw someone sitting on the step, but I was too far away to make out any facial features. I was pretty sure it was a man. I stepped back a bit, pulling Zanuck with me and I waved.

"Sorry!" I called, not wanting the person to feel that we were a threat or that we were intentionally trespassing. "Just out for a hike and got a bit off course!" I called, taking another step back. Zanuck growled again and moved to stand directly in front of me. The man stood up and I could see, even from my position down the hill from him, that he was tall and muscular. I squinted, trying to make out his face, but the setting sun was blinding my sight. Please don't have a gun, I thought; that would totally suck if I had to blow up such a nice cabin to keep from being shot. The man moved slowly down the stairs, coming out into the yard, the stream running like a vein between us. I still couldn't make out his face. Zanuck moved back to his haunches, his fur raised and his teeth barred. Maybe I should run, I thought. There was enough distance between us that I could get a pretty good head start. Suddenly, a gust of wind moved through the air, stirring the trees; I gasped out loud. The scent; *his* scent, it almost knocked me down cold. Moss and earth, musk and woods, honey and lemon—holy Christ! I looked at the man in the yard, trying to take in his blinding figure, but all I could see was that his hair was now blowing freely, swirling around his face in black strands of silk. At that moment, standing there seeing and not seeing, my mind became detached from my body and the only thing my body wanted to do was to run. I turned on the spot and bolted back into the woods, sprinting with Zanuck at my side. I ran all the way down the mountain, not stopping until I reached the porch of Noni's house where I proceeded to collapse on the wood floor.

"My bambina! My love, what is it? Why were you running?" Noni came out from the house and knelt down beside me, her face full of worry. Zanuck was pacing all around me and she reached out to pet down his flanks, soothing him. I laid there, my breath coming hard and shallow in my chest. I closed my eyes, not believing what I'd seen; not letting my mind register that it was Nathanial standing on that porch, in that yard. "Ana, what is it?" Noni was pulling me in a sitting position, her hands cupping my face. I sighed and closed my eyes.

"I think, I think that I just saw Nathanial in the woods, Noni," I said, the words sounding surreal to my ears. She sat back and tucked her legs under her.

"And you ran away from him, bambina?" she asked, her voice light.

"Well, I wasn't sure if it was him," I said, and that was true, mostly.

"Did he try to hurt you?" she asked, again her tone calm. I shook my head and moved to sit against the rocking chair. "So why did you run?" she asked me, her eyes following my every movement.

"Because, it's Nathanial. I don't want to see him. Why is he even here; it's been months since I left him in that stupid fire, why now does he choose to show up?" I exclaimed loudly, lifting my head off the back of the rocker. "Besides that, I'm pretty sure he was going to kill me, maybe he came back to finish the job!" I said, standing up.

"Is that what you truly believe my love, that he would take your life from you, from him? Is that who you know him to be?" she said, her eyes now closed.

"Noni, I can't talk about this now. I'm not ready to see him; I don't want to see him." I said quietly. I walked into the house, leaving her sitting on the porch.

For the next several days, I was completely on edge, not only about Nathanial, but also, I missed Stephen and I didn't want him to be angry with me. Emotionally, I was a mess and my nerves were just shot. Noni was kind enough not to press either issue and let me move through whatever it was that I needed to experience, but she would watch me, a lot. I felt her eyes follow me as I gazed up at the moon or toward the

174

mountains; when I would sit and listen to my favorite song over and over again on the porch, thinking about Stephen; she knew, but she kept her distance.

Noni was also worried about the upsurge in violence in some of the surrounding communities. Attacks on humans and Bonders were getting more and more frequent and I know she feared that the fragile peace our Reservation was maintaining was at risk of crumbling. Constant clouds and storms always seemed to be on the horizon and I struggled to remember the last sunny day we'd had—weeks, maybe?

The weather seemed fitting for my moods as of late. I drove home from work in a massive thunderstorm. It was after ten; one of my study sessions had run over an hour later than I expected and I was in a hurry to get home and have a cup of tea and a shower. The rain was coming down in sheets and not even the high-speed setting of my windshield wipers was helping me to see the road. I made the turn for the road up to Noni's and immediately I could see that the sudden downpour of water had caused a flash flood. I knew never to cross over a flooded road, so I attempted to steer my jeep over to the side, then hopefully, I could try and turn around. As I attempted a crude three-point turn, I heard my tires begin to squeal, and my jeep halted—I was stuck. I tried to back up, but the water from the flood was now spreading behind me, and any more movement would plunge the jeep into the water. Frick! I turned off the car and pulled my cell phone out. I scrolled through my contacts until I found Noni's number, but I paused as the name directly above hers made my heart skip—Nathanial. I still had his old cell phone contact. For a brief moment, I thought about calling him. I wondered if he still had the same number.

Lightening crashed around me, bringing me out of my musings and I hit Noni's number. She picked up in one ring.

"Bambina? Where are you?" She sounded nervous.

"I'm fine Noni, well actually, I'm stuck in the mud and there's a massive flash flood around the jeep. I can't actually get out at the moment..." I trailed off as my eye caught a blur of movement in the rearview mirror. I thought I heard Noni speaking to someone as the phone moved away from her mouth.

"We'll send someone right out love, stay put in the car," she said and again, I thought I heard someone else speak, a man maybe? Another blur appeared in the mirror and I turned around to look behind me. "Bambina? Are you alright?" Noni asked, her voice tense.

"Um, yeah. I'm fine. Thanks Noni. I'm on the side road, but I'm turning off the jeep so make sure who ever comes can see me," I said, my eyes now shifting back and forth out the side windows.

"Yes, love," she said, another voice spoke, it was a man, and I heard a door slam shut.

"Thanks Noni!" I said, hanging up the phone. I unbuckled my seat belt and tried to relax. It would take someone about twenty minutes to get out this far, with the storm, probably thirty, so I was going to be here for a bit. I left the headlights on; I had plenty of gas and the extra light helped to make my surroundings less frightening. I gazed around me, trying to see through the rain and the lightening, but there was nothing to see. I took a deep breath and leaned my head back against the seat and rubbed my eyes. When I looked up, there was a face staring back at me from the windshield. My heart stopped beating and I couldn't move. Adrenaline pulsed through my body and I could taste its metallic residue on my tongue. The face was a male; his skin was white and his eyes dark and inflamed. Rain was pouring over his neck and down his shoulders, but he didn't move, he did however, smirk at me. His lips curled over his teeth and I watched as he licked the rain from his mouth. A Vampire. I tried to focus, to clear my mind. This was unbelievable; was it ever going to stop, I thought, as I tried to allow the swelling of my skin to grow. I heard a deafening crash as he broke the windshield with one hit. I moved to open my door, but he had leapt on the hood of the car and was grabbing me around the neck, pulling me through the broken glass. I felt my flesh tear as the jagged pieces from the windshield grazed across my throat. The blood began to spill down my neck. I was disoriented and I couldn't concentrate. Massive amounts of rain pounded my face, making it hard for me to breathe. He threw me down on the ground and stood, leering over me, his eyes on fire. A low snarl erupted from his chest as he registered the blood now flowing freely from my throat. A flash of lightening and he was on top of me, pinning my hands down. He growled and snapped at my face as I tried to buck him off. My mind was racing and I couldn't get enough air into my lungs to use my innate force to throw him off of me; he was sitting on my chest. I gasped as he pressed down harder, flattening my lungs. Water crashed down over my eyes and I shook my head back and forth, trying to clear my vision. He head butted me, sending a wave of pain and shock so acute, that I gagged. My brain exploded, I was sure. I felt the back of my head hit the ground from his force and I saw black for a few seconds; that was all he needed. He lunged forward bringing his mouth to my neck, and in his bloodlust, his grip on one of my hands slackened. I broke one hand

177

free and gouged him in the eyes, making him scream. Then, suddenly, his body was ripped off of me, literally. His head detached from his neck and black ooze sprayed everywhere. I watched as each of his limbs was torn from the muscles and bones connecting them to his torso. Between my headlights and the extreme lightening, I couldn't see what was happening, who was doing this? I heard a high scream, a keening that made my gut heave. I looked up to see my attacker's body erupting into flames, exploding outward, showering me with blood and burning flesh. I tried to wipe the splatter from my face, but there was too much of it, my skin was dripping from the body and from the rain. I struggled to stand but the ground was leaning, curving inward. That didn't seem right. I started to fall to the side and someone caught me, propping me up against them. I wiped my face again and turned to see a pair of deep midnight blue eyes staring at me, eyes with stars that lined the rims. Then, I think I passed out.

Nathanial

I sat, watching her sleeping. How much more was she going to have to endure, before I lost her forever in either body or in spirit? Ana's Noni had put out a warning that the Reservation might be under attack. I wanted to get her and Ana away from whatever battle was to come, but Noni insisted that I take only Ana. After speaking with the old woman for several hours, I could see just where Ana got her stubborn streak—I was never going to win. I also doubted that Ana would allow herself to be taken away from this woman who raised her and certainly not by me. I sighed and moved to sit on the bed. I smoothed her hair and traced my finger along her cheek. She stirred and turned her face, her eyes open, the moon reflecting in their deep, bronze pools.

"Hey," she whispered, staring at me.

"Hey yourself," I said softly, still stroking her face.

"You came," she said, holding my hand to her face. I closed my eyes and tried to breathe. "That's a nice cabin you have," she said smiling at me. I opened my eyes and glared at her. She had the most inappropriate displays of humor. "What? It is," she said, smirking at me. "No, but seriously, thank you, thanks for saving me." She looked away from me, staring out the window. She was wondering if I did it out of guilt or just because I felt obligated.

"Neither," I said, turning her face back to me. "Although, guilt is something that I've been battling for some time now, but that's a different issue entirely." I heard the door crack and Noni came in with a cup of tea for Ana and one for me. I nodded and took the mug.

"Drink this bambina, it will help cleanse and replenish your blood." Noni whispered to Ana. Immediately Ana looked at me, her eyes filled with worry.

"He didn't get you," I said, smiling at her. Your wounds are more from him pulling you through the damn windshield, than anything else." My heart stopped for a moment as I recalled seeing him on top of her, blood pouring from her throat. I'd thought he'd bitten her for sure.

179

Noni caught my eye and motioned for me to follow her out into the hallway. I nodded and moved to get up off the bed.

"Leaving already?" Ana asked, she was smiling, but I caught a distinct current of sarcasm in her tone. I sighed.

"I'll be right back," I said, letting my hand run over her leg. She smiled and sat back to drink her tea. "And by the way, I wasn't the one who ran away upon seeing you after so many months," I said, my voice soft. She rolled her eyes and I turned to walk out into the hallway.

"Liam is waiting in the kitchen, my son." Noni looked sternly at me and grasped my shoulder with unusual strength and vigor for someone her age. I stared at her. "He is not what you remember, he is not what you have deemed him to be and if you want to understand Ana, if you want to know what it is that she has done, then you need to give him respect—you need to listen." I couldn't help but see the similarities between what Noni was telling me and what my uncle had said before I departed. They were joined souls and most likely right in their advice to me. I exhaled and walked down the hall. Liam was standing against the counter, his face in his hands. He looked up the minute I entered the room.

"Is she hurt Nathanial?" His voice sounded desperate and sad.

"She's scratched up a bit, but no, she's fine, she'll be fine." I moved to sit down at the table, running my finger along the rim of my mug. He was thinking about why she wasn't able to defend herself, why she couldn't fight him off. "I don't know," I said, meeting his gaze. "He hit her head pretty hard and he was crushing her chest; I'm guessing that she was disoriented, she couldn't focus…" Liam sighed and crossed the space between us to sit next to me at the table.

"Thank you Nathanial, if you weren't there, we might have lost her forever." Again his voice was somber and who was this "we" he was speaking of? "My family, of course," he said, studying me. "We all love her very much and all of us, all of us, owe Ana our entire lives; so to speak." He spoke with such passion and such reverence, that I couldn't help but look at him. He was referring to Lucie, I guessed. "Yes, of course; my daughter most likely would never have survived the fire that struck our home if Ana had not taken her to escape, but I was also speaking to Ana's relationship with me, my wife and of course, my brother." At the mention of Stephen, I felt my blood pressure rise and I tried to calm myself. Liam laughed quietly. "Nathanial, I would have never pegged you for the jealous type; you've always struck me as so refined and above such contrivances." He waved his hand and leaned back in his chair, his eyes on me.

"Well, you were wrong," I mumbled, lowering my gaze.

"No, I don't think that I am wrong, I just don't think that you anticipated that you could ever love someone as much as you love Ana." He touched my arm. I sighed and looked at him.

"So, what's the deal with your brother?" I asked, sounding like a petulant teenager, vying for the affections of some cheerleader in high school. Liam laughed.

"Yes, you do actually sound like that, and both your behavior and Stephen's is about equal to that of a teenage male; I'm sorry to say." He laughed again, but his face suddenly became smooth, his jaw tight.

181

"My brother has removed himself from Ana's life—for the time being; he's made a bit of a mess of things, not only with her, but for himself and he needs a bit of time to regroup."

"What the hell does that mean?" I asked, not liking the sound of that at all.

"I don't feel comfortable discussing the nature of their relationship, Nathanial. I think that is something that Ana will have to speak with you about, if she feels so compelled. I will say this. While I love my brother deeply and being with Ana is something that makes him the happiest that I have ever seen him, I do not think that he is the healthy choice for Ana—not right now; my brother has some personality traits that surface every now and again that do not make him very easy to live with." Liam smiled. "But beyond that, Stephen needs to learn accountability, he needs to learn to understand himself, in order to heal from his wounds; he's not ready to do that yet and that's why I do not think he is an apt choice for Ana at the moment."

"At the moment..." I repeated his words. "You mean, if Stephen reconciles whatever demons he has, if he comes to terms with his own problems, whatever they may be, that he might want to be with Ana? That she might want to be with him?" I asked, feeling on edge.

"I don't know, Nathanial. I can't speak for Ana and I can't really speak for my brother. I will say that I do know that they love each other and that they have a deep bond that even I can't understand. Stephen loves Ana and I'm guessing, if he finds redemption in himself, that he'd want to fight to get her back." He stared hard at my face. "What Ana

chooses in that moment, well…I guess we'll just have to wait and see."
He smiled and again touched my arm.

"Liam." I needed to ask…I had to ask. "Should I leave her? I mean, should I just let her be alone? Maybe…" I trailed off not wanting to even consider my life without her. Liam paused and leaned forward in his chair, his blue eyes flashing.

"No. No, I don't think you should disappear from Ana's life, especially now when the two of you have so much to say to one another, when there is so much that *needs* to be said. Ana is under some preconceived notion that you do not love her, not enough anyway. She's convinced herself that you were, in fact, going to kill her that night, that you saw no other choice and that you were not going to fight for her. Now, I like to think that none of that is true Nathanial, that my understanding of who you are, is not someone who would murder the woman they loved—of course, I've been wrong before." His eyes narrowed. "You have an opportunity to explain yourself, explain all of your choices and actions and to tell her just how deep your love runs; what she does after that, well—it's completely up to her isn't it?" He stood. "My daughter is waiting for me. Please tell Ana that I came by and remind her of my offer the last time we saw each other, and assure her that my coven will work to ensure that no other rogue Vampire attacks occur on the Reservation." He shook my hand and I nodded, wondering what offer he made to Ana. "That we would always protect her, and that all she had to do was call upon us and we would come to her—always." Liam gave me one more hard stare and then shimmered out of the kitchen.

Chapter Eight

Nathanial

I was desperate to speak with Ana. I wanted to ask her about Stephen, about their relationship; even though I was sure it would be difficult, I needed to get a sense of what she was feeling about him and about me. The conversation with Liam had me curious, well, it had me obsessing, if I was being honest and after two weeks, she'd finally agreed to meet with me. She suggested we go for a walk and I was waiting for her at the trailhead. I saw Zanuck come through the woods first, then Ana; she was smiling at me. I waved and walked to meet her.

"Thanks for this," she said quietly.

"Of course," I replied, watching her. "How was your day?" She laughed out loud and shook her head. I missed something. "What?" I stopped, staring at her.

"I'm sorry, it's just this, this moment; it's so redundant, just like so many things have been in my life the last two years." She turned her face to the sky.

"What's redundant about this moment?" I frowned.

"Doesn't it remind you of the time after I was recovering from that ridiculous suicide attempt and I would come over to your house for dinner..." She looked at me and shook her head. "It's just like that, but different—you're even more different now, than you were back then..." She trailed off, her voice going soft. I sighed and for some reason, I had to stifle the completely inappropriate urge to grab her and kiss her. I stepped back a few paces and moved to start up the trail. She followed, walking behind me. We didn't speak. I led us up the steep ravines and over the ledges of the mountain until we reached the highest overlook. I stood taking in the view and watching as the sun sank slowly behind the ridges and the moon rose on the horizon. I turned to see where she was. Everything was quiet except for the wind blowing the leaves. Ana was standing behind me, watching. She was so still, her hair billowing around her shoulders, skimming across her face, shielding her eyes. I held her gaze, not wanting to look away. I moved to stand directly in front of her and slowly, I reached out to brush a lock of her hair from her face. It was a familiar gesture, one that I had done many times, but it was also the very first time that I had ever touched her; in her car, when she had a panic attack about meeting me, about what was to be the inception of our journey together. I had touched her and in that moment, I knew my life was not, could not be a life without her—I just had no idea how lost I was to become from that knowledge, from that belief in us, in myself. Right now, as I stood before her on the mountain, I knew that nothing I could possibly explain, nothing that I could ever tell her, was more important than what I had always known, what I knew now and what she deserved to hear.

"Nathanial," Ana spoke, interrupting my thoughts. "There's something that you should know, something that I want to tell you." She stepped away from me and moved to stand on the edge of the overlook, her face to the moon.

"What?" I asked, coming to stand beside her, the memory of watching her fall from the deck that horrible night, was still to close to my heart. I reached to take her hand. She didn't pull away.

"Stephen offered to Change me. He asked me to be with him. He loves me, well, I think he may love me; I'm not actually sure at the moment," She said, squeezing my hand. My body tensed as I tried to process what she was telling me. I exhaled, trying to relax.

"I see," I said as calmly as I could. She looked at me. "What did you tell him?" God, I was going to be sick.

"That I needed some time, that I had come to love him in my own way but…" She stopped speaking and looked away.

"But what, Ana?" I pressed. She sighed.

"Apparently Stephen's motivations for changing me are not just because he loves me; he has some other issues…some very serious issues," she said. I thought about the conversation that I had had with Liam; Christ, what the hell was wrong with the guy? "But, that's not the only reason why I wanted some time," she whispered. "I guess I was hoping that maybe you would come back, not that I thought we would be together, but that just maybe we could tie up our loose ends, say goodbye properly….I don't know." She turned to face me, her eyes fierce. I met her gaze and swallowed.

"I don't want to say goodbye to you Ana; I'm not ready for *us* to say goodbye," I said, reaching to hold her other hand, turning her body toward me. "Is that what you want? Do you want for me, for us, to go our separate ways?" My voice shook. "I would follow you anywhere

Ana…but if you don't want me; if you've already made your decision, then I can respect that, but I won't let you say goodbye to me, I'll always want to be a part of your life." I could hear the tenor of my voice and it was rough and dark. "You said before you left, you said that you hoped that we would find our way back to each other and that you loved me. Are those things no longer true? Is what he is willing to give you, does that trump those sentiments?" I asked, holding her face in my hands. "Look at me Ana," I said, forcefully. She raised her eyes and bit her lip.

"No," she said softly. "No, nothing that Stephen said, nothing that anyone could say, would ever negate what I feel for you Nathanial," she whispered, pressing her face to my chest. I wrapped my arms around her and held her as closely as any being possibly could. For some reason, I was afraid that if I let go, Ana would disappear. We stayed on the overlook for hours, just talking. I wanted to know about her time with Stephen and Liam; she told me how much she loved Carmen and Lucie and how she also liked Micah, and that she felt it was because of him, that she was able to fight for herself that night, fight for us. I winced, remembering that horrible vision of her kneeling in front of me, but a thought crossed my mind as I listened to her talk about the fire in the hut. I knew from her thoughts, that she was thoroughly convinced that I would have taken her life and I couldn't imagine what in the world would ever make her think that, but she did, regardless. I waited for her to finish and then I turned to her.

"Ana, I want to show you something, I need you to see something," I said quietly. She looked at me and frowned.

"What?" she asked.

187

"I need you to concentrate and close your eyes, please," I instructed. I wasn't sure if it was possible for a human to be able to see into my mind, but Ana had always been the exception to the rule. Her eyes narrowed in skepticism. I raised my eyebrows at her; it was going to be a long road back for her to trust me. I sighed. "Please?" I asked, touching her top lip with my finger. She nodded and closed her eyes, taking a deep breath. I unbuttoned my shirt, exposing my tattoo. I placed her hand gently over the center, letting her feel the entwined metals and stone, letting her feel her inner eye; the eye that was now a permanent addition to both my mark and my heart. I reached my mind out to her letting the pictures of that night play as if they were a movie. She inhaled sharply, and I knew that she was watching. I let her see my plan. I showed her that I was prepared to kill that night, but not her, never her. I wanted her to know me in that moment, to know just how much I loved her; it was beyond any emotive capacity that one being or person could possibly withstand. She was embedded in me, and I in her. She gasped and pulled her hand away, breaking our connection. She stepped away from me, shaking her head.

"Christ, Nathanial! What am I supposed to do with that?" she asked, her tone more furious than I expected.

"What do you mean?" I asked, moving towards her, confused by her reaction.

"I mean, that it's too little, too late! I mean that when you came to Stephen's to see me and I told you how sorry I was, sorry for everything, sorry for that stupid fight, sorry for leaving you—I was sorry. You just stood there. I told you that I loved you and how much you meant to me and I had to watch you turn your back on me, and

188

now you show me this, you show me that you were going to do the valiant thing, you were going to try to protect me and what, what am I supposed to think or feel about any of that? I know that I hurt you when I left, I know that you hated that I went to Stephen for help; I know all of that, so maybe it's just too much for us, maybe we've hurt each other too much for us to ever be together again; maybe you're broken and I'm broken and that's just too many pieces for two people to put back together." She threw her hands in the air and went to sit in the grass, Zanuck at her feet. I stood gazing down on her, my arms folded across my chest.

"I don't believe that you are broken Ana and neither do you," I said, my tone commanding and harsh. She glared up at me. "I also don't believe that it will ever be too late for us, that none of those things that happened in the past, matter anymore—not for me, at least." I softened my voice and knelt down beside her. "I know that your faith in me, in us, has been shaken, but Ana, I swear to you, that I will prove to you just how much we belong together, how much we need each other and just how good I am for you. We need to be together Ana, and I will not walk away from you without fighting for what I want, for what I know you need—I won't do it," I said, looking at her face, my blood boiling; again the sudden urge to kiss her violently rose within me and I had to force myself to turn away from her face.

"Noni wants me to go with you, she thinks that a big fight is coming to the Reservation and she wants me to leave," Ana spoke quietly, lying back in the grass, her face gazing up at the stars. I wondered if she had registered anything that I had just said. I frowned at her, I didn't want to change the direction of our conversation, but it appeared that Ana was done with declarations for the evening. I indulged her reluctantly.

"I agree. I think that you should come with me; enough harm has come to you and I'd rather not see just how much you can endure," I said, still frowning at her. I was having trouble keeping my mind focused on our current conversation. The most inappropriate desire was beginning to flood my body and my thoughts. I had been away from her intimately for so long, that my need for her was now in overdrive. I could feel my scent hormones begin to change from their normally sweet and timid allure, to their more musky and seductive fragrance. I shifted my position so that I could create some space between us; I didn't trust myself. She exhaled, and I was glad that she didn't decide to take a deep breath in.

"I don't want Noni to fight alone; she's strong but…" Her voice trailed off.

"I've offered her refuge, along with any of her kin that also are in need of a safe place, but she refused. She did insist, however, that I not take 'no' for an answer from you." I laid my head on the ground and turned my face to watch Ana.

"Noni seems to think that I'm still three years old," she said, laughing lightly. "I wouldn't feel right leaving her by herself," she said, turning to meet my eyes. The current of heat coming off her skin was driving me crazy and my mind began to conjure memories of what it had felt like to taste her skin, to have her nourish my desires, to have her taste me. God, if we stayed out here any longer, I couldn't be accountable for what I might try to do to her. I stood up quickly and offered her my hand. She looked at me, startled by my sudden movement, but reached to grasp my arm, letting me pull her to her feet. "Are you ok?" she asked, putting the leash on Zanuck. I was grateful that the wind was blowing away from us, and that she couldn't detect just how much my fragrance was pouring out of my skin giving away my arousal.

"It's getting late," I said my jaw clenched. I dropped her hand and started back into the woods. I heard her sigh and mumble something about a personality disorder. I laughed to myself, if she only knew. My time in Peru had unearthed much more of my demonic nature than when I was residing with my brother and his coven. Being in the constant presence of Bonders and Bonders who were much less apt to display their humanistic tendencies, had caused a shift in my nature as a demon. I was much more aggressive and predatory in nature, especially when it came to the Human who was my Bond. She was mine and I wanted her; I wanted to dominate her and feel her and be in her. Being separated from Ana, and now being so close to her again, seemed to have triggered my inherent desire to mate. It was its own separate ritual, different from the initial Bonding that I had completed and different from my personal desire to engage in sex. This came after, after I had made my full change into a demon, after I had saved Ana with my blood. At some point all demons had the need to reproduce, and like with female Bonders, like with my own mother, it was extremely hard for a Human to become pregnant. While Ana and I had had sex numerous times, it was never out of a desire for her to conceive and I was able to make sure that the hormones that allowed for us to impregnate a Human, were not released during our intimate moments, but now, now things were different. I wanted her in a less Human way, and more out of a deep primal, demonic need and with a purpose. Unfortunately, the longer I went without mating, the more difficult it would become for me to control myself and the more aggressive the actual act would be, once it happened. I exhaled loudly.

"What's wrong, Nathanial? Are you upset or something?" Ana asked, stopping to tie her shoe. I turned to watch her stoop to the ground, her hair falling in front of her face.

"No, I'm not upset," I said, walking over to wait on her. She stood up, and whipped her hair back over her shoulder. I noticed that she had chills running over her skin. "Are you cold?" I asked, reaching to remove my pullover.

"A little, but you don't have to…" I cut her off, with a wave of my hand and I unzipped my sweatshirt holding it out for her to take. She was watching me; well actually, she was looking at my body. Her eyes were taking in my muscles and their bigger, more chiseled form. I knew that I looked different because I *was* different and I couldn't help but smirk at her gawking. She rolled her eyes and grabbed the pullover, zipping it up over her own t-shirt. When we got to the front porch, I surveyed the yard and asked Ana to let me in so that I could examine the inside of the house—since her attack, I didn't trust the safety of the Reservation anymore. Noni had left a note that she was attending an emergency Council meeting, but that Ana was not to come. I heard Ana sigh as she read the note over my shoulder. Her breath on my neck made my body tremble. I stepped away moving toward the front door.

"Is your number still the same?" she asked, cocking her head.

"What?" I replied, not sure of her question.

"Your cell number, is that the same as it's always been, or did you have it changed?" she asked, unzipping my pullover.

"The number is the same," I said quietly, watching her remove the shirt, her own muscles flexing under the movement.

"So, what's your deal? Are you just going to hang around here until you wear me down enough and get me to agree to leave with you?" she said, handing me the pullover.

"That's exactly what I'm going to do," I said, moving to stand closer to her. "And I'll win." I reached to touch her face.

"Humph. It must be nice to not have to work," she mumbled. I laughed and twirled a strand of her hair around my finger.

"I've told you before, you would never have to work unless you wanted to; that's the benefit of being Bonded to someone who's had over three hundred years to make money," I said, still laughing.

"That's not the only benefit," she said softly. "I never cared about your money Nathanial." She looked at me. I placed a finger on her bottom lip and traced back and forth.

"I know you didn't Ana," I spoke quietly, still moving my finger over her mouth, parting her lips. I stifled the groan that wanted to escape and moved back towards the door. "What about tomorrow? You have work no?" I asked, standing on the porch, the distinct smell of smoke filtering passed my nose. I saw Ana turn her head, clearly catching the scent.

193

"Um yeah, I work," she said, still gazing across the mountains looking for the source of the burning. I hoped it was just a campfire.

"Why don't you come by after you finish?" I suggested, not wanting her to feel obligated. She laughed.

"Redundancies," she said shaking her head. "Why don't you come here and have dinner with me and Noni; I'll cook for a change." I nodded and walked down the stairs.

"Goodnight, Ana," I said, smiling at her.

"Bye, and thanks again for hanging out with me today," she said, grinning wide. I chuckled and shimmered from her view.

I decided to go by the Council meeting. I had offered my assistance to Noni upon my arrival and I felt that I should be aware of any changes to the situation on the Reservation. I arrived a bit late, but found a seat near the back of the room. Immediately, I saw that both Liam and Christopher were also there and I quickly scanned the room for Stephen; after hearing what he'd proposed to Ana, I really wanted to kill him. He wasn't there. Liam nodded at me and I caught Noni's eye and smiled at her. I was glad that I decided to come. The Reservation was being turned into a refugee camp of sorts for the surrounding communities and states that were under threat from the Vampires. The Nez Perce had offered the protection of their land under the treaty that Ana and Stephen had negotiated and groups were due to arrive over the next few weeks. I offered my assistance in organizing the camp; this was something that I had done for most of my existence and from my work with Alec, over a century ago, I had learned how to efficiently set up and run camps for both military defense and for humanitarian need. The Council was quick to approve my participation and I was glad to have the distraction. My hormones needed a better outlet at the moment. Liam offered his coven as a protection escort to the caravans of people and Bonders who would be making the journey and I was actually glad to have his help. Liam was a powerful leader and an extremely gifted Vampire. He was both mentally strong and physically adept at handling the most difficult battle scenarios and I'd rather be fighting with him, than against him. I left with the offer of evaluating the best site to establish the camp and Noni instructed me to meet her at the house tomorrow morning. I agreed and set off for my cabin.

Once home, I settled in and poured myself a drink. I hadn't checked in with Micah for a while and I placed a call, hoping that he would answer. He didn't so I left a message, telling him that if he needed me, then I hoped he would call. I hadn't made any plans to return to Peru without Ana and he knew this, so I was guessing that he wouldn't contact me unless it was absolutely necessary. I sipped my drink and stared into the fire. My phone buzzed, I answered without looking at the number, expecting it to be Micah. A soft voice met me on the other end. Ana.

"Hey," she said, quietly. I took another sip of my drink, smiling.

"Hey to you," I said, trying not to laugh.

"I was just wondering if you wanted one of Noni's wolves up there with you? You're like in no man's land and you just never know…" she murmured and I could hear music playing in the background. It was a familiar song, one that I had been playing in Stephen's apartment when I had waited for her. I laughed, this time out loud. It was odd that she was worried about my safety. "I know that you can protect yourself Nathanial," she said, clearly annoyed at my response to her offer. "I just thought that maybe you would get lonely or something, and sometimes you don't always have your guard up; you could get taken by surprise too, you know," she replied, her voice stern. I laughed again.

"Well, if you are really concerned about my loneliness Ana, I can think of a possible solution that doesn't require a guard dog," I said purring, my voice low. I heard her chuckle softly.

"I'm sure you can, Nathanial, but I was just calling to make that specific offer." I heard her move the phone to her other ear.

"Hmmm. Alright, perhaps we can work on that." I took another sip from my glass. "When would I be getting this companion?" I asked, hoping that she would offer to bring the animal by this evening; I was fully immersed in my fantasies about being with her again and I wanted to see her; I needed to see her. There was silence on the other end, and I guessed she was debating with herself about what she wanted to do.

"What's a good time for you?" she asked, her tone wary. I resisted the urge to suggest that she come tonight. I was not in control of myself and I did not want to alienate her further.

"How about tomorrow? I'm coming by the house in the morning to see Noni, maybe when I come for dinner, we can go and pick a wolf out for me," I chuckled.

"She told me about the refugee camp. That's really nice of you to help. Let's hope that you run it better than your camp in Peru." I could tell she was smirking over the phone, but there was also an undercurrent of judgment to her tone. I inhaled.

"That camp was for prisoners Ana, for traitors; you were considered a prisoner, what type of accommodations would you have preferred?" I matched her tone. I didn't want to fight with her.

"I should go," she said, her voice tight. "I'll see you tomorrow for dinner."

"I'm glad you called, Ana." I heard her exhale. "Sleep well," I murmured, holding my breath.

"Thanks, you too." She laughed softly and I heard her end the call.

I spent the rest of the evening thinking of ways to convince Ana to have our baby; she'd never wanted to be a mother, but perhaps if she knew that we would be together, that I was willing to offer her a full life, perhaps she would reconsider, perhaps she would forget about Stephen and start a family with me; although that was going to be the least of my challenges with her. First I'd have to convince her to allow me to be back in her life as her lover and her partner; the idea of a baby was going to have to take a back seat for the moment—getting my hormones to oblige was also going to prove challenging. I hoped that I was up for the fight.

Ana had already left for work when I arrived at Noni's and I found myself quite disappointed at not being able to see her. My attention was quickly garnered by the time we arrived at the site that was to be the refugee camp. It was an abandoned summer camp that had been used during the 1980's. As far as campsites went, this was perfect. It was large and spanned over one hundred acres, with a lake and about a dozen cabins that could house at least twenty people apiece. The showers and bathrooms would need to be updated and the water lines fixed, we would need to build several more cabins and bring in a medic tent, but other than that, we had our site. Noni informed me that we would be expecting about a hundred people coming by the end of the month and then waves of fifty or so as the surrounding communities filtered in, over the coming months.

I spent the rest of the afternoon drawing up building plans and assessing what number of workers we had and how many more we would need. To accommodate the first group of people, we would need to fix the water main, get the cabins cleaned and assembled and the bathrooms up and running. I thought that Ana was always good at making even the worst places seem cozy and warm and I thought of asking her to help with the bedding and the cabin arrangement for the families. It was after eight when Ana texted me and Noni was nowhere near finishing with her team. She insisted that I leave and not keep Ana or the dinner she'd fixed, waiting. I was reluctant, but the thought of spending some alone time with Ana seemed to make the decision to leave an easy one. Upon pulling into the drive, I immediately felt my body tense, not from any alarm, but because physiologically, I was reacting to being so near to Ana. I had always been very aware of her cycles, and she was always very honest with me about how they might be affecting her from month to month. I also knew that Ana was vigilant about taking her birth control; fortunately for me, the hormones that Bonders excreted in order to facilitate the mating process overrode any medical device used to control reproduction, but I had to allow for those hormones to be released, and I was guessing that Ana should know what was happening.

I walked up the stairs to the porch and Zanuck howled at my appearance. I noticed that there was another wolf guarding the front door. The animal was large and deep gray with glints of silver running through its fur. I smiled; something about the wolf's coloring reminded me of Ana's metal tattoo. I pulled open the door and entered the kitchen. The stereo was at full volume and Ana had her back to me, arranging salads. I waved my hand, turning the sound down a few pitches, making Ana whip her head around. I stood, leaning against the chair, smiling at her.

"Clever little talent you got there." She joked and washed her hands under the sink. "Would you like a glass of wine?" She motioned to the bottle on the counter, my favorite Chianti; it was ridiculously expensive and I frowned at her. "What?" she said, slicing a tomato.

"You shouldn't be spending your money on my alcohol; you don't really even drink," I said, uncorking the bottle. She shrugged.

"Where's Noni?" she asked, handing me a glass.

"She's a bit over zealous with the crew." I laughed. "I have a feeling that they'll be at the site until everyone knows exactly what their responsibilities are." I said, taking a sip from my glass. "That reminds me," I said, moving so that I was leaning on the counter next to her.

"What?" she said, handing me an onion and a knife. I started chopping.

"I need some help and I thought of you," my voice lowering as I surveyed her.

"Sure, anything, what do you need?" she replied. I was amazed at her willingness to sign on to something that I had not made clear. I raised my eyebrows.

"Hmmm, are you sure you want to agree so quickly to help me; you have no idea what I'm asking?" I purred, making sure she knew what I was implying.

"What do you need, Nathanial?" Ana rolled her eyes. I laughed. I relished in how normal and easy we seemed to fall back into step. No matter what had happened between us, I knew that I was a weakness for her, that she wanted me. I just needed to be patient.

"Ok, ok, actually, I need someone to help get the cabins suitable for a family living space. Bedding, furniture…stuff like that," I said, handing her my onions.

"Of course, for sure. I can help with that. Do we have a budget?" she asked, carrying the plates out to the deck. I followed her outside, surprised at how nice she'd made our dining area. Tiny votive candles were lit on the table and along the railing of the deck, bathing the outside in a soft, luminous glow. There was a small fire pit, clearly made by her, with blue flames dancing along the rocks at the bottom. I watched her assemble the table settings, feeling my chest constrict. "Nathanial? Do we have a budget?" she asked again, pulling me out of my trance. I waved my hand and shook my head "no". I reached into my back pocket and pulled out my wallet. I took out a black credit card and handed it to her.

"Get whatever you need," I said, my eyes still on her body, her movements.

"Holy shit!" she exclaimed, her tone startled me and I looked around expecting to see something poised to attack us.

"What!" I said, my head whipping around in all directions.

"I've never known anyone who actually has an Onyx American Express Card. I'm clearly in the wrong profession," she said, reaching for the card and examining it as if it were a jewel. I exhaled and rolled my eyes at her.

"Just use it, please," I said, putting my wallet away.

She made a wonderful meal, my favorite, curry and rice; even though I didn't actually eat very much, it was nice to sit across from her and have dinner together. We chatted about her work and when she'd be able to come out to the site to help. Again, I was having difficulty concentrating on our dialogue. My body felt overheated and my arousal level was heightened. I didn't want to have to leave suddenly, but if things continued along this route, I was going to have to bail. Standing next to her, placing the dishes in the sink, I was immediately aware that she was ovulating. Christ! Could this be any more difficult? Her scent was potent and it hit me like a punch to the stomach. My muscles flexed and heat spread into my groin, making me grip the sides of the sink. I felt my skin grow warm and my own scent was released; there was nothing I could do to control it, my body knew that she was in reproduction mode and it was reacting accordingly. I saw her body go rigid as my fragrance registered with her. She turned to look at me, her eyes wide.

We stood staring at each other, not blinking. I was trying to override my biological reaction to her, but it was proving extremely difficult; her body was ready, whether she was or not. I perceived that tonight was the only day I had to mate with her, otherwise, I'd have to endure this hell for another whole month. I hated thinking about us coming together in such a technical way, but that was the mode I was in; I was being driven solely by my instincts. I moved to stand directly behind her, placing my hands on either side of the counter, blocking her inside my position. She turned to look at me and I could see that her face was flush and I felt heat pulsing off of her skin. I brought my face close to hers, my breath on her lips. She kept her eyes lowered, but I felt her move her body close to mine and the motion triggered a violent passion that I could no longer control. A low snarl reverberated in my chest, and her head snapped up, our eyes locked and I pressed her back hard against the counter, my mouth barely touching hers. She was breathing hard and another wave of her scent washed over me. I growled again and moved my hips against her, not kissing her. I wanted to drag out her anticipation, her longing. Since the change in my physiology and my psyche, any time I had thought of Ana, any time that I had allowed myself to fantasize about her, I had wanted to control her, to control her desire, her passion. I had this need to dominate her and the very thought of doing that now was making my body tremble. Suddenly, headlights flooded the kitchen and I stopped moving, my mouth inches from hers. Ana jumped and pushed me off of her. I took a deep breath, cursed under my breath and stood up, running my fingers through my hair and arranging myself casually next to Ana, by the sink. I growled low into her ear.

"Next time, we meet at my place," I said, as I reached to run my hands between her thighs, stroking her; she was hot. I growled again and moved toward the door. I saw Noni getting out of her truck, and I went over to say hello, desperately trying to quell the flood of hormones and compose my breathing.

"Good work today, son," Noni said, taking my hand as I closed her door. I laughed and moved toward my own vehicle.

"Nathanial, wait!" Ana called to me, from the porch, Noni smiled and walked into the house. Ana jumped down the stairs, the dark grey wolf at her side; she ran over to me smiling. "Don't forget Sheeba." She patted the large animal and it howled. My eyes went to the porch and I could see that Noni was making tea, her back to us. I pulled Ana against me, leaning myself back on my car door. I held her firmly around her hips; I was fairly confident that I could control myself.

"Tell me," I whispered, gazing into her eyes, "what would have happened if we hadn't been interrupted?" I asked. I was trying to gage her feelings for me, where they were and what she might be conflicted about—I couldn't tell at the moment. She smiled and shook her head, looking down.

"I'm not sure, Nathanial," she said. "You've always been a bit of a weakness for me, since the first time we were together at the beach." I felt heat rise in her skin and even through her clothes, I could sense the warmth of her blood. "I'm bound to you in so many different ways; they all make it hard for me to resist you—even if I wanted to," she said gently, her eyes still lowered.

"And do you want to, to resist me, I mean?" I asked, lifting her chin so that I could see her face. She smiled.

"Not really. I just don't know if I can emotionally handle becoming involved with anyone again; at least not for a while." She ran her fingers through her hair and exhaled. "My expectations are completely rattled. I mean, I went from being with you, to losing you, to finding you again, to leaving you, going for months without seeing you, to then saying goodbye, telling you that I loved you, that I was sorry, then thinking you were going to kill me, and now here we are." She was speaking very quickly and she sounded exasperated. "Not to mention all of the crap that happened in between, and yet..." She stopped and turned her face away from me.

"And yet what, Ana?" I probed, wanting to know what she was feeling. I couldn't get inside her mind; she had me blocked. She sighed, and stroked my face.

"And yet, I *want* you. I want to be with you. I've missed you desperately, ever since the last time we were together; I've missed you Nathanial. You affect me and not just because we are Bound by some stupid ritual, but because I still love you, and I would die first before I let anything ever happen to you." Her eyes turned fierce and she stepped away from me. My heart ached and I stopped breathing. "I'll see you tomorrow night at the camp," she said, turning to head back toward the house. "And yes, definitely next time, we meet at your house!" She laughed and waved and I watched my life, my soul, the very reason for my heart to beat, bound up the stairs and into her house.

I arrived at the camp around six in the morning and Noni already had the main projects up and running. I was surprised at the amount of volunteers she had managed to enlist and pleased to see how organized and diligent everyone seemed to be working. It was Fall and I would have liked for us to get the majority of the new construction done before the winter sets in. I was drawing up some blue prints when I noticed the date on the bottom of the plans; October 25th. Ana's birthday was just six days away. I had always mused that it seemed apropos that the day of her birth should come during a pagan holiday; Halloween. She loved Halloween, more than most humans I'd known, but she always preferred never to celebrate her birthday, opting instead for me to escort her to some ridiculous costume party given by one of her co-workers. It always ended up being more fun than I anticipated, mainly because Ana was fun and she could be silly, and I had always liked that part of her. I thought that I should give her something special this year, something symbolic, something that would keep me close to her. I rolled up the plans and headed out toward the lake to check on the water main.

It was after seven in the evening when we'd managed to get the water line to the cabins functioning and the second crew of the day was leaving. Our third shifters were now beginning to trickle in and I was waiting for Ana to arrive. I wasn't expecting for her to stay on all night; she'd been at work since early this morning and I was sure that she would be hungry and tired. I just needed her to get a feel for the living arrangements and then maybe she could decorate from there; that was my hope anyway. I heard tires squeal and gravel being pelted up in the air; I smiled, thankful that all of the horrific events in her life had not diminished her ability to operate a vehicle like a crazy person. She hoped out of her jeep and opened the back door for Zanuck. I walked over to meet her. A suddenly strong current of desire and need began tugging at my body and forced me to stop moving toward her. I watched as she put a leash on Zanuck, and tried to regulate my body's impulses. It was odd, I had thought that last night was our last chance to mate before having to wait another month, but for some reason, my hormones were again igniting and the drive to be with her was overwhelming. Perhaps her cycle was longer than average? I frowned, confused by my abnormal physiological reaction.

"What's the matter?" Ana was standing in front of me, her head cocked to the side. I looked at her and tried to smile, holding my breath. "Are you sick?" she asked, clearly concerned when I didn't respond.

"Nope," I said, still not taking any air in; I knew that if she was still within her cycle, her scent would make my actions towards her less than gentlemanly. I motioned for her to follow me and we walked down the hill to the first set of cabins. I had several people and Bonders working on the outside, repainting and installing gutter systems. A Bonder named Charlie was my main contractor. He was efficient and skilled and extremely loyal. He was also young, as far as Bonders went and he had yet to make a Bond with a human. He waved to me from his ladder and jumped down, trotting over to meet us.

"Charlie, this is Ana; Ana this is Charlie, he's my second in command." I winked at her and smiled. Immediately, I could see Charlie begin to conjure up images of Ana in his mind that were not to my liking. Apparently, I was not the only one experiencing a flood of hormones. I cleared my throat and jabbed him gently in the back.

"Hey Charlie," Ana said, putting out her hand.

"Ana," Charlie said, smiling widely at her and grasping her hand in his.

"So, I'll let Charlie show you around and then we can meet and discuss what you think can be done." I looked at her, hoping that she would want to stay a bit longer this evening. I noticed that Charlie had moved so that his arm was around Ana's shoulder, a smirk on his face. I shot him a look and a private warning message and then I turned to walk back toward the lake. Two hours later, I saw Ana heading down the hill towards me, a piece of paper in her hands and Charlie gazing after her. I rolled my eyes; it was like having a teenage, Human male on staff—of course, who was I to judge; I knew exactly how he felt.

"So, how'd it go?" I asked, bracing myself for the next onslaught of desire as her fragrance hit me in the gut.

"Good. I remember staying at one of the cabins when I was first on the Reservation; they're really quite nice as far as camp accommodations go." She smiled at me. "But I wouldn't think that you would care much for outfitting them with anything but the essentials; that's more your style these days isn't it?" She laughed, her eyes roaming over my fatigues and boots.

"Of course," I murmured, eyeing her. "But if anyone can make the essentials look elegant, it's you." I moved to put my arms around her, pulling her to me. I was being reckless, but I couldn't help myself.

"If I remember correctly, out of the two of us, it is you that has the best eye for all things decorative," she said, putting her hands on my chest and tossing her hair back. I knew she was remembering the renovations I had done to her house, a very small surprise for finishing her dissertation.

"Hmmm, yes, I suppose, but you have much more eclectic taste than I." I was running my hands up and down her back, pressing my fingers into her muscles. She was very tight and I'd guessed she might be experiencing a bit of stress.

"Is that code for 'strange'?" She laughed, but I heard her sigh as I reached up under her hair and began pressing on the muscles of her upper back.

"You're very tense," I said, looking at her face and continuing to work my hands into her flesh. I didn't feel safe, giving her the proper attention I wanted, not out here with so many people around and I hoped that my next question wouldn't be too presumptive. I reached into my pocket and pulled out the key to my cabin. I took her hand and pressed the metal piece into her palm. "Why don't you meet me at home and I can better tend to your stresses," I murmured, letting my lips caress over her ear.

"Do you really think that I'm that easy?" she said, pulling her head back from my mouth. I raised my eyebrows and smirked. She pulled my hair gently. "Well, I'm so glad that you think so highly of my virtue, Nathanial." And she tried to twist herself free from my grasp, laughing. I held her firm, squeezing her body to mine. "Fine, fine." She gasped, and I let my grip on her slacken. "But only to check on Sheeba, you're not known as a guardian of animals and they usually don't take to you very well," she said, grinning at me and breaking free from my hold. Just then, I felt my phone buzz in my pocket and I reached to pull it out. It was Micah. Ana waved to me and I watched her walk up the hill towards her jeep, whistling for Zanuck.

"Micah!" I said, my voice urgent. "How are you? I've been worried."

"Nathanial, you are a kind soul to worry and I have to say that your concerns are not without merit." His voice was quiet, contemplative.

"Micah, what's wrong, what's happened?" I pressed, fear growing in my heart.

"Nothing per se, my son, but I fear what is already in the works." I hated when my uncle spoke in riddles; it was maddening. I sighed, trying to quell my frustration.

"Micah!" I said, sternly, hoping that he wouldn't perceive my tone as disrespectful.

"They want retaliation, Nathanial," he said softly. My body tensed. "As soon as we can reclaim the land and the surrounding communities near the camp, there is a group that is hell bent on finding Ana and making her pay for what she did that night in the hut, for who she killed." He exhaled.

"What group Micah?" I asked, surprised at how calm my voice sounded.

"It's relatively small, Nathanial. Mainly followers of Nicholas, those who felt he was the strongest leader, but they are determined and impatient. I'm having them watched." I heard him shift the phone.

"What should I do?" I asked, not believing that Ana's life or our life together would ever be normal.

"Nothing at the moment, there's not much you can do. I know there was some discussion before you left about bringing Ana and her Noni to us, but that is clearly no longer an option. What is happening on the Reservation? I've been hearing things about refugees and outbreaks of violence." His voice sounded tight and quiet.

"Yes, all of that is true. Vampires have infiltrated two reservations and we are evacuating several more and the surrounding communities. We're setting up a camp…" I trailed off, my mind racing. "Micah, are you in danger?" I wondered if any in the group that was after Ana had known that he'd helped her; I wondered if his life was also forfeit.

"My son, do not worry yourself with what may or may not come to me. I am well prepared for either scenario and I see no use in troubling your mind with things that are unknown. Despair is for those who can say, beyond a shadow of a doubt, what the future holds and none of us have that luxury. Now tell me, how is your Ana?" I sighed. I knew from his tone, that my concern for his life was now no longer a part of our conversation.

"She's fine, but me, I'm a different story entirely." I laughed darkly.

"Why's that?" my uncle asked, laughing along with me.

"Something's occurred, something that wasn't part of our relationship before and I'm not doing well at handling this sudden change." I hoped that he would understand what I was alluding to; I wanted to spare my uncle the details of my animalistic sexual tendencies; he was family for Christ's sake. I heard him chuckle.

"Ahhh, you want a child; you're ready to mate!" He sounded more jubilant than I felt was appropriate. "You know, your mother came to me when she started to experience her urges; she was a mess, crying and laughing and more crying. I think your father was utterly confused by her range of emotions." Micah sighed and laughed heartily. I was absolutely sure that I did not want to hear about my mother's sexual mood swings; yes we were both Bonders, but there were just some things that a child should never know about their parents. "She knew the risks it would pose to her life, carrying a child. Bonder women have such a difficult time becoming pregnant, it can only happen once and they are lucky if they survive. Your mother was blessed; she got not only one child, but two and she lived for five years before her body shut down—amazing." He sounded sad, but also proud. "Does your Ana want children?" Micah asked, his voice shifting again to a happier tone. I sighed.

"She didn't when we were together; I'm guessing that hasn't changed," I said softly.

"Mmmm....well, you never know. Women sometimes change their minds when they know they are caring a child inside them; I saw the way Ana cared for Lucie, the way she protected her; she was ready to die for that little girl and she wasn't even hers. Perhaps she has a desire to be a mother and she herself does not realize it," he said gently. "Has Ana been responsive to your advances?" He sounded so clinical, that I had to laugh.

211

"A bit, but it's a trust issue with her, trust in herself and trust in me, I think," I said honestly.

"Of course it is," Micah exclaimed confidently. "Your journeys have continued to allow for the both of you to question how much you actually love each other; questions are good Nathanial, and I ask you now, do you know the answers? Do you know that your existence begins and ends with Ana? Have you forgiven her for whatever transgressions you perceived to be her fault? Have you forgiven yourself for your own ill-conceived decisions? Do you love her Nathanial?" His voice rang clear and commanding in my ears and just for a moment, I thought I could hear the sound of my mother's own voice speaking to my heart.

"Yes," I said quietly, resolutely.

"Well then, that's all you need to understand, everything else will happen as it is meant to; be patient with her and with yourself my son." He moved the phone again.

"Micah, where should I take Ana if the need arises?" I was still very concerned about this group he was having watched.

"I would take her abroad Nathanial. Avoid Central and South America, and of course Indonesia; let me contact a few of my kin in Europe and see if we can secure a safe place for you, should you need it." He sounded determined.

"Thank you Micah, for everything." I laughed softly.

"I'll be in touch as soon as I know anything. Goodbye my son."

"Goodbye Micah." I hung up the phone and walked up the hill to my car, feeling both lighter and heavier at the same time.

Upon arriving home, I was glad to see Ana's car in the drive, at least she hadn't reconsidered. I decided not to tell her about my conversation with Micah. Until we knew anything further, I saw no use in creating drama and worry where there needn't be. Plus, I had other things occupying my mind. I came into the living room to find Ana and Sheeba curled up on the couch, thumbing through a magazine, the fireplace was lit with Ana's trademark blue flames. I smiled, letting my natural urges surface. Hearing that my mother had encountered her own emotional and physical upheavals during her mating time made me feel a lot less guilty and resistant to experiencing this process.

"Why is it," Ana looked up at me, "that every place you own could be on the cover of Architectural Digest? Is it a Demon thing that all of you get to have nice places? I totally got shafted!" she exclaimed, flinging the magazine onto the coffee table. I laughed and poured myself a glass of wine.

"You know any time that you would like to take advantage of any demonic specific offerings, they are at your disposal," I said, raising my eyebrows at her and sipping my drink. She rolled her eyes and leaned back against the sofa.

"Have you always had this place?" she asked, watching me as I moved to stand near the fireplace.

"No," I said, simply. I wasn't sure if I wanted to get into discussing my activities after the attack at the University; we'd been down that road so many times before.

"When did you get it?" she pressed, stroking Sheeba, and still eyeing me.

"I got it after I left the first time," my voice quiet as I spoke. I turned to look at her, hoping she would let me end the discussion there.

"Oh," she whispered and I noticed that her fingers began to trace along the scar on her wrist, my scar. She smiled at me. "Well it's really nice, but it reminds me more of Patric's taste than your own." She laughed.

"You would know." I joked and she stuck her tongue out at me. I was glad, at least, that we could humor each other about my brother, knowing that we both missed him and that we both loved him. It was a comfortable place for us to be. I put my glass on the mantel and walked to stand behind her, sweeping her hair forward over her shoulders. She leaned her head back and looked up at me.

"You're quite presumptive about touching me, aren't you?" She laughed.

"You don't want me to touch you?" I asked, my voice soft and seductive. I could feel my body responding to the feel of her skin, her scent—her heat. I let my fingers press deeply into her muscles, sending my own warmth to penetrate her tension.

"Hmmm, I guess I do, otherwise I would leave," she murmured, leaning forward a bit.

"Why are you so tense?" I asked, kneading down her back.

"Who knows; I'm always like that," she replied softly and I felt her body begin to relax. I suddenly remembered how Andres had attacked Ana, how he'd almost raped her and I stopped moving. I didn't want my intimacy to frighten her, to make her uneasy. "What's wrong?" she asked, opening her eyes to look up at me. I pulled my hands away and moved to sit next to her on the couch. I took her hands in mine and stared at her face.

"Ana, you've never told me about what happened to you that night, the night that you were attacked by Andres." I studied her face, looking for any signs of distress.

"Is that why you stopped touching me?" she asked, shaking her head. "You're very considerate Nathanial, but really, I'm fine."

"How could you be fine?" I asked her, incredulous at her nonchalance. She shook her head again.

"Honestly?" she asked, returning my stare. I nodded. "Well, honestly, after you left me, when you attacked me; I thought about killing myself. I was so depressed. Of course then I did try to kill myself to help you and Patric and that backfired." She chuckled, but immediately stopped when she noticed me wince. "Sorry, but seriously, after everything that I've been through, Andres couldn't do any more damage than already existed, not to my heart at least." She waved her hand. "Plus, I totally kicked his ass," she said, reaching to smooth my hair down my shoulders. She turned her back to me and flipped her hair to the front. "Touch away!" She laughed. "Besides, do you know how much I would have to pay to get a massage

216

anywhere close to what you can do? That American Express card you gave me just might end up with a few extra charges on it," she said. I sighed and began running my hands along her back.

"You can have anything you want Ana," I said, caressing down her spine. "There's nothing that I wouldn't do *for* you or *to* you," I whispered into her ear, laughing gently. "But you know, this can actually work much better if you lie down," I purred, knowing that I might be crossing the line with her. She sat up straight and turned to face me.

"Massage only?" she asked, but I knew that it wasn't a question so much as a demand. I raised my hands up in the air.

"Of course." My tone dripped with contrived innocence. Her eyes narrowed and she bit her lip. She let me pull her up off the couch and I took her hand, leading her upstairs. I didn't want to lose her trust, so it was important that I be able to control the urges that my body needed me to indulge. If I had to wait another month before she felt comfortable being with me, then I would wait; I would wait forever for her, if that's what would make her feel safe to be with me again.

"Hey!" she said, coming into the room. Her excitement made me jump. "That's your mother's quilt, the one she gave your father when they got married. You still have it!" she said, walking over to the bed and running her fingers along the pattern. Besides Ana, the quilt was the most sacred, the most loved possession I had. Ana, of course, wasn't a possession, but the way I felt about her, well, no tangible object could ever come close to expressing that emotion. "I love this quilt," she said, looking at me as I turned the stereo on low. I ghosted to her

217

side and pulled her down so she was sitting next to me, the quilt folded between us.

"The turquoise thread is for Patric, of course," I said, smiling at Ana. "The midnight blue is for me," I traced her finger over the line that represented my own imprint, the mark of my mother, "the silver is for my father and these," I said, running her hands along brilliant golden threads stemming from Patric's symbol and mine, "these are for whomever is next," I said, my gaze turning to search her face, wondering if she understood.

"You mean children?" she asked, retracing the threads from Patric to me and back to Patric. She looked sad. I understood what she was feeling.

"We all make choices, Ana. With the exception of loving you, Patric made a series of very bad decisions." She looked up at me, her eyes wide. I laughed. "What, you didn't think that I knew my brother loved you, in his own bizarre and off center kind of way," I said, touching her face. She frowned. "What?" I asked, concerned that I'd said something to make her upset.

"Your mother, where is she in this? Your whole family is here, even potential children, but where is her thread?" I grinned; Ana missed nothing.

"Ahhh…" I whispered and I took her finger to trace along the deep red line that ran through all of our own threads. "She's here," I replied gently, moving Ana's finger along the thread. "That is her blood, her heart; she's right there." My voice became soft. "She's always there." Something wet hit my finger and I looked up to see tears coming down

Ana's face. I held her face in my hands. "Don't cry Ana. I'm not sad. I loved her very much and I knew that she loved me. She gave to me and to Patric her greatest gift, her life for ours, and I have always wanted to honor that. I haven't always done it well, but I have always tried and I know that she would be proud of me, of the being that I have chosen to become, and I know that she would have loved you like a daughter," I murmured, as I wiped Ana's cheeks. She smiled and nodded. I patted her leg. "Now, how about that massage?" I asked happily, moving to arrange the pillows for her.

"We have to move the quilt though," Ana said, her eyes wide and her face cringing. I laughed out loud at her reference for not wanting to disrespect my mother with what I was quite sure would be a very sensual massage. I pulled the quilt back to the end of the bed and patted the pillows, motioning for her to lie down. She eyed me again, but obliged. She had on a rather bulky sweatshirt and I frowned. "What?" she asked, looking down at the front of her shirt.

"Do you have anything on under that? I asked her and she rolled her eyes at me. She pulled the shirt over her head and I was glad to see that she was wearing a flimsy tank top. Actually, if she was going to be removing articles of clothing, I much preferred her to take off her jeans. My body tensed as I watched her lie down on my bed. Her movement stirred the air and her scent crashed over me, a surge of primal desire surfacing. I exhaled and stood over her. She let me lift up her shirt, exposing the muscles in her back and I began to massage deep into her skin.

"So, what do you want to do for your birthday this year?" I asked, trying to distract myself from the graphic fantasies that were now filling my head.

"It's not my birthday?" she said, puzzled. Quickly I did the math; it was.

"October thirty-first?" I asked, frowning.

"Yeah, but...frick!" she said, and I felt her body tense. I laughed. "I can't believe it's already here; I'd forgotten," she murmured, turning her face to the side. I pressed my fingers in deeper, moving them up and down her spine, letting the heat from my body release into her muscles and tendons.

"So, what do you want to do?" I asked her again, moving down to her lower back. I pressed gently. I knew that area was one, for Ana at least, that had a tendency to release quite a bit of arousal in her body; I didn't want to go too fast. She sighed and I hoped it was out of pleasure rather than annoyance at my questions.

"Hmmm; I don't care, this maybe." She chuckled to herself. I smiled.

"A massage? That's what you want to do for your birthday?" I asked, moving back up her spine stroking out to the side, letting my fingers gently graze the side of her breasts. I wondered if she'd let me take off her bra. I saw chills move over her skin. "Are you cold?" I asked, but knowing all along that it was her body's response to me and not the temperature. A surge of hormones released, heating my body and I knew my scent was also being dispersed. I heard Ana take a deep breath.

"No, I'm not cold," she murmured and I felt *her* scent release, but she seemed completely unaware. God, this was such an odd thing; it was like our bodies knew that we needed to come together, that we were both ready, both craving each other. I shuddered. Suddenly, she flipped herself over, letting her hair spill down her chest, her arms by her head. I inhaled and tried to step away from her, not willing to risk the foundations we were rebuilding in order to fulfill some biological need. I could see that her pupils were dilated, color began to fill her cheeks and the surge of heat and blood to her lips made them swell slightly... I rubbed my face, breathing hard. Suddenly and without warning, I lunged and was down on top of her with more force than I could have ever anticipated. I was stunned, but my body was not letting me process anything other than what I physically needed. I heard her gasp, but she didn't try to throw me off. I felt a snarl erupt from my throat. The most incredible wave of power washed over me and all I wanted to do was bind her hands; I had these unimaginable urges to watch her struggle to keep me from doing things to her body. I had never experienced this kind of desire before, not something so dark; it was demonic and domineering. I grabbed her wrists, holding her tightly. With my other hand I undid my belt, whipping it from the loops in one motion. I wrapped it around her hands and tied her to the headboard, securing the buckle. I moved my mouth to her ear and whispered to her.

"I'm not going to hurt you," I said, my tone seductive. "I want you to trust me. Do you trust me, Ana?" I took my tongue and traced along her ear, making her shiver.

"Yes," she moaned, closing her eyes. I breathed hard into her neck and with one slash, I had shredded her tank. I straddled her, ripping the remaining fabric from her body and raising her hips up so that I could undo her jeans. I cut the straps of her bra with my teeth and tore her underwear from her around her waist. She was naked and bound to my bed. Another growl escaped from somewhere deep in my chest and I removed my shirt and pants, tossing them to the side. I brought my face close to hers, she tried to bring her mouth to mine, but I turned my head, prompting her to pull back from me, her face puzzled.

"What, you don't kiss now either?" she asked, clearly referring to the bizarre physical code of some Vampires. I laughed softly and brought my forehead to hers, I was breathless. I reached up to undo the belt; I wanted to feel her wrists being bound by my own hands. I released her, but held her hands tightly, firmly.

"Kissing isn't exactly on the top of my list of things I want from you at the moment," I spoke, my voice rough and deep. I felt my eyes darken as my body tensed, my need to take her, to watch her as I moved inside her body, to hear her moan—I wasn't going to be able to make it a gentle experience for her. I ran my hands over her breasts and down her stomach, letting my fingertips barely caress her skin. Her eyes closed and she bit her lip and struggled against the feel of me. I stared at her, she was holding back and I knew it.

"Why are you resisting me Ana?" I murmured. "Your body wants this, you want this," I whispered in her ear and she shivered. I felt her breasts swell and I groaned, moving my mouth to run my tongue over each one, suckling hard on her tightened nipples. I let her hands go as I moved my body and my lips down by her thighs. I wanted to feel her hands on my head, pushing me. She tried to move me away, but I

222

wouldn't have it. I took her hands again and made a manacle with my fingers, binding her wrists tightly together.

"Stop," I said when she tired to free herself from my grasp. "Stop, Ana!" I said forcefully, but feeling her struggle against me, against what I knew she wanted; it created another surge of power in my body and I gripped her tighter, watching her body move and react—I wanted this. She was breathing hard and the electric current from the pulse in her groin was making my mouth water and my lips slick. I didn't hesitate. I took her into my mouth, letting my tongue move deeply inside of her. She moaned loudly and I felt her hands try to redirect me away from her. She was always so sensitive to me, to my movements inside of her, but this time she was going to have to let go, let me do what I wanted. I snarled at her and shook her off. "Stop fighting me!" I said, licking my lips. Her taste was flooding my mouth and I felt my hormones begin to break through whatever barriers I had in place. I gasped and my body shuttered. I rose up and hovered my body over hers. "You have to stop resisting me Ana," I spoke quietly, letting my hips press gently down on hers. "You have to let go. Let me control what you want, what you need; let me be with you," I said, running my fingers down between her legs; she opened them, accommodating me. "That's it," I said, my voice was dark, urgent. "That's what I want." I moved my mouth back down and took her again, feeling her press me deeply inside of her. Her body rocked and she groaned. "Relax, Ana," I said, pulling out and gently running my tongue over her most sensitive part, moving it slowly back and forth as I nipped and sucked. "Let me control you," I said, my voice snarling low; I barely recognized it. She let out another groan as I closed my lips over her, pulling gently, then not so gently. She tried to push me

223

away as she felt the tug, her pleasure beginning to peak. "Stop!" I said, but my body wanted to see her, wanted to watch her try to resist.

"Nathanial!" she groaned, trying to move her hips back. I held her down, gripping my fingers into her flesh. She arched, but she spread her legs wider and I shoved my mouth roughly inside of her. She wanted this, wanted me. I growled and moaned, as I tasted more and more of her; my body was craving her. I couldn't stop. I didn't want to stop. She screamed out, her body writhing under my grip. I felt fire begin to surge in my groin and I threw myself on top of her. My mind was racing, what did I want? How did I want her to be? My body knew and I immediately flipped her over bringing her up to her knees, her back to me. I moved my hands around and began massaging her forcefully between her thighs. She gasped and I held her tightly around the waist. I entered her from behind, and the force of my thrusting made me snarl so loudly that in that instant I felt more like an animal, a primal being than I had in my entire life. I became detached and all I wanted was to feel myself inside of Ana, to feel her come, to control her, to dominate her, to mate with her. I pushed her down and held her hair, as it cascaded down her back. The way she moved her hips, the way she pushed herself into me; Christ, I wanted her in the most brutal way. I felt her desire come and in a rush of heat and a surge of her scent, I violently thrust deeper wanting to feel the physical effects of her passion.

"Again," I said, my voice commanding and strong in her ear. "I want you to come again," I whispered forcefully in her ear. Each time she climaxed, the rhythm of my thrusting became so violent and so intense, that my own orgasms were hovering on the brink of painful.

My hormones were still coursing and I was waiting, I wanted to make sure that we released together; I wanted us to feel each other. I pushed harder and deeper inside of her, but then withdrew and moved below her, her hips over my mouth.

"What are you doing?" she gasped, breathless. "Nathanial, I don't think that…" Her voice trailed off as I started to taste her again, slowly. It was amazing. The release of her desire had also released a new scent, a new taste, one that was made for me, for what my body needed. Something deep inside of me moved, pushed forward and I knew that the final barrier for my hormones had been knocked down. I groaned and spun Ana hard onto her back, pinning her down. I pushed myself inside her, moving my hands between her legs. She moved my hands away and I felt her open her legs wider. I shuddered at the depth she was allowing and I ground into her, quicker. She held me to her, keeping my thrusts close inside her body. Suddenly, she moaned and I could feel her hold me tighter between her legs. I snarled and began pulsing and pushing hard, back and forth, the motion sending waves of animal desire through my body.

"I want it harder Ana," I gasped, it wasn't enough, the depth wasn't enough, the force wasn't enough; I needed more. She groaned, moving her hands to my back, pressing me against her. I yanked her up from the bed and wrapped her legs around my waist, not breaking our connection. I slammed her up against the wall and proceeded to fuck the hell out of her. It was the hardest and most forceful that I had ever done, especially with her and that was the best way I could describe what was happening between us. We weren't making love, that was for Humans. I didn't want to make love; I wanted to fuck her. There was nothing Human about what we were doing, we were

225

nowhere near Human; we were our animal selves and that's what I had wanted, what I had needed. Loud snarls echoed in the room and Ana screamed out in her pleasure. I slammed her body again, back against the wall as I drilled her, feeling everything from me enter her and I gasped, my breath leaving my lungs. I was panting and still thrusting roughly against her, not able to stop. I moved her from the wall and carried her back to bed. She was coated in sweat and I could smell the mingling of our mutual releases; her scent, mixed with mine, it was a potent combination and I greedily gulped in the air around me. I withdrew myself from her body and rolled onto the bed, my breath still coming in shallow bursts, energy pulsing between my legs. I turned to look at her. Her eyes were closed and I watched as her chest rose and fell in quick movements.

We didn't speak, we didn't move, we didn't touch each other. Hours passed and moonlight filtered through the window, bathing her skin in its celestial glow and it was me who finally broke the spell. I leaned forward and pulled my mother's quilt from the end of bed, wrapping both of us beneath its plush fabric. I pulled Ana close to me, so that our bodies were touching. She trembled and I put my arms around her shoulders, holding her.

"We never kissed," she spoke so quietly, that I wasn't even sure if the voice was coming from her. I dropped my chin and she raised her head, looking at me.

"What?" I said, thankful that my voice had returned to normal.

"We've never kissed each other, we haven't since you've been here," she said, her eyes on my face. I stared at her, wanting nothing more than to feel her lips on mine.

"Hmmm," I whispered. "We should remedy that." I pulled her so that her body was lying on top of me, the full contact of our skin sent a wave of convulsions up and down my body. I tried to breathe normally. She bent her head and pressed her lips gently to mine, letting her tongue linger and move with mine. I wound my hand to the back of her head and pressed her harder to me, kissing her deeply. Too quickly, she pulled away, laughing and breathless. "What?" I asked frustrated at her stopping us; for some reason my body didn't seem to be quite satiated with what we'd done. Apparently, I needed her again. She shook her head and nestled herself down, lying her head on my chest.

"And I thought the night we did that whole blood ritual thing was when you were at your most demonic. Clearly, that was just the tip of the iceberg," she said, looking up at me. Had I gone to far? Had I frightened her?

"Does that bother you?" I asked hesitantly. "When I'm that close to my truest form, I mean?" I shifted her so that she was lying next to me; I wanted to be able to see her eyes when she answered.

"Maybe it should bother me, but—no, it doesn't. I actually like that part of you," she said and I could feel a sudden release of heat from her skin as she stared at me. I touched her lips with my fingers, tracing their shape over and over again. Christ! If it was just up to me and my biological clock, I'd never let her leave this room or I would just manage to fuck her on every surface and in every space in the whole goddamn house, I thought to myself. Immediately, my body reacted to my contemplations and I felt another wave of hormones flood my system. What was wrong with me? I cleared my throat.

"Well, from where I'm sitting, I'm not the only one who seems to have tapped into their more demonic nature." I laughed quietly, still caressing her mouth.

"And what do you think about that, that part of me?" she asked, parting her lips. My heart started to beat faster and I moved my face close to hers.

"If it were up to me," I said, running my hands along the curves of her waist and hips, "I would have you like that all the time, every time," I murmured as my tongue traced along her bottom lip. She laughed, but again she pulled away, halting my movements.

"Nathanial," she said, looking at me, her face serious. "I know that we've shared this night together and that we are working on things between us; I want to work on things with us, but I also need to reconcile some other issues. I don't know what you want; if you want us to be together again and I'm not quite sure what I want either. I would never assume to speak for you...I don't know, I'm babbling." She grinned and turned to lie on her back.

"You mean with Stephen," I said, my tone even. We'd never really discussed the nature of her relationship with him, but from my conversation with Liam, I knew that the feelings they shared were incredibly strong. "The issues you are referring to are about him?" I asked, feeling the familiar surge of jealousy breaking through my composed façade.

"Yes. I miss him terribly and I don't like that he's not come back to at least talk to me, or to see me. I know that he's upset that I didn't allow for him to..." Her voice became quiet and she turned away from me. Jesus. Just the very thought of Ana being turned, becoming a Vampire; it made me sick, and then to picture her with *him*, knowing how I'm sure they would go about the transition. I knew they had had a bit of an intimate moment months ago; Ana was very honest with me and I was glad, but there was also a part of me that now had those images burned into my brain. It was odd, I didn't remember feeling this jealous when she told me about Patric. Maybe it was because I knew that he was largely responsible for triggering her emotional and physical state, whether she wanted to believe that or not; Ana was not acting of her own volition when she gave her blood to my brother, there was no way, but with Stephen...I just didn't know how much of what she was feeling was her and how much of Stephen's influence was at play.

"Ana, I would never dream of pressuring you into a relationship with me so soon, especially after everything that you've experienced. I will say this, I want you. I love you and I am confident that you will realize just how much we belong with each other, not just because of our ritualistic Bonding, but because we are truly mates. Being with you and loving you has altered my entire existence, both physical and emotional. There is not another soul in this world that can nourish me the way your body and your heart can, not a single soul. I understand that you have feelings for Stephen and that you love him, more as friend I feel, than anything else. However, you need to navigate through what you want; I can only tell you that I will not let you go easily." My voice turned rough. "I will not let you convince yourself that someone else, that Stephen or anyone else, is better for you than I am; they are not. I know you love me and I know that you feel bound to me by more than just symbolic threads; you need me, you need me to also nourish you, to indulge the many sides of who you are. You need me to show you how to be free, how to let go; you feel safe with me in spite of everything that has transpired between us. *I am what you want.*" And with that, I pulled Ana to me, kissing her forcefully, letting her feel everything that I had just said, and not giving her a chance to respond.

Ana

Both Noni and Nathanial had insisted that they get to do something special for my birthday. The only reason I agreed was that I felt guilty, guilty about Nathanial mainly, but not for the reasons I would have thought. I was feeling bad, not about what physically transpired between us, that was a whole other issue, but about me asking him for some time before I could make a full commitment to him again, that I was needing to sort through my feelings for Stephen and the way things had been left between us. I loved Stephen very much, but I wasn't sure what that meant; being with him was so very different than with Nathanial and Patric. Even though we'd never had sex, my physicality with Stephen seemed richer, more intense somehow as if my body and my soul were waiting to be ignited by him and with him. It was odd; with the exception of our time on the commune, most if not all of my intimate moments with Nathanial had always seemed so explosive and while he was caring with me and my body, tenderness wasn't the dominating quality. With Stephen, somehow I felt that I could have both, the roughness that my body desired, but also the gentleness that came from close intimacy and connection. His touches, both physically and emotionally, seemed to be willing to indulge all sides to my sexuality, all sides of who I saw myself to be. I sighed; my preoccupations with Nathanial had not led to me forgetting about Stephen. I missed him everyday and worried about his safety. Every hour, it seemed that the news would report on the communities in our area that were under attack from the Vampires and that the Bonders were launching their own vicious retaliations for the violence. Nathanial and I had gotten into a few discussions as of late, about the nature of attempting to quell violence with violence; we didn't see eye to eye on how to best handle the problem. Nathanial was much more in a military state of mind than I had ever seen him and his notions about war and violence were quite a bit different from when we'd first met. While I understood having to defend yourself against the annihilation of your species, I was always trying to see what middle ground, if any, could be reached before things became brutal, but then again, I also experienced first hand having to fight and kill for something, for someone that you loved, so maybe I understood him more than I thought.

Currently, I was scrubbing down the inside of one of the cabins. Nathanial had asked me to work on getting the living quarters in decent condition for the refugees and I was pretty sure that his idea of "decent" and my idea were slightly skewed. I had about an hour left before I would need to head home and get dressed for this ridiculous costume party that Nathanial, my friends and my students, were throwing for me. I did have to admit, I loved my costume. I was going as a Dominatrix and I hadn't told Nathanial; I thought he would appreciate my gesture. Since being with him this last time, I had noticed a distinct change in my physical reaction to him, more so than my usual arousal. Nathanial was the first being, or person that had made me feel safe enough to tap into my more "demonic" side, as he liked to put it and lately that's what seemed to surface any time I was around him. He'd been a bit hands off since our time together a week ago, but I could tell that it was also a struggle for him to control himself when I was near. Everything in my body felt hypersensitive; every touch he gave me, every look, every smell, god, his scent was becoming the biggest issue for me. Gone was the calm honey and lemon fragrance that he usually emitted, now he always smelled of musk, the richest and most seductive of his scents and the one that was expertly tuned to what attracted me the most. I had always been pretty comfortable with my level of sexual aggressiveness and as an adult, I had only had five partners including Nathanial and Patric, so I was definitely versed on what I liked, but this time, things were a bit different. I noticed that Nathanial was not trying to bury his Demonic persona. He was rougher, darker, commanding and more beautiful than I had ever seen him. I liked this side of him and with my mood as of late, it was a good fit. I frowned feeling slightly guilty and thinking about Stephen.

I finished mopping the floors and took to putting the sheets and blankets that I had bought on each of the bunks, making sure that the bedding was neat and looked inviting. I had tons of throw pillows, many that Noni had made, and I placed several on each of the beds, hoping that the families would feel like they were not refugees, but that they had come to a vacation home of sorts—it was wishful thinking. I was in the process of hanging a valance when I heard someone step into the space, more accurately, I *smelled* someone step into the space.

"This looks amazing, Ana," Nathanial said, standing with his arms across his chest looking solid and strong. I almost lost my footing on the stepladder, gawking at him. "Do you need some help?" he asked, noticing my slip. He moved to stand next to me, his hands on my lower back. I heard laughter out the open window and sighed; it probably wasn't the most professional behavior to jump Nathanial while I was on the job. I laughed to myself. I was just going to have to exercise some control. I jumped off the ladder and turned to grab the rest of the curtains from the table. Suddenly, I heard the door slam shut and the lock click in place. I whirled around, just as Nathanial came up behind me, wrapping his arms tightly around my waist, keeping me facing away from him. "You know what I find frustrating?" he said, as he swept my hair around to my right shoulder, still not letting me turn around.

"What?" I asked, breathing hard.

"I find it frustrating that you never seem to speak of your desires out loud. I always have to read through your mind to see what it is that you want." He moved one of his hands down the front of my jeans, undoing the button with one tug. My legs quickly became weak.

"I don't want you to think poorly of me," I whispered, feeling his fingers reach between my thighs. I moaned softly, leaning back against him.

"Now why would I ever think poorly of you Ana?" his voice purred in my ear. "I don't think there could be anything you could possibly come up with, any scenario that I wouldn't enjoy indulging." He moved just one of his fingers, barely massaging me. I felt his leg move in between mine, widening my stance. I groaned loudly.

"Nathanial, I'm going to have to sit down," I said breathlessly, my legs beginning to shake from desire. That was the other odd thing this past week. I was climaxing so quickly and the experience was so powerful and so intense that it was hard not to want to be in that mode all the time. Nathanial seemed to also enjoy pleasuring me; he liked being in control of my release and getting me to that point brought him in touch with his needs as a Demon. I groaned again as I felt him begin to caress me harder, stirring up my own body heat and making me gasp for air. He wrapped his free hand around my mouth, gently stifling the loud scream that was about to come. He held me off, moving his hand from the most perfect spot and laughed. I felt his breath in my ear.

"I think that's good for now," he said and I could feel him smirking. I was aghast. "We have a party to get to." He disentangled himself and turned me around to face him. My jaw was slack. "You should see your face!" He chuckled.

"You! You are so going to pay for that! You're such a tease, in the worst way!" I scowled, my voice low and dark. I punched him in the

234

stomach, harder than I actually wanted, my knuckles meeting with what felt like steel plating. He grabbed my fist and pulled me roughly against him.

"I'm sorry, you're right, that wasn't very fun for you was it?" He smiled at me. I'll make you a deal." My eyes narrowed. He laughed again. "You pretend that you actually are enjoying yourself at your party tonight, and I will make sure that I finish what I started here; in fact, I'll even up the ante a bit. We make it all about you, anything and everything you want, I will happily and gladly oblige but," he held up his finger and I wanted to bite him, "but, you actually have to *say* out loud what you want, no mind reading allowed." He shook his finger in my face. I grabbed his finger and bit down gently on the tip, drawing a single drop of blood. I took my tongue and moved his finger slowly around in my mouth, savoring the rich sweetness of his taste. I watched his face. He closed his eyes and a low growl thundered out from his chest. "I said," he groaned, his breath shallow, "that we were going to make it all about you." I watched as his chest rose and fell rapidly and I sucked more blood from his finger. I could thank Patric for this little skill I now had; it was quite intriguing. "Ana, what are you doing to me?" he moaned loudly and I ran my tongue over the puncture, tantalizing and teasing him. I was getting worked up, his taste, his moans; apparently I didn't need his hands anywhere near my body to become aroused by him. Thanks to Patric, I had a slight affinity for blood, and it served as a very powerful aphrodisiac for me. I bit down harder, drawing more blood from his finger and I heard him gasp, but I also noticed that his body was moving and his hips were pulsing. I backed him against the wall so that our bodies were touching and I ground against him as I slowly sucked his finger. He was breathing hard and so was I. "Ana, Christ!" He gasped and pushed harder against me. We were fully clothed, but I could feel him beneath his jeans and I pushed his finger further down my throat, pulling it in and out slowly. I was groaning as his blood entered my system; I was moving harder against him and I wanted him to go faster. He was growling louder and I saw his eyes darken. I was going to get what I wanted before our little deal came into play. He started to grind forcefully, the heat from his groin sending my body reeling. He reached to unbutton my jeans and I let him slide his finger, the one with the blood, down in between my legs. Upon touching me, he growled so loudly, I was sure someone would hear. My physical response to his blood made him come, fast. He gasped and moved his body against mine, thrusting his finger into me.

"God, Nathanial!" I groaned, wanting him to be harder with me. He obeyed and he brought his finger to his lips and bit down, drawing much more blood than I did. He massaged every area, saving the most sensitive for last. I was moaning and panting and he was moving so fast, I never wanted him to stop. I groaned loudly as he brought me to my release and instantly, I wanted to come again. I couldn't believe it. Nathanial pushed himself off of me and stared at my face, his eyes wide.

"What the hell was that?" he asked, his breath coming rapidly. I smiled and peeled myself off his body, taking a deep breath.

"I didn't feel like waiting for tonight." I smirked at him and walked over to plant a kiss on his cheek. "Thanks, that's just what I needed." I laughed and grabbed my purse and opened the door. "I'll see you at the party." I left him standing there to ponder just whom he thought he could mess with.

Nathanial

I was still trying to compose myself from Ana's little maneuver this evening; she was constantly surprising the hell out of me and she'd left me feeling slightly shaken at her level of desire. It was different, powerful and controlling, quite an extraordinary experience. I was also pondering the chances of us having actually conceived during our last evening together. I'd guessed that Ana would be able to know here in the next few weeks, but I had also noticed that my need to continue to mate with her, and her body's response to me, was as if we hadn't gotten enough of each other, that what our bodies were craving wasn't being satisfied. I wondered how long this could continue. I inhaled deeply as I pulled into the house of one of Ana's co-workers, a Bonder named Kyle who was also a youth counselor. Just by the looks of the front yard, Kyle and the rest of Ana's cohort had gone all out. Noni had given me her blessing and sent me with her gift for Ana; she was out at the camp overseeing the third shift construction. My present for Ana was back at the house; I'd left it for her wrapped in a large gift box. I hoped she would like it.

I wasn't much for costume parties, but Ana had insisted that I come wearing something that mimicked the theme— Masquerade of Demons and Dominatrix; it seemed fitting for both of our moods as of late. I grabbed my mask and walked around to the back deck. There were at least seventy-five people dancing, hitting a piñata, and bobbing for what looked like various sex toys. I couldn't help but smile; someone knew Ana's sense of humor, very, very well. I felt a hand on my shoulder and I turned to see Kyle, his costume not what I'd expected. He was decked out in some sort of bondage attire, with high motorcycle boots, a studded collar, leather vest and pants and carrying a whip. I laughed at the absurdity of the whole ensemble.

"I know, I know; it's a bit over the top." Kyle laughed and handed me a beer. "But I rarely get to exercise my alter ego, Charlotte isn't one for the rough stuff!" He laughed again and pointed to a young, Human woman, who compared to Kyle, was dressed rather conservatively. I supposed that I should count myself lucky; I didn't have to worry about experimenting with any of my alter egos with Ana, especially as of late. Kyle and I chatted for a bit, but I was getting restless and I wanted to find Ana. I seized my opportunity when a group of students came by to take pictures of Kyle and I scanned the deck for any sign of her. I noticed Charlie, my contractor, speaking to a young woman with long sleek hair, almost down to her waist. She was wearing tight leather shorts and boots that stretched up her muscular thighs. Her entire back was exposed except for an extremely low leather tie close to her tailbone. I smiled to myself. Charlie was a mess of hormones and this was the perfect place for him to indulge. He caught my eye and waved for me to come over. I did another quick scan of the deck and resigned myself to catching up with Ana later. I crossed the floor and made my way into the yard, headed for the tree where Charlie was standing. I was barely three feet in front of them, when the woman turned to look at me. I was stunned. It was Ana and I barely recognized her. Her hair was long and straight and it hung thick and full from underneath a leather cap, tilted sideways on her head. Like Kyle, she was also wearing some kind of studded collar, but unlike Kyle, her breasts were almost completely exposed. Thin leather straps weaved their way across her chest, covering her nipple area, but that was about it. Her stomach was exposed and I could see how chiseled and defined her abdominal area was. Her shorts skimmed up to her thighs, they were cut in a deep "V" shape down the very front, and had a diamond placed right above her pubic bone, drawing as much attention to the area as possible.

"Pretty spectacular, right?" Charlie laughed, clearly taking in my reaction to Ana's choice of costume. I was pretty sure that I hadn't blinked once since laying my eyes on her. She smiled at me and moved to put her arm through mine. I noticed that she had a whip holstered to her side. "I told her that it almost looks too natural for her! That maybe she should make this a full time profession." Charlie laughed again and sipped his beer. I didn't quite like just how much he was staring at her; he needed to rein it in just a bit. I put my arm around Ana's waist, feeling her skin and pressing my fingers into her side.

"You don't mind if I steal her away from you for a moment?" I looked at Charlie and smiled as much as I could; I wanted to rip his eyes out.

"Nah, I've got my eye on a very pretty and scantily dressed blond, most of the girls are all afraid of Ana and she's cramping my style!" he chortled, walking back toward the deck, waving. I waited for him to turn his back to us, and then I pulled Ana in front of me, trying to take in exactly what she was wearing.

"You like?" she said, strutting around in front of me. "The hair's a wig; I could never get mine this straight, but the rest is one hundred percent real!" She laughed, motioning to her breasts. I was at a loss for words; first her little seduction trick in the cabin this afternoon, now this? I was curious to find out just how far she was willing to go with this particular side of herself. "You're not saying anything. Do I look silly? You don't like it," she said, her face cringing; she bit her lip and stood back a few paces from me. "I've totally freaked you out!" she said, taking another step back. I noticed that the continuous blare of music had been replaced by one of Ana's favorite songs, one that was moderately slow, with dark, sensuous lyrics and rhythms; it seemed appropriate for the mood she was putting me in. Taking a deep breath in, I closed the distance between us in one step. I took her hand and led her over near the deck. I didn't want to isolate her from her friends, but I was struggling with my urge to be alone, just she and I.

"So," I said, pulling her close to me and winding her arms around my neck, "I would like to make a proposal, that at least once a week, you wear this outfit.," I spoke quietly in her ear, "sans the wig." She pulled back to look at me.

"Why no wig?" she asked, moving her hips closer against me. "Doesn't it give you the novelty of someone new?" She laughed as she kissed me gently on the mouth. At this rate, I was not going to be able to maintain any level of friendly, public affection for much longer. I kissed her back, harder.

"First," I murmured, biting down softly on her bottom lip, "I love *your* hair, and second…" I parted her lips and let my fingers run down the length of her back, pressing deeply on the spot just above her tailbone. Chills erupted over her skin. "Second, *you* are a novelty, everyday. I don't need anyone new Ana." I pulled back to hold her face in my hands. "Your birth has given me the very reason for my existence; no one else on the planet can offer me that gift." She shook her head and pressed her forehead to me. I heard people yelling her name and I turned to see a giant cake being wheeled out onto the deck. I reluctantly withdrew from our embrace and led her up the stairs. Ana spent the next several hours opening presents and surprisingly, taking a few shots of tequila, before she gracefully bowed out from the party. She hadn't gotten around to opening Noni's present so I slipped the tiny box into my coat and led us back to the car.

"That was fun," Ana murmured as she tried unsuccessfully to buckle her seatbelt. Alcohol was not something that she regularly consumed and she was definitely feeling the effects. I laughed as I reached over to snap the buckle in place. Our gazes locked.

"Hmmm," I said, barely touching my mouth to hers. "At this rate, I'm not sure how quickly we are going to get home." I kissed her gently and forced myself to start the engine. She moved to unzip her boots.

"Good god! I don't know how anyone could wear this getup full time; it's a bit high maintenance for me," she said, sliding a boot down her leg. "Frick!" She exclaimed, making me jump slightly.

"What?" I said, my eyes roaming over her face and body. "What's wrong?"

"My car, I took my own car to the party," she said, frowning at me. We were already on the road back to her house.

"I'll get it for you tomorrow morning. It's fine," I said, smiling at her. "Plus, there was no way I was going to let you drive in your condition." I smirked and glanced at her from the corner of my eye.

"You're very responsible," she said, leaning her head back against the seat. The next question out of her mouth was one that I wasn't expecting. "Hey, have you heard from Micah?" she asked, turning her head to look at me. My body tensed. I had made the decision to wait to discuss my conversation with my uncle; I didn't see any point in worrying her about things until we knew something more about the particular group of Demons. I was also a bit preoccupied feeling guilty not informing Ana that her birth control was no longer effective; at least not while I was still in mating mode. I wasn't exactly starting off on the most honest foot with her. I exhaled.

"Yes, I spoke with him earlier this week." I replied, keeping my eyes on the road.

"How is he?" she said, watching me.

"He's fine. He's safe." I knew that's what she was mainly concerned about. "He asked about you." I smiled, looking at her face. She nodded.

"That's nice of him. Ahh, yay, we're home." She laughed as she gathered her boots. The house was dark and Noni's car wasn't in the drive. That woman was a workaholic, I mused. "I've got to get this outfit off, are you ok with all the presents?" she asked, jumping down from the car.

"I think I can handle it." I rolled my eyes at her and watched as she headed for the porch, Zanuck howling in greeting. I piled the massive amount of gifts in my arms and went into the house.

"Hey, what's this?" she asked, carrying my present out into the kitchen. I surveyed her; she was wearing one of my t-shirts and a pair of sweatpants, also mine, and her hair was its normal long, curly self. I loved her best when she was like this.

"That's from me," I said, placing the last of her presents on the kitchen table.

"You didn't have to get me anything Nathanial." She was eyeing the box warily.

"It's not anything that's going to explode," I said, laughing at her expression. I took the box from her and motioned for her to follow me back down the hallway to her room. "You have one from Noni too, would you like to open it?" I asked, sitting on the bed.

"That's so nice of her," Ana whispered; I pulled the box from my coat. I had no idea what it held and I had to admit that I was curious. She came to sit next to me, pulling her legs under her. The box was hand carved wood, and I immediately recognized the symbol on the front; it was Ana's metal tattoo. I watched as she slowly traced her finger along the pattern. She opened the box to find a necklace nestled into a velvet pillow. She gasped as she withdrew the long leather cord, holding it in her palm. The amulet hanging down was one that I knew, although I had never seen it adorned on a Human before. The symbols were that of my species, ones that I had seen many times in books and on various sketches that my mother had done, but the intangible meaning behind the symbols had been greatly diminished; no one referred to such qualities amongst demons anymore, those were Human contrivances and I had never seen them entwined; they were always separated. The amulet was also hand carved in turquoise and unpolished silver and it somehow captured whatever light was in the room, reflecting it outward in a subtle, luminous glow. "What's it mean?" Ana asked quietly. "Do you know?" She looked at me, her eyes wide. Gently, I took the necklace from her hands and held it up, turning it from every angle. It was stunning in both its artistic craftsmanship and it's innate mystical qualities; I could feel its warmth running over my fingertips. I moved closer to her on the bed and placed the amulet into her palm.

"This," I said, pointing to the outward silver circle, "this is the sign for fire." I traced her finger along the rim. She pulled her finger away, startled.

"It's hot!" she said. I nodded, but took her finger back, placing it on the inside of the circle, to the oval that sat in the center of the main symbol.

"This is the sign for courage." I moved her hand around the shape. Inside the oval was a small pentagram, also carved in silver. "This represents forgiveness and this," I put her finger directly in the center of the amulet, to the turquoise stone, "and this, this is for redemption." I looked at her face. She took a shaky breath in, swallowing hard.

244

"Would you put it on me?" she asked, turning her back to me and holding her hair up. I slid the leather strand around her neck and fastened the clasp. A sudden white spark emitted from where the two parts of the necklace now met and I pulled back from Ana. "What was that?" She turned her head to look at me.

"I don't know," I whispered. She got up to look into the mirror. The amulet hung in the beautiful space between her collarbones and it looked as if it had melded itself to her flesh.

"It's really quite lovely," she spoke softly. She seemed sad. "So, it's going to be hard to compete with this!" She laughed and hopped back onto the bed, pulling my box into her lap. "It's heavy!" I shrugged and watched as she gently untied the fabric bow. "I like the wrapping." She smiled at me and I tousled her hair.

"Just open it please," I said, helping her to lift up the top. She peeled back the tissue paper and she gasped.

"Oh—my—god!" She looked up at me, her face showing total shock.

"I know you love it," I said quietly, pulling my mother's quilt from the depths of the box. "She would have wanted me to give it to you." I placed the blanket on her lap and watched her face. I'd hoped she wouldn't think that I was trying to solidify our relationship too quickly.

"Nathanial, I don't know what to say; there're just not enough words…" She trailed off as she spread the quilt out onto her bed, her fingers immediately tracing over the threads. "Are you sure you want to give this to me? I know how much you love having this part of your mother so near to you; it's important that you be able to experience her when you look at this," she said, her tone worried.

"Yes, I do love having something that my mother made, but Ana, I love you more and I know that she would have loved you as well. I want you to have this," I said, reaching to stroke her face. I stood up and walked over to the window. I was going to have to tell her; it was going to have to be now.

"Nathanial, what is it?" Ana asked, delicately folding the quilt so that it lie at the base of her bed. I bowed my head, my heart pounding in my throat. I didn't know where to start; how was I going to explain what was happening to me biologically, what I needed. This discussion had the potential to go very, very poorly. I turned to look at her.

"Ana, there's something that I need to tell you, something that you should know." I said, my voice quiet. She walked over to my place at the window and took my hands in hers.

"Tell me," she whispered.

Chapter Ten

Ana

I waited for him to speak. He looked upset, frustrated and I was worried.

"Ana, something has happened to me, something that affects you, affects us and I should have told you earlier; I'm so very sorry." His voice shook and I moved to stand closer to him; I couldn't imagine what he could possibly tell me that would affect us, not after everything we'd already been through.

"Well, out with it, Nathanial," I said, dropping his hands and moving to sit on my bed. He sighed and sat down next to me and started to speak quickly. For the next hour I listened to him attempt to explain this odd occurrence of mating in the Demon world and how it managed to rule every thought and action until there had actually been a conception; how he'd tried to fight it until he knew that I was feeling more comfortable with him, but apparently, my own body's cycles helped to drive his urges more. I was trying to follow his dialogue, which seemed to be half biology lecture and half on the mating secrets of Demons. I still wasn't getting why his tone seemed so regretful; I hadn't minded all of sexual assertiveness lately and in fact, I was wondering why I was so partial to us being together so often; I really couldn't see what the problem was. I told him this. He sighed and looked at me.

"Ana, you and I are..." He was struggling with his words, which I found rather humorous. "My mating cycle is attuned to yours and yours to mine; the reason you are feeling so 'in the mood' as of late, is directly correlated to what I am experiencing physiologically; my hormones trigger yours and vice versa, until we actually conceive," he whispered. "Your birth control is basically null and void and has been since that night at my house." He bowed his head. The conversation was about to take a very different turn and I felt my heart begin to race.

"What do you mean?" My voice was calm. He sighed and stood up, pacing.

"Any time before now, that you and I have been intimate, I have had the ability to make sure that the hormones that allow for me to...to impregnate you, that they didn't release during our...our time together, that whatever birth control you use, stayed effective." He shook his head, tossing his hair back over his shoulder. "But now, now that my natural need to mate has apparently surfaced, those hormones aren't really in my control any more and they make whatever precautions you take, obsolete." He turned to look at me, his eyes shifting rapidly over my face. I pressed my lips together and took a deep breath.

"So, what you're telling me is that you think that I might be pregnant?" I asked, my voice still even and calm. He nodded slowly. "And you're feeling guilty because you failed to mention any of this to me before we'd actually had sex that one night?" I said, the pieces falling into place. He nodded again, his face full of remorse. I shook my head and laughed softly; the irony was almost too much for me to handle. He looked confused at my reaction. "Nathanial, why of course I wish that you had been honest with me about what you were experiencing, but I'm not mad at you," I said quietly, knowing that what I had to tell him was much, much worse.

"You're not?" he asked, his face still puzzled.

"No, I'm not." I sighed and moved myself against the headboard, lying on the pillows.

"Why? I'd be mad if I were you. You could be pregnant and you don't want children, Ana; you have every right to be angry with me." He sounded incredulous. Again I shook my head.

"Maybe, if things weren't all that they seem," I said, looking away from him and out the window. He moved to lie next to me, turning my face to his.

"What are you talking about?" he asked his brow furrowed. I sighed and fingered my new necklace, wondering if this conversation would be the one to finally break the bond between Nathanial and me.

"I can't get pregnant Nathanial; it's impossible," I said flatly, looking him in the eye. He pulled back, his eyes full of questions. "You and I have never really discussed some of things that happened to me as a child; well we never were with each other long enough to go into much detail I suppose…" I laughed lightly. I smiled at him. I didn't think he needed to hear any specific details, but he needed to know the impetus behind some of my actions; he deserved to know. "The abuse that happened to me Nathanial, it was severe, very severe." He closed his eyes and I plowed forward. "The damage that was done, there was a lot of scarring…to much scarring. When the doctors checked me over, when Noni brought me to see someone after she found me bleeding one day, they told her that my uterus was too damaged to be able to carry a child; it just wasn't possible anymore." I took a deep breath in. "It wasn't too much of a big deal, even when I was fifteen, because I had never really wanted to be a mother so I didn't feel that much of a loss. It wasn't until I got older and began to have serious relationships with men, that I realized that my 'situation' could be a problem." Nathanial's eyes were watching me and I could see the storms begin to appear within their depths. "I was always really upfront with all of my boyfriends. I would tell them that I didn't want to have children, which was true, but I never mentioned to any of them that I *couldn't* have children, that my body was in effect useless in that capacity. Anyway, for the most part, that never became an issue until I met my ex fiancé. I kept myself on birth control, mainly to help with my cycles and we had discussed that neither of us really wanted children, but since I was marrying this man, I figured that he should know all about my medical history and what happened to me as a kid; he was to be my husband, my partner. If I couldn't be honest with him, what business did we have getting married. I suppose that the conversation really should have happened long before the engagement, but hey, hindsight is always twenty-twenty." I laughed, softly. "He was angry when I told him, but even more than that, he was disappointed. He said that even though he didn't want children then, that having that possibility was important to him, that we may change our minds and that he wanted to have his own child; he wanted that option. I took that away from him," I whispered. "He said that he wanted to be with someone who could give him a baby if that's what they decided. He didn't mention anything about the abuse or acknowledge that I offered to consider adopting, maybe one day. He said that he should be with someone who wasn't physically 'damaged'; it was important to him." I sat up on the edge of the bed, gazing out my window, remembering. "Anyway, obviously that relationship didn't work out; it was a bad choice really, but since then, I guess I've never felt safe telling men that I can't have children. I figured that Drew's feelings were somewhat universal and I suppose I actually began to believe that there was something wrong with me. I was going to tell you, when we were getting married, I wanted to tell you, but...I didn't want to lose you again." My voice choked and I swallowed thickly.

Nathanial sat up and leaned forward. I turned to look at him. "So, you see, I can't be mad at you; you'll never be able to get what you want... or what your body wants," I said, gazing back out the window. "At least not from me." I held the amulet in-between my fingers, wondering what he was thinking; wondering if this was going to be the end...

Nathanial

Jesus Christ. I didn't know what to think, what to feel; what Ana had just told me was overwhelming. She couldn't have children. She'd kept that information from me, but after everything I'd put her through, I really didn't care so much about that. However, I was wondering what that meant for me physically. Was I just going to be in this perpetual state of mating? That could get exhausting and the extreme fluctuations in my desire and arousal were difficult to control. My body didn't know that our coupling would never lead to producing offspring, but it seemed to know that each time we were together, that

251

we hadn't conceived; my body was remaining in the mating mode until we were successful. I couldn't get my head around things. I needed some time to figure out what we could do, how to be with her without this continuous urge and how to not try to mate with someone else—that would be devastating for Ana and for us. I needed to talk with Micah.

"Ana, I'm sorry, this is going to sound horrible, but can you give me some time with all of this. I'm not angry with you, it's important that you understand that. I love you more than anything." My tone was fierce; I needed for her to not think that I wanted to leave her. "There's just some, some more technical aspects that need to be navigated…" I wasn't even sure what those aspects were and I was hoping that Micah would be able to help. She kept her back to me.

"Of course Nathanial; take whatever time you need," she said quietly, still not looking at me. I moved to wrap my arms around her and I felt her entire body shudder at my touch. "Ana," I whispered, turning her face to me. I kissed her softly on the mouth. "I love you so much," I said, holding her face in my hands. "You have to know that, you must know that!" I said forcefully. I was desperate for her to understand. She nodded but I could see something shift deep in her eyes; something dark.

"Thanks." She kissed me on the cheek and stepped back from my embrace. "And thank you for the beautiful quilt; I promise to take good care of it, and I'm honored to be its guardian Nathanial." She moved back to her bed and I noticed she was fingering the thin golden threads leading from my symbol, the threads that represented children. "I'll be at the camp tomorrow morning," she said, still staring at the quilt. I felt the air shift around us; it felt cold.

"Ok," I said, moving to touch her hand. "I'll see you tomorrow then." I kissed her hand and walked out of the room. "You're car will be in the drive as well." I turned back, remembering.

"Great. Thanks." She raised her eyes; they looked flat. I nodded and left the house, feeling utterly terrified.

Unfortunately, the families were arriving earlier than expected with the encroaching winter and I had no time make a call to Micah. Two weeks passed before I'd even thought about contacting him. Ana was keeping her distance, interacting with me only at the camp and even then, she kept it to the bare minimum. I hadn't meant for her to avoid me. I'd just meant that I needed a bit of mental space to try to get my biological urges under control—I didn't want her to feel like she had to be away from me. I was rolling up a set of blue prints when I saw her walking toward me, Zanuck at her side.

"Hey," she said, standing further back from me than was needed. I sighed and moved to close the gap. "Is there any chance you could give me a ride home? I came with Noni and of course she's staying late." Ana reached down to stroke Zanuck, she lowered her eyes.

"Of course," I said, taking her hand. "I was just packing up to leave." She nodded and smiled. "How'd it go today?" I asked as we walked back up the hill to my car.

"Good. We got several families settled in and they seem to be coping alright so far," she said looking straight ahead. I opened the back door for Zanuck and threw my backpack and Ana's bag in after him. Ana was already in the front seat.

"I haven't seen much of you lately," I said as I eyed her. She should know that I wasn't completely oblivious to her avoidance tactics; I knew them well. She laughed quietly.

"I don't want to be intrusive Nathanial. You deserve to have your space, as much of it as you need." She turned to look at the setting sun. I studied her face, she seemed stoic, contemplative, but she wasn't letting me in. I turned up the road to her house and immediately I noticed a car in the drive.

"STEPHEN!" Ana shouted and before I could actually register what she'd said, she was leaping out of the car and running up the drive. Of course, I thought; of course he would chose this time to come back, when Ana was feeling vulnerable and unsure of herself and of us. I had to hand it to the guy, his timing was perfect and he didn't fight fair. I exhaled and parked the car, wondering just how much energy it was going to take for me to fight with a Vampire today. I came inside the house just in time to see Ana run to throw her arms around Stephen. My blood began to boil and I had to take a few deep breaths before moving into the kitchen. Immediately, I noticed that something wasn't right. Stephen's reaction to Ana was not what I had expected and even though she'd predicted that he was feeling angry with her, he hadn't seen her is months and I would have thought that he would have been able to quell his own selfish frustrations and be a friend. Stephen's head snapped up upon hearing my inner dialogue; his eyes were onyx. I watched as he pulled Ana away from his body and stepped back from her, looking stern. She seemed diminished. He shook his head and stared at me.

"Stephen? How are you? Why haven't you answered my calls?" Ana asked, her tone somber. I hadn't known she'd been trying to call him. Stephen laughed, still staring at me. "Stephen?" Ana asked again. He turned to look at her, his eyes roaming over her face.

"I didn't want to talk to you Ana." His tone was sharp. I didn't care for the way he was speaking to her. "I'm here as a favor to Liam; he was unable to come himself otherwise, believe me, I wouldn't be here." It took every ounce of self-control I had not to rip his head from his body. He was hurting her, I could feel it; she was devastated by his reaction to her.

"I'm sure you'll have your chance Nathanial," Stephen said, smirking at me. His voice was different from what I remembered; it was rougher and more sinister. "You're not the only one who's managed to embrace their true nature." He looked me over, glaring.

"What do you want Stephen?" I asked, moving to stand next to Ana. He eyed us both.

"Liam wanted me to inform you that the little group your uncle has been watching is on the move; they've organized themselves and they've grown in numbers." He moved to stand away from us, his eyes on me. Liam knew? How? I thought. "Liam will always be watching for anyone who wants to harm Ana, Nathanial—anyone," he said the last word looking straight at me.

"What are you talking about Stephen?" Ana asked, looking back and forth between us. Stephen laughed out loud.

"Oh, this is brilliant!" he chortled. " You haven't told her! Brilliant, bloody brilliant," he said, still laughing, Ana glared at me.

"Stephen, stop being such an ass! What the hell are you talking about?" Ana stepped toward him, her fists clenched at her sides. He set his jaw and looked at me.

"Well, it appears that the little stunt you pulled back in Peru, the fire and the killing of half a dozen Demons; it didn't appear to go over too well." Stephen turned back to stare at Ana. She exhaled.

"So?" she asked, looking at me now.

"So," Stephen replied, moving to lean against the counter, "they want revenge, and of course they don't think that you should have survived, so they also want to carry out the orders that you prevented Nathanial from completing." He motioned towards me, waving his hand.

"You knew about this?" Ana asked me quietly. I sighed, stepping away from her slightly.

"I only found out a few weeks ago and at that time, Micah and I didn't think we needed to worry you about the situation," I said, studying her face; she seemed amazingly calm. I couldn't get a read on her thoughts.

"Liam has asked me to offer you his protection and whatever services he can lend. Unfortunately, I am no longer bound to those offerings."

He stared at Ana and I saw a glint of blue return to his eyes. "I'm only here as a favor to my brother," he said quietly.

"What happened Stephen? Is something wrong?" Ana asked, relaxing her fists and taking another step toward him.

"That's no longer your concern Ana, nor what happens to me or with me." Stephen moved away from her, stopping Ana in her tracks. I tried to get through to his mind, but he, like Ana, was shut down.

"I was just asking," she murmured, her tone was so sad, but also frustrated.

"What do you want me to tell Liam the plan is?" Stephen looked to me.

"There is no plan," Ana said, her voice fierce. "And don't look at him, look at me!" She was angry now. "Tell Liam thank you and that I will always appreciate anything that he offers me, but there's nothing he can do; there's nothing I want him to do. I'm not going to run from everything that wants to kill me for the rest of my life." Her eyes turned to me. "You should go. You shouldn't be here if they come, they might not be as dedicated to you as you think." Stephen laughed. "And you!" Ana turned her attention back to Stephen. "I know that I hurt you Stephen, but you hurt me too by not telling me about what really happened to you in your life, by not being honest with me about why you wanted to Change me; I've forgiven you because I love you very much." I winced hearing her say those words, even though I knew they were true and even though I knew she loved me in a very different way than she loved Stephen—it still hurt. "You will always be one of my best friends and I will be forever grateful to you for fighting for me and Lucie that night—for protecting us. I suppose for you now, none of that matters; I suppose that I no longer matter to you." Her voice shook and I could see she was reaching her breaking point. "All I ever wanted Stephen was to make you see just how remarkable you are, that hopefully you would find a way to forgive yourself for everything you've done and to find the courage to love me without those ghosts. I wanted you to see yourself the way that I saw you, as a man, as my friend." She threw her hands up. "Oh Christ, whatever! I sound like a broken record. Do whatever you want, Stephen. I would never make the mistake of thinking that you would ever protect me again, or that you would ever *want* to protect me; you don't have to worry about that. I can take care of myself." She moved to open the screen door, holding it open. "Thanks for coming by. Tell Liam thank you and tell Lucie that I miss her every day and Carmen too…" She hesitated and took a deep breath; her body slacking under the weight of her emotions. "I miss you every day too Stephen…" she whispered.

Stephen's face was stricken and I could plainly see the pain and conflict washing over him. I sensed his desire to be with her, to hold her and I was surprised how sorry I felt for him in that moment, how much he actually wanted to be able to hug Ana, to repair their friendship, even their love.

Stephen turned to me, our eyes connecting. He bowed and walked toward the door that Ana was still holding. He stood in front of her and I saw that his eyes went to the amulet around Ana's neck. He looked back to me, then he reached into his coat pocket and pulled out a clear square case that held a small CD; he handed it to Ana. Pressing it into her palm, Stephen took a deep breath and turned and walked away. Ana came to sit down beside me at the table.

"What do you suppose he meant by he's no longer 'obligated' to Liam anymore?" she asked, her eyes on the tiny, jeweled CD. No more secrets, I decided.

"He's left his coven," I said, my eyes on her.

"What?" she exclaimed, looking stunned. "Why? How?"

"I couldn't gather all the details, he's about as versed as you at keeping me out, but it appears that Stephen felt he needed some time away from Liam; he's experimenting," I said, hoping to leave it at that.

"Experimenting with what?" she asked, meeting my gaze.

"With being a Vampire." I rose from my seat and went to start a kettle of water.

"But he's already a Vampire, he's been one for like five hundred years, what's there to experiment with?" she asked watching me.

"Vampires, like demons, are not singular in their experiences Ana; they and we evolve just like Humans do; you've had first hand knowledge of my...experimental phases." I raised my eyebrows at her. "It appears that Liam's softening about Humans has offered Stephen the opportunity to find a cause to belong to, one that is not in favor with his brother's new position—or rather Stephen has managed to experiment with all the ways that Humans can be used to satisfy his darker hungers." I was cautious. I didn't want Ana to know just how violent Stephen had appeared to become.

"So he's killing humans randomly now, because that's what he believes is the best thing?" she said sarcastically.

"Not quite," I murmured and poured us each a cup of tea. She sighed and held her mug in both of her hands.

"I think we should talk to Noni and make sure that we get her out of here. I don't want to put her life in danger because of me, or your life in danger either Nathanial." Her tone was commanding. I smirked at her.

"Well, that's very kind of you Ana and I'll definitely agree that Noni should be relocated, although it's highly unlikely that she'll go." Ana nodded and rolled her eyes. "However, the issue of my staying here with you is non-negotiable." I matched her tone.

"Great. So you, me and Noni will all die together, how lovely!" she mocked, putting her mug down on the table so hard that tea spilled over the top.

"I hardly think that will be the case," I said, taking a paper towel and wiping up her spill. I was already planning on calling Micah and asking him to send some of my brethren to Idaho; I had a lot of favors that I was willing to call due. "But I really wish that you would reconsider allowing me and Micah to relocate you; I hear Europe can be quite scenic this time of year." I smiled at her and reached to smooth her hair, when suddenly I was hit with a wave of desire so strong, that it knocked the breath out of me and I gasped.

"Nathanial! What's wrong?" Ana moved forward, her hands on my face. I swallowed and tried to breath normally. My body was tense and I could feel the now familiar surge of my hormones beginning to surface. Christ! I had to get away from her.

"I-have-to-leave, Ana," I choked out, scooting my chair back away from her. I stood and headed for the door.

"Oh," she said flatly. "It's ok. I'll see you tomorrow, I guess…" She was thinking about if she would be alive tomorrow; she was sad and worried about so many things. I wanted to go to her, to wrap my arms around her, to stay with her through the night; but I couldn't. I put my hand over my heart and looked at her face. "I'm fine, no worries." She laughed and looked away from me. "Hormones are a bitch, huh?" she said. I smiled at her and exited the same way Stephen had just left moments ago.

Ana

Well, it was a bummer that I was back to being a marked woman, but honestly, I really didn't have time to worry about it or about just how devastated I was with Stephen. His reaction to me was so cold and the familiar scene of broken tethers just seemed to keep playing out in my mind. More and more refugees would be coming into the camp as winter moved across the mountains, and I was in charge of all the families who came, getting them assigned a cabin, making sure they received their medical check-ups, getting their children whatever clothing and supplies that were needed—it was a ton of work. Just like Nathanial had predicted, Noni was not going to allow herself to be removed from the Reservation; she didn't seem frightened or concerned about the possibility that we all might be attacked. She was odd like that, worrying about the future was never something that

261

Noni spent time doing; she was a very "present moment" kind of woman and right now the present moment meant dealing with refugees.

My mind seemed to be having difficulty concentrating on so many things at once and several times during my day, I would find myself thinking about Stephen, then about dying, then about Nathanial and this whole baby situation, then back to the refugees. I couldn't get out of my own headspace. Seeing Nathanial on a daily basis didn't help much. I wanted to give him as much space from me as possible, as least as much physical space, but that was hard for me as well. I missed him, not only his companionship, but also our intimacy. I desired him very, very much and even if my own body was broken, the urges and need to be with him, those were still very much there. I had been watching him lately and I noticed something that I had never seen in Nathanial before, at least not while we were together. I noticed him looking at other women, human women. He wasn't leering at them in a disrespectful way, but he was definitely taking them in, especially when one of them would touch him or stand close to him; he noticed and I noticed. Oddly, I wasn't upset with him, it made sense to me and really, I felt more sorry for myself than I felt angry or jealous. There was nothing that I could do; I couldn't give him what he wanted and now he knew. I hated feeling sorry for myself; I never played the victim role, but this had always been a complicated issue for me. Dealing with the abuse alone was enough of a mental obstacle to overcome, but knowing that you loved someone whose biology wanted them to have something that you couldn't provide, well that was difficult to get a grip on.

Currently, I was watching one of our volunteers, a woman about my age, talking with Nathanial. She was standing very close to him and she was tossing her hair back and forth. She looked attractive, fit and obviously confident. I sighed.

"Hey Ana," someone spoke beside me; it was Charlie. I was still starring at the woman.

"Hey Charlie," I said, not breaking my gaze.

"What's going on there?" he asked, following my eye line over to Nathanial. I shrugged and looked away, my heart sinking.

"How are you?" I asked him, wanting to divert his attention. He was now watching them intently.

"She's a flirt Ana; I wouldn't worry about her. She's made the rounds once already today." He laughed and put his hand on my shoulder. "I'm sure Nathanial has seen everything she has to display many, many times; she's not offering him anything he wants." I felt my stomach turn. I wished that that were true. We walked up the hill, passing them as we went. Nathanial looked up and our eyes met. I cocked my head to the side and stared once more from the woman to him; I turned and let Charlie lead me back toward the registration tent. *There was nothing that I could do*; that phrase kept repeating in my head for the rest of the day and on my drive home; I had a feeling it would become burned into my very psyche at some point. I was hoping that Noni would be at the house, I had only seen her once in the last two weeks. She was traveling to the outer communities and to the other reservations, helping to evacuate any refugees. Vampire attacks were coming daily now, and getting as many people away from the violence

263

as possible was the primary goal. I wondered who would win this war, what segments of the world would be like if the Vampires returned to full power. I wondered how many humans would forsake their own humanity and allow for themselves to be turned, to be used and manipulated. It made me sad and it made me think of Stephen.

Over the next several weeks, I managed to keep myself busy, trying not to worry about being attacked, or about what was going to happen between Nathanial and myself; there was no point. I didn't have the luxury of knowing the future. He and I had chatted a bit. He would give me updates that he was getting from Micah, and it appeared that the group was waiting for something, what that was, no one knew.

I tried to stay out of Nathanial's way as much as possible, but our paths were always crossing. He needed me to be in communication with him about how many families I was registering and how many children needed medical care. It was impossible not to interact with him and presently, I was headed to the main tent to ask him to order more vaccinations. I sighed the instant I came up to the entrance. The woman was there, the one who'd been hanging out with him for weeks now, the one Charlie had said was a flirt. I noticed right away that she was an Indigenous American and she looked a lot like Nathanial. She had long, straight, dark hair, copper skin and beautiful dark eyes; actually, they made a nice couple, I laughed to myself, but I could feel my heart sinking again—it was doing that a lot lately. They were sitting side by side at a table, their bodies turned in toward each other and she was touching his hand. I felt the metals in my neck begin to shift, cutting into my flesh as they moved. Nathanial's head was leaning in as was hers; they looked like they were having a very intense conversation.

I cleared my throat as quietly as I could, not wanting to startle them. Nathanial's head jerked up and immediately, he pulled his hand out from under hers.

"I'm sorry to interrupt," I said, my voice coming out stronger than I would have expected, "but Dr. Taylor has requested some more vaccinations for the children, I just needed to clear the order with you," I said, trying to smile, but I suddenly felt sick and my heart hurt. Nathanial stood up and I noticed that he seemed flustered, his face was colored with a slight pink wash and he wasn't looking at me. "I'll just wait for you out here, there's no need to rush," I said, backing out of the tent. I stood watching the sunset, waiting for him. A few minutes later, the woman came out, tossing her hair in my face and walking past me without saying a word. Nice choice, I thought. He could at least flirt with someone who wasn't a bitch. Nathanial emerged from the tent and I rifled through the papers the doctor had given me; I really wasn't in the mood for awkwardness between Nathanial and me, I just wanted to get his signature and get the hell out of there. "Umm, let's see," I said, handing him an order form.

"Ana," he said quietly.

"I think this is the one he needs signed." I motioned to the line for Nathanial to put his name; I didn't want to talk to him about this; I wasn't angry with him, I just wanted to go. He stared at me for a moment; I lowered my eyes and motioned for him to sign the damn sheet of paper. He scribbled his signature across the bottom and handed it back to me. "Thanks, and this one too. This is for the vaccinations," I said, handing him another sheet of paper. He signed the space, but he was still staring at me.

"We haven't talked in a while," he said, his face showing worry. I shrugged, and waved my hand dismissively placing the papers back into the folder.

"We're busy," I said, hoisting my backpack over my shoulders. "Plus, you gave me an update a few days ago, unless something's changed?" I asked, finally meeting his gaze.

"No, nothing's changed, but I wasn't referring to the updates, Ana," he said quietly, his eyes narrowing. I shrugged again, not having the energy to discuss the matter of his mating behaviors and his seemingly new affinity for other women. I was tired. He bowed his head, clearly hearing my agitations. "We should talk," he said, not looking at me.

"Sure," I said, touching him on the shoulder. I wanted him to know that I didn't blame him for what he was feeling; I knew that his desire to mate was something that he had no control over; it wasn't his fault. "But I'm really tired and I have a massive headache. How about tomorrow, ok?" I said, letting my hand fall from his arm. I turned to walk past him.

"Tomorrow then," he said. I saw his gaze shift over my shoulder and I turned to see the dark haired woman watching us. I stared at him, waiting for his eyes to return to me, but they didn't. I sighed and turned my back on Nathanial, leaving him to his new muse.

Tomorrow turned into the next day and the next day turned into the next week. I had basically stopped speaking to Nathanial, not on purpose, but there was a heightened level of anxiety in the camp. A coven of Vampires had attacked one of the nearby communities, less than fifty miles from the Reservation and Noni and the elders were worried. She was waiting to hear back from Liam on which coven this was, and if they had acted on their own or under orders. I had hoped to see Liam as well; I missed Lucie terribly and I wanted to ask him about Stephen, about what had transpired between them; I just needed someone to talk to.

I was assembling my paperwork for the day, when Charlie approached me; he looked distressed. "What's up Charlie, you look upset," I said, smiling at him. He pulled out one of the folding chairs and sat down next to me.

"Look, I know it's none of my business, but you're a cool chick Ana, I like you and I consider you a friend," he said, his blond hair falling into his eyes. I frowned.

"We are friends Charlie and I think you're pretty cool as well." I laughed, waiting for him to tell me what had him so bothered. "But what's 'none of your business'?" I asked.

"It's Nathanial and Adrianna," he said, his brow furrowed. So that's what her name was; good to know I thought. "I mean aren't you two like together; I mean you're like Bonded to him right?" Charlie was a new Bonder, just having experienced the initial change within his own self and I knew he was struggling to understand the nature of his species and their relationship to humans.

267

"Technically, yes," I said quietly, now having noticed the source of his agitation. Adrianna and Nathanial were walking toward his car, her arm linked through his. I suddenly felt nauseous. I cleared my throat.

"I thought you guys were more than just 'technically', you know?" Charlie asked, his eyes on the two figures with their backs to us.

"Yeah, we seemed to have run into a few problems on that front." I tried to laugh, but I was pretty sure I was about to crumble.

"So?" Charlie turned to look at me, his brown eyes sad. I patted his hand. "So, everyone has problems; you work it out, you work on things. That's what people do or what demons do," he added, still looking at me.

"I know Charlie, and it seems as though that would make the most sense, but as I am sure you will come to find out, being a Bonder and a human for that matter, is a lot more complicated than it seems," I said gently, standing to leave. He shook his head, also standing.

"No, Ana, I don't think it is. I think if you claim to love someone as much as Nathanial claims to love you, then it's not complicated. You just make the decision that would never, ever cause the person you love to be hurt beyond repair or to not trust you anymore; to me, that's the easiest decision to ever make. There's nothing to think about." Charlie ran his fingers through his hair and glared at Nathanial. He was a sweet kid, I thought, naïve, but sweet. "I hope the person I find to be with, the person that becomes my Choice; I hope that she loves me as much as you love Nathanial, Ana. He's lucky you know." He nodded at me and I smiled.

"Thank you Charlie, you are very kind," I said, gathering my pack and wondering just how I was going to get to my car without having to see Nathanial. Charlie seemed to read my mind.

"You want me to walk with you?" he asked, hoisting his own pack over his shoulders. I laughed. It was nice to see that gentlemen were still present in this day and age.

"Nah, I'm fine. Besides, I'm pretty sure that my bicep is the size of one of her legs. I can put her down if need be!" I laughed and Charlie nodded vehemently. I exhaled and started up the hill toward my car. I forced myself not to look in their direction and I focused on getting my stuff in the seat as quickly as possible. I noticed the distinct smell of smoke drift passed my nose and I wondered if there had been another attack somewhere close. I closed my door and rolled down my window turning my stereo up as loud as it would go, hoping the music would drown the panic attack that was threatening to consume me. I didn't want to lose Nathanial. *There was nothing that I could do*. As I pulled out of my space, I looked up in time to see Adrianna slide into the passenger seat of Nathanial's car and close the door. Bile filled my mouth and I swallowed back the tears I knew I couldn't contain.

I went home to an empty house and decided to make myself some dinner. I was going to allow myself a few days to feel bad about my situation, but then I needed to get a grip and perhaps discuss with Nathanial just what he wanted to do. As desperately as I loved him and as much as I understood that he had no control over this whole mating thing, I knew that if Nathanial had a child with another woman, I just couldn't be with him; it would be too difficult. At least there would be some closure with that scenario.

I curled up on the couch with my dinner and listened to the stereo. I thought about calling Stephen, just to see if he would talk to me. I knew he wouldn't want to hear about my problems with Nathanial, but we had always had a good communication; he always listened. I decided instead to go to bed early and I called Zanuck from the front porch. The smell of smoke seemed to be getting stronger and I noticed a thin haze beginning to seep through the air. My body tensed. Zanuck bounded up the stairs howling and I ushered him through he door. I hoped that nobody's home was on fire. I lied awake for quite some time crying, sobbing, my anxiety not allowing my mind to welcome the sleep it needed, but eventually I think I dozed off. Then someone was shaking me, gently, but shaking me nonetheless. I startled and jumped immediately from my bed, my skin hot and my blood beginning to surge and boil.

"Relax Ana," a commanding voice spoke, cutting through my tension. Liam.

"Christ, Liam, you scared me to death. I almost ignited your ass. What are you doing here? Is something wrong?" I asked, moving to turn on the bedside lamp. Upon lighting his face I noticed how beaten up Liam looked. His skin was bloody and he had gashes on his arms and neck. He looked like he'd been in a street fight. He laughed.

"If only," he said, his voice turning dark. "Look, I don't have time to catch up Ana. I need you to tell me where I can find Nathanial." Liam looked at me, surveying what I was sure were my swollen and red eyes. "Are you alright?" Liam asked, forgetting his urgency for a moment. I waved my hand.

"Don't worry about it. Why do you need to see Nathanial?" I asked bowing my head; his scrutiny was oppressive. I knew he was reading my mind, seeing everything that I had seen over the last several weeks, the last image I saw of Adrianna getting into Nathanial's car—he missed nothing. I was too exhausted to try and keep him out; and I really didn't care to actually.

"Ana." Liam said moving toward me. I held out my hand to stop him.

"Don't worry about it Liam; I'm fine; I will be fine." My voice was stern and I met his gaze. "What can I do to help you, anything?" I said, my eyes begging him to not ask any more questions. He sighed, but looked upset.

"They're attacking the Reservation Ana; it's already begun and I need to get to Nathanial as soon as possible." I nodded at him and moved to take his shoulder. He looked at me, stunned.

"I'm going with you Liam, no arguments. Nathanial's at his cabin, let's go," I said, pulling on a sweatshirt. Liam nodded and together we shimmered out into the fire that was spreading across the land.

Chapter Eleven

Nathanial

Kissing Adrianna was an odd experience. I hadn't actually kissed anyone since being with Ana, not even on those occasions when there had been other women; some who had come by my own volition and some who had not. Regardless, I had never allowed myself to kiss any of them; it was too intimate. Unfortunately, my hormonal drive was dictating everything physical that I wanted and I wanted to kiss her, to feel her lips, to taste her. My mind and my heart knew that it was wrong, that it felt wrong. She tasted off, her scent was not to my liking and the very feel of her didn't seem to fit. Regardless, my body was responding to her fertility and the hormones she was emitting seemed to be overriding anything that my mind deemed uncomfortable. I wanted her. I slid down her underwear and pulled her on top of me. She moaned as I pressed myself against her and she lowered her head, undoing my belt and sliding down my jeans. I felt the sudden surge and heat of my own hormones release, and she spread her legs wide, grinding slowly against me as I started to penetrate her. A gust of cold air burst through the space and I stopped moving. Standing in front of me, her eyes wide and her jaw slack, was Ana and she wasn't alone. Liam was standing next to her and immediately he wrapped his arm around her shoulder, pushing her protectively behind him. I threw Adrianna off of me; oh Jesus...what had I done?

"Hey!" Adrianna said, glaring at me. Liam moved in front of her and gathered her clothes up, throwing them at her. He was absolutely furious.

"You need to leave please miss," he said, his eyes growing dark and he barred his teeth. Adrianna moved away from him, grabbing her clothes and heading for the door. Liam walked her out front and I heard him call for one of his guards to escort her home, leaving Ana and I alone. I pulled up my jeans and buttoned my shirt. She wasn't looking at me, but I could see that she'd started to hyperventilate. I heard the door shut and Liam returned to the living room. He glanced at me assembling my clothes, then at Ana, his eyes black flames. He moved to touch Ana on the back and almost immediately, her breath began to regulate. She clasped her chest and then the back of her neck, and I watched as her eyes locked with mine; they were dead, cold. I was going to vomit.

"The Reservation is under attack Nathanial. We need to go. The camp is at risk." Liam wasn't looking at me when he spoke, he was watching Ana. I let my eyes look towards her face, frightened by what I saw. She was frowning now, her head cocked to the side, her lips pressed in a solid line, her eyes lifeless. The image was almost the exact replica of when we'd first met, the day I had been waiting for her by her car after her class. I felt sick. Vomit surged in my mouth and I turned, heaving into the fireplace. "You can meet us at the camp Nathanial. I've already called in for fighters, but you may want to place a call to your uncle," Liam spoke, his voice not acknowledging my sudden purge. I wiped my mouth and spit into the fire.

"Bonders or Vampires?" I asked, referring to the group that was after Ana.

"Both," Liam said; his face smooth and composed. He took Ana's hand and looked into her eyes. She nodded at him and glanced back to stare at me. Then they disappeared.

Ana

Well, it was good to see that some decisions had been made for me. I didn't have time to worry what my life was going to be without Nathanial; I needed to be prepared to fight. I also needed to find Noni. I swallowed back the terrible sadness and disbelief that was threatening to consume me and I grasped Liam's hand as he led me through the massive amounts of people and Bonders that had gathered at the camp. He found several members of his coven and set about directing them to various locations around the area and ordering them not to attack the humans—he made no such order for the Bonder group that was after me or for the Bonders in general. I guessed some enemies would always be destined to destroy each other. I wondered if they would have a hard time fighting against their own species if they had to. Liam looked at me.

"We made an agreement Ana and that's all that matters," he said, gazing upon my face. "Can you fight?" he asked me. I blinked trying to steel my mind. I nodded, feeling the heat rise in my body. "Good girl!" Liam said. "Now listen to me, I don't care who appears to fight against

274

you, I don't care if you know them, if you like them; I don't care...you fight to kill Ana, you are to override whatever natural tendencies you have to show mercy; do-you-understand-me?" He was speaking very quickly and his voice was low and rough; it sounded strained. I nodded, again not quite getting the meaning behind what he was saying. I saw Nathanial appear at his side and he was watching us. Liam turned to Nathanial, looking angrier than I had ever seen Liam capable.

"He's not with us, you know this. He could kill her," I heard Liam say and a sudden wash of ice covered my body, but before I could process what I just heard, a monumental blast sounded from behind me shaking the ground, the force throwing me forward into Nathanial. We tumbled backward, rolling down the hill, wooden beams and scaffolding blowing past us. I felt him wrap his arms around me in a steel cage as we were catapulted down the hill towards the lake. I felt a surge of heat rush past my face and I opened my eyes to a ball of fire exploding in the sky. The screaming was getting distant as we crashed over the embankment and plunged through the ice into the water. The cold instantly paralyzed my lungs and I stopped breathing. I couldn't feel Nathanial's arms around me anymore—I couldn't feel anything. I tried to calm the wave of panic and attempted to gather all the heat within my own body. Within a few seconds, I found that I could move. I started to kick up as my head broke the surface. I scanned around the lake looking for Nathanial, but I didn't see anything, it was too dark. I swam yelling for him. I reached the gravel shore and pulled myself up out of the ice and water. I screamed for him again, my panic returning. He had to be ok. Nathanial was a superior swimmer, a good fighter, he could survive I told myself. I ran back up the embankment toward the fire, toward the screaming and charged into the crowd looking for Noni. Another explosion shattered the night and I hit the ground covering my head. I crawled toward one of the cabins that was not currently burning and got to the door, kicking it in and running inside. I froze mid stride.

Bodies were everywhere; women, children, men; all human and all dead. Dark red puddles were oozing and seeping from every corner. My eyes couldn't look away. I looked to the beds, blood dripped down from the sheets, leaving clotted splatters on the wood floors. There was an arm coming out from behind one of the beds in the corner and I saw a single lock of long white hair flowing over the skin. My breath stopped. I stepped over the mutilated bodies and toward the outstretched arm, knowing—my Noni was dead; her body was pristine except a single line of blood coming from her mouth. Her eyes were open and she was staring at me. I knelt down beside her and took her head in my lap, feeling wetness coat my fingers. I dropped her and pulled my hand away to find it covered in dark blood and pieces of her skull. I wiped the mess on my shirt and began sobbing, my bloodied fingers wiping the tears from my eyes. She was all I had left; she was the only family I'd known, the only one who loved me, who knew me. I was choking and I smelled smoke waft passed my nose. I didn't care if the place was on fire and I didn't care if I died; I wanted to die. I felt a sudden burning on my throat and I reached down to find my amulet glowing in bright flames. The outer most circle was ablaze as was the oval. I tried to tear it from my skin, but it wouldn't budge. The windows shattered around me as burning torches were thrown into the cabin. Still I sat, cradling Noni's head in my lap, not wanting to leave. Suddenly, I realized that I didn't want her to burn there; I didn't

276

want this horrible place to be her grave. I lifted her body into my arms and parted the now wall of flames that was surrounding my exit. I didn't even have to take the time to center myself, the action was so natural, so much a part of me now. I burst through the opening and out into the night air, holding her close to me. Chaos was exploding and I couldn't care less. I walked straight into the mass of people running, of Vampires killing, of death and fire. I walked, carrying Noni, my mother, my family, my savior. I headed deep into the woods, climbing up the steep terrain into the mountain trails. I couldn't return her to the meadow, but I could at least give her a sacred space in her beloved mountains. I would kill anyone who tried to stop me.

I didn't know how long I hiked. I didn't feel tired, just determined. I was pretty sure it was freezing, but my body didn't register the cold or how wet I was. I kept moving, letting the breath pull me, letting my heart guide me. I cleared the trail and came out of the forest to an overlook, one that had a western view of the mountains, where Noni could watch the sun set. It would have to do. I didn't want to bury her. I didn't want to risk someone coming and digging her body up and brutalizing her. I laid Noni down in the grass and sat next to her, closing her eyes. Suddenly my body tensed and I felt someone staring at me. I turned my head and saw a figure emerge from the shadows of the forest, from the trail we'd just climbed. It was Stephen.

Nathanial

Where the hell was she? I ran through the main part of camp, blasting away burning bodies and pieces of wood that were falling around me. People were screaming and running and I was grabbing up children and carrying them, trying to get to Liam who had several Vampires ready to transport the kids out of the camp. I had no idea how they were doing it, but I didn't actually care. Constantly, I was searching for Ana. I had seen Stephen as he and several of his new gang, burned and tossed torches into several of the cabins. I also saw him blur into the woods and I wondered who or what he was following. Someone grabbed me from behind and I whirled to stun them, but Liam blocked my hand and forced me backwards.

"He's found Ana!" His voice was clear and sharp, cutting through the screaming.

"Which way?" I yelled back, my heart stopping. He motioned toward the forest and I nodded. Of course, Stephen was after Ana; that's whom he'd been after this whole time, that's why he was here. I nodded and blurred over to the trail where I'd seen him enter.

Ana

He walked slowly toward me, his fists at his side, clenched. I bowed my head, finally understanding. This is what Liam had meant; I had known, but refused to acknowledge what he was saying, what he'd said to Nathanial before the explosion. Stephen came within feet of Noni's body and I saw his eyes scan over her face, over the blood and bits of skull that covered my shirt and my cheeks. He looked at me and I saw that his eyes were black and hollow, his cheeks were sunken in and he was pale. I turned toward the horizon letting the wind blow my hair around my shoulders; I felt the breeze caress my skin. I had no idea if Stephen was in any frame of mind to be reasoned with, but I just needed some time, then I would do whatever he wanted. I was not going to fight him, no matter what I had promised Liam. I turned to see that Stephen was now less than a foot in front of me; I met his gaze.

"I just need a moment," I said, my voice carrying on the wind. "I just need to say goodbye Stephen." I looked at him; he didn't move so I took that as a sign that he would wait to kill me, if that's what he intended. I stooped and picked up Noni, once again holding her against my chest. I bent my head and kissed her softly on each cheek, burying my head in her chest. I gasped and sobbed, but then a quiet calm filtered into my heart and the space where my amulet hung began to cool. I looked out toward the tops of the mountains; I knew that Stephen was watching me—waiting. With one breath, I heaved Noni's body over the cliff and watched as it cascaded down the side of the mountain into the ravine below. I whispered a blessing over her body and over the space that would allow her soul to be released and then slowly, I turned to face Stephen. We stood staring at each other, so similar in our postures as we were that night in the alley; again the redundancies of my life seemed never to fail to show themselves. He was in front of me in less than one heartbeat, his face close to mine, his hands on the sides of my neck, as if he were going to kiss me, but his eyes were black. Gone were the calming seas that I had kept in my memories and I was pretty sure that he was about to kill me. At that moment, I couldn't help but think of that song that we both liked, the one that had been playing that night the first time he had touched me in more than a casual way, the first time I realized just how much I'd come to depend upon him, and how much my feelings had grown for him. I supposed we were always destined to have this moment; he was after all supposed to have done this months ago.

I met his stare, he was waiting for me to reason through everything; he was allowing for me to remember. I closed my eyes and leaned my head against his shoulder; I didn't know what else to do. He didn't move, but I heard him take a deep breath in and I felt his arms begin to wrap around my waist. I heard rustling in the trees and my head snapped up. Out of darkness of the wood, emerged four Demons, they stood staring at us. Stephen whipped his head around and immediately he pushed me behind him. I swore, before my very eyes, Stephen grew, not only in height, but also in musculature. He was huge and I heard him make a sound so terrifying that fear encapsulated my entire being.

Nathanial

I blurred up the main trail, hoping that was the one Stephen and Ana had chosen. He had a head start, but I was also hoping that his conscience would allow for him to delay what he thought was the best solution for his sadness and regret. I stopped mid run and sniffed the air. Demons! At least four of them were also on the trail, just a few paces in front of me. Jesus! I knew they would kill Stephen and then Ana and just for a moment I had hoped that Stephen had gotten to her first. I knew Ana would never fight him, she loved him too much to be his executioner. Her compassion was finally going to be the knife that came down upon her heart. I raced up the trail and stopped just before emerging from the woods. I saw them. There were four Bonders and I also saw Stephen, at least I thought it was Stephen; the being looked absurdly large and stronger than any Vampire I had ever seen. I was behind the whole group, but I could plainly see that Stephen had Ana behind him, and he looked to be protecting her. A plan suddenly came to me, a plan that I knew had the potential to cost me everything with Ana, if I hadn't already done so, and a plan that would require me to trust Stephen with the very reason for my existence; I would have to trust him with my heart.

Ana

The group of Demons were now walking towards us and Stephen had moved directly in front of me, still pushing me back out of view. I could take them all if I had to, especially if they were going to harm Stephen. He quickly turned to look at me, processing my thoughts. He looked awestruck. I nodded to him. Suddenly, I saw another person emerge from the wood; it was Nathanial. Christ, we were all going to be fighting here in a moment. The Bonders moved closer, closing ranks. Everything seemed like it was happening in slow motion. I watched as

Nathanial also moved silently behind them. My blood began to stir, but Stephen whispered to me in a voice that I did not recognize.

"No, Ana." He wasn't looking at the Bonders, but at Nathanial; they seemed to be having some sort of conversation.

"I can protect us Stephen," I whispered back. He shook his head, keeping his back to me. My skin started to swell when one of the demons began speaking to Stephen.

"Either kill her or hand her over," his voice was low and even, but I could make out every word. Stephen folded his arms over his chest and stood with his legs apart, I felt heat surge from his body. Nathanial was now only a few paces behind and he looked to be growing out from the very earth, his body rising tall and grand in the moonlight. He was watching Stephen.

"Well, I was about to until you rudely interrupted," Stephen said, his voice calm, but deadly.

"Fine. Now you have an audience," one of the Bonders spoke stepping forward. The biggest one halted his pace and motioned for Stephen to continue what he'd started. I watched Nathanial rise up; my eyes widened. I saw Nathanial look at Stephen, then at me, and then he leapt straight into the air, sending himself hurdling down upon the group of Bonders. Stephen pushed me to the ground and started throwing blue-green flames from his hands. Screams pierced the air and smell of burning flesh made me gag. I tried to stand, but I was paralyzed; either Stephen or Nathanial had incapacitated me. I watched both of them dueling with the Bonders, at least the ones that weren't already on fire. I suddenly realized that they were fighting together, standing side-by-side. They were outnumbered, but they seemed to have the strength of an entire army between the two of them. Suddenly someone grabbed me around the neck, digging into the flesh and trying to tear the metal from my spinal cord. I screamed. I heard Nathanial shout and in a heartbeat, he was at my side, tackling a fifth Bonder that had appeared. The force of Nathanial's lunge sent all three of us tumbling near the edge of the cliff, and I landed with the Demon on top of me. Nathanial ripped him off of me and immediately he was hit in the head. I screamed for Stephen and I saw him slash the throat of the Bonder that was lunging at him, blood splattering onto Stephen's face. He moved to our side and sent the Demon flying off of Nathanial. I could move now and I crawled over to them, but the pain in my neck was excruciating. Nathanial looked at me and looked behind him. There were only two Demons left and they looked badly injured. I saw Nathanial turn back and stare at Stephen.

"Take her," he said. "Get her out of here, get her some place safe. I trust you Stephen and I'm trusting in your love for Ana—I'm trusting you to remember yourself." One of the Demons was rising up, growling. Nathanial whipped his head around. "Go!" he shouted. I looked at him, not believing what was happening. "GO!" Stephen grabbed my hand and jerked me up, crushing me against him. I looked once more at Nathanial and our eyes met. "I love you Ana and I'll come for you, I promise. I'm sorry for hurting you; I love you!" he shouted and grasped my other hand. There I stood, in the middle of two beings, both holding my hands, both holding my heart. I nodded at Nathanial and he dropped my hand and I saw him launch one last time into the air, colliding with the Demon. Just as Stephen whipped us away, I saw a giant explosion of fire blast high into the night, blackening the stars; then...nothing.

Part II

Chapter Twelve

Ana

Stephen's grip on me was so tight that I was sure he was going to crush my lungs. The act of shimmering normally took the breath out of me, but shimmering with Stephen made for an exceptionally rough experience. Despite the lack of air, I gasped trying to get my lungs to expand. The back of my neck was throbbing and the pain was spreading to the base of my skull. Finally, I felt the familiar shove through the air and we crashed together in the middle of what looked like someone's home. I gulped the air, relieved to have my lungs in working order. The pain from my mark heightened and I doubled over, dry heaving. Blood was streaming down my back and over my shoulders and I started to gag. I fell to my knees.

"Let me see," I heard Stephen speaking to me, his voice back to its normal tone. I couldn't move to help him. He scooped me up, carrying me over to the couch. He laid me facing away from him and I felt my hair being swept aside as he looked at the back of my neck. "Jesus," he whispered. He rolled me back over; I was shaking and my blood felt cold. I wondered if he was going to attack me, if the sight of my blood would be too much for him. Actually, I didn't care. He looked at me and then stood, pacing around the room. "What the hell did he expect me to do now?" I assumed Stephen was muttering to himself, his tone was distressed. He ran his fingers through his hair and came back over to the couch. "Well, you're lucky to be alive, Ana. That thing on your neck is barely still attached. I'm guessing that it will eventually re-embed itself, but what the fuck do I know about Bondings?" he cursed, his voice shaking. I tried to nod at him, but my convulsions were making it hard for me to control my own muscles. I watched as Stephen left the room and walked down the hall. He returned with a large blanket and draped it over my body. He then ran his fingers over the fireplace, igniting huge flames that immediately began to emit a pulsing heat. He stood with his palms bracing against the mantel, his back to me. "I have to go out," he whispered, turning to look at me. I tried to nod again. He shook his head and muttered under his breath, then, he shimmered out of the room leaving me alone and hoping not to die.

I had no sense of time or what day it was; I didn't even know how long I'd been on Stephen's couch or where we were. I was weak and exhausted. I was getting over heated, and I moved very slowly, pulling back the blanket and swinging my legs over the side of the couch to the floor. I tried to stand, but immediately the room tilted and my brain felt as if it was sloshing back and forth against my skull. Nausea washed over me and I collapsed back down on the couch. I took a deep breath through my mouth and waited for the room to stop spinning. I decided that standing up was a bit too advanced for me at the moment, so I settled for folding my legs up under me and pulling the blanket around my knees. I guessed I should just wait for Stephen to come back; *if* he came back. I zoned out. A strong gust of cold wind gathered in the room and as I snapped myself from my trance, I noticed a tall figure standing in the middle of the room.

"Hey," he said, not seeming to be alarmed by my presence. He was definitely a Vampire; I could tell just by looking at him. He was muscular, lean, with layered wavy black hair and gray eyes; it was a similar style to Stephen's. Of course, just like all Vampires, he was beautiful, rugged and lethal. "I'm Cillian," he said, in what sounded like a thick Irish accent that was not nearly as posh as Stephen's. "Right ya're!" He laughed and moved to sit down in the chair. "Don't look so frightened; I'm not goin' to hurt ya," he said, leaning forward to stare at me, his eyes flashed as if in recognition. He studied me for a moment. "I'm waitin' for Stephen; ya know where he's gotten off to?" I was guessing that it was typical for humans to hang out with Vampires in Ireland? Cillian chuckled. "Nah, not really, but our little group seems to attract quite a few of da lassies; ya know what I mean?" He winked at me. "We don't mind so much when da gentler sex wants to engage us." He leaned back in the chair, his eyes watching my face.

"What day is it?" I asked, trying to focus on the situation in front of me.

"Friday. Been on a bender have ya?" he said, winking at me again and I noticed that his eyes began to wander over my body. Friday, that meant I'd been here on the couch for three days! "Mus'ta been a good one!" Cillian laughed and stood up to stand near the fire. "I've only had a gal for two and dat was 'cause she was really too fucked up to actually leave." He chuckled to himself. I frowned at him; what the hell was he talking about? "Stephen holds da record, dat bastard; four whole days and he didn't even drain her, she was able to walk and everyting after, but man was he high as a kite! Didn't need to feed for a week, dat fucker!" I felt my eyes grow wide. Clearly, these Vampires were a bit of a different breed from Liam and Carmen, or at least the latter were sane enough to keep the details of their feeding preferences quiet. "Hey, ya know Liam?" Cillian turned to look at me. I nodded. "He's a good guy, didn't agree wit him sidin' wit your kind

288

dough, but besides dat, he's a good guy." He came to stand next to me. "Are ya sick? I have some vitamin B 12; I can give ya a shot," he said, again letting his eyes roam over my body. Why would I need a B 12 shot? "Ya know, to replenish da blood, especially if da two of ye have been goin' at it for tree days, yer bound to be feelin' a bit weak, yeah?" He raised his eyebrows and reached into his pocket. He pulled a tiny syringe and began thumping the vial.

"Umm, no, thanks; I'm alright," I said, eyeing the needle. Reality crashed over me. He thought that Stephen had been feeding on me—for three days! Christ, what the hell went on here? Cillian stared at me, his eyes narrowing.

"What da hell are ya doin' here if yer not here for Stephen?" he asked, his body tensing. Crap.

"She is here for me, just not in that capacity, at least not yet." Cillian and I both turned to see Stephen enter the room; he was carrying a bag of groceries, smirking slightly. Immediately, I saw Cillian relax and move away from me, but I noticed that his eyes flashed again, as if in some sort of recognition as he stared at me. His jaw set and I watched as he followed Stephen into the kitchen. I heard them talking.

"We need ya down at da club man. One of our gigs canceled and Eamonn asked if ya could fill in." They walked back to the living room, Stephen carrying two beers and a ginger ale. He put the soda down on the coffee table and nodded for me to take it. He sighed.

"Yeah, tell him I'll be there." Stephen looked at me and frowned.

"Excellent! We've got quite da crowd dis evenin' as well, lots of willing participants." Cillian winked at Stephen and sipped his beer. I felt a little sick. I finished my drink in one swallow; I was pretty sure that I hadn't had any fluid in my system for three days and I hoped that I could keep it down. Cillian looked at me and smiled. "You should come to. We'd love to have ya," he said, his tone hinted at something dark and I felt chills run up my spine.

"She's not well enough." Stephen looked at me, his eyes still dark and hollow. Cillian shrugged.

"Well, I'm pretty patient! Let me know when yer feelin' stronger den eh?" he said, standing and finishing his beer. "Well see ya tonight den." He patted Stephen on the back, smirked at me, snapped his fingers, then disappeared. Stephen walked back into the kitchen and returned with another ginger ale. He poured the soda in my glass and handed it back to me.

"Looks like you made some new friends," I said, eyeing him over my glass, wondering what the hell he'd gotten himself into.

"I told you before, it's none of your business," he said quietly. My chest began to hurt. I rubbed it trying to massage away the pain. Stephen watched me. "Are you hurt?" he asked, leaning forward. I shook my head, not trusting myself to speak again. He sat back and we stared at each other. I exhaled.

"I think that when I'm feeling better; I think that I should go," I said, looking into the fire.

290

"Hmmm, and just how do you think you are going to manage that?" he asked, closing his eyes and leaning his head back against the chair. "You have no clothes, no money, no job, no place to live…" He trailed off.

"Where are we?" I couldn't believe it had taken me so long to ask him. He opened his eyes and smirked at me.

"Ireland," he said quietly and our gazes locked… I thought that we were both remembering what we'd talked about that night at the cabin when he'd asked to Change me; I told him I'd wanted us to come back here, to be alone together in a place we both loved. I pulled myself out of the memory and back to reality. I could get a job easy enough, I still had my worker card from when I was a student; it was valid for ten years. The issue of money was definitely a problem. I hadn't taken a purse with me when Liam came to the house; I wasn't really thinking that I would be in need of anything like that at the camp and especially if I was having to fight.

"So, what do we do then? I mean I'm happy to work and save up some money and then we can go our separate ways. Nathanial didn't say that you had to stay with me Stephen." Just saying Nathanial's name flooded my mind with the memories of seeing him with Adrianna, seeing her on top of him, her eyes closed as she moved against him. I shook my head trying to clear the visions, trying to stop myself from remembering. Stephen's eye's flashed open and he jerked his head off the chair, leaning in to stare at me. He'd seen what I had just remembered. I cleared my throat and looked back toward the fire.

"Ana?" he whispered. I wiped the tears that were streaming down my cheeks and cleared my throat again.

"Don't worry about it Stephen; I know that you have no interest in hearing about my issues with Nathanial and it's a complicated story anyway," I murmured, not looking at him. "I'm fine; I will be fine." My voice shook. "That's our plan then," I said, determined to quell my panic and sadness. "I'll get a job. I'm not taking any money from you, and I'll get a place and that's it. I'll start over again…" I said, more to myself than to him. "I won't bother you, I won't use my stupid power unless it's a life or death issue and you can know that you did what Nathanial asked of you; you kept me safe until I could stand on my own." I closed my eyes and saw Noni's face; she was smiling. I heard Stephen shift in his seat and I opened my eyes; he was standing.

"I have to go…I'm…I have to go." He moved to get his coat. I nodded. "I bought you some food, fix whatever you want. Your bedroom is down the hall on the left." He motioned down the corridor.

"Thanks," I said, not looking at him. When I raised my eyes, he was gone.

Stephen

I was waiting to see Liam. I had to know what happened between Ana and Nathanial. The images I saw in her head, they couldn't be right; he wouldn't have done that to her—not after everything he'd experienced with Devon and Patric, with his own issues of depravity,

292

with how he'd hurt Ana. I was angry. Angry with Nathanial for dumping Ana on me, angry with myself for allowing myself to *feel* for her again; I was just angry. For a month Ana had been working and she'd refused to take any money I'd offered her. She was cutting ties with me and I felt sick in my soul knowing this, knowing that she was breaking herself off from me, from loving me. I had managed to keep most of my friends away from the house, but it was impossible to keep tabs on everyone who came and went. My place was somewhat of a gathering point for the rest of the group and whomever they chose to bring back with them. It had been my way of life for a little while now and it was hard to break the habit. I hoped that Ana wouldn't walk in on anything that might disturb her; she seemed a bit more fragile than was usual for her and I attributed it directly to whatever had transpired between her and Nathanial. But really, I didn't see why I should care about her fragility; she had made her choice.

I had hoped that Liam would answer my call and come back to Ireland. I wasn't in the mood to go gallivanting around chasing him and Carmen across the globe, but I was intrigued. There was something more to what Ana's visions were showing, a story there, and I wanted to understand; who knew, it might be something that I could use. My body felt weak and I needed to feed. I sighed. I had rarely indulged that side of my being when I was with Liam. We only fed when absolutely necessary, choosing our prey, not to kill, but only as hosts for our needs. For me, finding a Human woman who was willing to donate enough blood to satiate me was fairly easy—it actually didn't take much. I could make the experience pleasurable and they would barely feel a thing; but here, here things were different. The particular group I was now aligned with was involved in much darker rituals when it came to feeding. Benders, they would call them. They would keep women for a couple of days, having sex and taking their blood, leaving themselves gorged and the girls slowly weakened; sometimes they died. I had participated once, keeping a woman for four days, but that was after I had left Ana in Idaho, after Liam told me that he'd shared my past with her, that he'd told her that I wasn't really wanting to Change her out of love, but for revenge. I had binged then—it was easy not to feel anything but my need for blood. It was easy to picture her face every time I was with someone; I still did that, because I still wanted her, because I still loved her. I sighed and finished my drink, packed up my guitar and went to meet the young woman who had been waiting for me since the end of my set. I sighed and threw on my coat and walked to her side, grateful that Ana was working late tonight.

Ana

Crap! I had missed the first rail back to Bray and now I was going to have to wait another thirty minutes for the next train to arrive; so much for getting off early. I had found a job working with a cultural exchange program in Dublin and it required me to help new immigrants get settled into the city and the surrounding areas. I had worked with them while earning my first graduate degree and they seemed genuinely excited that I had returned to the country. I was so thankful that they offered me a job. I had enough money saved to put down on a small apartment or for a mutual housing situation. Some of my co-workers had used their connections and had arranged several showings for me this weekend; I was actually excited. I read the paper and waited for the rail to arrive.

I made it home by eight and was looking forward to a hot shower and getting to bed early. Stephen and I hadn't talked much since he'd seen some of what had happened with Nathanial and I was happy to avoid him and any member of his strange new gang. They were constantly shimmering in and out of the house, always with women on their arms; it was uncomfortable. I pushed the gate open and walked up the rocky drive. I liked Stephen's house very much. It was a traditional Irish cottage, made of stone and with a thatched roof. It was nestled into the cliffs overlooking the Irish Sea and you could see the rest of the tiny town below. The door was already ajar and I sighed. I wondered who was entertaining this evening. The scene in front of me could have been a flash back and for a moment, I thought I *was* having a flash back. Stephen was on the couch, a naked woman straddling his hips, her arms handcuffed behind her back, they were moving very fast and his face was buried in her neck. She was moaning and he was thrusting, she screamed and moved violently against him, they were breathing hard and I heard Stephen begin to growl. I saw him pull back and his lips were covered with copious amounts of blood and it dripped down his chin and neck. I gasped and he opened his eyes; they were on fire. I backed slowly out the door, not bothering to close it. I ran the rest of the way down the drive, stopping to throw up in the grass.

I made it to the city center and checked into a B & B, not wanting to go back to the house. Seeing Stephen like that, watching the woman on top of him; I couldn't help but think about Nathanial, about

295

Adrianna, about watching him hold her, kiss her. I curled up on the bed and tried to reason with myself. What I had seen wasn't anything that I hadn't known was already going on; I just hadn't seen Stephen doing it with anyone. It was a different image of him than the one that I had kept in my memory, the one of him playing the guitar, of him painting with me, of him singing in the car—it was the image of Stephen as a man, but he wasn't a man, he was a Vampire and that's what Vampires did, they fed. I could totally handle this, I just needed to get a grip on myself. It was really the issue with Nathanial that was causing my distress, not Stephen; he wasn't mine anymore...he was never really mine.

I got up the next morning and was grateful that I had an extra shirt and some make-up stashed in my backpack. I wanted to look somewhat presentable when I viewed my potential apartments. Just thinking that I might be moving out soon helped me to recover from the scene I had witnessed. Stephen and I really shouldn't be living together anymore. Four hours and six apartments later, I had put down the first months rent on a small loft space right off of the Temple Bar district. It would be loud, but the price was right and it was nicely furnished. I walked back up the driveway to the house, feeling good about being able to tell Stephen that he could have his house back again. I wasn't going to tell him where I would be living, not that he would care, but I just thought it best to keep as much distance between us as possible. I walked into the house and immediately heard voices in the living room. I halted my steps and listened. Two males. Thank god. I entered the room and exhaled; it was Liam.

"Liam!" I shouted and ran, jumping into his arms. He picked me up and I wrapped my legs around his waist, hugging him to me.

"Ana," he whispered in my ear. "Ana," he said again, putting me gently back on the ground. Immediately I could see that he was checking me over, looking for any signs of injury, I guessed. He held my hands and led me over to the couch, Stephen was sitting in the chair and he looked furious. I wondered why.

"Liam, are you alright? Are Carmen and Lucie ok? Is Nathanial...is he...is he well?" I asked, not sure if I wanted to know the answer to the last question. I distinctly heard Stephen grunt. I looked at him, our eyes meeting.

"I'm fine Ana, as are Carmen and Lucie—they send their love of course. We were able to save the camp, but the Reservation was pretty much destroyed. However, I think that any plans to have you killed have been somewhat disrupted. I cannot say for sure, but for the time being, it seems that you are safe," Liam said, but I noticed that he looked away from me and he hadn't mentioned anything about Nathanial—for some reason, hearing that there may be a reprieve on my life for a while didn't ease my tension. "Ana, were you able to find Noni? I sent several people back to the camp after the attack and to her home but we were unable to detect her presence anywhere." Liam looked at me and my hands shook in his.

"She's dead, Liam. I found her murdered in one of the cabins; they killed the children, they killed everyone," I said quietly, but I looked at Stephen. He averted his eyes.

"Oh Ana, I'm so very sorry. She was your only family, no?" Liam asked, rubbing my hands. I nodded, still watching Stephen. A thought occurred to me.

"Liam? Her house, all of her things; I should go back, someone should see that everything is safe…" I trailed off when I noticed that Liam and Stephen were staring at each other. "What? What is it?" I asked, suddenly feeling nervous.

"I don't think that's a good idea right now Ana," Liam spoke softly.

"Why?" I said, my voice urgent. "Is the house alright?"

"The house is fine, and I will make sure that we have guards watching the place every hour of every day until…until we can make other arrangements." Liam looked at me.

"Why can't I go back? I don't understand. I can protect myself if I need to and Nathanial is there; I'm sure he wouldn't let anything happen to me right? He said that he would come for me when it was safe…is it not safe?" I said standing up. Again I saw Liam and Stephen look at one another. My mind began to process what my heart couldn't. "He's not coming, is he?" I said, my voice barely a whisper. I never really expected him to, if I was being honest with myself. Stephen stood up and moved near the fire, he was watching me.

"Ana." Liam took my hand. "Please, come sit." He gently pulled me back down on the couch. I felt odd. Liam sighed and he took my face in his hands. "My dear Ana, my sweet, wonderful, beautiful girl." His voice shook and I looked at Stephen over his shoulder. "No, he's not coming; something's happened Ana." God was he dead? "No—" Liam stopped, mid sentence.

"She's pregnant Ana," I heard Stephen's voice cut through Liam.

"We, *think* she's pregnant," Liam corrected and I heard Stephen growl. My mark started to burn and I reached to finger the now warming metals.

"You mean Adrianna?" I asked, knowing of course that's whom they meant. Liam nodded.

"After the battle, she was wounded and I saw them together. Nathanial was tending to her and I heard her say that she was worried about the baby, about their baby..." Liam couldn't continue.

"But it happened so fast," I said, not understanding. "I just saw them..." Liam moved closer to me.

"I know. Things with Demons, conception issues, they happen faster than with Humans, things just happen faster..."

"Oh," I murmured. "Oh, well, he couldn't help it." My voice wasn't my own, it sounded distant, mechanical, dead. Stephen growled again and Liam shot him a lethal look. I withdrew my hands from Liam and moved to stand next to Stephen. "I found an apartment. I've already put down some money and I can be out of your way by the end of the week; I'm sorry for last evening..." I murmured. I felt as if I was disappearing, fading away into the very space that I occupied. Nothing seemed real. Stephen stared at me, his eyes stormy as he gazed at my face.

"Ana?" Liam looked worried by my stoic reaction. "I'm going to try to talk to Nathanial—"

"No!" I held up my hand, my voice shaking. "No, Liam. It's over. Nathanial is not coming for me; he's with someone else now. There's nothing I can do, there's nothing anyone can do. He couldn't help it, so no, I don't want you to speak to him. It-is-over," I said, moving away from the fire, away from Stephen. I crossed the room and gathered my purse. "Now, I would like for either you or Stephen to please take me back to Idaho. I need to collect some of my things and there are items that I need… that I want to have that were Noni's. If you won't take me, I think I might be strong enough to shimmer on my own…" I said, hoisting my pack and my purse around my shoulders.

"I'll take her." Stephen's eyes were on me.

"Stephen, do you really think that's a good idea? Nathanial is still there. *She* is still there." Liam sounded desperate in his need to protect me. Stephen looked to his brother, but crossed the room to stand next to me; he put his hand on my shoulder. Liam shook his head. "Ana, we're here if you need us. You're not alone, we…we love you." I saw tears fill his eyes and I nodded at him. I turned to look at Stephen.

"Let's go," I said quietly and I moved his hand from my shoulder and wound my fingers into his, holding him tightly. I took a deep breath, knowing that I would have to face the destruction of a Bond, of a love, of a life. Blackness swirled around me and Stephen pulled me close to him, making us disappear…making me, disappear.

Chapter Thirteen

Ana

For some reason, I missed Patric. It didn't make any sense, but as I sat rifling through some of Noni's things, I couldn't stop thinking about him and wondering what he would think about his brother, about all that had happened. I wondered what he would say to me. I exhaled and continued moving through the house. Stephen was sitting on the porch, trying to give me some privacy I guessed. I knew the elders would make sure that Noni's possessions were well guarded and that the house would be protected by Liam, so I was quick with my gatherings.

Noni had a jewelry box in which she kept all of her sacred pieces, ones that had been given to her by her kin over many generations. Those were the only things besides photographs that I wanted to take with me. I found the wooden box nestled in a drawer and I carefully removed it from its hiding place. I sat on her bed and smoothed the covers, letting my hands trace over the place where she'd laid her head. I pressed her pillow to my face and let the tears come. I shook my head, not wanting to grieve; I couldn't, not now. I exhaled and placed the box into my pack at the bottom. I moved into my room next, knowing what I was going to have to face. It was there, still folded neatly at the foot of my bed; Nathanial's quilt. Quickly, I went to my closet and began pulling sweaters, shirts and my favorite jeans out of the cubbies, stuffing them into my backpack. I grabbed my make-up and my best perfume, the one Noni made for me, and put those away in my purse. I took a deep breath and went to stand near my bed, wondering what to do.

"Ana?" Stephen had appeared in the doorway, his arms folded across his chest, his eyes still dark and hollow.

"I'm almost done," I said, wiping the tears from my cheeks. I thought he'd seen me cry way too much. I noticed something else on my bed, something that I had forgotten about in all of the chaos and in my own grief. A tiny plastic case was lying near my pillow; inside was a bright blue CD, Stephen's CD, the one he'd given me the last time he came to visit, to warn Nathanial. I reached, sliding it over the quilt and I tucked it inside my purse. The gift box that held the blanket was still on the ground and I picked it up and began folding the quilt to place it back inside.

"Was that a gift?" Stephen asked, coming a few steps into the room. I nodded.

"For my birthday," I said, running my fingers along the threads one last time.

"Who's it from?" he asked, standing still. I sighed and looked at him. "Ah." He nodded, his tone bitter.

"He can't help it Stephen," I said quietly, placing the top over the quilt and sealing the lid with the ribbon. Stephen laughed darkly.

"You know, you keep saying that Ana. It's bullshit and you know it!" His voice was rough and slightly loud. I looked up at him.

"It's not!" I said, matching his tone, but not his volume. "It's just part of who he is; it's something that Bonders do at some point in their lives. I don't understand it any more than you do Stephen, but I know that he can't help it." I flung myself on the bed, my body weak.

"Oh, I understand it more than you know Ana," he said, now standing directly in front of me. "See that's where Nathanial and I have something in common, except that I'm not a coward when it comes to my choices—most of them at least." He smirked at me. "Do you not think that every moment of every day that you were with me, that I didn't want to kill you? That I didn't want to take your blood? That my very inclinations to who I am, dominate my very existence? I need blood to live Ana; my very survival depends on my ability to feed on blood—Human blood, and yet here you stand, alive and relatively unharmed." He threw up his arms and began pacing around the room. "Do you not think that every time you were close to me, every time now, that you are close to me, that I don't have to make a choice? That I don't have to quell my instincts to survive? It is a choice Ana, and I'm pretty sure that Nathanial will not die if he doesn't produce a child, and yet you continue to defend him, to let him off the hook; he betrayed you Ana—again. How many more times is it going to take before you realize just how flawed he is?" He stared at me, his eyes pulsing; small embers began to appear in their depths.

"You're flawed too Stephen," I whispered, not looking at him. "I would defend you still, no matter what you've done," I said, fingering the gift box. He sighed.

"And that's another thing, Ana!" His voice began to rise. "I can't for the life of me understand why, after numerous times, after so many,

many times, why you still refuse to fight me for you life. Even after my own brother tells you to fight, to kill me if you have to; my own brother! Still, that night in my apartment, when you came back, when Liam pulled us away, the night in the alley, the overlook…still I could see that you weren't going to fight me and I was pretty sure that on several of those occasions—you might have been able to win!" He laughed bitterly. "I don't know why you continue to trust me; I could kill you now and yet here we are, together—you chose to let me take you here!" He seemed to be yelling about things he'd been holding in for a while, so I just sat there, not wanting to interrupt. He stopped talking, but he was looking at me, his eyebrows raised. "Well?" he said, putting his hands behind his head. Again, odd as it seemed, I thought about Patric and I couldn't help but notice some of the similarities in Stephen's line of thinking and what Patric had always thought about me—neither of them understood, but I had guessed that in the end, Patric came to realize that he didn't have to understand me, he just had to know that I believed he could be better, that he could, that he *would* make a different choice in the end. Stephen sighed, still waiting for me to answer. I was sure now in my response, as sure as I had been that night when the fire came to Liam's house and as sure as I was on the overlook, but I was also sure that it no longer mattered.

"I love you Stephen, very much. You are my best friend and I love you; different than what I felt for Patric, and in a different and perhaps more connected way, than I love Nathanial. I would never fight you for my life; I would never risk killing you, and I'm sorry that you can't understand that, that you don't understand *me* or perhaps even yourself, but there it is. I might as well be honest, here at the very end of so many things; I should be honest, not only with you, but with myself." I went over to my dresser and pulled out a small notebook. I tore a single sheet of paper out and scribbled a note, folded the sheet in half and slid it under the ribbon to the box that held the quilt. "Now, I need to do one more thing before we go," I said, meeting his gaze. His eyes were so dark, not a single inkling of the sea churned in their depths. He looked stunned. "I need you to take me to Nathanial's; I need to return this to him." My voice sounded shaky. "I don't need to see him—to see them; I'll just leave it on the porch…" I was whispering now.

"Are you sure?" he asked, his eyes on my face.

"Yes," I said, heaving my pack and purse over my shoulders. I put my hand on his shoulder, took one last look around the room and nodded at him. He clenched his jaw and whisked us away to Nathanial's cabin.

It was dark, and there were only a few lights on, but his scent hit me as soon as we landed in the yard. I wanted to scream; my heart felt as though it was being ripped from my chest. I knew that sometimes Bonders and their Bonds chose to live different and separate lives, to take other lovers and have families, but they were still a part of each other, still Bound by the sharing of their blood, still one. Something was different with me, with this situation. My mind was disconnecting from Nathanial and so was my heart. What had occurred, having to watch him as he desired another woman, having to see them together, knowing that she could give him what I never could; I had to break the Bond. I had to let him go. Stephen was listening to my thoughts and I could see his jaw clench even tighter, pulling his usually full lips into a thin, straight line. I saw Zanuck and Sheeba on the porch and they began howling as I approached. I turned to look at Stephen and he waved his hand, making them fall quiet. I placed the box with my note on the rocking chair, but I couldn't move away. I saw through the window, Nathanial on the couch, his head in his hands. My chest heaved and I started to raise my hand to knock.

"Ana." Stephen was there, lowering my arm. I nodded at him and glanced once more through the window. Nathanial looked up and I thought that our eyes met. He stood and I turned to Stephen. He grabbed my arm and pulled me once again into nothingness.

I spent the rest of the night in my room, not wanting to talk about anything, not wanting to feel anything and I really didn't want Stephen to play counselor; we no longer had that relationship. I didn't even know if he was still in the house. I was scheduled to move out soon and I hoped that I would be able to see him before I left, just to say goodbye. All my crying had made me thirsty, so I slowly raised myself off the bed and padded down the hall to the kitchen. Stephen's door was closed, but I could see the dim glow of a light under the crack at the bottom of the floor and I thought I could hear quite strumming of the guitar. I opened the refrigerator and pulled out a ginger ale and reached into the cupboard for a glass; as I strained my neck to get a hold of the cup—my head split open. I hit the floor pulling the entire shelf down with me in a loud crash of breaking stone and glass. I felt blood begin to pour from the back of my head and I vomited, heaving into the ground. My body writhed and liquid heat dripped down my shoulders, dark and red and on fire. I screamed, but I choked as more vomit filled my mouth. I heard someone come running into the kitchen.

"ANA!" Stephen screamed as he knelt down beside me. I couldn't look at him. "JESUS!" he shouted and I heard him fumbling for something. "You need to get here, now! She's dying, something's wrong! Now!" His voice sounded frantic, but I didn't have time to process who he was speaking to, the back of my neck split open, I was sure and more blood and fire began to ooze from my flesh. I tried to scream, but there was too much liquid in my mouth. It was salty and metallic, like someone had poured molten rust into my throat. I gurgled and spit, looking to see large chucks of dark red, splatter onto the floor. "CHRIST!" Stephen shouted. I felt a sudden blast of cold air and someone was carrying me. They laid me down on the floor near the fire, and I felt them move my head. I gasped at the pain.

"It's her mark," someone spoke, their voice sounded distant and it echoed in my ears. "Part of it is being absorbed back into her skin, look!" The voice spoke again; it sounded familiar. Liam.

"Is it going to kill her Liam?" Stephen shouted; it was Liam that he'd called. I groaned and turned my head to throw up.

"I don't know Stephen. I've never seen anything like this before, with a Bond, I mean." Liam reached to push my hair back and I felt something cool move over my face.

"Can you do anything? There's so much blood… Jesus Christ, she's losing so much blood." Stephen was bending over me now; I could smell him, his fragrance, the sea, the salt air, the sand. I tried to focus on it, to gather it into myself, to let it make whatever passing I may have coming, gentler. I sighed and took a deep breath in, either the pain seemed to be diminishing or I was just getting closer to dying. I didn't care, as long as I could keep the scent of him close to me. I found that I could open my eyes and I saw the brilliant blue of the ocean staring back at me. No longer were there the dark hollows that had been occupying Stephen's face for so long, now the seas swam before me, the tides crashing onto the shore, a bright horizon waiting in the distance. I couldn't look away; I didn't want to look away. My body heaved again and a tight pain shot through the back of my neck. I screamed. Another tremor of pain rocketed my body in the air and then slowly, I sank back into the floor—no longer feeling the pounding of my heart in my chest; it was broken, dead and I was grateful.

"What supplies do you have here?" Liam asked. "Do you have anything stored?" What was he talking about? I had to close my eyes; I was so tired and my body was mush, liquid… it was nothing.

"I have some, yeah, but I have no idea what blood type she is." I heard Stephen respond, his tone urgent.

"Well check!" Liam scolded him. "I'll call Carmen, and see what we have just in case."

"Liam," Stephen's voice was quiet. "Her taste, her scent…" he was whispering.

"I'm right here Stephen. I'm not going to let you lose control." Liam sounded stern, but comforting. I however, was beginning to feel slightly nervous, even in my exhaustion. What was going on? "Carmen? Please stay on the phone, we have a situation with Ana and I may need you." Liam had called Carmen. I felt Stephen bend his face close mine and wipe some blood off from my shoulder.

"No Stephen, it has to be a fresh blood supply. That's been out in the air and you won't be able to get an accurate read on her blood type," Liam instructed. I heard Stephen take a deep breath and then move his mouth to my ear.

"You won't feel anything Ana, I promise," he whispered. "I need to just get a little bit of blood from you, I'll take it from your wrist, alright?" He sounded like he was pleading with me, like I would be angry with him or something. I tried to nod, but my head felt disconnected from my body. I felt him take my right wrist, clearly he didn't want to make another scar over the one I had from Nathanial. His tongue began washing back and forth over the skin and immediately my arm began to cool and go numb. I wondered why Patric hadn't done it like this; it probably would've hurt a bit less. Stephen snorted in disgust and I heard him murmur under his breath, something to the effect that Patric had no idea what he was doing.

"Could you please hurry!" I heard Liam call to Stephen. "She's still bleeding out and we don't have time for your little internal dialogues." I saw Stephen grimace and lower his mouth to my wrist. His lips moved over my skin as if he were gently kissing me, then I felt pressure and a tugging sensation; not unpleasant, and somewhat familiar. Stephen's eyes were closed and I could hear that his breathing had picked up and color rose high in his cheeks. He opened his eyes and they were burning. Bright orange flames had ignited and they were leaping and pulsing, their heat starting to warm my face. A low, deep growl emitted from his chest and I felt him begin to tug harder and deeper into my vein. "Stephen, that's enough!" Liam came and put his face to Stephen's cheek, trying to gently pry his mouth from the wound. "We need to get her some blood, or she's going to die. Stop now, what blood type is she?" Liam's voice was very dark, and very hypnotic. Stephen moaned, his lips lingering on my skin. "Stephen!" Liam cut through the tension and he pulled his mouth away from me and I saw him lick his lips, they were dark red and swollen.

"AB negative," he said, his eyes not leaving my face.

"Do you have AB negative?" Liam asked. He was pulling Stephen to his feet, trying to snap him out of his bloodlust.

"I...I don't know." Stephen was moving back toward me, but Liam was holding his shoulders.

"Go and have a look then, won't you?" he ordered, his eyes locking onto to Stephen's and I saw Stephen nod mechanically, almost not of his own volition. "Carmen, do we have any AB negative on hand, check the safe please." Liam spoke back into the phone. It was exhausting trying to follow everything that was going on; I was just so tired. I heard Stephen come back into the room.

"Here...here this is AB neg." He tossed something to Liam and I tried to open my eyes. Liam bent over me, and I could see the mouthpiece for his phone around his ear. He was hooking up a tube to a plastic bag. I closed my eyes again, things were getting harder and harder to see, their faces seemed dimmed. "Hang on Ana, just hang on!" Liam's voice sounded so sad; I could hang on. I may not ever fight Stephen for my life, but I would hang on if Liam asked me to. Something sharp was jabbed into the crook of my arm and I gasped at the suddenness of the motion. "Sorry," Liam said, his tone apologetic.

"What now?" I heard Stephen ask. I was wondering that myself.

"We wait," Liam said, moving to stand up. "It shouldn't take very long and I think she'll only need one bag." I heard his footsteps move away from me. "No, Carmen, you don't need to come. I think she's going to be all right; yes, I promise. I will call you in a few hours, love." I smiled to myself. I was glad that Liam had taken my advice about being more affectionate with Carmen. It was nice to hear. I heard Liam laugh softly and I could feel the weakness in my bones begin to dissipate.

"Do we have to leave her on the floor?" Stephen asked, his voice sounded more distant than Liam's and I wondered if he was intentionally keeping space between us.

"Well, I can only pick her up if you can carry the IV, Stephen," Liam said sarcastically. I heard Stephen sigh. Liam stooped to slide his hands underneath my body, lifting me close to his chest. I watched as Stephen's eyes became wide, and he looked like he was holding his breath. He carried the IV and the bag of blood down the hallway, Liam going to the first open room, Stephen's room. He laid me on the bed and I wished I'd been strong enough to look around. I'd not seen the inside of this space since we arrived; he always kept the door shut. I turned my head, opening my eyes to look at him.

"So this is what it takes for a woman to get into your bed," I whispered, smiling at him. "Now I see why you keep the door closed." I croaked, my throat was so dry.

"Yes Ana, that's why I keep my door shut, because I like to have half dead and bloody women in my bed; it's such a turn on," he mocked me, but his face was tight and sadness creased across his beautifully

311

stunning eyes. Suddenly I was worried about all the blood in the house, in the kitchen and the living room; it was everywhere.

"That's what older, more experienced brothers are for Ana." Liam smiled down at me, but then he turned to Stephen. "The mess is nothing, consider it already gone," he said soothingly.

"I broke all of your glasses, even the ones for scotch," I said, thinking about how the entire shelf had come crashing down when I fell. Stephen had some really nice and expensive glassware. Stephen laughed and brushed his waves of hair from his eyes.

"Yes, well, I drink too much anyway. Not a huge loss." He smiled at me, but his eyes were serious and intent upon my face.

"Rest, Ana, you need to rest. We'll be back in to check on you in a few hours," Liam said, turning toward the door. I nodded, feeling very, very sleepy. I heard the door shut and that's the last thing I remember.

Stephen

I followed my brother back down the hallway and watched as he waved his hand, clearing the clots of blood and vomit from the wood floors. I sighed, wishing that I could help, but I was battling with my own desires to feed more upon Ana. It was horrible, but that was the truth. Her blood was like nothing I have ever experienced before and I was starting to understand just what the impetus behind both Patric

312

and Devon's obsessions had been. She was extraordinary in every way. I felt so nourished, so powerful; I felt high. Liam snorted and stood up, his face pulled into a frown.

"Am I right to worry about keeping her here with you Stephen?" Liam walked into the kitchen and I knew he was expecting me to follow.

"She's moving out," I said, flatly, thinking that now, letting her leave was going to be even more difficult.

"Yes, but she's only moving to Dublin, no?" He was picking up shards of glass and removing the last traces of blood from the counter and the floor. I nodded and handed him the wastebasket. "So you could easily find her," he said, dusting off his pants and throwing pieces of broken plates into the trash. I knew what he was getting at; he was expecting me to stalk her now, to make her my prey. He was right. "Were you able to keep your venom out of her bloodstream Stephen?" Liam was staring at me. "Because even a little bit…" I waved my hand, cutting him off.

"She's fine," I said, and she was fine; she hadn't taken any of my blood so the transformation could never happen. I heard Liam sigh.

"I don't think she's safe anymore with you Stephen. Your natural instincts are so close to the surface these days and while I know you would never mean to harm her, you might not be able to help yourself," Liam said, walking back out to the living room. It was at that moment when everything in my entire existence became clear, crystallized. That is how I was different from Nathanial, that is how I would show Ana that it *was* indeed about choice; that no matter what your inherent natural tendencies were to be, that if you were strong

313

enough and if you were lucky to love someone enough, you could override them—all of them. Nathanial had his opportunity to buck nature, to override what he was destined to do; he had the love of Ana and he chose to betray that gift for what he thought he needed; he did it time and time again and now he'd lost. He lost everything and I wouldn't want to be there when that reality came crashing down upon his heart; it was likely to destroy him. Emotion surged within my body and it was separate from the power I'd felt from Ana's blood; this was my own strength now, my own desire to fix her, to heal her, to be whatever she needed, even if that meant she needed to be alone.

"Ana will be fine, Liam," I said, walking to face my brother. "I swear to you, on my very existence in this world, as wretched as that may now be to you, I swear, I will not harm her." My voice was strong and my mind felt clear for the first time in so many months. Liam studied me, hard. I knew he was seeing into my mind, listening to what was in my heart. He nodded.

"Stephen, no matter what you do, no matter what you've done, your existence will never be wretched to me. You are my brother, my family and I love you. All I have ever wanted was for you to heal, to be happy—as happy as our kind can be. You will always have my guidance, my support and my love. I may not always agree with your decisions, but I will never invalidate our relationship because of them. However, if you hurt Ana, if you harm her in any way, physically, emotionally... consider our relationship to be forever altered." His eyes met mine and I smiled at him.

"Thank you Liam, for everything. You have my promise," I said walking to embrace him, something that we had not done since we were children. He kissed my cheek and patted my back.

"Call us and let us know how she's doing, how you're doing Stephen." Liam pulled back from me, his face serious. "What's happened to her, what's occurred between she and Nathanial, it's nothing to take lightly; the severing of a Bond has the potential to destroy individuals, even ones as resilient as Ana. I'm also not entirely sure that Nathanial will not eventually come to his senses, see his terrible mistake. I just don't want you to invest in something that is so fragile, so tenuous and for you to be disappointed." He searched my face. "I have no idea how this will affect Ana, how it will affect her ability to love, to be loved; he might have just managed to take that away from her—I don't know." My brother looked tearful and I could see just how much he loved Ana, how much she'd come to mean to him. I grasped his shoulders, a slight surge of hate beginning to surface at the mention of Nathanial.

"I know this Liam and I will give Ana whatever space she needs; I'm not in any hurry this time."

"Won't you consider coming back Stephen? Things are difficult right now, but we think that we can protect ourselves enough to start over somewhere else." I pulled back to look at his face. Worry flooding out the hatred.

"Liam, are you and Carmen in danger? Is the coven in danger?" I asked, my tone harsh. Liam sighed and stepped away from my hold.

"We don't know. Word of us assisting the Humans at the camp has spread and many of our brethren are not pleased with our choice, regardless of the treaties that were signed." He frowned. "We're working on making our case to as many covens that will listen, but it's a complicated ordeal. Most of the Vampires are fighting smaller battles and don't have the time or the luxury to listen to individuals they consider traitors." I didn't like what I was hearing.

"You could come here," I said, not quite sure why I was hesitant to return to my brother's coven. "I have many who will and can protect you Liam, Carmen and Lucie too," I said. Did I feel too embedded in the dark rituals that I was now accustomed? Did I like this side of myself too much to return to what I was sure would be a more diplomatic existence? Liam laughed.

"You've never really had the chance to explore much have you?" he said smiling. "You were always quite content to follow me around everywhere, staying by my side, doing what I asked of you. Perhaps you need a bit of a rebellion, a bit of an indulgence into the underground side of our species?" he said, still grinning. "Of course being five centuries old is a bit late to be experiencing your teenage years all over again, but…you were always more of an adult even when you were a child Stephen." He patted my face. "Just be careful not to get over zealous, what seems pleasurable at the time, usually just ends up being a very superficial, and cheap high." He chuckled. "Call us at the end of the week, please." I nodded and with that, he left me standing alone in the middle of the room.

Stephen asked me to delay my moving until the color returned fully to my face. After three weeks, I already thought that I looked better, but I wasn't in the mood to argue with him. I was returning from Dunne's Stores with some new bedding for Stephen. When Liam had laid me on his bed, I was still bleeding from my neck and my blood had gotten all over his very nice satin comforter and pillows. I also purchased some more gin glasses and dishes; it was the very least I could do. Surprisingly, I was actually feeling ok. I wasn't crying anymore and after Stephen explained what had happened to my mark, to Nathanial's symbol; after he'd told me that Nathanial's metal was now no longer a part of my Bond, I had felt lighter. I was glad that I still had Patric's stone and now his mark and mine were fully entwined. A less elaborate and smaller tattoo now adorned my neck, but it was still beautiful, and I was happy to have at least one part of Nathanial still with me, represented via Patric, even if he was no longer represented in my flesh.

I came home and set to putting Stephen's new décor in his room. I figured he wouldn't mind me going into his private space if it was to give him a gift. I had gotten him a satin duvet set the color of deep sea-blue. I found some interesting coordinating throw pillows in a lighter shade of blue with green swirls and waves woven across the fabric. I stood back to admire my selection.

"What's all this?" I heard a quiet voice from behind and I jumped. "Sorry." Stephen laughed and came into his room, throwing his keys on the dresser. He moved to look at the bed.

"Um, well, I felt bad that I had ruined your very nice bedding, so I thought I would get you something new. Is the color alright; I mean is it masculine enough?" Suddenly I worried that the color choice might not be to his liking. I bought it because it reminded me of his eyes, but maybe that was more to my taste than to his.

"Hmmm, masculine enough? Well, I don't know, you're a woman, if you saw this color in my room would you think it masculine enough?" He smirked at me. I frowned, but nodded. He laughed again and went over to sit on the bed. "It's really nice Ana, but you didn't have to do this." He reclined back, folding his hands on his stomach.

"Are you just getting home?" I checked my watch and saw that it was two in the afternoon. Had he been out all night?

"Hmmm…" he murmured, closing his eyes. "I played a double set at the club, then…went out for a bit." He sat up to look at me. I knew what he meant.

"Oh," I said, feeling a bit strange and awkward; I gathered up my shopping bags. "I got you some glasses too," I said quietly. "Cillian seems put out that he's had to drink his scotch out of a coffee mug." I moved toward the door.

"Cillian is a prat and he can drink out of whatever goddamned glass I give him," Stephen said, his tone joking. "Where are you going?" he asked, pulling himself up to look at me.

318

"I'm going over to the apartment; I want to get some of my clothes hung up and I need to buy some of my own bedding and dishware." I stepped out into the hallway, suddenly needing to leave his presence. He was sitting upright now, his face intent.

"Hmm… I wanted to know if you were interested in going out tonight?" he asked, his eyes flashing. I frowned at him.

"What do you mean? Going out where?" I was pretty sure that I wasn't going to be partial to any bizarre activity that Stephen and his cohort were usually up to during the evening hours. He chuckled.

"Nothing that you can't handle, but nothing too bizarre. It is at a club though." He rubbed his face.

"What kind of club?" My tone was wary. He sighed.

"A very tasteful S & M club run by Eamonn." He laughed, his eyes shinning."

"Those aren't words that usually go together Stephen." I was still frowning. He shrugged.

"I'm playing for a friend, a favor, and I thought you might like to get out in the city for an evening." He was lying on his side, tracing his hands along the satin duvet, not looking at me. It was an odd gesture considering his behavior towards me as of late, but I truly appreciated his effort.

"Do I have to wear anything particular?" I asked, hoping he knew what I meant. I hadn't bothered to bring the costume I'd bought for my birthday party.

319

"Yes, I saw that hanging in your closet back in Idaho. Very interesting and I wished I could have been around to see you in it." He laughed and looked up at me, his eyes shining. I sighed. "No, nothing special. What you're wearing is nice," he said. I looked down at my gray pullover and muddy jeans—I was sure that my current attire wouldn't be appropriate.

"Where's the club? Can I meet you there from the apartment?" I asked, I still hadn't told Stephen where I was moving; I was trying my hardest to keep my distance from him. Hearing my thoughts, he sat up, folding his hands in his lap.

"I know," he said quietly. "That's my fault. My attitude towards you over these last months has been less then deserving of your attention and your friendship Ana. I understand why you feel you need to put space between us...but I really wish you wouldn't," he whispered, his voice soft and deep. God, I missed him. I pursed my lips.

"I'm down in Temple Bar," I said, turning to walk down the hall. "I have a loft over a French Patisserie, right down from Barnacles Hostel," I called to him. "You can come and get me tonight." I heard him laugh and I left the house, hoping to find an outfit decent enough to wear to an S & M club, and actually, I was pretty relieved to get out for a bit. I needed to be out of my own headspace; I was having panic attacks daily now, mostly when I thought about Nathanial and the baby he was having. When I realized that he was no longer mine and I was no longer his, the anxiety would hit and I would have to stop everything I was doing and just breathe. Stephen had witnessed a few of my episodes and he always looked angry, not at me I guessed, but at Nathanial, at what he'd done. I was really ready to rebuild, to establish my own

320

foundations without him now. I had to. I wasn't giving myself a choice. There was no one to turn to; no Noni, no Alec, no Kai, no Patric, no Nathanial, possibly no Stephen, it had to be just me—alone.

Stephen

I was standing in the street waiting for her. It had stopped raining and I put my guitar down and leaned against the wall of the building, listening to music and parties now beginning to gather momentum. Temple Bar was always loud, always crowded with tourists and backpackers, drunks and musicians; it wasn't the most ideal place to have an apartment if you were looking for peace and quiet, but I had guessed that that was the last thing Ana was looking for these days— she seemed to need distraction. She was putting up a brave front, but I had caught her a few times in the kitchen, shaking, her fingers tracing along the metals in her neck. There was something else, something just beneath the surface as well that she was also experiencing; determination perhaps, maybe a bit of revenge? It was hard to decipher. I heard a door open and I watched her emerge from the awning. My eyes widened. She was wearing tight jeans with high-heeled boots tucked into the legs, accentuating the lines of her hips and the muscles in her thighs. Her hair was pulled up into a messy bun, exposing her long neck and the amulet that hung solidly around her throat. Her shoulders were bare and the blouse she was wearing flowed loosely around her chest and skimming to her waist. She was stunning. Just for a moment, I wished I hadn't made any promises to my brother about not trying to take her blood; it was moments like these that made me wish I had less of a conscience.

"Hey," she said, walking up to me, her gate strong and confident. I tried not to gawk at her.

"Hey. Ready?" I asked picking up my guitar. She nodded and we began weaving our way through the gathering crowd. The club was down a narrow side street off of O'Connell Street. It would take us a few minutes. We were quiet as we strode down the street together and I allowed myself to sneak a few looks at her from the corner of my eye. She seemed to be in good spirits.

"What are you playing tonight?" she asked, turning her face to me. "Stuff that I've heard?"

"Some, and some new material." I grinned at her.

"Cool," she replied. We walked the rest of the way in silence until we came to the entrance to the club. Ana looked cautiously around, and I had to admit, it was a bit of a sketchy location and yet the alley itself was familiar to me for some reason. I glanced at Ana and could see her eyes grow wide. I could see what she was remembering why the location was familiar to her as well. We were standing in a very similar place to when the two of us had been attacked, when I had attacked her, when she had saved my life. We stared at each other, both of us remembering. I reached past her shoulder, my eyes never leaving her face and knocked on the door.

"Hey man!" Cillian answered, heaving aside the metal lock. "Hey ya came Ana! dat's awesome." He threw opened the door and immediately wrapped his arm around Ana's shoulder. "We're going to have so much fun. Dis bastard is an amazing display of sexual energy and he's not too bad at playing da guitar eider." Cillian winked at me and I saw Ana shake her head. Perhaps this wasn't the best of ideas.

The club was already quite full and I scanned the room wondering if the scene was going to be too much for Ana. There were people dressed both casual like her, but there were also quite a few women who were dressed in extreme bondage attire, carrying whips and chains. I ran my fingers through my hair as I noticed there had been some changes in the décor since I'd been here last month. Adorning the walls were large hooks with handcuffs and scarves hanging down and people were in the process of tying each other up, laughing and drinking; no sex was allowed out on the main floor, but this was definitely the place to get in the mood.

"Hey man, you're on in like ten!" Cillian motioned toward the stage and I nodded; his arm was still around Ana. I pulled her away from him and whispered in her ear.

"Are you going to be alright if I leave you?" I knew that Cillian would never touch her; he wasn't like Devon, but his jovial nature and his love for everything hypersexual had a tendency to be overwhelming sometimes—even for me. Ana laughed and nodded, her brown eyes deep and penetrating.

"Yeah, I think I can handle him," she said, moving away from me and I sensed that being so close to me was difficult for her; there were feelings there, I could sense them running like swift currents beneath the surface of her mind and her body; she was trying to fight against their tides. "Have fun!" She turned back to Cillian who was holding out his arms, waiting to welcome her back. I shot him a look and turned to get my amp set up. I was playing with three other guys, a bassist, a drummer and another guitarist. They had a very strong sound, dark and somewhat violent, with very sexual lyrics and I was wondering how Ana would respond. She was used to my more acoustic, gentle rhythms; this was a different side that she hadn't experienced. I looked out into the crowd and noticed that Cillian had Ana at one of the round couches, sitting with various members of my brethren and some very scantily clad Human women. I hoped she would be ok. It took us about twenty minutes to set up, but eventually, we were ready. Everyone stood as I stepped in front of the microphone and introduced myself, apologizing that the band's usual lead singer was indisposed at the moment. The crowd laughed, understanding my innuendo and we started into our first set.

I noticed that almost immediately, Cillian pulled Ana up to dance and she caught my eye, shrugging. I was pretty sure that Ana could blow him to smithereens if she felt the need. She looked amazing out there, comfortable, dare I say happy even. I wondered what Nathanial was experiencing, if he was ready to be a father, if he missed her, missed her scent, her smile, the way she moved. I hoped he did. We finished the first set and we let the DJ continue with the mood we'd established. I put down my guitar and walked through the crowd toward Cillian.

"May I cut in?" I asked, but it really wasn't a question. He had his hand around her waist and I had to fight the growl that was threatening to erupt. He groaned, but pulled away.

"As soon as yer back on stage, she's back with me!" He laughed, winking at Ana. I moved to take his place, pulling her close to me, wondering if she would be comfortable with me touching her again, after so much time had passed. She wrapped her arms around my neck and smiled at me. We moved together, our bodies finding their natural rhythms; it felt amazing.

"Interesting new sound you've got there," she said, smirking at me. "Doing a little musical experimentation are we?" She laughed. I pulled her closer still, not letting any space between our bodies—my desire to feel her skin, her hips against mine; it was overwhelming. I couldn't believe that we'd never made love. I had stopped us that first time; god, I was stupid. I pressed closer to her, pushing her groin into me, moving with the beat of the music.

"You didn't like it?" I murmured in her ear. "I think I've heard that type of music coming quite loudly from your room at times, Mademoiselle." I breathed gently into her ear. I was getting too amped up, being this close to her again. I missed her so much.

"Hmmm; yes I suppose you're right." She pressed her face to the side of my cheek. I felt myself wanting to thrust against her, even through my jeans, the very motion of being so close was igniting a very deep arousal and the pulsing and throbbing music only served to accentuate my desires. I pulled my face back to look into her eyes.

"How are you, Ana?" I asked. Christ, my emotions were all over the place. I wanted her to talk to me again; I wanted us to be able to go back, go back to those nights when she would paint or I would play the guitar and I would sit and watch her, letting myself fall in love for the first time since Laura, since I'd forgotten myself and since I'd asked for my life to be forfeit. I didn't care about children, and I didn't care that Ana couldn't have a baby; loving Ana meant loving everything that she was, it meant honoring all of the horrors and traumas that she'd experienced. It meant loving her without conditions, without wanting her to be someone else—it meant letting her experience all of the redemption and grace that she allowed for all of us; it meant giving all of that back to her a thousand times. It meant doing what Nathanial could not, what he chose not to do. I heard Ana sigh and I remembered that I had asked her a question.

"Yeah, I'm good. I mean, some days are worse than others, but it's a grieving process I think. Unfortunately, it's running side-by-side to me grieving about Noni, so I get pretty overwhelmed at times…" she trailed off, smiling at me. "This club is interesting. Spend a lot of time here do you?" she purred in my ear, laughing.

"Nah; it's not as fun if you don't have someone to participate with you," I said, teasing her.

"I don't know Stephen, from the looks of the table you have me at, there are several women who I am sure would be more than excited to experiment with you!" She laughed and looked back toward Cillian who was now allowing himself to be fully straddled by one of his female escorts. "Take your pick," She said pulling away from me. I moved closer to her and let my hands wind tightly around her waist.

"You mean I get a choice?" I asked, staring at her.

"I would say so, except perhaps for the one giving the lap dance at the moment; Cillian doesn't seem to be one for sharing." She grinned at me and I felt that undercurrent of emotion in her that I had detected earlier; the determination was there, but also it now seemed, a bit of daring and slight abandonment of her inhibitions. Interesting. I was about to suggest something to her, when someone tapped me on the shoulder.

"We're on in five, man." My bassist moved back toward the stage. Ana dropped her hands from my chest and pulled away. I groaned, my body not wanting to part with her.

"Hey, are you not going to do any of your old stuff, like the acoustic songs?" she asked frowning. "Not the right crowd I guess…" she said eyeing the people who had begun to gather on the dance floor. I held her hand in mine and glanced at her, still wondering what she was feeling, where this new wave of emotion would lead her. I had my hopes.

"Something just for you. How about that?" I said, turning to look at the stage.

"Thanks," she said quietly and I saw Cillian get up from his lap dance and move toward us. I rolled my eyes.

"I think you have an admirer," I said, nodding toward Cillian.

"Great, cause we've seen how well that's worked out for me in the past," she mocked. Cillian came and linked his arm through hers, grinning madly at me.

"Go do yer ting mate; she's well cared for, I promise ya!" Cillian called to me as I left them standing together on the dance floor.

We finished our last set and I was looking forward to getting a drink and joining the table. Ana seemed to be in an intense discussion with one of the women and I saw the girl wipe her eyes on a napkin. I laughed. Ana was the only person that I had ever met in over five hundred years who could meet someone once and have them so emotional about their life and feeling so empowered to change whatever they didn't like, that I was in awe of her. I grabbed my scotch and slid into the booth across from Ana. Cillian was laughing loudly with Eamonn and I sipped my drink, content to watch Ana and her new friend. She finally caught my eye and I motioned for her to follow me out from the booth.

"Would you like a tour?" I said, taking her hand as she came to meet me by the bar.

"Of this place?" She looked wary and I laughed at her expression.

"Don't you trust me?" I said, pulling her into the crowd and to the back of the club.

"I didn't realize that getting a tour brought up issues of trust," she said, still eyeing me. I shrugged, knowing that I might be crossing a few lines. I stamped my thumb on a digital pad and opened a side door and led her into a dark stairway. "Special privileges, Stephen?" She was staring at me with a smirk on her face. I shrugged.

"Something like that," I said, pulling her down the corridor, hoping there would be at least one room free. I wanted some quiet. "This is the hallway," I mocked, waving my hand at the black velvet walls. She laughed. I noticed that several rooms were occupied, but the suite at the end of the hall was open. I pressed my thumb to another pad and the door clicked open. She looked at me as I held it for her. She walked through and I shut and locked it behind us.

Chapter Fourteen

Ana

It was pitch black, I couldn't see anything and I could feel panic begin to rise and my body start to tense.

"Relax Ana," Stephen whispered behind me. "I just need to find the light." Suddenly a dim glow began to filter into the room and I was able to make out shapes and shadows on the wall. It looked as if we had entered into someone's apartment, someone's very posh apartment.

"Does someone live here?" I asked, surveying the space. There was a large bar set back from the main room and a fireplace, a huge black leather sofa and chair and deep plush carpeting that looked like it was probably made from the softest fabric on earth.

"No," Stephen said, moving from behind me, the ice in his glass clinking as it settled. "It's more for...entertaining," he said, winking at me. He turned on the stereo and the music from the club began filtering into the room.

"Do you rent it out or something?" I asked, beginning to understand. He smiled.

"Yeah, by the hour or the night." He moved to the sofa and motioned for me to join him. He waved his hand the fireplace ignited.

"But you have...what, like special access or something, courtesy of Eamonn?" Eamonn owned this club and several others in the Dublin area. Stephen looked at me, his eyes deep and clear; they saw everything.

"Yes, the entire cohort has—special privileges. I just wanted some place a bit quieter for the moment," he said, sipping his drink. "Do you want anything?" he asked, gesturing toward the bar.

"I can get it." I stood and walked across the room. There were only expensive looking bottles of wine, so I chose a white Pinot and began hunting for the wine opener. I pulled open a tiny black drawer.

"Holy shit!" I said, laughing in my amazement.

"What?" Stephen stood, clearly alarmed by my expletive.

"There's like a ton of sex toys in here, like a whole bunch!" I said, pulling out what looked like a bondage scarf, but the material felt odd to me. Stephen laughed and walked to join me at the bar. "This is an S & M room!" I said, holding the scarf.

"You're just now figuring that out? That Ph.D. is really coming in handy," he scoffed, leaning over the counter to grab the scarf. I stuck my tongue out at him.

"Have you always been into this stuff; like when I met you down in West Papua, were you doing this then?" I asked, curious. Stephen always seemed so shy, when he wasn't in attack mode, and I was having a hard time getting my head around seeing him tying someone up. He laughed.

"I've been experimenting for a while now. When you met me I was just getting into a few things, mainly from hanging out with Devon, but it

331

was just basic stuff." I eyed him and immediately my brain conjured the image of Stephen on the couch with that woman, she was bleeding, handcuffed and they were having sex. I laughed to myself. I was way ahead of him on that front, sans the handcuffing, thanks to my stupidity and Patric's master manipulative skills. Stephen came around to stand next to me, taking the scarf from my hands and running it between his fingers.

"Hmmm, that's true Ana, I had forgotten about your little donation, but you shouldn't consider yourself stupid. You were hurting and I know you did feel something for Patric and he for you, very deeply, I might add." Stephen continued to play with the scarf, but he was watching me. I sighed.

"Why does that feel funny? Is it some kind of special fabric or something?" I thought about the scarf that Nathanial had kept in his bedside table, the black silk one and this didn't feel at all like that one.

"My goodness, you've done quite a bit of experimenting haven't you?" Stephen laughed as he saw my memories.

"Do you mind?" I said, sipping my wine. "Some of those things are private." He chuckled.

"Do a better job of burying them then, won't you?" he said, taking my glass and putting in down on the counter. He took my arm and began running the scarf over my skin; it felt like liquid and I looked down to make sure he hadn't poured something on me. He was watching my face. Suddenly, I felt the scarf begin to warm and it heated my skin gently, sending a soothing current of electricity through to my bones.

I gasped and looked at Stephen. His face was stoic. It was a wonderful feeling, soothing and relaxing me; I almost felt like I'd taken some kind of mood altering drug, but a good one. Stephen laughed softly and he continued to move the scarf over my arm and up toward my shoulder. I felt slightly drunk. I was still holding the corkscrew and I had become so relaxed that I hadn't noticed that the tip of my finger was poised directly over the pointed part of the opener. As Stephen began to move the scarf slowly around my neck, my finger slipped and the end of the screw nicked my finger. The damn thing was razor sharp. Immediately, Stephen stopped moving and I could see his jaw clench and his eyes darken.

Stephen

Her scent permeated my every pore and my body heaved with desire. I cursed myself for not feeding before we came tonight. I had been so cautious, making sure that I was always full, never hungry when we were alone together. How had I made such a mistake? I had tried to bury the memory of her taste, how my body had responded to the intake of her blood. How much I needed her; that night in the alley held nothing to the desire I now felt for Ana, for her blood, for her soul; I wanted to take her. That night was just unexpected; it had thrown me off. I had never wanted to kill her, even on the overlook or at my apartment; I had just wanted to be close to her; never would I have ever harmed her, but now, now after I had tasted so much of her, felt her blood inside of me--I was addicted. The things that she made me think about, the things I wanted to do; they were unholy, unsacred and now here we were alone and she was bleeding. I watched her bring her finger to her mouth and suck the blood from the wound and my mouth watered. She stepped away from me and I moved toward her.

"Stephen, seriously, get a grip; it's only a small amount of blood. What's your deal?" she said, her tone commanding and she almost snapped me out of my bloodlust, almost. "Besides, most women bleed every month, I do; you don't go all crazy then do you?" she asked as she moved putting the bar in between us.

"That's different," I said through my teeth.

"Why?" she asked, still sucking on her finger. "What's different, blood is blood right?" She was trying to distract me and I gave her credit; she'd asked a very interesting question.

"Because it is; it's…it's not the same kind of blood," I said, moving around the counter slowly.

"Yes it is!" she said sternly. "It is too the same. It's coming from me, from my body." I sighed and tried to hold my breath, but I was still moving, closing the distance.

"That blood, the blood from your cycle; it's not what we crave. That blood is considered untouchable to us; it has a purpose. It's there only as a means for you to be able to reproduce Ana," I said, now standing just feet from her.

"Oh," she said, lowering her hand to her side. "I guess it doesn't matter for me then really, you know, since I can't…since I can't have children… it really has no purpose then does it?" she asked and she finished the thought in her head; *like me* she spoke to herself. I was aghast and just for a moment I forgot my hunger and my thirst. She held out her hand to me as a small stream of blood trickled down her finger. "Here," she said, looking at me. "I trust you, I know you won't kill me, Stephen. I know it does something to you; it did for Patric...but I know your motives are pure." She laughed and stepped toward me. She *was* feeling daring, I had read her right. I stared at her, my eyebrows raised. I was still thinking about what she'd just thought, about her not having any purpose; unfortunately, having her blood within inches of my mouth was not allowing me to be terribly sympathetic. I checked my self-control. I could do this, if she really wanted me to.

"Ana, are you sure?" I asked, my voice rough, my arousal breaking through my composed façade. She nodded and smiled at me. "Hmmm, perhaps we should sit down." My legs felt a bit weak, but she seemed fine, oddly enough. I followed her over to the couch and we sat staring at each other.

"Honestly Stephen, it's not that big of a deal," she mused, looking at the blood dripping from her finger. "Here." She held out her hand. Clearly she thought her time with Patric had prepared her for what she was offering, but having your blood taken from a half-vampire was a vastly different experience than having it withdrawn by a full vampire and one that was completely and utterly aroused and addicted to your specific taste. I wasn't sure if she was ready for this, if *I* was ready for this. I took a deep breath, not believing what I was about to do.

"Ana, I don't think this is a good idea. You're not prepared; hell, *I'm* not prepared. You don't know what this means for us, what it would mean for me to do this with you, to you. I don't think that you're ready." She frowned at me.

"You did it with that woman in the house. Why am I any different? What's different?" she asked thoughtfully, sitting back from me. I sighed, trying to steady my need.

"Because you *are* different Ana; I didn't love that woman and I was pretty sure she didn't love me." I looked at her.

"You don't want to?" she asked, looking at the ceiling. She seemed frustrated and she also seemed to not be listening to me.

"Is that what I said?" I scolded her and pulled her back toward me. "Believe me Ana, my intentions with you this evening were less than pure and out of anything I could do in my existence, it would be to have that moment with you. To be with you in that way and for you to be with me…" I trailed off as I looked at her face.

"You said no before." She stood up and walked over to the fire. "Not about the blood, but to having sex; you stopped us at Liam's the night of the fire, we were together and you said you couldn't be with me like that. Remember?" She ran her fingers over the flames, letting them ignite her fingertips one at a time. I had forgotten her ability with fire and I was mesmerized watching her command the flames.

"But not because I didn't want you, Ana; that's never been the issue with us. In fact it's been the exact opposite. That night, it was wrong, the timing was wrong, you didn't know about me then, about what I

336

had done and I didn't feel right being so intimate with you...it wasn't right." I watched her play with the fire. She threw the flames back onto the logs and turned to face me, her hands on her hips.

"We have an odd relationship, don't you think?" she said, staring at me, her chin rose. I laughed.

"In what way?" I asked, curious. She shrugged.

"It's like we're attracted to each other—intensely; we love each other even... you're my best friend, we've kissed, we've come close to making love; you've tried to kill me on several occasions, I've saved your ass, but we've never been together, like together- together, you know?" She shrugged again. "Odd," she said moving back to the couch. I hadn't really thought about it like that, but she was right. Also, it was still so startling to her say that she loved me; I was having a hard time processing that knowledge.

"Hmmm...that's true. But in my defense, I asked you to be with me and you turned me down and, and you went back to that two-timing asshole," I said, leaning my head back against the couch. She sighed.

"Technically I did not turn you down Stephen. When Liam told me what you were going through, what you were trying to reconcile; I didn't think that it was the best time for you or me to be making decisions of life and death. I told him to tell you that when you could come to me, having been settled within yourself, having come to be accountable and not vengeful, then we might have a chance to be together, in what way I wasn't sure... but Nathanial knew, he always knew that you might come back, ready to be with me and that I might want to be with you; he knew, maybe that's why he did what he did;

337

maybe he always knew. I don't know…" She pushed herself back against the couch seeming to reconsider what she'd just offered to me. I looked at her and moved myself closer.

"And now Ana? What about now, what if I came to you free of my ghosts, free of my revenge and my guilt? What if I came to you wanting you to be with me, wanting to love you? What if I asked you again to give your life to me, to let me turn you, to let me have you, body and soul? What would you decide then Ana?" I could see her mind, see what she was experiencing. I saw pictures flash, pictures of her Noni, of her best friend Kai, of Alec, of Liam and Carmen, of Lucie, of Patric and Nathanial and finally of me; each one she still held sacred, each one she still loved, still missed. She closed her eyes and I saw her nod, slowly. My heart stopped. I touched her face. "Ana?" I asked her, not believing, not wanting to believe.

"Yes, Stephen, I might reconsider. I don't know how much good I'll be to you; I'm pretty broken, but I love you. However, I can't make any decisions about, about anything permanent right now—not with everything that's happened, it wouldn't be fair to you or to me, but maybe we could try to be together—just as we are now. Maybe, if we took things slow, maybe if I could heal…" she whispered, her eyes imploring, searching. I pulled her violently toward me, pressing my mouth to hers, forcing her lips open, kissing her deeply.

"God, yes, Ana. Of course, of course we can be together; you can have as much time as you need. I've always told you that," I said, my mouth moving quickly against hers. "I want you; I have always wanted you—in the most unholy of ways." She was kissing me back, laughing, her hands on my chest. I couldn't hold her close enough, couldn't feel enough of her body against me. "I promise to love you everyday, for my entire existence Ana. I promise to be everything you need, everything you want; I will prove to you just how much we belong together and I will spend lifetimes showing you what's in my heart; you have all of me," I was murmuring to her, my tongue tracing along her lips, tasting, savoring her. She kissed me forcefully and I pulled her back on the couch so she was lying on top of me, my arms holding her tight. She sighed and moved her head away and I pushed my mouth back to hers, not wanting to stop.

Ana

"One-Two-Three-Four! Come on, again! Your left side is weak!" Stephen called to me. Of course my left side was weak, we'd been going at this stupid boxing combination for over two hours; I was exhausted. I forgot all form and just decided to haul off and deck him in the face, sending his mouth guard flying. Stephen was the most amazing fighter I had ever gone up against and apparently he used to be quite a force of nature in the MMA world, but I could've cared less about that at the moment; he was pissing me off.

"There!" I said, smirking as he looked at me stunned. "Are we done now?" I asked, my hands on my hips. He growled, crouching.

"Not now, for sure!" He lunged at me and sent us both toppling to the mat, rolling so that I was on top of him. He held me close, tossing his mitts to the side and kissing me deeply, the taste of his sweat filling my mouth with his fragrance. I felt my hips begin to move and I pressed myself closer to him, moving my mouth to kiss down his throat. He laughed and pulled my head away. I sighed. Ever since we'd decided to take our time with each other, for me to heal emotionally from Nathanial, for us to try to be together first, before I made any decision about ending my life and being with Stephen; he had been adamant that we not have sex until I felt ready and until I could come to him without bringing the ghost of Nathanial to his bed. That was over two months ago. Stephen was being a perfect gentleman, but it was me who seemed to be having trouble controlling myself around him. Lately, all he had to do was look at me and every bone in my body turned to liquid. I wanted desperately to be with him, to experience him; he was so different from Nathanial. Stephen had a different kind of intensity, which I didn't think was possible, but on those rare occasions when he allowed for us to kiss—his movements, the way he touched me—making love with him might have just killed me.

Liam was the only one who knew that Stephen and I were somewhat together and when he'd heard that we were just *discussing* the matter of my transformation, Liam voiced his concerns. He was under the impression that with so many different types of blood already in my system, that taking Stephen's just might put me over the edge. Liam was concerned that my body might not be able to handle the Change and Stephen could end up killing me, thus our reasoning for being in the gym. Stephen wanted my body to be as strong as possible before he even thought about turning me and I could see that Liam's reservations had planted a seed of doubt in his mind. Both Stephen and Liam were also concerned about the broken Bond between Nathanial and me; none of us knew what that meant physically for me, if the blood he'd given me was still holding it's powers, or if through me severing ties with him, those powers were now lost.

It was odd, but I actually felt relieved to have a chance at a new life, a chance to be with Stephen, even if we were taking things slow, and to be part of a family with Carmen and Lucie; it meant so much to me and even though I was still devastated over losing Nathanial, I knew that I *could* have another choice, that I did have someone who loved me and who I loved deeply, someone who I might be able to build new foundations with; I was always better when I could be a partner to someone and I had spent enough of my life alone, lost and constantly searching. I knew that Noni would tell me not to be concerned with what others thought; if others would make a different choice, if other women might just go off and spend time by themselves, because it didn't matter what other people did or what choices other women made, this was my choice and I had been honest with Stephen. I had told him that I was shattered and that I could never stop loving Nathanial, that he would always be a part of who I was, but that I did love Stephen too, profoundly, and that I thought we could be together if he understood, if he acknowledged that I would need some time…Perhaps that's why he was waiting for us to be together physically; he wanted me to be able to move past my grief over losing Nathanial and Stephen deserved that; I deserved that.

Stephen was looking at me. I was sure he'd just heard everything that I reasoned through; it was nothing he hadn't heard before. I smiled at him and stood up, offering him my hand.

"One more round and then I promise I will draw you the nicest bath you've ever experienced," Stephen said, kissing me gently, but quickly on the mouth.

"Will you join me?" I said, my voice coy as I pulled him close to me, my gloves around his waist. He cleared his throat.

"Not the best of ideas." He smirked and I rolled my eyes, but kissed him on the nose. It never felt odd being affectionate with Stephen, he had always matched my enthusiasm just with his general nature and it was nice to be with someone who didn't mind me hugging on them as much as I did. Not that Nathanial had ever minded; it was just different. Demons and Vampires were different.

As promised, upon returning to his home, Stephen drew me a hot bath with extra bubbles and lit my favorite smelling candles; sea-spray fragrance. He also started dinner for me and I sunk into the water grateful to have the heat to warm my aching muscles. I heard Stephen in the kitchen doing the dishes and clattering pots and pans and I suddenly had a wave of emotion so strong that it knocked the breath out of me. It wasn't sadness exactly, but something deeper, a longing so great and vast that I felt a chasm open in my heart and I gasped. My body felt different, poised for something; my muscles were tense and every nerve ending seemed to be on fire. What was happening? I lifted myself out of the tub and dried myself off. Were we in danger? I heard Stephen come down the hall and I froze, not knowing why. He knocked on the door.

"Ana, ten minutes ok?" he said.

"Um, sure, great." I tried to sound normal and not so frightened and stiff, but he heard through my forced tone.

"Are you alright?" he asked and I saw him begin to turn the handle on the door. Frick, what the hell was wrong with me? The sudden upsurge of emotion was still there, but now it was pulsing strong and making me feel…well, it was making me feel intensely aroused. So much so, that I knew if Stephen opened the door, I might just physically attack him; that was so weird. "Ana, why aren't you answering me?" he said, opening the door slightly.

"I'm fine, Stephen… just, umm finishing up. Sorry. I zoned out there for minute." Frick! I was usually better at lying than this. He opened the door and I pulled the towel around me. I held my breath as he peered into the bathroom. His eyes roamed over my body, looking concerned. "See. I'm good, I swear." Another wave of arousal hit as we stared at each other and I saw his face change. He raised his chin in the air and looked as though he'd caught the scent of something; something he liked. His body went stiff and he came further into the room, walking toward me.

"Ana," he said, his voice low. "What's going on?" Again, his eyes moved over my towel clad body and I tried to bury what I didn't want him to see in my mind. He wanted to wait, he'd asked if we could wait to be together and I didn't want to mess that up for him, he had a plan. What was happening here? I was sexually aggressive, but I could most certainly restrain myself; it was never a problem for me. I saw Stephen raise his eyebrows. Frick! "Ana, is something going on with you?" he asked. I wasn't sure how to answer that. I stepped back from him as diplomatically as I could, not wanting to offend him.

"Um, I'm not sure exactly," I replied, which was true and I felt that I should at least be honest with him. Desire began coursing through my veins and the power it produced was almost painful. I bit the inside of my mouth to keep from gasping out loud.

"Jesus," Stephen whispered. His jaw tight and his nostrils flared.

"What?" I said, whipping my head around. Had he seen something? He shook his head and took a deep breath.

"Ana," he said softly and slowly. "I think...I think you are experiencing some sort of mating cycle." He looked at me, his eyes wide and I thought I saw the faintest hint of a smile appear across his face. What? That didn't make any sense; I wasn't a Bonder and my cycles were so off anyway that I never knew when I was ovulating, even if I had wanted to get pregnant—even if I could get pregnant.

"But you have both Bonder and half-vampire blood in your system Ana; perhaps the combination triggered a mating cycle of sorts in you," he spoke as if asking me the question. I cringed at him; how ironic I thought. Nathanial went and knocked some whore up because of his own desire to mate and now here I was trying desperately not to physically assault Stephen. Holy, frickin, Christ!

"Yeah, but I'm human Stephen, I don't have pronounced mating cycles and it's not like I want to mate with everybody," I said exasperated.

"What do you mean?" Stephen was now standing directly in front of me and he kept moving forward; I was running out of places to go.

"I mean, that...I'm not thinking about just, you know—wanting to jump random men; I...I want to be with you—specifically. At least that's

344

how it feels," I mumbled, feeling utterly embarrassed and extremely confused. "Plus, I can't have kids, so the whole process is sort of lost on me; if that's what my body is doing," I said, moving to the side. Stephen laughed. I glared at him. He held up his hands in surrender.

"I'm sorry Ana, this is no laughing matter, but I have to say that I'm quite intrigued by your—your particular affinity with me; I'm honored." He laughed again, but quickly worked to stifle his outburst. "And I don't think your ability to have children affects your desires to participate in the act of mating, at least not in this context. I mean, you have a cycle every month and that is strictly there to enable you to conceive; your body doesn't know that having sex for you can't lead to the production of children, possibly your situation is the same thing only intensified. It's really ok, Ana." Stephen mirrored my last movement and I was leaning back against the tub, the towel wrapped tightly around my body.

"How am I any different from Nathanial then?" I whispered. Stephen sighed.

"Well for one, as you just said, you seem to be selecting for the person you're already with—" I cut him off.

"Yes, but *you* can have children, maybe that's why I'm not searching to be with anyone else. My body knows that you can reproduce; it just doesn't know that I can't." My voice shook. Stephen's eyes looked suddenly sad and he lowered his head.

"That's just it Ana; I can't have children—no vampire can, at least none that I've known; it's impossible." His voice was so quiet that I had

345

to lean in close to him to hear what he'd just said. That was new information.

"You can't have children?" I asked, slightly shocked. "Are you sure?" I said, trying to process this entire scenario; I was getting slightly overwhelmed. He sighed and leaned against the sink.

"I'm pretty sure," he shook his head and laughed gently, "Otherwise I would have a ton a kids out there and my ass would be hauled in by the Irish Guarda for being a deadbeat dad." He chuckled. I bit my lip. Sometimes I forgot just how many women Stephen had been with; it made me feel slightly intimidated and a bit awkward. He stared at me, his eyes apologetic. "Something happens when we're Changed," he said, running his hands over his face. "I don't know the technical aspects of what actually occurs; I just know that being frozen in time has something to do with it and the influx of venom, apparently that kills our ability to produce sperm," he said, waving his hand. "I don't know." He shook his head again. "Liam was never one to give me the 'afterlife sex talk'; I kinda just went with the flow of things, I've never really thought about it, until now." He lowered his voice and his eyes found mine. I exhaled. I hadn't realized that I had been holding my breath. Stephen's fragrance hit me square in the chest and the current of desire raged. Quickly, I held my breath again and moved toward the door. I could totally handle this. I refused to do to Stephen, what Nathanial had done to me—it was horrible and I would never, ever want Stephen to experience those feelings. I was also glad that I had my own apartment, at least I could remove myself from being with him and I just hoped that I wouldn't begin to crave the company of other men; it wouldn't matter if I did—I would sequester myself until Stephen was ready to be with me; he was that important.

"Ana." Stephen was smiling at me, his palms against the counter—he looked strong. "You're not Nathanial and you have nothing to feel guilty or anxious about. I've pretty much seen it all after five hundred years and there's nothing that you could experience or desire, that would make me not want to be with you, even if you are trying very hard at the moment to not attack me." He laughed and moved to stand in the doorway. I nodded, still not prepared to breathe. "Would you please stop holding your breath? I think I can handle you," he mocked me and pinched my nose; I exhaled forcefully. "That's better, now how about some dinner; perhaps the oral fixation of chewing, will keep your mind off of other…more desirable acts," he said, sliding past me in the doorway, pressing me slightly against the wall; he was teasing me. He had no idea what he was doing. He laughed and I watched him saunter away from me, whistling.

Stephen

I wished that Ana wouldn't go out of her way to avoid me. It had been almost a month since she'd been over to the house and I missed spending time with her. Really, I was perfectly fine with her current state of physicality and I was more than happy that she seemed to just be focusing her desires on me; I wouldn't have it any other way. She was immensely considerate and I was regretting my ridiculous proposal that we wait to have sex until I felt she was healing from the whole Nathanial fiasco. God, what was I thinking? I wasn't the least bit inclined to be with anyone else now that Ana and I were attempting to formulate some kind of more intimate relationship and I had taken to utilizing my storage supply of human blood to satisfy my hunger; it was getting low.

While Ana seemed to be handling this new change in her body, I, on the other hand, was attempting to deal with my insane craving for her blood. The bizarre thing was, that my body seemed to recognize what was happening with Ana and my urges and my hunger to have her, to taste her, had amplified ten fold; I was wondering if there was some sort of connection there. I hopped off the bus and meandered over to stand in front of the Pennys department store to wait for her. She'd gotten off work early because Cillian was having some sort of gathering in which his only request was that Ana come. Jealously was my Achilles heel and it had caused me to make the most horrific mistake of my human life; I wasn't about to let it ruin whatever chance I had with Ana. I wanted her to see that I had changed and that I was good for her, that she needed me. Still, Cillian's unwavering interest in Ana pissed me off slightly and I wondered if it had to do with the uniqueness of her blood. I knew that both Patric and Devon were intensely drawn to her and I distinctly remember the dinner when I first met Ana. It had been hot and she'd wiped a drop of sweat off the back of her neck. Immediately, I'd pushed my chair away, trying to hold myself together; her scent was overpowering and what it did to my body, to my hunger, it was inexplicable. Devon had also been affected, but he was more drawn to the power of Ana's blood than what it was doing to him physically and sexually. I sighed upon remembering. It seemed like lifetimes ago.

We had missed Christmas because Liam and Carmen were unable to leave the protection of their current hiding place, but downtown

Dublin was still ablaze in decorations for various late winter festivals and swarms of people were shopping. Grafton Street was a permanent wall of tourists, but I actually loved it. I enjoyed being around so many Humans, it made me happy. Ana wasn't much for holidays; she was an atheist by most standards, as was I, but I loved Christmas time even if it was delayed, I had since I was a child and I had begged her to meet me so we could go shopping for Lucie. We were doing our own late "Christmas" celebration with Liam later in the week. Apparently, that was all I needed to say and Ana was good to go. I caught her scent, also something that was a new experience and usually only occurred when vampires decided to stalk our prey; I felt slightly guilty for that behavior, but I had also come to find it somewhat comforting that I could detect Ana easily from a crowed street. I could tell when she'd been in my house, in my room, when she'd touched my clothes—it made me feel like she was always with me. She waved excitedly at me as she crossed the street, narrowly missing getting hit by a bus. I shook my head; she was crazy.

"Howdy!" she said, as she reached me, pulling her hat down around her ears. She looked adorable. I was constantly amazed at how easily Ana could shift from one style to the next and look perfectly amazing in each one. Personally, I preferred her in the least amount of clothing possible, one of my shirts and just her underwear, but I was becoming more and more partial to the outfits she wore when she'd come to the club; they were extremely alluring.

"Howdy to you," I said, kissing her gently on the cheek. I felt her muscles tense and I laughed. "Still insanely attracted to me? Hmm…it's been a over a month." I pulled her hat down.

"I don't think that it's going away any time soon, I'm afraid." She sighed, hooking her arm in mine. "So what's the plan, shopping first then Cillian?" she asked, stopping to peer into a boutique window. Ana had refused to let me buy her anything and it frustrated me. I enjoyed picking various items out for her and I liked being able to give her things that would bring her joy, but Ana was a bit of a minimalist when it came to buying things for herself. She didn't feel that way when it came to me or Lucie or even her co-workers for that matter. She rarely splurged on herself and she always felt bad spending her money on clothes or things for her apartment—she was always feeling selfish and this seemed odd, considering she was the most unselfish being that I had ever come across in all my time on the earth.

"Cillian is for sure the last stop of the evening," I said, taking her gloved hand. "And Carmen sent me a list of things that Lucie has been asking for." I reached into my pocket and pulled out a copy of an email that Liam sent me a few days ago; they were somewhere in South Africa, still unsure of their safety and I was trying not to worry.

"Well let's have a look, shall we?" Ana pulled the list from my hand and immediately she devised a plan to hit the best stores for what we wanted. She was obsessively organized and I appreciated it, because I was not. We spent the next three hours buying everything on the list and several more items that Ana wanted to get Lucie, mostly books and art supplies. "Have you stopped painting?" she asked me as we carried out lot back to her apartment. I put the bags down on her floor and shrugged. "Is that a 'yes' or a 'no'?" She grinned, taking off her hat and shaking out her hair. I had stopped painting; I hadn't picked up a brush since I left her in Idaho. "Into darker stuff these days? Painting too tame for you?" she said, unbuttoning her coat.

"I guess," I murmured, studying her. She smirked at me.

"Do we have time for me to change? I don't really want to show up wearing a sweatshirt; everyone always dresses so nice at that club." She called as she walked across the vast space to her bed. "So, why don't you start painting again? I could use some art for my walls. I'll even pay you!" She laughed and opened up her wardrobe, pulling out a pair of tight leather pants and a blood red, backless silk top. She was killing me, very slowly, she was killing me; I mused.

"What kind of payment?" I asked, following her over to her bed, sitting on the edge. She shrugged as she stepped into the bathroom to change. I looked at the walls; they were nice, brick with various large surfaces ideal for some of my larger canvases.

"I don't know; you have *everything*," she called and I saw her pulling down her jeans. I sighed and ran my fingers through my hair—I wanted her. "And what you don't have, I guess you can just buy for yourself." She laughed. "I'll let you teach me how to play the guitar," she said, emerging from the bathroom. I exhaled. If I didn't know already that Ana was Human, I would have guessed that there was something supernatural about her; she was dark, seductive and looked more powerful than any Human or vampire woman I had ever been with. "I'm an excellent student and I actually practice," she said, coming to sit next to me on the bed, grabbing a pair of spiked heeled boots. I reached out to run my finger down the length of one of her curls, twisting it.

"Hmmm, I haven't actually taken on students for a while now; I'm not sure how that would go. We might be too distracted to actually get

351

any chords down," I murmured, pulling her closer to me. "Any other ideas?" I asked, knowing full well what I wanted to ask for. Her response prompted me to wonder if she was able to read minds now.

"Hey. I offered you the whole blood thing a while back and you gave quite an impassioned speech about the merits of such an activity and about what it would do to you and to me…" she mocked, smirking. I pressed my forehead to hers, my breath shallow.

"What if I've reconsidered?" I whispered, my mouth watering and my stomach contracting. She pulled back to stare at me.

"What do mean?" Her eyes narrowed and she frowned. I held her face and pulled her mouth to mine, biting down hard on her bottom lip.

"I mean," I breathed, "that I want to be with you; I want to taste you again Ana." I kissed her deeply. "I want your blood and I want your body; I want you." I was pushing her down on the bed.

"Whoa! Hang on a minute," she said, breathless; she tried to sit up. "You've changed your mind? Since when? I thought you wanted to wait; you said it was important to you," she asked, touching my face tenderly. She was so sweet to me, so kind and I was going to have to take her right now, if she didn't move away from me this instant. I pressed my lips to her throat and gripped her shoulders, massaging my fingers deep into her muscles.

"Since now, since weeks ago…" I gently bit her neck and ran my tongue over her throbbing pulse; she moaned softly, but she pushed me back.

"Really? You really want to do this? Stephen, are you sure?" Ana was whispering and I could feel her body responding to my hunger for her; what an amazing pair we were; physically we complimented each other, emotionally we restored each other—my mouth began to water violently.

"God, yes Ana. I promise it won't hurt, god I promise not to hurt you." Sex with a full vampire had a tendency to get quite rough and I didn't want her to be frightened or uncomfortable; I was pretty sure I could go slow. She was kissing me full on the mouth and I groaned as she moved her tongue in and out, teasing me. I felt her hands reach down between my legs and she began to stroke me, her movements matching the speed and depth of her kiss. I gasped, feeling shaken in my thirst, my hunger and my pleasure. Suddenly, there was a knock at the door.

"Hey, are you guys in dere? We're all waiting on yer asses—what da fuck is takin' ya so long?" Cillian. I would kill him. I would decapitate him and then burn his body. I was panting as Ana moved away from me, smoothing out her hair and trying to catch her breath.

"Hang on!" she called, leaving the bed and crossing the room to the door. I ran my fingers through my own hair and tried to calm my instincts to kill. "Hey!" she said so casually, that I was amazed at how composed she could be. Hmm…next time I would take more control; it was my style anyway. I saw Cillian standing in the doorway and I read his thoughts immediately. I rolled my eyes and stood to walk over next to Ana. I wrapped my arms around her waist and glared at him.

353

"Hmmm…looks like I've interrupted someting positively scandalous!" He laughed, winking at us. "Ok, well, we'll get started and da two of ya…finish up, den get down to da club; I hate celebratin' sans my favorite 'broter' and should a darker mood strike while yer dere, I've rented out all of da rooms for da entire evenin'!" He winked again and turned to leave. Ana shut the door, laughing. I shoved her against the closed door and pinned her hands above her head.

"He has terrible timing, don't you think?" I said, my voice turning rough. I began unbuttoning her pants.

"Uh…Stephen? I think we should hold off for a bit." She laughed and pushed me back gently. "Besides," she kissed my throat, then my lips, "we don't really want to rush, do we? I mean there's always the use of those rooms, if we just can't wait and Cillian made us a very nice offer don't you think?" She chuckled again and ran her hand across my groin, lingering. Was she serious? I had not exactly pegged Ana as the S & M type; I knew she was adventurous, but that could mean anything. I had gotten myself into quite a few precarious situations in those rooms and the very thought of having Ana there, of indulging my darkest fantasies about her, it was slightly overwhelming. I raised my eyebrows, staring at her.

"I had no idea you were interested in that mode of exploration," I said, watching her as she went to get our coats. She smiled as she buttoned herself up.

"I feel safe with you," she said, her eyes dark and intense. "It's weird, but even during those times when I thought you were going to kill me, I still felt safe having you there." She shook her head. "I'm pretty messed up!" She frowned and held the door open for me.

"I do messed up pretty well." I purred in her ear, grabbing her lobe in between my teeth. She sighed, actually she moaned and it took us another ten minutes just to make it down the stairs.

I had never seen the club so packed. Cillian must have invited every single vampire and Human he'd ever come across. The music was loud and throbbing and there was something very sexual and dark in the atmosphere. The smell of blood hit me as we crossed into the main space and I could see various couples, vampires and Humans, indulging their needs right at their tables. Christ. I hoped Ana wouldn't be sick. It was a lot to take in if you hadn't see it out in the open before. I steered her away from the most involved pairings and found Cillian's table near the back. I turned to look at her and she was watching me, her head cocked to the side. I smiled and slid into the booth next to her; she was keeping me out of her mind. Cillian came to greet us, bringing us drinks and more people to join the table. Of course, he chose a seat next to Ana. I immediately moved my hand to touch her leg under the table and I placed my arm around the back part of the booth, pulling her in towards me and away from Cillian. I noticed his lips were quite red and swollen and the woman next to him was clearly bleeding; I could smell it. I studied Ana. I wondered if this was a bad decision for the evening, but she actually seemed in good spirits. She was laughing with one of the other women and sipping on her drink. She was such an accommodating soul. I squeezed her thigh under the table and she placed her hand over mine, squeezing back.

355

I had been talking to one of my band mates when suddenly, I caught Ana's scent; it was different, but still distinctly her and it was coming in waves driving me to distraction. There was something heady about the fragrance, spicy, tangy and rich. Was she bleeding? Had she been cut? It was so strong and my body couldn't help but react. I waited for a break in my conversation and turned to look at her. She was tense. I scanned the table. It didn't appear that any of my brethren had caught this sudden release of scent; I exhaled, thankful. Was she emitting something that just I could detect? That would be odd. I caught her eye and smiled at her. She grinned back and I began stroking her thigh, trying to reassure her. Unfortunately, the movement seemed to trigger something in Ana and I felt her body tremble at my touch. Without thinking, I began pressing my fingers into her leg, deeply caressing her. Again, she trembled. Someone was talking to me and I turned to focus, all the while letting my hand travel up around her hip. I moved her knees apart and started to massage her between her thighs, over her pants. She was hot and her hips began to shift as I dug my fingers in between her legs. I also felt Ana's hand move down over my waist and I sucked in a deep breath as I felt her fingers begin to stroke, her hands working me slowly up and down feeling how hard I had become. I bit my tongue trying not to groan; her touch me, me touching her, they were creating such a friction between us that it was all I could do not to come right there at the table. I cleared my throat, and tried to listen to the woman who was speaking to me as I slowed Ana's movements between my legs. Someone came and tapped the woman on the shoulder, and gratefully she excused herself to go and dance. I turned back to Ana, my hand now moving slowly and deeply between her legs. She caught my eye and I motioned for her to get up. I took her hand and led her out to the dance floor where our interactions wouldn't get a single stare. There were couples and threesomes having quite the time with each other already. I pulled Ana close to me, whispering in her ear, my hands running over her chest.

"What's going on?" I asked, still wondering what that scent was. I wasn't objecting to it, I just wanted to know if she realized what she was doing to me.

"I'm not sure." She laughed. "My body felt all weird all of a sudden." She pulled back to look at me, her eyes intense. I held her hips and moved close to her, finding a wall to push her against. She groaned as I let my hand travel back down to her thighs, pressing deeply between her legs. I grunted low, feeling her and I wanted to pleasure her right there against the wall.

"Weird how?" I said, my mind was racing and I was thinking about what we could do to remedy this mounting situation. I started working her over her pants, feeling her heat spread across my fingers.

"Good weird," she panted and I suddenly felt her breasts begin to swell and her body felt hot. I took her face in my hands and stared at her.

"You want to try?" I asked her, hoping that I wouldn't scare her with my request.

"Yeah." She bit her lip and smiled. "But you'll have to go slow, I'm not quite used to all of the extra 'stuff'" she said, smiling. I had a feeling that she would be more comfortable with some of the things I wanted, than she thought.

I took her hands and pulled her to the back of the club and back down the same hallway we'd been before. Thankfully, the suite we'd also occupied was empty. I pressed my thumb to the door and led us inside the dark room. I hit the lights and worked the dimmer switch. I took Ana's hand and moved us to the sofa. She waved her hand and I watched in awe as the fireplace ignited in blue flames. I laughed and I sat down next to her, inhaling, letting her new chemical perfume drive my instincts. I had to be very, very careful. Any injection of my venom would serve to initiate the transformation process and then we only had two options; give her my blood and turn her, or let her die. No pressure. Of course, I had done this a thousand times with other women, but for some reason I felt this was different; I felt less in control of my need for Ana, less in control of my hunger and I wanted her so urgently; I wanted her blood, her soul. I stood and walked over to the bar, and began pulling out the drawer that Ana had fallen upon last time. I withdrew the dark purple scarf and motioned for her to join me. "You liked this, yes?" I said, running the fabric between my hands, warming it. "Perhaps we'll start there and see where it goes," I said, laughing as I wrapped the scarf around her neck and pulled her close to me. She frowned.

"That seems pretty mundane," she purred as she kissed me gently. "I mean you probably stopped using that ages ago." She was unbuttoning my shirt. I tossed my head back laughing as I shifted to let her undo my belt.

"And what would you suggest we start with?" I asked, my breath shallow. She was kissing me on the stomach and pushing me back against the counter, her lips beginning to move over me. I ran my fingers through her hair as she started to kneel down in front of me.

"I don't know, what do you like? You're the expert here," she said, running her tongue down between my legs and I groaned. Before I could even manage to move, she had me, fully working me into her mouth. I gripped the counter. Oral sex was not new to me, thousands of women had willingly pleasured me, but there was something distinctly powerful in Ana's movements, the way she caressed me, the way she moved her lips, how deeply she was able to push me…the feel of how hot and wet her mouth was; it suggested the other places that might just feel the same. She let her tongue trace slowly along the tip eventually going down hard and fast and I gritted my teeth together; I wasn't sure if coming in her mouth was something that she would want. "I think you're proving otherwise," I gasped, but I was wondering just how far she would want to go. I heard her moan and laugh as she spread my legs open and grasped my hips, letting her mouth do all the work. I started to thrust. She was too good and I was climaxing too fast. I pulled her up just before she managed to push me over the edge. "Jesus Christ," I panted, looking at her; she was frowning, clearly upset that I had stopped her from bringing me to come. I stood, my legs shaky, and moved over to a large black wardrobe positioned near the bed. I pulled open the doors revealing an array of whips, chains, ropes, blindfolds, lubricant, clamps, plugs, vibrators, candles and changes of sheets. Ana had appeared beside me.

"Wow!" she said, looking at me, her eyes wide. "That's a lot to chose from." She laughed, pulling out a pair of handcuffs and fingering a long satin rope. She wrapped her hands around my waist letting her fingers slide around my crotch; I was beyond firm and ready to come violently. I could feel it. She kissed my neck. "What do you want?" she whispered, making the surge of hunger rise rapidly in my body. If I was really being honest, what I wanted was to tie her up, feast on her blood, fuck the hell out of her and then feast on her some more; that's what I wanted. Not romantic in the slightest, but I didn't think that either of us was in this room for romance.

I took the rope from her and the blindfold. I had always thought sensory depravation was quite arousing; I would start with that. I moved to pull the blindfold over her head, and I gently lifted her hair over the strap. I winked at her as I let the black satin cover her eyes. I pushed her down on the bed and unbuttoned her pants, sliding them slowly down over her hips. I moved on top of her and whispered in her ear.

"Did you know," I said, kissing her throat, "that the tongue is one of the strongest muscles in the body?" I asked her, as I moved my hand down between her legs. She gasped and I pushed my fingers inside of her. "Fascinating, really. I mean, just think about what you could do; what pleasure you could actually have with just that one muscle." I pushed harder and she moaned. "Of course, you would really need to know what you were doing, otherwise it's just mundane oral sex and we know how much you don't want that." I laughed and began rubbing her, caressing her; she was hot and very aroused. Her body writhed and I was guessing that not being able to see what I was doing was driving her crazy. My body shuttered and I licked my lips. I enjoyed watching her. Ana knew how to move her body, especially when she was getting pleasured; she was so in tune with what she needed that the experience for me was just as arousing. Being able to look at her while I made her come; god, it made *me* climax without even penetrating her.

She groaned as I felt around inside. I wanted to wait until she was almost there, until she was on the very brink, then I would finish her off with my mouth. She was moving back and forth, thrusting against my hand and I withdrew, moving down her body, licking her, biting her, along the way. I pushed her chest back and I began running my tongue between her legs, pushing it barely in, then taking it away. She gasped and I groaned; I could feel my own pleasure rising and I wanted to taste her. Again I pushed my mouth against her, thrusting deep this time and she heaved forward, shocked by the depth of my penetration. I knew it felt good to her; I knew that I could make her feel amazing. I pulsed in and out, licking and sucking on her, bringing her forcefully into my mouth. I was beside myself, my desire and pleasure, reaching an unimaginable intensity. I came, suddenly and sharply, gasping and breathing hard.

"Don't stop!" Ana moaned. She was thrusting against me, pushing my mouth back into her—I wanted nothing more than to taste her and she was so close now. She gripped my head, running her fingers through my hair and I felt her tense in my mouth. She gasped and violently climaxed as I sucked her, still thrusting my tongue, wanting her to feel every ounce of pleasure. I moved to lie on top of her, our chests heaving in rapid breaths against one another. I wasn't done— not even close. That was a benefit of being a vampire. We needed no refraction period. We could orgasm hundreds of times in the same night, but of course, we needed to be cognizant of our Human partners; they made need a few moments of recovery before their bodies were able to become aroused again. We also had a trick to aid their recovery process.

"Ana," I whispered, kissing her deeply, letting her taste how delicious she was to me. "I want you again, but I know you may need a minute. Do you want me to help you?" I asked her, letting my lips move over her throat. She was breathing so hard and I was afraid she might hyperventilate.

"What?" she gasped, tearing off the blindfold and barely opening her eyes. I laughed and rose back to look at her.

"I can help you, help your body recover and we can...we can try other things, if you want?" I asked. I didn't want to assume that she would actually want to have sex with me; perhaps this was all she was craving. God, I hoped not. She nodded and I smiled, bringing myself to her side. I began to stroke over her stomach, running my hands up and down her skin, calming her nervous system. Once her breathing had slowed, I moved to look at her. "Don't be concerned, ok? This won't harm you and it's not going to interact with what you already have in your system." At least I hoped it wouldn't. I was taking a slight risk here, but my desire and my hunger seemed to be ruling my more logical inclinations. She looked at me her eyes wide.

"What are going to do?" she asked, sitting up now. I laughed and brought my wrist to my finger, slashing over the vein. She gasped and moved away from me as a single stream of black blood rose to the surface of my skin.

"Drink," I said, moving my wrist to her lips. "Slowly," I commanded her; I wanted to be able to monitor just how much she was taking, but that was going to be difficult; I would be climaxing—hard. It was a pleasant side effect. She stared at me and I nodded. She shook her head and took a deep breath in, pressing my wrist to her lips, gently. She was watching me and as I felt her begin to draw the blood from my veins, I closed my eyes and visions appeared, visions of Ana, of kissing her, of tasting her; I was breathing hard, but I also heard Ana breathing. She groaned as she let her mouth move forcefully over the wound and I felt her start to suck harder. I came, my pleasure rising quick and I growled, the force of my desire becoming uncontrollable. I had to come back to myself; Ana was getting too much, she was taking too much. "Stop!" I gasped, actually not wanting her stop. I was so close to my release again that I wanted to finish; this was amazing, having her take from me. I'd never experienced this with the other women. Ana seemed to want the blood, to crave it and if Patric were alive, I would hug him. "Ana, stop!" I said, forcing myself to pull away from her. She released me from her grip and I watched in awe as she casually wiped her mouth. Before I could recover, she was on me, kissing me and pushing herself against me. Desire racked my body and I moved, pulling her up off the bed. There were half a dozen hooks hanging from the marble pillars and they were not there for anything decorative. I pushed Ana against one of the large marble beams and with one wave of my hand, I lifted her up in the air. She looked alarmed at my sudden display of strength and that she was now dangling several feet off the ground, unsupported. "Relax, I've got you," I murmured, smiling up at her. She was easy to levitate. I rose up to meet her and I saw her eyes grow wide.

"Holy shit!" she said, staring at me. "When did you learn to do that?" She glanced down and I laughed.

"It's part of being a vampire, love." I backed her up against the marble and reached to take both of her arms. "You don't need to look down,

Ana. You're safe with me," I whispered as I secured the knot from the rope around the hook, binding her wrists. I took my finger and sliced open her blouse down the middle. "Now, you'll *have* to let me buy you some new clothes." I smirked and cut the remainder of the fabric leaving just her bra, hovering back to admire my work. She looked so sensual, the curves of her muscles, the way her body hung there, ready for me; I had no idea if I would be able to focus on her enough to give her pleasure. I hoped that the action of taking her blood would satisfy her body's cravings; it was usually enough for most women, but, then again, Ana wasn't most women. I flew back to her and slowly began running my fingers down over her body, letting them warm her skin, and super heating her blood. The taste was always more potent if the blood was close to scalding and the physical experience for her should be immensely arousing. She moaned and leaned her head back against the stone.

"I promised you, that it wouldn't hurt." I said, studying her reaction. "Does it hurt?" I asked, testing her threshold for the heat. She shook her head slowly and I smiled, kicking up the intensity. She gasped and groaned, twisting her body in the air. I checked the space between her wrists and the rope; plenty of room.

"What are you doing to me?" she murmured. I pressed my lips to her stomach, gently sliding down her underwear and letting them fall though the air to the ground.

"Just getting you warmed up," I said, spreading out her legs and moving my face in between her thighs. I exhaled, sending a current of heat surging through her groin.

"Stephen!" She moaned and arched her back. I laughed and moved back up her body stopping to kiss her throat. I pushed her legs up around my waist and I immediately felt her begin to grind against me. I growled and shoved myself closer to her, letting my pants fall and shrugging out of my shirt. We were both naked and hovering in the air; Ana bound, her scent coming out in full force.

"Let me have you, Ana; let me take you. I want your blood. I need it! God, I need it! I slid myself into her and she moaned. I pulled her hair back forcefully, exposing her throat. "Let me do this." My voice was dark and my lips became slick, my throat was on fire. I thrust deeply, feeling a surge of desire that made me push harder. She spread her legs wider and ground against me. I shoved her against the pillar still holding her head back. The marble cracked. I tore her from the rope and sent us flying through the air landing on the carpet, pinning her beneath me. I didn't have time to deal with the contrivances of sex toys. My hunger was overwhelming me and my bloodlust was driving my sexual pleasure to unimaginable places; I didn't need bondage tricks. She was gasping and moaning as I moved forcefully inside her. I saw fire behind my eyes and my need burst from my body as I took her, pushing and thrusting as hard as I could. I sunk my teeth into her throat and she cried out. I held her down; struggling just increased the chance that I would tear the wound. "Don't struggle Ana," I moaned. "Try and keep still. "Liquid heat ran down my throat and I drank greedily from her veins. The taste was more than I remembered and I felt myself have a physical release inside of her. I snarled and came again, not wanting to stop. The more I drank the more powerful my climax; I was addicted, consumed.

365

I heard Ana moan and I felt her hips rise each time I came. I pushed harder and deeper as I turned her head and bit her again. The feeling of penetrating new flesh, as I came inside of her, was intoxicating. I drank again, pulling and sucking. She was writhing under me and I pulled my mouth away, reluctantly. I watched as I moved forcefully over her, blood running down her chest and over her breasts. I lapped it up, every ounce and moved my mouth down in between her legs. "Do you trust me Ana?" My voice was clear and strong and I knew what I really wanted to do, where the best, most intense taste would be. She would be unable to control her desire and that would only serve to increase my own pleasure.

"Yes!" She tossed her head back and opened her legs. I laughed and moved my tongue inside of her as deep as I could possibly go, waiting for her. She came quickly and I took everything she had inside of me as I bit her in the most sensitive spot. My lips moved over her, trapping the blood and I sucked as much as I could. To my surprise, she came again and I felt a new release of her blood and her desire, run down my mouth quenching my darkest thirsts and awakening new hungers. I gasped at my own orgasm and I forced myself to penetrate her again fully, moving my lips back to her throat. This was too much. I didn't deserve to have this much of her; it was unthinkable what she was doing to me, what she made me crave; it was unholy and I wanted more. My body thrashed as I pounded deeper and harder, my muscles tightening against the thrusts and rippling with sweat. Her blood was all over my skin and I could feel its heat permeate my pores, absorb itself into my body. She pulled me down to her throat as she pressed me so far inside of her that I thought I would explode from what I was feeling. I grabbed her head and shoved it back, growling and snapping at her. She screamed out and I felt her come a third time, making my whole body rock and shake as I bit down and pulled her blood as she climaxed against me. I took one more deep drag and drilled into her, hard, releasing myself to her. "Ana!" I gasped as I felt something push forward and enter her body, something that I had no idea what, but it made me come so ferociously that I stopped breathing.

Chapter Fifteen

Ana

"Shit, shit! Christ! Ana, are you ok? God, I don't know what happened, something happened…I'm so sorry, god, did I hurt you? Are you hurt Ana?" Stephen was frantic and very, very panicked. I felt ok, considering what had just happened. Actually, besides feeling tremendously weak, my body felt amazing, nourished and I felt…deliriously happy. Stephen was pulling on his pants; blood covered his chest and neck. He was kneeling down beside me on the floor, his eyes bright and clear like the sea. I sighed and smiled at him. He put his hand on my forehead and smoothed my hair back. "What?" he whispered. "What is it?" He bent his head to kiss me.

"Thank you," I said, but I actually didn't know why I had spoken those particular words; it was as if that's what my body wanted to say…weird. Stephen pulled back, a look of worry and concern on his face.

"Did you say 'thank you'?" he asked, his eyes roaming over my body. I nodded and started to giggle. He raised his eyebrows, looking disturbed. "What's the matter with you?" His eyes narrowed. "Are you drunk?" A slight smile began to spread over his mouth. I started to laugh uncontrollably, tears rolling down my cheeks. I wasn't sad, but I had such a feeling of complete release and of joy that all my body could do was laugh and cry at the same time. Stephen waited for me to get myself contained.

"I'm sorry," I said, wiping my face. "I'm fine really; I feel great." He eyed me, distrusting my response. "Well, I mean I feel really, really weak, but just physically." I laughed again as I reached to stroke his face. He sighed and stood up to walk over to where he'd laid his coat. I saw him remove a small syringe full of black liquid and begin thumping out air bubbles. I had seen that before; he was going to stick me with something. Again, needles did not bother me, shots did not bother me; it was just the whole principal of inserting something into my veins that made me cringe; that was ironic considering what I'd just let him do, I thought. Plus, no nurse or doctor, shy of Alec, had ever had an easy time finding a vein to use. They always had to poke around making my arm swell and bruise. Stephen laughed and headed back toward my position on the floor.

"I thought you said you trusted me." He began swabbing my arm with alcohol.

"What are you giving me?" My eyes narrowed. I did trust him, just not with a needle. He laughed again as he tied a rubber band around the upper part of my arm, pulling it tight. "Are you a closeted heroin addict?" I asked, looking into the fire. "You seem to know your way around veins and the like," I said, turning back to watch him.

"Ana, after this evening, I will never need any form of artificial stimulant or drug in my system ever again," he said, his eyes flashing bright as he pressed on my arm, looking for a vein. The blood on his chest was now almost completely dried and I thought that we both might need showers. "This is a very small dosage of my blood, smaller than what you received from Patric when he was treating you," he said catching my alarm. Liam had been worried that too many different

369

blood types might kill me. Stephen nodded. "Too much of the blood is what we are worried about Ana, this is mostly a prescription vitamin mix with one or two drops of my own blood although, you certainly took a bit more than I anticipated already, but I still don't think it was enough." He frowned as he pressed down and I could feel that he'd found a good spot. I hoped that he was right.

"What's it going to do?" I asked, turning my head, not wanting to look.

"Help you feel stronger and replenish some of what you lost." He withdrew the needle and I wondered why he was stopping.

"What's wrong? Why didn't you give me the shot?" I asked, frowning. He smirked at me, and stood up tossing the syringe in the trash.

"I already did you silly girl; you didn't feel a thing did you?" he said and I saw him open a large door near the bed that I hadn't noticed before. "Ready for a shower?" He smiled and came over to help me stand.

Stephen

Liam, Carmen and Lucie were coming for our belated Christmas. I had begged Liam to leave South Africa and spend time with Ana and me and thankfully, he'd agreed. He said he had some matters to discuss with me and I was curious. Things with Ana were…well, they were pretty amazing. I was worried about her after what had transpired between us at the club, but that was a couple of weeks ago and she was anything but upset or disturbed with me, just the opposite actually. She couldn't keep her hands off of me, nor I her and it seemed that our coupling the first time made my addiction to her that much greater, if that was even possible. She'd allowed for me to take blood from her each time we made love and sometimes that was twice a day. My body was feeling so amped up that I was having a difficult time getting anything done. I was supposed to be wrapping some of Lucie's presents while Ana was at work, but her scent was all over the place. We already had a morning tryst, but it wasn't nearly enough for me and I was craving her again. I sighed and began taping up a small hand carved canvas stand; it was just the right size for a toddler to be able to stand and paint and Ana had insisted that we get it for Lucie as soon as we saw it.

I had just turned on the stereo and poured a drink, when I heard a key in the door. I exhaled, hoping that Ana wouldn't mind indulging me one more time this evening. I had a feeling that we wouldn't get much alone time with my family here.

"Hey!" she said; she was soaking wet. I frowned as I watched her strip off her raincoat and hang it on the hook by my door. I didn't know why we had to continue this nonsense of living apart; she hadn't thought about Nathanial in quite some time and I was pretty sure that her feelings for me were getting more and more solidified by the day. She stepped into the room and surveyed the complete disarray that I had created. I hadn't wrapped anything. "Stephen!" She glared at me. "What the hell, man? Why haven't you gotten any of Lucie's gifts wrapped? What've you been doing all day?" she said, her hands on her hips, her hat still on her head. Fantasizing, I thought…fantasizing a *lot*. I smiled at her and stepped over the mound of presents pulling her hat off. I ran my fingers through her hair, shaking it out and letting her fragrance fill my nose and mouth. She shook her head. "Seriously, what's the deal?" She was trying to sound fierce, but I could tell that my touch was making her voice go soft. I sensed an easy victory.

"We have time," I murmured, letting my lips find hers, parting them. "Several hours to be exact," I said, kissing her fully on the mouth.

"Hmmm…" She moaned gently I pulled her toward the couch.

"What do you want, love?" I asked as I slid her shirt over her head and moved so that she was straddling my lap, her hips spread wide. She pulled back from me and stared, her eyes looking slightly sad. "What's wrong? Are you feeling ok?" I said, thinking that I had missed the signs that she wasn't in the mood.

"How would you feel about the possibility of purchasing a new sofa?" she asked me, her lips pursed. I was thoroughly confused.

"What's wrong with my sofa?" I laughed as I took each of her fingers and sucked them gently, letting my teeth graze over the skin.

"Well, like nine thousand women have been on this thing, not only with you, but with Cillian and the rest of your group and I'm sure that if we shone a black light on these cushions, we would be disgusted at the amount of bodily fluid in the fabric. Besides all of that, every time we're on this thing, I think about that night that I came home from work and you were having sex with that woman." She swung her leg around and moved away from me. My god, Ana was jealous—she was too funny.

372

"Ana love, if you want me to get a new sofa, I will get a new sofa; I'm not attached to my furniture." I pulled her back toward me, wanting to see her eyes.

"Cool," she said, smiling. "Thanks." She stood up and I frowned, I was not ready for us to stop mid moment.

"Hang on," I said, grabbing her hand and pulling her back down. "I think we were just getting started," I said, caressing her neck and down her bare shoulders.

"Not on this couch!" She laughed as I pulled her across my lap and held her close to me.

In between our sexual experimentations, Ana and I managed to get all of Lucie's presents wrapped and under the tree with an hour left to spare. By the time Liam arrived, Ana and I had done it on every possible square inch in my home, cleaned up the blood, and I was ready to go again, if my brother had not been such a stickler for showing up to places on time. We were in the kitchen; I had Ana's pants down and was in the process of seeing how quickly I could pleasure her, when I heard a gust of wind out in the living room. I groaned and stood up, licking my lips.

"God, he's anal—and not in a good way!" I said, watching her button herself up, smile at me and smooth back her hair. She laughed and moved passed me running out into the living room. I stood back and watched as Lucie sprinted from my brother's side and launched herself into Ana's arms, screaming her name at the top of her lungs. My heart shook and I smiled at the scene; it was the closest thing to a real family that either Liam or I had experienced since we were children—the only person missing was my youngest brother. I sighed and saw Liam shake his head, he didn't want my guilt to spoil this time and he was right.

We spent the evening drinking and talking and I found myself wanting this to be my everyday life, to have my brother and his family and me and Ana together. Liam smiled at me and motioned for us to move to the kitchen. Ana and Carmen were having an intense discussion about some new immigration law that affected people in Carmen's home country; Ana was definitely the more intellectual of our pairing. I followed my brother out of the living room and we sat at the table sipping our drinks.

"It looks like things are going well for the two of you," he observed. "You seem very happy Stephen." He studied me over his glass and I shrugged. There was something to his tone that bothered me; he seemed cautious. Liam put his drink down. "There are some things that I think you need to know, but things that Ana does not need to know right now, so I tell you in strict confidence Stephen." I nodded. Liam cleared his throat. "The baby, the one from the girl that Nathanial was with, it's not his Stephen. The child was from another man, someone she'd been with just prior to…to her tryst with Nathanial." Liam sounded somewhat disgusted and it was unlike him to be so judgmental. "I can't help but judge; the whole situation is beyond my understanding. Both the girl's behavior and Nathanial's baffles me." I sat back, knowing there was more. "She lied to him of course, throughout the pregnancy, but once the baby was born the doctor confirmed it was one hundred percent Human and that's when she told him the truth. Of course he was struggling before then…." Liam looked at me.

"What do you mean?" I asked, already bored. I was hardly invested in what Nathanial was experiencing; he could die for all I cared.

"Funny you should think that, Stephen." Liam's voice became solemn and my eyes narrowed. "Apparently, after you and Ana returned to Idaho, shortly after, the baby was born, Nathanial tried to remove his imprint from his chest; he tried to kill himself," Liam said flatly. I sipped my drink casually, but something in my own chest shifted uncomfortably.

"So?" I said, not sure where Liam was going with this. "Is he still alive?" I asked, thinking about how I would have to tell Ana that Nathanial had died; she'd be devastated, I was sure.

"Yes, he's still alive; his uncle and myself were able to repair a significant portion of the damage, but it was a close call." I was stunned.

"You saved him?" I said, betrayal coloring my tone. Liam's eyes narrowed.

"Stephen, just because you love Ana and you are my brother, I am not about to allow for someone to whom Ana was Bound, to destroy their own existence, no matter what my feelings may be about his actions or his sense of right and wrong. He could have worked with the other Bonders the evening that you attacked the camp, but instead he fought with you and he trusted in you to care for the woman he loves; he put her heart in the hands of his very rival. He died that night and I didn't think allowing him to die again, was necessary." Liam's tone was firm and I knew that debating him, because I was terrified of losing Ana again, was not a noble cause.

"Where is he?" I asked, fear beginning to rise in my heart.

"Peru, he's with his uncle; who by the way, shares our complete disbelief at what transpired. According to him, he's never seen such behavior from a Bonder and especially not one so completely in love with their Bond." I didn't want to listen to anymore, it was too much. "I know this is hard for you to hear Stephen, but I warned you a while back that this situation with Ana was tenuous and that I anticipated that Nathanial would see the error of his choices and fight to get her back; I told you this." I started to interrupt but he cut across me. "But, but I also informed Nathanial that Ana was reestablishing her relationship with you and that it was on my best advice that he leave her alone, that he let her go now; the damage was too great— intentional or not—," I snorted, "intentional or not," Liam continued. "And that I felt that Ana had been through more than her share of chaos and recovery to last her many lifetimes." I exhaled.

"What'd he say?" I said sipping my drink, amazed that my brother came to my defense so easily.

"It wasn't just for you Stephen, it was also for Ana. You weren't there that night, the night she and I came to Nathanial's home. You didn't see what was in her mind; the impossible things she was thinking, the memories she recalled; you didn't feel the very essence of who she was, leave her body as she watched what was happening on that couch…" My mind was racing. That's why she'd wanted me to get a new sofa, because it reminded her of that night, of seeing him and it had brought it all back that evening when she'd seen me, with that woman. She'd felt betrayed by both Nathanial and me. Christ. "He altered her that night, changed who she thought she was, who she

376

thought she could be to someone. He did the worst thing anyone could do to someone like Ana; he made her question her value and he made her doubt her very existence on this earth." Liam spoke and I rubbed my face. It was all making sense now, why she wouldn't move in with me, why she was so agreeable for us to take things slow, why now after everything we'd shared, she still doubted my commitment to her, why she was so willing to indulge my hunger for her; she hoped that it would be enough to make up for her self-perceived deficiencies. She didn't trust that I would want to be with her as she is; she couldn't let herself trust me and she was waiting for the day that she came into my house and found me again, with another woman. Liam's head snapped up, hearing my thoughts.

"Please," I said, steamrolling over his judgment. "I think that me taking Ana's blood is really the least of our concerns at the moment, don't you?" My tone was bitter. "Is he coming back or not?" I said, my anger and my passion for Ana beginning to rise. Liam sighed.

"I don't know Stephen. The fighting is still very much active in South America and Nathanial's uncle is in dire need of his skills. There is a very powerful coven in the area and they have managed to take back over all the lands that the Bonders secured; it's quite a mess." I heard Lucie laugh and I sat back in my chair, staring at my brother. I knew the coven he was referring to. That was not going to be an easy fight for Nathanial to win.

"What do I do?" I asked, my anger giving way to desperation.

"Nothing Stephen; you live your life, you be with Ana; if Nathanial comes for her, it will be her and only her to make the decision on whether or not she wants to be with him. There's nothing you can do now except love her and let her love you." Liam grinned at me.

That night I was lying in bed awake; trying not to panic. Liam was right. All I could do was be with Ana, make her see that I was the better choice for her, that no matter what, I would never betray her love. Still… I turned up my stereo. There was a soft knock at my door.

"Come in," I said, not raising my head. I had left Carmen and Liam in the living room talking about their next move and Ana had put Lucie down before she went home; she said she didn't want to be intrusive with Liam and Carmen here. I begged her to spend the night with me, but she thought it best that she stay in her own apartment. I hoped it wasn't my brother coming to continue our conversation.

"Hey." It was Ana. She ghosted into the room.

"I thought you left," I said, my moodiness lifting at the sight of her.

"I forgot to give you your present," she said, biting her lip. I had gotten her something as well, but I wanted to wait until the company left; I wanted us to be alone.

"You didn't have to get me anything," I said, holding out my arms wanting her to come lie next to me. She rolled her eyes and sat across from me, tucking her legs up under her.

"So you know I'm not artistic in any way," she blushed as she pulled something from behind her, "but, I have a co-worker and he's been helping me; he's a really talented metal smith, anyway…" She pulled out a tiny box that was covered in dark leather. She took my hand and placed the box in my palm. "I know how much you love Christmas, how much it reminds you of your family; I wanted to get you something special," she said as I stared at her. "I made it," she murmured, still biting her lip. I took the box, holding my breath. I cracked open the top and my heart stopped beating. Nestled inside on a satin pillow was a ring. A stunning silver band with the symbols of both the coven of my brother and my family's Celtic crest woven intricately around the width of the circle. "Liam helped me with the patterns and he also told me your ring size; well he guessed, but I'm hoping he got it right!" She laughed. "Umm, do you like it? I mean I know you're not for too much for jewelry, but I thought..." her voice faded as she studied my shock. "It's too much; it's too serious for you," she said, pulling herself back from me.

"Ana," I said, finally able to form words. The conversation I had with Liam suddenly filtered into my mind and I knew what I had to do. "Ana. This is the most beautiful ring and the fact that you made it, makes it sacred to me, but I can't wear this, not yet," I said, my voice shaking. She stared at me, her eyes wide.

"Oh. Well, sure; I understand. It's too soon maybe..." She stood up. "You can keep it though right? Maybe you'll want to wear it someday." She gave me a slight smile and I shook my head. My brother was going to kill me.

"Ana, let me explain please," I implored her. She sighed and stood by the door, clearly wanting to leave. "I don't think you are over Nathanial—not completely; you never got closure from everything that happened, nor did he and you both deserve that; he needs to hear how he hurt you and you should...you should know that he still loves you." I couldn't believe that I was saying this. "I'm offering you the same conditions you offered me many months ago. I ask that you come to me having let Nathanial go, if that's what you so choose, and letting go all the doubt that he created in your heart. I'm asking you to trust in my love for you and in the love that I know you have for me; I'm asking you to chose me Ana, but only after you have said goodbye to Nathanial." I stood up and crossed the room to where she was standing. "I love you, and I do not want to exist in a world where you do not. It's as simple as that and I will wait for you forever," I whispered to her; she was crying and she looked angry and oddly, she looked diminished. She wiped the tears from her face and turned, leaving me holding the ring.

****

It had been over a week since I'd spoken with Ana, since she'd left my room after giving me her gift, a week since I'd risked losing her to do what I knew was right. Liam's response had surprised me; he was proud of me he'd said, proud that I had the courage to ask for what I needed, but to also give Ana the room she deserved to find her own sense of where she belonged, even if that didn't mean with me. I wasn't so sure that I'd done the right thing; I missed her every hour of every day and the longer I went without seeing her, without touching her, the darker my mood became. I had finally had enough. I was standing in the rain outside her apartment waiting for her to come home from work; I at least thought we should see each other and talk. I hadn't meant for us to stop being together, I just wanted her to know

380

where I stood and how I felt. I saw her round the corner and my heart jump-started; I loved her so much. She approached the door and I stepped out from the side, blocking her entrance.

"Hi," she said, her face shrouded by the hood of her raincoat. I hated not being able to see her eyes.

"May I come up?" I asked, moving to get a better view of her face. She looked tired, like she hadn't slept in days. She nodded and I followed her inside. She shrugged off her raincoat and took mine to hang and dry out.

"Do you want some tea?" she asked, and I noticed that her voice sounded distant and worried and her mind was closed. I didn't want her to be anxious around me, that's not at all the way I wanted her to feel. I sighed.

"Tea would be nice, thank you," I said, hating these polite gestures. I pulled out a chair in the kitchen and watched as she assembled our mugs.

"So how've you been?" she asked weakly, turning on the kettle. Horrible, wretched, depressed, suicidal, I thought to myself.

"Umm, good; I guess," I mumbled. "How are you?" This conversation was excruciating.

"Pretty, frickin, awful," she said and turned to stare at me. "I thought I was upset with you, but it turns out it's me that I'm pissed off with," she murmured pouring the water into our mugs. "You were right; everything you said, everything that you asked for, it was right. I'm not sure about the whole closure thing, though." She sat down across from me and sipped her tea. "I mean, seeing Nathanial, talking to him about what happened, I'm not sure if I really want to bother at this point, it doesn't matter now. Our Bond is broken and we're both free. I don't really see the practicality of dredging up past hurts; he made his choices and I've made mine." She stared at me, her eyes searching my face. I chuckled, remembering my conversation with Liam.

"I'm not sure that Nathanial would see things in quite the same way," I said, leaning back in my chair and holding her gaze. She shrugged, running her fingers through her hair.

"Well, that's for Nathanial to sort through then isn't it?" Her voice was stern. "However, I completely understand your position and I wouldn't want to ever make you think that you are a second choice, Stephen— because you're not, you never were." I looked at her, not quite willing to believe what she was saying; perhaps I had some trust issues of my own to deal with. She exhaled and took my hand. "I'm not sure what you want to do about us now, but I'm willing to give you your space, to take my own time away from you—if that's what you feel is best; whatever you want, Stephen." She squeezed my hand and I felt the heat from her skin, seep into my body.

"I don't want to be away from you," I said quietly, leaning my face in my hand. "I *can't* be away from you." I pulled her hand to me and kissed it, holding her palm against my cheek. "But..." I stared at her face.

"But...you want me to be sure," she whispered. I nodded, not able to speak. "Right then. Ok, so we'll just, like be friends or something." She pulled her hand away, laughing softly.

"Friends?" I asked, taking her hand back. There was no way that I could ever be *just* friends with Ana; I wanted her too much.

"Or not," she said, frowning. "Are you going to leave; like leave the country or something? Maybe you need some time away from me—from this place?" she asked, lowering her eyes. I hadn't thought about leaving Ireland; I had a home in the North, my mother's home, but I didn't really want to put so much distance between us; I didn't think that would bode well for my emotional wellbeing.

"No. No, I'm not leaving, Ana," I said, kissing her hand again. "I can't leave," I murmured, breathing her in. She closed her eyes and sighed.

"Well then, what do you suggest we do?" she whispered. I had a few ideas. I stood up pulling her close to me. I wound my fingers through her hair and brought my face close, breathing softly on her lips. "Hmmm…do you really think this is the best plan, considering our current circumstance?" She tried to speak as I began skimming my nose and mouth along her throat. Actually, I did.

"Just 'friends' isn't going to work for me Ana." I breathed into her ear and she gripped my shoulders, pushing me back gently.

"Maybe we should give it a try for a bit, otherwise we're just back where we were and nothing will be resolved; no closure." She smirked at me, reciting one of my suggestions I'd given her. I groaned and rolled my eyes.

"Fine. Friends, but I'm warning you, any time we spend alone together is not going to be 'friend-like'." I said, bringing my mouth to hers and kissing her hard and deep.

"No alone time, then," she said, breathless. "We'll have chaperones; Cillian perhaps?" She laughed and disentangled herself from the steel grip I had on her waist. At the mention of Cillian another thought began to cause a sense of anxiety in my heart.

"Will you be dating?" I asked, suddenly feeling a monumental case of jealousy coming on. She tossed her head back and laughed. I was failing to see the humor in such a relevant question.

"Uh…no!" She was emphatic. "I think that it's best for the population as a whole, that I withdraw myself from the entire dating scene. My love life has managed to cause enough mayhem and chaos to make it into some Bronte novel." She grasped the chair in front of her and shook her head, cocking it to the side. "Anyway, I'm waiting on you," she said, smiling. "Waiting on us…" she whispered, moving to kiss me on the cheek. "That is unless Cillian proposes an offer I can't refuse," She teased and hugged me tightly.

"I have a present for you," I said, pulling back to look at her.

"Oh. That's so nice, thank you, completely unnecessary, but nice." She smiled. "What is it?"

"It's a surprise. I'll bring it by this weekend, if that's ok." I put on my raincoat.

"Great! Hey, actually I did run into Cillian and he said that you were playing at the club tomorrow for some bash. Are you?" She opened the door for me. Christ. I had forgotten about that gig.

"Yeah, I guess I am." I sighed, not wanting to leave her apartment, her scent. "You should come," I said, staring at her, wondering if we had just made a huge mistake, not being together.

"Maybe. Or maybe I'll just spend a quiet evening at home, watch a movie and hang out in my sweats; you know, be very uncool!" She laughed, but actually I was thinking that sounded like the perfect way to spend an evening. "But you have…fun," her voice faded out and she stared at me, emotion filling her eyes. I felt a sudden rush of anxiety pulse out from her chest and I quickly scanned her mind before she could block me. She was thinking about the women at the club, about the girls that I'd been with or would be with, the blood I would be taking from them now that she and I were just friends. She wouldn't allow herself to ask what I'd be doing to satisfy my hungers; she didn't feel she had that right any longer. She cleared her throat and looked away from me. "So I'll see you this weekend, maybe," she murmured, still averting her eyes from my gaze.

"Yes." My throat felt dry and my chest ached. She smiled and waved as I stepped out into the hallway.

"See ya." She closed the door, leaving me to endure my own personal hell.

Ana

I hadn't decided if I was actually going to show up to the club for the latest bash. I was feeling emotionally and physically drained. All of the ups and downs between Stephen and I had me exhausted. He'd asked to come by on Sunday and I was thinking that was plenty soon enough. I just needed to process. I spent the rest of the week fixing up my apartment and enjoying a few days off from work; I was also doing a bit of research on the possibilities of maybe getting a job in Howth, a point North from Bray on the Rail. One of my co-workers had a boat that he'd kept and he was looking to do some studies on the impact that tourism was having on the ocean ecosystems. I thought it sounded interesting and spending some time at sea might just be what I needed. Even though I was tired, I wasn't sleeping; in fact I hadn't slept since I last saw Stephen. My mind was always racing and having to think about Nathanial and everything that happened, it was making me hurt all over again. I wondered what he was doing, if he was enjoying being a father, if he and Adrianna were together now. Life was so odd. At one point, I had hoped that Nathanial and I would be able to have a life together, but Stephen had entered into the background offering me a different choice, perhaps a steadier, more defined relationship—our journey had also been a significant one and it had brought us together in a different way than Nathanial and me. I had let Nathanial go and I did honestly feel that in time, Stephen and I could have a truly beautiful and committed relationship; that is what I wanted, what I needed, but now, even that prospect was seeming like less and less of a reality.

Sunday rolled around and I was in a bit of a mood, just sad and tired, but my body felt amped up, charged. I hoped that I wasn't experiencing another bizarre mating cycle, maybe just PMS. Stephen showed up in the early evening, apparently he didn't get in until this morning and I immediately felt a wave of panic and distress wash over me. I was sure that he had been with other women, that he would need to satisfy his hunger at some point. I buried my thoughts as I sensed him try to filter his way in.

"What's wrong, Ana?" he asked carrying a giant covered canvas through my door.

"What's that?" I asked, intentionally avoiding answering his question and trying to quell an odd sense of grief that had suddenly surfaced. He leaned the canvas against the wall and stood with his hands on his hips, visually scolding me. He looked so handsome today. He looked handsome everyday, but I especially liked the outfit he was wearing; distressed jeans, black boots, and a long sleeve deep blue sweater that showed off his perfect chest and shoulders and of course his eyes, they sparkled. He had a hat pulled down so that his chestnut waves peeked out and molded themselves around his ears and over his eyebrows, the lighter brown and caramel highlights swirling and shining against his skin. I sighed, thinking that perhaps I should have put on some actual clothes and not just my sweats. He was still staring at me. "What?" I asked, moving to stand near the canvas.

"Nothing." He relaxed his stance and strode into the room, sitting on my couch.

"You're not going to tell me what it is?" I asked, following him to the living room.

"It's your present, but you can open it later." He sounded agitated. Perhaps this whole friends thing wasn't going to be possible. Another wave of despair crashed over me and I had to bite the inside of my mouth to try and stop the tears. He rubbed his face and turned to look at me. "You didn't come to the club," he said, resting his head on one of my throw pillows and swinging one of his legs so that he was lying mostly horizontal. He seemed comfortable; maybe I had misjudged his mood.

"I wasn't really feeling up to it," I said, leaning away from him on the other side of the sofa. Really, I just hadn't mentally prepared myself to go to that stupid club and see Stephen sitting with other women; it made me feel weird and sad. He locked me into his vision and I knew that he'd heard my thoughts. I cleared my throat, trying to break his hold on me. "So, did you have a nice time?" That was a stupid question.

"Hmmm...it was fine. Nothing special," he said, not blinking. I bit my lip. "Are you going to talk to me or would you rather I just pick through your thoughts and make of them what I will?" he asked, his tone even but again, there was just a hint of agitation and I wondered if something had happened to him, if he was upset. "We're focusing on you for the moment, Ana," he spoke sharply, still keeping his eyes intent on my face.

"Nothing. I mean it's nothing, I'm just feeling a bit weird today, a bit off I guess." I could hear my voice shake; god I seriously needed to get a grip. This was never going to work. I was going to end up losing not only Nathanial, but Stephen too. Clearly, I wasn't the best fit for either of them, one because of my lack of fertility and the other, because he thought I was still in love with the first. Biology versus the heart, the soul; I was pretty damaged on all those fronts. I sighed and curled up on the couch, wanting to just disappear for a little while.

Stephen moved toward me, taking my hands and pulling me across the sofa onto his chest.

"I would be very upset if you disappeared Ana, even for a little while." He kissed the top of my head.

"Are you mad at me or something?" I asked, figuring that maybe he would be inclined to share. He laughed.

"No. No, I'm not mad. I'm just frustrated. I don't think I should have asked you to do any of those things, to sort out any of whatever you may or may not be still feeling for Nathanial; I should have trusted in your love for me...in your remarkable ability to be so self-aware. I'm afraid that I've now made you doubt me, doubt just what I feel for you..." His voice sounded tight and stern and I raised my head up to look at his face.

"Well actually, I was thinking that maybe you should find someone less human...I hear Vampire chicks are quite exciting." I laughed softly and buried my face in his chest, breathing in his scent. He sat up suddenly, jolting me out of my position against his body. He was shaking his head.

"That's what I mean." He looked at me, his eyes darkening. "That, right there, you thinking that I want someone else, that I *should* be with someone else. I've made you doubt me. I should have just listened to Liam; I shouldn't have tried to do the right thing. I can feel you distancing yourself from me Ana, I can feel it and it's making angry." He paced the room, running his hands through his hair, pulling off his hat.

"What's Liam got to do with any of this?" I asked, not sure why his brother would be so suddenly involved with our relationship. Stephen shook his head.

"Because he told me that I should just leave things alone, that I should continue with you as we were, moving forward and that if he came back, when he came back, that I needed to have faith in you to make the right choice the best choice for you, that the decision was not in my hands and all I could do, all I should do, was prove to you every moment of every day that we belong together and that you belong with me…" I wasn't exactly following his train of thought; my own mind was racing.

"Stephen, has Liam spoken with Nathanial? Is this what he wanted to discuss with you? Has something happened?" Surprisingly, my voice sounded even and calm. Stephen sighed and walked back over the couch.

"I'm really not at liberty to say, Ana. At least that's what Liam has advised; perhaps I should actually start listening to him," he muttered.

"Well, if that's what Liam has asked of you and he feels it best for me not to know, then you should oblige his request. I'm sure he has his reasons." I said, still, my voice was calm, but my heart was racing. Stephen laughed darkly.

"Aren't you the least bit curious, Ana?" His tone was acerbic and it took me aback. I stood up facing him, my stance rigid.

"No, Stephen, I'm not curious," I said quietly, but my voice now had a slight edge. "And I really don't appreciate your tone; I'm not a child and you standing there, questioning what I feel or what I want to know, it's insulting. If I was curious about anything that Nathanial was doing, I would ask Liam myself. Perhaps it's not just me that is having issues with trust here," I said, folding my arms across my chest. We stood facing each other, staring.

"You're right Ana. I'm sorry. I didn't mean to imply…I didn't mean anything. I'm sorry," he said, crossing to stand directly in front of me. "I do have some trust issues; I worry every day that he's going to come and steal you away from me, that your bond with Nathanial will transcend any love that you have for me, that I won't be enough to hold you." He looked so devastated, so broken—it was shocking that we were both feeling the same thing… that neither of us would be enough to hold the other.

"Stephen," I whispered, reaching to stroke his face. He closed his eyes and breathed in, his chest shaking. "Stephen." I moved to pull him to me. Slowly I brought my face to his. "Stephen," I whispered, feeling his breath on my lips. His hands secured my face and he closed his eyes. I pressed my mouth to his top lip, hesitantly.

"Ana." He kissed me back, gently, softly. I held his shoulders and pulled away, unsure if this was ok; if he felt this was right. " God, Ana." His voice was rough and quiet and I kissed him again, not able to resist. His hands ran down the sides of my neck, caressing me and I stepped closer to him. He took a deep breath and pulled himself away from my grasp, his lips still close to mine, speaking softly, "Christ…I have terrible timing. I have to go." I swallowed, trying to quell the massive desire that always came when we were close.

391

"Why?" I asked, breathless, and I kissed him a bit more forcefully, feeling his light trace of stubble rub my skin gently. He groaned and moved his mouth against mine, matching my intensity.

"We're having a meeting; some of the brethren are having a meeting," he whispered, his lips moving down my throat. It was my turn to groan. "God, you smell so good; it's been too long, Jesus it's been too long without feeling you..." He moaned, letting his tongue move slowly up and down my neck. Heat began to rise in my body and I pulled his head into my throat. "Oh Ana," he gasped and I felt his teeth begin to graze my flesh. He backed me up against the wall, pinning me with the strength of his hips. I was breathing hard—panting. Another soft growl escaped his throat and the next thing I knew, I was being lifted off the ground, my body still pressed against the wall. I wrapped my legs around his waist and held him close. Oddly, I felt a slight buzzing on his waist and I stopped mid-kiss to look at him. "Jesus, fucking, Christ!" Stephen breathed hard, lowering us gently back to the ground, his arms still holding me tightly against him. I heard his phone continue to buzz and I smiled at him. "What!" he answered the call, his eyes not leaving my face. "I'm on my way." He put the phone back in his pocket, still staring at me.

"Is everything ok?" I asked. I actually didn't know too much about the other Vampires that Stephen hung out with; none of them belonged to a coven and I had always considered them to be a bit rough and slightly unhinged. Stephen kissed me deeply and moaning, he pulled himself away and headed toward the door.

"Everything's fine," he said, but I detected an undercurrent of the agitation he'd had when he arrived this evening. He laughed. "No wonder you're such a good mediator; you don't have to read minds to understand every emotion in a room do you?" He pulled his raincoat on and grabbed his hat. I unlocked the door and slid it open for him. He touched my face and my throat and I saw his eyes flash. He was hungry. He chuckled and shook his head. "Tell you what." He stepped away from me and out into the hallway. "Why don't we make a plan to hang out tonight after my little gathering. We'll download a movie and I'll cook you something for dinner. What do you say?" He looked at me smiling.

"Well…is that on the 'acceptable things to do with friends' list?" I teased hanging on the door.

"Not in the slightest," he whispered, moving toward me. "And neither is this." He grabbed my finger and bit the tip, running his tongue over the prick, gently sucking the blood from the wound. I had to stifle the moan that wanted to erupt loudly from my throat. He closed his eyes and I felt him take another deep drag from my finger. His face flushed and he gasped softly, tilting his head back and swallowing slowly. He moaned and his body shuttered; watching his arousal seemed to ignite my own intense desire and I had to stop myself from asking him to do more. "Ana, you taste amazing." He looked at me, his eyes crystal clear. He licked his lips and kissed the tip of my finger, his tongue stopping the bleeding. I cleared my throat, still relishing in the desire he'd created, but feeling somewhat incomplete. "Don't worry, we'll remedy that this evening." He laughed and I watched him strut down the hall. Yeah, us being just "friends" wasn't going to be an option.

Stephen

"I'm not sure I understand what's going on," I said. I was sitting in the house of one of my brethren trying to follow the conversation. Granted, since leaving Ana's I'd been somewhat distracted and had, over the last hour, begun fantasizing about her, not paying attention to what was being said.

"They need extra fighters Stephen, at least that's what they're telling us," Eamonn told me, his tone quiet. Eamonn had always reminded me of Liam, steadfast, contemplative, but Eamonn also relished in his darker nature; he enjoyed his binges and he enjoyed being a vampire, something I never thought my brother was actually comfortable owning. Of course, unlike me, Liam didn't make the choice to become what he was now, he was bitten and had his life taken away against his will. I sighed.

"Why? I thought the South American coven had things under control; what's the problem?" I asked, taking a sip from my scotch.

"The Bonders have a strong leader; they have several strong leaders and their numbers have increased ten fold. They've come from all over to help Nathanial." Eamonn looked at me. My body tensed. Carlo's coven is very strong and very powerful, but they are no match for Nathanial and his fighters; Nathanial also has the support from the Humans—the ones that haven't been destroyed by Carlo, that is." Eamonn poured another drink. Carlo hated Humans and had made it his mission to kill and brutalize every one that crossed his path, but not until he'd taken what he'd wanted from them. Carlo was a very different vampire, different from me, different from Liam and not a single coven had been successful in usurping his rule in South America. Carlo was responsible for changing both Alec and Devon and he'd been the one to give Alec the ability to shape shift into a Bonder. His powers were of the darkest kind and rumor had it that Carlo had the ability to create illusions so real that even the most skilled and seasoned vampire could be seduced into believing the charade. He was ubiquitous, even if he was on a different continent; every coven, every vampire, was always aware of his presence. You didn't say no to Carlo when he came calling—at least not if you wanted to live.

"Obviously, Carlo understands that we need to keep some of the brethren here, just in case, but we need to decide who we are sending to meet with him." Shane added, looking at each one of us in turn.

"Stephen." Eamonn looked at me. "He's asked specifically for you." He lowered his head. Of course he had; Carlo was responsible for my ability to fight. He'd trained me after I had been turned, said I had potential after seeing me fight in the ring on one occasion. He was always recruiting, but I refused to join his coven in favor of staying with Liam and he was not pleased, but understood that family took precedent over potential; I was never under the impression that he actually was inclined to let me go, but whatever his reasons, I left with my existence in tact knowing that when he called the next time, I may not be so fortunate in my excuses.

"When?" I asked, running my finger along the rim of my glass, thinking about Ana.

"As soon as you can make arrangements," Eamonn replied.

"Just a meeting?" I asked, knowing that nothing was ever "just a meeting" with Carlo. Eamonn nodded.

"Yes, he's aware that we are loyal to no one and that we fight for ourselves only; that's been our creed here for centuries, but I'm sure he'll have some offerings for you to bring back to us…" Eamonn smiled and shook his head. Carlo was known to promise you everything you desired, things that you yourself didn't know you wanted. It was a dangerous and seductive gift.

"I can be there by the end of the week," I said, thinking that I wanted more time with Ana, more time to get things settled and right with us before I left. Eamonn nodded.

"I'll let him know." We adjourned and I headed for home hoping that Ana had not backed out of our plans. I arrived to my house an hour later, having stopped at the grocery and knowing that Ana was on her way. Immediately, I noticed something was off; there was a distinct scent in the room and one that was vaguely familiar, but I couldn't place its source. I eased into the room, surveying the space. Nothing seemed out of order. I pushed opened the door to the kitchen and saw him sitting in a chair, a large white box on the table.

"Stephen." Nathanial looked up, his eyes were black.

Ana

This couldn't be right. I pulled another test out of the packet and commenced to urinate on the tiny stick. This was the tenth one I had used. After Stephen left this afternoon, I had glanced at my calendar and noticed that I was supposed to have gotten my period a week ago; I did the math, but I wasn't concerned, until I started cataloging my symptoms as of late. The increased insomnia, the mood swings, the hormonal urges. I didn't know what made me think to take a pregnancy test, but for some reason my mind compelled me. Now, here I was in my bathroom staring at a digital screen that clearly stated that I was, in fact, pregnant. I frowned and put the test in the trash with the nine others, all reading the same thing. It had to be wrong; they all had to be wrong. Some sort of manufacture's defect, it was medically impossible for me to get pregnant; that's what the doctors had told Noni, that's what they had always told me. Were they mistaken? So many of them, could they all have been wrong? My heart began to race.

Stephen

"You look well," Nathanial said, as I crossed into the room, putting my bags on the table. I had been preparing for this moment. I glanced at the large box he had sitting on the table. "It's something for Ana; apparently she doesn't understand the meaning of a gift." He

397

chuckled darkly. I recognized the quilt from her bed, the one she'd returned to him the night we'd gone back to Idaho.

"I think she gave that back to you," I said, my tone even. "I think it was a symbolic gesture Nathanial," I said, turning my back to him, hoping to god that Ana wouldn't come walking in.

"You're expecting her," he said, fingering the threads of the blanket, clearly ignoring my last comment. I turned and leaned against the counter, my arms folded. I scanned his body. He looked the same; still strong, still confidant.

"Illusions, Stephen, all illusions," he whispered and I noticed that his fingers immediately began to caress the area over his heart. There was blood beginning to soak through his shirt. He caught me staring and he pulled his hand his away. "A constant reminder of my transgressions I think," he said, his voice returning to its normal bravado.

"What do you want Nathanial?" I asked, knowing full well why he was here.

"She's not the only reason I'm here although she's the main reason why I've come, but not for the reasons you think," he said, our eyes meeting. "I know you've been called to aid Carlo. I know that he wants a meeting with you and I know that you are obliged to go. I'm here to warn you Stephen, not that I have any obligation to you or to your life, but I still have one to Ana, even if she has broken her Bond with me, and this concerns her as well." My muscles tensed.

"I'm listening."

398

Ana

Christ. What the hell was I going to say to him? "Hey Stephen, I know that we're still trying to figure out what our relationship is going to be, but you know that time at the club; well, it looks like apparently our pairing can override both biology and Vampire constraints; I'm pregnant". He was going to flip out! I hadn't quite processed the whole thing yet and I was determined to get myself examined by a doctor before actually telling him. I couldn't get in until the end of the week, but that just seemed too long to wait. I wondered if I should tell him and get it out of the way. I was walking up the path to his house, my heart pounding and my mind felt slightly manic in its energy. I stopped to sit on the overlook before continuing up the road.

Stephen

Nathanial continued. "Unfortunately, before they died, both Devon and Alec had a meeting with Carlo, a meeting about something that Carlo has been searching for, for centuries. They informed Carlo that his quest was complete and the individual with the rare blood and the even rarer ability to call fire, the one who could not only provide him with nourishment, but with absolute power and the ability to command armies to come to his aid, the blood that my brother wanted, the blood that Alec wanted, the blood that Andres was willing to kill for, the power that warranted my Council to have me take Ana's life…it's still alive and her talents are unharmed, untainted. Her potential is almost too seductive for him to resist; she would be, could be, his ultimate weapon, if he doesn't kill her first." Nathanial stood, his body rising like some great stone god.

"Ana," I said, not believing. "He wants Ana." Everything about the meeting was now falling into place. Carlo didn't want me to fight; he wanted me to bring him Ana, to bring him the thing that he coveted the most and he would kill me, if I refused. Nathanial nodded. I wondered why Ana's blood didn't affect me like it had done with Patric; why when I drank from her, all I felt was complete love, complete joy. Nathanial cleared his throat, his eyes narrowing at my contemplations.

"Because your intentions, I'm guessing, are not to gain power, that you have no tangible greed or notions of coercion in your soul Stephen. By your very nature, you are a decent being, despite the sins of your past." Nathanial sounded just like Liam; maybe they should've been brothers, I mused.

"What do we do?" I asked him, not minding that he saw what had transpired between Ana and me. He laughed flatly and looked away.

"You think I'm here to offer you advice? You think that I have a plan to spare her life and possibly yours?" He waved his hand in the air. "I have nothing Stephen. Carlo is way beyond my ability to strategize around when it comes to this situation. I will tell you that if you *don't* bring Ana, that it can be guaranteed that both of you will die. Even if you refuse, even if every coven rallies to protect her, Carlo will find her; he will kill you and then he will come for her—it is his single mission. He's losing the battle and only a weapon such as Ana will allow for him to regain what he's lost, and then some. He will use her to defeat me, to rule you and extinguish or turn as much of the Human race he can. This is bigger than either of us; we can't protect her anymore."

Ana

I pushed open the gate and tried to steady my legs. I hoped that he would be happy; I was happy—I thought I was happy. If I knew that Stephen would be there, if I knew we were together, that we could be a family, the family he always wanted, then I could be at peace. I turned my key and stepped into the foyer. I choked. The smell hit me like a sickness and I fell over, pressing my palms to my knees. Honey, lemon, woods and musk; it was so strong, so pungent; it was making me nauseous. It must be my hormones; I must not be able to smell things correctly. He couldn't be here; he wouldn't come now, after so long, after everything that's happened. I wouldn't be able to handle this and the pregnancy news; I just couldn't do it. I rose up and tried to walk into the living room. I was breathing through my mouth, hoping not to vomit.

Stephen

Christ. She was here. I looked at Nathanial, not knowing what he
wanted to do.

Ana

I pushed open the kitchen door and stood, not believing, not trusting
myself to see him standing there.

Stephen

She was pregnant?

Chapter Sixteen

Ana

Immediately, I closed my mind, shutting down any possible thought about what was happening with me; I was pretty sure that Stephen had managed to hear what I'd been thinking before I got to the kitchen and I was hoping that now my Bond was broken with Nathanial, that he could no longer infiltrate my mind. I stood there, in the doorway, looking at both of them, Nathanial's face registering so many emotions, Stephen's face looking stoic, but there was just a hint of complete shock in his eyes; that's what told me he may have known about the pregnancy before I could shut him out.

"Nathanial," I said, moving to stand next to Stephen. I fingered my amulet, hoping for courage, for strength. Stephen touched my hand and I looked into his eyes. I didn't want him to be frightened; I didn't want him to doubt me. "I don't quite know what to say." I turned back to Nathanial, surveying his face.

"Nor do I Ana; actually, that's not true. I have so much to say…" His voice grew soft and I felt Stephen squeeze my hand.

"Why don't you take a moment and catch up," Stephen said eyeing me. I started to object, but he shook his head. "You should talk." He stared at Nathanial and then back to me, bent his head and kissed me softly on the cheek. "I'll be at the club, come find me when you're done." I nodded and watched him turn, leaving Nathanial and me in the kitchen. Strangely enough, I didn't feel anxious being alone with him again; I didn't feel angry or jealous, I didn't feel anything but perhaps a twinge of sadness for all that had happened. I opened a soda and pulled out a chair, pouring my drink into a glass.

"Can I get you anything?" I didn't know what else to say at the moment.

"No, I'm fine, thank you Ana." He stared at me and I noticed that he was bleeding, the space over his heart was seeping dark, red blood.

"Nathanial, are you hurt?" Without thinking I reached across the table and stretched out to touch him on the chest, my hand met with an invisible shield; I *couldn't* touch him. I pulled my hand away, looking startled. His body shook; closing his eyes, he put his head in his hands.

"You can't…you can't touch me Ana." His words were muffled as he ran his hands over his face. He was in a hundred kinds of pain.

"Why?" I whispered; I couldn't bear to see him like this, no matter what had happened between us—this was too much suffering.

"Our Bond…it's severed." His breath was shaky. "I'm not sure if you will ever be able to touch me again." He looked at me, our eyes meeting. His fingers traced over his heart and the back of my neck grew warm. I sighed. How symbolic, I thought. I eyed the box; it looked familiar.

"What's that?" I asked, sitting back from him, still wondering why a broken Bond would prevent me from touching him. It was odd.

"It's your birthday present. It was a gift Ana." His voice steadied as he stared at me.

"Well, I don't want it Nathanial. Besides, you should give it to Adrianna; she's the one who's having your child." I was surprised at how short my tone sounded; perhaps I wasn't quite out of the clear with my anger over what had occurred. He laughed bitterly and I wondered if he could in fact, still read my thoughts.

"Of course he didn't tell you," Nathanial said, his face growing dark, a shadow moving over his eyes. "Not that it matters…" he growled.

"Do you mind explaining what the hell you're talking about, Nathanial? I think we're past all of the pretenses at this point, don't you?" I sipped my drink and leaned toward him, my eyes fierce.

"The baby's not mine Ana. Adrianna was never pregnant with my child. The night you and Liam showed up; I hadn't…I was about to…" He trailed off, pain in his voice. "I wasn't sure if what we'd done would have been enough, but she insisted that it was mine…" Again, his voice grew shaky and I saw his body heave as more blood seeped out from his chest. I was contemplative. This is what Liam must have told Stephen not to tell me. I wasn't mad, Liam was always concerned about protecting me and I knew that he was furious with Nathanial for that night. I exhaled, feeling oddly sad.

"I'm so sorry Nathanial," I said, again reaching toward him, but again I was met with resistance from his barrier. His eyes grew wide and he pulled away from me.

"You're sorry Ana? *You're* sorry? Why the hell are you apologizing to *me*?" He rose from his seat and began pacing the kitchen.

"Because I know how much you wanted a child…or how much you…umm…" I was struggling for the right words. "How much your body needed you to have a child…" That didn't sound right. I frowned. "You risked everything to be with her…" I whispered, hearing the truth of my own words; he *had* risked everything and for what? He stared at me.

"You're right, Ana. You are so very, very right." He moved to stand close to me. I sighed. It didn't matter now anyway, things were so different; the possibilities for my life were now so completely altered, I had no where to go with Nathanial now, nothing left to really say to him.

"You can't read me anymore can you?" I asked looking up at him. His eyes penetrated my own and I felt something in my chest shift.

"No. I have no idea what you are thinking, what you are feeling…" He ran his fingers through the long strands of his hair.

"Are you still with her?" It was merely out of curiosity that I asked; I had no intention of repairing any relationship with Nathanial. I was too strong now, too confident in my love for Stephen to want anyone else ever again. He exhaled and turned away from me.

"No, Ana; I was never *with* her—she never had my heart…" he whispered. "And you? You are with Stephen now?" His back was still to me, but I could see that he was breathing hard.

"Yes. Yes, I love him," I said, my voice soft as I studied his form. He turned back to face me, pain so deep began to spread across his face that I found it hard to look at him.

"Are you...are you lost from me Ana; lost from me now—for good?" Tears were streaming down his face and I gasped at his sudden display of emotion. "I'm so sorry, Ana...I don't know what to say to you...I can't imagine my life now...I can't imagine living in the world without you, without your smile, without your touch....god, Ana." He was sobbing, his face in his hands. My heart broke. Whatever pieces I had managed to put back together, whatever repairs Stephen's love had mended, shattered in that one moment; watching his desperation, hearing his cries—I fell.

"Nathanial," I choked. "I can't do this anymore. You're different to me now. I can't stop picturing you, seeing you with her...everything's changed; I had-to-let-you-go." I was crying now, my tears coming so swift that I couldn't wipe them away. "I have to move on. I deserve that. I'm so very sorry, so sorry." I gasped and stood, wanting to go to him, wanting to wrap my arms around him; we were stuck, held between two worlds, between loving each other and moving on, between broken and repaired, lost and found and lost again; we were bleeding. "I love you Nathanial, no matter what happens now, I love you and I always will, but I can't do this, I can't be here with you, it's too much," I whispered backing away from him. "Too much has changed." I gasped again and ran from the room.

407

Stephen

I couldn't register what I had read in her mind. Was she pregnant? That couldn't be right; it wasn't possible. Christ. First Carlo, then Nathanial, now this; my emotions were numb from trying to process everything; I couldn't do it. I tossed back my drink and rubbed my face. It had been over two hours since I'd left them at my house; the waiting was making me sick. I wondered if I should call Liam; he'd most certainly want to know about Carlo. They knew each other quite well and I was sure he'd be more than concerned about my scheduled trip. I sighed, knowing that if I ever needed my brother, now was the time. I pulled out my phone, he picked up before the first ring even finished.

"Stephen. What's going on; Micah called and said that he thought Nathanial was headed to see you. What's happened?" I swallowed the last of my scotch and cleared my throat; where did I start?

"Liam." My tone sounded like that of a young boy, a boy who needed his father and his brother; for me, Liam was both… he had always been both. I knew that was all I needed to say.

"I'm on my way Stephen," he said, his tone forceful. I put my phone back in my pocket and signaled for another drink.

I was standing outside the club, trying to get a hold of myself. I didn't want Stephen to see me so upset; he was worried that I would leave him, that Nathanial coming back would be the end of our chance at a life together, but that would never be the case, not now, not ever. Of course, we also needed to discuss this issue of what could be a possible pregnancy. I wanted to know what he thought, what he wanted to do, because at this moment, I had no clue. I didn't really have the energy to evaluate my conversation with Nathanial, how I felt or what he'd said—it was just too difficult for me to navigate right now. I took a deep breath, wiped my eyes and knocked once on the large metal door. Eamonn answered.

"Hi Ana." He smiled at me, holding the door opened so I could pass through. "He's over in the back and he's on his third scotch; reel him in won't ya? We need him somewhat sober to perform tonight." Eamonn laughed and pointed me to the back of the club. Stephen was sitting on one of the red leather couches, his leg up and his back against the armrest. He had a drink in his hand and he was running his fingers through his thick waves. A sudden upsurge of emotion crashed over me and instantaneously, I reached to put my hands on my lower abdomen; I smiled. He looked up and our eyes met. I slid onto the couch next to him as he lowered his leg.

"Hey," I said, feeling the utter bizarreness of my greeting. I wanted to kiss him, but his body language seemed stiff and I thought better of it. He sipped his drink and studied my face, listening to my thoughts.

"Hey." His voice was soft and he looked away, breaking our gaze.

"So," I said, pursing my lips, not quite sure where to begin.

"So?" Stephen placed his drink on the table and rubbed his face.

"So, it appears that I may be pregnant." I had hoped to bring the news to him in a much more eloquent way, but Nathanial's appearance seemed to have diminished what I was hoping would be a somewhat joyous moment for us. Stephen turned fully to look at me, his eyes turbulent.

"How do you know?" He took my hand, tracing his finger along my palm. I laughed thinking about the ten tests that were now lying in my wastebasket at home.

"I took a bunch of tests after you left today," I said, watching his fingers entwine with my own. "Apparently, that venom of yours isn't quite potent enough to kill all of your sperm. Some Vampire you are," I said, pulling his face up so that I could look at him. "And I guess that five doctors and some of the best Healers didn't quite diagnose me correctly... or maybe it just took someone very unique to be able to allow for my body to...to be repaired," I whispered softly, holding his face in my hands. He brought my hand to his lips and kissed it gently.

"God, Ana. A baby; I can't believe it," he said, shaking his head and smiling. "I just never thought...not after everything I've done...all the horrible things that I've done, that I could...that this could..." His voice was tight and he was staring at me in such a way that made every nerve ending, every sense memory I had of him, ignite. He pulled me close and brought his face to mine, breathing deeply. "I love you so much; I love you Ana." He kissed me, his tears mingling with mine. I pulled back.

"I have an appointment with a doctor; I just think we need to be sure— you just never know…" I looked at him, not wanting him to get his hopes up prematurely.

"When?" he asked, moving his mouth against me, holding me tight.

"The end of the week," I said, breathless. He tensed. "What? Is that bad timing? What's wrong?" Just then, a felt a sudden blast of cold air and Liam appeared, standing a few feet away from the table. Stephen closed his eyes and shifted me to his side, wrapping his arm around my shoulder. "Liam? Is everything alright?" I asked, concerned at his sudden arrival. He looked to Stephen, then back to me, then back at Stephen.

"How is it possible?" he whispered, glancing again at this brother. "You're pregnant?" he asked, sliding into the booth next to me.

"We're not sure," I said, not wanting to alarm Liam, he seemed tense already. He frowned, looking to Stephen.

"Have you taken a test?" He glanced back at me, his eyes roaming over my face.

"Ten." I laughed at the similarities between Liam's question and Stephen's; they were definitely siblings. "All positive, but I have an appointment at the end of the week," I said. I saw Liam exchange a look with Stephen and something in both of their eyes sent chills into my very core. "Is something the matter?" I didn't want to intrude into

411

what I was sure was a very private conversation between them, but I was now very, very worried and I didn't know why.

"Nathanial came?" Liam asked, again looking toward his brother. I saw Stephen nod. Liam turned to me. "Does he know?" I shook my head, my throat beginning to tighten.

"We...I didn't...I didn't want him know," I said. "He can't read my mind anymore apparently and I can't—" my voice cut off as I saw Liam's eyes flash. "I can't seem to touch him any more either," I whispered. Stephen stroked the back of my head, letting his fingers rake through my hair. Liam nodded and sat back, his eyes seemed to be sorting through something very quickly.

"That's not all," Stephen said quietly and I saw him bow his head. "Carlo has called." Liam's face went dark as did his eyes and I saw a glimpse into just what kind of Vampire Liam actually was; utterly, bone chillingly, terrifying.

Nathanial

I couldn't stop the bleeding, not from my chest, not from my mark, not from my heart; it was too much for any one soul to endure. She couldn't be lost to me; it couldn't be over, not now, not when so much was at stake, when so many things were happening. I needed to be able to protect her, to keep her with me, to save her from what was coming. I wasn't ready for this to be the end; I wasn't ready to lose her forever. I wasn't ready.

Stephen

"Carlo and I have a very long history, Stephen. Perhaps I will accompany you to Argentina for this meeting." Liam and I were sitting in my home, trying desperately to figure out how to keep Ana away from Carlo, away from what he so deeply desired, what he'd been searching the world for…what he knew I had and loved. I shook my head, taking a deep drink from my glass.

"You can try Liam, but I don't think it will make much of a difference to him; he knows now that Ana is alive, he's surely heard about her attack on the Bonder Council and I'm sure he's more than just intrigued by her potential and her power. He'll want her, no matter what you or I or anyone can offer him." I exhaled, feeling helpless and sick.

"Does Nathanial know?" Liam asked, pouring more wine into our glasses. I nodded.

"He has no solutions either; he's convinced that there's nothing we can do but bring Ana to him, that Carlo will kill me if I don't, which personally I don't care if I die, but then what; she's spends the rest of her life trying to escape a psychopathic vampire who will stop at nothing to acquire her, her blood and her power? We can't win!" I slammed my drink down on the table, shattering the glass. My brother stood, sweeping the fragments of broken glass into his hand and placing them in the trash.

"What of the baby?" Liam asked, returning to his seat. Christ. The last thing I wanted to think about was Ana being pregnant and sitting across the table from Carlo, discussing her fate. My body clenched. I hated to admit it, but there was a very small part of me that was hoping she was wrong, that there had been some kind of mistake. The very idea of Ana having to possibly endure fighting for her life and the life of our child; it was too much—I didn't want to have that discussion with her. Liam sighed and touched my arm. "One thing at time Stephen. Ana has a lot on her mind right now and I know that you are wanting to be honest with her and discuss your upcoming trip, but let's wait to talk to Ana about Carlo once we've gotten an assessment on his requests, once I've been able to calibrate him out a bit." Liam's eyes searched my face.

Besides Carlo, my brother was one of the most powerful vampires within our entire species. He and Carlo had worked side-by-side many years ago, trying to acquire various lands that had once belonged to us. It was only when Carlo began to kill indiscriminately, that Liam broke from his coven in favor of starting his own. Like with me, it was a fairly diplomatic parting, but unlike with me, Carlo would never dream of calling upon Liam for anything. Of any vampire or Bonder, Carlo, I had always thought, was terrified of Liam. Liam was the only one who had powers that rivaled and possibly exceeded those of Carlo and he knew it, he feared it. Possibly having Liam there might not be such a bad idea.

"How was Ana's interaction with Nathanial?" Liam asked, a slight frown appearing across his face. I shrugged. Ana had been locked down tight when it came to whatever had transpired between them. I was trying to be respectful, but it was driving me crazy. Liam nodded.

414

"Let her process Stephen, she just needs some time." He was still frowning. I could see pictures of Ana, Carlo, Nathanial and oddly, Patric, running through his mind, but I couldn't get a read on what, if anything, he was trying to sort out. "One day at a time, for right now. Carlo isn't prepared to take action on anything as of yet; he's still trying to contend with Nathanial's forces. He's losing and most of his occupations are tied up in trying to salvage what little land and control he still has." Liam stood, staring at me intently. I heard Ana come in the front door and I sighed. "We'll be prepared to leave on Friday." Liam turned to greet Ana as she came through the kitchen door. He hugged her and kissed her head. "And how are we feeling?" he asked, moving his hands gently over her back and neck. I wasn't sure what he was checking for; Liam was quite a skilled Healer and I had always thought he would have made an amazing physician. "Thank you Stephen, but I find my current occupation as the proprietor of various S & M boutiques, vastly more intriguing." He laughed turning back to Ana, waiting for her to answer.

"I'm good," she said and she really seemed well. Of course, it had only been two days since she'd told me and since she'd seen Nathanial, but I was hoping both her mental and physical health would hold strong; it needed to hold strong. "So you guys are leaving on Friday, I guess?" She looked to me, smiling. Upon Liam's advice, we'd only told Ana that we were needed out in Argentina to possibly advise on some issues of military strategy; nothing about who Carlo was and who he was currently fighting seemed necessary to reveal to her at the moment. I hated keeping secrets from her, but I trusted my brother and I trusted him to always do what was best for Ana.

"Yes, we'll be leaving on Friday morning. When's you're appointment?" Liam asked, stroking Ana's hair. She grinned, and my heart melted.

"Friday, in the afternoon. Shall I call you and let you know how it goes? Will I be able to call?" She looked to me, frowning. I nodded and moved to stand up, placing my glass in the sink. "Cool. Well then, I guess I'll call on Friday." Liam hugged her again, turned to look once at me, then left Ana and I alone in the kitchen. We stood staring at each other. "Sooo…" she said, coming over to wrap her arms around my waist. "How are you?" She pressed her lips gently to mine, parting them. I didn't think it was possible, but ever since Ana told me that she might be pregnant, I wanted her even more; although taking a lot of blood from her now was not an option. She needed to be strong if she was going to be carrying a child. Still…I moved my lips to her throat, kissing down her neck to her chest. I felt her wind her fingers into my hair and pull me against her.

"I'm feeling much better now." I breathed heavy on her skin, lowering myself down the length of her body. She tasted amazing, even more delicious than she usually did and that was quite a feat.

"That's…good." She groaned, as I unbuttoned her jeans, pulling them roughly down over her hips and spinning her so she was now against the counter. I was on my knees—literally and figuratively.

"So, what's the result?" I asked, sitting with my feet in stirrups, having just gone through an intensive internal examine and trying to recover; they were always emotionally and physically painful for me from my past abuse. The doctor was a Bonder and I felt that at least, he was somewhat familiar with the oddities of mating between different species. He pulled his seat back and looked at me, his face puzzled, not something that you necessarily want to see from a man who has just been poking around all of your most delicate areas. He began rifling through my lab work, shaking his head.

"I've never seen anything like it," he muttered looking closely at my charts. He sighed and stared up at me. "Ana, have you ever been told what blood type you are?" he asked, not taking his eyes from my face.

"Umm, yes, AB Negative. I mean that's what I've always given when I've donated blood," I said, confused by the question. He sighed again.

"Well, yes, that's true, you are AB Negative, but you're also A Positive, A Negative, B Positive, B Negative...you're every blood type—all eight of them and two that are completely non-human—one from your former Bonder I'm guessing; that's ten blood types housed in one human being. I just don't see how that's possible." I shuttered at his mentioning of Nathanial. The doctor was staring at me.

"What about the baby?" I asked, not concerned with my own genetic defects. "Am I pregnant?" The doctor shook his head and my heart sunk.

"I can't tell...it's amazing really, but I can't tell." My eyes narrowed.

"What does that mean?" I asked, my tone sharper than I wanted. I took a breath and steadied myself. "I'm sorry, please, could you just explain?" I smiled at him.

"Your tests are showing both a negative and a positive result and your ultra sound and the exam...well, I can't get a good read on the ultrasound and..." he trailed off, gazing at me.

"What?" I asked, careful not too sound too agitated.

"Things feel different, they look different; your body feels different from other Human women Ana and it's hard for me to detect the usual signs of a pregnancy." He shook his head. Well, that seemed about right. I was never normal, nothing about me was ever typical, not my health, not my childhood, not who I loved... all vastly, far from normal. I exhaled.

"What do I do?" I was suddenly worried about telling Stephen, about disappointing him with this news, even though there wasn't really much to tell.

"I guess we wait. Vampire conceptions are a different animal from Bonder/Human breeding and they can sometimes be very difficult on the Human who is carrying the child. Gestation is normally shorter than with Human conceptions, but with you, with your genetic anomalies, I just can't say for sure." I sighed and swung my legs

418

around, dangling them off the end of the examination table. "I want you to come back next week and every week after that so that I can monitor you." His eyes roamed over my face, he seemed concerned. He went over to the desk and scribbled something down on the back of a card, handing it to me. "This is my personal number, you are to call me if anything feels out of sorts and I mean anything, Ana," he commanded. I nodded, holding the tiny card and wishing that for once, I could just be a normal woman. He raised his chin, his green eyes reminded me of Alec, of the way he used to look at me whenever I had thought badly about myself; of course Alec had been faking his love and concern for me, but Dr. Connelly seemed genuine in his sympathy. "I suspect that it is all of those rare conditions Ana, both physical and emotional, that make you quite extraordinary. He reached to finger the amulet hanging around my neck. "Those symbols rarely embed themselves to individuals unworthy to carry them. They only reflect the true nature of the soul that houses their powers, and these are pure and brilliant in their illumination. Whoever gave this to you, understood just how very unique you are." He smiled at me. Tears cascaded down my face. I nodded, swallowed back the panic and sadness that were now rising and slid off the table to get dressed.

"Stephen and Liam have arrived in Argentina Nathanial; I thought you might want to know." Micah and I were sitting in his house, drinking wine and staring at the fire. I gazed at the flames, seeing her face.

"What do you think he will want?" I asked, not averting my eyes from the fireplace. My uncle sighed.

"That's anyone's guess; he wouldn't dare ask anything from Liam, but Stephen is a different story entirely. He values Stephen, values his skills, and he won't be quick to forget that he allowed for Stephen to leave his coven to join Liam. I would suffice to say that Carlo would like very much to have Stephen to join him in his quest to defeat us, defeat you." I could see my uncle staring at me. Ever since he'd found out what happened with me and Adrianna, since he and Liam had saved me from trying to end my life, Micah was more distant with me, more contemplative and I knew that he was trying to understand, trying to know what I had been thinking, how I could have done something so horrible to the woman who was my life, my soul. I wished that I had a better answer. I was weak and stupid and driven by my own selfish desires, ones that I didn't even try to control, ones that I could no longer blame on the manipulations of others like Devon or Patric, but ones that were solely mine to choose and to exercise. I had devastated her; I made her doubt her own value as a Human being, as a breath in this world. I helped to reinforce everything that she had ever been told about her birth, about her not being wanted, about her not being enough to hold anyone to her. I made her watch, made her see what was happening with me; she knew what was coming and I let her stand, alone and scared, as it hit. Micah sighed, filtering my angst. "I've asked Liam and Stephen to come to Peru after they've met with Carlo." I turned, surprised at such a request.

"Isn't that a bit risky?" I asked. It didn't seem good military strategy to invite your potential enemies to your home after they've just been meeting with your most brutal rival. Plus, I actually respected Liam and I would hate for him to be seen as playing both sides of the fence; his life could be in danger.

"Yes, your concerns are valid, but Liam doesn't seem terribly worried and I think perhaps it might be of some help to hear what's been discussed. We may be able to develop a strategy to help your Ana, Nathanial," Micah spoke softly. I trembled and I felt fresh blood begin to seep from my chest at the mention of her name. I gasped as the tears began to fall.

Stephen

I was anxious for Ana to call. Her doctor's appointment should have been over hours ago and still, she hadn't called. I fingered my phone and thought about calling her myself, but we were walking up to Carlo's ranch, waiting to meet with him. I didn't have time. Carlo lived in the Mendoza Province on a thirty-seven million dollar ranch, sprawling over a couple thousand acres. The rivers of both the Rio Grande and the Rio Malargue were located inside the boundaries of the ranch. It was a grand place to say the very least. Oddly, I thought of just how much Ana would actually like it here. There was plenty of wildlife, hiking, mountains and beautiful indigenous communities—she would be happy.

Liam looked at me, his face solemn. "I want you to keep your temper in check Stephen. Carlo knows how to push your buttons and I'm sure he won't waste anytime trying to play on whatever guilt and regret you may still be holding onto over things that have happened in your life. You must not let him get to you. Do you understand me?" Liam scolded, his eyes dark. I sighed. Carlo saw everything, everything that you've ever done, in both lives, everything that you've ever felt, desired, coveted, hated—loved, and he knew how to use those things to get what he wanted from you. A guard met us on the sprawling front porch and motioned for us to come inside the main foyer. Liam glanced once more at me and I rolled my eyes, but nodded and followed my brother inside the house. For such a massive ranch, the main house itself was cozy and welcoming. The bones may have at one time been a large barn, but Carlo had renovated the structure so that the original integrity and feel remained, but the space was now completely residential.

Carlo himself was someone to be admired, but unlike his accommodations, he was scaled back, contemplative, thoughtful. He was difficult to read and a master of diplomacy; I actually thought that he and Ana would get along quite well, if under different circumstances. Carlo was always very careful to make you feel as though you were chatting with an old friend, but one who was keeping tabs on your every move and your every thought. He was subtly lethal.

Liam and I stood in the hallway as the guard announced our arrival. I watched my brother for any sign of distress or agitation; there were none. My mind was racing and I was having difficulty concentrating. I thought about Ana, about what might have happened with the doctor and I hoped she was alright; I missed her terribly. The guard motioned for us, and Liam and I walked slowly into the living room where Carlo was sitting, relaxed and pouring three glasses of cognac.

Ana

I was waiting to call Stephen. I had no idea when their meeting was supposed to be taking place, but I thought I would hold off for a bit. I needed to regroup from the doctor's visit. I had already been to the gym, the grocery, back and forth on the rail, and now I was sitting in my apartment, chewing on my fingernails. Again, since the whole fiasco with Nathanial, for the second time since that happened, I was thinking about Patric. He had always been so honest with me, never minimizing the truth in order to protect my feelings. It was brutal at times and I also knew now that some of the actions I took with him were not of my own choosing, that he had manipulated me; still—I felt that Patric believed in me and in my capacity for resilience, but it all made me wonder what he would think of me now, of what his brother had done, of what was happening with my body. Patric was an amazing Healer and I remembered Nathanial having said that his brother had inherited that skill from both their mother and their father, allowing him to tap into both the supernatural and the spiritual

423

sides of the body, but perhaps for now, what I needed was a psychologist or a friend. I picked up the phone and waited.

"Carmen?" I asked, hoping that she would come.

Chapter Seventeen

Stephen

"How fortunate I am to have both Byrne brothers in my presence; it's a good day I think." Carlo stood, his hands on his hips, smiling wide. He was a few years older than me, more around Liam's Human age of forty-two, but as far as his vampire age, Carlo was close to a thousand years old. He was tall, six foot or so and his Argentinean heritage was pronounced. Even for a vampire, Carlo was extraordinary to look upon. His stance radiated power as did his musculature and his black hair was thick, glossy and wavy, sweeping down over his shoulders. The extreme coloring of his skin added a distinctly unearthly appearance. He was ivory colored, not pale, but luminous and no matter which way he turned, his skin seemed to capture even the dimmest light in the room and project it outward. However, it was in his eyes, that his true powers lie. They were an odd shade of rich brown, light in some areas, deep and penetrating in others and upon seeing them again after so many years, I immediately thought of Ana.

"Carlo." Liam crossed the room and they embraced. "It's good of you to have us. You look well." Liam smiled and I watched him survey Carlo, taking in his god-like appearance.

"Yes, yes; I'm well. Please sit and let's have a drink shall we?" He motioned for us to join him on the back terrace. I sighed, welcoming the sudden surge of alcohol into my system. A table had been set, with four chairs and various adorned casks of what I could only assume, held Human blood. Carlo laughed and put his hand on my shoulder. "Now what sort of host would I be if I didn't offer my guests a small refreshment?" He winked and decanted one of the bottles. The smell hit and immediately my stomach clenched. Ana had been the only one with whom I had taken to indulging my needs with as of late and the freshness of new blood was a bit shocking to my system. I saw Carlo's eyes darken as he read my thoughts and I quickly shut down my mental dialogue; I wanted to protect Ana from him in every possible way. He smirked and poured me a glass of thick, red liquid. We settled in around the table and I was anxious to get the discussion going. "Still a bit impatient are we?" Carlo's eyes flashed and he smiled. "You should take a lesson from your brother; there are many rewards in learning the art of equanimity." Carlo chuckled and nodded toward Liam.

"Are we waiting for another guest Carlo?" Liam asked, eyeing the extra chair. Carlo took a long drag from his glass and licked his lips slowly. He smiled, but his face seemed tense.

"Yes, actually we are, but not until this evening. You have another meeting to attend later no?" Christ, he knew about our scheduled trip to see Micah. I felt sick. "Relax Stephen; I'm not concerned about your visit with the Bonders. I know that Ana seems to have everyone across species, concerned for her wellbeing and that it is only fair that the individuals who love her, know what is to become of her fate." Again, Carlo smiled and I felt my brother's energy make a sudden shift. He wasn't worried, he was angry. "Besides, I actually like Nathanial and Micah. Pity that I can't seem to get them to change to the better side, particularly Nathanial, now that he's so devastated, it seems the right time to perhaps make a change." Carlo grinned, his eyes finding mine. I met his stare. I couldn't imagine Nathanial being so far gone that he would actually consider working with us, with Carlo; he would never betray his family or his code as a Bonder, Patric maybe, but never Nathanial. Carlo's eyes flashed. Liam was sitting up straight and I could see him working Carlo out in his mind.

"Speaking of Ana, Carlo; I'm assuming that's what you brought us here to discuss?" Liam asked pushing both of his glasses aside and staring across the table. Carlo laughed.

"See, that's why I've always liked you Liam, you don't tolerate my musings as much as others do…" He took another sip from his glass, gazing at my brother. "Yes, I do wish to talk about Ana; such an extraordinary story there, from what I've been told, and to hear that she's with one of *us*!" He motioned in my direction and I gritted my teeth. "Well, that's even more unusual is it not?" Liam shifted forward in his seat.

"My family owes Ana our lives Carlo; besides her great love for my brother, we all owe Ana for her capacity to place a group of vampires' lives over her own, the life of my child over her own; it's not unusual, it's awe-inspiring." Liam's voice was quiet, but clear and commanding and I saw Carlo's face shift from cocky to subdued. It was my turn to smirk.

"Of course Liam. I had not intended to invalidate the measures that Ana has taken for you and your family. I meant to merely imply that her choices are somewhat non-traditional as far as Humans go." I couldn't argue with him there; Ana was non-traditional in every, single way.

"What would you like to propose Carlo?" Liam spoke again. I admired his unwillingness to be sidetracked in debating Carlo; he wanted him to get to his point—quickly. Carlo nodded.

"Not much. I had hoped that your brother would be willing to bring Ana for a visit, perhaps show her where he got his start?" Carlo grinned, but the smile did not reach his eyes.

"You wish to speak with Ana?" Liam asked, again not willing to deviate from the discussion at hand.

"Liam, I have no intentions of harming Ana if she were to come; what sense would that make if I'm interested in what she has to offer? Killing her would be counterproductive, no? At least for the time being." His chin rose and he turned to gaze out at the mountains.

"What then are your intentions?" Liam cocked his head to the side and I could see his wheels turning, but he was keeping me out. Carlo waved his hand nonchalantly and sipped his drink.

"I'm intrigued by her. She's a fascinating case study. A Human who can call fire from within her, command it, strengthen it, control it's very properties to either protect or harm—it's quite amazing. Vampires and Bonders alike have only been able to utilize fire as a very insignificant fighting tactic—well at least most vampires and Bonders. We certainly cannot take it within, and we cannot, by any means, breathe life into such an object. Fire, by it's very physical property, is not truly alive, but Ana, well, she seems to have the odd talent of giving it its own breath, a breath that she takes from her own self without any harm coming to her—extraordinary. I believe that the only other being that I have witnessed who even came close to commanding such a talent was Patric, Nathanial's brother." I saw Carlo's face register an emotion I couldn't place; it looked like fear, but that couldn't be right. He again turned to stare at the horizon. "Then of course we have the novel concept of her blood." My head snapped up and I felt my brother reach down and press on my leg—hard. I clenched my jaw.

"Your knowledge of Ana is barely subsurface Carlo. However, if there is something more that you would like to understand, Stephen and I are willing to indulge your inquiries. Is bringing Ana here really necessary? Unless of course you have something that you wish to propose to her in person?" Liam's tone was smooth and calm, but even I could detect an undercurrent of darkness and agitation. Suddenly I felt my phone buzz in my pocket and without thinking I reached down to pick it up. Liam's hand shot out from under the table and immediately the phone fell quiet. What if she was in trouble? *She's not.* Liam answered my worry, sending his voice cutting through my mental blockade against Carlo.

"I hear that many months ago, Ana came to you with a proposal of her own, no?" Carlo turned his focus to me, his eyes clear. I nodded, keeping my hand on my phone. "And you chose not to honor her request?" he asked me.

"Yes; I didn't think that was the best choice for her," I said, trying to control my temper.

"So you thought that killing her would be a better option?" Carlo licked his lips again, taking a sip from his glass and swallowing slowly, closing his eyes. Again, Liam squeezed my leg, clearly in tune with my need to lunge across the table and decapitate Carlo.

"My coven was debating the merits of her request when she was captured, along with my child, by a group of Bonders. They were taken to Peru, held prisoner and Ana was sentenced to die by the Council," Liam spoke before I could, his tone flat.

"Ahh…yes, Nathanial's Council, how very apropos. Her escape was, shall we say, awe-inspiring." Carlo leered at my brother. "And now, now that she lives, what does your coven plan on doing with her presently?" Again Carlo turned to stare at me. "You are together no?" His eyes flashed.

"Ana and Stephen have made a decision that when she is ready, she will be allowed to have the Change initiated, that she and my brother will be a mated pair and then Ana will join my coven." Liam did not blink, he did not move and his voice was unfamiliar to me, menacing and chilling. Carlo smiled, but I could see a shadow fall across his face.

"And what makes you think that your coven deserves access to such power Liam; when did your coven begin to make decisions for the rest of us?" Carlo sat back, folding his arms across his chest.

"Ana is not a commodity Carlo. Her life is not to be bought and sold, no matter what she thinks of herself, no matter what she originally proposed; I owe Ana the life of my daughter and the life of my brother—many times over. Ana loves Stephen and her decision to be with him for the rest of his existence—is her own. She is my family and while I would hope that Ana would want to live out her life as Human, her commitment to my brother leaves them with few options. Ana is not inclined to use her power, nor are we inclined to allow her to utilize those skills until she's been properly trained. She is not a threat to you or to any other coven and her existence, while intriguing to you, is not a bargaining tool for war." Liam's tone was venomous and I felt my whole body tense upon hearing his words. Carlo's face flashed and he stood suddenly, demonstrating a rare display of anger. Liam sat back, sipping his cognac, watching.

"Why not offer her a choice?" Carlo said, quickly composing himself.

"A choice of what?" I asked, wondering what he was planning. He looked at me, shifting his eyes from Liam's face.

"Let me train her, let me show her how to fight, how to harness her powers. If she's to be turned anyway, why not allow for her to come and be exercised here? Her life will be in no danger if she agrees to come, but of course if she doesn't, I can make no such guarantees. Unfortunately for Ana, I would much rather see her dead, than be trained by any other coven than my own. It's a personal sacrifice, I know, but I think that's the only option I have now." Carlo's tone was calm, but I could see flames begin to ignite in his eyes.

"And you would allow for her to leave at the end of her training, for her to return to me and my brother so that they can be married and complete Ana's transition?" I looked at Liam. How had he known that I was going to ask Ana to marry me; I had been keeping it a secret for months now. Jesus, was nothing sacred to Liam? I heard my brother chuckle softly.

431

"If she so chooses." Carlo smirked. "But I have a feeling that she might grow accustom to the accommodations and the company that I have here." He looked at me and I frowned, suddenly feeling uneasy. What the hell was he talking about? "Of course Stephen, I wouldn't dream of keeping you away from Ana; you have always been welcome here and I would relish in the chance to train you as well; even skilled vampire assassins need reconditioning no?" He winked at me and I exhaled.

"Is that your proposal then?" Liam asked, rising from his seat. "We agree to send Ana here, with Stephen, she trains with you and at the end of that training, she returns to be married and join my coven?" Carlo rose to meet Liam's stance. He nodded.

"It's a reasonable compromise, for the time being. Of course, I ask that you acknowledge that Ana has the right to decide if she would like to stay." He smirked and again I felt a wave of uneasiness wash through my body. "Contrary to rumor, I am always partial to mediation and of course I'm always open to renegotiations."

"I don't think that will be necessary Carlo," Liam said, putting out his hand. Carlo looked to my brother and I could see awe in his eyes; he was giddy at the prospect of entering into a deal with Liam. I didn't like what I was seeing.

"I guess we'll see won't we?" Carlo said, grasping my brother's hand. "I'm looking forward to our meal this evening; it's bound to prove at the very least, entertaining. Please send my regards to Nathanial and Micah. I'll be very interested to hear about their reactions to our little negotiations. Nathanial is still very much in love with Ana is he not?" Carlo turned to stare at me. My blood boiled.

"Thank you for your hospitality Carlo," my brother said, clearly ignoring Carlo's last remark. "We look forward to dining with you this evening upon our return. Good afternoon." Liam bowed, put his hand on my shoulder and shimmered us off the back deck.

Ana

Carmen had been quick to come and she'd brought Lucie. It was nice to be able to talk to a woman, to have her understand, however neither of us could figure out what to do about my possible pregnancy or the oddities with my blood. Carmen thought that Liam would be particularly interested in hearing about my lab results and that he may have a better gage on what was happening with my body; still, I was ill at ease. Carmen, being direct and also extremely perceptive, had asked about Nathanial and it threw me. She had wanted to know if I was still in love with him and from her perspective that it was possible to love more than one person and that I shouldn't feel guilty if I still had feelings for him. I did love Nathanial, but I wasn't sure if I was *in* love with him anymore. I also knew, beyond a shadow of a doubt, that I both loved Stephen and I was in love with him— completely. My heart didn't feel so much torn as it was fallen, fallen from what I thought I knew about Nathanial, from what I thought I knew about myself; I just felt as though I was in this perpetual free-fall, wondering when, if ever, I would hit solid ground.

Carmen also allowed for me to talk about Patric and Alec, even Kai. Even through my tears, it was nice to be able to recall their memories, to conjure their faces in the presence of someone I felt safe with, someone who I knew would not judge me for my feelings or my emotions. To my surprise, Carmen reveled that she'd always liked Patric, mainly before he'd lost himself completely; she thought him to be strong willed, independent, but also constantly at war with himself… at war with what he wanted to be and what he thought he was capable of. She thought he housed quite a bit of self-doubt, something she didn't fail to mention that she saw also in me. Perhaps that's why I had always felt connected to Patric. Even beyond his mental coercions of me, I had always thought that when Patric looked at me, he understood why I was making some of the choices I made, even if they seemed reckless or stupid at the time. He could see that perhaps it was out of my own desire to better understand myself, to know that in the face of so much loss, confusion, love or desire, that my choices would only serve to make my own journey more complete and if I was lucky, to give someone else the courage to complete theirs. I also wondered what Patric would say to Nathanial about what he'd done, and where Patric's perspective would have fallen. I would never know.

Nathanial

I wasn't sure if I was ready to see Stephen again. Every part of my being felt hijacked by the loss of her and laying eyes on the individual with whom she now held herself to, it might just serve to put me over the edge. Micah sensed my unease and poured me a glass of wine. We didn't speak. A gust of chilly air suddenly filled the space. I blinked once and Liam and Stephen were standing in front of me.

"Liam!" my uncle exclaimed. "It's so good of you to come, of you both to come." He moved to grasp Liam's hand, bowing.

"Of course, Micah. We have no ill will towards you; we're happy to be here," Liam spoke and I heard Stephen snort. We locked eyes. I wanted to vomit.

"We don't want to keep you; it's at great risk to you and your family that you are here, so please, tell us—what has been decided about Ana?" Micah moved toward the sofa, motioning for Liam and Stephen to sit across from us. Liam sighed and looked over to me, his eyes drifting to the blood over my chest.

"We've made a deal of sorts, albeit a tenuous deal, but her life is protected for the time being," Liam spoke and while his eyes were on Micah, I felt that his voice was in my head, pulling me out of my own revelry, Micah exhaled.

"What kind of deal Liam?" he asked, looking concerned. Carlo was not one to make deals, not without clauses, loop holes. I saw Stephen rub his face; he looked wrecked and I felt fresh blood begin to seep from my metal tattoo.

"Ana is to visit with Carlo, train with him, let him see her power, her potential. If she comes, of course he has promised not to kill my brother or her." I saw Stephen's head snap up; apparently this was new information to him. Liam didn't miss a beat. "Stephen will accompany her to Argentina. Carlo is under the impression that Ana will not want to leave and he's offered to initiate the Change in her himself should she decide to stay." Again, I watched Stephen glare at his brother; was Stephen not at the meeting? "I assured him that won't be necessary. My brother and I have agreed to Change Ana ourselves and once her training is complete, Ana will join my coven, my family." Liam paused. I was furious. Had they not seen the problem here? How stupid were they? Liam turned to face me. My temper and desperation exploded.

"Do you honestly think that once Carlo gets within millimeters of Ana, that he's going to let her go, that he's just going to allow for her walk to away from him and take her power and her blood with her? Are you insane?" I stood, rubbing my chest. "She'll never get out of there alive! He'll kill her before he lets you or your coven benefit from Ana; he'd rather see her dead Liam, he'd rather see her dead than with you!" I heaved forward, pain fracturing my heart; blood came pouring from my wound. Micah moved to put his hand on my back. I shook my head. "I'm fine!" I shrugged him off. Liam stood, his voice calm.

"Your concerns are valid Nathanial, but I do not think they will come to pass. I think that once Carlo meets Ana, that he will want her too much to sacrifice her life, that the draw of her power, the very possibility of what she can offer him; it will prove too tempting for him. In fact, I'm counting on that being the case." Liam was watching me, but I was watching Stephen. He looked utterly confused and angry. What was going on?

"I don't understand Liam." My uncle turned away from me and moved toward the fire. "You mean to use Ana somehow? Have her negotiate for her life?" Micah sounded appalled

"Not exactly, Micah. I don't think that Ana will have to convince anyone that she deserves to live, that she should be allowed to return to her life with my brother, with my family. In fact, I think that the very person who will be making the decisions about her fate will want her to leave." Every eye in the room was on Liam.

"Isn't Carlo the one who will be making that decision, Liam? Micah dared to ask.

"No, he is not," Liam said quietly. "Carlo is not the presence you think. I would never underestimate him of course; he is still very powerful and quite a force within our species, but he has been offering you an illusion, many illusions in fact—some that are serving to baffle even me…" he trailed off, his eyes focusing on my face. I could tell from his tone that the discussion was over for the time being. As if on cue, Liam stood and bowed. "We must be returning now, we have a dinner to attend. I will of course, keep you abreast of any developments and we will let you know as soon as we have spoken to Ana about what has been decided. You needn't worry. Her life is protected." Liam held my gaze. He bowed again, nodded toward Stephen and with that, they disappeared.

Stephen

"What the fuck, Liam! What the hell do you think you're doing? What's going on?" I grabbed my brother as we landed outside Carlo's ranch. I was infuriated. Liam kept walking. "Liam!" He rounded on me, his eyes piecing.

"Stephen, we don't have time to play catch up at the moment," Liam scolded. "I need you to trust me right now. There are things at work here that are beyond your knowledge, beyond your abilities, you need to calm down and trust me." His face was stoic and his tone gave me no alternative but to submit. We started walking toward the house. He was muttering to himself. I started to ask what he was saying, but thought better of it and continued to fall in step beside him. When we approached the front porch, Liam turned to me, holding my shoulder. "If what I think has happened, if what I read in Carlo's mind is, in fact true, then Stephen you must hold it together. I cannot afford to be trying to help you to control your temper or your emotions this evening. You need to keep your mouth shut and let me concentrate. Am I understood?" His eyes were stormy and the conviction in his voice gave me chills. I nodded, feeling slightly sick. "Turn off your phone please." I started to object but Liam cut across me. "Ana is fine Stephen, Carmen was with her not but a few hours ago. You can call her later." He raised his eyebrows as I huffed, silencing the device in my pocket. We stepped up onto the porch and waited to be escorted into the house.

The circular table outside was still set for four, although gone were the casual place settings of this afternoon. Now, our seats were adorned each with a small chalice filled copiously with red liquid set atop rustic coasters. In the middle of the table stood three larger chalices, each looking more antiquated than the next and I was sure that for our "dinner" Carlo had brought out his best and most valued Human blood supply. Liam and I were instructed to take our seats by one of the house tenders and I noticed that Liam did not sit next to me; instead, he chose to sit directly across placing himself in the middle of the two empty seats. He seemed slightly on edge, but his body language spoke only of peace and calm. I sighed. I hated waiting.

"Gentleman! You're back. Wonderful, now our evening can begin." Carlo appeared, looking as powerful and relaxed as ever and I thought about what my brother had spoken at Micah's, about Carlo giving us illusions— if so then they were quite good. "I take it your time with Micah and Nathanial proved productive. I'm interested to hear what they made of our little arrangement. Let's wait for a moment though, we have one more and he won't want to miss this discussion, I am sure." Carlo smiled and I saw Liam clench his jaw. What the hell was going on? Suddenly, I saw a figure emerge from the house and I stopped breathing.

"Stephen, Liam. It's so good to see you both again," a solemn voice spoke as his deep turquoise eyes roamed over the table. Patric stood before me, alive and looking more powerful than I could have ever imagined. I tried to exhale as I watched him move to pull out his seat. This had to be an illusion, one of the best ones that I had ever seen. The entire incident with Devon, Ana, Alec and Patric; it was epic and we'd all heard about how Patric had sacrificed himself to save his brother and Ana; just what the fuck was going on here? I turned, dumbfounded to Liam. His response only continued to add to my disbelief.

"Patric." Liam rose from his seat and bowed his head. His tone not surprised, but thoughtful. Christ; Liam was right, this was all so beyond me.

"Well, I'm sure by now you are quite captivated at such a development." Carlo motioned toward Patric. "And I assure you, you will have plenty of time to hear about Patric's resurrection, but for now, I'd like hear about what the Bonders had to say about our negotiations this afternoon. Liam?" I watched as Carlo placed his chalice to his lips and drank slowly, the scent from the blood making my stomach heave; I wasn't hungry. Liam moved to sip from his own glass, his hands steady and his gaze moving between Carlo and Patric; he was assessing.

"Naturally, they are wary of our settlement, Carlo. Their interest in Ana is not for her powers or for her blood; both Micah and Nathanial love Ana and their only concern is for her wellbeing," Liam said, turning his gaze to Patric. I still wasn't sure if that's who was sitting at our table; it just didn't seem possible. I saw Liam and Patric exchange what looked to be a private dialogue and I wondered what Liam was sharing with him; I wondered if he was telling Patric about his brother's betrayal. Patric's eyes turned to me, and his chin rose. Clearly that was *not* what Liam was explaining. This should be interesting. I sighed and fingered my glass. Carlo laughed.

"Well, of course they are concerned for Ana; everybody seems to be don't they?" Carlo looked to me, his eyes flashing; I was watching Patric. "I hope you were able to reassure them that all I want is to meet Ana, to allow her an opportunity to train like no Human has ever been granted and then...we'll see." Again, he was staring at me and I felt a slight pressure in my head—he was trying to get in. I set my jaw. Liam turned to Patric, his eyes black.

"Am I right to assume that your brother is not aware of your return Patric?" Liam asked, sitting back in his seat. Patric matched his movements, leaning away from the table, tossing his hair over his shoulder. I couldn't help but notice just how much he now mirrored Nathanial in physical appearance. They were twins, but Patric seemed to always go out of his way to delineate from his Bonder brother and his heritage, in favor of the more rugged and worn look of the vampires. Oddly, this was not the present case. Patric's hair was long, sweeping, and loose and had shifted in tone to a soft black, not as dark as his brothers, but with the same reflective qualities that you don't normally see in black hair. His skin tone was also deeper, more copper in color and it served as a sharp contrast to his strangely colored eyes. He was a bit shorter than Nathanial's six foot two frame and his muscles were leaner, but impressive nonetheless. He looked to be hovering between two worlds, neither providing him with a defined sense of identity.

"Yes; you would be correct, Liam," Patric answered, his voice distinctly deeper and rougher than I had remembered. Patric's eyes looked distant and I wondered if he was thinking about Nathanial... or Ana.

441

"Are you planning on revealing yourself, or are you content to let him continue thinking that his only sibling has died?" Liam's tone was condescending and I couldn't help but think that he might be taking Patric and Nathanial's relationship a bit too personally; they weren't like Liam and me. They've always had a difficult tie to one another; Liam and I were rare in that we had managed to maintain our bond from our childhood, from the events that I caused with our younger brother, and carry that through to our afterlives—we were lucky.

"Yes you are Stephen," Patric whispered, staring at me. Carlo cleared his throat, clearly uncomfortable with the direction the conversation had taken.

"Well now, perhaps we should be discussing when you would be bringing Ana to begin her training. I was hoping to enjoy her company by the end of the month, will that do?" Carlo turned to Liam, and I saw Patric stiffen in his seat at the mention of Ana coming. I couldn't imagine what she would think or say when she saw him…or when he saw her. A slight twinge of jealousy flooded through my heart. I knew that Ana cared for Patric very much; she believed in him, in the potential of him and I had always been under the impression that despite his corrosive nature, that Ana was the first person that really affected him, that he possibly allowed himself to care for, even if he had manipulated her for his own greedy purposes. Patric and I locked gazes and he nodded subtly.

"Carlo, the situation with Ana is a very delicate one. She has suffered through a myriad of traumas as of late, the most recent was having to see Nathanial after such horrific events occurred." Patric's eyes flashed at Liam's reference to Nathanial and a veil filtered down, diluting their perfect clarity and depth. God, he would probably kill Nathanial if he knew. "I think it only fair that Ana be allowed to absorb what is being asked of her and to be able to come to you in understanding about who you are and what you are offering. I also fear that this new development," he gestured toward Patric, "I fear that it might open some very serious wounds. Ana, by ritual, is actually still Bound to Patric. It's an odd occurrence for either species, but it happened and I am sure that that Bonding is still firm, for both of them." Liam was looking at Carlo, but I could see that Patric's head was bowed; he suddenly looked diminished. Was this what my brother was counting on? Was he hoping that Patric would still be willing to protect Ana from Carlo and from a fate that was worse than death; was Liam so willing to gamble the life of woman that I loved, on a traitor, on a half-breed, on a coward? Surely this couldn't be his plan; surely he had something else. Suddenly, a glass shattered, startling the table with the noise. I saw Patric's hand was bleeding, the shards from his chalice gripped between his fingers. He had heard me.

Carlo snapped his finger and a servant came to swipe the broken glass for a new one; it didn't appear that Carlo had heard my inner monologue. Patric was always a master at infiltrating others, perhaps even more so than Carlo.

"Hmmm...yes I had forgotten about the Bonding between Patric and Ana, quite an interesting scenario." Carlo looked at Patric, his eyes bright. I hear that her imprint even holds your stone Patric, how truly lucky you are I think—she's quite a catch." Carlo laughed and I felt Liam reach under the table and hold my arm; I was about to lunge. A large guard appeared at the table and whispered something in Carlo's ear. "I'm so sorry, I'm needed for a moment, something with your

Bonder I think." He stood, pushing his chair back and I saw Patric lock eyes with Carlo; Carlo nodded and left us alone at the table. I lost any sense of decorum that Liam had asked of me and I rounded on Patric.

"What the fuck is going on? You were killed; what the hell are you trying to pull?" I leaned in toward him, my muscles tense and my blood boiling.

"Stephen," Liam said quietly, pushing me gently back into my chair. I shrugged him off.

"No, Liam, no! This is crazy. Do you know what this is going to do to Ana? And how about Nathanial, and Micah? This is fucking unbelievable. I'm not bringing Ana here, there's no way; she'll fall apart. She's not ready for this, she won't understand. Hell! I don't even understand!" I stood, pacing around the deck.

"Stephen, sit down." Patric stared at me, his voice even. I exhaled and remained standing, my hands on the back of my chair. Patric looked to Liam. "What's happened to Ana, Liam; what's happened to her and my brother?" Patric's voice had a slight edge to it and his desperation to know about her could not be hidden.

"I don't think you get to know anything about Ana, Patric!" I hissed at him. "Not until you tell us exactly what the fuck you are doing here working with Carlo and what you are doing alive! Then, then maybe we will be so inclined to indulge your quires about Ana and your god-forsaken brother!" I was near my boiling point. This was too much.

444

"Christ, Stephen. I had forgotten what a temper you have. I think it in your best interest to calm down, don't you?" Patric sipped from his glass, watching me.

"Stephen." Liam glared and I sighed, pulling out my chair and collapsing into the seat. Liam turned to Patric.

"Patric, unfortunately, the story is too long for words, would you be so inclined to allow for me to show you what's happened since you left?" I had no idea why Liam was asking permission from Patric for anything; who was he to us? Patric chuckled.

"It seems that your brother is not quite up to speed on some of the things that have transpired with me as of late; interesting that you would chose to keep him in the dark." Patric took another sip from his chalice and smirked at me. There it was, the old Patric, the cocky sonofabitch that I remembered. Suddenly, Patric had his hands around my throat and he was lifting me in the air. I flipped myself over, escaping his grip with ease and crouched, ready to lunge. Before I could even breathe, Liam was between us his posture erect and his eyes on fire.

"ENOUGH!" he hissed, growling at me. I ran my fingers through my hair and stepped back a few feet. "Sit down, both of you." Liam's tone was cold and his face furious. He was going to kill me the instant we were alone. Patric returned to his seat and gulped down the remaining blood in his glass, wiping his mouth and breathing hard.

"Get on with it." He motioned to Liam. "I'm quite sure that whatever it is that my brother has done, it won't surprise me in the least," Patric spat, his tone bitter.

"I wouldn't be so sure," I muttered and Patric snarled. It was Liam's turn to growl and I would have preferred to go the rest of my existence having to never hear him make that sound again. He scared the shit out of me. I put my head in my hands and waited for Liam to show Patric just what devastation and trauma his brother had managed to cause. Liam and Patric locked eyes and I knew it had started.

Watching Patric's reaction as my brother replayed all the events in Ana's life since his supposed death was a very disturbing visual experience. Patric had been so sure that nothing that Liam could show him would be surprising, nothing could be so beyond his knowledge of his brother to cause him any anger or despair—how very wrong he was. I too was subjected to the replay, having noting else to do; I wasn't allowed to call Ana and I began to become quite depressed. Christ, she had endured so much, too much and now we were going to have to return to Dublin and tell her that her life was yet again, in danger. I tuned out until I saw pictures that I had not come to know. They were pictures of Nathanial, images of him attempting to end his life. I sucked in a sharp breath as I watched what appeared to be a shadow, climbing up a steep mountain to an overlook. I didn't recognize him; he looked ghostlike. His eyes were clouded in a thick film and his skin was ashy, gray in color. His body was emaciated and I could see the blood from his chest seeping thick and heavy through his t-shirt. He fell to his knees sobbing and I gasped; his pain was too close, too real for me. He couldn't breathe and he was choking. I watched as he removed his shirt, revealing a skeleton, his bones cutting like knives through his skin. Blood poured over his fingers as he began stroking the metal tattoo over his heart, stepping closer to

446

the edge of the cliff. I then witnessed what was sure to be, the single most devastating and violent act that a being could do to themselves. I watched as Nathanial, this great godlike creature, this being of strength and power, of a great capacity for love because he loved Ana and he loved his brother; this man, this Demon, tore his Bond from his chest and fell, screaming so violently, that I heard my own scream erupt, as I watched him succumb to his death.

Ana

I awoke screaming, my breath coming in torrid pulses, tears streaming down my face in uncontrollable waves. I was having a nightmare, a horrible, horrible nightmare. I saw them each dead; lying, their bodies bloodied, not moving, their eyes opened. Nathanial, Stephen, Patric, Kai, Alec and Noni—all dead, all silent. Nathanial's heart ripped from his chest, Patric's body part ash, part solid mass, Kai, bloated and decapitated, Alec's neck broken, and Noni, her head bleeding. All of them were waiting for me to find them, to see that I was alone, that nothing I could do now would ever bring them back. They had fallen, gone to a place that I couldn't follow—it was over and I was alone.

I heaved over the deck, vomiting blood and spit. I couldn't breathe. I gasped and turned back to Liam; he was now sitting and watching, not Patric, but me; his eyes roaming over my face, feeling my utter despair. My body shuddered and I tried to steady myself, not wanting to ever close my eyes again.

"Patric?" Liam, still looking at me, addressed Patric who seemed to be handling things better than myself. He was stoic, unmoving, unblinking, and his hands gripped the sides of the table.

"I want to see Ana. Bring her to me immediately Liam." Patric's tone was soft, but there was an urgency that made my heart beat out of rhythm. I looked to Liam, shocked.

"As you wish Patric. Stephen, we need to take our leave." Liam rose. I didn't understand. What was happening? He was going to bring Ana to Patric? She would die; her heart would be shattered. What was he thinking? Patric wasn't looking at either of us; his eyes were still closed and I was suddenly thankful that Carlo was not here to bear witness to what we'd just experienced. Liam was pulling me, dragging me off the deck. I stumbled and he caught me, holding me up, our eyes meeting. He knew what I was about to do and he knew that Ana would need him, that I would need him. In a breath, he shimmered us back to her, back to the truth, back to what she needed to know, back to the fight of her life.

Chapter Eighteen

Ana

Liam and Stephen had returned and I was walking up the drive to Stephen's house, trying to brace myself for what I had to tell them about the pregnancy and my stupid blood types. I hoped Stephen wouldn't be too upset. There was still a chance for us, for us to have a family. I was so exhausted. My nightmare from last night rattled me into such a state, that I hadn't slept. I hadn't actually slept since Stephen left two days ago; I missed him.

I put my raincoat on the hook in the foyer and moved slowly down the hall, my legs feeling stiff. Stephen and Liam were sitting on the sofa, drinking wine by the fire. Upon my entrance, Stephen locked his eyes on me, but he didn't smile, he didn't move to greet me, he just sat there staring. I felt sick; something was wrong, terribly, terribly wrong.

"Ana." Liam stood, his hands out, but I was staring at Stephen. Something about that look he was giving me, resonated; I had seen it before. The sickness it produced in my chest was familiar and instantly I thought of Nathanial, when I'd seen him at the camp with Adrianna, when he would look at me after I had watched them together, when I'd realized that it was over and that I had, in fact, lost him. My heart froze. My blood froze. "Ana," Liam said again. I forced myself to look away from what I knew was happening. I started to back out of the room, not wanting to understand, not wanting to hear an explanation. I didn't care anymore. How much could one person take? How many times could one heart be shattered, repaired, and shattered again before it just stopped beating entirely? I quickly became angry. Angry with Stephen for doing what I knew he was about to do, angry with Liam for being here when it happened, angry with myself for thinking that I could rebuild my life, angry with Nathanial for tearing down my foundations and leaving me with nothing, angry for all the death and despair that seemed to always find their way into my life, and angry for the love as well. It shouldn't be there. I should've never allowed for it to be a part of my life; it was destroying me from the inside out. "Ana; why don't you and I go for a walk?" Liam was now standing directly in front of me, blocking Stephen from my view.

"No," I whispered, moving around Liam and coming back into the room. "No, I want him to tell me. I want him to look at me and tell me that it's over. That something happened on this trip and he's changed his mind and that we're done. I want to stand here and I want him to say it." I was quiet, but my body was quivering. Stephen's head was in his hands. "Look at me!" I shouted at him. "Look at me and say it!" I clutched my heart, it was cracking, one last fissure to destroy an already fragile repair.

"I have to Ana," Stephen said softly, his face still covered. "You don't know, you don't understand. He loves you, more than I could ever have known. Not being with you, it's...it's killing him; literally, he's dying. I can't be the one to destroy him, I can't, not after everything that I've done, not after what I did to Laura and my brother. I won't kill him, even if not being with you... kills me; our love, it's not the same..." He was choking and I didn't understand. I couldn't process. I kneeled down in front of him, taking his hands from his face.

"What are you talking about Stephen; who's dying?" I was trembling and all I could do was hold on to him.

"Nathanial, Ana; Nathanial is dying." Stephen's eyes met mine. I shook my head.

"No, he's not, I just saw him; we both just saw him. He's hurting Stephen, but he's not dying," I cried, still not comprehending.

"Liam?" Stephen called to his brother, his gaze drifting away from my face. I turned, having forgotten that Liam was in the room.

"Stephen, I don't think that's necessary…"

"Do it," Stephen commanded. " She needs to see, especially now." Stephen's face froze and his eyes went flat. Liam came to stand next to me, pulling me gently to my feet and away from Stephen. I turned back to him worried but he wasn't looking at me.

"Close your eyes, Ana," Liam said quietly, his voice tight and heavy. Liam took my hands and pictures began to filter into my mind. My nightmare was real; the dream I had had of Nathanial, with his chest torn open—it was real, it had happened. I pulled away from Liam and moved to kneel back down by Stephen.

"It doesn't matter Stephen, it doesn't matter," I cried, laying my head on his legs. "He survived, he'll repair himself, he'll be ok!" Yes, what Liam showed me was horrible, but what was I supposed to do about it? I wasn't responsible for Nathanial and while I was truly sorry that he was in such devastating pain, it wasn't enough to make me stop loving Stephen, to go to Nathanial and want to fix our relationship. I loved

Stephen and now I was fighting not to lose him. Stephen shook his head and pushed me away.

"No Ana, no. You do love Nathanial, you are Bound to him and he to you. His very existence is dependant upon you being together; that's what is so different about you, what makes you so special. You transcend what everyone could possibly think they know about loving you, about what it means to love. It's not just about a Bond, it's about a complete alteration of a life or an existence. Without you, there is neither." He was speaking so fast that I couldn't take everything in. I shook my head.

"But I want *you*! I love *you*! You promised that we could have a life together; you promised that we would be together, that we might be able to have a family! You-you…you promised Stephen." I was breaking; slowly, he was killing me. "Please." I took his hands and placed them over my heart. "Please Stephen, don't do this. We can get through this together. Please, don't leave me." My stomach heaved and suddenly I was throwing up, violently.

"ANA!" Stephen shouted, bracing my fall to the ground. Sharp pains shot through my abdomen and I heaved again, gagging and choking. "LIAM!" Stephen shouted. Liam knelt beside me, pushing my hair out of my face.

"The—doctor!" I tried to call out. "Call—the—doctor—in—my—purse!" I screamed as another wave of vomit spilled from my mouth and I felt something contract. I heard Liam talking quickly to someone and I gasped, the air leaving my lungs.

452

"What's happening Liam?" Stephen's voice sounded fierce and I felt him take me in his arms, holding me close. A cold gust of wind filled the room and I heard a familiar voice.

"Ana, it's Dr. Connelly. I'm going to help you, you're going to be ok." I felt him pull me away from Stephen and I cried out, knowing that if I left him, he would be gone to me forever. I felt someone bend close to my ear and whisper.

"I'm not going to leave you Ana. I love you and I'm not going to leave you." Stephen kissed my cheek as the doctor picked me up whirling me away from the being that held my heart and my soul.

Stephen

Liam was glaring at me. We were sitting in the waiting room at a private hospital in Dublin. Ana was in a room somewhere being poked and prodded and I wasn't allowed anywhere near her.

"Do you really think that was necessary, Stephen?" Liam spoke quietly, his eyes black and furious. I shook my head.

"I didn't know what else to do Liam. Seeing Nathanial like that, seeing what was happening to him; what else was I supposed to do?" I said, meeting his gaze, but immediately looking away. "I thought you knew what I was thinking," I muttered.

453

"Your inclinations to allow Ana some additional time before you asked her to marry you, were the only thoughts that you were allowing me to see Stephen. If I had known what you were actually planning, the stupidity of it, then I would have knocked you out until you returned to yourself," Liam hissed at me, flames appearing in his eyes. "What you made that woman endure back there, what you made her beg for, plead for—I'm disgusted. That was far from noble behavior Stephen, no matter what your intentions behind the act were—you were so far over the line that you couldn't even see it anymore!" he spat at me and stood up, pacing. "I mean honestly, Stephen!" Liam continued, scolding me. "I appreciate your compassion for Nathanial and your sudden surge of humanity for his pain, but do you really think that breaking up with Ana is the best way to help her through what is about to come? Is that what you really want; you want to leave her? You think that once you do, that she'll go running back to Nathanial— that's not what will happen and you know it! She'll be gone from you, from us—forever!" He was so furious; the last time my brother had ever yelled this much at me was after I came to tell him that I requested to be Changed, to end my life. He was beside himself in his anger. I rubbed my face.

"I know. I know. I just…it was too much. Patric, Nathanial, Carlo, it was too much. I snapped," I muttered. "I really do think that it might serve her to at least let Nathanial explain what happened; she didn't give him that chance I don't think…" Liam snorted.

"And how do you propose to fix the damage that you've inflicted on Ana? She thinks you've left her, that it's over between the two of you and I'm sure she's more than confused at such a sudden turn of events. So now, thanks to your melodramatic upheaval, we not only

454

have to deal with telling her about Patric and Carlo, but now she will have to listen to you apologize for almost making the biggest mistake of your afterlife—not to mention whatever is happening with the baby!" Again, Liam hissed and I felt my chest cave in. So I wasn't the best at making emotional judgment calls; I would fix it. "I can't wait to see you try," Liam huffed. Just then the doctor returned, looking drained.

"What's happening, Dr. Connelly?" Liam composed himself and gave his full attention to the doctor.

"From what Ana tells me, she's not had the time to discuss with you my findings during her first exam." Dr. Connelly looked to us both, his eyebrows raised. Liam and I shook our heads. The doctor sighed. "Ana is very rare indeed. Her physical make up is not anywhere close to Human, Bonder or Vampire. She's her own unique genetic composition, beyond the normal variances between the species of course," he paused, shaking his head, "she possesses ten blood types in her system, ten that seemingly work together, ten that don't cause her any harm and ten that allow for her body to continue to work as it should, to be strong and healthy despite the past abuse that she has endured. I exhaled.

"Ten blood types," Liam spoke softly, his eyes churning. Dr. Connelly nodded. "And what of the baby?"

"Well, that's the other part of this story. Until now, it has been damn near impossible for me to tell whether or not Ana is pregnant." I sucked in my breath and Liam put his hand on my shoulder. "It appears that she is," Dr. Connelly said, quietly.

"There's more isn't there?" Liam said, looking hard at the doctor.

"Despite Ana's incredible health and her capacity to heal, this pregnancy is not conducive to her biological environment. It is my fear that at the very least, she will miscarry or the child will be stillborn. Liam sighed and squeezed my shoulder.

"Is her life in danger?" Liam asked the question that I could not.

"Yes."

"What do you recommend we do?" Liam's voice was determined. Dr. Connelly sighed.

"Liam, Stephen; I feel that in such a case as extraordinary as this one, that we must terminate the pregnancy if we are to save Ana's life. I realize that this will be an extremely difficult decision to make and of course my medical advice is only that, advice. But it is quite clear to me, that Ana is an important force in both of your lives and I would suspect that sparing her life for that of a barely formed embryo and one that will most certainly not be carried to term and that will most likely kill her…that's not a risk you both are willing to take." He raised his eyebrows and looked sternly at both my brother and myself. There was no doubt in my mind; of course we save Ana, of course that's what we do. I had never thought about us having children and it was not an important factor to me in how much I loved her; it was never a factor—nor would it ever be.

"Does she know?" I asked. I wasn't sure how much Dr. Connelly had told Ana or what condition she was currently in.

456

"No, she doesn't know. We had to administer quite a bit of pain medication, so she is pretty sedated. Would you like for me to speak with her?" The doctor looked between Liam and myself.

"I'll talk to her," I spoke, my voice certain. Liam looked at me, his eyes narrowing. Clearly he didn't trust my capabilities to be helpful to Ana at the moment; I was sure he was thinking that I would possibly see this as an appropriate time to break her heart—again. "Liam, I can do this; it should be from me," I said, meeting his stare. He nodded and I followed the doctor down the hall to her room.

Dr. Connelly left me by the window looking into Ana's bed. He turned to me, put his hand on my back and spoke quietly.

"This is the right decision Stephen. I've never seen anything like Ana in all my centuries on this earth; to lose her would mean losing whatever fraction of humanity could be salvaged for us all, I think. She's come through too much for her life's journey to be made in vain. She'll need support, she'll need reassurance; can you give that to her Stephen?" Dr. Connelly turned to stare hard into my eyes and for a moment, just a moment, I saw Nathanial's face gazing at me. Losing Ana to this would most certainly push him over the edge; he would find a way to follow after her and not even Liam would be able to save him. Whatever feelings I had about Nathanial, no matter how much I have resented him, been jealous of him, hated him, I owed him this much. I owed him the chance to see Ana again, to allow for her to make whatever decisions she needed to, in order to have the life that she deserved, and I truly hoped that she would still want to have that life with me. I nodded to the doctor and pushed the door opened, stepping inside the tiny room. Ana was lying in the bed, her hair spread out in waves and curls, dark against the stark whiteness of the pillow. Her breathing was coming in shallow bursts and I watched as her chest rose and fell beneath the sheets. She had various IV's attached to her arms and a small breathing tube looped around her ears to her nose. I moved to sit on the edge of the bed, taking her hand and running my thumb over her skin. Her eyes found mine and immediately, thick tears began falling down her cheeks. She turned away from me, sliding her hand out, breaking my touch, my connection.

"Ana," I said softly, watching her face. "What happened earlier, what I said…I didn't mean any of it…"She cut me short.

"Yes you did or you wouldn't have been looking at me like you did; you wouldn't have insisted that Liam show me those horrible images of Nathanial," she whispered, still turning her face away. "I should have listened to you the night that I gave you that stupid ring; you were saying the same things then and I should have listened. I should have left Dublin, left Ireland and disappeared from you, from Nathanial and started my life without either of you. We three can't exist with each other, and no matter how much I tell you that I love you; you knowing that I will always love Nathanial, it will always serve to bring you doubts about me, about when and if he comes back, will I want to leave, will he manage to say the right thing to make me want to leave you… You asked me to get closure, but you were really asking me for time. You needed time to make sure that I was what you wanted, if you could live with the idea of him, the place he would always have in my soul. You were asking me to leave you until you could make your own decisions about us, about me." She turned her face back to me, the tears continuing to stream down her face.

"Ana," I said, my voice shaking. She shook her head.

"It's ok Stephen; really it is. I understand. I know that you love me, I truly do and maybe that has to be enough for now. I hope you know that I love you as well, more than my own life." She was still crying, but she reached up to stroke the tears from my face. " You know, I have this opportunity to go out to sea for a while, maybe I'll do that." She looked distant and I could feel her shutting down from me, from us. I wanted to throw up.

"Ana, we need to talk about something," I said, not wanting to believe what was happening in this room, what she was saying and what she knew I was feeling—it wasn't real.

"It's the baby right? I can't keep her can I?" I looked at her, surprised.

"I know it was stupid to assign a gender, but I couldn't help it; I was thinking about Lucie and Maria, you remember her? You told me that's when you knew I was special, that day when I was holding her; you said you could see what it was that I wanted, what I needed. You were right, Stephen; even then, you were right about me." I nodded and touched her lips. She sobbed and I brought my face to hers, wrapping my hands gently around her neck. We stayed like that, for hours I think, just holding each other, our tears mingling, our sobs becoming one. Finally, I reached into my pocket and pulled out a small leather box. I lifted her chin and kissed her eyes, waiting for her to open them. Slowly, I lifted the lid showing her not one ring, but two, the Celtic band that she had given me, and one that I had made for her. A smaller, delicate version of mine with a sea-blue stone melded in the center and her own symbol, her metal tattoo, with Nathanial's and Patric's emblems embossed on the inside of the band.

"Stephen, it's beautiful; I don't understand, why do you have these?" She asked struggling to sit up. I slid my band out of the satin loop and placed it on my left ring finger; I then took her ring and held her hand in mine.

"I want us to wear these Ana. I want us to wear these until we can find our way back to each other. It's my promise to you that I will not move through this world without you and that I know we will not be lost to each other for long. We won't have fallen far from what we promise now, from who we are to each other; I won't let it happen. You wear yours and I will wear mine and we will remember that we have a life together, a life that is ours to share and a love that is ours to nurture and to hold sacred." My hands trembled as I slid the ring on her finger, taking her hand and kissing it. "I love you Ana and I promise you, I will find you again and we will be together. Do you promise me?" I asked, tears coming heavy and fast down my face. She nodded and laid her head against my chest.

"Ana." Liam's voice cut through my grief. "They need to take you to the operating room now." I turned to look at my brother and I saw that tears were brimming in his eyes. I held Ana's face in my hands. "I'll be here when you wake up Ana," Liam said, knowing that I had to leave, I had to go now or I would never be able to part from her bedside again. Ana gasped and looked at me, her eyes wide and scared.

"You won't forget about me will you?" She stroked my face. "And you'll remember that I love you, that I love you Stephen, please

460

remember." Liam drifted over to her side and I saw him run his fingers over her back, quieting her nerves, easing her pain. She took a deep breath in and I saw her fall gently back against the pillow, her eyes closing.

"Go." Liam turned to me. "She'll be ok Stephen. I'll escort Ana to Argentina; I'll let you know what's happening; you won't be left out unless that is what you want." Liam stared at me and I shook my head "no". He nodded and moved away from Ana to my side. I heaved forward, my hands on my knees. "It's not over Stephen; I don't honestly believe that it is. Remember yourself, remember your love for her and her love for you; it's not over." He brought me back up and pulled me against his chest, holding me as my body shook violently.

Ana

I was trying to decide what to bring. I had never been to South America for a visit or even an extended amount of time; of course, I wasn't counting my stint in Peru. Liam had been with me in my apartment since I'd come home from the hospital; he was concerned about my physical and mental health. I'd guessed and he wasn't inclined to leave me alone, especially now. I was completely numb. Stephen leaving me had cut the final tether; all that I was doing was falling and waiting to collide with the earth below, for the impact to shatter what was left of my soul.

According to Liam, I was yet again being asked to display my powers to a very particular coven in Argentina, a coven that Liam knew well and had a history with; someone by the name of Carlo had requested to see me. Liam assured me that Carlo was in no position to cause me any harm and that it was typical of him to be intrigued by someone with my particular talents, but I sensed that Liam wasn't telling me the whole truth, that he was protecting me from something. I sighed and attempted for the third time, to light my fireplace. I waved my hand over the logs and waited for the blue flames to ignite. Nothing. I waved again and again, still nothing.

"What's wrong Ana?" Liam appeared at my side.

"I can't light this damn thing," I said, moving my hand rapidly back and forth across the space. Ever since I'd come home from the hospital, since Stephen had left Dublin, I had no fire to conjure—it wasn't there. I thought it was the surgery, that perhaps my body needed some time to recover, but it had been a month now and still, I couldn't use my power. Liam stopped my hand and held in his own.

"It's alright Ana; you've been through some very serious trauma these last weeks. I suspect that your ability to utilize your power is tied to how you are feeling." He studied my face. I threw my hand in the air and exhaled.

"Well, a lot of good that's going to do me with this Carlo person," I said, pulling away from Liam. "He's called me down to his stupid ranch so that he can see what I'm capable of, clearly I'm guessing he has some sort of plan in the works for me, and now look, I have nothing to show him, nothing to offer." I was frustrated.

"Carlo is well aware of what your capabilities are Ana; he's had more than enough time to study you and what you've been able to accomplish to date. I've made him aware that you have been quite ill and that this may affect your ability to 'perform', shall we say. He's just interested in speaking with you," Liam said, but his voice grew tight.

"About what?" I asked. Liam sighed; clearly annoyed that I kept asking him about Carlo. Liam moved to sit on my couch, his head resting on the back of the cushions. He looked so much like Stephen in that moment that I suddenly felt my chest compress and I had to work at swallowing the tears that were coming. Liam watched me.

"He's interested in making you an offer Ana," Liam spoke quietly. This was new information. I stood near the fireplace, my eyes narrowing.

"What kind of offer?" I didn't know this man and he most certainly didn't know me; why on earth would he feel compelled to make me any offer?

"He knows enough. He knows how unique your are, how special; he also knows how valuable your blood has been to so many of our brethren." Ahhh…now things were falling into place. I had come full circle yet again. It was back to my blood, back to what it could offer someone who was greedy enough to corrupt it's potential. He wanted my stupid blood, blood that could nourish Vampires, just not a child. Liam exhaled, looking sad. "Actually Ana, Carlo wants you, not just your blood." Again Liam's voice was soft, barely audible to my ears and I moved to stand closer to him.

463

"He wants me for what? I'm not a Vampire and you've told me how much he hates humans, why would he want a human?" Liam smirked, a rare gesture for him and it made me feel slightly on edge.

"He's willing to take you up on your offer, the one you first brought to Stephen. He's willing to Change you himself in exchange for your loyalty to him and his coven." Liam's eyes were closed and I felt my heart begin to race.

"Wait a minute. You've agreed to bring me to a Vampire who has offered to Change me and who's expecting me to then join some coven that I know nothing about, to lose my life to become a Vampire and to do what?" I didn't understand how Liam could come to agree to such an arrangement.

"Not quite," Liam said, his eyes still closed. "Carlo is offering you a choice, as much as he can. He's hoping that you will want to stay with him, that the training and the 'company' he's willing to offer you will be enough of a draw for you to want to join him. I have told Carlo that of course the choice is yours, but that should you refuse, you are to be allowed to leave under the condition that I Change you myself and that you join my coven." I thought that Liam seemed to be missing a giant hole in this ridiculous plan.

"And you think Carlo is going to allow for you to then benefit from my powers, to have those be part of your coven and not his? Don't you think he'd rather see me dead, after he's taken what he can from me, than see me join with you?" I was shocked at the lack of attention to detail that Liam seemed to be displaying; it wasn't like him to fall short on negotiations.

"I don't think that will be a problem for us Ana," Liam replied, his eyes finding mine.

"Why?" I said, my tone sharp.

"Because while Carlo has the power to make you an offer, he does not have the authority to order you to be killed and he wouldn't risk causing his position in the coven to go against the individual who does have that power. Now, I think you need to finish your packing, yes?" The conversation was over.

Nathanial

I was getting worse; I could feel it. My body was weakening and I could barely get out of bed. Micah was doing his best to stave off the inevitable, but I knew that things were now in a very critical state. The only shred of luck I was having, was that for the time being, Carlo had offered a break in the fighting. The deal had come out of the blue and was offered only a day after Liam and Stephen had come; I wondered what had happened at that dinner of theirs. I heard Micah enter the room. I turned my face to see him sit on the edge of the bed, his eyes full of worry.

"Ana and Liam have arrived on Carlo's ranch. They came this morning." Micah put a damp cloth to the now bloody mass that was my imprint. I winced at the gesture.

"Where's Stephen; I thought he was supposed to escort Ana?" I whispered, licking my lips; they were so dry. A shadow passed over my uncle's face and I suddenly felt very cold. "What, Micah? What's happened?" Micah tucked my mother's quilt up around my shoulders.

"I don't know all the details Nathanial; Liam felt that things were too personal for him to share with me at the moment, but Stephen has left. He's left Ireland, I think for the North; he and Ana came to a mutual understanding of sorts…" Micah trailed off, looking at my face.

"What sort of understanding?" I asked, my voice shaking from the bout of chills that I was now experiencing.

"That they should be apart for the time being, that they love each other, but there are things that they both need to reconcile before they can come together, before anything permanent can happen between them."

"You mean before he'll Change her?" I said, knowing that's exactly what he meant.

"Yes, but Stephen wants to marry Ana and Liam is under the impression that no matter how much time they spend away from one another, his brother will always want to be with her." My chest shuddered and fresh blood began to ooze from my heart. Micah took the damp cloth and began pressing gently, trying to quell the clots of dark red puss.

466

"I don't see the problem; if they love each other, then they should just be together, they should just get married and be done with it," I spat. The quicker this was over, the sooner I could die.

"Yes, well, as much as I know you are hoping to pass from this world, Nathanial, Ana's situation is not that clear cut I'm afraid." Micah's tone was scolding and his eyes flashed. "There are other factors in the mix," he said quietly and I closed my eyes, feeling exhausted.

"Like what?" I murmured.

"Like you, my son," Micah spoke, his voice firm and clear. I opened my eyes, staring. "Stephen and Liam both think that Ana is still very much in love with you, no matter how deeply she's buried those feelings, no matter that she's broken her Bond with you; they both see that she has yet to really let you go Nathanial."

Ana

Liam and I were walking up a dirt path and had been for quite some time. I didn't understand why he just didn't shimmer us to the front door. I was anxious and as beautiful as the scenery was, I was in no mood to appreciate it. Liam chuckled and stopped walking, pausing near a fence to watch several stallions gallop past.

"We need to talk for a moment Ana.," he said, reaching out to stroke one of the horses through the fence. I waited. "I won't be able to stay with you here in Argentina after today. I have to return to South

Africa, Carmen and Lucie need me and the covens there have offered us their protection. I don't wish to leave you, not for a moment, but…" He turned to look at me.

"That's ok Liam. I understand. I would feel terrible if you continued to put your life and the lives of your family at risk to stay here with me; that seems stupid." I smiled at him and touched his arm.

"Ana, there are things here, things that you are not prepared for, that I couldn't prepare you for…it's imperative that you try to get past whatever shock and disbelief that you may experience and you listen to what's being asked of you; your powers are not only of the physical kind, Ana. You know people; you can read people and an environment. You can assess the emotional tenor of a room. It's those powers that you need to harness here; the fire comes not from any physical strength that you house. Your fire is from your capacity for courage, from forgiveness and redemption." I fingered my amulet, wondering how Liam knew. He smiled at me. "I have always known Ana, from the first time we ever talked; I knew it then and I know it now." I bowed my head.

"Ok Liam," I said, not knowing how else to reply. I was scared now.

"Don't be scared Ana; I actually think that you may be very surprised at yourself and what you are able to accomplish. Your ability for honesty, to be upfront and direct, should be a source of courage for you. You have never held any illusions about yourself Ana or your life and you have very little patience for those who hide behind them. I think that will serve you well." Liam smiled and we continued to walk along the path. I linked my arm in his, not trusting myself to stand on my own just yet. Carlo's ranch rose in the distance, the setting sun bathing the landscape in a wash of brilliant gold and red fire. "Ready?" Liam asked, pulling me toward him. I nodded and he whirled us up the path to the front door.

Nathanial

I watched the sun set out my bedroom window, thinking of her. She didn't love me anymore, I didn't care what Liam or Stephen or even Micah thought—she didn't love me; she couldn't. I wished that I would be able to see her one more time, to tell her that I never meant to hurt her, that her soul and her heart were the most precious things to me in this world. That, for reasons I couldn't explain, I had fallen, but no matter how lost I became, no matter what she believed, that I would never, ever want her to doubt just who she was and just how much she had altered my life in such a beautiful and extraordinary way, that she was perfect, flawless even in her missteps, in her mistakes; she was more beautiful for them, stronger because of them, more loving, more willing to be loved—she was my hero, my Choice, my Bond—my salvation when I couldn't and shouldn't have been saved.

I stood with Liam on the back of some massive deck that overlooked the mountains and a winding river. I was trying to breathe. I turned my face to the now rising moon and thought of Noni. Liam stiffened beside me and I shifted to look at him.

"Ana, Liam," a soft voice spoke from behind us, a voice I knew, a voice I had been desperately trying to recall, desperately trying to play out what he would think, what he would say. Liam put his hand on my back and I tried to take air into my lungs. Slowly, I turned from the horizon, Liam at my side. Patric stood before me, his eyes bright turquoise, scanning my face. I gasped loudly and without thinking, I ran, crashing into him, into his arms…sobbing like a child. Vanilla, musk and sandalwood filtered into my bones as I touched his face, stroking over his eyes. He wasn't real. He couldn't be real. I pressed my face into his neck, letting my tears soak his skin. His body shuddered and gently he pulled me back, gazing into my eyes. I choked and sobbed, trying to see him through my crying.

"Patric is Carlo here?" Liam asked, piercing through my trance, my utter emotional release and disbelief. Patric's eyes didn't leave my face.

"He'll be here shortly," Patric whispered, pulling me back further but still not releasing me from his gaze. I felt a breeze move over my skin and Liam pulled me away from Patric just as another person shimmered onto the deck. I could only assume from the look of him, that it was Carlo. Quickly, I wiped my eyes and steadied my breath, still staring at Patric. The back of my neck grew hot, scalding, and I reached to stroke my now smaller metal tattoo. I had to be dreaming or maybe I had finally snapped; I hoped that I was dreaming. I felt Liam entwine his fingers with mine and stand closer to me, his energy calming my nerves and quelling my tears. Patric was watching me, his gaze steady and penetrating.

"Ana! What an honor it is to meet you." Carlo moved toward me, reaching to shake my free hand. "I am Carlo Rios. Of course, I'm sure Liam has already told you. I'm very glad you came." His accent was thick, but he spoke English with an impeccable cadence and articulation and like all Vampires, he was stunningly beautiful. He was wearing a ranch style hat, jeans and boots. A loose, bright blue shirt provided a stark contrast to his skin, which was somewhat pale for what I had always thought quite a few Argentinean people usually displayed. His hair was dark, long and billowed out in waves over his chest, but it was his eyes that were the most intriguing. They were brown, but a much lighter shade than his hair and they gave him a somewhat mystical appearance, very similar to Patric and Nathanial, but perhaps a bit more sinister in what I was sure he was hiding in their depths. Patric caught my eye and I thought that I saw him smirk. Clearly, he had been monitoring my internal assessment of Carlo. At least that connection wasn't broken. Carlo winked at me; he had heard my reaction to him as well.

"Why don't we sit?" He motioned for us to join him at the table. He waved his hand and immediately, someone brought out a plate of fruit and cheeses and a ginger ale. I raised my eyebrows and glanced quickly at Patric. I wondered if he too was recalling that horrific

471

dinner at his villa in West Papua. "Ana, I hope this is to your liking. I can get you anything you like." He smiled at me.

"Oh, no, this is wonderful, thank you so much Carlo." I was surprised at how steady my voice sounded. My mind was racing. How was Patric alive? Did Nathanial know? Maybe Patric could help Nathanial, help him to heal if he was as sick as Stephen thought. I saw Patric stiffen and I felt a familiar pressure in my head. *Ana, you will need to do a much better job at burying your mental dialogues. Carlo is assessing you as we sit; he's looking for chinks, vulnerabilities in your armor. Your emotions are not allowing you to block his penetration into your mind and he can see far deeper than most. We'll have a chance to talk later, just you and I, but for now, you need to keep your concerns for me and my brother out of your head.* The voice disappeared and I took a shaky breath in. Liam squeezed my hand under the table and I tried to center myself, tried to calm the rise of panic and anxiety that my body wanted to succumb to. I let my mind go blank, filling all space with darkness; brick, by brick, I rebuilt the wall that I had used so many times in my life. I just had to do it a lot quicker this time.

"Eat, eat, Ana. You must be hungry." Carlo stared at me as he sipped his wine, his eyes flashing.

"Carlo, unfortunately, I have to return to my family." Liam stood, squeezing my hand again as he felt my panic returning. I couldn't believe that he was leaving me here, with Patric and with Carlo; this was horrible. Liam turned to stare at Patric. "I can entrust that you of course will honor our agreement?" Liam wasn't asking at all; I knew that tone.

472

"Yes, yes, of course Liam." Carlo stood, laughing. "Ana will visit with us, hopefully enjoy herself and when she's ready, all she needs to do is call you." Carlo turned to wink at me again. Christ. Liam nodded and his eyes went to Patric. They were having a conversation.

"Ana." Liam pulled me from my seat and moved me away from the table. "Remember what we've discussed. Remember what you need to do while you are here. I know you are in shock over Patric, but he is prepared to tell you everything; the situation is not as it seems." Liam's eyes were urgent upon my face. "You are not in any danger, Patric will see to that." I was doubtful. Liam shook his head. "He knows everything Ana. He knows about you and Nathanial, he knows that his brother is dying; he knows. I have not told him about you losing the baby, that's not information for me to hand out. You have the right to keep that to yourself. Carlo is also not privy to any of the information Patric has about you, although he is aware that Nathanial is in a very weakened state. I promise you on my own existence Ana that I would not leave you here if I thought you were to be killed. I promised Stephen that I would protect you always." At hearing Stephen's name, I ran my finger over the ring on my hand, trying not to cry. "Listen to me, your ability to shimmer is part of who you are now, it doesn't just go away. If you need to, you can do it again. You come to South Africa and Carmen and I will be there to meet you. Do you understand me?" Liam was holding my face in his hands. If I wouldn't be in any danger, why would I need to shimmer? "Because you may need to make some decisions while you are here, decisions that not only involve your life, but possibly the life of someone else, things are not what they seem here Ana, remember that please." Jesus, he was just like Noni, talking in riddles. I sighed and nodded. He

473

kissed my cheeks and pressed a small device into my palm. It was the smallest phone I had ever seen. "There are two numbers on this phone, one for me and one for Stephen. You call and we will be to you in less than a heartbeat." I had a phone number for Stephen? Liam shook his head. "Let him be Ana; you both need time." I nodded again and tucked the phone in my pocket.

"How long do I have to be here?" I asked, not sure if I wanted to know.

"I'm not sure exactly, that depends on Patric. He'll need to assess the situation, assess Carlo; he wants you to remain safe, I'm sure of it." Liam was frowning.

"Ok, then, so I'm here in Argentina. Umm… what do I do about my bills and my apartment and my job?" I asked Liam. It was just like when Stephen told me that I couldn't leave his house after coming to him. He'd offered to pay for everything. Liam smiled and took my hands.

"Ana, I took care of all those things weeks ago." Liam laughed.

"What, so you just like paid off my bills and told my landlord that I wouldn't be coming back?" I was stunned. I was pretty sure that I owed over a hundred thousand dollars in student loans alone. Liam waved his hand.

"It's odd just how practical you are amidst some very bizarre situations." He grinned. "Your apartment will be there when you return, if you so wish," he said quietly. Did he think that I would want to stay? Liam shook his head. "I'm not sure Ana; I can't see the future, but I have the utmost belief in your ability to do what you feel is best—to make the choice that will give you the beautiful life that you so very much deserve." He kissed the top of my head and pointed to the phone in my pocket. I nodded. He turned and bowed to Patric and to Carlo, then shimmered away leaving me on the deck to ponder my fate.

Part III

Chapter Nineteen

Ana

Frick, this totally sucked! I sighed and looked at Patric and Carlo, both who had been watching me intently as Liam spoke before leaving me alone. Oddly, I thought that my current situation wasn't any scarier than the one I had with Stephen or what had happened in Peru or with Andres or even at the camp in Idaho and especially with me having to terminate my pregnancy. Sadly, this just didn't seem to be that big of a deal if I could get past the whole Patric coming back from the dead thing and the fact that I didn't seem to be able to use my power with fire anymore… maybe I would make it through. I wanted Liam to be proud of me. I would want him to know that I at least held it somewhat together despite what seemed to be falling apart around me.

"Ana, why don't we sit and you can have something a bit more substantial than just fruit." Patric motioned for me to come back to the table and I stared at him. He looked just like Nathanial; it was so strange. They were in fact, twins, but Patric was a master at altering his appearance and he rarely displayed the visual characteristics that reminded him of his ties to Nathanial and to their family. His eyes were the same, they were his mother's eyes and I was betting that he liked having at least that part of her close to him; like Nathanial's quilt. I nodded and returned to my seat. Carlo stood and waited for me to slide in my chair.

"What can I get you for dinner Ana?" he asked, leaning in toward me and grasping my hand. Instantaneously, an electric pulse shot through my fingers and Carlo pulled away, having been shocked, I was sure.

"I'm so sorry!" I said, looking aghast as a force of electricity coursed through my veins. "Are you alright?" It was a silly question to ask a Vampire, but that was just typical for me; I tended to apologize for things beyond my control and to worry about everything. Carlo laughed.

"I'm fine Ana, no harm done. But I can see you have an energy about you, yes?" He laughed again, tossing his hat to the side and running his fingers through his hair. The action reminded me a bit of Stephen and it made my heart skip a few beats. I wondered where he was, what he was doing. Since he'd left me at the hospital, I had no idea where he'd gone or if he would ever come back. I slowly turned the ring on my finger, rubbing the marine-blue stone in the center of the band.

"Ana, how about some chicken and rice perhaps?" Patric cut through my grief and I nodded to him.

"That's fine, but I don't want to put anyone out," I said. "I really hate eating when no one else does." I forced myself to smile.

"Nonsense." Carlo smiled back. "You need to eat and of course while you are staying here, you will have access to a chef and all of our freshest meat and vegetables; whatever you desire, it's yours." Carlo sat back, folding his arms across his chest, his eyes scanning over my face. He waved his hand and a small young woman suddenly appeared at his side. I hadn't noticed her before. "Ana, this is Esther. She runs all of the main house and the guest quarters where you will be staying. She will get you anything that you need and make sure that you are comfortable and well taken care of when I am not here to see it done myself, of course." He smiled at me and cocked his head to the side. I stood and reached to take both of Ester's hands in mine.

"Gracias por su bondad," I spoke, hoping that I had not butchered her language too poorly. She smiled, her eyes shining.

"Usted son bienvenidas!" she replied and I leaned in to kiss her on both her cheeks. I sat back down as Carlo instructed her what to prepare me for my meal.

"You speak Spanish so well Ana!" Carlo poured himself and Patric glasses of wine.

"Not as well as I should," I mused, sipping my drink and wondering how long these pleasantries were going to last. At Patric's instruction, I had been preventing either of them from seeing into my thoughts; I just hoped that I was doing a good enough job. Carlo was a tough read. He was a talker and he seemed quite content to yammer on and on about his ranch and organic farming and migrant workers, all while I tried to eat without throwing up. Patric had yet to say a single word and I wondered just what he must have been thinking; he looked to be assessing every move I made and every question that Carlo asked me. The questions themselves were pretty mundane; what kind of work did I do, how long did I take me to get my Ph.D., what did I study, did I enjoy living in Ireland—all things I had been asked many, many times. My answers were standard by this point. He was getting me warmed up, I could tell. I humored him as much as I could, given my current situation, but I knew he wanted to ask me about the whole fire thing and possibly about what had happened in Peru with the Bonders. I wasn't about to offer any information without prompting. I would let him come and get it himself.

Esther cleared out plates and brought me out a kettle of tea—Matè, my favorite. I looked again to Patric and I saw that he was studying me, my face, my eyes. It made me self-conscience. I sipped my tea, waiting.

"So, tell me Ana." Here it comes. "I'm don't mean to pry at all, but Liam seemed to think that you've been experiencing some effects from your illness—you were sick for a bit, no?" Carlo's eyes met mine and another surge of electricity rocketed through my body—not from him, I was sure, but from me. I placed my mug back in its coaster and met his gaze.

"Yes, that's correct," I offered, again I wanted him to work for the information. Carlo nodded and leaned across the table.

"If you don't mind me asking, what kind of illness did you endure?" The sound of the question struck me as odd; perhaps it was the vernacular used or perhaps it was just the word "endure", it seemed ironic somehow. Liam had told me that it was my honesty that would be of most use to me, my ability to level the emotional playing field, so to speak; I hoped he was right.

"I lost my baby," I said. "I had to terminate my pregnancy because I was about to lose my life." Silence. I sipped my tea.

"My god, I'm so very sorry Ana." Carlo's eyes deepened and he frowned. "I had no idea." I shook my head.

"Liam has always been very respectful of me, Carlo. He would never assume that I would want anyone to know unless I told them myself." I folded my hands on the table.

"If you don't mind me asking; who is the father?" Carlo's eyes studied me. I hoped Stephen wouldn't mind.

"Stephen is...he was the father." I corrected myself. Carlo sat back in his chair and sipped his wine, actually he swallowed the entire glass in one sip.

"And you think that this loss...that it has affected your abilities?" Patric spoke and the sound of his voice startled me—it was so very dark and low; I almost thought that it wasn't coming from him at all. I sighed.

"Yes," I replied, meeting Patric's gaze.

"Why do you think that is Ana?" Carlo was watching the interaction between Patric and me; I guessed he was also assessing things. I cleared my throat and looked Carlo in the eyes, my tone fierce and almost as dark as Patric's.

"Because I have nothing left to fight for anymore Carlo. I've lost everything, everyone. I lost a child—or what could have been a child; I lost my two best friends; one killed the other, I lost the only family that I have ever known; she was brutally murdered. I lost three people that I loved desperately, all for very different reasons; my life has been forfeit so many times and somehow I've always managed to escape, but I'm guessing that I've run my course now. See, you can't offer me anything that I could want Carlo, because I've been lucky. I've been able to love and to be loved, to have the potential for a family and a life beyond what I could ever dream I deserved. I've had it all in front of me, waiting, but here's the rub; you can't take away anything that I haven't already lost, and you can't give any of it back. It's gone now, lost to me forever I am quite sure." My heart was pounding and the reality of the situation, of everything that I had just said, was crashing down around me. "I have nothing left to lose now and if you think that my life is important to me; if you think that living in this world without the people that I love, without having them love me or want me, is a life that I would want to live, well you have been sorely mistaken." I stared at him unblinking, moving forward in what I needed to say. "I'm broken Carlo, shattered and I'm guessing that you were hoping that I would be able to provide you with a sense of power, of strength, but how could I possibly do that for you when I have none for myself—they don't exist in me anymore. I've disappeared and what you are wanting, it is no more; it's a shadow that your are chasing, a misted dream that has no tangible form. I'm sorry, but I cannot give you what you want." I sat back, my body heavy from the weight of my life. Esther suddenly appeared at my side.

"Ana, Esther will take you to your room, your bags are already there." Patric was staring at me, his eyes dark. I nodded, knowing that my little rant was probably going to put a slight dent in whatever plans Carlo had hoped to carry out. I didn't care, he needed to know and if he still thought that I was worthy of being turned, well then maybe I would just let him or he could kill me; I honestly didn't care anymore. I had been down this road so many times that I truly wished there would be some sort of resolution to my journey—for good or ill.

Of course my room was stunning, rustic and cozy with a large bed, a fireplace and a huge private bath. It also appeared that, besides Patric, I would have the entire guest quarters to myself. I had a terrace that looked out onto the river flowing through the ranch and the mountains rising against the deep black of night. My bags had been neatly unpacked with the few clothes I'd brought hanging neatly in the closet. A plush black robe had been set out on the bed with matching slippers placed on the throw rug beside the fire. I wondered if I could ask Esther to light the fireplace for me. I unpacked my travel kit and set about taking my shower. At least it was a nice room. I put on my sweats and turned down the bed, not wanting to believe that I would actually have to wake up here tomorrow, alone. I wanted to call Liam, to tell him to come back, that I couldn't do this, not now. Absently, I rubbed my lower abdomen, thinking. A soft knock broke through my revelry and I suddenly realized that I had been crying. I wiped my eyes.

"Come in," I said, my voice breathy. I watched as Patric drifted silently into the room, looking ethereal and strong. I settled back against my pillows. "Wow, man, just when you think you've seen it all. I had no idea that resurrections were actually possible; perhaps being an atheist isn't the right path for me after all," I said sarcastically, staring out the window. Patric moved to block my view of the terrace; his arms folded across his chest.

"That was quite an impassioned speech you gave this evening," he said, his eyes flashing and churning. "However, I'm inclined to think that it's bullshit." His tone was condescending. I laughed softly.

"Well, I don't know what to say then, that's the truth and I'm sorry that you can't seem to wrap your head around what's happened to me Patric, but really, it's not for you to understand. I'm sorry that I've disappointed you, ruined your plans and what not...but you haven't been here, you haven't been part of my life in a very long time and I'm different now, so many things have happened; too many things have happened..."My voice softened and the metals in my neck started to burn. He came to stand next to the bed. "You're welcome to sit if you want," I said, still gazing past him out the window. He sighed and sat on the bed. "So what's the deal with you? I saw you explode right in front of me; I saw your ashes fall..." My mind was reliving the moment at my house and I saw myself crawling over to the remains of Patric's body, his ash covered the ground. I saw myself sobbing into the grass, not believing that I had lost him too, so soon after Kai and Alec. I remembered Nathanial's face, knowing that his only sibling was dead, gone from his world forever. Suddenly, I became angry. I sat up staring at Patric. His eyes were closed. "Well?" I said, jostling him out of his trance. "Would you like to explain?" I said, holding his shoulder.

"It's complicated Ana," he said, turning to look at my hand.

"Well uncomplicate it, Patric," I hissed at him, removing my hand from his body. He sighed again and turned the full force of his eyes on me. I met his stare.

484

"I thought you had died," he began speaking, his voice low and rough. "I saw you fall from the deck, I saw your body fall backward. I knew, I knew immediately when I got your package at the villa, I knew that you had figured it out and that you would try to save Nathanial, and me if you could. I just never would have dreamed that you would have sacrificed your own life to give us a chance; I should have known that's what you would do though…" He looked at me, his eyes clear and bright now. I waited for him to continue. "Alec was there on the deck of your bungalow, in West Papua of course, and others came as well having seen your fall; I was captured and Devon ordered me to be taken to Carlo. I, unlike the rest of the vampires, am not afraid of Carlo, I never have been. Perhaps it's my arrogance at work, but he's never intimidated me. His powers have never impressed me and I have always thought him to be weak and overly concerned with perceptions; he's an illusionist at best."

"Liam seemed to put his powers in high regard and Liam isn't impressed or afraid of much either," I said, fiddling with the tie on my robe. Patric chuckled.

"Liam is cautious by nature and he remembers what Carlo once was, a reasonably powerful and somewhat talented vampire. Liam is the master diplomat; he never takes things for granted and is always assessing situations for depth and truth. He's not arrogant and he's certainly not pursuing respect or power for that matter; he doesn't need either. Liam also knows that he could defeat Carlo in an instant, and Carlo knows this, that's why Liam is certain that Carlo will not harm you. Liam will kill him if you are ever touched while you are here." Patric touched my hand and stopped me from worrying the tie on my robe to shreds. Our eyes met and I felt my skin grow warm.

"So, what happened when you were brought to Carlo?" I asked, eager to know how he'd managed to fake his own death. It reminded me of something that would happen on a cheesy soap opera. The favorite character that everyone loves or loves to hate, suddenly dies in some massive explosion, but then miraculously, he reappears to avenge those who tried to kill him; it's a good story, if you liked those kinds of things. Patric laughed and I guessed I had let a few bricks in my wall displace. He could hear my thoughts again. He raised his head and shook his hair, letting it cascade down his back in a soft curtain of dark waves.

"I was to be killed for my treachery and Carlo was going to be the one to do it." Patric sighed and leaned back against the post on my bed.

"Treachery for what? For trying to kill Devon that night on the deck?" I asked. He shook his head.

"No, I had Carlo and Devon up in arms long before then." He grinned at me.

"For what?" God, it was like pulling teeth. Out with it already, I thought. Patric laughed again, but his face turned smooth and contemplative once he began speaking.

"For not bringing you to Carlo after Nathanial's attack at the University. For keeping you for myself, for taking your blood, for allowing you to get to me, for having an intimate relationship with you…take your pick," he said, his voice soft. "Like me, he thought you to be dead and that's that. I was going to be killed and he'd just continue fighting his wars against Humans and Bonders and the story's over. He didn't realize that the individual he was fully

486

embroiled with when I was brought to him was my uncle, Micah. I saw this as an opportunity to gain a bit of leverage and possibly spare my life; I'm not nearly as unselfish in my gestures as you are Ana." Patric stared up at me from under his thick frame of dark lashes. "Plus, Carlo is fascinated by anomalies and my combined bloodlines were something that proved intriguing to him. I offered my help against my uncle. Both Nathanial and I have always been excellent military strategists; we get that from our father, I think. Both of us have always had an affinity for commanding troops, to getting individuals to fight for a cause; it's just natural for us," he paused and his eyes grew distant, "anyway, I was able to make myself useful and put off my imposed death sentence. Carlo eventually became dependent upon me, upon my advice and guidance and in a very short period of time, I became his most trusted advisor. Of course during this entire process, I was learning everything I could about Carlo, about his history, his powers, what he feared, what he was tempted by, what he hated. I came to find that he actually hated Devon, that his existence was that of a petulant child, in Carlo's eyes." Patric stared at me.

"What?" I asked, wondering why he was looking at me so intently.

"Nothing. It's just that I was remembering you dancing with him that night at the restaurant. I think that was the first time that I realized that I had the capacity to be possessive over a woman." Patric laughed.

"If I remember correctly," I said sitting up fully now, "you had a serious attitude problem with me that whole trip. You were commanding me to do this and that and not to tell Alec this and that, even though I now know that you were all working together, and you wanted me to lie to

487

the authorities about those god forsaken murders. You were horrible," I said the blood rushing to my cheeks. "So what, you were all there to get to me; were you supposed to bring me to Carlo or something?"

"No. I mean I wasn't part of that plan actually. That was something that Devon and Alec had devised; they had been keeping tabs on you after Nathanial and I left you at the beach. Carlo was intrigued by your existence; he learned a lot about you from Alec of course and he wanted you watched. I would call Alec from time to time and let him know how you were doing and what your reaction was to seeing Nathanial again. I had no idea that Devon was poised to take your blood and neither did Alec. Devon went out on his own once he...once he got to know you." Again Patric stared at me, his eyes fierce. "So then the ultimate chance arrived for Carlo and myself I guess. I just happened to be in the room when Alec arrived to tell us that somehow, beyond all reason, you had survived that insane fall from the deck; that you were in fact alive. I was in disbelief, but Alec showed us the images from his memory and there you were, alive and thankfully in the care of my brother. Alec wouldn't dare touch you while Nathanial was around."

"Humph," I said, thinking a lot of good that did me. Alec turned out to be a psychopath.

"Yes, well that was an unforeseen behavior. Alec was ordered not to touch you Ana, but he and Devon were supposed to bring you to Carlo here in Argentina, to kidnap you I guess. To Alec's credit, I don't think he expected you to fight back as much as you did or be willing to tap into your more violent nature, shall we say." He raised his eyebrows at me.

"I get that from you," I muttered. Patric tossed his head back and laughed loudly.

"No way Ana, I'm not letting you blame me for you sadistic fighting style; that's all you." He eyed me.

"Ok, so now Carlo knows I'm alive, and he sends Devon and Alec to kidnap me; when do you come into the mix?" I asked, waiting for some resolution to all this absurdity. Patric shifted so that he was lying beside me on the bed, putting one of my pillows behind his neck.

"I made a proposal of sorts to Carlo. I suggested that if he wanted Devon out of the picture that now would be the opportune time to do it. I volunteered to finish what I started that night on the deck in West Papua. We devised a plan to make Devon think that Carlo wanted him to use me as bait for my brother and for you and that Devon would be in control of whatever fight Nathanial decided to launch. Of course, we were all still under the impression that Devon would be taking you back to Carlo. Even after Nathanial killed Alec, you were supposed to be taken away from the house and from my brother—you weren't to be harmed. But Devon is a predator and he was obsessed with you and with your blood and the lure of you was just too great for him. He betrayed Carlo for a second time, so the plan to kill him seemed apropos." Patric took a deep breath and turned to glance at my face.

"Was that you at the battle or not?" I asked getting frustrated; this was taking too long for me, my patience with things was not what it used to be.

489

"Yes and no," Patric said, his eyes still on my face.

"What the hell does that mean? Did you attack Devon with me when we fought together, was that you?" I asked, desperately wanting it to have been the two of us fighting, needing it to have been him standing there next to me. Slowly, I watched as Patric brought one finger up to my face and gently stroked my cheek, warming my skin with his touch. I felt so sad, so empty and his touch was so familiar that I wanted to cry.

"Yes Ana, we fought Devon together; in that moment we were together," he said softly, taking his hand away. Something occurred to me.

"When Devon and I were facing each other, when I had sent Nathanial back against the tree and I had you protected in my fire; you were really quiet back behind me. I remember thinking that and I remember that I had wanted to look at you to make sure you were ok. What happened to you?" I asked, somewhat in awe of how much I was allowing myself to recall. Patric shook his head, smirking.

"God, those stupid flames. Do you know that they almost actually cost me my life, that I may have had to fight off Devon?" He looked at me, his eyes deep in color and vast in their knowing. "You wanted to save me Ana." His voice became quiet and he again looked distant. He sighed. "At the last moment before I actually arrived to your house, Carlo decided against having me kill Devon myself; he didn't want to risk me losing my life and him losing the best military strategist he had; we made a switch of sorts, one of Carlo's most interesting abilities and one you were able to bear witness to with Alec." Patric stroked my arm, absently.

"A shape shifter?" I asked, stunned, but also seeing how it was now possible for Patric to be sitting next to me. He nodded.

"A sacrificial lamb of sorts; we made the exchange when you were confronting Devon." I shook my head.

"But you were talking to me, I heard you when Devon was showing me all those images of Nathanial with those women, you were screaming at me not to listen to him."

"Yes, that was me; I wanted to stay just in case you or Nathanial needed me, just in case things did not go as planned, and no, I did not want you to listen to what Devon was saying," Patric scolded me and I couldn't help but think that he might have resented me a bit for leaving Nathanial over that whole issue. I was sure that Liam had showed him what the impetus was behind me going to Stephen in the first place. Patric huffed out loud, but he didn't seem agitated with me.

"So that wasn't you that I pulled from the fire?" I looked at him awestruck.

"No," he said, leaning back against the pillow.

"So you didn't actually sacrifice your life to help save mine and Nathanial's?" I said quietly; feeling slightly stupid for all those times that I had defended Patric against criticism that he was selfish and unredeemable. I heard him sigh and I searched his face.

491

"No, Ana I didn't." He met my gaze.

"Oh. But that night on the deck in Papua when you came, when you found me; that was you. You were going to help me, you didn't want me to die." My voice sounded desperate.

"No Ana, I didn't want you to die; I've never wanted you to die. Christ I've made some extremely bad decisions and my behavior towards you and towards my brother has been enough to get me bound by my own chains, by my own sins for the rest of my miserable existence. I did everything wrong; I failed in so many ways and I am so ashamed of who I allowed myself to become. It was me who made those choices and it was me who decided to cast away everything that my mother and father hoped I could be; I betrayed them and I have dishonored the sacred life of my mother. She died loving me and I have given her nothing in return except a son who chose to be selfish, greedy, arrogant and bitter—all the things she wasn't." Patric moved off the bed and stood near the window, his hands on his hips.

"Well, I never thought those things about you; I mean I always thought you had a bit of an attitude problem, but I would never think that your mother or your father would not love you Patric. They might be disappointed in the life you decided to live, but that's only because they knew that you deserved better, that you could be better, that you could be happy. I think that's what parents might feel—I don't know..." My voice faded and I stroked my stomach. Patric turned from the window and came to sit on the bed again.

"Ana, I'm so sorry; I'm so sorry that you lost...that you had to..." He was struggling.

"It's ok; it's not like I would have wanted Stephen to stay with me if I had been able to continue with the pregnancy; we needed to be apart I guess. He needed to be apart from me." My chest shook and Patric raised his chin.

"And that brings us back to your speech this evening I think." His tone contemplative and suddenly I thought about what Liam had said about things not being what they seemed. Something about the way Patric and Carlo were acting this evening and the information that Patric had now just recalled for me, about how much Carlo had trusted and needed Patric…it made me wonder.

"Patric? Are you in charge here? I mean have you usurped Carlo for control of his coven?"

"Yes," he said, studying my face.

"And that means that you are still fighting Micah."

"Yes."

"Which means that you are fighting Nathanial," I said, connecting the threads.

"Yes."

"And he doesn't know that you're alive."

"No."

"Are you planning on telling him?" I asked.

"I haven't decided yet," Patric responded. I sighed, Lucie had a better response capability than Patric at the moment.

"Do you know what happened with him, with the Council and the fire and me and Lucie and what happened with the girl he was with?" I wasn't sure just how much Liam had told Patric.

"Yes."

"Do you know that he tried to kill himself; do you know that I can't touch him anymore and that he can't read my mind?"

"Yes."

"Liam thinks he's dying. Is he?"

"Yes."

"So you know everything then?" I asked, somewhat grateful that I wouldn't have to recount all of those horrible moments when I had to watch Nathanial and Adrianna, not with Patric; I didn't want him to see how hurt I was or how awful his brother's behavior had been, intentional or not.

"Yes, Ana, I know everything." Patric's eyes were hard to look at; they seemed to be the only thing that I still had a connection to, the two things that perhaps still knew me.

"So what do we do now?" I asked, still very unsure of what I was supposed to be doing here. Patric reached to stroke my face again, his thumb holding my cheek.

"Why don't we focus on getting your power back for right now. Liam is very concerned about your emotional health…" His eyes searched mine as his voice went soft.

"How do we do that?" I couldn't help but meet his gaze.

"By getting you to heal, to relax, to regain your confidence," he said, stroking down the length of my cheek to my jaw, his eyes roaming over all the new bite marks I had in my flesh. "Hmmm…are these from Stephen?" he asked, fingering my wounds gently. I nodded, looking away from him. He pulled back and smiled.

"Patric? Liam promised that I wouldn't be hurt here, that I would be doing some sort of training, learning to use my power. Was he right? I have no idea who you are now, not that I care if you decide to kill me; it would be just nice to know." I bit my lip.

"Ahh…yes, I'd forgotten that you are subscribing to a complete disregard for you life these days." He studied my face, smirking slightly. "That stupidity aside, no, you will not be harmed while you are here. Carlo wouldn't dare risk his position with me to get to your blood or anything else he desires." Patric's eyes flashed. "But me, well now, that's a completely different story." He grinned as he ran his finger down the bridge of my nose. "Rest assured, you have nothing to worry about; perhaps apropos to our past together, I haven't decided just want to do with you yet." Patric laughed and I found myself smiling, remembering the first time he came to my room, nearly two years ago now. He rose off the bed and opened my bedroom door.

"Hey, guess what? I called after him. He turned to look at me.

495

"What?" He hung on the doorframe looking way too powerful.

"I have ten different blood types in me. Can you believe that?" I asked, pursing my lips. I laughed.

"Actually Ana, I can most certainly believe that." He winked at me and shut the door.

****

I had no idea what time it was when I awoke the next day. I felt wrecked and groggy. I shook out my curls and splashed some water on my face, brushed my teeth, but kept on my sweats. Patric had not mentioned any particular plan for me today, so I had no idea what to expect. I headed downstairs to the guest kitchen to find Esther chopping up large bowls of mangos.

"Buenos tardes Miss Ana." She smiled as I approached. Frick! What the hell time was it, the afternoon already? "Mr. Arias has left you a note and some maps for your travels." She pointed to a small breakfast nook that was set with a glass of orange juice and a coffee mug.

"You speak English beautifully Esther," I said, walking to stand beside her as she chopped. She shook her head.

"I could be much better. Maybe with you here, I will improve, no?" She laughed.

"Only if you teach me Spanish first," I said, getting a knife.

"No, no, miss Ana. I have breakfast for you. Have your coffee and look at your maps. Sit please." She shooed me out of the main kitchen and over to the table.

"Fine, but you must stop calling me 'Miss Ana' Esther; I think we are the same age and you are not my servant!" I teased her as I sat down to examine the note left for me on my plate. The stationary was very elegant; not exactly what I would have pictured Patric to use, but hey, it'd been awhile since I'd seen him.

Dear Ana,

Per our conversation last night; I have set out several maps for you incase you would like to explore the area a bit. Eduardo has offered to take you horseback riding if you wish and will be waiting for you in the stables at 1pm. Carlo would also like to see you for an aperitif at 6 and I hope to be back for dinner around eight. Enjoy yourself today and please try not to tempt anyone with your blood, your body or anything else that seems to be getting you into trouble these days!

Best,

Patric

I finished my very late breakfast and with directions from Esther, I headed off to the main stables. I hated to admit it, but in some ways, I felt as though I was on a retreat of sorts, an offering of perhaps some

497

peace and healing for all of my wounds, but like with everything in my life, I wasn't expecting that peace to hold for long.

I entered the stables trying to figure out who Eduardo was exactly; Patric didn't say. I figured if he was a Vampire, I would know immediately. I scanned the vast space, thinking the accommodations for the horses were just as nice as my guest quarters, when a figure appeared to my left. I turned to see a man sauntering slowly towards me, leading a very large and very black stallion on a rope.

"You must be Ana," he spoke, his accent similar to Carlo's but with a distinct inflection difference. He laughed and held out his hand. "I am from the North, Carlo is from the South; the inflection you hear is not the only difference between us no?" he mused, shaking my hand. I looked at his face and I could see even before our eyes met, that yes, he was in fact, a Vampire. Christ, I really wish I would be able to get my power back; I might just feel a bit better being alone with so many of them. "We're going to work on that." Eduardo smiled at me. "First, though, we ride." He winked and handed me the rope attached to the stallion. It had been years since I'd ridden a horse and I had forgotten just how liberating it could be galloping across a vast landscape, seeing the mountains rise in the distance; I felt strong and free.

"Ahh...you are a natural no? We'll have to talk to Carlo about getting you out to play Polo sometime; or perhaps learning how to wrangle in the cattle." Eduardo and I were back in the stables brushing down the horses; I had also forgotten how meditative it was to have the honor of grooming such beautiful animals. I smiled at him. I had learned today that Eduardo would be in charge of most of my physical training. I had no clue what that meant and the idea that there seemed

498

to be a distinct delineation between my physical and my mental training had me concerned. Eduardo shook his head. "No, no. No concern Ana. You are strong; you won't need to worry. We'll start slow. I know that you have been ill and we don't want to overdue things too quickly. I hear you like boxing, perhaps we'll start there yes?" He watched me as I cleaned the hoof of my horse, Bastion. I smiled and nodded, wondering if Patric had told Eduardo about my physical fitness preferences.

By the time I finished up in the stables, it was after five and I ran back up to the guesthouse. I needed a shower before meeting with Carlo and I didn't want to come into his home, sweaty and smelling like manure. I sprinted upstairs and jumped into the bath, not bothering to wash my hair; it had been in a ponytail all day and I was hoping with a few tweaks, I could make it presentable. I had no idea what you wore to aperitifs with an Argentinean Vampire, but I had not packed for anything special, so cargos and my favorite turquoise tank would have to do. I made it to the main house by five after six and Carlo was already sitting on the back deck waiting.

"I'm so sorry I'm late," I said, coming to join him at the table. He stood upon my arrival and I could see his eyes move over my face, searching. Immediately, I put my mental wall back together and hoped that it would be strong enough to hold.

"You're not late Ana. You look beautiful; I can see that being with the horses is good for you yes?" He pulled out my chair and I nodded.

"Yes, it was wonderful. You are very lucky to have so much property for them to be able to run so freely. I'm pretty sure that a PhD in

Ecology won't get you anything this nice." I laughed as he poured some fruity looking cocktail into a thick crystal glass. I eyed it warily. I rarely drank and I never drank around people I didn't know.

"It's like a Sangria," Carlo said, clearly seeing my hesitation. "My family's recipe, very low alcohol." He smiled and handed me my drink. "The land, yes, it's very nice, but the more you have the more you want; at least that's my problem." He surveyed me over his glass. I wondered if he was upset with me over our conversation the other night; his current mood suggested just the opposite and I tried to settle into mediation mode. Even mood, even temper—diplomatic. Everything Liam said I could do well. Even knowing that it was Patric who was actually in charge here, I was falling more along the lines of Liam and not taking anything for granted. I didn't know Carlo and I had not had the privilege of a history with him. To me, he was someone to be cautious around, at least for the time being. For the next hour, he continued with his questions from last night.

"Carlo, really, I hate talking about myself," I said, sitting back in my chair. "We haven't discussed you or your life or anything other than me; I feel a bit selfish." I laughed, but it was true. I had never felt comfortable being the focus of a conversation; I always thought other people were way more interesting than me.

"Nonsense Ana, that is why you are here. I want to learn all about you." He smiled. I wondered if the rest of the coven knew that it was Patric running the show now or if they were being kept in the dark on purpose. "So tell me, you and Patric, you are Bonded yes?" I looked up, my eyes narrowing. That was an interesting question for him to ask.

"Yes," I said simply, not knowing what else to say. Carlo sipped his drink, his eyes roaming over my face and neck.

"You exchanged blood then?" His focus was now clearly on the various bite marks that adorned my skin.

"I received blood from Patric as a medical treatment," I said, my body tense now. "It was a very small amount to keep me alive." I watched him from across the table.

"Yes, yes, you were attacked by Nathanial, of course. You were going to die." Carlo's eyes flashed and my chest heaved at the mention of Nathanial. I nodded, wondering where he was going with this. "But you, you gave your blood to Patric voluntarily did you not?" Carlo smirked at me and I could see the wheels turning in his head, his desire, his bloodlust. I started to respond when someone interrupted.

"Not quite Carlo." Patric had suddenly appeared behind me and I couldn't help but think that he'd been listening to our conversation the whole time. Carlo smiled as Patric approached the table, pulling out a chair and sitting beside me. "I had done quite a number on Ana's psyche, if you remember, and I'm quite sure that she would have never willingly volunteered her blood to help me achieve my goals. But that's ancient history." Patric poured himself a glass of Sangria and sat back in his chair, looking positively mellow. I, however, was getting angry. I didn't like Patric speaking about our time together as if I had absolutely no control over what I was doing or feeling, that what happened between us was all of his doing and his coercion. I had of course come to understand that Patric might have pushed me in the right direction to offer him what he wanted, but to make it seem as though my mind and my heart had been hijacked by his mental prowess; that wasn't fair. I felt something squeeze my leg under the table and realized that it was Patric; he'd sensed my agitation. I shoved him off.

"Perhaps, but it is evident that you are still relishing in the effects; would you disagree?" Carlo mimicked Patric's body language and I suddenly felt as though I was watching a chess game, a very, deadly chess game. Patric shrugged. Carlo laughed. "And what of your Bond; is that too ancient history?" Carlo looked to me, his eyes flashing.

"No," I said, feeling the metals of my mark surge with heat. "Patric will always be with me, even when I thought he was dead, he was still with me..." I whispered, suddenly feeling very overwhelmed and tired. Carlo met my gaze and he raised his chin slightly, assessing me.

"But you are no longer Bound to Nathanial; am I correct in that assumption, that Bond has been broken?" Again, Carlo's eyes flashed as he studied my face. I felt Patric's eyes on me as well and I sighed.

"Yes, you are correct," I said, not wanting to continue this conversation.

"And the powers you received from your original transaction; the blood you received from him to complete your Bond, are those gone as well?" Carlo's voice was a bit too excited for my taste and I began to feel suddenly ill at ease. I wasn't actually aware of any particular powers that I had gotten from my Bond with Nathanial except the normal ones that every human gets from their Bonder; long life span, slow aging process, ability to ward off even the most deadly of diseases. Actually, I wasn't sure if those effects were still even accessible any more. Carlo's question was a good one. I looked at Patric, wondering if he knew.

"I would imagine whatever Ana received from my brother, whatever skills or biological attributes that he's given her; I would have to say they are still very much a part of who she is." Patric sipped his drink. How did he know? Carlo frowned.

"But perhaps that is why you can no longer use your gift then? Perhaps your ability with fire is directly tied to your Bond with Nathanial?" Carlo looked at me, his face smooth, but his eyes were curious. I shook my head.

"My ability with fire does not come from Nathanial," my voice held steady, "it comes from Patric and a small amount from me, I've been told…" I smiled softly remembering my conversation with Micah the night I had to demonstrate my powers in that stupid hut. "But it doesn't appear to matter much for the moment, does it? I'm unable to conjure any remnants of that ability and I'm guessing for good reason; I shouldn't have ever been allowed to have such a power, not as a human any way; perhaps it's run its course," I said, desperately wanting to change the focus of the discussion or leave. "I'm sorry, I don't mean to be rude, but I'm really not feeling well and I should very much like to retire for the evening if that's acceptable. I looked at Carlo, hoping that Patric wouldn't think I was being disrespectful.

"Of course, Ana. It's been a long day for you. Please, get some rest and I will see you tomorrow." Patric's eyes twinkled and I exhaled,

503

grateful to be able to leave the discussion. Any influx of positive feelings that I had acquired from my time with the horses today, had suddenly plummeted during the course of the evening and I was now beginning to feel as if a massive weight was pressing on my heart. I felt sick and alone and very, very depressed.

Chapter Twenty

Patric

For three weeks now, I had been observing Ana, watching her mood, her body language, watching everything. Something was wrong. She wasn't eating, she wasn't sleeping and it appeared that she had, in fact, given up. I knew she was upset about losing both Stephen and having to terminate her pregnancy, and I knew that she was constantly thinking about my brother, worrying if he was going to die, she was wary of me, scared of Carlo and desperate for Liam. She was disappearing in front of me. I was starting to think that calling her here was not the best option, that Carlo's suggestion that we try to get Ana to help us against Nathanial was a mistake. I was also contemplating the possibility that Carlo had no incentive to have Ana help us in our war with the Bonders, but that he was so obsessed with Ana and her blood and her powers, that he had really no intention of using Ana's abilities for the greater purpose of war, but that he wanted to acquire her, convince her to be Changed, make her his prized possession. I had seen his mind. Every time he looked at her, I could see his attraction building, his desire boiling over. I understood those feelings quite well. Even I was struggling with keeping my need for her under control. Having her so close to me again was proving a significant challenge to my self-restraint, but she was so vulnerable, so lost, that the last thing I wanted to do was to cause her more confusion and more heartbreak. I cared for Ana very much and I needed her in more ways than I was ready to extrapolate upon for the time being.

I was headed to meet her in an isolated clearing near the river. I wanted to gage just where her powers might be and if we might be able to bring them to the surface again, but not for any particular reason, at least not yet. I wasn't interested in using her to fight my brother, not any more. I just wanted her to be whole again. It seemed wrong not to see her smile, not to hear her laugh; I wanted to fix her. I approached her while she was sitting in the grass. She had been crying again and I watched her wipe her face as I came to settle next to her. My eyes scanned her face and I could clearly see that the month without sleep was doing a number on her. She was pale and she had dark bruise-like circles under eyes, making them hollow. Her hair was limp from her lack of nutrition and her clothes hung loose and shapeless on her thin frame. The once brilliant copper and bronze glow of her brown eyes had gone and her gaze looked slightly manic, as if she was constantly searching for something or someone.

"I'm calling Liam to come and get you," I said quietly, lying back in the grass, feeling the breeze stir around me.

"Why?" she said. Christ, even her voice sounded sad.

"Because you're a mess, you're falling apart and I can't bare to watch it Ana; it's too much." I lifted my head up toward the sun, thinking.

"I didn't think I had a choice; I thought I was supposed to be here and then I would be allowed to be Changed, either by you or by Liam..." She trailed off and I heard the tears in her throat.

"Yes, well, I don't think being here is the best plan for you anymore, do you?" I sat up to look at her.

"So are you going to kill me?" She sounded like a child; a small girl wondering what was going to happen to her if she didn't do what she was asked.

"No," I said, reaching to rub her back. "I'm pretty sure that if you die, my brother dies and as much as I want to kill him for what he's done to you, I'm not quite ready to let either of you go just yet." I laughed.

"I hurt him too," she whispered and I felt her body begin to shake.

"Perhaps, but it doesn't excuse what Nathanial did; it doesn't make it ok, Ana." I pulled my fingers through her curls, which were a lot less springy and shimmery than they used to be.

"I don't think he could help it. I mean, I tried to be understanding. I tried to let him go after I saw...after I saw that he was starting to lose interest in me, but then that night we went to his house, that night he was with her—it was too horrible for me. I just didn't know how to work around that; it seemed impossible and I was never going to be able to give him what he needed..." She bowed her head. "I really just wanted him to be happy." She turned to look at me, her eyes wide and scared.

"Ana, you did nothing wrong and regardless of whether or not Nathanial's behavior was intentional, he made a mistake and I'm not inclined to let him off the hook in favor of blaming biology. He devastated you and I happen to believe that if he had shown a bit more resolve and more courage, he could have worked around his natural urges; he could have dealt with his need and not betrayed you." I sat up.

"But what if you're wrong; what if everything he did he couldn't help? I mean, I forgave him before when he was with you and he had all of those women, when he'd told me he had been drugged, manipulated by Devon and then Stephen told me that wasn't true…that was hard to hear and I left him then. I left him and went to Stephen because Nathanial had given his blood to strangers over me…I was so angry, but maybe he couldn't help either of those situations…" Her voice was rising and she was speaking quickly. I had forgotten about Nathanial and those women when he was with me; he was so wrecked. He was beside himself and vulnerable to any manipulation. It was partially his fault and partially Devon's for taking advantage of his weakened state. My brother never made good decisions when he was angry and hurt and he was both during those months we'd spent together, angry with me and angry with himself—it was a devastating combination.

"Ana, my brother is no saint and he, just like the rest of us, has to learn accountability for every action, *every* action—no matter what seems to be ruling his mental and physical make-up. What he did, it had repercussions; his actions set things in motion and now he's suffering the consequences. You are not obliged to save him from himself; you are not accountable for fixing his mistakes. You made a decision to not subject yourself to a relationship where someone had effectively betrayed you, where there was a distinct possibility of a child being produced from that betrayal and you chose to leave that situation in favor of finding a better life for yourself…I'm just sorry that it has not had the happy ending that you deserve." I was staring at her face, trying to get her to see, to understand.

"I don't really have anywhere to go at the moment or anything to do. I don't think Liam is prepared to take me back so soon; he has a lot to contend with and I don't really want to burden him. Can't I just stay here for a while and try to recover? I'm happy to help out with things and maybe work on getting my power back, but I'm not ready to leave; I'm not ready to be out there alone—not yet." She met my gaze and bit her lip. I studied her thoughts. I had never seen Ana like this; she was so diminished and frail. I felt terrified and I felt guilty.

"Fine, but if you don't start eating, I swear Ana, I'm calling Liam and I'm having him haul your ass out of here. We also need to keep up the pretense that you are here for training to possibly help us against Nathanial. The coven has been ordered not to touch you during this process, but if they caught wind that I was keeping you here to protect you and help you heal, all bets are off and we'd be fighting for your life, yet again. I really don't have the energy or the time to try and prevent an entire coven from killing you." She gave me just a hint of the smile that I loved. One down, one to go, I mused. The latter of the two was going to be a bit more difficult. I was not only fighting against time, but a mental frame of mind that had given up; Nathanial wanted to die.

Nathanial

I felt her move under me, her body warm and her arms holding me close. Her lips caressed my neck and I heard myself whisper her name. Ana. I suddenly felt very warm and I pulled away from her. She

509

continued to kiss me, deeper and harder as my skin started to burn. I screamed out as my flesh erupted into flames and I saw her face one last time before my body ignited. I gasped and opened my eyes, my body shaking and sweating.

"It was just a dream my son, just a dream." I saw my uncle sitting on my bed, a compress held in his hand. He placed the towel to my damp, hot skin and instantly, I felt cooler; I started to shiver.

Ana

I had promised Patric that I would work hard at trying to recover not only my power with fire, but also just my general mental health. I had been here for almost two months and I was determined to get my strength back; at the very least I owed Liam for always doing so much, for believing in me—I might be able to recover for him. Eduardo had me riding horses in the morning and working out with him in the afternoon. Evenings were spent with Patric and Carlo, trying to conjure my power to the surface. I was exhausted, overwhelmed and extremely grateful to have the distraction; I needed to get out of my own headspace. All three of us—me, Carlo and Patric were currently down by the river practicing some sort of fire wall that Patric was able to produce; it moved and shifted and grew and I was pretty sure that I could do one better, if I could just concentrate enough. Having Carlo watching me was proving to be a bit nerve racking. I felt like I was being evaluated and judged; It made me nervous.

Vampires had to get their fire from a source, either one close to them or they mentally drew upon the constant fire that was lit at their coven's main house and that fire was there for that purpose only; it was their main choice for a weapon. This was new information to me, but Carlo had been offering me all sorts of Vampire trivia over the last months and I was pretty fascinated. Currently, we had a small fire burning between Patric and me, for his purposes only; I didn't need a source to call fire—it came from within, something that both Carlo and Patric had been surprised to learn. Of course, I could also manipulate an already burning fire like I had done that night in front of the Council; I could create a storm if I wanted.

"Ana! Would you please concentrate; you're zoning out and it's starting to piss me off," Patric called across the field, clearly annoyed that I wasn't paying attention to him. He had a huge wall of dark blue flames erected in front of him and I watched as it hovered several feet off the ground. I wasn't impressed.

"Fine," I called back to him, taking a sip of water. "What do you want me to do?" I asked, standing with my hands on my hips; Carlo laughed behind me.

"I want you to do what I ask. Now try again." Patric came out from behind his wall and stood facing me, his arms crossed. Sheesh, he could be such an asshole sometimes. It must have sucked having to deal with him as a teenager, I mused.

"ANA!" Patric yelled.

"Ok, ok!" I said, squaring my stance and facing him down. I was annoyed and I let my emotions drive the heat under my skin to the surface. I felt my mind grow calm and silent, one of the few times when I wasn't constantly thinking and worrying about something, and I felt my blood seethe and course rapidly through my veins. The internal breeze that always preceded the fire began to shift and move, creating wind where there was none. My hair swirled around my face and I stepped forward, bringing the image in my mind, to life. Instantly, a giant wall of different shades of blue flames erupted in front of me and I watched as Patric took his place back behind his own wall. He moved his forward, and I mirrored the gesture. He moved his up and so did I; to the side, I matched him. I was getting bored. Suddenly Patric sent his fire hurdling towards me and I hit the ground, barely missing getting my head blown off.

"WHAT THE FUCK!" I yelled, angry at his retaliation for my boredom. I leapt to my feet and sent my own fire heading straight for him, tumbling in a giant cloud of lightening and flame. I also moved him, hitting him square in the chest with one wave of my hand; a trick I still had no idea where I'd obtained it from, but it seemed to have developed along side my abilities with fire. I sent both Patric and my firestorm right into the river, watching as his body hit the water and the flames plummeted in after, making a huge cloud of smoke rise against the dark sky, veiling the starlight and the moonlight. Carlo came to stand beside me, putting his hand on my shoulder.

"You seem to have a bit of a temper Ana," he murmured in my ear and I distinctly felt him breathe deeply. I stepped away from him, still angry.

"Well, if he quit doing stupid shit like that, I wouldn't have to get so angry, now would I?" I said, watching as Patric leapt from the river, perfectly dry and laughing his ass off.

"That was pretty good Ana, but I think you could do a lot better!" Patric blurred over to me, his dark hair whipping behind him and his eyes glowing bright, reflecting the flames from the fire; he looked mystical, beautiful. I rolled my eyes and went to grab my water and my pack.

"We're not done." Patric grabbed my arm and took my backpack off of my shoulder.

"Oh yes we are," I said, grabbing my stuff forcefully from him, sending him stumbling a few feet. "You effectively brought this session to an end with your petulant behavior. If you weren't three hundred years old, I would think that I was dealing with a teenager!" Patric smirked at me as I went over to Bastion and untied his lead rope; I was riding him everywhere these days.

"I'm sorry Ana, that was uncalled for, but honestly, your internal monologues are going to get you into trouble; you are constantly thinking about everything." He smiled at me and leaned against the tree.

"Well excuse me; I had no idea that you would retaliate for me thinking about things. I didn't realize that it would be such a problem for you considering our history. Perhaps you should just resort to possessing me like you did before, since, according to you, I apparently don't have the capacity to think for myself." I was still upset with him for making it seem that I had not intended to be with him that night in my room when I had let him take from me, that I had not wanted to be close with him, to help him. He was making me feel so stupid. I hoisted myself on Bastion and looked down at Patric and Carlo, who had come to witness our argument. "Carlo, it's been a pleasure as always. Thank you for the dinner earlier and I will see you tomorrow I am sure." He nodded at me, smiling. I nudged Bastion and galloped back toward the guesthouse.

After my shower, I decided to sit out on my terrace. It was a nice evening, not too cold and the moon was shining full and bright. Suddenly, Patric appeared, levitating over my balcony railing. I gasped and fell backward in my seat, hitting my head on the bamboo deck. He was over to me in less than a single breath.

"Good god, you're jumpy," he said, helping me back into my chair. I rubbed my head, glaring at him. "Let me see." He began to move his hand over the back of my skull, but I pulled away.

"What do you want?" I hissed at him, repositioning myself next to my little side table. He sat down in the seat next to me, putting his feet on the railing.

"I came to apologize for this evening." He looked at me, his eyes dark and pulsing outward with their familiar pull on my chest.

"Since when do you levitate?" I scowled at him, thinking about Stephen suddenly. He caught my eye and shrugged.

"Since always I guess." He was still staring at me.

"I thought only full Vampires could levitate." I looked back out at the moon, rubbing my head and my chest.

"I've always been the exception to the rule Ana...just like you." His voice was low and soft and I turned to glance at his face.

"You know what's always bothered me about you?" I asked him, holding his stare.

"No, what?" He smirked.

"It's like you don't even want to acknowledge that you are a Bonder by birth, that you've done everything you can to diminish that part of who you are to be more like a Vampire. Your mother was a Bonder Patric; don't you ever feel that by not owning that part of you, that you are invalidating her somehow, invalidating her sacrifice for you and Nathanial? I mean it's not like she was a horrible mother who beat you or something, then maybe you would have an excuse to shed that as part of your life—but she was a good mother and your father seems like he was also a good man, that he loved you. You were lucky and it makes me angry because I wasn't lucky. I didn't have a mother who thought I was important enough to sacrifice herself; she didn't want me and her decisions led to me having to experience some of the worst trauma in my life. My father, he couldn't have cared less; he never told me I was beautiful or special in anyway and I'm guessing that both of your parents made you feel loved, extraordinary even. You were so lucky and it makes me angry to see you in this role, this illusion of who you are trying to be, when I'm quite sure that Patric the Bonder would have been even more wonderful and more extraordinary because of the love you had from two people who actually wanted you!" My head was starting to hurt and I rubbed what was a now forming knot on the back of my skull. Patric stared at me, his eyes looking deep into mine.

"You're right Ana," he said quietly. "I cannot imagine having to endure some of the things that you were allowed to face; you should have been protected. You should have always been made to know just how unique and beautiful you truly are." I rolled my eyes.

"We're not talking about me Patric," I said, frustrated that he seemed to be missing the point of my rant. "I think that you should go to Nathanial; I think he needs to see that his only sibling is alive. Perhaps it might give him the impetus to fight for his life," I muttered, my chest and my head beginning to throb. "Don't you want to see him?" I asked, sipping from my mug of tea. Patric shifted his gaze from me to the moon, closing his eyes and breathing deeply.

"Do you?" he asked, keeping his face toward the sky. Odd that he should ask that; I had just been thinking about Nathanial and wondering if I could go to Peru and just talk to him. I didn't like the way that I had left things in Dublin when he came and now, now things were so dire. I was torn. "So am I Ana." Patric opened his eyes and moved to rock his chair back.

"Yes, but he's not my sibling; he's not my flesh and blood, he's your brother."

"I would have to disagree with you there, Ana. Nathanial is your blood; he has yours and you have his… you are just as much tied to him as I am, perhaps even more." I stared at Patric; he was right.

"We should go together then. I think you and I should go to see Nathanial together Patric; I need to see him and so do you," I whispered. Patric nodded.

"When?" I asked, feeling the ache in my heart grow.

"The day after tomorrow. I'll call Micah and let him know." Patric stood and pulled me to my feet so that we were standing side by side, looking out over the night horizon. I put my hand around his waist.

"You have to know Patric, that I wanted to be with you that night; I wanted us to be together. I thought you were just that special. I wasn't expecting you to marry me or anything, but I thought we truly had a bond, something beyond this stupid metal tattoo. I thought you were one of the only people who understood who I was and why I made some of the decisions I made. I valued you, even with your flaws and even if you didn't want me back. All I wanted was to give you a choice. I wanted you to maybe see yourself as I saw you, as your mother saw you and even as Nathanial truly saw you. I'm sorry if you believed that I didn't truly care for you." I bowed, resting my head against his shoulder.

"Ana, being Bound to you is the only good thing that I have done in all my existence and it wasn't even me who made it happen. It was all you, because of what you gave to me, because of what you were willing to sacrifice for me, because you were courageous enough to know that you cared for me. If I wasn't so sadistic and arrogant, I would have wanted us to be together; hell, I may have even considered marrying you." He turned and kissed the top of head.

"Well that's very nice Patric, thank you. I would have been honored." I laughed, but his face was serious, his eyes not blinking. He reached to stroke my face, running his finger down my cheek and caressing his original bite marks on my neck. He bent his head and pulled me closer to him and for a moment, I thought he was going to kiss me, but he suddenly shook his head, exhaling loudly.

"Jesus Ana, even after all this time; I'm still drawn to you, to how you feel, how you smell. You're like an addiction that I can't break, that I don't want to break," he murmured, still shaking his head. He took a deep breath and stepped back leaving me slightly weak in the knees. "Esther is going to the market tomorrow, you should go with her, it's your kind of place." He laughed and jumped over the railing of the terrace hovering gently in the air. "I kicked your ass tonight; you need to work harder!" he called to me as he drifted down to the ground and disappeared into the darkness.

Patric

Needless to say, my uncle was in a bit of a shock when I called. He was under the impression that it was some sort of trick and I had to rattle off several incidental facts about my childhood and my mother that only Nathanial or I would know. I was going to see my brother first, without Ana. Her mental state was fragile and if Nathanial was as critical as my uncle said, then I wanted to make sure that seeing him would not push her or my brother over the edge. I was trying to make it back before dinner with Carlo. For weeks now, I was becoming more and more uneasy with his inclinations toward her and leaving her alone to fend for herself was not something that gave me comfort. Carlo could be seductive, alluring and Ana was already feeling slightly unhinged by Stephen and Nathanial; I didn't want her to do anything reckless.

I arrived at my uncle's feeling anxious for many reasons, but mainly I was scared for my brother. The images that Liam had shown me of Nathanial had terrified me; I had never seen my brother in such a diminished state. He looked dead, barely clinging to life and I was sure that he had just continued to fall even further into darkness. I hadn't seen my uncle in a very long time and I suddenly felt very guilty for fighting against him for so many months. He was a good man and he and my mother were the closest that I have ever seen two siblings be, and he loved us very much. It was startling to see him; the resemblance between he and my mother and between he and I, was something that I had forgotten. We all shared the same turquoise eyes, clear and deep, with flecks of silver around the rim. No one knew where Nathanial got his eye color, my father's had been black; perhaps it was a perfect blending of my two parents. Upon my arrival, my uncle hugged me, holding my face in his hands. Christ, the situation must have been critical; he was acting as if I was his long lost child.

"In a way, perhaps Patric, in way you are." Micah scanned my face, reading every thought I was processing. "It's good that you are here, although I am afraid he might not even recognize or remember you my son." My chest felt tight.

"What do you mean, how bad has he gotten?" I asked, not sure if I really wanted to know. Micah sighed, and for a moment, I thought I caught a glimpse of my mother's face in his eyes and she looked frightened—terrified.

"I'm afraid that we've run out of time, I think. He's given up Patric and the wounds seem too deep to ever be repaired." Micah was standing near the fire, his head bowed. I swallowed hard.

"Where is he?" I whispered. My uncle motioned for me to follow him down the hall. I approached the bedroom, but before I could enter, my uncle turned to me, tears in his eyes.

"Do you think she will come?" he asked, gripping my hand. "He's been asking for her, do you think she will come?" I couldn't breathe and I couldn't speak. I nodded. Micah bowed and opened the door. I braced myself against the frame, not prepared for what my eyes fell upon. My brother was a barely living skeleton. His face wasted away to cheekbones and teeth. The body that lie beneath the sheets was barely visible, the outline a crumbled mess of bones. His hair was gray in tone and gone were the rich sheen and sparkle that usually filled the strands. Nathanial's breath was labored, and I counted three whole minutes between gasps. My body was paralyzed by grief and shock. I couldn't move forward. My brother was dying. I pushed through my despair and went to his bedside, sitting gently next to him. I took his hand in mine and touched his face. His eyes opened and they focused on me. He gasped and shuttered.

"Shhh, Nathanial, shhh… it's ok, it's me." I tried to calm his anxiety. My tears were coming fast and I wiped them away, not understanding why this was happening to him, why we couldn't help him.

"Patric?" Surprisingly, his voice was clear and strong.

"Yes," I said, moving closer to him.

"I thought you were dead," he said, his eyes losing their focus.

"It's a long story Nathanial; you'll have to hear it sometime. I'm sure that even you will be astounded by my ability to execute a plan." I laughed softly.

"Patric?" Nathanial's eyes found mine again and tears were forming, falling slowly down his cheeks. "Ana; is she alive?" he asked me, his chest heaving and his breath slowing.

"Yes, she's alive and she's coming to see you Nathanial; she wants to see you," I said, watching him struggle to breathe, feeling helpless.

"When?" he asked, his eyes closing.

"Now, I'll get her now ok?" I asked him, and he nodded his head. "Hold on ok? Nathanial? Nathanial?" He wasn't moving. "MICAH!" I yelled and my uncle appeared at my side.

"He's sleeping Patric, but you should hurry; I don't think he can last in this world too much longer. He's yearning to move on my son." Micah was crying. I nodded and shimmered immediately back to Carlo and Ana.

Ana

I was just returning from yet another intensive Q & A with Carlo at dinner when Patric suddenly appeared in my room; he looked shattered.

521

"Patric!" What's the matter, what's wrong?" I ran to him, his eyes were wet and he was breathing hard.

"Ana you need to come with me now," he gasped taking my hand. I nodded and let him pull me close to him as we shimmered away from my room. We landed in Micah's house and I froze. I wasn't ready for this, why was he bringing me here now; I needed a day to prepare.

"We don't have a day Ana. Nathanial cannot hold on for a day; we're losing him," Patric whispered to me. He took my hand and led me down a dark hallway. Suddenly, the back of my neck erupted in fire and I sucked in a sharp breath. "What?" Patric looked at me as I doubled over grabbing my metal imprint.

"It's ok," I said and I let Patric push the door open to a bedroom. My eyes roamed over the bed and I choked. My heart stopped beating as I watched Patric cross into the room and stand near his brother. I forced myself to move, to walk, to breathe. I came to the bed and reached to touch Nathanial's hand, but I was forced backward. I gasped. I couldn't touch him; I had forgotten. I looked to Patric who seemed confused.

"You can't touch him—not even now?" he asked me, struggling to understand what I already knew. I shook my head averting my eyes from Nathanial's face. Patric rubbed his eyes. "Christ, I thought that now you might be able to..." He sounded so desperate. He sat on the bed and held his brother's pale hand. I couldn't look; I was beyond terrified and I felt sick, not a physical sickness, but a deep and penetrating soul sickness, as if my very core was slowly being shredded, ripped from the very source of my being, I knelt down

522

beside him and put my head on the covers, seeing the familiar golden threads of his mother's quilt.

"Ana," a voice spoke, pulling me from my despair. I looked to find Nathanial staring at me, his eyes clouded by a milky fluid. I swallowed the bile that was filling my mouth.

"Please," I moved closer to him, but again I was met with invisible resistance, "Please, Nathanial, you can't leave me. I know you are hurting, I know I hurt you, but you can't leave me. I need you; I need you to stay. PLEASE!" I was screaming now, my body shuddering and shaking.

"Ana." Nathanial said again and tears filled his eyes. "I love you."

"NO! NO! You stop this right now! You stop this Nathanial, I won't let you do this, I won't let you leave me, not now, not after everything that's happened, not when we've fought so hard. NO!" I was angry now. He was giving up, letting go and that wasn't fair. He was being selfish. A knowledge flooded into my bones, an understanding that I buried so deeply that I had forgotten it was still with me, but of course it was; it was always there waiting for me to acknowledge what it already knew, what it proved two years ago, what it was proving now; that I loved Nathanial, that we were Bound, not by metal and stone, but by the eyes that knew each other, by the hearts that beat for each other, by the blood that ran in our veins. I would always love Nathanial and I knew that a world without his breath would be a world that would never manage to exist; he had to survive. I stood and faced Patric. "Listen very carefully to me," I said, my voice growing dark and low. Patric stiffened. "I need you to take one of my jewels from my mark," I said, moving to kneel down in front of him.

"What?" Patric looked shocked.

"My jewels, I need you to take one off of my tattoo Patric. I can't do it myself," I said, my voice stern.

"Ana, that might kill you. Removing something from your mark, it could kill you," he said, his eyes brimming with tears.

"Just do it!" I yelled at him, the force of my voice, startling him. Micah appeared at my side and took my hand.

"Patric, my son, we must trust in Ana. We must trust in her now." Micah looked at me and I saw a picture of Nathanial and I embracing in a whirl of fire, a picture of us on a mountaintop, a picture of Nathanial waiting by my jeep, a picture of my wedding dress, a picture of us together, his mother's quilt lying on my bed. I nodded to Micah and grasped his hand. Patric's hands were trembling as he moved to stand behind me. I heard Nathanial gasp, as his eyes grew wide. I looked at him.

"I love you too Nathanial; I always have," I said. "Patric!" I called to him, "Do it now."

I felt Patric dig his fingers into the back of my neck grasping the metal and stone embedded in my flesh. Flames burst through my skin as he pulled one of my stars away from its tiny universe. I heaved forward as the pain took me. Blood gushed from the back of my head and I crashed forward onto the bed, onto Nathanial. I could feel him, smell him, touch him and I forced myself to reach for Patric.

"Give it to me!" I stretched my hand out and he placed the tiny piece into my palm. I clawed my way through the dizziness, through the blood, through my utter and complete grief, and I tore open his shirt reveling a bloodied mass of puss and bone. I choked from the smell; rancid and putrid death threatened to consume me and I held my breath as I pressed my jewel to his heart, to my inner eye, to the part of me he knew. Nathanial's body shuddered and he gasped. I held out my wrist to Patric one last time. "Patric!" I shouted to him.

"Ana, I can't, I can't do this to you, you're bleeding…Christ you're bleeding so much." I was bleeding; it was streaming down my neck and over my shoulders and I was getting weaker by the minute.

"Micah!" I said, turning to him, knowing that Patric was too far-gone in his grief to help now. Micah nodded and took my hand; he whispered a prayer and then sliced through my flesh with his finger. I sucked in a breath and held my wrist to Nathanial's mouth, blood spilling down onto his face. "Nathanial!" I yelled at him as his body began to quiver and pulse violently. I forced his lips open and I poured my blood down his throat, tipping his head back, his hair falling out in clumps in my hand. Nathanial lurched forward vomiting blood, but I held my wrist to him, pressing his lips to my skin. I felt him begin to pull from my veins and the pain was horrific, like I was being hacked and slashed by a dull knife. He was gasping and choking and continuing to vomit, but he was still taking my blood. I held on for as long as I could until I felt someone gently pull me back, releasing Nathanial's grip on my arm. I collapsed down upon him and I felt him breathe in once, then fall silent and my heart stopped beating.

I awoke in a large bedroom and it was dark. Only the dim light from the moon shone in through the window and I blinked trying to orient myself. Nathanial. Was he alive? Had I done enough? I tried to sit up, but my body felt a bit wonky, like jelly. I had to get to him; I had to know. My heart jumped. There was someone in the far corner of the room sitting in a chair, they were sleeping, and their head slumped back against the wall. Micah. "Micah?" I whispered, not wanting to startle him. He sat up immediately looking alarmed.

"Ana. Are you alright; is something the matter?" He blurred to my side and put his arms around my shoulders.

"Nathanial. Is he dead; did he die Micah?" It was better if I just knew. I was never good with the in between of things. Micah held my face in his hands, his eyes glowing as they shifted and pulsed. He closed them and breathed deeply. My heart sank.

"My beautiful, beautiful girl, our Ana, our precious gift. Nathanial is alive. He is alive and you have saved him. You have brought him back and his life has been restored." I felt numb surprisingly. I was in shock I guessed.

"Is Patric alright?" I knew he'd been quite upset at what I had asked him to do and I was worried that he might be angry with me or something. Micah laughed.

"No Ana, Patric is far from angry with you; in fact I believe that he is in awe of what you have done for his brother.

"I would do the same thing for him if he needed me to," I mumbled.

"I know that you would Ana," a solemn voice spoke from the door and Patric stood looking at his uncle and me. Micah rose and patted me on the shoulder.

"I will sit with Nathanial for a while. He's anxious to see you Ana, when you are ready." Somehow I figured that Micah sensed my apprehension about Nathanial; it was weird, but I didn't have another word that I could use to describe how I was feeling. Patric nodded to his uncle and drifted into the room, coming to sit on the bed next to me.

"Are you ok? I asked him, still worried that he might be upset. Patric raised his eyebrows at me, a look of complete disbelief washing over his face.

"Yes, Ana, I am fine, thank you for asking. Although I must admit, it's been quite a while since I've removed anything from someone's mark; quite disturbing I have to say." He smirked at me.

"You did a good job," I said, holding his hand. "He's alive; that's all that matters now," I whispered. That was true. I had no idea what was going to happen next, but to know that Nathanial would still be a force in this world, still be someone that I could see and touch if I wanted, that was right, it just seemed right. Patric held my hand firmly.

"He wants to see you Ana." I sighed, still not knowing why I was so hesitant to visit with him. Patric tilted my head up so that our eyes met. "You don't need to make any decisions about anything at all Ana. You don't need to make any promises or declarations; you just need to talk to each other—you still have so much healing to do and now is not the time to be trying to sort our your feelings." It was weird having

Patric give me relationship advice, but he was right and hearing those words from him, seemed to ease my anxiety just a bit. Patric helped me off the bed and I leaned on him as we walked down the hall. It had been two days since I saw Nathanial last and I suddenly thought of Carlo; wouldn't he wonder where we were? Patric laughed. "Don't worry about Carlo, Ana... I've got things under control." He winked at me and opened the bedroom door.

Nathanial was propped up against several pillows and his transformation was mind-boggling. Gone was the skeleton-like figure, the gray hair and ashen skin; gone were the milky eyes and gone was the hole over his chest. He still looked exhausted, but he was luminous and stunning. His hair was its beautiful glossy black satin, hanging long and straight over his shoulders. His skin shimmered with a fiery copper sheen that I had not witnessed before, not to that degree, but it was his eyes that were the most startling. They were still deep midnight blue, but now in the center there was a distinct ring of dark coppery brown, with tiny flecks of gold, bronze and silver. He looked like some fallen angel, mystical and slightly terrifying in his beauty. I stood staring, not quite sure he was real, that he was truly alive. My world stood still and just for a moment, I felt that we were the only two people left standing, left breathing, left loving.

"Ana," his voice moved through my soul, coursed through my veins, made my blood surge with incredible heat; I didn't know that voice, it was new to me with its perfect tone and its deep roughness; it was unfamiliar. I moved slowly, feeling like a ghost inside a dream. He remained still and quiet, waiting. I stood close to him wondering if I should touch him, if I *could* touch him. He raised his arm, reaching for my hand and I felt an electric current so vast and strong race between

528

us that I was scared to move for fear of breaking the connection. "Don't be scared Ana." Our fingers barely touched and I tried to breathe, tried to take in his scent. It was different, yet very familiar and safe, but there was definitely something more now, something deeper and layered; not just honey, lemon, woods and musk, but now there was a rich and fragrant spice, an undercurrent of heady perfume that was intoxicating and my lungs seemed to contract— wanting more, needing more. I uttered a quiet sob as a wave of emotion so penetrating and deep, crashed violently over my heart.

"Nathanial," I cried. "Nathanial." He threaded his fingers in mine, his eyes seeing things I had kept buried, things that were no longer needing to stay hidden, things that I needed for him to understand. Neither of us moved; we stayed holding hands and staring at each other as the world turned, painting the next horizon and the next and the next…

Nathanial

I was watching her sleep. She hadn't wanted to, but I had insisted, as did Patric and Micah; she'd been through quite a bit over these last three days and needed to rest. A cool breeze shifted the air around me and Patric appeared at my side. He studied Ana, his eyes moving over her face. He gently stroked her cheek and I was surprised at my brother's display of affection. He laughed quietly. "How is she?" I asked him, knowing that he understood exactly to what I was referring. He turned his eyes on me and motioned for us to leave the

529

room. I followed him down the hall to the living room and poured us two glasses of wine. Patric nodded and sat down on the couch.

"She has her good days and her bad days, more bad than good it seems." He sipped his drink and stared into the fire.

"Can't you just send her back to Liam and Stephen? She doesn't have to stay with you anymore does she Patric; they had planned on turning her anyway, you can't honestly still be thinking that she'll be killed? The covens are too occupied fighting me," I said, finding it somewhat odd that I was now speaking to the individual responsible for the battles that I was currently trying to win. Patric shook his head and tossed his drink back, finishing it off in one swallow.

"Send her back to what?" he whispered, his voice rough. "There is no Liam, there is no Stephen, Nathanial; it's over. What do I do, leave her on her own somewhere? Tell her to go back to Dublin, to Idaho, to Indonesia—there's nothing left for her in those places and to ask her to start over again someplace new…you don't understand what's happened." He stood and poured another drink. I didn't understand.

"What do you mean there's no Stephen or Liam; Liam promised that he would come for her when she was ready, that she and Stephen were to be together…" My brother was shaking his head again.

"Liam and Carmen are in hiding Nathanial. Things for them have taken a very serious turn and their lives are in danger. I have been trying to help as much as I can, but I'm not ubiquitous; I can't account for what every coven does and when they do it." Patric's tone was icy and he was frustrated. He waved his hand. "And Stephen; Stephen's not exactly in the picture anymore. Ana will say that it was a mutual decision, but he really didn't give her much of a choice and she wasn't in any condition to argue with him at the time." He stood, moving to stare out the window. I was thoroughly confused. Patric laughed bitterly. "Try being Ana for a day," he said, rounding on me, our eyes meeting.

"What happened with Stephen?" I'd always known how much he'd loved Ana, how much his existence had been transformed by knowing her, by her loving him. It seemed odd that he would choose to no longer be a part of her life. Patric leaned against the window, surveying me. I was still having a difficult time getting used to the fact that my brother was alive, that he was standing in the same room with me, that we were existing together in the world. Patric bowed his head and exhaled.

"I suppose it doesn't matter if I tell you; you can read Ana's thoughts again now and this is something that she's not had the capacity to bury from anyone anyway…" His voice faded and he turned away from me. "Ana and Stephen were to have a baby, nothing short of a miracle I'm told, but there it is." I stopped breathing. "Liam and Stephen came to dinner a few months back, after they had been to see you and Micah I believe and Liam offered to show me what you had been experiencing; what you had done." I winced. "I had assumed that Stephen was already aware of everything that Liam was recounting, but I was wrong; he had not seen what you tried to do to yourself, what you almost succeeded in doing." Patric's body shuddered and I rose to stand next to him at the window. "Stephen was beside himself watching your grief, your despair and he'd made a decision to leave Ana alone; having you in her life, knowing just how much your very soul depended on being with her, it was too much for him. He tried to end things with her when they arrived back to Dublin, but Ana's body started to shut down, quickly and Stephen and Liam had to make the decision to terminate her pregnancy or lose Ana forever." I braced myself against the window frame, not comprehending. "The baby would never have been able to be carried to term and if it had, the doctors most certainly thought it would have been stillborn." Patric sighed and turned to face me, his eyes searching my face. "Stephen told Ana that they couldn't be together, not now, that he needed time to make sure that he could live with the fact that you would always be a part of Ana, a constant presence in her thoughts and in her heart. Of course Ana agreed; she's not one to ever really fight for herself is she? She only seems to find the will to go on when there is someone else she thinks deserves to live more than she, then she'll fight, she'll fight for them." Patric's eyes flashed as our gazes locked. He chuckled darkly and turned his back to me. "You know what she said when she arrived at Carlo's? You know what she said to him, this vampire that she'd never met, who had never met her…she told him that there was nothing that he could take from her that she hadn't already lost and nothing that he could promise to give her that she'd hadn't already experienced. He asked her why she thought her power was not working and she looked at him and without hesitation, she told him that she had nothing left to fight for anymore and nothing left to lose and that her life meant nothing; she was broken, shattered and if that's what he wanted, then he could have her…" He swallowed hard and I could tell he was fighting back his anger and his tears. He took a deep breath. "Of course then there's the matter of Carlo," he said, his tone sarcastic and black.

"What about him?" I was starting to feel overwhelmed.

"I've been watching him for the last two months, studying his mind, his movements. He's obsessed with her, but he's subtle because he knows I'm aware of him. He thinks about her constantly, his desire is nauseating. I've even caught him coming to her room at night to watch her sleep!" Patric's voice was rising and his tone was deadly. He knows not to touch her, that I would kill him if he ever touched her, but my relationship with Carlo is an odd one. While I've managed to push out his rule over the coven, he's still able to garner enough fear from some of the brethren that I'm beginning to wonder if he's not planning something." Patric stood over the fire, capturing the flames in his hands and bringing them close to his face.

"Can you not see what he's thinking?" I asked, watching him move the fire back and forth over his hands. He shook his head.

"I can only get feelings right now, nothing has been decided; he's restless and agitated, and Ana is easy prey right now..." He exhaled and threw the flames back onto the logs, running his hands through his hair. "I'm also fairly sure that Carlo is behind this ridiculous pursuit of Liam; he's the only one that Carlo has ever really feared and he knows that by keeping him on the run, Ana most likely will stay with us." I rubbed my face. I didn't know just where to place my rage, with Carlo, with Stephen, with Ana...there were too many things to be angry about, too many things to worry about. I wanted to scream.

"What about us?" I turned to face my brother, his face mirroring mine so much now, that I almost had forgotten we were twins. He smirked, his eyes glowing bright against the fire.

"What *about* us Nathanial?" he said, watching me.

533

"Are we just going to continue fighting each other, killing, pursuing, destroying?" I asked quietly, putting my hand on his shoulder. "Is that how we want to spend our time now?" I thought we had a second chance, my brother and myself; we could find our way back to who we were to each other as children. We could be a family—it's what our parents would have wanted.

"One step at a time Nathanial." My brother laughed. "I'm still trying to decide if I should kill you for what you did to Ana," he said, his tone turning serious. "In fact, if I'm going to be killing people; I'd also like to kill Stephen and Carlo and anyone who's ever hurt Ana—including myself," he scoffed and moved away from me. "I'll call a moratorium on the fighting for now; we'll need to negotiate a treaty of sorts before anything permanent can be put in place." Patric turned back to the couch. "I'll need to be taking Ana back to the ranch," he said, staring at me.

"And do what with her?" I asked, unsure of what my brother had planned. He sighed.

"Try to get her confidence back, try to get her to see that she should always fight for herself, that she's that important, that extraordinary, try to get her to remember who she is and what she's capable of...unfortunately, I don't think that I'm skilled enough to accomplish any of those tasks." Patric laughed, tossing his hair back. "Rising from the dead seems like child's play next to all of that." He looked at me and seeing his eyes made me sad; I missed my mother and I yearned to have Patric as my twin pillar again, as my brother. "You should talk to Ana a bit before we leave. I would tell you that you're welcome on the ranch to see her, but I'm pretty sure that Carlo would try and kill you the moment you stepped foot on the land." Patric chuckled. "I will be in contact with you and you will know how she's doing Nathanial; I can promise you that. I can also promise you that while she's with me, she won't be harmed. I'm not planning on leaving the ranch now that I know what Carlo's been pondering. I won't leave her." Patric crossed the room and put his hands on my shoulders; he felt strong, stronger than me at the moment.

Chapter Twenty-one

Ana

I was helping Esther in the garden. We'd been out there since the morning and I was enjoying being with her and being outside. I felt better knowing that Nathanial was going to be ok, that he wasn't dying anymore and I was trying to relax myself a bit. I missed Liam and often I would find myself fingering the tiny phone I always carried with me, and then of course my mind would automatically go to Stephen. I kept his ring on and I had hoped that he had kept his. I wasn't expecting us to ever be together again; I didn't get the impression from him that that would be what he would want and I thought he was just trying not to hurt me too terribly by saying that we would find each other again—I knew that we were over, but having something that he gave me, something that I could keep close, it made me feel less sad. I hoped he hadn't forgotten about me.

We finished in the garden and I had to rush to meet Patric who was waiting for me at the gym. Eduardo was traveling, buying more horses and Patric had been my main trainer and companion for several weeks. In fact, Patric seemed to be everywhere, all the time. Even when I couldn't see him, I thought every so often that I could smell his fragrance on the air and it seemed that perhaps, he was watching me, out of sight. Carlo was also a constant presence and I had enjoyed our meals together as of late. Carlo liked to debate and he was engaging to listen to, even more so when Patric would oblige his arguments. It was like watching a very intense tennis match, with a never-ending volley, where you were just waiting for someone to lower the boom. I rarely participated; it wasn't my style to debate matters that I had no knowledge of and since both of my dining companions had thirteen hundred years between them, I figured they knew a lot more about the world than I did, so why bother.

I made it to the gym on time and saw that there was someone else also there. He was standing with his back to me, grabbing various weights and placing them onto the floor. I hung back not wanting to disturb him. I looked around the space for Patric. The gym was huge and you couldn't see all the way down from one end to the other. It was like that on purpose; they needed the space for when they practiced taking each other down in mid air—it was visually stunning to watch; like acrobats who could kill you. I went over to fill up my water bottle and suddenly I was struck by a familiar scent, vanilla, musk and sandalwood, Patric's scent. Had I missed him? I whirled around to see the guy near the weights staring at me, smirking.

"Patric?" I asked, hesitantly walking back near the entrance.

"Were you expecting someone else?" He laughed, tossing his now short, wavy hair out of his eyes.

"You cut your hair!" I exclaimed, moving to stand next to him.

"Yeah, I needed a bit of a change," he said, eyeing me. He looked amazing. I loved his long locks but this… this was really flattering. Patric had always had thick wavy hair and when it was long, I was constantly jealous. Like Nathanial, Patric's hair was perfect. I would have paid thousands of dollars for his waves. The short style suited him and I couldn't help but be reminded of Stephen; his hair was cut in a similar fashion. Patric's hung loose and shaggy around his ears and it looked expertly "undone" in its texture. "Wow! I had no idea that a single hair cut would make such an impression Ana; you're really into hair." He laughed and I fingered my own ponytail, feeling the mass of curls and frowning; I hated my hair. Patric chuckled and shook his head.

"Did you go somewhere to get it done?" I asked, not sure if Patric was one to see a stylist to achieve his very rugged and perfect look.

"I cut it myself," he said, handing me a pair of weight gloves, his eyes roaming slowly over my face. I thought that perhaps Patric should consider becoming a master stylist; it might be a more enduring career than trying to rule over a rampant coven of Vampires. "Maybe, maybe that will be my next life," he said, smirking.

"Would you cut mine?" I couldn't remember the last time I had my hair done; it must have been in Dublin, maybe.

"You want to cut your hair?" Patric asked, as he placed forty-five pound plates on either side of the squat rack. I guessed that was going to be my warm up set.

"Just a trim. It really needs a trim." I said eyeing him. He looked so different; it was a bit unsettling. He came and stood behind me, both of us facing the large mirrors in front of the weights. He ran his hand down the length of my plait, twisting the curls around his fingers. I felt a jolt of electricity run through my metal tattoo and my skin grew warm; different hair, same Patric, I mused. He laughed softly and I could see him watching me in the mirror, his eyes pulsing in their familiar rhythm.

"I can trim it for you if you want," he said, stepping out from behind me and leaning on the rack. "If you trust me." He nodded for me to take my place at the bar and I put on my gloves.

"I trust you; I've always trusted you," I said, cocking my head to the side.

"You are a very, very stupid woman." He laughed as I started my squats.

We finished with our weights and moved onto grappling. I was a much better stand up fighter than on the ground and like Stephen, Patric was a master at both. It wasn't fair. He had just finished flipping me so hard over his head, that if it wasn't for the super soft padding from the mat, I was sure he would have broken every bone in my body.

"Christ Patric, I'm not a Vampire, I can still be injured. Would you calm the fuck down already!" I yelled at him as I tried to turn myself over, wondering if I was going to have to crawl out of the gym today or be carried.

"Language, language," he scolded as he stood over me waiting for me to get to my feet. I was thinking that it was probably safer if I just stayed down.

"I don't understand the purpose behind me doing any of this; are you expecting me to join the UFC or something?" I said, standing to face him.

"Are you questioning the methods of an individual who is over three hundred years your senior? I'm thinking that's not the best way to make sure you get out of here with all of your limbs in working order," he said and then he lunged, hurdling both of us up in the air and slamming me against one of the padded walls, ten stories off the ground. I stared at him, my eyes wide.

"ARE YOU INSANE!" I yelled, trying not to look down. "IF YOU DROP ME, I SWEAR, PATRIC…" He snickered.

"You swear what, Ana? If I drop you, and that's highly unlikely, we'll have to take you to the emergency room and I don't think you will be in any sort of condition to seek revenge." He laughed, pressing me harder against the wall. Suddenly I felt something push through my body and before I could even register what was happening, Patric was flying backward with such force that he looked like a bullet, whirling through the air. He stopped himself, just before he crashed into the opposite wall and hovered, looking stunned. I hadn't moved; I hadn't fallen. I was still pressed up against the wall. I froze. Holy shit, what was happening to me?

"Patric!" I yelled and the sudden wave of panic seemed to have broken whatever connection I was experiencing in my body and I felt myself begin to fall from the air. "PATRIC!" I screamed as I saw the mat on the ground getting closer and closer. Just as I was about to hit the ground, Patric grabbed me from underneath, rolling me so that I was lying on top of him. He landed us gently onto the mat, his arms wrapped tightly around my back.

"You're ok Ana, you're ok," he said, as my body shuddered and heaved. Adrenaline was coursing so fast through my body that my muscles were involuntarily contracting and releasing, the movement becoming painful. I collapsed against his chest, trying to catch my breath. "Shhh, breathe, breathe." Patric stroked my back. "It's ok," he said holding me close. I was suddenly sobbing, my face buried against him; violent cries were escaping my chest and I screamed out in my utter sadness and despair—my emotions were so fragile these days; I was a mess. He let me cry, he let me stay against him, he held me and he kept me close, he made me safe.

****

After dinner with Carlo and Patric, I was lying in bed holding my ring from Stephen between my fingers, turning it over and over again and playing my stereo loudly.

"That's a nice ring." I startled and saw Patric leaning against the doorframe, a tiny black case in his hand. I put the ring back on my finger. "Was that a gift?" he asked, drifting into the space, turning down my stereo a few notches. He and Nathanial, they both hated loud music. He laughed. "I don't hate loud music, it's just not fitting for my mood at the moment," he said, still eyeing my ring.

"What's in the case?" I asked, ignoring his question about my ring.

"You first." He raised his eyebrows at me and swept his hair off his forehead. I sighed.

"Stephen gave it to me; it matches the one that I gave him for Christmas last year," I said, feeling slightly childish and stupid for the whole thing now.

"Ahhh...." Patric murmured as he took my hand and traced his finger along the silver band. "Were you to be married?" he asked, not looking at me. I laid my head back concentrating on the slow music now playing.

"Maybe, at one point. He never really said." I shrugged.

"You gave him a ring first?" Patric lifted his eyes to mine, his face contemplative.

"Yep; totally stupid of course, but yes, I did." I inhaled deeply, closing my eyes.

"Why do you think it was stupid Ana?" he said, touching my eyelids gently, wanting me to look at him.

"Because it was, it just was. He said he couldn't wear it when I gave it to him, that he felt I still needed closure with Nathanial, that I still loved him and that Nathanial still loved me and Stephen was struggling with that. He was unsure and untrusting of me and of himself and because it was just stupid of me," I said, my voice rough.

"But he gave you a ring as well," Patric said, staring at me. "He must have felt that he could move past his insecurities for him to give you something so precious." I tossed my hair back and frowned.

"I think he felt guilty at that point Patric. I was about to go into surgery and our child was to be lost to us forever; he had seen what had happened to Nathanial and he was at war with himself; I think it was a nice gesture—that's all," I whispered. I couldn't hold him, I thought to myself; I couldn't hold anything or anyone anymore. Patric pulled me up towards him, holding my face in his hands, his eyes

542

moving furiously, searching mine. A heartbeat passed and for the second time since I'd been here, I thought he was about to kiss me. He pressed his forehead to mine and breathed heavily in and out, still holding my face.

"How about a hair cut," he whispered, pulling back and smiling.

"A *trim*," I corrected him. He rolled his eyes and unzipped the little black case he brought. "Here?" I said, thinking that I didn't want to be sweeping up tiny hairs off my floor for the next week. He looked around the room.

"The terrace, but we need to wet your head down a bit." He smiled and pulled me off the bed toward the bathroom. I flipped my hair over into the sink as he started the water. "Is it too hot?" he asked as I felt his fingers begin to rake through the wet strands.

"Nope, it's perfect." I closed my eyes and let him massage my scalp. I smelled something familiar begin to permeate the air around me, sandalwood and vanilla and I saw lather appear in the sink. "What's that?" I asked, wondering if he could get me a bottle of whatever shampoo he was using. He laughed.

"Something that I make myself," he said as his hands moved gently over my scalp. I forgot that Patric was a Healer by profession and he spent most of his life studying herbs and holistic medicine, like his father before him.

"Can you make me a bottle?" I asked, suddenly feeling very relaxed and calm.

"You like it?" he asked, rinsing my hair.

543

"Yeah, it's nice," I said, flipping my hair back over as he handed me a towel.

"What do you like about it?" he asked, patting down my hair. I smiled at him; he hadn't changed in some ways, he was still very seductive.

"The scent, it's yours. I've always liked it," I said, grinning at him. He studied me as he led me out to the terrace and pulled out a chair for me to sit. He took a comb and began gently untangling my hair. It was an odd gesture for him, I thought. Patric had always struck me as so masculine and rugged, that for him to be combing through my hair with such a delicate hand, it seemed contradictory, not that one couldn't be masculine and still be gentle... I'd just never experienced that side of Patric.

"I can be gentle Ana, if that's what's required, if that's what is needed." His voice was soft and I suddenly felt overwhelmed, my emotions rising to the surface swift and heavy, like they were prone to do these days. "I used to brush my mother's hair before she died; she and I would sit on her bed and she would give me her brush and I would sit next to her and brush her hair and she would sing. Sometimes Nathanial would be there, wrapped in her quilt, watching us..." Patric's voice faded softly and I could tell that he was remembering.

"That's a very sacred moment that you have in your memory; it's good for you to have that, to keep it close," I said quietly, not wanting to disturb his recollections. I felt him begin to cut the strands of my hair and I tensed.

"Just a trim," he said, laughing softly. He worked quietly for a while and I wondered if he was still thinking about his mother. "I'm thinking that you have a ton of hair," he said, coming to kneel down in front of me, pulling the sides of my hair over my shoulder, measuring the length. Our eyes met and I suddenly felt shy around him; he knew me so well that I couldn't hide, couldn't pretend. He bowed his head and stood to move back behind me. "You have a new addition to your mark I see," he noted as he swept the lose hair from the back of my neck.

"You mean that stupid eye thing," I said, I hated that addition; even with my broken Bond to Nathanial that thing still remained, right in the center; Patric's turquoise stone running through, piecing it like a knife.

"The color shifts," he murmured and I felt him trace his fingers over the ever-changing eye.

"Yeah I know," I said quietly, running my hand along the imprint, my fingers touching Patric's. He held our touch, tracing my fingertip down the length of his stone. My heart skipped and Patric softly laughed, hearing the glitch. I felt a sudden whoosh of warm air swirl around my head and shoulders and my hair was dry, the curls hanging in perfect spirals down over my chest and shoulders. Patric came to stand in front of me. "People would pay you good money for your skills," I said, feeling how soft my hair was. "Are you sure you want to stick with this whole mining business and rallying covens of Vampires to fight in wars?" I stood matching his posture. He lowered his head, his own hair capturing the light from the stars and shimmering and swirling in waves around his face.

"I'm an essentially selfish creature Ana; I've told you that before. I don't much care for helping others out if I don't get something in return." His chin rose and he surveyed me.

"You've helped me; you've been helping me and I'm pretty sure I haven't done much for you since I've gotten here except be a colossal basket case," I murmured, biting my lip. Patric came to stand closer to me and I could see the familiar, tiny embers beginning to dance in the depths of his eyes.

"Well that's simply not true. You have a distorted perception of yourself like always," he scolded. "You *have* helped me Ana; I have gotten something from you, something that I never deserved to take, something that wasn't mine to have and something that has forever altered my existence in this world." He took my hands in his and pulled me closer to him.

"Altered in a good way?" I said, unsure if having my blood in fact caused Patric to be more ambitious and power hungry; if that was the case, then I wasn't sure I wanted to be held responsible for being the impetus behind such motivations. His fingers traveled up the length of my arms, making my skin erupt in chills.

"Some good and some bad," he murmured softly, his eyes finding mine. I frowned. "But trust me when I say that anything bad that has come from our exchange was all my doing; I am accountable for my actions, not you." His hands rested on my shoulders and he smiled. "What do you think of Carlo?" he asked. That was an odd question and somewhat out of the blue. He nodded still smiling. "I know. I'm trying to distract myself." He shook his head. I pursed my lips.

546

"I don't like him," I said, holding onto his hands. "I think he's shallow, manipulative, narcissistic and hides behind what he thinks will be the most frightening and intimidating to others. I'm quite sure that he's very powerful, but I am also quite sure that his weakness for all things unsubstantial in life, will serve to betray him at some point." I exhaled and looked at Patric, whose eyebrows were raised.

"Tell me how you really feel, Ana." Patric laughed and pulled me into a hug. "You don't find him alluring, or attractive?" he asked, running his hands over my back. I pulled my face away frowning at him again.

"Well, all of you guys are attractive; Demons, Vampires... its part of who you are, but attractiveness only gets you so far. An individual's journey is what speaks to who they truly are and how they've traveled that journey can prove to be just as attractive and alluring as, say, a nice hair cut." I smiled at him. "But then again, I'm a girl and we tend to be a lot more substantial in who we choose to be with; men, not so much," I said, hugging him forcefully. "Why do ask?" I tilted my head up to look at him.

"Because Carlo wants you Ana." Patric's voice was dark and I pulled away from him, stepping back a few feet.

"What do you mean he 'wants me'?" I asked, my body tensing. Patric sighed and leaned against the terrace.

"He's very attracted to you, not just your blood—that's another issue, but he's attracted to your honesty, your willingness to not hide who you are from him. He finds your Bond to me intriguing and your Bond to Nathanial fascinating and your love for both of us, utterly baffling. He's amazed by what you did that night in the hut when you

547

escaped with Lucie; Liam's love for you stuns him and the sheer fact that you seem to be so willing to give him what he wants without a fight—well he's beside himself in his lust for you." Patric's eyes were dark now and I suddenly felt very, very frightened.

"He wants to kill me?" I asked, stepping back another few steps from Patric. For some reason, he was making it hard for me to trust him in this instant. I had no idea how close Patric and Carlo were, and while I was pretty sure that Patric would never harm me, I just didn't trust any one anymore except Liam. I pressed on the tiny phone in my pocket, my mind racing. Patric stayed put, but I could see that he was watching my every move, hearing my every thought.

"No, I don't think he actually wants to kill you. I think that he would much prefer for you to be his mate and for the two of you to accomplish some of his most desired ambitions. He's hoping that you will want to be Changed, that in your grief and your despair over Stephen, over what happened with you and Nathanial, with losing the baby, that you will come to him and ask to have your deal that you brought to Stephen, fulfilled, that you end your life as a Human and you begin your Afterlife with him. Of course all of that won't happen until you give him your blood; that's a whole separate prize." Patric had moved a fraction of an inch toward me and I was suddenly feeling as if I was facing Devon or Andres all over again.

"And you? What do you want for me Patric?" I asked, stepping back incrementally. Patric rubbed his mouth and moved forward again, closing the distance.

"I know that I don't want you to be with Carlo, that's for sure," he said continuing to get closer to me. "I know that I don't think that my brother or Stephen are the best choices for you right now and I know that you're vulnerable, you're weak and you've given up. You're the easiest kind of prey Ana, because you think you have nothing left to lose and that you are beyond repair." His voice was coming from behind me! I whirled to see him standing so close that we were barely touching. How had I missed him? I shook my head and turned my back to him, not caring at this point.

"I know Patric, but what do you want me to say? That's the truth and I don't think trying to pretend that I am something more, something stronger will make much of a difference. I've been as strong as I can be and I'm tired now. I did what Stephen asked, I did what Liam asked; I helped Nathanial, I forgave you. I've tried to love, I've tried to hope, tried to have courage and now it's done. It's over. I have nothing left." I felt him wrap his arms around my waist and pull me back against him. He turned me violently around so that we were facing each other. He kissed me—hard. I was caught off guard by the roughness of the motion and it took me a few seconds for my brain to register what was happening. I didn't know what to do; it felt strange and yet somewhat familiar and safe at the same time. His hands wove themselves into my hair and he grasped the back of my neck, pulling me closer still, his mouth moving swiftly against mine. I couldn't breathe and he wasn't letting me surface. We were moving. Slowly he was stepping me back toward the door and I felt my feet leave the ground. He was kissing me so passionately that it was hard for me to be responsive; I was confused by his affection for me and unsure of my feelings for him. He laid me gently down on my bed, his body hovering above mine.

549

"I want you to stop thinking Ana and *feel*. You're numb, you've been numb and I want you to feel something, anything!" His tone was harsh, and he was staring, his gaze penetrating every part of my soul.

"I'm sorry...Patric...I'm sorry. I don't know what you want," I stammered. He rolled over and stood, his hands on his hips.

"Jesus Christ, what's the matter with you? I want *you* Ana! I want the woman who I stood side-by-side and fought with; I want the woman who came to my house and shook me to my core with the intensity of her passion, her love! I want the woman I made love to, the woman who looked at me like I was the only person in the world who mattered! I want the woman who resurrected me, who redeemed me, who believed in me." I shook my head. "Don't shake your head!" he yelled, his eyes on fire. "I'm calling Liam tomorrow. I'm tracking him down and I'm getting you out of here as soon as possible. I won't watch you disappear; I won't watch you fall apart! I can't do it Ana, I can't!" He slammed open my door and left me lying on my bed, shocked and terrified.

Patric

I hung up the phone, my body tense and my heart racing. Presumed dead. What was I going to tell her? Liam and Carmen and possibly Lucie were all missing and thought to have been killed, their home torched by an ambush. No one had been able to identify the burned bodies effectively to say for sure, but they were nowhere to be found. There was no news about Stephen; no one knew whether or not he had been in the home, if he too had been killed. It had Carlo's signature all over this horrific event and now he would know that Ana's last refuge was gone; he'd know that she would have no where else to turn, no one else to offer her protection from those who wanted her power and her blood. She would be desperate and grief-stricken and that's when he would strike. I had to get her out of here. I picked up the phone and called the one person who I had no right to call.

I met my brother at my uncle's house, leaving Ana with Eduardo who had orders to kill Carlo if he got anywhere near Ana. I could trust Eduardo more than most and I knew that I was waiting to shimmer Ana here to Peru after Nathanial and I had forged a plan; I hoped it wouldn't take too long.

"Patric." Nathanial opened the door to greet me, his eyes bright and his body back to its muscularity and strength. I nodded at him and pushed my way past. "Is it Ana? Has something happened Patric?" Nathanial's jaw set as we moved into the living room.

"Liam and Carmen are thought to be dead Nathanial. Their home in South Africa was ambushed and set on fire; none are thought to have survived, not even the little girl," I said, my heart and my mind racing. "Carlo's behind it I'm sure. He knows that Liam was Ana's only safe haven left; that he'd promised to take her and to Change her, make her part of his family and his coven. With him dead, he knows she's on her own, she has no protection, nowhere to go. She'll be afraid, grief-stricken and that's what he wants," I spat. My brother braced himself against the sofa, his body tense and his jaw locked.

551

"Does she know?" he asked.

"I didn't know what to say to her? How to tell her? She's beyond a mess right now and I can't snap her out of it." I threw my hands in the air. "I have to get her out of there Nathanial. I have to get her away from Carlo. I can't be seen protecting her, otherwise the peace agreement between you and me, it won't hold. It will be all out war against you if the coven realizes that we're working together to save her and to put an end to the violence." My chest hurt and I was having trouble breathing.

"Where is she Patric?" Nathanial was looming in front of me, looking more like our father than I had ever seen him.

"She's with Eduardo." I paced back and forth.

"Bring her here," Nathanial said, his eyes stern. I looked at him. "She needs to know now Patric." I sighed and found Ana in my mind; this trick was sure to scare the hell out of her. Instantly Ana crashed into the room. She landed on her back, but leapt lithely to her feet, ready to fight it seemed.

"What the fuck Patric?" she yelled rounding on me. It took her a moment to realize where she was. "Why the hell am I here?" she cursed at me, her eyes not leaving my face.

"We need to speak with you Ana," Nathanial said quietly from behind her, his face solemn, but I could also see just what it did to him when he saw her, he glowed. She stepped back from him and moved so that we both were in her eye line—she glared.

"About what?" she asked, her eyes narrowing. She looked angry and if the situation wasn't so serious I may have commended her on the amount of feeling she was allowing herself. This was the Ana that I remembered. Nathanial motioned for her to sit on the couch and she cocked her head, defiant. I watched as she and Nathanial stared each other down; it was a tad frightening. Clearly Ana still had some issues with my brother.

"We think that Liam and Carmen are dead. They were attacked last night."

"Nathanial!" I hissed at him. I had hoped he would have been a bit more delicate when he told Ana the news. Christ, what was the matter with him? He held up his hand to silence me and suddenly Ana wasn't the only one in the room staring him down.

"What?" she asked, stepping away from us both. "What are you telling me Nathanial? Are you saying that you think Liam is dead?" Her voice shook and I could see that her body was quick to follow. Nathanial nodded, keeping his stoic glare on her face. "Lucie?" She was trembling.

"We don't know but we think, yes—Lucie too." Nathanial didn't move and I saw something odd happen to Ana's form, she actually began shimmering back and forth, her shape changing from solid to ghostlike so swiftly, it was dizzying.

"Stephen, is he...is he dead?" she asked, returning to her sold mass. Nathanial looked to me. I stepped forward.

"I don't know Ana; it doesn't appear that he was at the house when the attack happened. We're not even sure if he knows yet," I said quietly, watching her. She nodded to me.

"I have to go," she said, looking to me. "I have to find Lucie if she's alive.

"Ana I don't think—" Nathanial spoke, she cut him off.

"Patric, I need to go. Will you come with me, both of you? We need to go; I need you both," she said, her voice was strange to me; it was dark and sounded…it sounded weary. We stared at each other not blinking and for a moment I was returned to that night in her room, that night we'd been together and she had looked into my eyes and told me that she loved me, that she wanted me, the night that I betrayed her. I looked to my brother and he nodded. She nodded back and came to stand next to me, taking my hand. Nathanial crossed the room and stood on her other side, weaving his fingers through hers. Together, we shimmered away as one.

The house was still burning upon our arrival and immediately Nathanial and I could sense whether there were any other Bonders or Demons in the space. It seemed clear. Ana bolted as soon as we landed and we blurred to catch up. The front entrance was ablaze in black flames, a Carlo trademark. Just as I was about to force the flames back, I watched as Ana parted the burning wall and leapt into fire, holding the space for Nathanial and me. I looked at my brother and I thought I saw him smile. Jesus. The house was consumed and there were dozens of charred bodies strewn about. The smell was horrendous. Burning flesh and blood dripped down the walls. I was worried about Ana, about her seeing such a scene, but I found her kicking heads and picking up torched limbs with her bare hands. The fire was consuming the entire room and I looked to Nathanial; we needed to hurry or we were going to be burned to death, I could control only so much.

"Ana!" I heard him shout. "The fire," he said their eyes locking. She nodded and I suddenly saw the flames begin to shape and morph into what looked like a giant black cloud. Thunder rumbled from somewhere and I watched as lightening began forming at the base of the black flames. I turned to see Ana standing in the middle of the room, her body still, but her hair was blowing back off her face. She looked huge and utterly terrifying. The fire rolled, tumbled and expanded into a storm of flames and smoke. Ana turned her face to the sky and I stood in awe as she commanded the storm to propel itself upward and out through the open space in the roof. I heard a fierce explosion and then silence. She didn't miss a beat and instantly she was running through the house calling for Lucie. I didn't see Nathanial until I blurred into the kitchen and found him standing over a body that looked like Liam. Next to him was a woman, possibly Carmen. We stared at each other, both wondering if this would be it, the one last thing that left Ana thinking she had no one and that she'd truly lost everything and everyone she had ever loved. Cries pierced the silence and Nathanial and I whirled around. A little girl was crouched in the corner in a tiny hidden cubby. She was screaming. Nathanial blurred to her side and scooped her up, holding her close. She was hysterical.

"ANA!" he yelled. "ANA!" I heard footsteps as Ana crashed through the hole in the wall.

"LUCIE! LUCIE!" she screamed and the tiny girl soared through the air as if propelled by some otherworldly force and leapt into Ana's arms. She shielded the girls face in her chest as I saw her find the two bodies on the ground. She closed her eyes and held Lucie close to her, whispering in the girl's ear. Ana mesmerized me. She was more magnificent than I had ever seen her and more breathtaking than I could get my head around.

"Nathanial!" She rounded on us. "You and Patric take Lucie back with you. Keep her in Peru. I need to find Stephen, he doesn't know and I need to find him." She was giving us instructions and it didn't sound at all out of the ordinary. Nathanial nodded and reached to take Lucie from Ana's arms. Lucie screamed, holding out her hands for Ana. "It's ok baby! It's ok! I'm coming right back. I'll be right back Lucie. I love you. Stay with Nathanial now ok? Hold tight love and I'll be right back." I was stunned. Right before my eyes, Ana became not only a protector and a fighter, but also a mother. I was awestruck. "Patric, can you deal with Carlo until I can get back? I don't want your life to be at risk, you can come with me if you want," she said, her eyes searching my face.

"It's fine Ana. I'll be fine. Go." She nodded and with one quick glance back at Nathanial and me, she disappeared.

I landed just outside of Belfast; I wasn't entirely sure that I had commanded the right location. I wasn't even sure this is where he would be; I just tried to conjure his face and I hoped that I got close enough. I was on a narrow side street with small and cozy houses that lined the walk. I tried to remember what the house looked like from Stephen's paintings, but everything was so similar. My heart was thundering in my chest. Liam and Carmen were dead. Lucie was alive; Stephen didn't know I was guessing. How was I going to do this? How was I going to see him again, to tell him that his brother had been killed? I paused on the street and scanned up and down the road, looking for anything familiar. Suddenly I saw what looked like a familiar figure go into a house across the street. Cillian. I ran across the road and reached the door just as it shut. I heard loud music coming from inside and the smell of blood hit me square in the gut. I opened the door, holding my breath. I would have taken the scene at Liam's house over what I had just walked in to—it was a disgusting. A large table was erected and there were various Vampires gambling and drinking. The pile in the center held liquor, casks of blood and what appeared to be an assortment of jewelry. The women at the table were being fed upon, their wrists and necks dripping blood, some were bound and gagged, unable to move away from the bloody assaults on their bodies. I walked slowly over to the table and Cillian looked up, his eyes showing complete surprise.

"Ana! Holy shit! I can't fuckin' believe it!" he shouted, as he tossed the girl, who he'd just been drinking from, onto the floor. I scanned the table and noticed something shiny and familiar lying in the pile. I reached across the blood and the liquor and picked up a thick silver band, Stephen's ring. I held it up and in that instant every string that was attached to my heart, was severed. Cillian was staring at me.

"Where is he?" I said, my voice barely a whisper.

"Ana." Cillian took my arm, his eyes brimming with sadness.

"Where is he?" I said again, pocketing the ring. Cillian motioned to the back of the house. I walked slowly down the hallway and heard soft music coming from one of the bedrooms; it was the song that always played when Stephen and I were together. I fingered my amulet, feeling it suddenly surge with heat. I pushed opened the door and found Stephen. He was with a woman, he was feeding on her and they were having sex. Blood was everywhere and the smell from their coupling made me gag. I steadied myself and thought of Noni, of what she would want me to do, how she would want me to not be lost from myself, no matter how much I was grieving; she would want me to hold on, just a little longer.

"Stephen," I said, my voice trembling slightly as I watched him move over her. He stopped mid-motion. "Stephen," I said again, closing my eyes, not wanting to look anymore. I heard the woman moan and the bed creak. I took a deep breath and opened my eyes.

"Ana?" Stephen was staring at me, his face and chest bloody and coated in sweat.

"I need to speak with you for a moment; it's very important or I wouldn't have come," I said, not meeting his eyes.

"I'll be right out," he said, looking shocked. I nodded and closed the door and walked back down the hallway and out the front entrance. It was raining and I let the cold and the damp settle into my bones, numbing me even further. I heard a door open and shut and Stephen was standing in front of me. I stepped back from him.

"Stephen," I took a deep breath, "Liam and Carmen are dead; they were killed last night in a fire at their home. Patric, Nathanial and I have just come from the scene and we have Lucie, she's alive, she's with Nathanial." The rain was streaming down my face, soaking my hair. I sounded mechanical, robotic. Stephen didn't move. He was staring at me, his eyes shifted from coal black to deep and beautiful blue; the clearest and purest waters moved swiftly over my face. "Stephen did you hear me?" I said, as a clap of thunder shook the sky.

"Ana," he said, his voice shaking and I smelled alcohol on his breath. He was wrecked. I sighed.

"Listen to me Stephen. Your brother, he's dead, so is Carmen. I have Lucie, but I'm also with Carlo and I just don't know how much longer I'm going to be able to fend him off. Lucie needs you; she needs her uncle. Are you hearing me?" I was shouting over the thunder and the pounding rain, feeling returning to my voice. "STEPHEN!" I shook him, pushing him back a few feet.

"Ana, I can't. I'm not in any shape to deal with this now. I can't," he whispered to me.

"Are you kidding me? Are you crazy? This is your brother we're talking about, your niece—your family! I'm so sorry that I interrupted your feeding frenzy and your alcohol binge; I'm sorry if my presence is not conducive to your little party and that perhaps your brother could have picked a more suitable time to have been murdered, SO THAT YOU WOULDN'T BE INCONVENIENCED!" I screamed at him and shoved him down to the ground. He lunged at me, sweeping my legs out from under me and throwing me to the pavement. I hit him in the face and sent him staggering backward. "ARE YOU CRAZY! I screamed. "WHAT THE FUCK ARE YOU DOING?" Cillian suddenly appeared.

"Ana, he's messed up, dis isn't da best time." Cillan was helping me to stand up. Stephen was still lying on the ground, breathing hard. I looked at Cillian.

"Liam is dead Cillian. Lucie is in Peru with Nathanial. Carlo is waiting to either kill me or turn me and there isn't anyone who can protect me for much longer. That little girl needs her uncle. You tell Stephen to get his fucking ass to Peru and take care of Lucie." I wiped the rain off my face and stepped over to Stephen. "You selfish sonofabitch!" I said, spitting the rain from my mouth. "You don't have to love me anymore Stephen; you don't owe me anything, but Lucie has just lost her parents and you're the only family she has left. If you have any shred of kindness and love in your soul, any love at all—she deserves to have it;" I locked eyes with him, tossing his ring to the ground before I disappeared.

I gambled and retuned to Patric first. I was uneasy leaving him to deal with Carlo and I figured that between Nathanial and Micah, Lucie would be well tended to until I could make other arrangements for her. I made it back to my room and heaved myself on the bed, wet clothes and all. I clutched my abdomen and curled up in a ball, sobbing and choking. I was crying because I had lost Stephen, crying because I had lost Liam and Carmen, crying for Noni, for Kai, for Nathanial, for Patric, for the baby I never got to hold and for Lucie. All my bonds were broken now, they all faded away like ghosts; like mists over the mountains; they had nothing to hold them any more, and I had nothing to hold on to. I clutched my ring from Stephen, tearing my own from my finger. It was over. I was done. Lucie was my last act of grace, my last sacred thing I could do for Liam and for Carmen. I had saved Nathanial, given him a chance to rebuild his life. I had gone to Stephen, knowing that his love for was no more. I had seen Patric alive. I had been able to tell him that I didn't hate him and that I wanted him to be happy; the game had played itself out. I sat up wiping my face. I stood and put my ring on my dresser and walked out of the room.

Patric's suite was located two floors above mine and it was the size of my apartment in Dublin, Stephen's house and Noni's house, combined. I stood outside, seeing a soft glow coming from under the door. I hoped he was alone. I took a deep breath and knocked. The door swung open and I saw Patric sitting at his desk, reading. It was such a normal image that I almost forgot he was a lethal Vampire, at least partly. He closed the book and surveyed me as I entered the room. I sensed a weird energy coming from him and I wondered if he was angry for my leaving him and Nathanial at Liam's house. He didn't say anything; he just stared.

"Umm, hey," I said, completely aghast by my own lack of oratory skills. "I'm sorry to bother you," I said, looking at the stack of books and maps that covered his desk. He leaned back in his chair, his eyes

561

roaming slowly over my face; he was reading my thoughts, seeing everything that I had just worked through, everything that had happened with Stephen; he was seeing it all. "As soon as I can find suitable arrangements for Lucie, as soon as Stephen comes, if he comes; I want to leave. I don't know how we can make that happen. I'm guessing we'll have to engage in some sort of deadly battle for my soul or something and that Carlo will not be happy, but I can't stay here anymore I have to go." Patric's eyes flashed and he moved forward, his face glowing deep and smooth in the light of the candle he had lit. His gaze shifted over my shoulder and I turned to see Nathanial coming from the hallway. Great, now I was going to have to deal with both of them. What the hell was he doing here; he was going to get himself killed and I was pretty sure that even I wouldn't be able to bring him back from that fate. Nathanial grinned and sauntered into the room; I had never seen him saunter before, that was more Patric's Stephen's style. My heart felt dislodged. I ignored him and turned back to Patric. "What do you want me to do?" I asked, figuring that he would be the one I would have to convince to help me get the hell out of here.

"Things didn't go well with Stephen I take it," Patric finally spoke, moving out from behind his desk and pouring two glasses of wine and opening a ginger ale for me. Christ, they must have been expecting me. I took the soda and stood as far away from the two of them as I could. I was so tired.

"No, things did not go well at all. I'm not even sure if he heard anything that I said," I murmured. I touched the now empty space where my ring once sat and I saw Nathanial watching me.

"Was something wrong with him?" Nathanial asked, his eyes still on my ring finger.

"You could say that," I replied, sipping my drink and wanting to die. I felt so stupid and I wasn't even sure why, maybe because somewhere deep inside I always thought that Stephen would find me again, that he would want to find me again, that he wouldn't forget about me; clearly that was not the case. I thought about his ring, sitting in the middle of that blood soaked table; I felt sick. Both Patric and Nathanial were staring at me. "What?" I said, my agitation surfacing.

"We're working on trying to find you a safe location to go to Ana. Micah is using all of his contacts to find you and possibly Lucie, a place you can escape." Patric's voice was low and his eyes were dark. I shook my head, they didn't understand.

"That's very nice of your uncle, but I don't want an escape. I don't want your protection or your contacts; I don't want anything from either of you. I just want to be allowed to leave, for you to help me one last time get the hell out of this place and I will never bother either of you again. I don't want you to know where I am or where I'm going or if I'm alive or dead. I don't care. I don't care if the minute I step foot off this land, I'm killed. I don't want you to help me!" I started to shout, my drink sloshing around in the glass. "God! We've been through so much, aren't the two of you just a little bit tired of trying to decide what to do with me, what to do with yourselves? Aren't you exhausted from all the loss and the grief and the love and despair and the stupid Bonds and the blood? None of it has made any difference, none of it has mattered in the least; nothing in me has survived that is in any shape or form capable of holding on to anything anymore or anyone.

563

We've all hurt each other so much, so much damage has been done and for what, for whom? Aren't you ready to end things now, to get on with your lives? We go our separate ways, we have our memories and we live knowing that we were lucky enough, I think, to have had each other for as long as we did. The two of you have a chance now, you have a chance to make different choices, to be the individuals that your mother believed you to be, the men that she died for, the men that she loved. Our fates have been tied to each other for far too long and at some point one of us has to cut the rope." I bowed my head, my heart breaking one last time.

"I agree Ana and I must say that you are quite an impassioned speaker," Carlo's voice came from behind me. I closed my eyes and exhaled. Could this day get any worse?

Chapter Twenty-two

Nathanial

I rose to stand next to my brother as we watched Carlo come into the room. He was smiling. Immediately I shut my mind and I could feel Patric do the same.

"Well, it looks like negotiations are going well. It is nice to see the two of you working together again, not at all like that last time we tried to hash out a treaty; that did not end well at all for us, not well at all." Carlo positioned himself next to Ana and I could feel Patric tense. He was going to have to stay calm. Carlo turned to Ana who bizarrely seemed relatively unflustered. "Ana, I hear that you've had quite an upsetting day. I'm so very sorry to hear about Liam and his wife. You were able to rescue their daughter no?" Carlo asked, his eyes bright and gleaming as he looked at Ana. I watched in awe as Ana took a sip from her glass and nodded her head.

"Thank you Carlo. Yes, we were able to find Lucie and get her away from the house. I've contacted her uncle and I'm waiting for him to arrive to escort her back to Ireland." Ana's voice was calm and I had to look at her just to make sure she actually didn't have some sort of mental break under all of the stress she was carrying. She appeared normal. Carlo put his arm around Ana and stared at her, his face registering some emotion that I could not decipher. "I hope you won't mind if I leave to check on her; she's very important to me and I don't want her to be frightened over what has happened to her parents." Ana smiled at Carlo, but I knew that tone; that was her "don't fuck with me" tone, her "I have nothing left to lose" tone and it was chilling. Carlo eyed Ana and I could see him trying to sort her out. She was locked down and every wall that she had ever built from childhood until now was up and strong and no one was getting through.

"Of course Ana, anything you want. You can even bring Lucie here if you wish." I saw Ana's eyes flash and I almost laughed. She wouldn't dare put Stephen at risk; she knew he and Carlo had a history and even after everything she just experienced with him, still she would try to protect him if she could.

"Thank you Carlo, you are very kind. I think she's fine with Micah for the time being, but I will of course keep your offer in mind should her uncle not have the capabilities to come for her in a timely manner." I thought it odd that she kept referring to Stephen as "uncle" it was as if she couldn't bring herself to say his name.

"Good, good," Carlo said, smiling down at Ana as he pulled her close. Again, I felt my brother tense, his body rigid. "Now I hear that you would like to leave Ana, that these boys are giving you all sorts of grief, is that correct?" Carlo eyed me and I met his stare, my chin raised. Ana laughed and I turned my gaze to her. Had she cracked?

"Yes, Carlo I would like to leave. Not that you haven't been the most gracious, the most hospitable host I have ever had the pleasure of meeting, but I think that I have caused quite enough distraction and trouble here to last several lifetimes. I'm pretty sure that I am in dire need of therapy and some quality time to myself. Plus, I would actually like to use the degree that I paid a hundred thousand dollars in student loans to acquire." She laughed again staring at Carlo, her eyes shinning. Carlo scanned her face and I could see just how intrigued he was by Ana, how much he desperately wanted to know her. I understood those feelings quite well.

"Nonsense Ana, you've been nothing but a pure delight to host and your appreciation for everything that I have here, for everything that I have to offer; well I don't deserve it." Carlo held her hand in his and now it was my turn to tense. "However, there is the matter of our little negotiation that I made with Liam before his untimely death." Carlo looked to Patric, but it was Ana who spoke.

"Ah yes, the matter of my blood, the matter of turning me; the matter of my powers." Carlo turned back to her; actually we all did. "I'm happy to give you what you want blood-wise Carlo. Patric has my blood and so does Nathanial; I'm sure one more offering won't be over doing it. Although I should tell you that, with the exception of Nathanial, it doesn't seem to be doing much good for any one as of late. I wouldn't hesitate to say that it's cursed." She laughed, but her eyes didn't leave Carlo's face. "Let's see, my ability with fire...well I would absolutely give you that as well; in fact I wish you would just take it. I hate fire, always have. I was almost killed by the damn stuff as a kid, so if you could find a way to negate that power then, please by all means, you wouldn't have to fear it anymore—it would be gone, no one would have it and we're back to a somewhat level playing field." She paused, taking another sip of her drink and I was pretty sure that I heard Patric start to growl. "So that brings us to the matter of Changing me. Well, if you already have some of my blood and you benefit from those properties, and we just forget about the fire, then really what's the point of transitioning me? I've already said I would give you the thing that the other two people in this room already have, the thing that Andres tried to rape and kill me for, the thing that made Patric betray himself and me for, the thing that I know you want Carlo." She paused again watching him, assessing him. I was just trying not to tell her to shut up. I couldn't believe what she was saying, what she was offering. Apparently I wasn't alone. Carlo was beside himself. He stepped away from her and paced the room, in shock.

"Ana, are you offering me your blood, freely? I don't understand." He seemed genuinely confused. She smirked and stepped forward.

"Everything has a price Carlo." Ana's voice had changed, it was dark and seductive and I had never heard her speak in such a sensuous manner before. She also seemed to be changing her appearance right in front of us. Her hair shone from some invisible light and it was swirling and billowing out around her shoulders except there was no wind, no breeze; the air was still and quiet. Patric growled again, this time not so quietly. I shot him a deadly look. Carlo appeared just as caught off guard by the change in her tone as I was and he stopped pacing to stare at her.

"You wish to negotiate?" Carlo asked, moving back a few feet.

"Yes, you like making deals, I know this, so this is what I am offering," she moved forward towards him, making me very nervous, "you get my blood, just enough to help you out with whatever it is you want to do." She waved her hand nonchalantly as if she couldn't possibly care less why he wanted her blood. "I get to leave, unharmed and unchanged and so do they, if they so wish and Stephen too." She motioned towards us and I tried to catch her eye, but she looked right past me. "You go out into the world and you do whatever it is that powerful,

568

Argentinean Vampires do, but you don't come for me Carlo and you don't come for Patric or Nathanial or Micah or Stephen or Lucie." Ana seemed to grow before me and I had to hold in a gasp as I saw her feet leave the ground slightly. I turned to Patric, who unlike me didn't seem surprised by this sudden turn in Ana's abilities. Carlo however, was sharing in my disbelief. She stared at him. "If you do, if I ever hear that you have caused any of those people harm, if I catch even a hint that you are trying to propagate violence or revenge," she paused and her eyes caught fire, they pulsed and burned outwards heating the room, "I will kill you." She stayed hovering off the ground, her eyes turned black and flames burned brightly in their depths. I was absolutely terrified. "Do we have a deal?" she asked, watching him, her voice hypnotic. Carlo looked at me and then at Patric, then back to Ana, his face unrecognizable.

"What makes you think that I just won't kill you now," Carlo said, floundering in his attempt at bravado. Ana laughed, but this time it was not a genuine laugh, not a deep laugh that came from her heart; this was a deadly laugh, sinister and bone chillingly evil. Patric stepped back taking me with him. Ana was on Carlo in less than a heartbeat. I watched as she appeared to soar in the air, grabbing him around the throat and pushing him back against the wall, hovering him there while her feet remained firmly planted on the ground.

"Try," she said, tightening her grip. Carlo seemed immobilized; it was odd to see him unable to move at Ana's hand. "I told you the first night we met that I have nothing left to lose. You can't take anything from me that I haven't already lost and that includes my life. Try, but one of us isn't getting a second chance at redemption. Do you really want to gamble and take your chances because I have no problem playing the odds Carlo." She squeezed tighter and I heard him gasp. "Now, do we have a deal?" she asked, her tone icy. I was stunned, terrified at what I was observing; the violence coming from Ana was so tangible, so palpable, that the depths of my very soul felt her pain, her anguish.

"Yes," Carlo said and Ana surveyed him, turned to my brother and I saw him nod slightly. What the hell was going on here? She dropped him to the ground, grabbed her drink and turned to leave the room. "As soon as Stephen comes to take Lucie then you get what you want; you try any sooner and the deal's off!" She didn't look back and I watched as she drifted out of the room, leaving us to revel in our shock at what had just transpired.

Ana

Well that went better than I thought. I started the shower and tried to calm my nerves. I hoped that everything I had been told months ago was correct—it had to be. I tugged on my pajamas, combed through my wet hair and tried not to think about anything. I wondered if Patric could make me something to help me sleep. I crawled into bed and tried to relax, but I was suddenly terrified that Carlo would somehow try to murder me in my sleep. I knew my reaction may seem strange to some after my behavior this evening, my mind was always over active at night and I tended to have most of my panic attacks while trying to sleep. I rose from my bed and walked out into the hall and back up to the second story. Patric's door was closed and I wondered if

Nathanial was still here. I knocked softly and waited. The door opened without prompting and I peeked into the room. Patric was sitting, his head on the back of the sofa, a glass in his hand. He looked like he was sleeping. I started to back out towards the hallway, but he suddenly spoke.

"Can't sleep?" he asked, his eyes still closed. I stepped closer to him, shutting the door.

"Yeah, can I come and hang out with you for awhile?" I asked, sounding like a scared child after a horrible nightmare. He laughed and raised his head to look at me.

"Be my guest Ana." He patted the seat and I curled up next to him.

"Thanks for your help tonight," I whispered, watching him. He was breathing softly and his scent was filling the room with its warm, rich fragrance. He turned his face to me, his eyes so clear it made me not want to look away, but I did.

"I wish I could take credit for what occurred this evening Ana, but alas, I cannot. I didn't help you; you didn't need my help or Nathanial's for that matter… it was all you." He turned his face back and looked at the ceiling.

"I can't immobilize people, not yet anyway; that was you. You've always helped me when I've needed it, when I didn't think I could muster enough strength to use my own powers; you've always been there, standing beside me even when I thought you were dead…" I whispered. "Everything that I can do, everything that I am able to create and control and use—it comes from you, from the first time

571

that you gave me your blood to keep me alive; it's always been you, Patric." Patric turned to stare at me, his eyes wide as they searched my face. He shook his head and exhaled.

"Ana." He laughed softly and sipped his drink. "What are we going to do with you?" he said, shifting in his seat so that he was angled in towards me. "Do you really want to cut the rope from Nathanial and from me Ana? Is that what you think is best, that no one will know where you are or what you are doing, if you are alive or dead? Is that really how you feel about things now?" His face was contemplative, but his eyes were moving swiftly back and forth as he took me in. I took a deep breath.

"I don't think that we really have a choice anymore Patric. I don't know where to go from here. My Bond is broken with Nathanial, but he's alive and safe; Stephen…well the life that I thought we were going to have…that's no longer, and you're alive as well now and that's good, that's wonderful." I sighed, not knowing what else to say or how to explain to him just how broken I was, how far I had fallen and that I had finally hit the ground and shattered. After seeing Stephen this last time—I shattered. I rubbed my abdomen gently.

"Hmmm…do you really think that Stephen has forgotten about you Ana, that the love he had for you just evaporated? Do you really think so little of him to judge him at a time of desperation and confusion?" Patric studied me, processing my thoughts.

"No, but I think he knows what he wants and what he doesn't Patric. He may have been confused and uncertain about Nathanial, but he had a point. I would find it hard to be with someone who was

572

constantly thinking about someone else, constantly grieving for the ending of a Bond and of a life that may have been; he deserved better then and he deserves better now. He's an amazing being and I love him very much," I said, trying not to cry for the millionth time.

"You love my brother too." Patric was still focusing on my face, on my eyes.

"Always," I said, smiling at him. "I love you as well, just in a more complicated and bizarre way than the other two." I laughed softly and swept his hair out of his eyes.

"Interesting that someone who believes themselves to be so broken and shattered, can have the capacity to offer so much love to so many people. Why do you think that is?" He touched my face, stroking my cheek.

"Oh, no Patric," I said, rolling my eyes. "Reverse psychology doesn't work on me. I've had years of therapy trying to discover the paradigms that make up who I am; your question will never have an answer." I pulled back from him and bit my lip. He touched his finger to my mouth and frowned. "What?" I asked.

"Where do I fit into all of this? I just wonder sometimes what would have developed between us if I hadn't been so greedy, so manipulative and if my brother had not, in fact, returned." Patric was now tracing his finger gently over my bottom lip, his gaze holding me.

"But that's what did happen Patric; it really serves no purpose to dwell on 'what might have been'," I said, breathing out gently. "As far as where you fit in, well I suppose that's up to you. We're actually

Bonded and I feel quite terrible about that; you might have chosen someone else for yourself—a supermodel perhaps!" I laughed. "I like to think that we will always have a connection to one another, beyond just what we have out of ritual. It makes me happy to know that you and I exist in the world at the same time and that you know me—I think there is something sacred about our relationship. I mean you were the first person that I gave my blood to in such an intimate way… that counts for a lot in my book. However, it wasn't the most romantic evening I've had." I smiled at him. He grinned.

"No, I guess it wasn't was it?" He pulled his hand away and glanced sideways at me. I could see he was thinking about something. "I should have made it better for you Ana; I should have made you feel as extraordinary as you truly are. Instead, I just left you there alone and bleeding. Christ, how is it that you can even stand to be next to me?" He seemed sad and angry. I didn't want him to feel either of those things. It was over now and it didn't matter to me. I took his face in my hands and forced him to look at me.

"Because Patric, because I never truly believed that that's who you were that night, that that's all you were capable of. I was thinking about the person who sat in my kitchen so many nights after Nathanial left and talked to me or just listened, if that's what I needed. I was thinking about the man who would watch me make dinner and who would tease me about what I was eating. I was thinking about the fact that you chose to keep me alive and that even though you were using me, I couldn't honestly believe that you wanted to see me die. Maybe there was some small part of you that grew to appreciate me and you recognized just how much I was hurting after Nathanial left and at that time I'm guessing you could foresee just how betrayed I was going to feel about Alec. I can sit here next to you Patric, because you were with me the night Lucie and I had to escape from Liam's house and you were with me the night that I was sure that Nathanial was going to kill me. You allowed me to believe enough in what we had given each other, to not only save your brother and Lucie, but to also save myself. You, in all of your missteps and horrible decisions, you redeemed me," I said, feeling the truth of that knowledge. I hadn't thought about it in those terms and suddenly the memory of Noni's vision in the meadow came flooding back. I had thought that she of course was speaking about someone who was still alive, at that time, someone who still needed to complete their own journey and that I still needed to help. I hadn't thought about Patric in that moment or even myself, but perhaps Noni knew. Perhaps she knew that my journey couldn't be complete without Patric nor his without me, that I was so busy trying to save everyone else from themselves that I failed to notice what was occurring in the background. That all the while, Patric had been with me, waiting, waiting to not only prove himself worthy of his mother's sacrifice, but also waiting to save me—to be my redemption. I gasped and looked up to see Patric, tears coming from his eyes.

"Yes Ana," he said softly. "I fell in love with you that night, more deeply than I could have ever thought possible, but I was selfish and couldn't see past my own ambitions, my own greed, to see that you were, in fact, offering me a different choice, a chance at a life that would have made my mother happy, that would have made me happy and I tossed it away, discarded it as worthless. I discarded you Ana and I put your very life in danger. I kept you balancing on the edge of a knife that I held and I lowered the blade." His head was bowed and I could see drops of tears falling onto his jeans, sending small puffs of mist into the air as they hit. "I have always wanted you; I have always believed in you and I am so very sorry for causing you pain, for hurting you so deeply." I tucked my finger under his chin and brought his face to the light. I studied him, wanting to fall deep into his eyes and I did…

Nathanial

I left Lucie with Micah and instructions to not let Ana or Patric know where I was going. This business with Stephen had to stop. He needed to do what Ana asked of him and because it's what that little girl deserved. His confusion and angst over he and Ana's relationship wasn't an excuse and my patience for his petulant behavior had run its course. I landed in Dublin, Micah having used his contacts to relocate Stephen. He had left his mother's house in Belfast shortly after Ana's visit and was now back in his old home and I wasn't expecting a warm reception.

He needed to know what Ana had done for him, how she still found a way to protect him, to keep him safe, even after he'd made her feel as though she was forgettable, after he's tossed a beautiful symbol of her love, to the wind, after he'd had the honor of her choosing him to be her mate and conceiving a child—I couldn't understand how he would throw it all away because he was jealous. Jealous of me, of someone who continuously stumbled over themselves, killing Ana with each misstep, with my lack of courage, with each spineless decision.

He had an opportunity to prove to her that he was the better choice and that he would care for her, love her, cherish her and he turned away, turned her away. I was disgusted and disbelieving. I wanted an explanation, so at least I could return to Ana when I pleaded with her to take me back, knowing that I had given him one last chance, that I would bow out of her life as a partner and let them be together. I would love her from a distance and hope that she would still find a way to have me as a friend and companion. This was it. If he didn't step up now, all bets were off and I wouldn't stop short of killing him to get Ana back, no matter how much it hurt her.

I paused at the door and listened. Quiet music was playing and after the images that Ana brought back from her last visit, I was hoping for Stephen's sake, that those images were not going to be reality; I wasn't inclined to be as diplomatic as Ana. I shimmered through the door and stood in the hallway. A deep darkness hung in the air and I moved slowly down the corridor toward the living room, listening. His back was to me and I could see that he was playing his guitar. Canvases and paints were strewn about and images of Ana were hanging everywhere, in photographs, in paintings and drawings; Jesus, if I didn't know Stephen better, I'd say he was beginning to fit the profile of a stalker. The music stopped, but he kept himself turned away. I leaned against the wall.

"Are you coming to get your niece Stephen?" I asked quietly, sensing his grief over his brother and for Ana. He shook his head and started playing again. I waved my hand and sent his guitar crashing against the fireplace, splintering into millions of pieces. He rubbed his face and I crossed the room to stand in front of him. "So that's it then? You're done? That's how you are choosing to honor your brother Stephen, to not come for his daughter, to not see to it that she's taken care of by the only remaining family she has? Are you that selfish? Perhaps Ana has been blinded by her love for you, that she couldn't see what waste of space you actually are. Perhaps in her undying belief in people's capacity to be resilient, she was mistaken when it came to you. Perhaps you manipulated her, used her, broke her!" My voice was deadly as I watched his disinterest. He stood and took a sip from a large liquor bottle near the fire.

"What would you like me to do Nathanial?" he asked, wiping his mouth. I ran my fingers through my hair; it was like trying to reason with a child.

"I want you to come and get Lucie; I want you to tell Ana that you love her and I want you to stop acting like a goddamned, sonofabitch for Christ's sakes!" I said, taking a step closer to him. He looked at me, his eyes red and swollen.

"Lucie is better with Ana; she's a good mother. Lucie loves her," he said, taking another drink from his bottle. I laughed bitterly.

"Ana has gotten herself into quite a little negotiation with Carlo, Stephen. She's not expecting to be around for much longer and she's asked that Lucie is taken care of before Ana leaves or before she's killed, whichever happens to come first." Stephen's eyes flashed once but then dimmed.

"What sort of a deal?" he asked collapsing on his couch. I stood facing him; he was pathetic. "What sort of a deal Nathanial?" Stephen said again, hearing my internal judgment of his current condition.

"She's offered him what he wants; her blood. Well, that's the main thing he wants, but it also appears that he's very attracted to her and I'm sure he would prefer having her as an intimate companion," I scoffed. "But beyond any of that, Ana has managed to scare the shit out of Carlo and by doing so she has mediated for her protection, mine and my brother's protection and yours Stephen. By tapping into Carlo's need for power and his desire to acquire much sought after things, Ana has offered him her blood in exchange for all of our lives." I stood in front of him, my arms folded across my chest. "She also took things one step further and threatened to kill him if he ever touched you or any one else that she cares about; she's ready to leave all of us Stephen, to cut the rope as she so aptly put it, having Lucie is not part of her plan." I exhaled and sank down beside him on the couch.

"She threatened to kill Carlo?" Stephen asked, running his fingers through his hair and rubbing his eyes.

"Yes, and quite terrifyingly so. It appears that her time back with Patric seems to have reawakened some of her deeper, more sinister attributes, shall we say." I put my hands behind my head. "I wouldn't want to cross her and I most certainly wouldn't want to make her angry." I chuckled. " Two things that I seemed to have done quite well in the past, unfortunately." Stephen turned to me, his eyes flat and lifeless.

"When? I mean when is she supposed give Carlo…" He trailed off, not able to say the words. I was sure that the very thought of Ana giving someone her blood that didn't love her and that she also didn't love, was a sickening idea to him, it was to me.

"She's agreed to go about the transaction as soon as you've come for Lucie or until we can make other arrangements for her. She's waiting on you. For some reason, she's still under the impression that despite your dismissal of your relationship, that you would want to come and help Lucie." Stephen turned on me, his face violent.

"I didn't dismiss our relationship Nathanial. It was never going to work, not while she was still so in love with you. I just did what I knew would eventually happen. I knew that she would do whatever it took to save you, to bring you back from whatever hell you were going through and I was right wasn't I? Here you sit, fully restored in your sense of self, in your heart and your soul; she saved you because she loves you and she always will." He swigged more from his bottle and tossed his head back.

"You're an idiot," I said, staring at him. "We both are, for different reasons, but idiots all the same." I leaned forward turning to face him. "So that's it then; you're done with Ana?" I asked, wondering if he truly understood just how much she loved him, and how much she's given up on herself.

"I don't doubt that Ana loves me Nathanial. In fact I know that she loves me very deeply, but that still does not change the fact that I cannot deal with her love for you or yours for her; if we are being honest. I'm selfish Nathanial and ultimately, I don't want to share Ana's heart or her soul, with anyone else. I want her to be mine fully and I want her forever," he whispered. I shook my head.

"Then you truly don't love Ana, Stephen. If you did, you would know that loving Ana means you respect and honor just how extraordinary her capacity to love really is and that her ability to take all of us into her life, to love each and every one of us for our flaws, for our betrayals, for our weakness; her capacity to believe in our redemption, in our strength to make the other choice, the one that's more difficult, but the one that will ultimately reveal who she knows us to be; that is only some of what it means to love Ana and between the two of us, we've failed miserably. Ironic that the one person who instigated a myriad of chaos and disaster in her life is the one person who seems to have figured that all out," I said, my voice going soft.

"Whose that?" Stephen asked, his eyes open wide now. I exhaled, not believing that I didn't see it before.

"My brother. He's known all along how to love Ana even when he betrayed her. He's always known because she was the first person who ever loved him at his very worst and she changed the very core of who he is. He fought against it, he fought her every step of the way, but he was always there, always believing in her because she believed in him. She defended her affection for him against everyone, against me, against Alec and Kai, and against you. Patric loves Ana and I'm guessing that he's not going to let her slip through his fingers again, that he wants to redeem himself for the pain he's caused her and he wants to prove to himself, that he is worthy of her love, of being loved." Christ. This added something new to the mix.

"You're brother is in love with Ana?" Stephen asked, his tone incredulous. "But he knows that you love her; doesn't that go against some sort of sibling code or something?" Stephen bowed his head thinking of Liam. I laughed.

581

"Patric has never been one to follow any code, not for himself and certainly not when it comes to me," I said.

"You think he's going to try to take her away from you?" Stephen seemed anxious all of sudden and I was wondering if having Patric as competition was enough to raise his emotions for Ana.

"She's not mine to take Stephen. Ana has her own choices to make and it looks like my brother might want to add his heart into the ring." I wasn't entirely sure whether that was what Patric wanted, but if it helped get Stephen to at least talk to Ana, then what the hell did I have to lose. "Listen Stephen, I want you to know that if you love Ana and you want to be with her, then you need to go to her. You need to beg and plead and I won't stand in your way. If that's what she truly wants, I will let her go. I will always be a presence in her life, that's something that you will just have to deal with, but if she chooses you and you can offer her the life that she deserves, if you are willing to die for her, to go to the ends of the world to see that she feels loved and cherished, then I will not make it difficult for either of you. I will let it happen as she so wishes. But know this, the instant that you hurt her, the instant that you cause her to doubt her value, her heart; the instant that you betray her love, I will come for her and then I will come for you." I stood and offered him my hand. He stared at me, tears in his eyes. He nodded. "Good. Then we need to go; the longer Carlo has to wait for Ana, the more I'm sure he's tempted to take her by force," I said. Stephen and I stood side-by-side, both of us wondering just who Ana would choose and how either of us would survive existing in a world without her by our side.

582

I was waiting for Nathanial to return from somewhere; Micah had been vague with his whereabouts, but I was happy to spend some time with Lucie. We read and colored and snuggled together on the couch and I wanted her to know how much she was loved. Micah was very good at explaining what had happened to Liam and Carmen. He'd told her a great Inca story of gods and goddess who fall to earth for a time being. They come to love and to be loved and that Lucie was their great love and that at some point they have return to their own place in the world, but they leave all of their joy, hope and love with her, so that she never has to feel alone because they can always see her and listen to her…I had to leave the room because I started to cry.

I was leaving the bathroom, wiping my eyes when I heard voices coming from the hall, it was Lucie and she was laughing. I walked into the living room and saw Nathanial sitting on the couch and Lucie jumping into Stephen's arms. I exhaled and tried to quell my anger at his complete disregard for his niece, making her wait while he sobered himself up. Nathanial caught my eye and he raised his eyebrows. I stood back, away from the whole scene, feeling separated somehow.

"Ana, look!" Lucie called to me as she jumped down from Stephen and bolted over to me. "Look, it's uncle Stephen; look Ana!" She was so excited and I scooped her up, holding her against me. I felt cold. I walked further into the room and stood beside Micah; he seemed to be the best bet out of the other people currently available.

"Ana." Stephen looked at me. He looked horrible, worse than he did after our attack in the alley. My eyes narrowed as I took in his disheveled appearance. His current state did not speak to someone capable of taking in a little girl.

"No way!" I said, staring at him. "No way am I sending her with you." I stood back against the wall handing Lucie to Micah and watching them as he ushered her out of the room.

"Ana." Nathanial rose from the couch, his voice firm. I glared at him.

"NO! Look at him, he's barely alive and he looks drunk! Are you drunk?" I asked him, taking a step forward. "Oh, no, I'm sorry, or is it that Nathanial just disturbed you while you were feeding on one of your many whores that you entertain. Perhaps you're high from the blood!" My tone was icy. Stephen flinched. "Or, he interrupted one of you gambling sessions; what, did you run out of things to put into the pot Stephen, couldn't find any more jewelry to ante up?" I was surprised at the level of anger that I was experiencing. I knew that I was definitely crushed at what I had found at his house, but I didn't realize that I was so mad. My blood started to boil.

"Ana." Nathanial touched me on the shoulder and I shrugged him off.

"Just leave Stephen. Liam would be appalled at the condition that you've come to get his daughter. I don't want you taking Lucie. I'll figure something else out. Carlo will just have to wait a bit longer," I trailed off, trying to think. Stephen took a step toward me and I could see that his eyes were red and swollen; he looked like he'd been crying for years. I didn't care; he'd said his goodbyes to me and now it was my turn.

584

"Not much longer, Carlo is asking for you Ana." Patric had suddenly appeared in the room, looking like he'd just come from the gym. I sighed. I walked over to stand next to Patric. Ever since I had come to his room that night, since he'd told me how sorry he was and how much I had meant to him, he was the only one that I could currently tolerate. I turned to Stephen.

"You, leave," I said pointing my finger at Stephen. "Sober up and get your shit together. Come back when you can deal with life. You," I pointed to Nathanial, "can you take care of Lucie for just a bit longer, until Stephen gets back?" Nathanial nodded, his lips pressed in a straight line. "Good, then we all have our work to do," I said, taking Patric's hand. "Let's go," I said, meeting his gaze and not looking at Stephen or Nathanial as Patric shimmered us out of the room.

"What was that all about?" Patric asked as he landed us back in the training gym.

"Nothing. Nathanial thinking he was doing the noble thing by bringing Stephen to his house so that we could see each other; of course he brought back a drunk and totally wrecked Stephen. I yelled at him and told him he wasn't in any shape to take Lucie and well, you showed up for the rest," I said, lying back against the mat on the floor.

"I'm sorry I came late." He laughed, rubbing my arm gently. "Although, that was nice of my brother trying to get you back together." He smirked.

"There's nothing nice about it Patric. You pride yourself on being the manipulative one in the family, but Nathanial doesn't play fair; he's waiting for me to choose between the two them and he's hoping that I will be too pissed at Stephen to listen to anything he has to say," I huffed and rolled on my stomach.

"Are you?" Patric asked, coming to lie next to me, his face aligned with mine. He was smiling.

"Yes, but that doesn't mean that I want to be with Nathanial," I said, staring at him, wishing that I had turquoise eyes, they were so much cooler than plain brown. Patric laughed.

"There's not a thing about you Ana, that could ever be described as 'plain'." He reached to smooth my hair off my neck.

"So what does Carlo want? " I asked, feeling more and more depressed.

"Nothing in particular, he's just been inquiring into your whereabouts." Patric propped himself on his arm and stared down at me.

"What did you tell him?" I asked, tucking my arms underneath my sides.

"I told him that you were trying to make arrangements for Lucie and that I would be escorting you out this evening so not to expect you for dinner." Patric grinned at me. I sat up arching my back.

"What?" I wasn't sure if I had heard him correctly.

"I'm taking you out tonight. You've been here for three months and you haven't seen much of the country and it's beautiful; plus I think it would do you good to get dressed up and have a nice night out, don't you?" He cocked his head, searching my face. I cringed; I really wasn't in dress up mode and Patric, like his brother, always looked impeccable. I was starting to think that this wasn't such a good idea.

"And Carlo just agreed to this?" I asked, sitting up.

"He wouldn't dare do anything to test the validity of your threats Ana, he's ambitious, but not stupid." Patric laughed and put his hands up as if in surrender. My eyes narrowed.

"I don't have anything to wear out with you. Maybe we should reschedule when I can go shopping," I said, watching him as he stood up, pulling me with him.

"I've taken care of everything Ana." He smirked at me and shimmered us back to the guesthouse.

****

Patric had provided me with the most exquisite dress that I had ever seen. It was deep teal with a subtle silver shimmer illuminating from the fabric and it was sleeveless and form fitting on top. The neckline was deep, almost to the navel and it was full on the bottom, the skirt portion hitting just above my knee. The slit on the side came up to mid thigh and I was pretty sure that sitting down was going to be a challenge. The dress fit perfectly and I wondered how Patric had gone about getting my measurements; maybe I didn't want to know.

There was also a pair of shimmery gray heels that reminded me of the shoes that professional ballroom dancers wore. They were pretty and comfortable. My amulet was my only jewelry I was opting for these days since I'd taken off my ring from Stephen and I hoped that I looked dressy enough. I tied my hair into a low ponytail twisted at the nape of my neck, less to worry about. There was also a tiny gray clutch just perfect to fit some makeup and my favorite lip balm hanging behind my door. Jesus, he'd thought of everything. I had never pegged Patric to be so posh. I sighed and walked down the stairs to meet him.

He had his back to me and he was leaning on the railing on the outside deck. I slid open the door and almost dropped my bag. I didn't recognize him. I mean, it was him, but his attire and his face were memorizing, different. He was wearing loose deep black pants that fit perfectly on his waist. His shirt was form fitting, black as well, with a very subtle turquoise pattern threaded throughout. The top was long sleeved, but it seemed to hit ever muscle in his arms in just the right places. He had the first several buttons undone and I could clearly see his amulet hanging around his neck. It looked familiar, but I wasn't close enough to make out the symbols. My eyes traveled to his face and I could see a distinct difference in the tone of his skin. He was a deep bronze, darker than he usually was and I wondered if he'd been out in the sun. He still maintained his rugged hair and dark five o'clock shadow, which only seemed to make him more entrancing. His skin glowed, but not with the copper sheen of Nathanial; Patric's skin looked as if someone had crushed pearls over the surface. There were many different tones and shades of luminescence radiating from his body and I blinked to make sure that he wasn't an illusion.

"You look so amazing Patric," I said, walking to meet him. "Really, you're incredible," I said, smiling widely. I was glad to see him happy, particularly after I had witnessed him looking so shattered the night I came to his room.

"Hmmm…that's very generous of you Ana, but I do not think that there is a soul in this world that glows as beautifully as you do tonight and every night for that matter." His tone seemed solemn and I wondered if something was bothering him.

"Thank you for the dress and the shoes and the bag; it's a little much." I laughed.

"Oh, that's right, I had forgotten just how much you hate people spending money on you; I'm guessing you're not going to be too happy with the arrangements I've made this evening." He winked at me and took my hand as Esther snapped off a few photos; I felt like we were going to the prom. Patric stared down into my face, his eyes brilliant and deep as they searched mine. I took a deep breath and let him lead me out into the night.

Patric

I wasn't feeling nearly as guilty as maybe I should for taking Ana out. I was pretty sure that Nathanial wouldn't have looked to favorably upon my actions, but I really just couldn't endure having Ana waiting around to decide when she and Carlo would be following through with their deal. I had seen his mind and he wasn't, in any way, wanting a simple vial of Ana's blood. He wanted *her*. He had his hopes set on extracting Ana's blood in the way that most vampires fed, most male Vampires anyway. He was addicted to the high that came from engaging in both sex and the blood release and since first laying eyes on Ana, having that moment with her, it was all he'd been fantasizing about. He was going to up the ante on their deal and make her a counter offer. She would be allowed to leave if she completed the exchange in the way he wanted, otherwise he wouldn't make any guarantees for the safety of Nathanial or me or Stephen...or Lucie. I didn't much care about my own protection. I had more followers and more respect than Carlo and I was sure that I could have him killed or kill him myself if need be, but Nathanial I wasn't sure about and Stephen seemed too preoccupied to be able to fight off someone as skilled as Carlo. Nathanial had no idea about this new development and I was holding off telling him for fear that he would go ballistic and do something rash. The very thought of Ana having sex with Carlo to protect all of us, I was sure would drive him over the edge; I was going to have to tell her this evening.

I had made reservations at an outdoor bistro in the heart of Buenos Aires; it was of my favorite places to dine in the whole world. The restaurant was family owned, intimate and the atmosphere definitely hinted at more of the romantic and passionate side of the Argentinean culture. The music was rhythmic and sensual, but not intrusive and I thought that Ana would like to sit out on the patio and enjoy watching the people dance and play drums in the streets. She seemed in awe of my ability to provide some semblance of a normal evening out and I found it humorous that she kept saying it was like a real date, something that she and I had never gotten to experience.

"You don't think that I go out on dates?" I asked, as I pulled out her chair. I hadn't failed to observe that every man and vampire in the room turned to stare at her when she'd walked by; she didn't even notice or she did notice and couldn't care less. She shrugged.

"Well I guess you do date right? I mean it would be odd if you just sat around planning out military strategies all day and what new lands to mine and never hooked up with anyone." She grinned. "By the way, how is your mining company, still digging up on protected refuges?" She smirked. The server came with a bottle of wine and poured two glasses. The food was simple and I knew exactly what Ana would like and what she could eat so I ordered for us both. She shook her head; clearly I wasn't appreciative of a woman's ability to order for herself. I smirked and sipped my wine.

"I sold the company," I said, studying her amulet, wondering when she would notice.

"Good," she said. "That was the most horrific thing that I have ever had to do and I was so angry with you; you were such a jerk." I was amused at how much she still seemed to be upset with me. She was right, my behavior in West Papua had been appalling and how I treated her was beyond repose.

"Yes well, that may have been true, but at least you didn't have to watch me fling myself off a cliff and plummet to my death," I replied. Her eyes narrowed and her internal dialogue disturbed me; things *wouldn't* have been less complicated had she actually died, things would have been so much worse. I glared at her.

591

"Whatever." She looked away from my gaze. "So, are you seeing anyone?" She sipped her wine and leaned forward, her plait of hair falling softly over her shoulders and down her chest.

"Why, are you interested in checking out the competition?" I teased, reaching across the table for her hand. I suddenly felt an overwhelming sadness radiate from deep inside her heart and it startled me with its intensity. *I can't hold anyone, I can't hold anyone, I can't hold anyone. I tried and it didn't matter. I tried and everyone disappeared. I tried and everyone chose something or someone different. It doesn't matter; it doesn't matter...* She was repeating those words over and over in her head. She was gazing out into the streets watching a young couple dancing, their two children along side them, laughing and singing. I saw her reach and touch her abdomen, something that I had observed her doing many, many times since coming to the ranch.

"Ana," I said stroking her hand.

"Hmm...? Oh, sorry. I'm sorry Patric, I zoned out for a minute." She turned back to me and smiled. "Competition you asked? Well, I'm guessing your choice for companionship is not quite bottom of the barrel, now seeing just how well you clean up; I should be quite honored that you have decided to 'slum it' with me this evening." She laughed and grabbed my hand. Our meals arrived and we ate and talked about Lucie and how much I sold my company for and whether or not I would have hired her to work at the company had she been in support of mining on sacred indigenous lands. I sighed, not wanting to take the conversation where it needed to go.

"Ana, there's something that I need to discuss with you." I stared at her, feeling sick.

"What?" she asked, pushing her plate aside and watching me.

"It's Carlo. He's wanting to renegotiate your deal," I said, fingering my own amulet, my eyes focusing on her face.

"What does he want now?" She sounded agitated. I exhaled, hoping that she wouldn't make me have to explain in detail what it was he desired.

"You," I said, raising my eyebrows.

"How do you mean?" Christ this was uncomfortable.

"He wants you to be with him, in an intimate way," I said, feeling the oddness of my words. Her eyes flashed.

"You mean he wants me to sleep with him," she stated, sipping her wine. I nodded. "Why?" she asked. I almost laughed. Why? She was asking "why".

"Oh I don't know Ana, it couldn't be that he finds you intriguing, seductive, beautiful, powerful, intelligent or that he's seen you in my mind and knows to a very little extent, just what you are like in bed?" I allowed myself to laugh; she was ridiculous sometimes. She rolled her eyes. "Don't you roll your eyes at me," I scolded her. "You know I'm right." I said, my mind replaying the first night I came to her room, the night she came to my house and the last night we were together—none of those moments were about her, none of them were me making sure that Ana felt special or beautiful or amazing; they had all been about me, about what I wanted from her; in those moments, I was no different from Carlo. I exhaled, at war with myself as usual, at war with what I needed to do and what I truly wanted, at war with my choices and I knew that tonight, I was making the wrong one.

"I'm guessing his conditions are that if I don't sleep with him, all our lives are forfeit. Am I right?" She took another sip of her wine and closed her eyes. I nodded again. "Well, I have to hand it to him, he knows how to play ball." She laughed. I thought she was taking this amazingly well. Her eyes were staring at my chest so intently that I felt my amulet start to warm. "Hey!" she exclaimed, startling me. "Your symbols, they're the same as mine!" Her eyes were wide.

"I know Ana," I murmured, tracing my finger along the outer ring of my necklace.

"But how's that possible? My Noni made this for me. How can you and I have the same amulet?" she asked, her chin was bent and she was looking at her own necklace. "Wait, yours is a bit different; I don't have that diamond thing in the center—what's that from?" she asked, her eyes sparkling. For someone who was so perceptive, she had a tendency to miss anything that had to do with her. I sighed.

"It's part of our Bond Ana; it's one of your jewels from your mark," I said quietly. "As far as our amulets go, I happen to know that Noni was a very gifted Seer, perhaps the symbols came to her in vision and she thought you would benefit from having them. The symbol was one of my mother's, something that she created for me. Nathanial's mark was also given to him by her and of course now we both have an additional representation," I mused. Perhaps Ana's Noni also knew just how connected Ana and I actually were, even more so than either of us realized.

"Does yours move?" she asked, picking up her necklace and letting it fall back against her throat before it solidified into her skin again. I smiled.

"No. It's embedded permanently into my flesh." I sipped my wine.

"Why?" She was still staring at my chest, frowning.

"Because we're Bonded Ana and we have been since that night in your room; it's my own version of your metal tattoo." I leaned forward, and gently touched my fingertips to hers. "It would have to be ripped away from my body now, for it to be removed," I said, finding her eyes. I hoped at some point that by choosing me, Ana's amulet would also become permanently embedded in her flesh; I had a feeling I was going to have to wait for quite some time, if ever. I had put something in motion now that I couldn't stop. Even with my great love for Ana, my ambitions and my greed had surfaced; maybe I didn't want to stop it, maybe I wanted things to play out and for that, maybe I would never deserve Ana or her love. We stared at each other until the waiter came to tell us that there was someone here asking for me. I apologized and excused myself, leaving Ana to ponder her feelings for me. I liked that I was in her mind, even if I had to occupy the space with my brother and Stephen. The waiter motioned outside and I stepped into the street.

Chapter Twenty-three

Ana

It was odd, this sudden realization about Patric and me, how connected we were; I hadn't realized it and my emotions were all over the place. I looked out upon the street and watched as couples danced close and music swirled in the air. I felt as though I was catching a glimpse into another world, one where I didn't belong or couldn't belong, one where people were happy and together, where they felt safe and loved and not alone. Lifetimes moved through my mind and I was eight again, terrified, a victim of the worst kind of torture and of course, I was left alone to endure. I sighed and felt someone touch me on the shoulder. Patric had returned.

"Why don't we go for a walk; it's a nice night." He smiled and held out his arm for me to take. We strolled out into the lively streets, feeling the vibrations of life and music and love, all entwined in the air, all bound in one furious storm of breath and heat; the passion was palpable. Patric was quiet as we walked and I wondered if he could sense my struggle to understand our history and my feelings for him. I sighed and he turned to look down upon my face, his eyes flashing. We turned down a quiet side street and the music and laughter from the city center began to fade. He stopped us in front of what looked like the ruins of ancient house. The stone was slightly crumbled, but as I looked closer I could see that someone had renovated the basic structure to something nothing shy of magnificent. I was reminded of the old temples that monks were usually housed in during the middle ages, dark and ominous, but with a sacred energy that permeated from every crack and each hand placed stone.

"What is this place?" I asked, turning to Patric.

"Do you like it?" He was staring at me, his eyes deep and luminous.

"It's stunning; it looks so ancient," I said and he laughed. He opened the gate and held it open for me to walk through. We stood in a garden, a perfectly landscaped area full of flowers and trees and the fragrance in the air was heady with a rich floral perfume that floated around my body and sank deep into my pores. The scent was so strong that I could no longer smell Patric's familiar perfume. "Is this yours?" I asked, following him up to the front door, watching curiously as he pulled a skeleton key from his pocket and unlocked the entrance. There were candles lit all along the dark foyer and beautiful stone tiles were beneath our feet, each one looking as if someone had hand painted the intricate pentagram patterns. Patric took my hand and led me down the hall into a living room of sorts; a roaring fire was ablaze and there was a plush black leather sofa and matching chairs filling the space without getting lost in the vastness of the room. More candles illuminated the mantel and each windowsill, bathing the room in such a powerful glow that I could almost feel the pulse from each flame deep within my own body. Had he planned all of this? I turned back to see Patric standing near one of the windows watching me, his stance relaxed and casual.

"What do you think?" he asked me, his face reflecting the shadows from the candlelight.

"It's beautiful," I said, trying to see his eyes; they were hidden. "I had no idea that you had such a magnificent home. Do you live here?" I asked. I had always been under the impression that Patric had lived with Carlo in the guest quarters. Patric laughed.

"I don't live with Carlo, Ana." He smirked. "The ranch is mine; I bought it from him," he said and his tone suddenly became dark. "We did a bit of an exchange. He bought out the mining company and I got the ranch." Again, his voice hinted at some sort of bitterness and I wondered if he felt shafted by the deal. Patric was a very keen businessman and perhaps losing such a profitable and influential company was something that made him upset.

"Oh. Why didn't you tell me?" I inquired, wondering what else Patric was keeping me in the dark about and why.

"I'm good at secrets Ana, good at illusions; it's what I do best," he said, his voice deep.

"Not always," I said slightly defiant. "You were always honest with me about most things. I always knew where I stood with you and you never made me any promises about us at all, you never gave me any illusions that we would ever be anything more to each other…" My voice faded. The use of the word "illusion" was striking me as familiar, but I didn't know why. I watched as Patric moved from out of the shadows and crossed the room to the sofa. His posture was fluid and graceful; usually Patric's gate was strong and powerful, his stance always commanding a sense of solidness. My heart kicked up a notch and I frowned—again, there was something familiar tugging at the corners of my mind and for some reason, my instincts told me to put

598

up my wall, to shut Patric out for the time being. I also noticed that now we were indoors, that I still couldn't smell him. I frowned. He was pouring us each a glass of wine and I moved to stand in front of him. He reached to give me my glass and his hand trembled. I checked his eyes, they were vibrant and moving very swiftly back and forth over my face. "Thank you, I said, still watching him. He smiled at me and cocked his head to the side. Suddenly, a wash of memory flooded through me and I heard Liam's voice the last night that I ever saw him. *Nothing is as it seems here Ana...you have always been able not to be fooled by the illusions of others...nothing is as it seems here.* My heart stopped and I found myself trying very hard not to take a step back from Patric. I didn't want him to think that something was wrong because I wasn't actually sure that anything *was* wrong. Patric sat down on the sofa his arms spread wide across the spine; he was watching me.

"Ana?" he said, motioning for me to join him. I shook my head, betrayal sinking so deep into my soul, I was sure I was going to cry out.

"You," I said, taking a step back. "It's always been you." I was breathing hard. "It wasn't Carlo who wanted me to come; it was you. You called Stephen and Liam for the meeting, you brought me here." I was stunned. "You're working so hard to get my powers back because you want to use them, not Carlo..." Wait, that wasn't right, that couldn't be right; I was missing something. If it had in fact been Patric who was wanting me here, then why would he have helped me to save Nathanial and Lucie; why would he have a desire to have my blood, he already had it...no, something was off. *Nothing is as it seems here.* Liam's voice again reverberated in my head. I remained standing, trying frantically to sort through everything that I had ever heard Liam say, everything that I knew about Vampires, everything that I had experienced with Devon, Andres, Stephen, Patric…Alec…Alec; why was he an issue?

"Ana, is something wrong? Are you unwell?" Patric asked me, his eyes moving over my body. Patric stood from the sofa and moved, placing himself directly in front of me, blocking my view of the window. His response to my outburst seemed wrong; he should be upset or at least asking me what the hell I was talking about.

"I'm just a bit tired," I said, forcing my voice to hold steady. "The thing with Stephen today has been a bit overwhelming for me." I tried to smile, my heart beginning to pound.

"Hmmm…well perhaps you just need to let that go for tonight; let Stephen go for the time being." Patric reached to stroke my face, his fingers moving slowly down my cheek to my throat. He was so close and again, I realized that I still couldn't smell him; his fragrance was absent. It was never absent and especially when we were close. Alec, illusions, nothing being what it seemed…I took a step back, the pieces falling into place.

"You," I said, pushing Patric's hand away, except it wasn't Patric who was touching me now; it was Carlo. He laughed and I saw his eyes change from deep turquoise to Carlo's odd light brown shade and before I could take my next breath, Patric had disappeared and Carlo was now standing before me, looking smug and quite pleased with himself.

I had managed to finally free myself from Carlo's paralysis, but I had lost time and I couldn't get a read on where he'd taken her. I needed help; I didn't want to do this anymore. I shouldn't have ever used her; she would never forgive me if she ever found out. I would lose her forever. I shimmered, crashing into the living room where Micah, Nathanial and Stephen were sitting. I didn't have time to explain and I couldn't let them see what I had planned, what it was that I had wanted to do; they could never know. "He has Ana. She doesn't know it's him, he has her and she doesn't know!" I shouted. Nathanial rose from his seat, his eyes locking with mine.

"Where are they?" he asked, as he crossed the room to where I stood.

"I can't get a read on him, he's done something to lock us out; I have no idea where he took her." I was furious at my stupidity, at my complete arrogance that I would always be able to outsmart Carlo. My memories surged from the moment that I stepped into the street and knew I'd been deceived, knew I'd been too arrogant this time...

As my foot had hit the ground, I'd felt a sharp pain hit me in the back and I'd gasped; I couldn't move, couldn't yell. Something or someone had immobilized me with such force that it was impossible for me to break the hold. I was slammed up against the wall of the side alley and my breath returned, just in time to see Carlo emerge from the street. He was smirking.

"I really have a problem with patience," he'd said, pacing back and forth in front of me while I tried to release myself from his invisible grasp. "I think that Ana and I are in need of a little time together. You've been quite selfish with her, trying to keep her away from me and I'm not terribly happy about that," he'd said, standing in front of me, his arms folded across his chest. "You needn't worry about her safety Patric; I have no desire to kill her. I made a deal with Ana and after her display of power the other night, I'm not inclined to go back on my word." He'd moved closer to me and I'd watched as he reached to finger my necklace. "I merely want to experience what you were so fortunate to share with her. She's a very passionate being and I can only imagine what it must be like to engage in...well, I should be a gentleman here shouldn't I? I think you know to what it is I'm referring." He'd smiled and I felt my chest and throat surge with heat from his touch. "I'm thinking of course that Ana is quite selective in her mates and I am hoping that a little incentive will make her less choosy." He was going to threaten to kill all of us if she didn't comply

"She'll kill you," I'd gasped, still trying to release myself from against the wall.

"Perhaps, but I think that I may just be able to give her the attention she deserves and the pleasure she should experience, to make her reconsider." He'd laughed as I tried to lunge for his throat. "Of course, I cannot make any guarantees that I will be able to keep my venom from penetrating her system; I have a feeling that self-control with Ana might be a bit of a challenge for me." He'd snickered as I snarled loudly. "Now, what do you say that you stop moving so I can get on with my evening?" He'd waved his hand and I became *completely paralyzed, stunned into watching him take on a perfect version of me, before my very eyes....*

" Patric?" Stephen's voice broke me from the memory. "He has a home in Buenos Aires; that's where you were tonight?" Stephen turned to me, his face smooth, but his eyes were pitch black; he'd been keeping tabs on Ana and this was one time when I was grateful, not jealous.

"Yes, but there's something else, something that you need to know." Christ, did I have time to explain, to tell them what he wanted from her, what he was going to threaten to take away. "He'll kill us if she doesn't agree to sleep with him and give him her blood. He wants the opportunity to Change her during the act and he knows that he has a better chance of her not fighting back if...if she's distracted." I wanted to throw up, even saying the words were making my stomach heave. "He wants to Change her." I gasped and that wasn't even the half of it, that was just Carlo's part in all of this; I had played my part as well. Nathanial turned to Stephen.

"Doesn't she need to take his blood in order for the transaction to work?" he said, his tone even. Stephen nodded.

"Yes, but you can do that without your victim actually participating, it's not done that much anymore because it takes up so much of our energy..." He trailed off, looking as angry as I was feeling.

"What do you mean Stephen?" Nathanial was standing directly in front of him, they towered against each other, both looking like giant pillars, both looking ready to crumble.

"Carlo can inject his blood directly into Ana's veins once he's bitten her. He can excrete along with his venom, a significant amount, copious amounts of his own blood, and inject it into her open wound. It takes skill and energy like I said, but it can be done; it has been done," he said rubbing his face.

"Jesus, fucking, Christ!" I yelled. She won't come back from that; WE'LL LOSE HER!" I shouted, wondering what we all were still doing standing here.

"Calm down Patric." My brother moved to stand next to me. "Do you think that Ana is likely to give Carlo what he wants, that she won't fight to kill him first before he can get to her?" Nathanial was contemplative. I shook my head.

"You don't understand; she thinks Carlo is me! She won't figure it out in time and he'll be able to get close to her, close enough to catch her off guard, to dominate her; she won't be able to fight. He knows her powers are intermittent at best these days. She's weak and grieving and he knows this, it's what he's been counting on," I said, the gravity of the situation crashed down over my soul. I looked at my brother and Stephen and for a brief moment, I wanted to kill them both and myself. I wanted them to die for what they each had made Ana experience and I wanted to go right along with them. I was angry. Stephen and Nathanial both caught my eye; they knew I was right, they just didn't know to what extent.

I exhaled, knowing that my plan was to be executed a bit sooner than I had wanted. I wasn't expecting Carlo to shape shift, that, I had not made allowances for. "What do you want Carlo?" I asked, keeping my tone even and my stance relaxed.

"I think you know Ana," he said, taking me around the waist. "I think Patric was explaining exactly what it is that I want, before he became indisposed." Carlo grinned at me and ran the back of his hand over my arm.

"Did you kill him?" I asked, wondering if he would tell me the truth.

"No. I promised you that no harm would come to him or any of the other beings you care about, but I've decided that my part of the deal seemed to be a bit lacking." His eyes swept over my neck and chest and suddenly, Carlo reminded me of Devon, a much stronger and more powerful Devon. I pulled away from him.

"Have I given you the impression that I'm some sort of whore Carlo, that I will sleep with anyone who offers?" I said, glaring at him, but keeping my tone calm.

"Of course not Ana, I would never dream of placing such a derogatory association with someone like yourself." He moved closer to me, blurring to my side so quickly that my eyes barely registered the movement.

"Then what in the world makes you think that I would ever have sex with you Carlo?" I said, my hands on my hips, my stance firm. He smirked and reached to trace his finger down between my breasts; my skin surged with heat.

"Because if you don't, I have five of my closest and most loyal followers standing by to kill each and everyone that you love; including that little girl. They're waiting for my signal," he said, pulling me close to his chest, his mouth barely touching mine. "It only takes a second, less than an heartbeat for me to give the order so any interest that you may have to fight me, would be in vain. You may kill me, but everyone else will also be dead." He moved his mouth, kissing my top lip slowly. I shuddered, trying not to vomit. At his touch, my mind went foggy and I felt my wall beginning to slip; he was doing something to me. He was trying to mentally drug me. I fought back, pushing him out of my memories, my thoughts, but he grasped me harder.

"I don't think you want to do that Ana; a mental tug of war with me just won't do." A surge of heat blasted into my brain and I could feel every defense, every capability to protect myself, shatter. "That's better," he purred, tracing his tongue along my mouth. "I'm not normally one to kiss, but my god, your taste is intoxicating." He bit down on my lower lip and I felt him pull and run his tongue back and forth. It was a dizzying movement and my body began to break down against his mental coercion. He had filtered his way in, dominating my own will for what I wanted or didn't want in this case. He laughed upon hearing my thoughts.

"I think you actually like being dominated Ana; I think it's arousing for you. In fact, I know it's arousing for you," he murmured as he took my arms and locked them behind my back, holding me against him. He pressed his mouth deeply against my neck and an involuntary moan escaped from my throat. "Hmmm, I think I actually enjoy hearing you moan Ana; it's a beautiful sound." He swept his tongue over all my bite marks and my body heaved with desire I didn't want. I gasped. I felt him reach up under my dress and slide down my underwear, tearing it off before it hit the ground. His fingers found Patric's other wounds and Stephen's as well and he pulled back. "What's this? You let one of us get your blood from such an intimate place? My goodness, you are quite the lover aren't you. You are completely unselfish in your own desires. Perhaps we should make sure that you are satisfied as well this evening, no?" Carlo began to slide his fingers between my thighs and I groaned as he massaged me, making my legs weak. "Does that feel good Ana? I want you to feel good," he purred as he kissed me deeply, still holding my hands behind my back. I felt outside of myself, as if I was drifting above this scene. I had always heard that rape victims sometimes felt that way, that their minds were protecting them from what was happening. I hadn't been so lucky during my own abuse from my brother—I experienced the entire event, wholly present. Carlo pulled back starting at me his fingers pushing themselves forcefully inside of me. "I hardly think that what we are doing here constitutes a parallel with rape or abuse Ana; I'm merely helping you to express what it is you want, what you desire. You still have your free will," he said, pressing deeper; I moaned again feeling desire and pleasure begin to rise in my body. That was a lie, he'd hijacked my free will; I had no means of defense against him. He growled and withdrew his hand raising me up in the air and sending me crashing to the floor on my back. He was on top of me, pining my hands over my head. Even if I could muster the force to fight him it didn't matter, he would just kill Lucie anyway, I was trapped and he knew it. "That's right Ana; I will kill her so you should just let yourself go, let me have you." His hips ground against mine, and the rhythm was so intense, so perfect with what my own body responded to, that I felt almost relieved that perhaps this wouldn't be a violent exchange. "It doesn't have to be Ana; I can be gentle with you, if that's what you truly want. I'm partial to the rougher acts of sex myself and I think you are as well, but perhaps you are needing something a bit gentler this evening, yes?" he spoke and his voice turned low and dark and his hand moved up the slit on my dress, tearing it away with one finger.

"Carlo, stop. Stop for a minute." I breathed and broke one of my arms free and pushed his hand away from my thigh. He pulled back staring at me, his eyes fierce in their desire.

"What is it Ana?" He sounded frustrated and I could tell that he was struggling to keep up his calm façade. I felt a brick return to my wall, and another and another. I continued to speak.

"If we do this; if you and I are together, how will I know that Lucie and Stephen and the rest will be safe? How do I know that once you've had me, once you have my blood and my body, that you won't order all of them to be killed? What guarantees do I have that you will keep your side of the deal?" He couldn't make any guarantees; I knew it and he knew it. I was stalling, stalling for one more brick, for one more hope that maybe I could hold him off taking my blood like this. Carlo smiled and bent his head close to my face, his lips skimming my cheek.

"Because Ana, I'm not too keen on fighting you and I believe that you made yourself perfectly clear that you will kill me if I touched your pathetic group of friends. I have no desire or patience to spend my energy on them once I've gotten what I want from you, but I suppose it ultimately comes down to trust, does it not?" He kissed me hard. Another brick. I let him kiss me again as I tested my physical strength; my limbs no longer felt weak and I sensed the fog in my mind start to clear. He used his knee to spread my leg out to the side and I could feel him begin to move on top of me. My body was tense, no longer under his mental control for its physical desire; I came back to myself. I didn't want to fight him. In fact, my whole plan depended on me *not* fighting Carlo. I actually needed him to take my blood—it was crucial. If the doctor was correct, if what Dr. Connelly had told me the night I had my surgery was in fact the truth, then I would need to get Carlo to take as much blood from me as possible. I wished he'd just let me give him a damn vile and be done with this already; I was getting annoyed at how difficult things were becoming.

Carlo growled at my lack of response. I was going to have to fake it. I forced myself to kiss him, as rough and deep as I could tolerate and hoped that's what he liked.

"Much better Ana," he murmured, as I let him move his lips down across my throat. He stopped just where my pulse was the strongest and he bit lightly down, his teeth grazing my flesh. His body quivered and he pressed his hips down, moving them in rhythm with his mouth on my neck. He shoved up my dress and pressed my legs apart. I was hoping to get him to take the blood before any sex actually occurred and the only way I could think of to get him off top of me was to guide him down. I cringed, but thought of Lucie; if I could save her, then none of this would matter in the end. I could make it a memory, part of the collective nightmare that had been my life for so many years. I wove my fingers into his long hair and slowly pushed his head down from my throat, guiding him. He ran his tongue down my body and I could feel that his bloodlust just might be out competing his sexual desire. I ran my fingers over the bite marks in my groin and then traced my hand over his lips, hoping that he would understand what I wanted. He grasped me hard around the waist forcing my back to arch and my hips to rise off the ground. He was moaning and breathing hard. His lips found my groin and I braced myself against what I was sure to be a less than delicate extraction; there was no love between us, no intimacy, no knowledge of each other's journey's. He had no reason to be gentle or kind and neither did I. He snarled once and plunged his teeth deep into my flesh.

Nathanial

We landed on a somewhat deserted street after getting Stephen a map so he could get us as close to a location on Carlo's house as possible. I scanned the road. The only thing that remotely resembled a house was looming just a few paces behind us, it looked like an old abbey or monastery.

"That's it!" Stephen yelled as he blurred over to the house.

"Are you sure?" Patric was next to him looking frantic and doubtful.

"Yes." Stephen was already leaping over the gate. "There are candles in the window," he called quietly as my brother and I stood together watching as Stephen surveyed the house. "And I can smell her," he said, looking around the garden. My heart sank; she was here and so much time had passed, we were sure to be too late. Suddenly, a large crash came from the house and we all moved back several feet, startled. I heard glass shatter and I looked up to see Carlo come smashing out from the window, his face bloodied and most of his flesh dripping in chunks off of his body. He stumbled toward us and I quickly realized that he was melting, from the inside. Bile filled my mouth at the putrid odor coming off his skin and I saw Patric and Stephen begin to gag. Carlo continued to fall forward, snarling and gasping as black blood splattered out from his eyes and mouth. I turned my face as a spray from his nose hit my shirt and neck, instantly scalding my skin. What the fuck was going on? I saw him stretch out his arm, reaching for Stephen and in one quick movement, Stephen lunged at him grasping Carlo's chest and ripping his heart clean out from his body, sending an eruption of black blood, flesh and bone shattering in the air. Stephen stood holding Carlo's heart in his hand, the arteries and veins still attached and Carlo still standing, still moving forward. In all my centuries on this earth, I had never once witnessed one Vampire kill another, and I hoped that I would go many more before I ever had to witness something so disgustingly violent and brutal. I did not know Stephen in that moment; he was a Vampire and any shred of humanity that he had managed to cling to during his existence was gone in the instant he pulled the still beating heart from Carlo's chest. I was stunned. Stephen tossed the heart to my brother and my eyes widened. How did Patric know what to do; this seemed beyond him, even for all of his time with Vampires. I couldn't imagine that my twin would understand this kind of sheer, primal brutality. I watched as Stephen ripped Carlo's head from his body and tossed it in the air while at the same time my brother took Carlo's heart and plunged his teeth, fangs at this point, right into the center. At that exact moment Carlo's body exploded and so did his heart, spraying all of us in a thick coating of blood and flesh and death. I was beside myself, but before I could even wrap my head around what I had just witnessed, Stephen was flying through the air kicking in the door. Patric and I blurred to his side, none of us prepared for what we were to find.

Stephen

Blood was everywhere. It dripped in thick clots on the floor both red and black in color and instantly, I could smell that some of it was Ana's. I flew into the living room, following the dark liquid lines on the stone floor. A large leather sofa was facing the fireplace and I leapt over its frame landing in a large pool of black blood. Ana was lying face down, her hair spilling over her head and her blood seeping and oozing out from her body. She was shivering and trembling, convulsing violently. I knelt down beside her. Nathanial and Patric came to stand near me, their faces dark in their despair. We were too late. Patric and Nathanial didn't move, they didn't breathe and I was sure that every heart in the room had stopped beating.

"Stephen." Nathanial looked at me, his face anxious and I could see that he was worried about what having so much of Ana's blood around me, would do.

"I'm fine Nathanial," I spoke as I gently turned Ana over, her body twitching and rocking on the floor. It was hard to see just where the initial bite marks were; her neck was covered in blood. I tried to wipe as much of the skin off as a possible, but still, I couldn't see any wounds. "I can't find the marks!" I spat. We were losing time; if she had been bitten, if there had been blood exchanged, the transition was already underway.

"Her legs! Stephen, they're bleeding!" Patric was at Ana's side, pushing up her dress. I saw him close his eyes and run his hands over his mouth, streaking his skin with her blood. My eyes shifted and I could see, just below Patric's original marks and my own, a fresh new set of punctures adorned her body. He'd bitten her.

"Did he bite her?" Nathanial was standing back, his body gripped with fear. I met his gaze and nodded my head. "Venom?" he was asking the worst of the questions; had Carlo managed to inject his venom before his own death, which we all were still wondering how that happened.

"I don't know. I'd have to...I'd have to..." I didn't want to say what it was that I would have to do in order to tell if there was venom or any of Carlo's blood in Ana's system.

"Do it." Patric's eyes were fierce as he studied my thoughts and I turned to look at Nathanial. I wasn't sure why, but I felt as though I needed to ask his permission. He nodded. I exhaled and bent my face close to Ana's groin; so many memories came flooding back to me at

613

once; not memories of sex or lust or passion, but memories of her smiling, pulling her hat down over her ears, of her curled up on my couch sipping tea, of us walking hand in hand on the wet streets of Dublin. I shuddered as I let my lips gently caress her skin. The wound was icy and an acute bitterness filled my mouth, numbing my tongue. Christ, he'd done it; he'd injected his venom. Desperation racked my heart and I doubled over gasping for air that wouldn't come.

Nathanial

"Stephen, what can we do? Does she have any of his blood in her system? Can you tell?" my voice was flat as I watched Stephen and my brother hovering over Ana; I couldn't look at her.

"I'm not sure," Stephen replied looking to Patric. "Can you tell?" he asked, his voice full of frustration. I watched as my brother bent close to Ana's leg and I had to close my eyes.

"There's nothing; I can't tell if there's any other blood in her system." Patric rose wiping his lips off franticly. Stephen bowed his head and I knew things were at their worst. Carlo had left Ana to die, to be poisoned to death, slowly.

"Stephen." Patric was staring hard at Stephen, his eyes pleading, begging.

"NO! I can't, I won't Patric, not like this!" Stephen gasped; I didn't understand.

"What!" I found my voice. "What!" I said looking to my brother. Patric ran his fingers through his hair. Ana gasped and choked.

"Stephen can complete the Change," Patric said, his eyes not moving from Stephen's face. "He can save her, not from this life; that's over, but he can Change her. I can't do it...I'm not able, it has to be a full vampire..." Patric's voice was solemn. I took a step back, not wanting to believe that it had come to this, that Ana's life was over, that she would be forever changed, altered into some sort of being that I wouldn't know, wouldn't understand; she was dead.

Patric

I didn't' understand what we were waiting for. Ana as a Vampire was going to be better than a dead Ana. I wouldn't have it; it wasn't going to happen. "Stephen, do it!" I shouted at him, trying to break through his grief and guilt over what he would be responsible for—he was falling apart. "Nathanial?" I looked to my brother; he was standing so far away, his eyes closed. Christ, what was the matter with the two of them? The very woman they claimed to love so much was dying if not already dead and she could be saved! We could give her a second chance; she'd be different, but she'd still be Ana, still be the extraordinary soul that we loved and that we betrayed. I saw my brother's body tremble and he opened his eyes. They glowed so brightly that for a minute I was stunned; I couldn't see his face through their glare.

"Do it Stephen," his voice rang through the violent scene, clear and strong. Stephen looked back to me, shaking his head. Nathanial came to stand next to him, putting his hand on his shoulder and a wash of heat entered through the space between all of us. "Do it," he said calmly, bending to whisper in Stephen's ear. Ana's legs stopped twitching and panic overwhelmed me.

"STEPHEN!" I shouted at him; we didn't have time now. We didn't have time for guilt or anger or panic; he needed to save her. He owed her that much. Stephen turned his face to mine, his eyes bright and brimming with tears. He took her wrist in his hand, inhaled and bit down hard, piercing through Nathanial's scar, sending a cascade of fresh blood flooding out from her veins. She heaved and gasped and I tried to hold her down, but she was thrashing and sputtering blood all over my face. "Nathanial!" I shouted and Nathanial was at my side, helping me, holding Ana in his arms as Stephen began to inject his venom and blood. There we all were, lying in pools of blood, each holding the woman we loved and who had loved each of us, who had redeemed us, who had given us life and warmth and strength and courage. We were there, bent over her body as she hung in the worst of all balances, still not knowing all of her secrets, still not knowing why she constantly sacrificed herself for the three of us; men, beings who were constantly selfish, confused, ruled by instincts and not by their hearts. Each of us had taken from her and each of us had left her, abandoned her because we were all cowards in our own way; cowards of greed, of lust, of our past sins in our past lives. All of us now were here, a collision of all of Ana's choices and all of her love, her loyalty, her grief, her patience, her life and now her death. I heard Stephen choke and I pulled myself from my revelry. Her wrist lie in his lap, his lips coated with her blood and his own, mingled together in their now permanent, forged connection.

Nathanial

I pulled Ana away from Stephen and Patric and held her in my arms, close to my chest. She was so cold and her body was trembling. I pressed my face to hers and kissed her cheeks, her eyes, her lips. I saw nothing, no one and for the second time in all my knowing Ana, I held her broken body. This time there was no beach, no sand, no water, no falling from a cliff, no Alec. There was just her and me, lost to each other, found, fallen, lost again and now here she was, back in my arms where she always belonged. I rocked her back and forth, my chest heaving against hers. I touched her face, smoothed her hair and I watched as she took a breath, shuddered, gasped and fell silent.

Chapter Twenty-four

Nathanial

After shimmering Ana back to Micah's, Patric couldn't stay. The death of Carlo was sure to quickly filter its way down through the various covens in Argentina and Patric couldn't allow for any power vacuums to be created. He would need to re-establish that he was still in charge. Stephen was too beyond himself in his grief over what he had to do to Ana, that I told him to go back to Dublin, that I would take care of Lucie and I would find him as soon as Ana came to, if she came to. He was sick and very weak from the injection of his venom and his blood; he was sick in his soul, we all were.

I had no idea what to expect from a Change. Stephen had told me upon leaving, that Ana wouldn't be breathing, she wouldn't be moving and she would be very, very cold and that she might bleed out, her old blood being replaced by her new blood. That if the transition took, it could take days or even a week for her to regain consciousness and if she remained unresponsive, there really wasn't any way to tell if she would be experiencing pain or suffering while her human body died. I felt helpless. I kept her in my bed, lying beside her still body, watching. I had changed her clothes, and tucked my mother's quilt up around her shoulders. She didn't *feel* cold. Micah would come in at consistent intervals, bend over Ana, stand back, bend over her again, touch her face and then leave the room. I had no idea what was going on in his head; he was keeping me out and I was nervous. Micah entered the room for the third time in less then an hour and stood by Ana. I could hear Lucie playing in her room. She'd been so worried and had sat with me on the bed earlier in the day, stroking Ana's hair and nuzzling herself next to her body. My heart broke.

"What is it Micah?" I asked, getting frustrated with my uncle now. He didn't look at me, but spoke softly.

"What happened to Carlo, Nathanial?" he asked, studying Ana's face.

"He died," I said, frowning. That was true, but the nature of his death was still a mystery. Micah shook his head.

"No, I mean what did it look like?" Micah asked, his fingers moving gently over Ana's arm. That was an odd question. I sighed, exasperated.

"I don't know Micah, he looked like he was melting from the inside," I said, the image of my brother tearing Carlo's heart apart with his teeth appeared fresh in my mind. Micah shook his head and then he bent very close to Ana, sniffing her. "What the hell are you doing?" I said sharply, my tone almost a snarl.

"Curious," Micah whispered, sniffing all along Ana's body and around her neck. "Curious," he said again. I rose off the bed and pulled him away from her.

"Micah!" I growled this time, full and rough. I wasn't inclined to let anyone, anyone, get that close to Ana and not tell me what they were thinking, not let me into their mind. Micah sighed and put his hand on my shoulder and I instantly returned to myself. "I'm sorry Micah, forgive me," I said, looking at Ana's face.

"My son, no forgiveness is needed," Micah said, ushering us out of the room. I stopped to peek in on Lucie and found her playing with her paints and crayons; she seemed content. She smiled up at me and waved a piece of paper in the air. I came into the room and crouched down beside her.

"What's this?" I asked, taking the paper from her. She giggled and crawled next to me.

"That's me and Ana; we're on a boat," she said, pointing to her sketch. The detail was startling as were her use of form and shape. Apparently half-Vampire children were amazingly gifted and Lucie was half of a Vampire. She was bitten and left to die, but Carmen and Liam had decided to not Change her completely; together they had given her only a bit of blood and no venom in order to save Lucie's life and to keep her partially human. Couldn't Stephen have done the same thing? Couldn't he have given Ana some of his blood to save her life, not injecting his venom and keeping her part human?

"No," Micah's voice spoke from behind me.

"Why not?" I asked, not able to hide my hopefulness. Micah sighed and motioned for me to leave Lucie. I followed him into the living room. "Why?" I asked again.

"Because the situations between the state Lucie was found and the state of your Ana are completely different," Micah replied, his eyes roaming over my face. "Lucie was found having been bitten, not in the process of being Changed; no venom was injected into her system, she was bleeding to death. There was already venom in Ana's system; it had already begun to kill her human self. You didn't have the same choices as Liam. Liam's options were to Change Lucie completely or to give Lucie some of his and Carmen's blood and venom, saving Lucie's life, but also making her similar to them—it's not unlike the Bonding exchange that we perform for Humans, the exchange that Ana asked you for. It makes Lucie have the ability to grow up, but she is free from the diseases and sickness that plague so many Humans; her aging process will be slow and she will have a very long life and of course she has some special abilities." Micah laughed. "The difference is, that by taking blood from two whole Vampires, her parents, she becomes essentially a Vampire; where in our Ritual, the Human does not become a Bonder, instead they become a better or worse version of themselves, but they are still very much Human." I frowned; I hadn't understood the concept in quite the same way.

"And what of the matter with immortality? We can offer that, the same as the Vampires can we not?" I asked, thinking of the argument Ana and I had had the night she left me and went to find Stephen. Micah cocked his head to the side, surveying me.

"To a degree, yes we can. But as you so recently experienced, our species cannot avoid the death of the heart or of the soul. Vampires cannot be affected by such emotional upheavals and therefore the immortality that they grant is to a different degree and more permanent than ours, Nathanial." I thought of Stephen; he looked like he could be affected by emotional upheavals. Micah's eyes grew deep. None of this really mattered; if Ana survived, she would be a Vampire, her full immortality in tact. Micah looked at me again, his eyes stormy; he was thinking. "Nathanial, I don't mean to get too personal, but if you don't mind me asking my son, you've taken some of Ana's blood have you not?" I was stunned. That was beyond private. Besides my episode at the University, everything that Ana and I had shared, blood-wise, came out of some extremely intimate and passionate moments. Micah laughed quietly and shook his head. "I don't need details Nathanial, and if your brother was here, I would ask the same question," he said, coming to stand next to me, his hands on my shoulders.

"Yes," I said, my mind not allowing for me to remember those times with her or what I saw transpire between her and Patric after I left. Micah nodded.

"And what did it taste like?" he asked, now pacing the floor, his hands on his hips.

"Excuse me?" I said; his question unnerved me.

"What did it taste like Nathanial; what could you taste in the blood?" he asked, turning to me. This was sacrilege, to be discussing how the woman I loved, *tasted*. My uncle had now managed to make me more uncomfortable than I had ever been. "Objectively, I mean Nathanial; objectively what did the blood taste like to you?" Objectively? "Forget the emotions Nathanial, be objective."

"It tasted different," a quiet voice spoke from behind and I turned to see Patric standing in the hall.

"Different how?" Micah asked, his voice urgent. Patric came to stand beside me; he looked horrible; exhausted, depleted, grief-stricken and something else, something stronger than all of those emotions...it was guilt... but why?

"I tasted different blood in her system, not just Nathanial's or mine but several others as well." Patric bowed his head. He was feeling uncomfortable having to recount his intimate moments with Ana with me in the room. It was a huge shift from the last time; he had wanted me to see what they had done, what she'd been like with him, he was arrogant in his acquisition of her and in his greed to get back at me, to make me hurt. I stared at him, truly not caring anymore.

"Curious," Micah said again. "Could you tell how many different types Patric?" Micah asked, watching us stare at each other. Patric tore his eyes away from me and exhaled.

"I wasn't exactly paying attention, Micah." Patric seemed embarrassed and frustrated as well and he was frowning. "Jesus Christ!" he said, his eyes flashing. "Jesus Christ!" he said again, freezing Micah in his tracks. Patric was shut down so I had no idea what he was thinking. "Ana told me on her first night with me at the ranch, that she'd learned something about herself, that she'd had ten different blood types in her system, two of them from me and Nathanial and the others were all Human, but that she had them all—a genetic anomalie, she was thinking." Patric's voice was frantic and I was missing why he was so urgent. "The doctor must have told her, he must have told her before she had her surgery." Patric was pacing around the room. "Do either of you know who the doctor was that treated Ana?" he asked, moving down the hall to where Ana was lying. Micah and I followed. "Her purse…" he said, shimmering away, leaving us bewildered and not giving us a chance to answer. He returned almost immediately, holding Ana's familiar messenger bag that she used as her purse. He emptied the contents, spilling lip balm, notes, pens, make-up…all things Ana, out onto the bed. He dug through various compartments, finding a small CD, several photographs and a single appointment card. He flipped it over, pulled out his phone and dialed the number. I held my breath.

"Dr. Connelly, this is Patric Arias; I am a friend of Ana's. Something has happened to her and we need your help; we need some information," my brother spoke, his voice commanding and calm. "Can you tell me what the issue is concerning Ana's blood types?" he asked, his eyes finding Ana's face. We waited. "And she knew this, you told her before she had her surgery?" Patric took Ana's hand in his; he looked strong by her side, stronger in himself. "And what would happen if that should occur?" I wondered what the doctor was telling Patric to make him ask that question. He ran his fingers through his hair and rubbed his face. "I see. Would that cause some effects in her should she have been bitten?" Patric was now staring at Ana so intently that he was making me frightened; the fierceness in his eyes was acute and penetrating. "And why wouldn't it have affected me or my brother in the same way?" Patric asked turning his gaze to me, another pause. "And Stephen? Genetically compatible…as a mate, yes, I see." Patric was now peering over Ana; I was having trouble following the conversation. "And you think that might be a possibility because of her blood make up?" Patric stood and paced the room. Micah and I exchanged glances, both of us wondering what the information the doctor was passing along. I wished my brother would let his wall down, let me in; I was going insane. "No, he's not currently here." Patric looked at me and mouthed the question "Stephen?" I shook my head. "Is he aware of any of this information?" Patric asked, now standing by Ana's side, stroking her hair absently. It was odd to watch my brother being so tender with someone; he was never

624

partial to affection, not even from our mother except in very rare moments when she'd asked him to brush her hair. To witness him as he caressed Ana's face, seeing the gentleness behind the gesture, it left me slightly awestruck. "Well thank you, that's very kind and you've been most helpful to us Dr. Connelly." Another pause as the doctor spoke. Patric was now sitting on the bed, listening intently. "Yes, I know. Yes, Ana is very exceptional and I assure you, she is very much loved…I know he was. No she's never wanted to discuss that with me or my brother I don't think…Yes, I was aware that had happened, I just didn't know that you had spoken to her after… I see. Well, I am sure she was quite upset." Patric rubbed his eyes and I saw a shadow pass over his face. "Thank you. Of course, I will call you as soon as we know anything and thank you again for all of you help and for taking such good care of Ana." Patric ended the call and sat starring at the phone. A faint smile crossed his lips and I saw him turn to look at her.

"What is it Patric?" I said, moving to stand in front of him. "What's going on?" My tone was dark and I was tired of not knowing his mind.

"She knew the whole time," he whispered. "She had a plan the entire time, just like when we were on the island with Devon; she'd had plan. Jesus, fucking Christ!" he said, standing to look at her. He then looked to me. "Ana's blood is not conducive for any vampire to take because of her different blood types, anyone who draws blood from her will die." I started to object, but he continued holding up his hand. "You were her original Bond Nathanial, so you were never at any risk; nor are any other Bonders for that matter, including myself. I am a Bonder by blood first so I too was protected. Stephen is a bit of a mystery, his blood wasn't showing up in her composition, but it was in

625

the fetus. The doctor thinks Stephen was protected because Ana chose him as a mate, possibly even before she knew it herself and her body wasn't going to kill off the potential father to her child. Unfortunately, it is also her blood types that prevented her from carrying the child to term." Patric stared at Ana, his eyes full of wonder and sadness. "The doctor told Ana of this before taking her into surgery. Apparently, Stephen doesn't have the best timing for things and had managed to break things off with Ana just prior to her having to terminate the pregnancy. She was beside herself, hysterical and Dr. Connelly was trying to calm her down; he wanted her to know what he'd figured out, he wanted Ana to know just how special she was and that it wasn't her fault. There was nothing horrible about her that prevented her from becoming a mother and that the very blood that may not be able to nourish new life, is the very same blood that had the potential to bring back those lives already on the brink." Patric looked at me and I could see he was remembering how close I was to losing my own existence and how Ana's blood and her soul, had saved me. "He also told her that because of her unique make up, that he suspected that she may have some added protections from outside assaults, like venom." Patric stood near Ana, his eyes roaming over her body and her face. "He told her what he'd suspected about her blood having the potential to kill anyone who was not bound to her, either in ritual or by her own choice and she was counting on him being right, she wanted Carlo to take her blood all along." Patric exhaled and collapsed on the bed, rubbing Ana's leg.

"Patric, does this mean that the Change that Stephen initiated, that it may not have taken?" said Micah who hadn't said a word until now; he'd been absorbing and processing… understanding.

"I don't know Micah. It's hard to tell right now, but that's what I think the doctor was saying…we won't know until she wakes up…if she wakes up." Patric bent his head to hers and kissed her forehead. "I have to go back; things are somewhat of a mess right now and I need to make sure that the covens are doing what I ask of them, that they are honoring the treaty that we've established." Again, I felt a sudden wave of guilt surge over my brother and I stared, trying to filter the source. He stood and turned and beckoned for me to follow him to the hallway. He cocked his head to the side and leaned up against the wall, staring at me.

"What?" I asked, mimicking his stance.

"I know you went to find Stephen; I know that you went to tell him to fight for Ana, that you would let them be together. I saw it in his mind and in Ana's." He surveyed me, again his gaze somewhat frightening in its depth and perception. "Is that what you truly want Nathanial; you want Ana to be with Stephen?" he asked, his eyes flashing as he spoke.

"I want Ana to have the best life possible Patric; I want her to be happy and loved and to know how special and how desired she is," I said, feeling somewhat defiant in his questioning of me. Patric shook his head.

"Stephen can't be with Ana, Nathanial, not now anyway. He's full of vengeance for his brother's murder and he's leaving to track down those responsible for killing Liam and Carmen. He loves Ana, but he has some personality traits that for whatever reason, won't allow him to make a commitment to her. Had you come to him and Liam had not

627

been murdered, I'm quite sure that Stephen would have taken you up on your offer to remove yourself from the picture and while he labored over his decision, he's opting for revenge over love at this time." Patric bowed his head and took a breath.

"Why are you telling me this?" I asked, my eyes narrowing.

"Honestly Nathanial, because I don't think that you are ready to let Ana go; I don't think that you would be ok without having her to touch and to hold and to be with; I think it would kill you. With Stephen gone, for now, you may just be able to salvage the connection the two of you had. It's still there, it's still palpable and perhaps you won't screw it up this time." He glared at me and I looked away. "But you should know that I also love Ana very much and while I respect you as my brother, I cannot get past your behavior and what you subjected Ana to in Idaho. I'm happy to sit back and let you try and repair the damage, but I also know that Ana and I have a connection and it's different from you and different from Stephen and I'm inclined to let her explore the feelings that I know she has for me; it's her right."

"What are you saying Patric?" I asked, suddenly feeling as though we were thirteen again, playing chess and trying to calculate each other's next move.

"I'm saying that you need to give Ana some leeway, that no matter what state she is in when she comes out of this, that she doesn't feel overwhelmed, that she doesn't feel as though she's being given ultimatums, that you let her be who she needs to be and not hold it against her later." He eyed me, raising his chin. I smiled in spite of myself.

"Patric, if I didn't know any better, I would say that it sounds as if you are placing the needs of someone else over the needs of yourself; it almost sounds like you really do care for Ana," I said, grinning slightly at his sudden protective nature. He leaned forward, watching me.

"Not care for, Nathanial, *love*; I'm in love with Ana," he replied, speaking as if that was the only truth he'd ever known, that anything that he had been told about the world up until that point was irrelevant and that this, this one truth, was the only principal in his entire existence worth knowing. I nodded more complete in my understanding of my brother than I had ever been, he nodded back and then he shimmered away.

Five days passed, then seven, then ten and still no movement from Ana. I sat holding her hand and contemplating the last discussion I had with Patric; listening to him declare his love for her, while unnerving because of my own desires to be with her, it also made me somewhat pleased that he had allowed himself to be so affected by another soul and that he was willing to share with me just how much he wanted her. I wondered if she knew. I leaned back against the pillows watching the moonrise and I closed my eyes, letting my mind drift. My body felt hot, very, very hot and I awoke from my sleep feeling sweat soaking my shirt; I didn't perspire. I sat up and looked at Ana. He face was flush and her skin was damp and I could see, even in the dark, that she was shivering. I pressed my hand to her head, heat scorched my fingers and I pulled away. She started to choke and I grabbed her arms, heaving her upright. White foam seeped from her mouth and I yelled for Micah. He entered just in time to see her projectile vomit clear across the room. Foam and blood splattered against the wall and she gagged.

"MICAH! I shouted as she started to convulse in my arms. My uncle came to my side and tried to clear the vomit from her mouth. "ANA!" I shouted to her, desperate to help, not wanting her to die. Suddenly I saw her eyes open; they were wide and full of fear. "Ana!" I said, holding her face in my hands. "Ana!" Her gaze was unfocused. She threw up, this time on me as blood and spit soaked my shirt and pants.

"Oh god Nathanial! I'm so sorry!" Ana's voice rang out clear, but soft and I looked at her completely startled and in disbelief. She was looking at me, her eyes apologetic and now very focused and she was trying to move herself away from me.

"Ana?" My uncle was rubbing her back and trying to look at her. "Ana are you alright?" he asked, his eyes brimming with emotion. She turned to him.

"I'm sick; I feel sick." She dry heaved and panted as my uncle held her hair back. She rose and looked back at me, her face cringing as she assessed my blood soaked clothes. Micah approached her and gently pushed her back against the pillows, wiping her mouth with a damp cloth. I still couldn't speak.

"Ana, do you know where you are or what's happened to you?" Micah was frowning as he pressed the washcloth to her face. She glanced back at me, and then she turned to Micah, swallowing and licking her lips.

"Peru. But I wasn't here before; I mean I was with Patric, we were out at a restaurant...he'd taken me out," he voice trailed off and I could see Micah's mind racing. "He bought me a nice dress..." she said, looking out the window, she now seemed a bit out of it.

630

"What else do you remember Ana? Do you remember anything from that evening?" Micah pressed her and I was worried that she would become overwhelmed, plus I thought we should be checking to see if she was, in fact, a Vampire.

"Our amulets are the same," she said, fingering the necklace that lay on her chest.

"Whose amulets are the same?" Micah asked her.

"Mine and Patric's, we discovered that they were the same," she whispered, still tracing her finger around the outer symbol of the metals. Micah stared at me, his eyes full of questions and something else, some realization. I shrugged, my eyes wide; I had no idea.

"Ana, do you remember meeting Carlo? Do you recall seeing him the night that you were with Patric?" Micah was now kneeling down in front of her and she was smiling weakly at him.

"Carlo? No, I don't remember seeing him; why?" she asked, and I took a sharp breath in. She didn't seem to be recalling any events from that evening; at least none that had to do with Carlo. "Does he know that I'm sick? He'll be worried if I don't come back and he might be upset with Patric." Her tone was full of worry and she turned back to look at me. I found my voice finally.

"Patric's fine Ana, and you don't have to worry about Carlo. Tell me, how do you feel?" I was surprised at my level of decorum and how impersonal my tone sounded; I wanted to grab her and hold her and not let her go—ever.

"I feel tired and I really hate throwing up, but other than that, I guess I feel alright." She frowned and wiped her hair from her face.

"Nathanial, I'm going to call Patric, he might be able to help us out a bit here," Micah whispered as he left the room. I nodded.

"Why, what's wrong?" Ana asked sitting up.

"Nothing Ana, Patric's an excellent Healer and we would just feel better if we had him check you over a bit." I smiled at her and she nodded.

"I'm really sorry about your clothes Nathanial; those jeans look expensive…" She closed her eyes. I moved so that I was leaning over her head. I pushed her hair aside and bent my mouth to her ear.

"It doesn't matter," I said, echoing her mantra that she'd been saying for months, possibly years now. Her eyes opened and she stared at me, understanding.

Patric

"She doesn't remember what happened in that house?" I had arrived at Micah's to the news that Ana was awake, but didn't seem to remember what had transpired between she and Carlo. Neither Nathanial or my uncle could tell if Ana was now a vampire; it wasn't hard if you were already one or half of one like me. We had distinctive scents, predatory scents and I should be able to tell if Ana's had changed from her normal fragrance that I knew.

"She remembers that she was out with you and she mentioned something about a dress and that your amulets were the same, but when Micah asked her if she remembers seeing Carlo that night, she said no." My brother was sitting on the sofa, a glass of wine in his hand. I nodded. When my Change had occurred, after I awoke, I had no memory of what had happened prior to the event. I had to work hard to recall memories of my mother and even memories of Nathanial. It was arduous work and to this day, there were still gaps, but Ana not being able to remember events didn't necessarily mean that she had been Changed, it could just mean that her mind wasn't allowing her to recall such horrors. I stared at my brother as his thoughts permeated my mind. He was hoping that she would forget everything bad that had transpired between them; he wouldn't be that lucky. He frowned at me. I walked down the hall to her room, leaving Nathanial to tend to Lucie. Ana was curled up under my mother's quilt and she looked to be sleeping, but the minute I walked into the room, her eyes opened.

"Patric!" she called and sat up. I smiled and took a deep breath; I didn't smell anything unusual aside from Ana's normally intoxicating and arousing fragrance; it was all her. Maybe we would get lucky, maybe Dr. Connelly would be right.

"I heard you're not feeling very well," I said, sitting down on the bed next to her and opening my medicine bag.

"Nauseous, mainly," she said, eyeing me. "You know the last time I was in your care, you ended up giving me an affinity for blood and the ability to blow things up." Yeah, Nathanial was shit out of luck—memory in tact. I grinned and began crushing some herbs with a mini pestle. She seemed just like her old self, the only way I could tell now, would be to test her blood—it would be black. "Is that going to make me feel better?" she asked, touching my arm and staring at me, her eyes clear and deep; they were beautiful.

"It should," I said, meeting her gaze, not wanting her to look away from me.

"Hmmm…" she murmured and she reached to touch my face. "I'm sorry that I ruined our evening; it was so nice and you planned everything so beautifully and you looked so handsome," she said, frowning. "I'm bummed, I hadn't been out in quite a while." She pursed her lips, twisting them to the side. She seemed to think that she'd just gotten sick while out with me; that story might work for a bit, I pondered.

"Open," I said, touching her lips, they were warm and full of color. She obliged and I placed a pinch of the herb mixture on her tongue. "Close," I said, thinking. "Well, how about when you are feeling better, we try again?" I smiled and waited for the medicine to dissolve. She nodded, but then started to cringe and turn her head back and forth.

"God Patric; this is disgusting. I'm already sick to my stomach and the taste of this crap isn't helping." She gagged as she swallowed. I laughed.

"Give it a minute please," I instructed. "Maybe we'll try a different restaurant," I mused, wondering if any of her memory would come back; for her sake, I hoped it wouldn't. "Can you hold out your

634

finger?" I asked, withdrawing a tiny needle from my bag. I could just bite her, but if she were still human, the taste of her blood would most definitely conjure up a mood in me that was nowhere near appropriate for her current condition.

"Why?" she asked, still trying to swallow her medicine. "Can't you give me some water or something; it's sticking in my throat." I shook my head.

"Water dilutes the properties and then we'll just have to do it all over again. Finger please." I stared at her. She stuck out her finger, I took it and jabbed the tip of the needle into the tip; fresh, deep red blood rose to the surface and Ana's familiar scent hit me except it was powerful, so much so that I had to lean away from her. It was filling the room, absorbing every molecule of air and I had nowhere to turn, my body started to tremble and I gasped staring at her. The scent was predatory. It was still hers, but now it seemed to be serving her purposes rather than something that *I* would use to stalk *her*. It was luring me to her, making my mind and body react with such an intense need to have her want me, for me to give her what she desired. Jesus.

"What's wrong with you?" she asked, looking startled by my reaction, clearly unaware of what she was doing to me. I rose off the bed, hovering over and pressing my palms deep into the mattress, trying not to be hypnotized into getting any closer to her. Prey that suddenly could lure a predator; what the hell was going on? I cleared my throat.

"Umm, I just need to go and talk to Nathanial for a minute Ana," I choked out, heading for the door.

"What the hell Patric?" I heard her call as I bolted from the room, my own reaction surprising even me; usually I had much more control around her. Nathanial and Lucie were sitting on the couch reading and Lucie looked up, smiling widely at me.

"Uncle Patric, did you know that uncle Nathanial has a boat?" she asked, jumping off the couch to come and stand by me. I was trying to breathe regular. Nathanial was eyeing me, his face concerned. I steadied myself and gulped the fresh air, but the taste of her was still in my mouth. I regained as much control as I could, using Lucie as a distraction.

"Yes, in fact I did know that, but did you know that he doesn't know a thing about boats; he can't tell the stern from the portside," I said, laughing, regaining my full composure.

"What's a portside?" she asked, putting her arms up to me. I picked her up. I wasn't used to being around kids, but seeing just how much Ana had done for this little girl, how she was prepared to die for her. I couldn't help but love Lucie, we all did. "Have uncle Nathanial try and explain it to you and let's just see how far he gets," I said, throwing her high in the air. She screamed and laughed as I caught her. I nodded to Nathanial and he looked to Micah who immediately took Lucie from me and carried her away, tickling and kissing her under the chin.

"What's wrong with you?" my brother asked. Christ, he and Ana were so similar sometimes. He smirked.

"She appears to be Human." I exhaled sitting down beside him.

"What does that mean, she *appears* to be human?" he asked, uncertainty in his voice. I cleared my throat and turned to face him.

"She seems to be a bit more predatory in her behavior than before." I was trying not to laugh. I had no idea why this was striking me as funny, but there it was nonetheless.

"Predatory? You mean like she's…she's…she's what?" Nathanial was confused.

"Hmmm…" I chuckled. "She's releasing a very potent version of her scent, one that only vampires release when they are stalking their prey," I said, grinning.

"You mean their *Human* prey?" he reasoned. I shrugged.

"Ana's body and instincts don't seem to care; prey is prey to her at the moment and she wants what she wants," I said, pressing my lips together.

"Is something amusing to you Patric?" Nathanial's tone was curt, which seemed to make it that much harder for me not to laugh. I shook my head. "Let me guess, she released this scent while in your presence and you are feeling somewhat honored that she seems to have turned her attention to you," he said, again his tone was slightly mocking and short.

"Nathanial, I'm trying to communicate to you that the woman you love appears to be relatively unharmed and quite possibly won't remember any of the atrocities that Carlo subjected her to; do you really want to dwell on the fact that Ana may or may not be displaying some

637

mechanism of attraction to me?" My tone was serious, but I wasn't beyond gloating.

"So who's going to tell her?" Nathanial asked, glaring at me.

"Tell her what?" I asked. I wasn't inclined to tell Ana anything about Carlo, at least not yet. She needed to recover and I was keen to observe the physical affects of what her body experienced.

"You're content to let her wonder why she thinks she's been ill? And what do we do about Stephen? I'm sure she's going to want know if he's coming back for Lucie. Do we tell her that he's gone and that he's most likely done with their relationship? She still loves him, you have to know that." My brother sounded frustrated and on edge. I sighed.

"Well, I suppose someone should tell her about Stephen, considering how much she wants Lucie to be with family, but I'm not sure if we should be the ones to discuss Stephen's feelings about her, with her." I wasn't big into letting Ana know that a person she loved just couldn't seem to handle a relationship, even though his prime competition had volunteered to step aside so they could be together, and that he had decided to commit himself to hunting down and killing various covens of vampires, rather than have a life with her. It was just to depressing.

"Coward," Nathanial said, rising from the sofa. I shrugged.

"She's all yours for the time being." I also rose.

"What do you mean 'for the time being'? You can't possibly expect to be taking Ana back to the ranch with you; it's too dangerous." Nathanial rounded on me.

"What danger? Carlo's dead and I've been running his coven for months now; there is no danger," I said, my hands on my hips.

"You may have control over Carlo's coven, but what about the others; what about the ones who know about Ana's powers and about her blood? Can you protect her from them?" he asked, his voice rising.

"Can you?" I replied, taking a step forward. Nathanial and I were now face to face, barely a fracture of light between our stances.

"Umm…excuse me!" A fierce voice sounded from the side of the room. We both turned to see Ana standing in her sweats and tank glaring at us. "I don't need to be protected thank you. I didn't realize that Carlo was dead so I think that actually, I will be safe. He was the one that Liam was the most concerned about and now he's no longer an issue—for whatever reason; I don't really care to know," she said, leaning against the doorframe. "I'm taking Lucie and I'm chartering a boat from a friend; we're going to have a bit of a vacation I think." She sighed and came into the room, facing us. "I heard what you said about Stephen, so I guess he's not coming back for me or for Lucie." She ran her fingers down the length of her hair. "Well…there's not much I can do about that can I? He knows that I love him, but he's accountable only to himself now, he's made that quite clear. I'm not so pathetic that I would put my entire life on hold for the hope that some guy was going to realize what he's missing and come and rescue me— we've seen that that little fairy tale doesn't hold true, at least not for me. I'll be returning to the ranch to get my things and call my friend. I will be returning to Ireland with Lucie and together we will spend a few months sailing and enjoying ourselves—she needs to heal and so do I." Ana stared hard, daring either of us to challenge her.

"Of course Ana, we wouldn't dream of preventing you and Lucie from taking some time away; whatever you want." My brother met her gaze, but I could sense that the tenor of his emotions were bordering on depression; he didn't want to be away from her, especially since their moments together after she'd saved him. He wanted to talk to her, to explain things. I sighed. Ana looked at me; my body heaved forward uncontrollably as her scent knocked the breath out of my lungs. I grasped the back of the sofa trying to regain my balance.

"Patric? What is the matter with you?" Ana asked looking annoyed and concerned. I heard my brother growl lowly. "Is there something wrong with me? You keep doing that whenever I look at you. What's going on?" She turned to Nathanial, her eyes questioning.

"It's nothing you need to be concerned about Ana. Patric just needs to get himself under control that's all." Nathanial glared at me. I tried to breathe through my mouth, but I could taste her so much that my mouth was watering and I wanted to be close to her; I wanted her to want me. "Would you shut up!" Nathanial snarled at me, his voice so low that Ana couldn't hear. Ana rolled her eyes and walked out of the room.

"Patric, I'm feeling better, can you take me back tomorrow? I just want to stay in bed one more day," she called down from her room.

"Yeah!" I called back, exhaling loudly. Nathanial was headed down to her room. "Hey!" I started after him. He breathed deep, but kept his back to me. "Are we agreed that we don't tell her that she was bitten by Carlo and by Stephen?" I asked, my voice low; I was still trying to regulate my breathing. I turned him toward me. His eyes pulsed with their strange new coloring.

"Fine, but if she asks, or if her memory suddenly comes back, she gets to know—everything," he said raising his chin. "And if you notice anything in her behavior or her health, you are to summon me immediately, are we clear?" he commanded. I laughed. "And keep your hands off of her." He snarled at me.

"Sure thing," I said, still smirking. There was no way that was going to happen.

Nathanial

I wanted to kill him. His inability to control his reaction to whatever it was that Ana was putting out there was inexcusable. She was vulnerable and sick and the last thing she needed was to be fending off his hypersexual advances. I stood in the door watching her crawl back into bed, pulling my mother's quilt up over her shoulders.

"I've sort of taken over your room I guess." She smiled at me. "I'm sorry." She leaned back against the pillows. I walked hesitantly into the space, not wanting to assume that she would want me to come in. "Are you scared of me or something? You look slightly petrified." She laughed. Did I? I didn't think I was scared of her; maybe I was scared of being so close to her again knowing that she was leaving. I sat down on the bed taking her in.

"I didn't know that you were leaving," I said softy, reaching to touch her hand. She took my fingers and weaved them with hers. I sighed.

"I think it's best for the time," she said, staring at me. "Lucie needs to get away."

"Lucie?" I asked, finding her eyes.

"And me," she said, bowing her head. I pushed her hair back from hiding her face.

"When will you come back?" I lifted her chin.

"When I'm ready." Her breath was shallow and she swallowed hard. I moved my face closer to her.

"When you're ready," I whispered, I breathed softy on her lips. She closed her eyes.

"Nathanial." She sighed my name.

"Ana," I whispered, my mouth barely touching her hers.

"I love you so much," she whispered. "I thought I'd lost you. I thought you were going to die." Her body trembled as I stroked her face. "Why didn't you want me Nathanial, why didn't you try to stay with me, try to work things out?" She was shaking her head. "I couldn't hold onto you; I couldn't hold onto to Stephen; what's wrong? Why are things so complicated?" She shuddered, but she kept her face close to mine. I could feel the heat from her breath in my mouth. I swallowed, tasting her emotion. I pulled her close, wrapping my arms around her. "I'm sorry that I couldn't have a baby; I'm sorry that my body is broken. I'm sorry that I couldn't be what you wanted, what you needed... I'm sorry." She sobbed, putting her head on my chest. "I lost too, Nathanial; I lost too. I didn't get away unpunished, I lost so much. I lost a child and I lost you and I lost Stephen. I haven't been redeemed at all..."She cried. "I have nothing left and yet I have to find something, find anything to give to Lucie; she's lost so much too, Nathanial." She pulled back, her eyes searching mine. I couldn't form words. Hearing her ask me those questions, hearing her ask why I didn't want her, why I had subjected her to so much agony, watching me pursue someone else. I was gutted. I had nothing, no mechanism to explain, no way to justify what I had put her through, no way to repair so much damage. She was everything that I needed, everything that I had always wanted and yet I had proven to her that that wasn't the case, that I lusted after someone else, not because I didn't want her, but because I was weak. I didn't bother to try to understand what was happening in my body, I didn't try to fight.

There was now nothing that I could offer her to keep her with me, to make her choose me. I didn't deserve her love, her passion, her heart or her soul. I had squandered all of those things away and still she saved me, still she choose to bring me back, to keep me in this world, even if that meant being separate from hers for a while—or forever. I had to let her go. I could only hope that when she came back, I would be the one she wanted and I would be waiting, waiting to give her the life and the love she deserved, that she needed and that she had given me so unselfishly. I loved her and I had to let her go—for now.

I had insisted that Ana and Lucie remain at the ranch for a few weeks just until I could assess how she was doing physically and mainly emotionally. The last thing I wanted was for her to be out at sea in the middle of nowhere and memories of Carlo came rushing back. Nathanial seemed to be in agreement, but I wasn't fooled; he wasn't ready for Ana to leave and having her somewhere he now had access to, well, it was good for him. My brother had taken my advice and backed off from his desire at an attempt to repair his relationship with Ana; she didn't need to be subjected to having to sort though such complicated feelings and I could tell just from her reactions to Nathanial, that she wasn't inclined to go down that path with him, at least not yet.

Ana had confided in me and no one else apparently, that she wanted to take Lucie to Italy, that her friend who owned the boat was planning on setting her up with a small touring yacht once they arrived in Rome and she and Lucie would leave from there. I felt honored that she entrusted me with this information considering that she'd made it perfectly clear that she didn't want any of us to know where she would be going. I had spent centuries sailing myself around the world and I knew boats and the sea quite well and I had offered to help her chart the most scenic routes for her and Lucie to explore. She seemed grateful and I was happy to help, to be included.

Being around her was proving a bit of a challenge, but I was managing. She still didn't seem aware of her predation of me and I found it amusing that she remained clueless while I was trying every minute of every day, not to allow myself to by hypnotized by her scent. I wanted Ana, but I also wanted her to come to me to explore her feelings. I, unlike Stephen, didn't mind if she brought Nathanial with her into whatever relationship she wanted with me. I could care less because loving him, for her, only served to make her that much more extraordinary, that much more alluring in her passion and I would never think for a moment of diminishing that journey or those feelings. I also knew that she was fighting against me, against the pull that I had always created in her, the immense attraction that we had always shared even beyond my own manipulations of her. Ana and I had always shared a very sexually charged relationship, a very intensely passionate connection that just seemed to have become more substantial since she first arrived in Argentina. I sighed, thinking as I poured over a map of Greece. There was a knock at my door.

"Come in," I said, knowing immediately that it was Ana; I could smell her. She pushed the door open, carrying a bowl of cereal. I smiled. "Is Lucie in bed?" I asked standing to greet her. She nodded, munching quietly. She looked healthy all things considered. I went to sit on my couch and beckoned for her to join me.

"So what are you going to do now that Carlo's dead?" she asked, putting her bowl on the coffee table and settling back against the sofa. I sighed. The ranch was an extremely large operation to run, beef cattle, prize winning stallions, a winery, an organic farm...I had plenty to keep me busy and distracted until Ana returned—if she returned. I glanced at her face; visions of us together in her old room, visions of me kissing her, of me holding her, were filling her mind and I was somewhat startled at the details she was allowing herself to experience. I exhaled.

"I have plenty to do," I said, quietly, remembering along side her. She looked at me and frowned.

"Are you in any danger at all Patric?" She seemed sad suddenly and the images of my death, of my body exploding into ashes, now flooded her memory. I reached and pulled her close to me, feeling the warmth of her body and inhaling her scent, letting it course through my veins.

"No," I replied, my voice rough.

"Promise?" she asked, gazing at my face, at my eyes.

"I promise Ana." I bent my head and allowed myself to reach for her forehead, but she shifted her face and brought her lips to mine, pressing them softly on my mouth. I inhaled. She pulled away, her eyes searching mine; she was asking me, asking for my permission, asking if she should, if she could, asking me to remember her love for my brother, her love for Stephen, to remember the love that she had for me; she was asking to be with me, asking for what I knew she needed. I held her face and stared hard into her eyes. I stood, lifting her to her feet and I took her hand, leading her to my bed. I pulled her toward me, embracing her body; she pressed her face to my chest and breathed me in, deeply. "Ana," I said, moving away slightly. "I'm in love with you," I said, feeling the sudden release of what I had always known, what I had been fighting for years now and what I never thought I would be allowed to say to another living soul. It was a secret that I never knew how to tell.

"Be with me Patric," she whispered, stroking my face. "It's ok now; we know now, we both know the secrets we never knew how to express, to ourselves or each other." My eyes widened. She had heard my thoughts. Ana nodded and moved closer to me. "It's ok...it's ok." She kissed me. So forceful was her emotion that I felt the very essence of who I knew myself to be... fall. In it's place was a man, a man that I knew, a man that I had forgotten, that I had lost and now here he stood, holding a woman that he loved, that he would die for; a woman that had allowed him to fall and she had followed, knowing all along that they would catch each other, that hitting the ground did not have to mean shattered or broken bonds or even despair; it could mean courage, forgiveness... redemption. I took Ana to my bed honoring her journey and she honoring mine, and I told her all my secrets knowing that they were protected, that my heart was safe. I kissed her tears as we moved together, softly, gently, our eyes never leaving each other, our amulets glowing bright and hot as we held one another close. My breath became hers and flames ignited against our flesh, melding us together, forging our bond, not in ritual, not in obligation, but in love and friendship and the sacredness of Spirit that my mother gave to me. We released everything to each other as I explored her body through my new eyes, seeing her for the first time. Our passion consumed us, enveloping our joining in heat and fire and we fell away, just the two of us drifting together, tied, held...bound.

Nathanial

My blood boiled and my heart shattered; I had been betrayed. I stood watching them moving together, whispering, sharing, loving each

647

other. Ana I understood, I could forgive; she was weak, tired, grieving for so much, but Patric—he knew. My brother knew how much I loved Ana, how much I needed her for my own survival. I didn't care about his redemption or his realization about his feelings toward her; I loved her. I loved her first and she was mine. I would fight him. I would fight him for her and I was prepared to use every tactic I had to eliminate him from her life, from her heart. I grabbed the charted map off his desk and tucked it in my pocket. I turned once more to my betrayer watching him as he kissed the very reason for my heart to beat, for my breath to move; I watched as he stroked her face and moved his mouth to her throat. I watched once more knowing that in the end, Ana would be mine and I would destroy him.

End of Book II

Made in the USA
Charleston, SC
21 July 2015